The Inheritance Cycle:

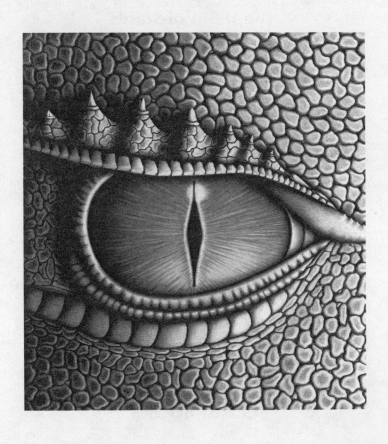

INHERITANCE

or

The Vault of Sands

THE INHERITANCE CYCLE
BOOK FOUR

Christopher Paolini

CORGI BOOKS

TRANSWORLD PUBLISHERS
61-63 Uxbridge Road, London W5 5SA
A Random House Group Company
www.transworldbooks.co.uk

INHERITANCE
A CORGI BOOK 978 0 552 15862 6

First published in Great Britain in 2011 by Doubleday,
an imprint of Random House Children's Publishers UK
A Random House Group Company
Corgi children's edition published 2012
Corgi edition published 2013

A CIP catalogue record for this book is available from the British Library

Addresses for Random House Group Ltd companies outside the UK
can be found at: www.randomhouse.co.uk
The Random House Group Limited Reg. No. 954009

The Random House Group Limited supports The Forest Stewardship Council® (FSC®), the leading
international forest-certification organisation. Our books carrying the FSC label are printed on
FSC®-certified paper. FSC is the only forest-certification scheme supported by the leading
environmental organisations, including Greenpeace. Our paper procurement policy can be found at
www.randomhouse.co.uk/environment

Set in Goudy
Printed and bound in Great Britain by CPI Group (UK), Croydon CR0 4YY

2 4 6 8 10 9 7 5 3 1

As always, this book is for my family.
And also for the dreamers of dreams:
the many artists, musicians, and storytellers
who have made this journey possible.

CONTENTS

In the Beginning:
A History of *Eragon, Eldest,* and *Brisingr*

In the beginning, there were dragons: proud, fierce, and independent. Their scales were like gems, and all who gazed upon them despaired, for their beauty was great and terrible.

And they lived alone in the land of Alagaësia for ages uncounted.

Then the god Helzvog made the stout and sturdy dwarves from the stone of the Hadarac Desert.

And their two races warred much.

Then the elves sailed to Alagaësia from across the silver sea. They too warred with the dragons. But the elves were stronger than the dwarves, and they would have destroyed the dragons, even as the dragons would have destroyed the elves.

And so a truce was struck and a pact was sealed between the dragons and the elves. And by this joining, they created the Dragon Riders, who kept the peace throughout Alagaësia for thousands of years.

Then humans sailed to Alagaësia. And the horned Urgals. And the Ra'zac, who are the hunters in the dark and the eaters of men's flesh.

And the humans also joined the pact with the dragons.

Then a young Dragon Rider, Galbatorix, rose up against his own kind. He enslaved the black dragon Shruikan and he convinced thirteen other Riders to follow him. And the thirteen were called the Forsworn.

And Galbatorix and the Forsworn cast down the Riders and burnt their city on the isle of Vroengard and slew every dragon not their own, save for three eggs: one red, one blue, one green. And from each dragon they could, they took the heart of hearts—the Eldunarí—that holds the might and mind of the dragons, apart from their flesh.

And for two-and-eighty years, Galbatorix reigned supreme among the humans. The Forsworn died, but not he, for his strength was that of all the dragons, and none could hope to strike him down.

In the eighty-third year of Galbatorix's rule, a man stole from his castle the blue dragon egg. And the egg passed into the care of those who still fought against Galbatorix, those who are known as the Varden.

The elf Arya carried the egg between the Varden and the elves in search of the human or elf for whom it would hatch. And in this manner, five-and-twenty years passed.

Then, as Arya traveled to the elven city of Osilon, a group of Urgals attacked her and her guards. With the Urgals was the Shade Durza: a sorcerer possessed by the spirits he had summoned to do his bidding. After the death of the Forsworn, he had become Galbatorix's most feared servant. The Urgals slew Arya's guards, and before they and the Shade captured her, Arya sent the egg away with magic, toward one who she hoped could protect it.

But her spell went awry.

And so it came to pass that Eragon, an orphan of only five-and-ten years, found the egg within the mountains of the Spine. He took the egg to the farm where he lived with his uncle, Garrow, and his only cousin, Roran. And the egg hatched for Eragon, and he raised the dragon therein. And her name was Saphira.

Then Galbatorix sent two of the Ra'zac to find and retrieve the egg, and they slew Garrow and burnt Eragon's home. For Galbatorix had enslaved the Ra'zac, and of them only a few remained.

Eragon and Saphira set out to avenge themselves on the Ra'zac. With them went the storyteller Brom, who had once been a Dragon Rider himself, ere the fall of the Riders. It was to Brom that the elf Arya had meant to send the blue egg.

Brom taught Eragon much about swordsmanship, magic, and honor. And he gave to Eragon Zar'roc, that had once been the sword of Morzan, first and most powerful of the Forsworn. But the Ra'zac slew Brom when next they met, and Eragon and Saphira only escaped with the help of a young man, Murtagh, son of Morzan.

During their travels, the Shade Durza captured Eragon in the city of Gil'ead. Eragon managed to free himself, and as he did, he freed Arya from her cell. Arya was poisoned and gravely wounded, so Eragon, Saphira, and Murtagh took her to the Varden, who lived among the dwarves in the Beor Mountains.

There Arya was healed, and there Eragon blessed a squalling infant by the name of Elva, blessed her to be shielded from misfortune. But Eragon spoke badly, and without realizing it, he cursed her, and his curse forced her to instead become a shield for others' misfortune.

Soon thereafter, Galbatorix sent a great army of Urgals to attack the dwarves and the Varden. And it was in the battle that followed that Eragon slew the Shade Durza. But Durza gave Eragon a grievous wound across his back, and Eragon suffered terrible pain because of it, despite the spells of the Varden's healers.

And in his pain, he heard a voice. And the voice said, *Come to me, Eragon. Come to me, for I have answers to all you ask.*

Three days after, the leader of the Varden, Ajihad, was ambushed and killed by Urgals under the command of a pair of magicians, twins, who betrayed the Varden to Galbatorix. The twins also abducted Murtagh and spirited him away to Galbatorix. But to Eragon and everyone in the Varden, it looked as if Murtagh had died, and Eragon was much saddened.

And Ajihad's daughter, Nasuada, became leader of the Varden.

From Tronjheim, the seat of the dwarves' power, Eragon, Saphira, and Arya traveled to the northern forest of Du Weldenvarden, where live the elves. With them went the dwarf Orik, nephew of the dwarf king, Hrothgar.

In Du Weldenvarden, Eragon and Saphira met with Oromis and

Glaedr: the last free Rider and dragon, who had lived in hiding all the past century, waiting to instruct the next generation of Dragon Riders. And Eragon and Saphira also met with Queen Islanzadí, ruler of the elves and mother to Arya.

While Oromis and Glaedr trained Eragon and Saphira, Galbatorix sent the Ra'zac and a group of soldiers to Eragon's home village of Carvahall, this time to capture his cousin, Roran. But Roran hid, and they would not have found him if not for the hatred of the butcher Sloan. For Sloan murdered a watchman so as to let the Ra'zac into the village, where they might take Roran unawares.

Roran fought his way free, but the Ra'zac stole from him Katrina: Roran's beloved and Sloan's daughter. Then Roran convinced the villagers to leave with him, and they journeyed through the mountains of the Spine, down the coast of Alagaësia, and to the southern country of Surda, which yet existed independent of Galbatorix.

The wound upon Eragon's back continued to torment him. But during the elves' Blood-oath Celebration, wherein they celebrate the pact between the Riders and the dragons, his wound was healed by the spectral dragon the elves invoke upon the conclusion of the festival. Moreover, the apparition gave Eragon strength and speed equal to those of the elves themselves.

Then Eragon and Saphira flew to Surda, where Nasuada had taken the Varden to launch an attack against Galbatorix's Empire. There the Urgals allied themselves with the Varden, for they claimed that Galbatorix had clouded their minds, and they would have their revenge against him. With the Varden, Eragon met again the girl Elva, who had grown with prodigious speed because of his spell. From a squalling infant to a girl of three or four she had become, and her gaze was dire indeed, for she knew the pain of all those around her.

And not far from the border of Surda, upon the blackness of the Burning Plains, Eragon, Saphira, and the Varden fought a great and bloody battle against Galbatorix's army.

In the midst of the battle, Roran and the villagers joined the

Varden, as did the dwarves, who had marched after them from the Beor Mountains.

But out of the east rose a figure clad in polished armor. And he rode upon a glittering red dragon. And with a spell, he slew King Hrothgar.

Then Eragon and Saphira fought the Rider and his red dragon. And they discovered the Rider was Murtagh, now bound to Galbatorix with oaths unbreakable. And the dragon was Thorn, second of the three eggs to hatch.

Murtagh defeated Eragon and Saphira with the strength of the Eldunarí that Galbatorix had given him. But Murtagh allowed Eragon and Saphira to go free, for Murtagh still bore friendship for Eragon. And because, as he told Eragon, they were brothers, both born of Morzan's favored consort, Selena.

Then Murtagh took Zar'roc, their father's sword, from Eragon, and he and Thorn withdrew from the Burning Plains, as did the rest of Galbatorix's forces.

Upon completion of the battle, Eragon, Saphira, and Roran flew to the dark tower of stone, Helgrind, that served as the Ra'zac's hiding place. They slew one of the Ra'zac—and the Ra'zac's foul parents, the Lethrblaka—and from Helgrind rescued Katrina. And in one of the cells, Eragon discovered Katrina's father, blind and half-dead.

Eragon considered killing Sloan for his betrayal, but rejected the idea. Instead, he put Sloan into a deep sleep and told Roran and Katrina that her father was dead. Then he asked Saphira to take Roran and Katrina back to the Varden while he hunted down the final Ra'zac.

Alone, Eragon slew the last remaining Ra'zac. Then he took Sloan away from Helgrind. After much thought, Eragon discovered Sloan's true name in the ancient language, the language of power and magic. And Eragon bound Sloan with his name and forced the butcher to swear that he would never see his daughter again. Then Eragon sent him to live among the elves. But what Eragon did not tell the butcher was that the elves would repair his eyes if he repented of his treason and murder.

Arya met Eragon halfway to the Varden, and together they returned, on foot and through enemy territory.

At the Varden, Eragon learned that Queen Islanzadí had sent twelve elven spellcasters, led by an elf named Blödhgarm, to protect him and Saphira. Eragon then removed as much of his curse as he could from the girl Elva, but she retained her ability to feel the pain of others, though she no longer felt the compulsion to save them from their misery.

And Roran married Katrina, who was pregnant, and for the first time in a long while, Eragon was happy.

Then Murtagh, Thorn, and a group of Galbatorix's men attacked the Varden. With the help of the elves, Eragon and Saphira were able to hold them off, but neither Eragon nor Murtagh could defeat the other. It was a difficult battle, for Galbatorix had enchanted the soldiers so that they felt no pain, and the Varden suffered many casualties.

Afterward, Nasuada sent Eragon to represent the Varden among the dwarves while they chose their new king. Eragon was loath to go, for Saphira had to stay and protect the Varden's camp. But go he did.

And Roran served alongside the Varden, and he rose through their ranks, for he proved himself a skilled warrior and a leader of men.

While Eragon was among the dwarves, seven of them tried to assassinate him. An investigation revealed that the clan Az Sweldn rak Anhûin was behind the attack. The clanmeet continued, however, and Orik was chosen to succeed his uncle. Saphira joined Eragon for the coronation. And during it, she fulfilled her promise to repair the dwarves' cherished star sapphire, which she had broken during Eragon's battle with the Shade Durza.

Then Eragon and Saphira returned to Du Weldenvarden. There Oromis revealed the truth about Eragon's heritage: that he was not, in fact, Morzan's son but Brom's, though he and Murtagh did share the same mother, Selena. Oromis and Glaedr also explained the concept of the Eldunarí, which a dragon may choose to disgorge while living, though this must be done with great care, for whosoever owns the Eldunarí may use it to control the dragon it came from.

While in the forest, Eragon decided that he needed a sword to replace Zar'roc. Remembering the advice he had gotten from the werecat Solembum during his journeys with Brom, Eragon went to the sentient Menoa tree in Du Weldenvarden. He spoke with the tree, and the tree agreed to give up the brightsteel beneath its roots in exchange for an unnamed price.

Then the elf smith Rhunön—who had forged all of the Riders' swords—worked with Eragon to make a new blade for him. The sword was blue, and Eragon named it Brisingr—"fire." And the blade burst into flame whenever he spoke its name.

Then Glaedr gave trust of his heart of hearts to Eragon and Saphira, and they made their way back to the Varden, while Glaedr and Oromis joined the rest of their kind as they attacked the northern part of the Empire.

At the siege of Feinster, Eragon and Arya encountered three enemy magicians, one of whom was transformed into the Shade Varaug. And with Eragon's help, Arya slew Varaug.

As they did, Oromis and Glaedr fought Murtagh and Thorn. And Galbatorix reached out and took command of Murtagh's mind. And with Murtagh's arm, Galbatorix struck down Oromis, and Thorn slew Glaedr's body.

And though the Varden were victorious at Feinster, Eragon and Saphira mourned the loss of their teacher, Oromis. But still the Varden continued, and even now they march deeper into the Empire, toward the capital, Urû'baen, wherein sits Galbatorix, proud, confident, and disdainful, for his is the strength of the dragons.

INHERITANCE

INTO THE BREACH

The dragon Saphira roared, and the soldiers before her quailed. "With me!" shouted Eragon. He lifted Brisingr over his head, holding it aloft for all to see. The blue sword flashed bright and iridescent, stark against the wall of black clouds building in the west. "For the Varden!"

An arrow whizzed past him; he paid it no mind.

The warriors gathered at the base of the slope of rubble Eragon and Saphira were standing upon answered him with a single, full-throated bellow: "The Varden!" They brandished their own weapons and charged forward, scrambling up the tumbled blocks of stone.

Eragon turned his back to the men. On the other side of the mound lay a wide courtyard. Two hundred or so of the Empire's soldiers stood huddled within. Behind them rose a tall, dark keep with narrow slits for windows and several square towers, the tallest of which had a lantern shining in its upper rooms. Somewhere within the keep, Eragon knew, was Lord Bradburn, governor of Belatona—the city the Varden had been fighting to capture for several long hours.

With a cry, Eragon leaped off the rubble toward the soldiers. The men shuffled backward, although they kept their spears and pikes trained on the ragged hole Saphira had torn in the castle's outer wall.

Eragon's right ankle twisted as he landed. He fell to his knee and caught himself on the ground with his sword hand.

One of the soldiers seized the opportunity to dart out of formation and stab his spear at Eragon's exposed throat.

Eragon parried the thrust with a flick of his wrist, swinging Brisingr faster than either a human or an elf could follow. The soldier's face grew slack with fear as he realized his mistake. He tried to flee, but before he could move more than a few inches, Eragon lunged forward and took him in the gut.

With a pennant of blue and yellow flame streaming from her maw, Saphira jumped into the courtyard after Eragon. He crouched and tensed his legs as she struck the paved ground. The impact shook the entire courtyard. Many of the chips of glass that formed a large, colorful mosaic in front of the keep popped loose and flew spinning upward like coins bounced off a drum. Above, a pair of shutters banged open and closed in a window of the building.

The elf Arya accompanied Saphira. Her long black hair billowed wildly around her angular face as she sprang off the pile of rubble. Lines of splattered blood striped her arms and neck; gore smeared the blade of her sword. She alit with a soft scuff of leather against stone.

Her presence heartened Eragon. There was no one else whom he would rather have fighting alongside him and Saphira. She was, he thought, the perfect shield mate.

He loosed a quick smile at her, and Arya responded in kind, her expression fierce and joyous. In battle, her reserved demeanor vanished, replaced by an openness that she rarely displayed elsewhere.

Eragon ducked behind his shield as a rippling sheet of blue fire appeared between them. From beneath the rim of his helm, he watched as Saphira bathed the cowering soldiers in a torrent of flames that flowed around them, yet caused them no harm.

A line of archers on the battlements of the castle keep let fly a volley of arrows at Saphira. The heat above her was so intense that a handful of the arrows burst into fire in midair and crumbled to ash, while the magical wards Eragon had placed around Saphira deflected the rest. One of the stray arrows rebounded off Eragon's shield with a hollow *thud*, denting it.

The plume of flame suddenly enveloped three of the soldiers, killing them so quickly, they did not even have time to scream. The other soldiers clustered in the center of the inferno, the blades of their spears and pikes reflecting flashes of bright blue light.

Try though she might, Saphira could not so much as singe the survivors. At last she abandoned her efforts and closed her jaws with a definitive *snap*. The fire's absence left the courtyard startlingly quiet.

It occurred to Eragon, as it had several times before, that whoever had given the soldiers their wards must have been a skilled and powerful magician. *Was it Murtagh?* he wondered. *If so, why aren't he and Thorn here to defend Belatona? Doesn't Galbatorix care to keep control of his cities?*

Eragon ran forward and, with a single stroke of Brisingr, lopped off the tops of a dozen polearms as easily as he had flicked off the seed heads of barley stalks when he was younger. He slashed the nearest soldier across the chest, slicing through his mail as if it were the flimsiest of cloth. A fountain of blood arose. Then Eragon stabbed the next soldier in line and struck the soldier to his left with his shield, knocking the man into three of his companions and bowling them over.

The soldiers' reactions seemed slow and clumsy to Eragon as he danced through their ranks, cutting them down with impunity. Saphira waded into the fray to his left—batting the soldiers into the air with her enormous paws, lashing them with her spiked tail, and biting and killing them with a shake of her head—while, to his right, Arya was a blur of motion, every swing of her sword signaling death for another servant of the Empire. When Eragon spun around to evade a pair of spears, he saw the fur-covered elf Blödhgarm close behind, as well as the eleven other elves whose task it was to guard him and Saphira.

Farther back, the Varden poured into the courtyard through the gap in the castle's outer wall, but the men refrained from attacking; it was too dangerous to go anywhere near Saphira. Neither she nor Eragon nor the elves required assistance in disposing of the soldiers.

The battle soon swept Eragon and Saphira apart, carrying them to opposite ends of the courtyard. Eragon was not concerned. Even without her wards, Saphira was more than capable of defeating a large group of twenty or thirty humans by herself.

A spear thudded against Eragon's shield, bruising his shoulder. He whirled toward the thrower, a big, scarred man missing his lower front teeth, and sprinted at him. The man struggled to draw a dagger from his belt. At the last moment, Eragon twisted, tensed his arms and chest, and rammed his sore shoulder into the man's sternum.

The force of the impact drove the soldier backward several yards, whereupon he collapsed, clutching at his heart.

Then a hail of black-fletched arrows fell, killing or injuring many of the soldiers. Eragon shied away from the missiles and covered himself with his shield, even though he was confident his magic would protect him. It would not do to become careless; he never knew when an enemy spellcaster might fire an enchanted arrow that could breach his wards.

A bitter smile twisted Eragon's lips. The archers above had realized that their only hope of victory lay in somehow killing Eragon and the elves, no matter how many of their own they had to sacrifice to do so.

You're too late, thought Eragon with grim satisfaction. *You should have left the Empire while you still had the chance.*

The onslaught of clattering arrows gave him the chance to rest for a moment, which he welcomed. The attack on the city had begun at daybreak, and he and Saphira had been at its forefront the whole while.

Once the arrows ceased, Eragon transferred Brisingr to his left hand, picked up one of the soldiers' spears, and heaved it at the archers forty feet above. As Eragon had discovered, spears were difficult to throw accurately without substantial practice. It did not surprise him, then, when he missed the man he was aiming for, but he *was* surprised when he missed the entire line of archers on the battlements. The spear sailed over them and shattered against the castle wall overhead. The archers laughed and jeered, making rude gestures.

A swift movement at the periphery of his vision caught Eragon's attention. He looked just in time to see Arya launch her own spear at the archers; it impaled two who were standing close together. Then Arya pointed at the men with her sword and said, "Brisingr!" and the spear burst into emerald-green fire.

The archers shrank from the burning corpses and, as one, fled from the battlements, crowding through the doorways that led to the upper levels of the castle.

"That's not fair," Eragon said. "I can't use that spell, not without my sword flaring up like a bonfire."

Arya gazed at him with a faint hint of amusement.

The fighting continued for another few minutes, whereupon the remaining soldiers either surrendered or tried to flee.

Eragon allowed the five men in front of him to run away; he knew they would not get far. After a quick examination of the bodies that lay sprawled around him to confirm that they were indeed dead, he looked back across the courtyard. Some of the Varden had opened the gates in the outer wall and were carrying a battering ram through the street leading to the castle. Others were assembling in ragged lines next to the keep door, ready to enter the castle and confront the soldiers within. Among them stood Eragon's cousin, Roran, gesturing with his ever-present hammer while he issued orders to the detachment under his command. At the far end of the courtyard, Saphira crouched over the corpses of her kills, the area around her a shambles. Beads of blood clung to her gemlike scales, the spots of red in startling contrast to the blue of her body. She threw back her spiky head and roared her triumph, drowning out the clamor of the city with the ferocity of her cry.

Then, from inside the castle, Eragon heard the rattle of gears and chains, followed by the scrape of heavy wooden beams being drawn back. The sounds attracted everyone's gaze to the doors of the keep.

With a hollow *boom,* the doors parted and swung open. A thick cloud of smoke from the torches within billowed outward, causing the nearest of the Varden to cough and cover their faces. From somewhere in the depths of the gloom came the drumming of iron-clad hooves against the paving stones; then a horse and rider burst forth from the center of the smoke. In his left hand, the rider held what Eragon first took to be a common lance, but he soon noticed that it was made of a strange green material and had a barbed blade forged in an unfamiliar pattern. A faint glow surrounded the head of the lance, the unnatural light betraying the presence of magic.

The rider tugged on the reins and angled his horse toward Saphira, who began to rear onto her hind legs, in preparation for delivering a terrible, killing blow with her right front paw.

Concern clutched at Eragon. The rider was too sure of himself, the lance too different, too eerie. Though her wards ought to protect her, Eragon was certain Saphira was in mortal danger.

I won't be able to reach her in time, he realized. He cast his mind toward the rider, but the man was so focused on his task that he did not even notice Eragon's presence, and his unwavering concentration prevented Eragon from gaining more than superficial access to his consciousness. Withdrawing into himself, Eragon reviewed a half-dozen words from the ancient language and composed a simple spell to stop the galloping war-horse in his tracks. It was a desperate act—for Eragon knew not if the rider was a magician himself or what precautions he might have taken against being attacked with magic—but Eragon was not about to stand by idly when Saphira's life was at risk.

Eragon filled his lungs. He reminded himself of the correct pronunciation of several difficult sounds in the ancient language. Then he opened his mouth to deliver the spell.

Fast as he was, the elves were faster still. Before he could utter a single word, a frenzy of low chanting erupted behind him, the overlapping voices forming a discordant and unsettling melody.

"Mäe—" he managed to say, and then the elves' magic took effect.

The mosaic in front of the horse stirred and shifted, and the chips of glass flowed like water. A long rift opened up in the ground, a gaping crevice of uncertain depth. With a loud scream, the horse plunged into the hole and pitched forward, breaking both of its front legs.

As horse and rider fell, the man in the saddle drew back his arm and threw the glowing lance toward Saphira.

Saphira could not run. She could not dodge. So she swung a paw at the dart, hoping to knock it aside. She missed, however—by a matter of inches—and Eragon watched with horror as the lance sank a yard or more into her chest, just under her collarbone.

A pulsing veil of rage descended over Eragon's vision. He drew upon every store of energy available to him—his body; the sapphire set in the pommel of his sword; the twelve diamonds hidden in the belt of Beloth the Wise wrapped round his waist; and the massive store within Aren, the elf ring that graced his right hand—as he prepared to obliterate the rider, heedless of the risk.

Eragon stopped himself, however, when Blödhgarm appeared, leaping over Saphira's left foreleg. The elf landed on the rider like a panther pouncing on a deer, and knocked the man onto his side. With a savage twist of his head, Blödhgarm tore open the man's throat with his long white teeth.

A shriek of all-consuming despair emanated from a window high above the open entrance to the keep, followed by a fiery explosion that ejected blocks of stone from within the building, blocks that landed amid the assembled Varden, crushing limbs and torsos like dry twigs.

Eragon ignored the stones raining on the courtyard and ran to Saphira, barely aware of Arya and his guards accompanying him. Other elves, who had been closer, were already clustering around her, examining the lance that projected from her chest.

"How badly— Is she—" Eragon said, too upset to complete his sentences. He yearned to speak to Saphira with his mind, but as long as enemy spellcasters might be in the area, he dared not expose his consciousness to her, lest his foes spy on his thoughts or assume command over his body.

After a seemingly interminable wait, Wyrden, one of the male elves, said, "You may thank fate, Shadeslayer; the lance missed the major veins and arteries in her neck. It hit only muscle, and muscle we can mend."

"Can you remove it? Does it have any spells that would keep it from being—"

"We shall attend to it, Shadeslayer."

Grave as priests gathered before an altar, all the elves, save Blödhgarm, placed the palms of their hands on Saphira's breast and, like a whisper of wind ghosting through a stand of willow trees, they sang. Of warmth and growth they sang, of muscle and sinew and pulsing blood they sang, and of other, more arcane subjects. With what must have been an enormous effort of will, Saphira held her position throughout the incantation, though fits of tremors shook her body every few seconds. A thread of blood rolled down her chest from the shaft embedded within.

As Blödhgarm moved to stand next to him, Eragon spared a glance for the elf. Gore matted the fur on his chin and neck, darkening its shade from midnight blue to solid black.

"What was that?" Eragon asked, indicating the flames still dancing in the window high above the courtyard.

Blödhgarm licked his lips, baring his catlike fangs, before answering. "In the moment before he died, I was able to enter the soldier's mind, and through it, the mind of the magician who was assisting him."

"You killed the magician?"

"In a manner of speaking; I forced him to kill himself. I would not normally resort to such an extravagant display of theatrics, but I was . . . aggravated."

Eragon started forward, then checked himself when Saphira uttered a long, low moan as, without anyone touching it, the lance began to slide out of her chest. Her eyelids fluttered and she took a series of quick, shallow breaths while the last six inches of the lance emerged from her body. The barbed blade, with its faint nimbus of emerald light, fell to the ground and bounced against the paving stones, sounding more like pottery than metal.

When the elves stopped singing and lifted their hands from Saphira, Eragon rushed to her side and touched her neck. He wanted to comfort her, to tell her how frightened he had been, to join his consciousness with hers. Instead, he settled for looking up into one of her brilliant blue eyes and asking, "Are you all right?" The words seemed paltry when compared with the depth of his emotion.

Saphira replied with a single blink, then lowered her head and caressed his face with a gentle puff of warm air from her nostrils.

Eragon smiled. Then he turned to the elves and said, "Eka elrun ono, älfya, wiol förn thornessa," thanking them in the ancient language for their help. The elves who had participated in the healing, including Arya, bowed and twisted their right hands over the center of their chests in the gesture of respect peculiar to their race. Eragon noticed that more than half of the elves assigned to protect him and Saphira were pale, weak, and unsteady on their feet.

"Fall back and rest," he told them. "You'll only get yourselves killed if you stay. Go on, that's an order!"

Though Eragon was sure they hated to leave, the seven elves responded with, "As you wish, Shadeslayer," and withdrew from the courtyard, striding over the corpses and rubble. They appeared noble and dignified, even when at the limits of their endurance.

Then Eragon joined Arya and Blödhgarm, who were studying the lance, a strange expression on both their faces, as if they were uncertain how they ought to react. Eragon squatted next to them, careful not to allow any part of his body to brush against the weapon. He stared at the delicate lines carved around the base of the blade, lines that seemed familiar to him, although he was not sure why; at the greenish haft, which was made of a material neither wood nor metal; and again at the smooth glow that reminded him of the flameless lanterns that the elves and the dwarves used to light their halls.

"Is it Galbatorix's handiwork, do you think?" Eragon asked. "Maybe he's decided he would rather kill Saphira and me instead of capturing us. Maybe he believes we've actually become a threat to him."

Blödhgarm smiled an unpleasant smile. "I would not deceive myself with such fantasies, Shadeslayer. We are no more than a minor annoyance to Galbatorix. If ever he truly wanted you or any of us dead, he only needs to fly forth from Urû'baen and engage us directly in battle, and we would fall before him like dry leaves before a winter storm. The strength of the dragons is with him, and none can withstand his might. Besides, Galbatorix is not so easily turned from his course. Mad he may be, but cunning also, and above all else, determined. If he desires your enslavement, then he shall pursue that goal to the point of obsession, and nothing save the instinct of self-preservation shall deter him."

"In any event," said Arya, "this is not Galbatorix's handiwork; it is ours."

Eragon frowned. "Ours? This wasn't made by the Varden."

"Not by the Varden, but by an elf."

"But—" He stopped, trying to find a rational explanation. "But no elf would agree to work for Galbatorix. They would rather die than—"

"Galbatorix had nothing to do with this, and even if he did, he would hardly give such a rare and powerful weapon to a man who could not better guard it. Of all the instruments of war scattered throughout Alagaësia, this is the one Galbatorix would least want us to have."

"Why?"

With a hint of a purr in his low, rich voice, Blödhgarm said, "Because, Eragon Shadeslayer, *this* is a Dauthdaert."

"And its name is Niernen, the Orchid," said Arya. She pointed at the lines carved into the blade, lines that Eragon then realized were actually stylized glyphs from the elves' unique system of writing—curving, intertwined shapes that terminated in long, thornlike points.

"A Dauthdaert?" When both Arya and Blödhgarm looked at him with incredulity, Eragon shrugged, embarrassed by his lack of education. It frustrated him that, while growing up, the elves had enjoyed decades upon decades of study with the finest scholars of their race, and yet his own uncle, Garrow, had not even taught him his letters, deeming it unimportant. "I could only do so much reading in Ellesméra. What is it? Was it forged during the fall of the Riders, to use against Galbatorix and the Forsworn?"

Blödhgarm shook his head. "Niernen is far, far older than that."

"The Dauthdaertya," said Arya, "were born out of the fear and the hate that marked the final years of our war with the dragons. Our most skilled smiths and spellcasters crafted them out of materials we no longer understand, imbued them with enchantments whose wordings we no longer remember, and named them, all twelve of them, after the most beautiful of flowers—as ugly a mismatch as ever there was—for we made them with but one purpose in mind: we made them to kill dragons."

Revulsion overtook Eragon as he gazed at the glowing lance. "And did they?"

"Those who were present say that the dragons' blood rained from the sky like a summer downpour."

Saphira hissed, loud and sharp.

Eragon glanced back at her for a moment and saw out of the corner of his eye that the Varden were still holding their position before the keep, waiting for him and Saphira to retake the lead in the offensive.

"All of the Dauthdaertya were thought to have been destroyed or lost beyond recovery," said Blödhgarm. "Obviously, we were mistaken. Niernen must have passed into the hands of the Waldgrave family, and they must have kept it hidden here in Belatona. I would guess that when we breached the city walls, Lord Bradburn's courage failed him and he ordered Niernen brought from his armory in an attempt to stop you and Saphira. No doubt Galbatorix would be angry beyond reason if he knew that Bradburn had tried to kill you."

Although he was aware of the need for haste, Eragon's curiosity would not let him leave just yet. "Dauthdaert or not, you still haven't explained why Galbatorix wouldn't want us to have this." He motioned toward the lance. "What makes Niernen any more dangerous than that spear over there, or even Bris—" he caught himself before he uttered the entire name, "or my own sword?"

It was Arya who answered. "It cannot be broken by any normal means, cannot be harmed by fire, and is almost completely impervious to magic, as you yourself saw. The Dauthdaertya were designed to be unaffected by whatever spells the dragons might work and to protect their wielder from the same—a daunting prospect, given the strength, complexity, and unexpected nature of dragons' magic. Galbatorix may have wrapped Shruikan and himself in more wards than anyone else in Alagaësia, but it is possible that Niernen could pass through their defenses as if they don't even exist."

Eragon understood, and elation filled him. "We have to—"

A squeal interrupted him.

The sound was stabbing, slicing, shivering, like metal scraping against stone. Eragon's teeth vibrated in sympathy and he covered his ears with his hands, grimacing as he twisted around, trying to locate the source of the noise. Saphira tossed her head, and even through the din, he heard her whine in distress.

Eragon swept his gaze over the courtyard two separate times before he noticed a faint puff of dust rising up the wall of the keep from a foot-wide crack that had appeared beneath the blackened, partially destroyed window where Blödhgarm had killed the magician. As the squeal increased in intensity, Eragon risked lifting one of his hands off his ears to point at the crack.

"Look!" he shouted to Arya, who nodded in acknowledgment. He replaced his hand over his ear.

Without warning or preamble, the sound stopped.

Eragon waited for a moment, then slowly lowered his hands, for once wishing that his hearing were not quite so sensitive.

Just as he did, the crack jerked open wider—spreading until it was several feet across—and raced down the wall of the keep. Like a bolt of lightning, the crack struck and shattered the keystone above the doors to the building, showering the floor below with pebbles. The whole castle groaned, and from the damaged window to the broken keystone, the front of the keep began to lean outward.

"Run!" Eragon shouted at the Varden, though the men were already scattering to either side of the courtyard, desperate to get out from under the precarious wall. Eragon took a single step forward, every muscle in his body tense as he searched for a glimpse of Roran somewhere in the throng of warriors.

At last Eragon spotted him, trapped behind the last group of men by the doorway, bellowing madly at them, his words lost in the commotion. Then the wall shifted and dropped several inches—leaning even farther away from the rest of the building—pelting Roran with rocks, knocking him off balance, and forcing him to stumble backward under the overhang of the doorway.

As Roran straightened from a crouch, his eyes met Eragon's, and in his gaze Eragon saw a flash of fear and helplessness, quickly followed by resignation, as if Roran knew that, no matter how fast he ran, he could not possibly reach safety in time.

A wry smile touched Roran's lips.

And the wall fell.

HAMMERFALL

"**N**o!" shouted Eragon as the wall of the keep tumbled down with a thunderous crash, burying Roran and five other men beneath a mound of stone twenty feet high and flooding the courtyard with a dark cloud of dust.

Eragon's shout was so loud, his voice broke, and slick, copper-tasting blood coated the back of his throat. He inhaled and doubled over, coughing.

"Vaetna," he gasped, and waved his hand. With a sound like rustling silk, the thick gray dust parted, leaving the center of the courtyard clear. Concerned as he was for Roran, Eragon barely noticed the strength the spell took from him.

"No, no, no, no," Eragon muttered. *He can't be dead. He can't, he can't, he can't.* . . . As if repetition might make it true, Eragon continued to think the phrase. But with every repetition, it became less a statement of fact or hope and more a prayer to the world at large.

Before him, Arya and the other warriors of the Varden stood coughing and rubbing their eyes with the palms of their hands. Many were hunched over, as if expecting a blow; others gaped at the front of the damaged keep. The rubble from the building spilled into the middle of the courtyard, obscuring the mosaic. Two and a half rooms on the second story of the keep, and one on the third— the room where the magician had expired so violently—stood exposed to the elements. The chambers and their furnishings seemed dirty and rather shabby in the full light of the sun. Within, a half-dozen soldiers armed with crossbows were scrambling back from the drop they now found themselves standing by. With much pushing and shoving, they hurried through the doors at the far ends of the rooms and vanished into the depths of the keep.

Eragon tried to guess the weight of a block in the pile of rubble; it must have been many hundreds of pounds. If he, Saphira, and the elves all worked together, he was sure that they could shift the stones with magic, but the effort would leave them weak and vulnerable. Moreover, it would take an impractically long time. For a moment, Eragon thought of Glaedr—the golden dragon was more than strong enough to lift the whole pile at once—but haste was of the essence, and Glaedr's Eldunarí would take too long to retrieve. In any case, Eragon knew that he might not even be able to convince Glaedr to talk with him, much less to help rescue Roran and the other men.

Then Eragon pictured Roran as he had appeared just before the deluge of stones and dust had hidden him from view, standing underneath the eaves of the doorway to the keep, and with a start, he realized what to do.

"Saphira, help them!" Eragon shouted as he cast aside his shield and bounded forward.

Behind him, he heard Arya say something in the ancient language—a short phrase that might have been "Hide this!" Then she had caught up to him, running with her sword in hand, ready to fight.

When he reached the base of the rubble, Eragon leaped as high as he could. He alit with a single foot upon the slanting face of a block and then jumped again, bounding from point to point like a mountain goat scaling the side of a gorge. He hated to risk disturbing the blocks, but climbing the pile was the fastest way to reach his destination.

With one last lunge, Eragon cleared the edge of the second story, then raced across the room. He shoved the door in front of him with such force that he broke the latch and hinges and sent the door flying into the wall of the corridor beyond, splitting the heavy oak planks.

Eragon sprinted down the corridor. His footsteps and his breathing sounded strangely muted to him, as if his ears were filled with water.

He slowed as he drew near an open doorway. Through it, he saw a study with five armed men pointing at a map and arguing. None of them noticed Eragon.

He kept running.

He sped around a corner and collided with a soldier walking in the opposite direction. Eragon's vision flashed red and yellow as his forehead struck the rim of the man's shield. He clung to the soldier, and the two of them staggered back and forth across the corridor like a pair of drunk dancers.

The soldier uttered an oath as he struggled to regain his balance. "What's wrong with you, you thrice-blasted—" he said, and then he saw Eragon's face, and his eyes widened. "You!"

Eragon balled his right hand and punched the man in the belly, directly underneath his rib cage. The blow lifted the man off his feet and smashed him into the ceiling. "Me," Eragon agreed as the man dropped to the floor, lifeless.

Eragon continued down the corridor. His already rapid pulse seemed to have doubled since he entered the keep; he felt as if his heart were about to burst out of his chest.

Where is it? he thought, frantic as he glanced through yet another doorway and saw nothing but an empty room.

At last, at the end of a dingy side passage, he caught sight of a winding staircase. He took the stairs five at a time, heedless of his own safety as he descended toward the first story, pausing only to push a startled archer out of his way.

The stairs ended, and he emerged into a high-vaulted chamber reminiscent of the cathedral in Dras-Leona. He spun around, gathering quick impressions: shields and arms and red pennants hung on the walls; narrow windows close under the ceiling; torches mounted in wrought-iron brackets; empty fireplaces; long, dark trestle tables stacked along both sides of the hall; and a dais at the head of the room, where a robed and bearded man stood before a high-backed chair. Eragon was in the main hall of the castle. To his right, between him and the doors that led to the entrance of the keep, was a contingent of fifty or more soldiers. The gold thread in their tunics glittered as they stirred with surprise.

"Kill him!" the robed man ordered, sounding more frightened than lordly. "Whosoever kills him shall have a third of my treasure! So I promise!"

A terrible frustration welled up inside Eragon at being delayed once again. He tore his sword from its scabbard, lifted it over his head, and shouted:

"Brisingr!"

With a rush of air, a cocoon of wraithlike blue flames sprang into existence around the blade, running up toward the tip. The heat from the fire warmed Eragon's hand, arm, and the side of his face.

Then Eragon lowered his gaze to the soldiers. "Move," he growled.

The soldiers hesitated a moment more, then turned and fled.

Eragon charged forward, ignoring the panicked laggards within reach of his burning sword. One man tripped and fell before him; Eragon jumped completely over the soldier, not even touching the tassel on his helm.

The wind from Eragon's passage tore at the flames on the blade, stretching them out behind the sword like the mane of a galloping horse.

Hunching his shoulders, Eragon bulled past the double doors that guarded the entrance to the main hall. He dashed through a long, wide chamber edged with rooms full of soldiers—as well as gears, pulleys, and other mechanisms used for raising and lowering the gates of the keep—and then ran full tilt into the portcullis that blocked the way to where Roran had been standing when the keep wall collapsed.

The iron grating bent as Eragon slammed into it, but not enough to break the metal.

He staggered back a step.

He again channeled energy stored within the diamonds of his belt—the belt of Beloth the Wise—and into Brisingr, emptying the gemstones of their precious store as he stoked the sword's fire to an almost unbearable intensity. A wordless shout escaped him as he drew back his arm and struck at the portcullis. Orange and yellow sparks sprayed him, pitting his gloves and tunic and stinging his exposed flesh. A drop of molten iron fell sizzling onto the tip of his boot. With a twitch of his ankle, he shook it off.

Three cuts he made, and a man-sized section of the portcullis fell inward. The severed ends of the grating glowed white-hot, lighting the area with their soft radiance.

Eragon allowed the flames rising from Brisingr to die out as he proceeded through the opening he had created.

First to the left, then to the right, and then to the left again he ran as the passage alternated directions, the convoluted path designed to slow the advance of troops if they managed to gain access to the keep.

When he rounded the last corner, Eragon saw his destination: the debris-choked vestibule. Even with his elflike vision, he could make out only the largest shapes in the darkness, for the falling stones had extinguished the torches on the walls. He heard an odd huffing and scuffling, as if some sort of clumsy beast were rooting through the rubble.

"Naina," said Eragon.

A directionless blue light illuminated the space. And there before him, covered in dirt, blood, ash, and sweat, with his teeth bared in a fearsome snarl, appeared Roran, grappling with a soldier over the corpses of two others.

The soldier winced at the sudden brightness, and Roran took advantage of the man's distraction to twist and push him to his knees, whereupon he grabbed the soldier's dagger from his belt and drove it up under the corner of his jaw.

The soldier kicked twice and then was still.

Panting for breath, Roran rose from the body, blood dripping from his fingers. He looked over at Eragon with a curiously glazed expression.

"About time you—" he said, and then his eyes rolled back into his head as he fainted.

SHADOWS ON THE HORIZON

In order to catch Roran before he struck the floor, Eragon had to drop Brisingr, which he was reluctant to do. Nevertheless, he opened his hand, and the sword clattered against the stones even as Roran's weight settled into his arms.

"Is he badly hurt?" Arya asked.

Eragon flinched, surprised to find her and Blödhgarm standing next to him. "I don't think so." He patted Roran's cheeks several times, smearing the dust on his skin. In the flat, ice-blue glare of Eragon's spell, Roran appeared gaunt, his eyes surrounded by bruised shadows, and his lips a purplish color, as if stained with the juice from berries. "Come on, wake up."

After a few seconds, Roran's eyelids twitched; then he opened them and looked at Eragon, obviously confused. Relief washed over Eragon, so strong he could taste it. "You blacked out for a moment," he explained.

"Ah."

He's alive! Eragon said to Saphira, risking a brief moment of contact.

Her pleasure was obvious. *Good. I will stay here and help the elves move the stones away from the building. If you need me, shout, and I'll find a way to reach you.*

Roran's mail tinkled as Eragon helped him onto his feet. "What of the others?" Eragon asked, and gestured toward the mound of rubble.

Roran shook his head.

"Are you sure?"

"No one could have survived under there. I only escaped because . . . because I was partially sheltered by the eaves."

"And you? You're all right?" Eragon asked.

"What?" Roran frowned, seeming distracted, as if the thought had not even occurred to him. "I'm fine. . . . Wrist might be broken. It's not bad."

Eragon cast a meaningful glance at Blödhgarm. The elf's features tightened with a faint display of displeasure, but he went over to Roran and, in a smooth voice, said, "If I may. . . ." He extended a hand toward Roran's injured arm.

While Blödhgarm labored over Roran, Eragon picked up Brisingr, then stood guard with Arya at the entrance in case any soldiers were so foolhardy as to launch an attack.

"There, all done," Blödhgarm said. He moved away from Roran, who rolled his wrist in a circle, testing the joint.

Satisfied, Roran thanked Blödhgarm, then lowered his hand and cast about the rubble-strewn floor until he found his hammer. He readjusted the position of his armor and looked out the entrance. "I've about had my fill of this Lord Bradburn," he said in a deceptively calm tone. "He has held his seat overlong, I think, and ought to be relieved of his responsibilities. Wouldn't you agree, Arya?"

"I would," she said.

"Well then, let's find the soft-bellied old fool; I would give him a few gentle taps from my hammer in memory of everyone we have lost today."

"He was in the main hall a few minutes ago," Eragon said, "but I doubt he stayed to await our return."

Roran nodded. "Then we'll have to hunt him down." And with that, he strode forward.

Eragon extinguished his illuminating spell and hurried after his cousin, holding Brisingr at the ready. Arya and Blödhgarm stayed as close beside him as the convoluted passageway would allow.

The chamber that the passageway led to was abandoned, as was the main hall of the castle, where the only evidence of the dozens of soldiers and officials who had populated it was a helmet that lay on the floor, rocking back and forth in ever-decreasing arcs.

Eragon and Roran ran past the marble dais, Eragon restricting his speed so as not to leave Roran behind. They kicked down a door just to the left of the platform and rushed up the stairs beyond.

At each story, they paused so that Blödhgarm could search with his mind for any trace of Lord Bradburn and his retinue, but he found none.

As they reached the third level, Eragon heard a stampede of footsteps and saw a thicket of jabbing spears fill the curved archway in front of Roran. The spears cut Roran on the cheek and on his right thigh, coating his knee with blood. He bellowed like a wounded bear and rammed into the spears with his shield, trying to push his way up the last few steps and out of the stairwell. Men shouted frantically.

Behind Roran, Eragon switched Brisingr to his left hand, then reached around his cousin, grabbed one of the spears by the haft, and yanked it out of the grip of whoever was holding it. He flipped the spear around and threw it into the center of the men packed in the archway. Someone screamed, and a gap appeared in the wall of bodies. Eragon repeated the process, and his throws soon reduced the number of soldiers enough that, step by step, Roran was able to force the mass of men back.

As soon as Roran won clear of the stairs, the twelve remaining soldiers scattered across a wide landing fringed with balustrades, each man seeking room to swing his weapon without obstruction. Roran bellowed again and leaped after the nearest soldier. He parried the man's sword, then stepped past his guard and struck the man on his helm, which rang like an iron pot.

Eragon sprinted across the landing and tackled a pair of soldiers who were standing close together. He knocked them to the ground, then dispatched each of them with a single thrust of Brisingr. An ax hurtled toward him, whirling end over end. He ducked and pushed a man over a balustrade before engaging two others who were trying to disembowel him with billed pikes.

Then Arya and Blödhgarm were moving among the men, silent and deadly, the elves' inherent grace making the violence appear more like an artfully staged performance than the sordid struggle most fights were.

In a rush of clanging metal, broken bones, and severed limbs, the four of them killed the rest of the soldiers. As always, the combat exhilarated Eragon; it felt to him like being shocked with a bucket of cold water, and it left him with a sense of clarity unequaled by any other activity.

Roran bent over and rested his hands on his knees, gasping for air as if he had just finished a race.

"Shall I?" asked Eragon, gesturing at the cuts on Roran's face and thigh.

Roran tested his weight on the wounded leg a few times. "I can wait. Let's find Bradburn first."

Eragon took the lead as they filed back into the stairwell and resumed their climb. At last, after another five minutes of searching, they found Lord Bradburn barricaded within the highest room of the keep's westernmost tower. With a series of spells, Eragon, Arya, and Blödhgarm disassembled the doors and the tower of furniture piled behind them. As they and Roran entered the chambers, the high-ranking retainers and castle guards who had gathered in front of Lord Bradburn blanched, and many began to shake. To Eragon's relief, he only had to kill three of the guards before the rest of the group placed their weapons and shields on the floor in surrender.

Then Arya marched over to Lord Bradburn, who had remained silent throughout, and said, "Now, will you order your forces to stand down? Only a few remain, but you can still save their lives."

"I would not even if I could," said Bradburn in a voice of such hate and sneering derision, Eragon almost struck him. "You'll have no concessions from me, elf. I'll not give up my men to filthy, unnatural creatures such as you. Death would be preferable. And do not think you can beguile me with honeyed words. I know of your alliance with the Urgals, and I would sooner trust a snake than a person who breaks bread with those monsters."

Arya nodded and placed her hand over Bradburn's face. She closed her eyes, and for a time, both she and Bradburn were motionless. Eragon reached out with his mind, and he felt the battle of wills that was raging between them as Arya worked her way past Bradburn's defenses and into his consciousness. It took a minute, but at last she gained control of the man's mind, whereupon she set about calling up and examining his memories until she discovered the nature of his wards.

Then she spoke in the ancient language and cast a complex spell designed to circumvent those wards and to put Bradburn to sleep. When she finished, Bradburn's eyes closed and, with a sigh, he collapsed into her arms.

"She killed him!" shouted one of the guards, and cries of fear and outrage spread among the men.

As Eragon attempted to convince them otherwise, he heard one of the Varden's trumpets being winded far off in the distance. Soon another trumpet sounded, this one much closer, then another, and then he caught snatches of what he would have sworn were faint, scattered cheers rising from the courtyard below.

Puzzled, he exchanged glances with Arya; then they turned in a circle, looking out each of the windows set within the walls of the chamber.

To the west and south lay Belatona. It was a large, prosperous city, one of the largest in the Empire. Close to the castle, the buildings were imposing structures made of stone, with pitched roofs and oriel windows, while farther away they were constructed of wood and plaster. Several of the half-timbered buildings had caught fire during the fighting. The smoke filled the air with a layer of brown haze that stung eyes and throats.

To the southwest, a mile beyond the city, was the Varden's camp: long rows of gray woolen tents ringed by stake-lined trenches, a few brightly colored pavilions sporting flags and pennants, and stretched out on the bare ground, hundreds of wounded men. The healers' tents were already filled to capacity.

To the north, past the docks and warehouses, was Leona Lake, a vast expanse of water dotted with the occasional whitecap.

Above, the wall of black clouds that was advancing from the west loomed high over the city, threatening to envelop it within the folds of rain that fell skirtlike from its underside. Blue light flickered here and there in the depths of the storm, and thunder rumbled like an angry beast.

But nowhere did Eragon see an explanation for the commotion that had attracted his attention.

He and Arya hurried over to the window directly above the courtyard. Saphira and the men and elves working with her had just finished clearing away the stones in front of the keep. Eragon whistled, and when Saphira looked up, he waved. Her long jaws parted in a toothy grin, and she blew a streamer of smoke toward him.

"Ho! What news?" Eragon shouted.

One of the Varden standing on the castle walls raised an arm and pointed eastward. "Shadeslayer! Look! The werecats are coming! The werecats are coming!"

A cold tingle crawled down Eragon's spine. He followed the line of the man's arm eastward, and this time he saw a host of small, shadowy figures emerging from a fold in the land several miles away, on the other side of the Jiet River. Some of the figures went on four legs and some on two, but they were too far away for him to be sure if they were werecats.

"Could it be?" asked Arya, sounding amazed.

"I don't know. . . . Whatever they are, we'll find out soon enough."

KING CAT

Eragon stood on the dais in the main hall of the keep, directly to the right of Lord Bradburn's throne, his left hand on the pommel of Brisingr, which was sheathed. On the other side of the throne stood Jörmundur—senior commander of the Varden—holding his helmet in the crook of his arm. The hair at his temples was streaked with gray; the rest was brown, and all of it was pulled back into a long braid. His lean face bore the studiously blank expression of a person who had extensive experience waiting on others. Eragon noticed a thin line of red running along the underside of Jörmundur's right bracer, but Jörmundur showed no sign of pain.

Between them sat their leader, Nasuada, resplendent in a dress of green and yellow, which she had donned just moments before, exchanging the raiment of war for garb more suited to the practice of statecraft. She too had been marked during the fighting, as was evidenced by the linen bandage wrapped around her left hand.

In a low voice that only Eragon and Jörmundur could hear, Nasuada said, "If we can but gain their support . . ."

"What will they want in return, though?" asked Jörmundur. "Our coffers are near empty, and our future uncertain."

Her lips barely moving, she said, "Perhaps they wish nothing more of us than a chance to strike back at Galbatorix." She paused. "But if not, we shall have to find means other than gold to persuade them to join our ranks."

"You could offer them barrels of cream," said Eragon, which elicited a chortle from Jörmundur and a soft laugh from Nasuada.

Their murmured conversation came to an end as three trumpets sounded outside the main hall. Then a flaxen-haired page dressed in a tunic stitched with the Varden's standard—a white dragon holding a rose above a sword pointing downward on a purple field—marched through the open doorway at the far end of the hall, struck the floor with his ceremonial staff, and, in a thin, warbling voice, announced, "His Most Exalted Royal Highness, Grimrr Halfpaw, King of the Werecats, Lord of the Lonely Places, Ruler of the Night Reaches, and He Who Walks Alone."

A strange title, that: He Who Walks Alone, Eragon observed to Saphira.

But well deserved, I would guess, she replied, and he could sense her amusement, even though he could not see her where she lay coiled in the castle keep.

The page stepped aside, and through the doorway strode Grimrr Halfpaw in the shape of a human, trailed by four other werecats, who padded close behind him on large, shaggy paws. The four resembled Solembum, the one other werecat Eragon had seen in the guise of an animal: heavy-shouldered and long-limbed, with short, dark ruffs upon their necks and withers; tasseled ears; and black-tipped tails, which they waved gracefully from side to side.

Grimrr Halfpaw, however, looked unlike any person or creature Eragon had ever seen. At roughly four feet tall, he was the same height as a dwarf, but no one could have mistaken him for a dwarf, or even for a human. He had a small pointed chin, wide cheekbones, and, underneath upswept brows, slanted green eyes fringed with winglike eyelashes. His ragged black hair hung low over his forehead, while on the sides and back it fell to his shoulders, where it lay smooth and lustrous, much like the manes of his companions. His age was impossible for Eragon to guess.

The only clothes Grimrr wore were a rough leather vest and a rabbit-skin loincloth. The skulls of a dozen or so animals—birds, mice, and other small game—were tied to the front of the vest, and they rattled against one another as he moved. A sheathed dagger protruded at an angle from under the belt of his loincloth. Numerous scars, thin and white, marked his nut-brown skin, like scratches on a well-used table. And, as his name indicated, he was missing two fingers on his left hand; they looked to have been bitten off.

Despite the delicacy of his features, there was no doubt that Grimrr was male, given the hard, sinewy muscles of his arms and chest, the narrowness of his hips, and the coiled power of his stride as he sauntered down the length of the hall toward Nasuada.

None of the werecats seemed to notice the people lined up on either side of their path watching them until Grimrr came level with the herbalist Angela, who stood next to Roran, knitting a striped tube sock with six needles.

Grimrr's eyes narrowed as he beheld the herbalist, and his hair rippled and spiked, as did that of his four guards. His lips drew back to reveal a pair of curved white fangs, and to Eragon's astonishment, he uttered a short, loud hiss.

Angela looked up from the sock, her expression languid and insolent. *"Cheep cheep,"* she said.

For a moment, Eragon thought the werecat was going to attack her. A dark flush mottled Grimrr's neck and face, his nostrils flared, and he snarled silently at her. The other werecats settled into low crouches, ready to pounce, their ears pressed flat against their heads.

Throughout the hall, Eragon heard the slither of blades being partially drawn from their scabbards.

Grimrr hissed once more, then turned away from the herbalist and continued walking. As the last werecat in line passed Angela, he lifted a paw and took a surreptitious swipe at the strand of yarn that drooped from Angela's needles, just like a playful house cat might.

Saphira's bewilderment was equal to Eragon's own. *Cheep cheep?* she asked.

He shrugged, forgetting that she could not see him. *Who knows why Angela does or says anything?*

At last Grimrr arrived before Nasuada. He inclined his head ever so slightly, displaying with his bearing the supreme confidence, even arrogance, that was the sole province of cats, dragons, and certain highborn women.

"Lady Nasuada," he said. His voice was surprisingly deep, more akin to the low, coughing roar of a wildcat than the high-pitched tones of the boy he resembled.

Nasuada inclined her head in turn. "King Halfpaw. You are most welcome to the Varden, you and all your race. I must apologize for the absence of our ally, King Orrin of Surda; he could not be here to greet you, as he wished, for he and his horsemen are even now busy defending our westward flank from a contingent of Galbatorix's troops."

"Of course, Lady Nasuada," said Grimrr. His sharp teeth flashed as he spoke. "You must never turn your back on your enemies."

"Even so . . . And to what do we owe the unexpected pleasure of this visit, Your Highness? Werecats have always been noted for their secrecy and their solitude, and for remaining apart from the conflicts of the age, especially since the fall of the Riders. One might even say that your kind has become more myth than fact over the past century. Why, then, do you now choose to reveal yourselves?"

Grimrr lifted his right arm and pointed at Eragon with a crooked finger topped by a clawlike nail.

"Because of him," growled the werecat. "One does not attack another hunter until he has shown his weakness, and Galbatorix has shown his: he will not kill Eragon Shadeslayer or Saphira Bjartskular. Long have we waited for this opportunity, and seize it we will. Galbatorix will learn to fear and hate us, and at the last, he will realize the extent of his mistake and know that we were the ones responsible for his undoing. And how sweet that revenge will taste, as sweet as the marrow of a tender young boar.

"Time has come, human, for every race, even werecats, to stand together and prove to Galbatorix that he has not broken our will to fight. We would join your army, Lady Nasuada, as free allies, and help you achieve this."

What Nasuada was thinking, Eragon could not tell, but he and Saphira were impressed by the werecat's speech.

After a brief pause, Nasuada said, "Your words fall most pleasantly upon my ears, Your Highness. But before I can accept your offer, there are answers I must have of you, if you are willing."

With an air of unshakable indifference, Grimrr waved a hand. "I am."

"Your race has been *so* secretive and *so* elusive, I must confess, I had not heard tell of Your Highness until this very day. As a point of fact, I did not even know that your race *had* a ruler."

"I am not a king like your kings," said Grimrr. "Werecats prefer to walk alone, but even we must choose a leader when to war we go."

"I see. Do you speak for your whole race, then, or only for those who travel with you?"

Grimrr's chest swelled, and his expression became, if possible, even more self-satisfied. "I speak for all of my kind, Lady Nasuada," he purred. "Every able-bodied werecat in Alagaësia, save those who are nursing, has come here to fight. There are few of us, but none can equal our ferocity in battle. And I can also command the one-shapes, although I cannot speak for them, for they are as dumb as other animals. Still, they will do what we ask of them."

"One-shapes?" Nasuada inquired.

"Those you know as cats. Those who cannot change their skins, as we do."

"And you command their loyalty?"

"Aye. They admire us . . . as is only natural."

If what he says is true, Eragon commented to Saphira, *the werecats could prove to be incredibly valuable.*

Then Nasuada said, "And what is it you desire of us in exchange for your assistance, King Halfpaw?" She glanced at Eragon and smiled, then added, "We can offer you as much cream as you want, but beyond that, our resources are limited. If your warriors expect to be paid for their troubles, I fear they will be sorely disappointed."

"Cream is for kittens, and gold holds no interest for us," said Grimrr. As he spoke, he lifted his right hand and inspected his nails with a heavy-lidded gaze. "Our terms are thus: Each of us will be

30

given a dagger to fight with, if we do not already have one. Each of us shall have two suits of armor made to fit, one for when on two legs we stand, and one for when on four. We need no other equipment than that—no tents, no blankets, no plates, no spoons. Each of us will be promised a single duck, grouse, chicken, or similar bird per day, and every second day, a bowl of freshly chopped liver. Even if we do not choose to eat it, the food will be set aside for us. Also, should you win this war, then whoever becomes your next king or queen—and all who claim that title thereafter—will keep a padded cushion next to their throne, in a place of honor, for one of us to sit on, if we so wish."

"You bargain like a dwarven lawgiver," said Nasuada in a dry tone. She leaned over to Jörmundur, and Eragon heard her whisper, "Do we have enough liver to feed them all?"

"I think so," Jörmundur replied in an equally hushed voice. "But it depends on the size of the bowl."

Nasuada straightened in her seat. "Two sets of armor is one too many, King Halfpaw. Your warriors will have to decide whether they want to fight as cats or as humans and then abide by the decision. I cannot afford to outfit them for both."

If Grimrr had had a tail, Eragon was sure it would have twitched back and forth. As it was, the werecat merely shifted his position. "Very well, Lady Nasuada."

"There is one more thing. Galbatorix has spies and killers hidden everywhere. Therefore, as a condition of joining the Varden, you must consent to allow one of our spellcasters to examine your memories, so we may assure ourselves that Galbatorix has no claim on you."

Grimrr sniffed. "You would be foolish not to. If anyone is brave enough to read our thoughts, let them. But not her"—and he twisted to point at Angela. "Never her."

Nasuada hesitated, and Eragon could see that she wanted to ask why but restrained herself. "So be it. I will send for magicians at once, that we may settle this matter without delay. Depending on what they find—and it will be nothing untoward, I'm sure—I am honored to form an alliance between you and the Varden, King Halfpaw."

At her words, all of the humans in the hall broke out cheering and began to clap, including Angela. Even the elves appeared pleased.

The werecats, however, did not react, except to tilt their ears backward in annoyance at the noise.

AFTERMATH

Eragon groaned and leaned back against Saphira. Bracing his hands on his knees, he slid down over her bumpy scales until he was sitting on the ground, then stretched out his legs in front of him.

"I'm hungry!" he exclaimed.

He and Saphira were in the courtyard of the castle, away from the men who were laboring to clear it—piling stones and bodies alike into carts—and from the people streaming in and out of the damaged building, many of whom had been present at Nasuada's audience with King Halfpaw and were now leaving to attend to other duties. Blödhgarm and four elves stood nearby, watching for danger.

"Oi!" someone shouted.

Eragon looked up to see Roran walking toward him from the keep. Angela trailed a few steps behind, yarn flapping in the air as she half ran to keep up with his longer stride.

"Where are you off to now?" Eragon asked as Roran stopped before him.

"To help secure the city and organize the prisoners."

"Ah . . ." Eragon's gaze wondered across the busy courtyard before returning to Roran's bruised face. "You fought well."

"You too."

Eragon shifted his attention to Angela, who was once again knitting, her fingers moving so quickly, he could not follow what she was doing. *"Cheep cheep?"* he asked.

An impish expression overtook her face, and she shook her head, her voluminous curls bouncing. "A story for another time."

Eragon accepted her evasion without complaint; he had not expected her to explain herself. She rarely did.

"And you," said Roran, "where are you going?"

We're going to get some food, said Saphira, and nudged Eragon with her snout, her breath warm on him as she exhaled.

Roran nodded. "That sounds best. I'll see you at camp this evening, then." As he turned to leave, he added, "Give my love to Katrina."

Angela tucked her knitting into a quilted bag that hung at her waist. "I guess I'll be off as well. I have a potion brewing in my tent that I must attend to, and there's a certain werecat I want to track down."

"Grimrr?"

"No, no—an old friend of mine: Solembum's mother. If she's still alive, that is. I hope she is." She raised her hand to her brow, thumb and forefinger touching in a circle, and, in an overly cheerful voice, said, "Be seeing you!" And with that, she sailed off.

On my back, said Saphira, and rose to her feet, leaving Eragon without support.

He climbed into the saddle at the base of her neck, and Saphira unfolded her massive wings with the soft, dry sound of skin sliding over skin. The motion created a gust of near-silent wind that spread out like ripples in a pond. Throughout the courtyard, people paused to look at her.

As Saphira lifted her wings overhead, Eragon could see the web of purplish veins that pulsed therein, each one becoming a hollow worm track as the flow of blood subsided between the beats of her mighty heart.

Then with a surge and a jolt, the world tilted crazily around Eragon as Saphira jumped from the courtyard to the top of the castle wall, where she balanced for a moment on the merlons, the stones cracking between the points of her claws. He grabbed the neck spike in front of him to steady himself.

The world tilted again as Saphira launched herself off the wall.

An acrid taste and smell assaulted Eragon, and his eyes smarted as Saphira passed through the thick layer of smoke that hung over Belatona like a blanket of hurt, anger, and sorrow.

Saphira flapped twice, hard, and then they emerged from the smoke into the sunshine and soared over the fire-dotted streets of the city. Stilling her wings, Saphira glided in circles, allowing the warm air from below to lift her ever higher.

Tired as he was, Eragon savored the magnificence of the view: the growling storm that was about to swallow the whole of Belatona glowed white and brilliant along its leading edge, while farther away, the thunderhead wallowed in inky shadows that betrayed nothing of their contents, save when bolts of lightning shot through them. Elsewhere the gleaming lake and the hundreds of small, verdant farms that were scattered across the landscape also commanded his attention, but none were so impressive as the mountain of clouds.

As always, Eragon felt privileged to be able to look upon the world from so high above, for he was aware of how few people had ever had the chance to fly on a dragon.

With a slight shift of her wings, Saphira began to glide down toward the rows of gray tents that composed the Varden's camp.

A strong wind sprang up from the west, heralding the imminent arrival of the storm. Eragon hunched over and wrapped his hands even more securely around the spike on her neck. He saw glossy ripples race across the fields below as the stalks bent under the force of the rising gale. The shifting grass reminded him of the fur of a great green beast.

A horse screamed as Saphira swept over the rows of tents to the clearing that was reserved for her. Eragon half stood in the saddle as Saphira flared her wings and slowed to a near standstill over the torn earth. The impact as she struck knocked Eragon forward.

Sorry, she said. *I tried to land as softly as I could.*

I know.

Even as he dismounted, Eragon saw Katrina hurrying toward him. Her long auburn hair swirled about her face as she walked across the clearing, and the press of the wind exposed the bulge of her growing belly through the layers of her dress.

"What news?" she called, worry etched into every line of her face.

"You heard about the werecats . . . ?"

She nodded.

"There's no real news other than that. Roran's fine; he said to give you his love."

Her expression softened, but her worry did not entirely disappear. "He's all right, then?" She motioned toward the ring she wore on the third finger of her left hand, one of the two rings Eragon had enchanted for her and Roran so they might know if one or the other was in danger. "I thought I felt something, about an hour ago, and I was afraid that . . ."

Eragon shook his head. "Roran can tell you about it. He got a few nicks and bruises, but other than that, he's fine. Scared me half to death, though."

Katrina's look of concern intensified. Then, with visible struggle, she smiled. "At least you're safe. Both of you."

They parted, and Eragon and Saphira made their way to one of the mess tents close to the Varden's cookfires. There they gorged themselves on meat and mead while the wind howled around them and bursts of rain pummeled the sides of the flapping tent.

As Eragon bit into a slab of roast pork belly, Saphira said, *Is it good? Is it scrumptious?*

"Mmm," said Eragon, rivulets of juice running down his chin.

MEMORIES OF THE DEAD

"**G**albatorix is mad and therefore unpredictable, but he also has gaps in his reasoning that an ordinary person would not. If you can find those, Eragon, then perhaps you and Saphira can defeat him."

Brom lowered his pipe, his face grave. "I hope you do. My greatest desire, Eragon, is that you and Saphira will live long and fruitful lives, free from fear of Galbatorix and the Empire. I wish that I could protect you from all of the dangers that threaten you, but alas, that is not within my ability. All I can do is give you my advice and teach you what I can now while I am still here. . . . My son. Whatever happens to you, know that I love you, and so did your mother. May the stars watch over you, Eragon Bromsson."

Eragon opened his eyes as the memory faded. Above him, the ceiling of the tent sagged inward, as loose as an empty waterskin, after the battering it had received during the now-departed storm. A drop of water fell from the belly of a fold, struck his right thigh, and soaked through his leggings, chilling the skin beneath. He knew he would have to go tighten up the tent's support ropes, but he was reluctant to move from the cot.

And Brom never said anything to you about Murtagh? He never told you that Murtagh and I were half brothers?

Saphira, who was curled up outside the tent, said, Asking again won't change my answer.

Why wouldn't he, though? Why didn't he? He must have known about Murtagh. He couldn't not have.

Saphira's response was slow to come. Brom's reasons were ever his own, but if I had to guess, I imagine he thought it more important to tell you how he cared for you, and to give you what advice he could, than to spend his time talking about Murtagh.

He could have warned me, though! Just a few words would have sufficed.

I cannot say for certain what drove him, Eragon. You have to accept that there are some questions you will never be able to answer about Brom. Trust in his love for you, and do not allow such concerns to disturb you.

Eragon stared down his chest at his thumbs. He placed them side by side, to better compare them. His left thumb had more wrinkles on its second joint than did his right, while his right had a small, ragged scar that he could not remember getting, although it must have happened since the Agaetí Blödhren, the Blood-oath Celebration.

Thank you, he said to Saphira. Through her, he had watched and listened to Brom's message three times since the fall of Feinster, and each time he had noticed some detail of Brom's speech or movement that had previously escaped him. The experience comforted and satisfied him, for it fulfilled a desire that had plagued him his entire life: to know the name of his father and to know that his father cared for him.

Saphira acknowledged his thanks with a warm glow of affection.

Though Eragon had eaten and then rested for perhaps an hour, his weariness had not entirely abated. Nor had he expected it to. He knew from experience that it could take weeks to fully recover from the debilitating effects of a long, drawn-out battle. As the Varden approached Urû'baen, he and everyone else in Nasuada's army would have less and less time to recover before each new confrontation. The war would wear them down until they were bloody, battered, and barely able to fight, at which point they would still have to face Galbatorix, who would have been waiting for them in ease and comfort.

He tried not to think about it too much.

Another drop of water struck his leg, cold and hard. Irritated, he swung his legs off the edge of the cot and sat upright, then went over to the bare patch of dirt in one corner and knelt next to it.

"Deloi sharjalví!" he said, as well as several other phrases in the ancient language that were necessary to disarm the traps he had set the previous day.

The dirt began to seethe like water coming to a boil, and rising out of the churning fountain of rocks, insects, and worms, there emerged an ironbound chest a foot and a half in length. Reaching out, Eragon took hold of the chest and released his spell. The ground grew calm once more.

He set the chest on the now-solid dirt. "Ládrin," he whispered, and waved his hand past the lock with no keyhole that secured the hasp. It popped open with a *click*.

A faint golden glow filled the tent as he lifted the lid of the chest. Nestled securely within the velvet-lined interior lay Glaedr's Eldunarí, the dragon's heart of hearts. The large, jewel-like stone glittered darkly, like a dying ember. Eragon cupped the Eldunarí between his hands, the irregular, sharp-edged facets warm against his palms, and stared into its pulsing depths. A galaxy of tiny stars swirled within the center of the stone, although their movement had slowed and there seemed to be far fewer than when Eragon had first beheld the stone in Ellesméra, when Glaedr had discharged it from his body and into Eragon and Saphira's care.

As always, the sight fascinated Eragon; he could have sat watching the ever-changing pattern for days.

We should try again, said Saphira, and he agreed.

Together they reached out with their minds toward the distant lights, toward the sea of stars that represented Glaedr's consciousness. Through cold and darkness they sailed, then heat and despair and indifference so vast and so great, it sapped their will to do anything other than to stop and weep.

Glaedr . . . Elda, they cried over and over, but there was no answer, no shifting of the indifference.

At last they withdrew, unable to withstand the crushing weight of Glaedr's misery any longer.

As he returned to himself, Eragon became aware of someone knocking on the front pole of his tent, and then he heard Arya say, "Eragon? May I enter?"

He sniffed and blinked to clear his eyes. "Of course."

The dim gray light from the cloudy sky fell upon him as Arya pushed aside the entrance flap. He felt a sudden pang as his eyes met hers—green, slanted, and unreadable—and an ache of longing filled him.

"Has there been any change?" she asked, and came to kneel by him. Instead of armor, she was wearing the same black leather shirt, trousers, and thin-soled boots as when he had rescued her in Gil'ead. Her hair was damp from washing and hung down her back in long, heavy ropes. The scent of crushed pine needles attended her, as it so often did, and it occurred to Eragon to wonder whether she used a spell to create the aroma or if that was how she smelled naturally. He would have liked to ask her, but he did not dare.

In answer to her question, he shook his head.

"May I?" She indicated Glaedr's heart of hearts.

He moved out of the way. "Please."

Arya placed her hands on either side of the Eldunarí and then closed her eyes. While she sat, he took the opportunity to study her with an openness and intensity that would have been offensive otherwise. In every aspect, she seemed the epitome of beauty, even though he knew that another might say her nose was too long, or her face too angled, or her ears too pointed, or her arms too muscled.

With a sharp intake of breath, Arya jerked her hands away from the heart of hearts, as if it had burned her. Then she bowed her head, and Eragon saw her chin quiver ever so faintly. "He is the most unhappy creature I have ever met. . . . I would we could help him. I do not think he will be able to find his way out of the darkness on his own."

"Do you think . . ." Eragon hesitated, not wanting to give voice to his suspicion, then continued: "Do you think he will go mad?"

"He may have already. If not, then he dances on the very cusp of insanity."

Sorrow came over Eragon as they both gazed at the golden stone.

When at last he was able to bring himself to speak again, he asked, "Where is the Dauthdaert?"

"Hidden within my tent even as you have hidden Glaedr's Eldunarí. I can bring it here, if you want, or I can continue to safeguard it until you need it."

"Keep it. I can't carry it around with me, or Galbatorix may learn of its existence. Besides, it would be foolish to store so many treasures in one place."

She nodded.

The ache inside of Eragon intensified. "Arya, I—" He stopped as Saphira saw one of the blacksmith Horst's sons—Albriech, he thought, although it was difficult to tell him from his brother, Baldor, because of the distortions in Saphira's vision—running toward the tent. The interruption relieved Eragon, as he had not known what he was going to say.

"Someone's coming," he announced, and closed the lid of the chest.

Loud, wet footsteps sounded in the mud outside. Then Albriech, for it was Albriech, shouted, "Eragon! Eragon!"

"What!"

"Mother's birth pains have just begun! Father sent me to tell you and to ask if you will wait with him, in case anything goes wrong and your skill with magic is needed. Please, if you can—"

Whatever else he said was lost to Eragon as he rushed to lock and bury the chest. Then he cast his cloak over his shoulders and was fumbling with the clasp when Arya touched him on the arm and said, "May I accompany you? I have some experience with this. If your people will let me, I can make the birth easier for her."

Eragon did not even pause to consider his decision. He motioned toward the entrance of the tent. "After you."

✦ ✦ ✦

WHAT IS A MAN?

The mud clung to Roran's boots each time he lifted his feet, slowing his progress and making his already-tired legs burn from the effort. It felt as if the very ground were trying to pull off his shoes. Thick as it was, the mud was also slippery. It gave way under his heels at the worst moments, just when his position was the most precarious. And it was deep, too. The constant passage of men, animals, and wagons had turned the top six inches of earth into a nigh on impassable morass. A few patches of crushed grass remained along the edges of the track—which ran straight through the Varden's camp—but Roran suspected they would soon vanish as men sought to avoid the center of the lane.

Roran made no attempt to evade the muck; he no longer cared if his clothes stayed clean. Besides, he was so exhausted, it was easier to keep plodding in the same direction than to worry about picking a path from one island of grass to the next.

As he stumbled forward, Roran thought of Belatona. Since Nasuada's audience with the werecats, he had been setting up a command post in the northwest quarter of the city and doing his best to establish control over the quadrant by assigning men to put out fires, build barricades in the streets, search houses for soldiers, and confiscate weapons. It was an immense task, and he despaired of accomplishing what was needed, fearing that the city might erupt into open battle again. *I hope those idiots can make it through the night without getting killed.*

His left side throbbed, causing him to bare his teeth and suck in his breath.

Blasted coward.

Someone had shot at him with a crossbow from the roof of a building. Only the sheerest of luck had saved him; one of his men, Mortenson, had stepped in front of him at the exact moment the attacker had fired. The bolt had punched through Mortenson from back to belly and had still retained enough force to give Roran a nasty bruise. Mortenson had died on the spot, and whoever had shot the crossbow had escaped.

Five minutes later, an explosion of some sort, possibly magical, had killed two more of his men when they entered a stable to investigate a noise.

From what Roran understood, such attacks were common throughout the city. No doubt, Galbatorix's agents were behind many of them, but the inhabitants of Belatona were also responsible—men and women who could not bear to stand by idly while an invading army seized control of their home, no matter how honorable the Varden's intentions might be. Roran could sympathize with the people who felt they had to defend their families, but at the same time, he cursed them for being so thick-skulled that they could not recognize the Varden were trying to help them, not hurt them.

He scratched at his beard while he waited for a dwarf to pull a heavily laden pony out of his way, then continued slogging forward.

As he drew near their tent, he saw Katrina standing over a tub of hot, soapy water, scrubbing a bloodstained bandage against a washboard. Her sleeves were rolled up past her elbows, her hair tied in a messy bun, and her cheeks flushed from her work, but she had never looked so beautiful to him. She was his comfort—his comfort and his refuge—and just seeing her helped ease the sense of numb dislocation that gripped him.

She noticed him and immediately abandoned her washing and ran toward him, drying her pink hands on the front of her dress. Roran braced himself as she threw herself at him, wrapping her arms around his chest. His side flared with pain, and he uttered a short grunt.

Katrina loosened her hold and leaned away, frowning. "Oh! Did I hurt you?"

"No . . . no. I'm just sore."

She did not question him but hugged him again, more gently, and looked up at him, her eyes glistening with tears. Holding her by the waist, he bent and kissed her, inexpressibly grateful for her presence.

Katrina slipped his left arm over her shoulders, and he allowed her to support part of his weight as they returned to their tent. With a sigh, Roran sat on the stump they used for a chair, which Katrina had placed next to the small fire she had built to heat the tub of water and over which a pot of stew was now simmering.

Katrina filled a bowl with stew and handed it to him. Then, from within the tent, she brought him a mug of ale and a plate with a half loaf of bread and a wedge of cheese. "Is there anything else you need?" she asked, her voice unusually hoarse.

Roran did not answer, but cupped her cheek and stroked it twice with his thumb. She smiled tremulously and laid a hand over his, then returned to washing and began to scrub with renewed vigor.

Roran stared at the food for a long time before he took a bite; he was still so tense, he doubted he could stomach it. After a few mouthfuls of bread, however, his appetite returned, and he began to consume the stew with eagerness.

When he was done, he placed the dishes on the ground and then sat warming his hands over the fire while he nursed the last few sips of beer.

"We heard the crash when the gates fell," said Katrina, wringing a bandage dry. "They didn't hold for very long."

"No. . . . It helps to have a dragon on your side."

Roran gazed at her belly as she draped the bandage over the makeshift clothesline that ran from the peak of their tent across to a neighboring one. Whenever he thought of the child she was carrying, the child that the two of them had created, he felt an enormous sense of pride, but it was tinged with anxiety, for he did not know how he could hope to provide a safe home for their baby. Also, if the war was not over by the time Katrina gave birth, she intended to leave him and go to Surda, where she might raise their child in relative safety.

I can't lose her, not again.

Katrina immersed another bandage in the tub. "And the battle in the city?" she asked, churning the water. "How went it?"

"We had to fight for every foot. Even Eragon had a hard time of it."

"The wounded spoke of ballistae mounted on wheels."

"Aye." Roran wet his tongue with ale, then quickly described how the Varden had moved through Belatona and the setbacks they had encountered along the way. "We lost too many men today, but it could have been worse. Much worse. Jörmundur and Captain Martland planned the attack well."

"Their plan wouldn't have worked, though, if not for you and Eragon. You acquitted yourself most bravely."

Roran loosed a single bark of laughter: "Ha! And do you know why that is? I'll tell you. Not one man in ten is actually willing to attack the enemy. Eragon doesn't see it; he's always at the forefront of the battle, driving the soldiers before him, but I see it. Most of the men hang back and don't fight unless they are cornered. Or they wave their arms about and make a lot of noise but don't actually do anything."

Katrina looked appalled. "How can that be? Are they cowards?"

"I don't know. I think . . . I think that, perhaps, they just can't bring themselves to look a man in the face and kill him, although it seems easy enough for them to cut down soldiers whose backs are turned. So they wait for others to do what they cannot. They wait for people like me."

"Do you think Galbatorix's men are equally reluctant?"

Roran shrugged. "They might be. But then, they have no choice but to obey Galbatorix. If he orders them to fight, they fight."

"Nasuada could do the same. She could have her magicians cast spells to ensure that no one shirks their duty."

"What difference would there be between her and Galbatorix, then? In any case, the Varden wouldn't stand for it."

Katrina left her washing to come and kiss him on the forehead. "I'm glad you can do what you do," she whispered. She returned to the tub and began scrubbing another strip of soiled linen over the washboard. "I felt something earlier, from my ring. . . . I thought maybe something had happened to you."

"I was in the middle of a battle. It wouldn't be surprising if you had felt a twinge every few minutes."

She paused with her arms in the water. "I never have before."

He drained the mug of ale, seeking to delay the inevitable. He had hoped to spare her the details of his misadventure in the castle, but it was plain that she would not rest until she knew the truth. Attempting to convince her otherwise would only lead her to imagine calamities far worse than what had actually occurred. Besides, it would be pointless for him to hold back when news of the event would soon be common throughout the Varden.

So he told her. He gave her a brief account and tried to make the collapse of the wall seem more like a minor inconvenience rather than something that had almost killed him. Still, he found it difficult to describe the experience, and he spoke haltingly, searching for the right words. When he finished, he fell silent, troubled by the remembrance.

"At least you weren't hurt," said Katrina.

He picked at a crack in the lip of the mug. "No."

The sound of sloshing water ceased, and he could feel her eyes heavy upon him.

"You've faced far greater danger before."

"Yes . . . I suppose."

Her voice softened. "What's wrong, then?" When he did not

answer, she said, "There's nothing so terrible you can't tell me, Roran. You know that."

The edge of his right thumbnail tore as he picked at the mug again. He rubbed the sharp flap against his forefinger several times. "I thought I was going to die when the wall fell."

"Anyone might have."

"Yes, but the thing is, I didn't *mind.*" Anguished, he looked at her. "Don't you understand? *I gave up.* When I realized I couldn't escape, I accepted it as meekly as a lamb led to slaughter, and I—" Unable to continue, he dropped the mug and hid his face in his hands. The swelling in his throat made it hard to breathe. Then he felt Katrina's fingers light upon his shoulders. "I gave up," he growled, furious and disgusted with himself. "I just stopped fighting. . . . For you . . . For our child." He choked on the words.

"Shh, shh," she murmured.

"I've never given up before. Not once. . . . Not even when the Ra'zac took you."

"I know you haven't."

"This fighting has to end. It can't go on like this. . . . I can't . . . I—" He raised his head and was horrified to see that she too was on the verge of tears. Standing, he wrapped his arms around her and held her close. "I'm sorry," he whispered. "I'm sorry. I'm sorry. I'm sorry. . . . It won't happen again. Never again. I promise."

"I don't care about *that,*" she said, her voice muffled against his shoulder.

Her reply stung him. "I know I was weak, but my word still ought to be worth something to you."

"That's not what I meant!" she exclaimed, and drew back to look at him accusingly. "You're a fool sometimes, Roran."

He smiled slightly. "I know."

She clasped her hands behind his neck. "I wouldn't think any less of you, regardless of what you felt when the wall came down. All that matters is that you're still alive. . . . There wasn't anything you could do when the wall fell, was there?"

He shook his head.

"Then you have nothing to be ashamed of. If you could have stopped it, or if you could have escaped but you didn't, then you would have lost my respect. But you did everything you could, and when you could do no more, you made peace with your fate, and you didn't rail needlessly against it. That is wisdom, not weakness."

He bowed and kissed her on the brow. "Thank you."

"And as far as I am concerned, you are the bravest, strongest, kindest man in all of Alagaësia."

This time he kissed her on the mouth. Afterward, she laughed, a short, quick release of pent-up tension, and they stood swaying together, as if dancing to a melody only they could hear.

Then Katrina gave him a playful push and went to finish the washing, and he settled back on the stump, content for the first time since the battle, despite his numerous aches and pains.

Roran watched the men, horses, and the occasional dwarf or Urgal slog past their tent, noting their wounds and the condition of their weapons and armor. He tried to gauge the general mood of the Varden; the only conclusion he reached was that everyone but the Urgals needed a good sleep and a decent meal, and that everyone, including the Urgals—especially the Urgals—needed to be scoured from head to foot with a hog's-hair brush and buckets of soapy water.

49

He also watched Katrina, and he saw how, as she worked, her initial good cheer gradually faded and she became ever more irritable. She kept scrubbing and scrubbing at several stains, but with little success. A scowl darkened her face, and she began to make small noises of frustration.

At last, when she had slapped the wad of fabric against the washboard, splashing foamy water several feet into the air, and leaned on the tub, her lips pressed tightly together, Roran pushed himself off the stump and made his way to her side.

"Here, let me," he said.

"It wouldn't be fitting," she muttered.

"Nonsense. Go sit down, and I'll finish. . . . Go on."

She shook her head. "No. You should be the one resting, not me. Besides, this isn't man's work."

He snorted with derision. "By whose decree? A man's work, or a woman's, is whatever needs to be done. Now go sit down; you'll feel better once you're off your feet."

"Roran, I'm fine."

"Don't be silly." He gently tried to push her away from the tub, but she refused to budge.

"It's not right," she protested. "What would people think?" She gestured at the men hurrying along the muddy lane next to their tent.

"They can think whatever they want. I married you, not them. If they believe I'm any less of a man for helping you, then they're fools."

"But—"

"But nothing. Move. Shoo. Get out of here."

"But—"

"I'm not going to argue. If you don't go sit, I'm going to carry you over there and tie you to that stump."

A bemused expression replaced her scowl. "Is that so?"

"Yes. Now go!" As she reluctantly ceded her position at the tub, he made a noise of exasperation. "Stubborn, aren't you?"

"Speak for yourself. You could teach a mule a thing or two."

"Not me. I'm not stubborn." Undoing his belt, he removed his mail shirt and hung it on the front pole of the tent, then peeled off his gloves and rolled up the sleeves of his tunic. The air was cool against his skin, and the bandages were colder still—they had grown chill while lying exposed on the washboard—but he did not mind, for the water was warm, and soon the cloth was as well. Frothy mounds of iridescent bubbles built up around his wrists as he pushed and pulled the material across the full length of the knobby board.

He glanced over and was pleased to see that Katrina was relaxing on the stump, at least as much as anyone could relax on such a rough seat.

"Do you want some chamomile tea?" she asked. "Gertrude gave me a handful of fresh sprigs this morning. I can make a pot for both of us."

"I'd like that."

A companionable silence developed between them as Roran proceeded to wash the rest of the laundry. The task lulled him into a pleasant mood; he enjoyed doing something with his hands other than swinging his hammer, and being close to Katrina gave him a deep sense of satisfaction.

He was in the middle of wringing out the last item, and his freshly poured tea was waiting for him next to Katrina, when someone shouted their names from across the busy way. It took Roran a moment to realize it was Baldor running toward them through the mud, weaving between men and horses. He wore a pitted leather apron and heavy, elbow-length gloves that were smeared with soot and were so worn that the fingers were as hard, smooth, and shiny as polished tortoise shells. A scrap of torn leather held back his dark, shaggy hair, and a frown creased his forehead. Baldor was smaller than his father, Horst, and his older brother, Albriech, but by any other comparison, he was large and well muscled, the result of having spent his childhood helping Horst in his forge. None of the three had fought that day—skilled smiths were normally too valuable to risk in battle—although Roran wished Nasuada had let them, for they were able warriors and Roran knew he could count on them even in the most dire circumstances.

Roran put down the washing and dried his hands, wondering what could be amiss. Rising from the stump, Katrina joined him by the tub.

When Baldor reached them, they had to wait several seconds for him to regain his breath. Then, in a rush, he said, "Come quickly. Mother just went into labor, and—"

"Where is she?" asked Katrina in a sharp tone.

"At our tent."

She nodded. "We'll be there as fast as we can."

With a grateful expression, Baldor turned and sprinted away.

As Katrina ducked inside their tent, Roran poured the contents of the tub over the fire, extinguishing it. The burning wood hissed and cracked under the deluge, and a cloud of steam jetted upward in place of smoke, filling the air with an unpleasant smell.

Dread and excitement quickened Roran's movements. *I hope she doesn't die,* he thought, remembering the talk he had heard among the women concerning her age and overlong pregnancy. Elain had always been kind to him and to Eragon, and he was fond of her.

"Are you ready?" asked Katrina as she emerged from the tent, knotting a blue scarf around her head and neck.

He grabbed his belt and hammer from where they hung. "Ready. Let's go."

✦ ✦ ✦

THE PRICE OF POWER

T"here now, Ma'am. You won't be needing these anymore. And good riddance, I say."

With a soft rustle, the last strip of linen slid off Nasuada's forearms as her handmaid, Farica, removed the wrappings. Nasuada had worn bandages such as those since the day she and the warlord Fadawar had tested their courage against one another in the Trial of the Long Knives.

Nasuada stood staring at a long, ragged tapestry dotted with holes while Farica attended to her. Then she steeled herself and slowly lowered her gaze. Since winning the Trial of the Long Knives, she had refused to look at her wounds; they had appeared so horrendous when fresh, she could not bear to see them again until they were nearly healed.

The scars were asymmetrical: six lay across the belly of her left forearm, three on her right. Each of the scars was three to four inches long and straight as could be, save the bottom one on the right, where her self-control had faltered and the knife had swerved, carving a jagged line nearly twice the length of the others. The skin around the scars was pink and puckered, while the scars themselves were only a little bit lighter than the rest of her body, for which she was grateful. She had feared that they might end up white and silvery, which would have made them far more noticeable. The scars rose above the surface of her arm about a quarter of an inch, forming hard ridges of flesh that looked exactly as if smooth steel rods had been inserted underneath her skin.

Nasuada regarded the marks with ambivalence. Her father had taught her about the customs of their people as she was growing up, but she had spent her whole life among the Varden and the dwarves. The only rituals of the wandering tribes that she observed, and then only irregularly, were associated with their religion. She had never aspired to master the Drum Dance, nor participate in the arduous Calling of Names, nor—and this most particularly—best anyone in the Trial of the Long Knives. And yet now here she was, still young and still beautiful, and already bearing these nine large scars upon her forearms. She could order one of the magicians of the Varden to remove them, of course, but then she would forfeit her victory in the Trial of the Long Knives, and the wandering tribes would renounce her as their liegelord.

While she regretted that her arms were no longer smooth and round and would no longer attract the admiring glances of men, she was also proud of the scars. They were a testament to her courage and a visible sign of her devotion to the Varden. Anyone who looked at her would know the quality of her character, and she decided that meant more to her than appearance.

"What do you think?" she asked, and held out her arms toward King Orrin, who stood framed in the open window of the study, looking down at the city.

Orrin turned and frowned, his eyes dark beneath his furrowed brow. He had traded his armor of earlier for a thick red tunic and a robe trimmed with white ermine. "I find it unpleasant to look at," he said, and returned his attention to the city. "Cover yourself; it is inappropriate for polite society."

Nasuada studied her arms for a moment longer. "No, I don't think I will." She tugged on the lace cuffs of her half sleeves to straighten them, then dismissed Farica. She crossed the sumptuous dwarf-woven rug in the center of the room to join Orrin in inspecting the battle-torn city, where she was pleased to see that all but two of the fires along the western wall had been extinguished. Then she shifted her gaze to the king.

In the short while since the Varden and the Surdans had launched their attack against the Empire, Nasuada had watched

Orrin grow ever more serious, his original enthusiasm and eccentricities vanishing beneath a grim exterior. At first she had welcomed the change, for she had felt he was becoming more mature, but as the war dragged on, she began to miss his eager discussions of natural philosophy, as well as his other quirks. In retrospect, she realized these had often brightened her day, even if she had sometimes found them aggravating. Moreover, the change had made him more dangerous as a rival; in his current mood, she could quite easily imagine him attempting to displace her as leader of the Varden.

Could I be happy if I married him? she wondered. Orrin was not unpleasant to look at. His nose was high and thin, but his jaw was strong and his mouth was finely carved and expressive. Years of martial training had given him a pleasing build. That he was intelligent was without doubt, and for the most part his personality was agreeable. However, if he had not been the king of Surda, and if he had not posed such a great threat to her position and to the Varden's independence, she knew that she would never have considered a match with him. *Would he make a good father?*

Orrin put his hands on the narrow stone sill and leaned against it. Without looking at her, he said, "You have to break your pact with the Urgals."

His statement took her aback. "And why is that?"

"Because they are hurting us. Men who would otherwise join us now curse us for allying ourselves with monsters and refuse to lay down their weapons when we arrive at their homes. Galbatorix's resistance seems just and reasonable to them because of our concord with the Urgals. The common man does not understand why we joined with them. He does not know that Galbatorix used the Urgals himself, nor that Galbatorix tricked them into attacking Tronjheim under the command of a Shade. These are subtleties that you cannot explain to a frightened farmer. All he can comprehend is that the creatures he has feared and hated his whole life are marching toward his home, led by a huge, snarling dragon and a Rider who appears more elf than human."

"We need the Urgals' support," said Nasuada. "We have too few warriors as it is."

"We do not need them as badly as all that. You already know what I say is the truth; why else did you prevent the Urgals from participating in the attack on Belatona? Why else have you ordered them not to enter the city? Keeping them away from the battlefield isn't enough, Nasuada. Word of them still spreads throughout the land. The only thing you can do to improve the situation is to end this ill-fated scheme before it causes us more harm."

"I cannot."

Orrin spun toward her, anger distorting his face. "Men are *dying* because you chose to accept Garzhvog's help. My men, your men, those in the Empire . . . dead and *buried.* This alliance isn't worth their sacrifice, and for the life of me, I cannot fathom why you continue to defend it."

She could not hold his gaze; it reminded her too strongly of the guilt and recrimination that so often afflicted her when she was trying to fall asleep. Instead, she fixed her eyes on the smoke rising from a tower by the edge of the city. Speaking slowly, she said, "I defend it because I hope that preserving our union with the Urgals will save more lives than it will cost. . . . If we should defeat Galbatorix—"

Orrin uttered an exclamation of disbelief.

"It is by no means certain," she said, "I know. But we must plan for the possibility. If we should defeat him, then it will fall to us to help our race recover from this conflict and build a strong new country out of the ashes of the Empire. And part of that process will be ensuring that, after a hundred years of strife, we finally have peace. I will not overthrow Galbatorix only to have the Urgals attack us when we are at our weakest."

"They might anyway. They always have before."

"Well, what else can we do?" she said, annoyed. "We have to try to tame them. The closer we bind them to our cause, the less likely they will be to turn on us."

"I'll tell you what to do," he growled. "Banish them. Break your pact with Nar Garzhvog and send him and his rams away. If we win this war, then we can negotiate a new treaty with them, and we will be in a position to dictate whatever terms we want. Or better yet, send Eragon and Saphira into the Spine with a battalion of men to wipe them out once and for all, as the Riders should have done centuries ago."

Nasuada looked at him with disbelief. "If I ended our pact with the Urgals, they would likely be so angry, they would attack us forthwith, and we cannot fight both them and the Empire at the same time. To invite that upon ourselves would be the height of folly. If, in their wisdom, the elves, the dragons, and the Riders all decided to tolerate the existence of the Urgals—even though they could have destroyed them easily enough—then we ought to follow their example. They knew it would be wrong to kill all the Urgals, and so should you."

"Their wisdom— Bah! As if their *wisdom* has done them any good! Fine, leave some of the Urgals alive, but kill enough of them that they won't dare leave their haunts for a hundred years or more!"

The obvious pain in his voice and in the strained lines of his face puzzled Nasuada. She examined him with greater intensity, trying to determine the reason for his vehemence. After a few moments, an explanation presented itself that, upon reflection, seemed self-evident.

"Whom did you lose?" she asked.

Orrin balled up a fist and slowly, haltingly, brought it down upon the windowsill, as if he wanted to pound it with all his strength but did not dare. He thumped the sill twice more, then said, "A friend I grew up with in Borromeo Castle. I don't think you ever met him. He was one of the lieutenants in my cavalry."

"How did he die?"

"As you might expect. We had just arrived at the stables by the west gate and were securing them for our own use when one of the grooms ran out of a stall and stabbed him right through with a pitchfork. When we cornered the groom, he kept screaming stuff and

nonsense about the Urgals and how he would never surrender. . . .
It wouldn't have done the fool any good even if he had. I struck him
down with my own hand."

"I'm sorry," said Nasuada.

The gems in Orrin's crown glittered as he nodded in acknowledgment.

"As painful as it is, you cannot allow your grief to dictate your
decisions. . . . It isn't easy, I know—well I know it!—but you must
be stronger than yourself, for the good of your people."

"Be stronger than myself," he said in a sour, mocking voice.

"Yes. More is asked of us than of most people; therefore we must
strive to be better than most if we are to prove ourselves worthy of
that responsibility. . . . The Urgals killed my father, remember, but
that did not prevent me from forging an alliance that could help
the Varden. I won't let anything stop me from doing what is best for
them and for our army as a whole, no matter how painful it might
be." She lifted her arms, showing him the scars again.

"That is your answer, then? You will not break off with the
Urgals?"

"No."

Orrin accepted the news with an equanimity that unsettled her.
Then he gripped the sill with both hands and returned to his study
of the city. Adorning his fingers were four large rings, one of which
bore the royal seal of Surda carved into the face of an amethyst: an
antlered stag with sprigs of mistletoe wound between his feet standing over a harp and opposite an image of a tall, fortified tower.

"At least," said Nasuada, "we didn't encounter any soldiers who
were enchanted not to feel pain."

"The laughing dead, you mean," Orrin muttered, using the term
that she knew had become widespread throughout the Varden.
"Aye, and not Murtagh nor Thorn either, which troubles me."

For a time, neither of them spoke. Then she said, "How went
your experiment last night? Was it a success?"

"I was too tired to assay it. I went to sleep instead."

"Ah."

After a few more moments, they both, by tacit agreement, went to the desk pushed against one wall. Mountains of sheets, tablets, and scrolls covered the desk. Nasuada surveyed the daunting landscape and sighed. Only half an hour earlier, the desk had been empty, swept clean by her aides.

She concentrated upon the all-too-familiar topmost report, an estimate of the number of prisoners the Varden had taken during the siege of Belatona, with the names of persons of importance noted in red ink. She and Orrin had been discussing the figures when Farica had arrived to remove her bandages.

"I can't think of a way out of this tangle," she admitted.

"We could recruit guards from among the men here. Then we wouldn't have to leave quite so many of our own warriors behind."

She picked up the report. "Maybe, but the men we need would be difficult to find, and our spellcasters are already dangerously overworked. . . ."

"Has Du Vrangr Gata discovered a way to break an oath given in the ancient language?" When she answered in the negative, he asked, "Have they made any headway at all?"

"None that is practical. I even asked the elves, but they have had no more luck in all their long years than we have these past few days."

"If we don't solve this, and soon, it could cost us the war," said Orrin. "This one issue, right here."

She rubbed her temples. "I know." Before leaving the protection of the dwarves in Farthen Dûr and Tronjheim, she had tried to anticipate every challenge the Varden might face once they embarked on the offensive. The one they now confronted, however, had caught her completely by surprise.

The problem had first manifested itself in the aftermath of the Battle of the Burning Plains, when it had become apparent that all of the officers in Galbatorix's army, and most of the ordinary soldiers as well, had been forced to swear their loyalty to Galbatorix and the

Empire in the ancient language. She and Orrin had quickly realized they could never trust those men, not so long as Galbatorix and the Empire still existed, and perhaps not even if they were destroyed. As a result, they could not allow the men who wanted to defect to join the Varden, for fear of how their oaths might compel them to behave.

Nasuada had not been overly concerned by the situation at the time. Prisoners were a reality of war, and she had already made provisions with King Orrin to have their captives marched back to Surda, where they would be put to work building roads, breaking rocks, digging canals, and doing other hard labor.

It was not until the Varden seized the city of Feinster that she grasped the full size of the problem. Galbatorix's agents had extracted oaths of loyalty not only from the soldiers in Feinster but also from the nobles, from many of the officials who served them, and from a seemingly random collection of ordinary people throughout the city—a fair number of whom she suspected the Varden had failed to identify. Those they knew of, however, had to be kept under lock and key, lest they try to subvert the Varden. Finding people they could trust, then, and who wanted to work with the Varden had proved far more difficult than Nasuada had ever expected.

Because of all the people who needed to be contained, she had had no choice but to leave twice the number of warriors in Feinster that she had intended. And, with so many imprisoned, the city was effectively crippled, forcing her to divert much-needed supplies from the main body of the Varden to keep the city from starving. They could not maintain the situation for long, and it would only worsen now that they were also in possession of Belatona.

"A pity the dwarves haven't arrived yet," said Orrin. "We could use their help."

Nasuada agreed. There were only a few hundred dwarves with the Varden at the moment; the rest had returned to Farthen Dûr for the burial of their fallen king, Hrothgar, and to wait for their clan chiefs to choose Hrothgar's successor, a fact that she had cursed countless times since. She had tried to convince the dwarves to appoint a regent for the duration of the war, but they were as stubborn as stone and had insisted upon carrying out their age-old ceremonies, though doing so meant abandoning the Varden in the middle of their campaign. In any event, the dwarves had finally selected their new king—Hrothgar's nephew, Orik—and had set out from the distant Beor Mountains to rejoin the Varden. Even at that moment, they were marching across the vast plains just north of Surda, somewhere between Lake Tüdosten and the Jiet River.

Nasuada wondered if they would be fit to fight when they arrived. As a rule, dwarves were hardier than humans, but they had spent most of the past two months on foot, and that could wear down the endurance of even the strongest creatures. *They must be tired of seeing the same landscape over and over again,* she thought.

"We have so many prisoners already. And once we take Dras-Leona . . ." She shook her head.

Appearing suddenly animated, Orrin said, "What if we bypass Dras-Leona entirely?" He shuffled through the slew of papers on the desk until he located a large, dwarf-drawn map of Alagaësia, which he draped over the scarps of administerial records. The tottering mounds underneath gave the land an unusual topography: peaks in the west of Du Weldenvarden; a bowl-like depression where the Beor Mountains lay; canyons and ravines throughout the Hadarac Desert; and rolling waves along the northernmost part of the Spine, born of the rows of scrolls below. "Look." With his middle finger, he traced a line from Belatona to the capital of the Empire, Urû'baen. "If we march straight there, we won't come anywhere near Dras-Leona. It would be difficult to traverse the whole stretch all at once, but we *could* do it."

Nasuada did not need to ponder his suggestion; she had already considered the possibility. "The risk would be too great. Galbatorix could still attack us with the soldiers he has stationed in Dras-Leona—which is no small number, if our spies are to be trusted—and then we'd end up fending off attacks from two directions at

61

once. I know of no quicker way to lose a battle, or a war. No, we must capture Dras-Leona."

Orrin conceded the point with a slight dip of his head. "We need our men back from Aroughs, then. We need every warrior if we are to continue."

"I know. I intend to make sure that the siege is brought to an end before the week is out."

"Not by sending Eragon there, I hope."

"No, I have a different plan."

"Good. And in the meantime? What shall we do with these prisoners?"

"What we have done before: guards, fences, and padlocks. Maybe we can also bind the prisoners with spells to restrict their movement, so that we don't have to keep watch over them so closely. Other than that, I see no solution, except to slaughter the whole lot of them, and I would rather—" She tried to imagine what she would not do in order to defeat Galbatorix. "I would rather not resort to such . . . *drastic* measures."

"Aye." Orrin stooped over the map, hunching his shoulders like a vulture as he glared at the squiggles of faded ink that marked the triangle of Belatona, Dras-Leona, and Urû'baen.

And so he remained until Nasuada said, "Is there anything else we must attend to? Jörmundur is waiting for his orders, and the Council of Elders has requested an audience with me."

"I worry."

"What about?"

Orrin swept a hand over the map. "That this venture was ill conceived from the start. . . . That our forces, and those of our allies, are dangerously scattered, and that if Galbatorix should take it in his head to join in the fight himself, he could destroy us as easily as Saphira could a herd of goats. Our entire strategy depends upon contriving a meeting between Galbatorix, Eragon, Saphira, and as many spellcasters as we can muster. Only a small portion of those spellcasters are currently among our ranks, and we won't be able to gather the rest into a single place until we arrive at Urû'baen and meet with Queen Islanzadí and her army. Until that happens, we remain woefully vulnerable to attack. We are risking much on the assumption that Galbatorix's arrogance will hold him in check until our trap has sprung shut around him."

Nasuada shared his concerns. However, it was more important to shore up Orrin's confidence than to commiserate with him, for if his resolve weakened, it would interfere with his duties and undermine the morale of his men. "We are not entirely defenseless," she said. "Not anymore. We have the Dauthdaert now, and with it, I think we might actually be able to kill Galbatorix and Shruikan, should they emerge from within the confines of Urû'baen."

"Perhaps."

"Besides, it does no good to worry. We cannot hasten the dwarves here, nor speed our own progress toward Urû'baen, nor turn tail and flee. So I would not let our situation trouble you excessively. All we can do is strive to accept our fate with grace, whatever it might be. The alternative is to allow the thought of Galbatorix's possible actions to unsettle our minds, and *that* I won't do. I refuse to give him such power over me."

✦ ✦ ✦

RUDELY INTO THE LIGHT ...

A scream rang out: high, jagged, and piercing, almost inhuman in pitch and volume.

Eragon tensed as if someone had stabbed him with a needle. He had spent the better part of the day watching men fight and die—killing scores himself—yet he could not help but feel concern as he heard Elain's cries of anguish. The sounds she made were so terrible, he had begun to wonder if she would survive the birth.

Next to him, beside the barrel that served as his seat, Albriech and Baldor squatted on their hams, picking at the tattered blades of grass between their shoes. Their thick fingers shredded each scrap of leaf and stalk with methodical thoroughness before groping for the next. Sweat glistened on their foreheads, and their eyes were hard with anger and despair. Occasionally, they exchanged glances or looked across the lane at the tent where their mother was, but otherwise they stared at the ground and ignored their surroundings.

A few feet away, Roran sat on his own barrel, which lay on its side and wobbled whenever he moved. Clustered along the edge of the muddy lane were several dozen people from Carvahall, mostly men who were friends of Horst and his sons or whose wives were helping the healer Gertrude attend to Elain. And towering behind them was Saphira. Her neck was arched like a drawn bow, the tip of her tail twitched as if she were hunting, and she kept flicking her ruby-red tongue in and out of her mouth, tasting the air for any scents that might provide information about Elain or her unborn child.

Eragon rubbed a sore muscle in his left forearm. They had been waiting for several hours, and dusk was drawing near. Long black shadows stretched out from every object, reaching eastward as if striving to touch the horizon. The air had turned cool, and mosquitoes and lace-winged damselflies from the nearby Jiet River darted to and fro around them.

Another scream rent the silence.

The men stirred with unease, then made gestures to ward off bad luck and murmured to one another in voices intended only for those closest to them but which Eragon could hear with perfect clarity. They whispered about the difficulty of Elain's pregnancy; some solemnly stated that if she did not give birth soon, it would be too late for both her and the child. Others said things like "Hard for a man to lose a wife even in the best of times, but 'specially here, 'specially now," or "It's a shame, it is. . . ." Several blamed Elain's troubles on the Ra'zac or on events that had occurred during the villagers' journey to the Varden. And more than one muttered a distrustful remark about Arya being allowed to assist with the birth. "She's an elf, not a human," said the carpenter Fisk. "She ought to stick with her own kind, she should, and not go around meddling where she's not wanted. Who knows what it is she really wants, eh?"

All that and more Eragon heard, but he hid his reactions and kept his peace, for he knew it would only make the villagers uncomfortable if they were aware of how sharp his hearing had become.

The barrel underneath Roran creaked as he leaned forward. "Do you think we should—"

"No," said Albriech.

Eragon tugged his cloak closer around him. The chill was beginning to sink into his bones. He would not leave, though, not until Elain's ordeal was over.

"Look," said Roran with sudden excitement.

Albriech and Baldor swiveled their heads in unison.

Across the lane, Katrina exited the tent, carrying a bundle of soiled rags. Before the entrance flap fell shut again, Eragon caught a glimpse of Horst and one of the women from Carvahall—he was not sure who—standing at the foot of the cot where Elain was lying.

Without so much as a single sideways glance at those watching,

Katrina half ran and half walked toward the fire where Fisk's wife, Isold, and Nolla were boiling rags for reuse.

The barrel creaked twice more as Roran shifted his position. Eragon half expected him to start after Katrina, but he remained where he was, as did Albriech and Baldor. They, and the rest of the villagers, followed Katrina's movements with unblinking attentiveness.

Eragon grimaced as Elain's latest scream pierced the air, the cry no less excruciating than those previous.

Then the entrance to the tent was swept aside for a second time, and Arya stormed out, bare-armed and disheveled. Her hair fluttered about her face as she trotted over to three of Eragon's elven guards, who were standing in a pool of shadow behind a nearby pavilion. For a few moments, she spoke urgently with one of them, a thin-faced elf woman named Invidia, then hurried back the way she had come.

Eragon caught up with her before she had covered more than a few yards. "How goes it?" he asked.

"Badly."

"Why is it taking so long? Can't you help her give birth any faster?"

Arya's expression, which was already strained, became even more severe. "I could. I could have sung the child out of her womb in the first half hour, but Gertrude and the other women will only let me use the simplest of spells."

"That's absurd! Why?"

"Because magic frightens them—and I frighten them."

"Then tell them you mean no harm. Tell them in the ancient language, and they'll have no choice but to believe you."

She shook her head. "It would only make matters worse. They would think I was trying to charm them against their will, and they would send me away."

"Surely Katrina—"

"She is the reason I was able to cast the spells I did."

Again Elain screamed.

"Won't they at least let you ease her pain?"

"No more than I already have."

Eragon spun toward Horst's tent. "Is that so," he growled between clenched teeth.

A hand closed around his left arm and held him in place. Puzzled, he looked back at Arya for an explanation. She shook her head. "Don't," she said. "These are customs older than time itself. If you interfere, you will anger and embarrass Gertrude and turn many of the females from your village against you."

"I don't care about that!"

"I know, but trust me: right now the wisest thing you can do is to wait with the others." As if to emphasize her point, she released his arm.

"I can't just stand by and let her suffer!"

"*Listen* to me. It's better if you stay. I will help Elain however I can, that I promise, but do not go in there. You will only cause strife and anger where none are needed. . . . Please."

Eragon hesitated, then snarled with disgust and threw up his hands as Elain screamed yet again. "Fine," he said, and leaned close to Arya, "but whatever happens, don't let her or the child die. I don't care what you have to do, but don't let them die."

Arya studied him with a serious gaze. "I would never allow a child to come to harm," she said, and resumed walking.

As she disappeared inside Horst's tent, Eragon returned to where Roran, Albriech, and Baldor were gathered and sank back down onto his barrel.

"Well?" Roran asked.

Eragon shrugged. "They're doing all they can. We just have to be patient. . . . That's all."

"Seemed as if she had a fair bit more than that to say," said Baldor.

"The meaning was the same."

The color of the sun shifted, becoming orange and crimson as it approached the terminating line of the earth. The few tattered clouds that remained in the western sky, remnants of the storm that had blown past earlier, acquired similar hues. Flocks of swallows swooped overhead, making their supper out of the moths and flies and other insects flitting about.

Over time, Elain's cries gradually decreased in strength, fading from her earlier, full-throated screams to low, broken moans that made Eragon's hackles prickle. More than anything, he wanted to free her from her torments, but he could not bring himself to ignore Arya's advice, so he stayed where he was and fidgeted and bit his bruised nails and engaged in short, stilted conversations with Saphira.

When the sun touched the earth, it spread out along the horizon, like a giant yolk oozing free of its skin. Bats began to mingle among the swallows, the flapping of their leathery wings faint and frantic, their high-pitched squeaks almost painfully sharp to Eragon.

Then Elain uttered a shriek that drowned out every other sound in the vicinity, a shriek the likes of which Eragon hoped he would never hear again.

A brief but profound silence followed.

It ended as the loud, hiccuping wail of a newborn child emanated from within the tent—the age-old fanfare that announced the arrival of a new person into the world. At the sound, Albriech and Baldor broke out grinning, as did Eragon and Roran, and several of the waiting men cheered.

Their jubilation was short-lived. Even as the last of the cheers died out, the women in the tent began to keen, a shrill, heart-rending sound that made Eragon go cold with dread. He knew what their lamentations meant, what they had always meant: that tragedy of the worst kind had struck.

"No," he said, disbelieving, as he hopped off the barrel. *She can't be dead. She can't be. . . . Arya promised.*

As if in response to his thought, Arya tore back the flap to the tent and ran toward him, bounding across the lane with impossibly long strides.

"What's happened?" Baldor asked as she slowed to a halt.

Arya ignored him and said, "Eragon, come."

"What's happened?" Baldor exclaimed angrily, and reached for Arya's shoulder. In a flash of seemingly instantaneous movement, she caught his wrist and twisted his arm behind his back, forcing him to stand hunched over, like a cripple. His face contorted with pain.

"If you want your baby sister to live, then stand aside and do not interfere!" She released him with a push, sending him sprawling into Albriech's arms, then whirled about and strode back toward Horst's tent.

"What *has* happened?" Eragon asked as he joined her.

Arya turned to face him, eyes burning. "The child is healthy, but she was born with a cat lip."

Then Eragon understood the reason for the women's outpouring of grief. Children cursed with a cat lip were rarely allowed to live; they were difficult to feed, and even if the parents could feed them, such children would suffer a miserable lot: shunned, ridiculed, and unable to make a suitable match for marriage. In most cases, it would have been better for all if the child had been stillborn.

"You have to heal her, Eragon," said Arya.

"Me? But I've never . . . Why not you? You know more about healing than I do."

"If I rework the child's appearance, people will say I have stolen her and replaced her with a changeling. Well I know the stories your kind tells about my race, Eragon—too well. I will do it if I must, but the child will suffer for it ever after. You are the only one who can save her from such a fate."

Panic clutched at him. He did not want to be responsible for the life of another person; he was already responsible for far too many.

"You have to heal her," Arya said, her tone forceful. Eragon reminded himself how dearly elves treasured their children, as well as children of all races.

"Will you assist me if I need it?"

"Of course."

As will I, said Saphira. *Must you even ask?*

"Right," said Eragon, and gripped Brisingr's pommel, his mind made up. "I'll do it."

With Arya trailing slightly behind, he marched over to the tent and pushed his way past the heavy woolen flaps. Candle smoke stung his eyes. Five women from Carvahall stood bunched together close to the wall. Their keening struck him like a physical blow. They swayed, trance-like, and tore at their clothes and hair as they wailed. Horst was by the end of the cot, arguing with Gertrude, his face red, puffy, and lined with exhaustion. For her part, the plump healer held a bundle of cloth against her bosom, a bundle that Eragon assumed contained the infant—although he could not see its face—for it wriggled and squalled, adding to the din. Gertrude's round cheeks shone with perspiration, and her hair clung to her skin. Her bare forearms were streaked with various fluids. At the head of the cot, Katrina knelt on a round cushion, wiping Elain's brow with a damp cloth.

Eragon hardly recognized Elain; her face was gaunt, and she had dark rings under her wandering eyes, which seemed incapable of focusing. A line of tears streamed from the outer corner of each eye, over her temples, and then vanished underneath the tangled locks of her hair. Her mouth opened and closed, and she moaned unintelligible words. A bloodstained sheet covered the rest of her.

Neither Horst nor Gertrude noticed Eragon until he approached them. Eragon had grown since he had left Carvahall, but Horst still stood a head taller. As they both looked at him, a flicker of hope brightened the smith's bleak expression.

"Eragon!" He clapped a heavy hand on Eragon's shoulder and leaned against him, as if events had left him barely able to stand. "You heard?" It was not really a question, but Eragon nodded anyway. Horst glanced at Gertrude—a quick, darting glance—then his large, shovel-like beard moved from side to side as his jaw worked, and his tongue appeared between his lips as he wet them. "Can you . . . can you do anything for her, do you think?"

"Maybe," said Eragon. "I'll try."

He held out his arms. After a moment's hesitation, Gertrude deposited the warm bundle in his hold, then backed away, her demeanor troubled.

Buried within the folds of fabric was the girl's tiny, wrinkled face. Her skin was dark red, her eyes were swollen shut, and she appeared to be grimacing, as if she was angry at her recent mistreatment— a response that Eragon thought was perfectly reasonable. Her most striking feature, however, was the wide gap that extended from her left nostril to the middle of her upper lip. Through it, her small pink tongue was visible; it lay like a soft, moist slug, occasionally twitching.

"Please," said Horst. "Is there any way you can . . ."

Eragon winced as the women's keening struck a particularly shrill note. "I can't work here," he said.

As he turned to leave, Gertrude spoke up behind him, saying, "I'll come with you. One of us who knows how to care for a child needs to stay with her."

Eragon did not want Gertrude hovering about him while he tried to mend the girl's face, and he was about to tell her just that when he remembered what Arya had said about changelings. Someone from Carvahall, someone the rest of the villagers trusted, ought to bear witness to the girl's transformation, so that they could later assure people that the child was still the same person as she had been before.

"As you wish," he said, stifling his objections.

The baby squirmed in his arms and uttered a plaintive cry as he exited the tent. Across the lane, the villagers stood and pointed, and Albriech and Baldor started toward him. Eragon shook his head, and they stopped where they were and gazed after him with helpless expressions.

Arya and Gertrude took up positions on either side of Eragon as he walked through the camp to his tent, and the ground trembled under their feet as Saphira followed. Warriors in the path quickly moved aside to let them pass.

Eragon strove to keep his steps as smooth as possible, in order to avoid jostling the child. A strong, musty aroma clung to the girl, like the smell of a forest floor on a warm summer day.

They had almost reached their destination when Eragon saw the witch-child, Elva, standing between two rows of tents next to the path, solemn-faced as she stared at him with her large violet eyes. She wore a black and purple dress with a long veil of lace that was folded back over her head, exposing the silvery, star-shaped mark, similar to his gedwëy ignasia, on her forehead.

Not a word did she say, nor did she attempt to slow or stop him. Nevertheless, Eragon understood her warning, for her very presence was a rebuke to him. Once before he had tampered with the fate of an infant, and with dire consequences. He could not allow himself to make such a mistake again, not only because of the harm it would cause, but because if he did, Elva would become his sworn enemy. Despite all his power, Eragon feared Elva. Her ability to peer into people's souls and divine everything that pained and troubled them—and to foresee everything that was about to hurt them—made her one of the most dangerous beings in all of Alagaësia.

Whatever happens, Eragon thought as he entered his dark tent, *I don't want to hurt this child.* And he felt a renewed determination to give her a chance to live the life that circumstances would have denied her.

A CRADLE SONG

Faint light from the dying sun seeped into Eragon's tent. Everything within was gray, as if it were carved from granite. With his elf vision, Eragon could see the shape of objects easily enough, but he knew that Gertrude would have trouble, so for her sake he said, "Naina hvitr un böllr," and set a small, glowing werelight floating in the air by the peak of the tent. The soft white orb produced no discernible heat but as much illumination as a bright lantern. He refrained from using the word *brisingr* in the spell, so as to avoid setting the blade of his sword on fire.

He heard Gertrude pause behind him, and he turned to see her staring at the werelight and clutching at the bag she had brought with her. Her familiar face reminded him of home and Carvahall, and he felt an unexpected lurch of homesickness.

She slowly lowered her gaze to his. "How you have changed," she said. "The boy I once sat watch over as he fought off a fever is long gone, I think."

"You know me still," he replied.

"No, I don't believe I do."

Her statement troubled him, but he could not afford to dwell on it, so he pushed it out of his mind and went to his cot. Gently, ever so gently, he transferred the newborn from his arms onto the blankets, as carefully as if she were made of glass. The girl waved a clenched fist at him. He smiled and touched it with the tip of his right forefinger, and she burbled softly.

"What do you intend to do?" asked Gertrude as she sat on the lone stool near the tent wall. "How will you heal her?"

"I'm not sure."

Just then, Eragon noticed that Arya had not accompanied them into the tent. He called her name, and a moment later, she answered from outside, her voice muffled by the thick fabric that separated them. "I am here," she said. "And here I shall wait. If you have need of me, you have but to cast your thoughts in my direction and I shall come."

Eragon frowned slightly. He had counted on having her close at hand during the procedure, to help him where he was ignorant and to correct him if he made any mistake. *Well, no matter. I can still ask her questions if I want to. Only this way, Gertrude will have no reason to suspect that Arya had anything to do with the girl.* He was struck by the precautions that Arya was taking in order to avoid arousing suspicion that the girl was a changeling, and he wondered if she had once been accused of stealing someone's child.

The frame of the cot creaked as he slowly lowered himself onto it, facing the infant. His frown deepened. Through him, he felt Saphira watching the girl as she lay on the blankets, now dozing, seemingly oblivious to the world. Her tongue glistened within the cleft that split her upper lip.

What do you think? he asked.

Go slowly, so that you do not bite your tail by accident.

He agreed with her, then, feeling impish, asked, *And have you ever done that? Bitten your tail, I mean?*

She remained silently aloof, but he caught a brief flash of sensations: a medley of images—trees, grass, sunshine, the mountains of the Spine—as well as the cloying scent of red orchids and a sudden painful, pinching sensation, as if a door had slammed shut on her tail.

Eragon chuckled quietly to himself, then concentrated on composing the spells he thought he would need to heal the girl. It took quite a while, almost a half hour. He and Saphira spent most of that time going over the arcane sentences again and again, examining and debating every word and phrase—and even his pronunciation—in an attempt to ensure that the spells would do what he intended and nothing more.

In the midst of their silent conversation, Gertrude shifted in her seat and said, "She looks the same as ever. The work goes badly, doesn't it? There is no need to hide the truth from me, Eragon; I have dealt with far worse in my day."

Eragon raised his eyebrows and, in a mild voice, said, "The work has not yet begun."

And Gertrude sank back, subdued. From within her bag, she removed a ball of yellow yarn, a half-finished sweater, and a pair of polished birch knitting needles. Her fingers moved with practiced speed, quick and deft, as she began to knit and purl. The steady clacking of her needles comforted Eragon; it was a sound he had heard often during his childhood, one that he associated with sitting around a kitchen fireplace on cool autumn evenings, listening to the adults tell stories while they smoked a pipe or savored a draught of dark brown ale after a large dinner.

At last, when he and Saphira were satisfied that the spells were safe, and Eragon was confident that his tongue would not trip over any of the strange sounds of the ancient language, Eragon drew upon the combined strength of both their bodies and prepared to cast the first of the enchantments.

Then he hesitated.

When the elves used magic to coax a tree or a flower to grow in the shape they desired, or to alter their body or that of another creature, they always, so far as he knew, couched the spell in the form of a song. It seemed only fitting that he should do the same. But he was acquainted with only a few of the elves' many songs and none of them well enough to accurately—or even adequately—reproduce such beautiful and complex melodies.

So, instead, he chose a song from the deepest recesses of his memory, a song that his aunt Marian had sung to him when he was little, before the sickness had taken her, a song that the women of Carvahall had crooned to their children from time immemorial when they tucked them under the covers for a long night's sleep: a lullaby—a cradle song. The notes were simple, easy to remember, and had a soothing quality that he hoped would help keep the infant calm.

He began, soft and low, letting the words roll forth slowly, the sound of his voice spreading through the tent like warmth from a fire. Before he used magic, he told the girl in the ancient language that he was her friend, that he meant her well, and that she should trust him.

She stirred in her sleep, as if in response, and her clenched expression softened.

Then Eragon intoned the first of the spells: a simple incantation that consisted of two short sentences, which he recited over and over again, like a prayer. And the small pink hollow where the two sides of the girl's divided lip met shimmered and crawled, as if a dormant creature were stirring beneath the surface.

What he was attempting was far from easy. The infant's bones, like those of every newborn child, were soft and cartilaginous, different from those of an adult and thus different from all of the bones he had mended during his time with the Varden. He had to be careful not to fill the gap in her mouth with the bone, flesh, and skin of an adult, or those areas would not grow properly along with the rest of her body. Also, when he repaired the gap in her upper palate and gums, he would have to move, straighten, and make symmetrical the roots of what would become her two front teeth, something he had never done before. And further complicating the process was the fact that he had never seen the girl without her deformity, so he was uncertain how her lip and mouth ought to appear. She looked like every other baby he had seen: round, pudgy, and lacking definition. He worried, then, that he might give her a face that appeared pleasant enough at the moment, but that would become strange and unattractive as the years passed.

So he proceeded cautiously, making only small changes at a time and pausing after each one to ponder the result. He started with the deepest layers of the girl's face, with the bones and cartilage, and slowly worked his way outward, singing all the while.

At a certain point, Saphira began to hum along with him from where she lay outside, her deep voice making the air vibrate. The werelight brightened and dimmed in accordance with the volume of her humming, a phenomenon that Eragon found exceedingly curious. He resolved to ask Saphira about it later.

Word by word, spell by spell, hour by hour, the night wore on, though Eragon paid no attention to the time. When the girl cried from hunger, he fed her with a trickle of energy. He and Saphira tried to avoid touching her mind with theirs—not knowing how the contact might affect her immature consciousness—but they still brushed against it occasionally; her mind felt vague and indistinct to Eragon, a thrashing sea of unmoderated emotions that reduced everything else in the world to insignificance.

Beside him, Gertrude's needles continued to clack, the only interruption in the rhythm coming when the healer lost count of her stitches or had to tink back several knits or purls in order to correct a mistake.

Slowly, ever so slowly, the fissure in the girl's gums and palate fused into a seamless whole, the two sides of her cat lip pulled together—her skin flowing like liquid—and her upper lip gradually formed a pink bow free of flaws.

Eragon fiddled and tweaked and worried over the shape of her lip for the longest while, until at last Saphira said, *It is done. Leave it,* and he was forced to admit that he could not improve the girl's appearance any more, only make it worse.

Then he let the cradle song fade to silence. His tongue felt thick and dry, his throat raw. He pushed himself off the cot and stood half crouched over it, too stiff to straighten up entirely.

In addition to the illumination from the werelight, a pale glow pervaded the tent, the same as when he had started. At first he was confused—surely the sun had already set!—but then he realized that the glow was coming from the east, not the west, and he understood. *No wonder I'm so sore. I've been sitting here the whole night through!*

And what about me? said Saphira. *My bones ache as much as yours.* Her admission surprised him; she rarely acknowledged her own discomfort, no matter how extreme. The fighting must have taken a greater toll on her than had first been apparent. As he reached that conclusion, and Saphira became aware of it, she withdrew from him slightly and said, *Tired or not, I can still crush however many soldiers Galbatorix sends against us.*

I know.

Returning the knitting to her bag, Gertrude stood and hobbled over to the cot. "Never did I think to see such a thing," she said. "Least of all from you, Eragon Bromsson." She peered at him inquiringly. "Brom *was* your father, wasn't he?"

Eragon nodded, then croaked, "That he was."

"It seems fitting, somehow."

Eragon was not inclined to discuss the topic further, so he merely grunted and extinguished the werelight with a glance and a thought. Instantly, all went dark, save for the predawn glow. His eyes adjusted to the change faster than Gertrude's; she blinked and frowned and swung her head from side to side, as if unsure of where he stood.

The girl was warm and heavy in Eragon's arms as he picked her up. He was uncertain whether his weariness was due to the magic he had wrought or to the sheer length of time the task had taken him.

He gazed down at the girl and, feeling suddenly protective, murmured, "Sé ono waíse ilia." May you be happy. It was not a spell, not properly, but he hoped that maybe it could help her avoid some of the misery that afflicted so many people. Failing that, he hoped it would make her smile.

It did. A wide smile spread across her diminutive face, and with great enthusiasm, she said, "Gahh!"

Eragon smiled as well, then turned and strode outside.

As the entrance flaps fell away, he saw a small crowd gathered in a semicircle around the tent, some standing, some sitting, others squatting. Most he recognized from Carvahall, but Arya and the other elves were also there—somewhat apart from the rest—as well as several warriors of the Varden whose names he did not know. He spotted Elva lurking behind a nearby tent, her black lace veil lowered, hiding her face.

The group, Eragon realized, must have been waiting for hours, and he had not sensed anything of their presence. He had been safe enough with Saphira and the elves keeping watch, but that was no excuse for allowing himself to become so complacent.

I have to do better, he told himself.

At the forefront of the crowd stood Horst and his sons, looking worried. Horst's brow knotted as he gazed at the bundle in Eragon's arms, and he opened his mouth as if to say something, but no sound came forth.

Without pomp or ceremony, Eragon walked over to the smith and turned the girl so that he could see her face. For a moment, Horst did not move; then his eyes began to glisten and his expression changed to one of joy and relief so profound, it could have been mistaken for grief.

As he gave the girl to Horst, Eragon said, "My hands are too bloody for this kind of work, but I'm glad I was able to help."

Horst touched the girl's upper lip with the tip of his middle finger, then shook his head. "I can't believe it. . . . I can't believe it." He looked at Eragon. "Elain and I are forevermore in your debt. If—"

"There is no debt," Eragon said gently. "I only did what anyone would if they had the ability."

"But you were the one who healed her, and it's to you I'm grateful."

Eragon hesitated, then bowed his head, accepting Horst's gratitude. "What will you name her?"

The smith beamed at his daughter. "If it's agreeable to Elain, I thought we might call her Hope."

"Hope . . . A good name, that." *And don't we need some hope in our lives?* "And how is Elain?"

"Tired, but well."

Then Albriech and Baldor clustered around their father, peering at their new sister, as did Gertrude—who had emerged from the tent soon after Eragon—and once their shyness faded, the rest of the villagers joined them. Even the group of curious warriors pressed close to Horst, craning their necks in an attempt to catch a glimpse of the girl.

After a while, the elves unfolded their long limbs and approached as well. Seeing them, people quickly stepped out of the way, clearing a path to Horst. The smith stiffened and pushed his jaw out like a bulldog's as, one by one, the elves bent and examined the girl, sometimes whispering a word or two in the ancient language to her. They did not seem to notice or mind the suspicious stares that the villagers cast at them.

When only three elves were left in line, Elva darted out from behind the tent where she had been concealing herself and joined the end of the procession. She did not have to wait long before it was her turn to stand before Horst. Although he appeared reluctant, the smith lowered his arms and bent his knees, but he was so much taller than Elva, she had to rise up on the tips of her toes in order to see the infant. Eragon held his breath as she gazed at the formerly deformed child, unable to guess her reaction through her veil.

After a few seconds, Elva dropped back onto her heels. With a deliberate pace, she started down the path that ran past Eragon's tent. Twenty yards away, she stopped and turned toward him.

He tilted his head and lifted an eyebrow.

She nodded, a short, abrupt movement, then continued on her way.

As Eragon watched her go, Arya sidled up to him. "You should be proud of what you have accomplished," she murmured. "The child is sound and well formed. Not even our most skilled enchanters could improve on your gramarye. It is a great thing, what you have given this girl—a face and a future—and she will not forget it, I am sure. . . . None of us will."

Eragon saw that she and all the elves were regarding him with a look of newfound respect—but it was Arya's admiration and approval that meant the most to him. "I had the best of teachers," he replied in an equally low voice. Arya did not dispute his assertion. Together they watched the villagers mill around Horst and his daughter, talking excitedly. Without taking his eyes off them, Eragon leaned toward Arya and said, "Thank you for helping Elain."

"You're welcome. I would have been remiss not to."

Horst turned then and carried the child into the tent so that Elain might see her newborn daughter, but the knot of people showed no signs of dispersing. When Eragon was fed up with shaking hands and answering questions, he said farewell to Arya, then slipped off to his tent and tied the flaps closed behind him.

Unless we're under attack, I don't want to see anyone for the next ten hours, not even Nasuada, he said to Saphira as he threw himself onto his cot. *Will you tell Blödhgarm, please?*

Of course, she said. *Rest, little one, as will I.*

Eragon sighed and draped an arm over his face to block the morning light. His breathing slowed, his mind began to wander, and soon the strange sights and sounds of his waking dreams enveloped him—real, yet imaginary; vivid, yet transparent, as if the visions were made of colored glass—and, for a time, he was able to forget his responsibilities and the harrowing events of the past day. And all through his dreams, there wound the cradle song, like a whisper of wind, half heard, half forgotten, and it lulled him, with memories of his home, into a childlike peace.

NO REST FOR THE WEARY

Two dwarves, two men, and two Urgals—members of Nasuada's personal guard, the Nighthawks—were stationed outside the room in the castle where Nasuada had set up her headquarters. They stared at Roran with flat, empty eyes. He kept his face equally as blank as he stared back.

It was a game they had played before.

Despite the Nighthawks' lack of expression, he knew they were busy figuring out the fastest and most efficient ways to kill him. He knew, because he was doing the same with regard to them, as he always did.

I'd have to backtrack as fast as I could . . . spread them out a bit, he decided. *The men would get to me first; they're faster than the dwarves, and they'd slow the Urgals behind them. . . . Have to get those halberds away from them. It'd be tricky, but I think I could—one of them, at least. Might have to throw my hammer. Once I had a halberd, I could keep the rest at a distance. The dwarves wouldn't stand much of a chance, then, but the Urgals would be trouble. Ugly brutes, those. . . . If I used that pillar as cover, I could—*

The ironbound door that stood between the two lines of guards creaked as it swung open. A brightly dressed page of ten or twelve stepped out and announced, louder than was necessary, "Lady Nasuada will see you now!"

Several of the guards twitched, distracted, and their stares wavered for a second. Roran smiled as he swept past them and into the room beyond, knowing that their lapse, slight as it was, would have allowed him to kill at least two before they could have retaliated. *Until next time*, he thought.

The room was large, rectangular, and sparsely decorated: a too-small rug lay on the floor; a narrow, moth-eaten tapestry hung from the wall to his left; and a single lancet window pierced the wall to his right. Other than that, the room was devoid of ornamentation. Shoved into one corner was a long wooden table piled high with books, scrolls, and loose sheets of paper. A few massive chairs—upholstered with leather fastened with rows of tarnished brass tacks—stood scattered about the table, but neither Nasuada nor the dozen people who bustled around her deigned to use them. Jörmundur was not there, but Roran was familiar with several of the other warriors present: some he had fought under, others he had seen in action during battle or heard tell of from the men in his company.

"—and I don't care if it does give him a 'pain in his goiter'!" she exclaimed, and brought her right hand down flat on the table with a loud *slap*. "If we don't have those horseshoes, and more besides, we might as well eat our horses for all the good they'll do us. Do I make myself understood?"

As one, the men she addressed answered in the affirmative. They sounded somewhat intimidated, even abashed. Roran found it both strange and impressive that Nasuada, a woman, was able to command such respect from her warriors, a respect that he shared. She was one of the most determined and intelligent people he had ever known, and he was convinced that she would have succeeded no matter where she had been born.

"Now go," said Nasuada, and as eight men filed past her, she motioned Roran to the table. He waited patiently as she dipped a quill in an inkpot and scribbled several lines onto a small scroll, then handed it to one of the pages and said, "For the dwarf Narheim. And this time, make sure you get his reply before you return, or I'll send you over to the Urgals to fetch and clean for them."

"Yes, my Lady!" said the boy, and sprinted off, half frightened out of his wits.

Nasuada began to leaf through a stack of papers in front of her. Without looking up, she said, "Are you well rested, Roran?"

He wondered why she was interested. "Not particularly."

"That's unfortunate. Were you up all night?"

"Part of it. Elain, the wife of our smith, gave birth yesterday, but—"

"Yes, I was informed. I take it that you didn't stand vigil until Eragon healed the child?"

"No, I was too tired."

"At least you had that much sense." Reaching across the table, she picked up another sheet of paper and scrutinized it before adding it to her pile. In the same matter-of-fact tone she had been using, she said, "I have a mission for you, Stronghammer. Our forces at Aroughs have encountered stiff resistance—more than we anticipated. Captain Brigman has failed to resolve the situation, and we need those men back now. Therefore, I am sending you to Aroughs to replace Brigman. A horse is waiting for you by the south gate. You will ride fast as you can to Feinster, then from Feinster to Aroughs. Fresh horses will be waiting for you every ten miles between here and Feinster. Past there, you will have to find replacements on your own. I expect you to reach Aroughs within four days. Once you have caught up on your rest, that will leave you approximately . . . three days to end the siege." She glanced up at him. "A week from today, I want our banner flying over Aroughs. I don't care how you do it, Stronghammer; I just want it done. If you can't, then I'll have no choice but to send Eragon and Saphira to Aroughs, which will leave us barely able to defend ourselves should Murtagh or Galbatorix attack."

And then Katrina would be in danger, thought Roran. An unpleasant feeling settled in his gut. Riding to Aroughs in only four days would be a miserable ordeal, especially given how sore and bruised he was. Having to also capture the city in so little time would be compounding misery with madness. All in all, the mission was about as appealing as wrestling a bear with his hands tied behind his back.

He scratched his cheek through his beard. "I don't have any

experience with sieges," he said. "Leastways, not like this. There must be someone else in the Varden who would be better suited to the task. What about Martland Redbeard?"

Nasuada made a dismissive motion. "He can't ride at full gallop with only one hand. You should have more confidence in yourself, Stronghammer. There are others among the Varden who know more about the arts of war, it's true—men who have been in the field longer, men who received instruction from the finest warriors of their father's generation—but when swords are drawn and battle is joined, it's not knowledge or experience that matters most, it's whether you can *win*, and that's a trick you seem to have mastered. What's more, you're lucky."

She put down the topmost papers and leaned on her arms. "You've proven that you can fight. You've proven that you can fol-low orders . . . when it pleases you, that is." He resisted the urge to hunch his shoulders as he remembered the bitter, white-hot bite of the whip cutting into his back after he had been disciplined for defying Captain Edric's orders. "You've proven that you can lead a raiding party. So, Roran Stronghammer, let us see if you are capable of something more, shall we?"

He swallowed. "Yes, my Lady."

"Good. I am promoting you to captain for the time being. If you succeed in Aroughs, you may consider the title permanent, at least until you demonstrate that you are deserving of either greater or lesser honors." Returning her gaze to the table, she began to sort through a morass of scrolls, evidently searching for something hid-den underneath.

"Thank you."

Nasuada responded with a faint, noncommittal sound.

"How many men will I have under my command at Aroughs?" he asked.

"I gave Brigman a thousand warriors to capture the city. Of those, no more than eight hundred remain who are still fit for duty."

Roran nearly swore out loud. *So few.*

As if she had heard him, Nasuada said in a dry voice, "We were led to believe that Aroughs's defenses would be easier to overwhelm than has been the case."

"I see. May I take two or three men from Carvahall with me? You said once that you would let us serve together if we—"

"Yes, yes"—she waved a hand—"I know what I said." She pursed her lips, considering. "Very well, take whomever you want, just so long as you leave within the hour. Let me know how many are going with you, and I'll see to it that the appropriate number of horses are waiting along the way."

"May I take Carn?" he asked, naming the magician he had fought alongside on several occasions.

She paused and stared at the wall for a moment, her eyes unfocused. Then, to his relief, she nodded and resumed digging in the jumble of scrolls. "Ah, here we are." She pulled out a tube of parchment tied with a leather thong. "A map of Aroughs and its environs, as well as a larger map of Fenmark Province. I suggest you study them both most carefully."

She handed him the tube, which he slipped inside his tunic. "And here," she said, giving him a rectangle of folded parchment sealed with a blob of red wax, "is your commission, and"—a second rectangle, thicker than the first—"here are your orders. Show them to Brigman, but don't let him keep them. If I remember correctly, you've never learned to read, have you?"

He shrugged. "What for? I can count and figure as well as any man. My father said that teaching us to read made no more sense than teaching a dog to walk on his hind legs: amusing, but hardly worth the effort."

"And I might agree, had you stayed a farmer. But you didn't, and you're not." She motioned toward the pieces of parchment he held. "For all you know, one of those might be a writ ordering your execution. You are of limited use to me like this, Stronghammer. I cannot send you messages without others having to read them to you, and if you need to report to me, you will have no choice but to trust one of your underlings to record your words accurately. It makes you easy to manipulate. It makes you untrustworthy. If you hope to advance any further in the Varden, I suggest you find someone to teach you. Now begone; there are other matters that demand my attention."

She snapped her fingers, and one of the pages ran over to her. Placing a hand on the boy's shoulder, she bent down to his level and said, "I want you to fetch Jörmundur directly here. You'll find him somewhere along the market street, where those three houses—" In the midst of her instructions, she stopped and raised an eyebrow as she noticed that Roran had not budged. "Is there something else, Stronghammer?" she asked.

"Yes. Before I leave, I'd like to see Eragon."

"And why is that?"

"Most of the wards he gave me before the battle are gone now."

Nasuada frowned, then said to the page, "On the market street, where those three houses were burned. Do you know the place I mean? Right, off you go, then." She patted the boy on the back and stood upright as he ran out of the room. "It would be better if you didn't."

Her statement confused Roran, but he kept quiet, expecting that she would explain herself. She did, but in a roundabout way: "Did you notice how tired Eragon was during my audience with the werecats?"

"He could barely stay on his feet."

"Exactly. He's spread too thin, Roran. He can't protect you, me, Saphira, Arya, and who knows who else and still do what he has to. He needs to husband his strength for when he will have to fight Murtagh and Galbatorix. And the closer we get to Urû'baen, the more important it is that he be ready to face them at any given moment, night or day. We can't allow all of these other worries and distractions to weaken him. It was noble of him to heal the child's cat lip, but his doing so could have cost us the war!

"You fought without the advantage of wards when the Ra'zac attacked your village in the Spine. If you care about your cousin, if you care about defeating Galbatorix, you must learn to fight without them again."

When she finished, Roran bowed his head. She was right. "I'll depart at once."

"I appreciate that."

"By your leave . . ."

Turning, Roran strode toward the door. Just as he crossed the threshold, Nasuada called out, "Oh, and Stronghammer?"

He looked back, curious.

"Try not to burn down Aroughs, would you? Cities are rather hard to replace."

◆   ◆   ◆

DANCING WITH SWORDS

Eragon drummed his heels against the side of the boulder he was sitting on, bored and impatient to be gone.

He, Saphira, and Arya—as well as Blödhgarm and the other elves—were lounging on the bank next to the road that ran eastward from the city of Belatona: eastward through fields of ripe, verdant crops; over a wide stone bridge that arched across the Jiet River; and then around the southernmost point of Leona Lake. There the road branched, one fork turning to the right, toward the Burning Plains and Surda, the other turning north, toward Dras-Leona and eventually Urû'baen.

Thousands of men, dwarves, and Urgals milled about before Belatona's eastern gate, as well as within the city itself, arguing and shouting as the Varden tried to organize itself into a cohesive unit. In addition to the ragtag blocks of warriors on foot, there was King Orrin's cavalry—a mass of prancing, snorting horses. And strung out behind the fighting part of the army was the supply train: a mile-and-a-half-long line of carts, wagons, and wheeled pens, flanked by the vast herds of horned cattle the Varden had brought from Surda and supplemented by what animals they had been able to appropriate from farmers along their path. From the herds and the supply train came the lowing of oxen, the braying of mules and donkeys, the honking of geese, and the whinnies and neighs of draft horses.

It was enough to make Eragon want to plug his ears.

You would think we would be better at this, considering how many times we've done it before, he commented to Saphira as he hopped down off the boulder.

She sniffed. *They ought to put me in charge; I could scare them into position in less than an hour, and then we wouldn't have to waste so much time waiting.*

The thought amused him. *Yes, I'm sure you could. . . . Be careful what you say, though, or Nasuada might just make you do it.*

Then Eragon's mind turned to Roran, whom he had not seen since the night he had healed Horst and Elain's child, and he wondered how his cousin was doing and worried about leaving him so far behind.

"Blasted fool thing to do," Eragon muttered, remembering how Roran had left without letting him renew his wards.

He's an experienced hunter, Saphira pointed out. *He will not be so foolish as to allow his prey to claw him.*

I know, but sometimes it can't be helped. . . . He had best be careful, that's all. I don't want him to come back a cripple or, worse, wrapped in a shroud.

A grim mood descended upon Eragon, then he shook himself and bounced up and down on his feet, restless and eager to do something physical before spending the next few hours sitting on Saphira. He welcomed the opportunity to fly with her, but he disliked the prospect of being tethered to the same twelve or so miles for the whole day, circling vulture-like over the slow-moving troops. On their own, he and Saphira could have reached Dras-Leona by late that very afternoon.

He trotted away from the road to a relatively flat stretch of grass. There, ignoring the looks from Arya and the rest of the elves, he drew Brisingr and assumed the on-guard position Brom had first taught him so long ago. He inhaled slowly and settled into a low stance, feeling the texture of the ground through the soles of his boots.

With a short, hard exclamation, he swept the sword up around his head and brought it down in a slanting blow that would have halved any man, elf, or Urgal, regardless of their armor. He stopped the sword less than an inch above the ground and held it there, the blade trembling ever so slightly in his grip. Against the backdrop of the grass, the blue of the metal appeared vivid, almost unreal.

Eragon inhaled again and lunged forward, stabbing the air as if it were a deadly enemy. One by one, he practiced the basic moves of sword fighting, focusing not so much on speed or strength but on precision.

When he was pleasantly warm from his skill work, he glanced round at his guards, who stood in a semicircle some distance away. "Will one of you cross swords with me for a few minutes?" he asked, raising his voice.

The elves looked at one another, their expressions unreadable; then the elf Wyrden stepped forward. "I will, Shadeslayer, if it pleases you. However, I would ask that you wear your helm while we spar."

"Agreed."

Eragon returned Brisingr to its sheath, then ran to Saphira and clambered up her side, cutting the pad of his left thumb on one of her scales as he did so. He was wearing his mail tunic, and his greaves and bracers too, but he had stowed his helm in one of the saddlebags, so that it would not roll off Saphira and become lost in the grass.

As he retrieved the helm, he saw the casket that contained Glaedr's heart of hearts wrapped in a blanket and nestled at the bottom of the saddlebag. He reached down and touched the knotted bundle, silently paying tribute to what remained of the majestic golden dragon, then closed the saddlebag and swung down from Saphira's back.

Eragon donned his arming cap and helm as he strode back to the greensward. He licked the blood off his thumb, then pulled on his gauntlets, hoping that the cut would not bleed too much into the glove. Using slight variations of the same spell, he and Wyrden placed thin barriers—invisible, save for the faint, rippling distortion they caused in the air—over the edges of their swords, so they could not cut anything. They also lowered the wards that protected them from physical danger.

Then he and Wyrden took up positions opposite each other,

91

bowed, and raised their blades. Eragon stared into the elf's black, unblinking eyes, even as Wyrden stared at him. Keeping his gaze fixed on his opponent, Eragon felt his way forward and tried to inch around Wyrden's right side, where the right-handed elf would have more difficulty defending himself.

The elf slowly turned, crushing the grass beneath his heels as he kept his front oriented toward Eragon. After a few more steps, Eragon stopped. Wyrden was too alert and too experienced for Eragon to flank him; he would never catch the elf off balance. *Unless, of course, I can distract him.*

But before he could decide how to proceed, Wyrden feinted toward Eragon's right leg, as if to skewer him in the knee, then in midstroke, changed directions, twisting his wrist and arm to slash Eragon across his chest and neck.

Fast as the elf was, Eragon was faster still. As he spotted the shift in Wyrden's posture that betrayed his intentions, Eragon retreated a half step while bending his elbow and whipping his sword up past his face.

"Ha!" shouted Eragon as he caught Wyrden's sword on Brisingr. The blades produced a piercing *clang* as they collided.

With an effort, Eragon shoved Wyrden back, then leaped after him, battering him with a series of furious blows.

For several minutes, they fought upon the sward. Eragon landed the first touch—a light rap on Wyrden's hip—and the second as well, but thereafter, their duel was more equally matched, as the elf got the measure of him and began to anticipate his patterns of attack and defense. Eragon rarely had the opportunity to test himself against anyone as fast or strong as Wyrden, so he enjoyed the contest with the elf.

His pleasure, however, vanished when Wyrden landed four touches in quick succession: one on Eragon's right shoulder, two on his ribs, and a wicked draw cut across his abdomen. The blows smarted, but Eragon's pride smarted even more. It worried him that the elf had been able to slip past his guard so easily. If they had been fighting in earnest, Eragon knew that he would have been able to defeat Wyrden in their first few exchanges, but that thought was of little comfort.

You shouldn't let him hit you so much, observed Saphira.

Yes, I realize that, he growled.

Do you want me to knock him over for you?

No . . . not today.

His mood soured, Eragon lowered his blade and thanked Wyrden for sparring. The elf bowed and said, "You're welcome, Shadeslayer," then returned to his place among his comrades.

Eragon planted Brisingr in the ground between his boots—something he never would have done with a sword made of ordinary steel—and rested his hands on the pommel while he watched the men and animals jostling within the confines of the road that led from the vast stone city. The turbulence within the ranks had diminished substantially, and he guessed that it would not be long before the horns signaled the Varden to advance.

In the meantime, he was still restless.

He looked over at Arya, where she stood next to Saphira, and a smile gradually spread across his face. Resting Brisingr on his shoulder, he sauntered over and motioned toward her sword. "Arya, what about you? We've only sparred together that one time in Farthen Dûr." His grin widened, and he flourished Brisingr. "I've gotten a bit better since then."

"So you have."

"What say you, then?"

She cast a critical glance toward the Varden, then shrugged. "Why not?"

As they walked to the level patch of grass, he said, "You won't be able to best me quite so easily as before."

"I am sure you are right."

Arya prepared her sword, then they faced each other, some thirty feet apart. Feeling confident, Eragon advanced swiftly, already knowing where he was going to strike: at her left shoulder.

Arya held her ground and made no attempt to evade him. When he was less than four yards away, she smiled at him, a warm, brilliant smile that so enhanced her beauty, Eragon faltered, his thoughts dissolving into a muddle.

A line of steel flashed toward him.

He belatedly lifted Brisingr to deflect the blow. A jolt ran up his arm as the tip of the sword glanced off something solid—hilt, blade, or flesh he was not sure, but whatever it was, he knew that he had misjudged the distance and that his response had left him open to attack.

Before he could do much more than slow his forward momentum, another impact dashed his sword arm to the side; then a knot of pain formed in his midsection as Arya stabbed him, knocking him to the ground.

Eragon grunted as he landed on his back and the air rushed out of him. He gaped at the sky and tried to inhale, but his abdomen was cramped as hard as a stone, and he could not draw air into his lungs. A constellation of crimson spots appeared before his eyes, and for a few uncomfortable seconds, he feared he would lose consciousness. Then his muscles released, and with a loud gasp, he resumed breathing.

Once his head cleared, he slowly got back to his feet, using Brisingr for support. He leaned on the sword, standing hunched like an old man while he waited for the ache in his stomach to subside.

"You cheated," he said between gritted teeth.

"No, I exploited a weakness in my opponent. There is a difference."

"You think . . . that is a *weakness?*"

"When we fight, yes. Do you wish to continue?"

He answered by yanking Brisingr out of the sod, marching back to where he had started, and raising his sword.

"Good," said Arya. She mirrored his pose.

This time Eragon was much more wary as he closed with her,

and Arya did not stay in the same place. With careful steps, she advanced, her clear green eyes never leaving him.

She twitched, and Eragon flinched.

He realized he was holding his breath and forced himself to relax.

Another step forward, then he swung with all his speed and might.

She blocked his cut to her ribs and replied with a jab toward his exposed armpit. The blunted edge of her sword slid across the back of his free hand, scraping against the mail sewn onto his gauntlet as he slapped the blade away. At that moment, Arya's torso was exposed, but they were too close for Eragon to effectively slash or stab.

Instead, he lunged forward and struck at her breastbone with the pommel of his sword, thinking to knock her to the ground, as she had done to him.

She twisted out of the way, and the pommel went through the space where she had been as Eragon stumbled forward.

Without knowing quite how it had happened, he found himself standing motionless with one of Arya's arms wrapped around his neck and the cool, slippery surface of her spell-bound blade pressed against the side of his jaw.

From behind him, Arya whispered into his right ear, "I could have removed your head as easily as plucking an apple from a tree."

Then she released her hold and shoved him away. Angry, he whirled around and saw that she was already waiting for him, her sword at the ready and her expression determined.

Giving in to his anger, Eragon sprang after her.

Four blows they exchanged, each more terrible than the last. Arya struck first, chopping at his legs. He parried and slashed crosswise at her waist, but she skipped out of reach of Brisingr's glittering, sunlit edge. Without giving her an opportunity to retaliate, he followed up with a looping underhand cut, which she blocked with deceptive ease. Then she stepped forward and, with a touch as light as a hummingbird's wing, drew her sword across his belly.

Arya held her position at the conclusion of the stroke, her face mere inches from his. Her forehead glistened and her cheeks were flushed.

With exaggerated care, they disengaged.

Eragon straightened his tunic, then squatted next to Arya. His battle rage had burned itself out and left him focused, if not entirely at ease.

"I don't understand," he said quietly.

"You have become too accustomed to fighting Galbatorix's soldiers. They cannot hope to match you, so you take chances that would otherwise prove your undoing. Your attacks are too obvious—you should not rely on brute strength—and you have grown lax in your defense."

"Will you help me?" he asked. "Will you spar with me when you can?"

She nodded. "Of course. But if I cannot, then go to Blödhgarm for instruction; he is as skilled with a blade as I am. Practice is the only remedy you need, practice with the proper partners."

Eragon had just opened his mouth to thank her when he felt the presence of a consciousness other than Saphira's pressing against his mind, vast and frightening and filled with the most profound melancholy: a sadness so great, Eragon's throat tightened and the colors of the world seemed to lose their luster. And, in a slow, deep voice, as if speaking was a struggle of almost unbearable proportions, the golden dragon Glaedr said:

You must learn . . . to see what you are looking at.

Then the presence vanished, leaving behind a black void.

Eragon looked at Arya. She appeared as stricken as he was; she had heard Glaedr's words as well. Beyond her, Blödhgarm and the other elves stirred and murmured, while by the edge of the road, Saphira craned her neck as she tried to look at the saddlebags tied to her back.

They had all heard, Eragon realized.

Together he and Arya rose from the ground and sprinted over

to Saphira, who said, *He will not answer me; wherever he was, he has returned, and he will not listen to anything but his sorrow. Here, see. . . .*

Eragon joined his mind with hers, and with Arya's, and the three of them reached out with their thoughts toward Glaedr's heart of hearts, where it lay hidden within the saddlebags. What remained of the dragon felt more robust than before, but his mind was still closed to outside communication, his consciousness listless and indifferent, as it had been ever since Galbatorix slew his Rider, Oromis.

Eragon, Saphira, and Arya tried to rouse the dragon from his stupor. However, Glaedr steadfastly ignored them, taking no more notice of them than a sleeping cave bear might of a few flies buzzing around his head.

And yet Eragon could not help but think that Glaedr's indifference was not as complete as it seemed, given his comment.

At last the three of them admitted defeat and withdrew to their respective bodies. As Eragon returned to himself, Arya said, "Perhaps if we could touch his Eldunarí . . . ?"

Eragon sheathed Brisingr, then hopped onto Saphira's right foreleg and pulled himself into the saddle perched on the crest of her shoulders. He twisted round in his seat and began to work on the buckles of the saddlebags.

He had unfastened one of the buckles and was picking at the other when the brazen call of a horn rang forth from the head of the Varden, sounding the advance. At the signal, the vast train of men and animals lurched forward, their movements hesitant at first, but becoming smoother and more confident with every step.

Eragon glanced down at Arya, torn. She solved his dilemma by waving and saying, "Tonight, we will speak tonight. Go! Fly with the wind!"

He quickly rebuckled the saddlebag, then slid his legs through the rows of straps on either side of the saddle and pulled them tight, so he would not fall off Saphira in midair.

Then Saphira crouched and, with a roar of joy, leaped out over the road. The men below her ducked and cringed, and horses bolted as she unfurled her huge wings and flapped, driving herself away from the hard, unfriendly ground, up into the smooth expanse of the sky.

Eragon closed his eyes and tilted his face up, glad to finally be leaving Belatona. After spending a week in the city with nothing to do but eat and rest—for so Nasuada had insisted—he was eager to resume their journey toward Urû'baen.

When Saphira leveled off, hundreds of feet above the peaks and towers of the city, he said, *Will Glaedr recover, do you think?*

He will never be as he was.

No, but I hope that he will find a way to overcome his grief. I need his help, Saphira. There are so many things I still don't know. Without him, I have no one else to ask.

She was silent for a while, the only sound that of her wings. *We cannot hurry him,* she said. *He has been hurt in the worst way a dragon or Rider can be. Before he can help you, me, or anyone else, he must decide that he wants to continue living. Until he does, our words cannot reach him.*

✦ ✦ ✦

No Honor, No Glory, Only Blisters in Unfortunate Places

The belling of the hounds grew louder behind them, the pack of dogs howling for blood.

Roran tightened his grip on the reins and bent lower over the neck of his galloping charger. The pounding of the horse's hooves rolled through him like thunder.

He and his five men—Carn, Mandel, Baldor, Delwin, and Hamund—had stolen fresh horses from the stable of a manor house less than a half mile away. The grooms had not taken kindly to the theft. A show of swords had been sufficient to overcome their objections, but the grooms must have alerted the manor guards as soon as Roran and his companions had departed, for ten of the guards had set out after them, led by a pack of hunting dogs.

"There!" he shouted, and pointed toward a narrow strip of birch trees that extended from between two nearby hills, no doubt following the path of a stream.

At his word, the men pulled their horses off the well-traveled road and headed in the direction of the trees. The rough ground forced them to slow their headlong pace, but only slightly, despite the risk that the horses would step in a hole and break a leg or throw a rider. Dangerous as it was, allowing the hounds to catch them would be more dangerous still.

Roran dug his spurs into the sides of the horse and shouted "Yah!" as loudly as he could through his dust-clogged throat. The gelding leaped forward and, stride by stride, began to gain on Carn.

Roran knew that his horse would soon reach a point where it could no longer produce such bursts of speed, no matter how hard he jabbed it with his spurs or whipped it with the ends of his reins. He hated to be cruel, and he had no desire to ride the animal to death, but he would not spare the horse if it meant the failure of their mission.

As he drew level with Carn, Roran shouted, "Can't you hide our trail with a spell?"

"Don't know how!" Carn replied, barely audible over the rush of wind and the sound of the galloping horses. "It's too complicated!"

Roran swore and glanced over his shoulder. The hounds were rounding the last bend in the road. They seemed to fly over the ground, their long, lean bodies lengthening and contracting at a violent rate. Even at that distance, Roran could make out the red of their tongues, and he fancied he saw a gleam of white fangs.

When they reached the trees, Roran turned and began to ride back into the hills, staying as close as he could to the line of birches without hitting low-hanging branches or fallen logs. The others did likewise, shouting at their horses to keep them from slowing as they raced up the incline.

To his right, Roran glimpsed Mandel hunched over his speckled mare, a feral snarl on his face. The younger man had impressed Roran with his stamina and fortitude over the past three days. Ever since Katrina's father, Sloan, had betrayed the villagers of Carvahall and killed Mandel's father, Byrd, Mandel had seemed desperate to prove himself the equal of any man in the village; he had acquitted himself with honor in the last two battles between the Varden and the Empire.

A thick branch hurtled toward Roran's head. He ducked, hearing and feeling the tips of dry twigs snapping against the top of his helm. A torn leaf tumbled down his face and covered his right eye for a moment; then the wind snatched it away.

The gelding's breathing became increasingly labored as they followed the rift deeper into the hills. Roran peeked under his arm and saw that the pack of hounds was less than a quarter mile away. Another few minutes, and they would surely overtake the horses.

Blast it, he thought. He raked his gaze back and forth across the densely packed trees to his left and the grassy hill to his right, searching for something—anything—that could help them lose their pursuers.

He was so fuzzy-headed from exhaustion, he almost missed it.

Twenty yards ahead of him, a crooked deer trail ran down the side of the hill, crossed his path, then disappeared into the trees.

"Whoa! . . . Whoa!" Roran shouted, leaning back in his stirrups and hauling on the reins. The gelding slowed to a trot, though it snorted with protest and tossed its head, trying to get the bit between its teeth. "Oh no you don't," Roran growled, and tugged on the reins even harder.

"Hurry!" he called to the rest of the group as he turned his horse and entered the thicket. The air was cool under the trees, almost chilly, which was a welcome relief, hot as he was from his exertion. He only had a moment to savor the sensation before the gelding pitched forward and began to stumble down the side of the bank toward the stream below. Dead leaves crackled under its iron-shod hooves. In order not to fall over the horse's neck and head, Roran had to lie almost flat against its back, his legs stuck out straight in front of him, knees locked.

When they reached the bottom of the gorge, the gelding clattered across the stony creek, splashing wings of water as high as Roran's knees. Roran paused at the far side to see whether the others were still with him. They were, riding nose to tail, down through the trees.

Above them, where they had entered the thicket, he could hear the yapping of the dogs.

We're going to have to turn and fight, he realized.

He swore again and spurred the gelding away from the stream, climbing the soft, moss-covered bank as he continued along the faintly marked trail.

Not far from the stream was a wall of ferns, and beyond that, a hollow. Roran spotted a fallen tree that he thought might serve as a makeshift barrier if it could be dragged into place.

I just hope they don't have bows, he thought.

He waved at his men. "Here!"

With a slap of the reins, he drove the gelding through the bracken and into the hollow, then slid out of the saddle, though he kept a tight hold on it. As his feet struck the ground, his legs gave out beneath him, and he would have fallen if not for the support. He grimaced and pressed his forehead against the shoulder of the horse, panting as he waited for the tremors in his legs to subside.

The rest of the group crowded around him, filling the air with the stink of sweat and the jingle of harnesses. The horses shuddered, their chests heaving, and yellow foam dripped from the corners of their mouths.

"Help me," he said to Baldor, and motioned at the fallen tree. They fit their hands under the thick end of the log and heaved it off the ground. Roran gritted his teeth as his back and thighs screamed with pain. Riding at full gallop for three days—combined with less than three hours of sleep for every twelve spent in the saddle—had left him frighteningly weak.

I might as well be going into battle drunk, sick, and beaten half out of my senses, Roran realized as he let go of the log and straightened upright. The thought unnerved him.

The six men positioned themselves in front of the horses, facing the trampled wall of ferns, and drew their weapons. Outside the hollow, the hunting cries of the hounds sounded louder than ever, their overeager yelps echoing off the trees in a raucous din.

Roran tensed and lifted his hammer higher. Then, interspersed with the barking of the dogs, he heard the strange, lilting melody of the ancient language emanating from Carn, and the power contained within the phrases caused the back of Roran's neck to prickle with alarm. The spellcaster uttered several lines in a short, breathless manner, speaking so quickly, the words melded together into an indistinct babble. As soon as he finished, he gestured at Roran and the others and said in a strained whisper, "Get down!"

Without question, Roran dropped to his haunches. Not for the first time, he cursed the fact that he was unable to use magic himself. Of all the skills a warrior could possess, none was more useful; lacking it left him at the mercy of those who could reshape the world with nothing more than their will and a word.

The ferns in front of him rustled and shook; then a hound pushed its black-tipped snout through the foliage and peered at the hollow, nose twitching. Delwin hissed and raised his sword, as if to behead the dog, but Carn made an urgent noise in his throat and waved at him until he lowered his blade.

The dog furrowed its brow, appearing puzzled. It scented the air again, then licked its jowls with its engorged, purplish tongue, and withdrew.

As the fronds sprang back over the dog's face, Roran slowly released the breath he had been holding. He looked at Carn and raised an eyebrow, hoping for an explanation, but Carn just shook his head and placed a finger over his lips.

A few seconds later, two more dogs wiggled their way through the undergrowth to inspect the hollow; then, like the first one, they backed out after a short while. Soon the pack began to whine and yip as they cast about among the trees, trying to figure out where their prey had gone.

As he sat waiting, Roran noticed that his leggings were mottled with several dark blotches along the inside of his thighs. He touched one of the discolored areas, and his fingers came away with a film of bloody liquid. Each blotch marked the location of a blister. Nor were they his only ones; he could feel blisters on his hands—where the reins had chafed the web of skin between his thumbs and forefingers—and on his heels, and in other, more uncomfortable places.

With an expression of distaste, he wiped his fingers against the ground. He looked at his men, at how they crouched and knelt, and he saw the discomfort on their faces whenever they moved and the slightly twisted grips with which they held their weapons. They were in no better condition than he was.

Roran decided that when they next stopped to sleep he would have Carn heal their sores. If the magician seemed too tired, however, Roran would refrain from having his own blisters healed; he would rather endure the pain than allow Carn to expend all of his strength before they arrived at Aroughs, for Roran suspected that Carn's skills might very well prove useful in capturing the city.

Thinking of Aroughs and of the siege he was somehow supposed to win caused Roran to press his free hand against his breast to check that the packet containing the orders he could not read and the commission he doubted he would be able to keep were still safely tucked in his tunic. They were.

After several long, tense minutes, one of the hounds began to bark excitedly somewhere in the trees upstream. The other dogs rushed in that direction and resumed the deep-chested baying that meant they were in close pursuit of their quarry.

When the clamor had receded, Roran slowly rose to his full height and swept his gaze over the trees and bushes. "All clear," he said, keeping his voice subdued.

As the others stood, Hamund—who was tall and shaggy-haired and had deep lines next to his mouth, although he was only a year older than Roran—turned on Carn, scowling, and said, "Why couldn't you have done that before, instead of letting us go riding willy-nilly over the countryside and almost breaking our necks coming down that hill?" He motioned back toward the stream.

Carn responded with an equally angry tone: "Because I hadn't thought of it yet, that's why. Given that I just saved you the inconvenience of having a host of small holes poked in your hide, I would think you might show a bit of gratitude."

"Is that so? Well, I think that you ought to spend more time working on your spells *before* we're chased halfway to who-knows-where and—"

Fearing that their argument could turn dangerous, Roran stepped between them. "Enough," he said. Then he asked Carn, "Will your spell hide us from the guards?"

Carn shook his head. "Men are harder to fool than dogs." He cast a disparaging look at Hamund. "Most of them, at least. I can hide us, but I can't hide our trail." And he indicated the crushed and broken ferns, as well as the hoofprints gouged into the damp soil. "They'll know we're here. If we leave before they catch sight of us, the dogs will draw them off and we'll—"

"Mount up!" Roran ordered.

With an assortment of half-muttered curses and poorly concealed groans, the men climbed back onto their steeds. Roran glanced over the hollow one last time to make sure that they had not forgotten anything, then guided his charger to the head of the group and tapped the horse with his spurs.

And together they galloped out from under the shadow of the trees and away from the ravine as they resumed their seemingly never-ending journey to Aroughs. What he would do once they reached the city, though, Roran had not the slightest idea.

MOONEATER

ragon rolled his shoulders as he walked through the Varden's camp, trying to work out the kink in his neck that he had acquired while sparring with Arya and Blödhgarm earlier that afternoon.

As he topped a small hill, which stood like a lone island amid the sea of tents, he rested his hands on his hips and paused to take in the view. Before him lay the dark spread of Leona Lake, gleaming in the twilight as the crests of the shallow waves reflected the orange torchlight from the camp. The road the Varden had been following lay between the tents and the shore: a broad strip of paving stones set with mortar that had been constructed, or so Jeod had informed him, long before Galbatorix had overthrown the Riders. A quarter mile to the north, a small, squat fishing village sat close against the water; Eragon knew its inhabitants were far from happy that an army was camped on their doorstep.

You must learn . . . to see what you are looking at.

Since leaving Belatona, Eragon had spent hours pondering Glaedr's advice. He was not certain exactly what the dragon had meant by it, as Glaedr had refused to say anything more after delivering his enigmatic statement, so Eragon had chosen to interpret his instruction literally. He had striven to truly *see* everything before him, no matter how small or apparently insignificant, and to understand the meaning of that which he beheld.

Try though he might, he felt as if he failed miserably. Wherever he looked, he saw an overwhelming amount of detail, but he was convinced there was even more that he was not perceptive enough to notice. Worse, he was rarely able to make sense of what he *was* aware of, like why there was no smoke rising from three of the chimneys in the fishing village.

Despite his sense of futility, the effort had proved helpful in at least one regard: Arya no longer defeated him every time they crossed blades. He had watched her with redoubled attention—studying her as closely as a deer he was stalking—and as a result, he had won a few of their matches. However, he still was not her equal, much less her better. And he did not know what he needed to learn—nor who could teach him—in order to become as skilled with a blade as she was.

Perhaps Arya is right, and experience is the only mentor that can help me now, Eragon thought. *Experience requires time, though, and time is what I have the least of. We'll be at Dras-Leona soon, and then Urû'baen. A few months, at the most, and we'll have to face Galbatorix and Shruikan.*

He sighed and rubbed his face, trying to turn his mind in other, less troubling directions. Always he returned to the same set of doubts, worrying at them like a dog with a marrow bone, only with nothing to show for it other than a constant and increasing sense of anxiety.

Lost in rumination, he continued down the hill. He wandered among the shadowy tents, heading generally toward his own, but paying little attention to his exact path. As it invariably did, walking helped calm him. The men who were still about moved aside for him when they met and clapped a fist against their chests, usually accompanied by a soft greeting of "Shadeslayer," to which Eragon responded with a polite nod.

He had been walking for a quarter hour, stopping and starting in counterpoint to his thoughts, when the high-pitched tone of a woman describing something with great enthusiasm interrupted his reverie. Curious, he followed the sound until he arrived at a tent set apart from the rest, near the base of a gnarled willow tree, the only tree near the lake that the army had not chopped down for firewood.

There, under the ceiling of branches, was the strangest sight he had ever seen.

Twelve Urgals, including their war chief, Nar Garzhvog, sat in a semicircle around a low, flickering campfire. Fearsome shadows danced on their faces, emphasizing their heavy brows, broad cheekbones, and massive jaws, as well as the ridges on their horns, which sprouted from their foreheads and curved back and around the sides of their heads. The Urgals were bare-armed and bare-chested, except for the leather cuffs on their wrists and the woven straps they wore slung from shoulder to waist. In addition to Garzhvog, three other Kull were present. Their hulking size made the rest of the Urgals—not one of whom was under six feet tall—appear childishly small.

Scattered among the Urgals—among and *on* them—were several dozen werecats in their animal forms. Many of the cats sat upright before the fire, utterly still, not even moving their tails, their tufted ears pricked forward attentively. Others lay sprawled on the ground, or on the Urgals' laps, or in their arms. To Eragon's astonishment, he even spotted one werecat—a slim white female—resting curled atop the broad head of a Kull, her right foreleg draped over the edge of his skull and her paw pressed possessively against the middle of his brow. Tiny though the werecats were compared to the Urgals, they looked equally savage, and Eragon had no doubt whom he would rather face in battle; Urgals he understood, whereas werecats were . . . unpredictable.

On the other side of the fire, in front of the tent, was the herbalist Angela. She was sitting cross-legged on a folded blanket, spinning a pile of carded wool into fine thread using a drop spindle, which she held out before her as if to entrance those who were watching. Both werecats and Urgals stared at her intently, their eyes never leaving her as she said:

"—but he was too slow, and the raging, red-eyed rabbit ripped out Hord's throat, killing him instantly. Then the hare fled into the forest, and out of recorded history. However"—and here Angela leaned forward and lowered her voice—"if you travel through those parts, as I have . . . sometimes, even to this day, you will come across a freshly killed deer or Feldûnost that looks as if it has been *nibbled* at, like a turnip. And all around it, you'll see the prints of an unusually large rabbit. Every now and then, a warrior from Kvôth will go missing, only to be found lying dead with his throat torn out . . . always with his throat torn out."

She resumed her former position. "Terrin was horribly upset by the loss of his friend, of course, and he wanted to chase after the hare, but the dwarves still needed his help. So he returned to the stronghold, and for three more days and three more nights the defenders held the walls, until their supplies were low and every warrior was covered in wounds.

"At last, on the morning of the fourth day, when all seemed hopeless, the clouds parted, and far in the distance, Terrin was amazed to see Mimring flying toward the stronghold at the head of a huge thunder of dragons. The sight of the dragons frightened the attackers so much, they threw down their weapons and fled into the wilderness." Angela's mouth quirked. "This, as you can imagine, made the dwarves of Kvôth rather happy, and there was much rejoicing.

"And when Mimring landed, Terrin saw, much to his surprise, that his scales had become as clear as diamonds, which, it is said, happened because Mimring flew so close to the sun—for in order to fetch the other dragons in time, he had had to fly *over* the peaks of the Beor Mountains, higher than any dragon has ever flown before or since. From then on, Terrin was known as the hero of the Siege of Kvôth, and his dragon was known as Mimring the Brilliant, on account of his scales, and they lived happily ever after. Although, if truth be told, Terrin always remained rather afraid of rabbits, even into his old age. And *that* is what really happened at Kvôth."

As she fell silent, the werecats began to purr, and the Urgals uttered several low grunts of approval.

"You tell a good story, Uluthrek," Garzhvog said, his voice sounding like the rumble of falling rock.

"Thank you."

"But not as I have heard it told," Eragon commented as he stepped into the light.

Angela's expression brightened. "Well, you can hardly expect the dwarves to admit they were at the mercy of a rabbit. Have you been lurking in the shadows this whole time?"

"Only for a minute," he confessed.

"Then you missed the best part of the story, and I'm not about to repeat myself tonight. My throat is too dry now for talking at length."

Eragon felt the vibration through the soles of his boots as the Kull and the other Urgals got to their feet, much to the displeasure of the werecats resting on them, several of whom uttered yowls of protest as they dropped to the ground.

As he gazed at the collection of grotesque horned faces gathered around the fire, Eragon had to suppress the urge to grasp the hilt of his sword. Even after having fought, traveled, and hunted alongside the Urgals, and even after having sifted through the thoughts of several of them, being in their presence still gave him pause. He knew in his mind that they were allies, but his bones and his muscles could not forget the visceral terror that had gripped him during the numerous occasions when he had confronted their kind in battle.

Garzhvog removed something from the leather pouch he wore on his belt. Extending his thick arm over the fire, he handed it to Angela, who set down her spinning to accept the object with cupped hands. It was a rough orb of sea-green crystal, which twinkled like crusted snow. She slipped it inside the sleeve of her garment, then picked up her drop spindle.

Garzhvog said, "You must come to our camp sometime, Uluthrek, and we will tell you many stories of our own. We have a chanter with us. He is good; when you listen to him recite the tale of Nar Tulkhqa's victory at Stavarosk, your blood grows hot and you feel like bellowing at the moon and locking horns with even the strongest of your foes."

"That would depend on whether you have horns to lock," said Angela. "I would be honored to sit story with you. Perhaps tomorrow evening?"

The giant Kull agreed; then Eragon asked, "Where is Stavarosk? I've not heard of it before."

The Urgals shifted uneasily, and Garzhvog lowered his head and snorted like a bull. "What trickery is this, Firesword?" he demanded. "Do you seek to challenge me by insulting us so?" He opened and closed his hands with unmistakable menace.

Wary, Eragon said, "I meant no harm, Nar Garzhvog. It was an honest question; I've never heard the name of Stavarosk before."

A murmur of surprise spread among the Urgals. "How can this be?" said Garzhvog. "Do not all humans know of Stavarosk? Is it not sung of in every hall from the northern wastes to the Beor Mountains as our greatest triumph? Surely, if nowhere else, the Varden must speak of it."

Angela sighed and, without looking up from her spinning, said, "You'd best tell them."

In the back of his mind, Eragon felt Saphira watching their exchange, and he knew that she was readying herself to fly from their tent to his side if a fight became unavoidable.

Choosing his words with care, he said: "No one has mentioned it to me, but then I have not been with the Varden for very long, and—"

"Drajl!" swore Garzhvog. "The lack-horned betrayer does not even have the courage to admit his own defeat. He is a coward and liar!"

"Who? Galbatorix?" Eragon asked cautiously.

A number of the werecats hissed at the mention of the king.

Garzhvog nodded. "Aye. When he came to power, he sought to destroy our race forever. He sent a vast army into the Spine. His soldiers crushed our villages, burned our bones, and left the earth black and bitter behind them. We fought—at first with joy, then with despair, but still we fought. It was the only thing we could do. There was nowhere for us to run, nowhere to hide. Who would protect the Urgralgra when even the Riders had been brought to their knees?

"We were lucky, though. We had a great war chief to lead us, Nar Tulkhqa. He had once been captured by humans, and he had spent many years fighting them, so he knew how you think. Because of that, he was able to rally many of our tribes under his banner. Then he lured Galbatorix's army into a narrow passage deep within the mountains, and our rams fell upon them from either side. It was a slaughter, Firesword. The ground was wet with blood, and the piles of bodies stood higher than my head. Even to this day, if you go to Stavarosk, you will feel the bones cracking under your feet, and you will find coins and swords and pieces of armor under every patch of moss."

"So it was you!" Eragon exclaimed. "All my life I've heard it said that Galbatorix once lost half his men in the Spine, but no one could tell me how or why."

"*More* than half his men, Firesword." Garzhvog rolled his shoulders and made a guttural noise in the back of his throat. "And now I see we must work to spread word of it if any are to know of our victory. We will track down your chanters, your bards, and we will teach them the songs concerning Nar Tulkhqa, and we will make sure that they remember to recite them often and loudly." He nodded once, as if his mind was made up—an impressive gesture considering the ponderous size of his head—then said, "Farewell, Firesword. Farewell, Uluthrek." Then he and his warriors lumbered off into the darkness.

Angela chuckled, startling Eragon.

"What?" he asked, turning to her.

She smiled. "I'm imagining the expression some poor lute player is going to have in a few minutes when he looks out his tent and sees twelve Urgals, four of them Kull, standing outside, eager to give him an education in Urgal culture. I'll be impressed if we don't hear him scream." She chuckled again.

Similarly amused, Eragon lowered himself to the ground and stirred the coals with the end of a branch. A warm, heavy weight settled in his lap, and he looked down to see the white werecat curled up on his legs. He raised a hand to pet her, then thought better of it and asked the cat, "May I?"

The werecat flicked her tail but otherwise ignored him.

Hoping that he was not doing the wrong thing, Eragon tentatively began to rub the creature's neck. A moment later, a loud, throbbing purr filled the night air.

"She likes you," Angela observed.

For some reason, Eragon felt inordinately pleased. "Who is she? I mean, that is, who are you? What is your name?" He cast a quick glance at the werecat, worried that he had offended her.

Angela laughed quietly. "Her name is Shadowhunter. Or rather, that is what her name means in the language of the werecats. Properly, she is . . ." Here the herbalist uttered a strange coughing, growling sound that made the nape of Eragon's neck crawl. "Shadowhunter is mated to Grimrr Halfpaw, so one might say that she is queen of the werecats."

The purring increased in volume.

"I see." Eragon looked around at the other werecats. "Where is Solembum?"

"Busy chasing a long-whiskered female who is half his age. He's acting as foolish as a kitten . . . but then, everyone's entitled to a little foolishness once in a while." Catching the spindle with her left hand, she stopped its motion and wound the newly formed thread around the base of the wooden disk. Then she gave the spindle a twist to start it spinning again and resumed drafting from the batt of wool in her other hand. "You look as if you are full to bursting with questions, Shadeslayer."

"Whenever I meet you, I always end up feeling more confused than before."

"Always? That's rather absolutist of you. Very well, I will attempt to be informative. Ask away."

Skeptical of her apparent openness, Eragon considered what he would like to know. Finally: "A thunder of dragons? What did you—"

"*That* is the proper term for a flock of dragons. If ever you had heard one in full flight, you would understand. When ten, twelve, or more dragons flew past overhead, the very air would reverberate around you, as if you were sitting inside a giant drum. Besides, what else could you call a group of dragons? You have your murder of ravens, your convocation of eagles, your gaggle of geese, your raft of ducks, your band of jays, your parliament of owls, and so on, but what about dragons? A *hunger* of dragons? That doesn't sound quite right. Nor does referring to them as a *blaze* or a *terror*, although I'm rather fond of *terror*, all things considered: a terror of dragons. . . . But no, a flock of dragons is called a thunder. Which you would know if your education had consisted of more than just learning how to swing a sword and conjugate a few verbs in the ancient language."

"I'm sure you're right," he said, humoring her. Through his ever-present link with Saphira, he sensed her approval of the phrase "a thunder of dragons," an opinion he shared; it was a fitting description.

He thought for a moment longer, then asked, "And why did Garzhvog call you Uluthrek?"

"It is the title the Urgals gave me long, long ago, when I traveled among them."

"What does it mean?"

"Mooneater."

"Mooneater? What a strange name. How did you come by it?"

"I ate the moon, of course. How else?"

Eragon frowned and concentrated on petting the werecat for a minute. Then: "Why did Garzhvog give you that stone?"

"Because I told him a story. I thought that was obvious."

"But what is it?"

"A piece of rock. Didn't you notice?" She clucked with disapproval. "Really, you ought to pay better attention to what's going on around you. Otherwise, someone's liable to stick a knife in you when you're not looking. And then whom would I exchange cryptic remarks with?" She tossed her hair. "Go on, ask me another question. I'm rather enjoying this game."

He cocked an eyebrow at her and, although he was certain it was pointless, he said, *"Cheep cheep?"*

The herbalist brayed with laughter, and some of the werecats opened their mouths in what appeared to be toothy smiles. However, Shadowhunter seemed displeased, for she dug her claws into Eragon's legs, making him wince.

"Well," said Angela, still laughing, "if you *must* have answers, that's as good a story as any. Let's see. . . . Several years ago, when I was traveling along the edge of Du Weldenvarden, way out to the west, miles and miles from any city, town, or village, I happened upon Grimrr. At the time, he was only the leader of a small tribe of werecats, and he still had full use of both his paws. Anyway, I found him toying with a fledgling robin that had fallen out of its nest in a nearby tree. I wouldn't have minded if he had just killed the bird and eaten it—that's what cats are supposed to do, after all—but he was torturing the poor thing: pulling on its wings; nibbling its tail; letting it hop away, then knocking it over." Angela wrinkled her nose with distaste. "I *told* him that he ought to stop, but he only growled and ignored me." She fixed Eragon with a stern gaze. "I don't *like* it when people ignore me. So, I took the bird away from him, and I wiggled my fingers and cast a spell, and for the next week, whenever he opened his mouth, he chirped like a songbird."

"He *chirped?*"

Angela nodded, beaming with suppressed mirth. "I've never laughed so hard in my life. None of the other werecats would go anywhere near him for the whole week."

"No wonder he hates you."

115

"What of it? If you don't make a few enemies every now and then, you're a coward—or worse. Besides, it was worth it to see his reaction. Oh, he was angry!"

Shadowhunter uttered a soft warning growl and tightened her claws again.

Grimacing, Eragon said, "Maybe it would be best to change the subject?"

"Mmm."

Before he could suggest a new topic, a loud scream rang out from somewhere in the middle of the camp. The cry echoed three times over the rows of tents before fading into silence.

Eragon looked at Angela, and she at him, and then they both began to laugh.

Rumors and Writing

It's late, said Saphira as Eragon sauntered toward his tent, beside which she lay coiled, sparkling like a mound of azure coals in the dim light of the torches. She regarded him with a single, heavy-lidded eye.

He crouched by her head and pressed his brow against hers for several moments, hugging her spiky jaw. *So it is,* he said at last. *And you need your rest after flying into the wind all day. Sleep, and I'll see you in the morning.*

She blinked once in acknowledgment.

Inside his tent, Eragon lit a single candle for comfort. Then he pulled off his boots and sat on his cot with his legs folded under him. He slowed his breathing and allowed his mind to open and expand outward to touch all of the living things around him, from the worms and the insects in the ground to Saphira and the warriors of the Varden, and even the few remaining plants nearby, the energy from which was pale and hard to see compared with the burning brilliance of even the smallest animal.

For a long while, he sat there, empty of thoughts, aware of a thousand sensations, the sharp and the subtle, concentrating on nothing but the steady inflow and outflow of air in his lungs.

Off in the distance, he heard men talking as they stood around a watchfire. The night air carried their voices farther than they intended, far enough that his keen ears were able to make out their words. He could sense their minds as well, and he could have read their thoughts had he wanted, but instead he chose to respect their innermost privacy and merely listen.

A deep-voiced fellow was saying, "—and the way they stare down their noses at you, as if you're the lowest of the low. Half the time they won't even talk to you when you ask them a friendly question. They just turn their shoulder and walk away."

"Aye," said another man. "And their women—as beautiful as statues and about half as inviting."

"That's because you're a right ugly bastard, Svern, that's why."

"It's not my fault my father had a habit of seducing milkmaids wherever he went. Besides, you're hardly one to point fingers; you could give children nightmares with that face of yours."

The deep-voiced warrior grunted; then someone coughed and spat, and Eragon heard the sizzle of moisture evaporating as it struck a piece of burning wood.

A third speaker entered the conversation: "I don't like the elves any more than you do, but we need them to win this war."

"What if they turn on us afterward, though?" asked the deep-voiced man.

"Hear, hear," added Svern. "Look what happened at Ceunon and Gil'ead. All his men, all his power, and Galbatorix still couldn't stop them from swarming over the walls."

"Maybe he wasn't trying," suggested the third speaker.

A long pause followed.

Then the deep-voiced man said, "Now, there's a singularly unpleasant thought. . . . Still, whether he was or wasn't, I don't see how we could hold off the elves if they decided to reclaim their old territories. They're faster and stronger than we are, and unlike us, there's not one of them who can't use magic."

"Ah, but we have Eragon," Svern countered. "He could drive them back to their forest all by himself, if he wanted to."

"Him? Bah! He looks more like an elf than he does his own flesh and blood. I wouldn't count on his loyalty any more than the Urgals'."

The third man spoke up again: "Have you noticed, he's always freshly shaven, no matter how early in the morning we break camp?"

"He must use magic for a razor."

"Goes against the natural order of things, it does. That and all the other spells being tossed around nowadays. Makes you want to hide in a cave somewhere and let the magicians kill each other off without any interference from us."

"I don't seem to recall you complaining when the healers used a spell instead of a pair of tongs to remove that arrow from your shoulder."

"Maybe, but the arrow never would have ended up in my shoulder if it weren't for Galbatorix. And it's him and his magic that's caused this whole mess."

Someone snorted. "True enough, but I'd bet every last copper I have that, Galbatorix or no, you still would've ended up with an arrow sticking out of you. You're too mean to do anything other than fight."

"Eragon saved my life in Feinster, you know," said Svern.

"Aye, and if you bore us with the story one more time, I'll have you scrubbing pots for a week."

"Well, he did. . . ."

There was another silence, which was broken when the deep-voiced warrior sighed. "We need a way to protect ourselves. That's the problem. We're at the mercy of the elves, the magicians—ours and theirs—and every other strange creature that roams the land. It's all well and fine for the likes of Eragon, but we're not so fortunate. What we need is—"

"What we need," said Svern, "are the Riders. They'd put the world in order."

"*Pfft.* With what dragons? You can't have Riders without dragons. Besides, we still wouldn't be able to defend ourselves, and that's what bothers me. I'm not a child to go hiding behind my mother's skirts, but if a Shade were to appear out of the night, there isn't a blasted thing we could do to keep it from tearing our heads off."

"That reminds me, did you hear about Lord Barst?" asked the third man.

Svern uttered a sound of agreement. "I heard he ate his heart afterward."

"What's this now?" asked the deep-voiced warrior.

"Barst—"

"Barst?"

"You know, the earl with an estate up by Gil'ead—"

"Isn't he the one who drove his horses into the Ramr just to spite—"

"Aye, that's the one. Anyway, so he goes to this village and orders all the men to join Galbatorix's army. Same story as always. Only, the men refuse, and they attack Barst and his soldiers."

"Brave," said the deep-voiced man. "Stupid, but brave."

"Well, Barst was too clever for them; he had archers posted around the village before he went in. The soldiers kill half the men and thrash the rest within an inch of their lives. No surprise there. Then Barst takes the leader, the man who started the fight, and he grabs him by the neck, and with his bare hands, he pulls his head right off!"

"No."

"Like a chicken. And what's worse, he ordered the man's family burned alive as well."

"Barst must be as strong as an Urgal to tear off a man's head," said Svern.

"Maybe there's a trick to it."

"Could it be magic?" asked the deep-voiced man.

"By all accounts, he's always been strong—strong and smart. When he was just a young man, he's said to have killed a wounded ox with a single blow of his fist."

"Still sounds like magic to me."

"That's because you see evil magicians lurking in every shadow, you do."

The deep-voiced warrior grunted, but did not speak.

After that, the men dispersed to walk their rounds, and Eragon heard nothing more from them. At any other time, their conversation might have disturbed him, but because of his meditation, he remained unperturbed throughout, although he made an effort to remember what they said, so that he could consider it properly later.

Once his thoughts were in order, and he felt calm and relaxed, Eragon closed off his mind, opened his eyes, and slowly unfolded his legs, working the stiffness out of his muscles.

The motion of the candle flame caught his eye, and he stared at it for a minute, enthralled by the contortions of the fire.

Then he went over to where he had dropped Saphira's saddlebags earlier and removed the quill, the brush, the bottle of ink, and the sheets of parchment that he had begged off Jeod several days before, as well as the copy of *Domia abr Wyrda* that the old scholar had given him.

Returning to the cot, Eragon placed the heavy book well away from him, so as to minimize the chances of spilling ink on it. He laid his shield across his knees, like a tray, and spread the sheets of parchment over the curved surface. A sharp, tannic odor filled his nostrils as he unstoppered the bottle and dipped the quill into the oak-gall ink.

He touched the nib of the feather against the lip of the bottle, to draw off the excess liquid, then carefully made his first stroke. The quill produced a faint scratching sound as he wrote out the runes of his native language. When he finished, he compared them to his efforts from the previous night, to see if his handwriting had improved—only a small amount—as well as to the runes in *Domia abr Wyrda*, which he was using as his guide.

He went through the alphabet three more times, paying special attention to the shapes that he had the most difficulty forming. Then he began to write down his thoughts and observations concerning the day's events. The exercise was useful not only because it provided him with a convenient means of practicing his letters, but also because it helped him better understand everything he had seen and done over the course of the day.

Laborious as it was, he enjoyed the writing, for he found the challenges it presented stimulating. Also, it reminded him of Brom, of how the old storyteller had taught him the meaning of each rune, which gave Eragon a sense of closeness with his father that otherwise eluded him.

After he had said everything he wished to say, he washed the quill clean, then exchanged it for the brush and selected a sheet of parchment that was already half covered with rows of glyphs from the ancient language.

The elves' mode of writing, the Liduen Kvaedhí, was far harder to reproduce than the runes of his own race, owing to the glyphs' intricate, flowing shapes. Nevertheless, he persisted for two reasons: He needed to maintain his familiarity with the script. And if he was going to write anything in the ancient language, he thought it wiser to do it in a form that most people were unable to understand.

Eragon had a good memory, but even so, he had found he was starting to forget many of the spells Brom and Oromis had taught him. Thus he had decided to compile a dictionary of every word he knew in the ancient language. Although it was hardly an original idea, he had not appreciated the value of such a compendium until very recently.

He worked on the dictionary for another few hours, whereupon he returned his writing supplies to the saddlebags and took out the chest containing Glaedr's heart of hearts. He tried to rouse the old dragon from his stupor, as he had so many times before, and as always, he failed. Eragon refused to give up, however. Sitting next to the open chest, he read aloud to Glaedr from *Domia abr Wyrda* about the dwarves' many rites and rituals—few of which Eragon was familiar with—until it was the coldest, darkest part of the night.

Then Eragon set aside the book, extinguished the candle, and lay down on the cot to rest. He wandered through the fantastic visions of his waking dreams for only a short while; once the first hint of light appeared in the east, he rolled upright to begin the whole cycle anew.

◆ ◆ ◆

AROUGHS

It was midmorning when Roran and his men arrived at the cluster of tents next to the road. The camp appeared gray and indistinct through the haze of exhaustion that clouded Roran's vision. A mile to the south lay the city of Aroughs, but he was able to make out only the most general features: glacier-white walls, yawning entryways containing barred gates, and many thickly built square stone towers.

He clung to the front of the saddle as they trotted into the camp, their horses near to collapsing. A scraggly-looking youngster ran up to him and grabbed the bridle of his mare, pulling on it until the animal stumbled to a stop.

Roran stared down at the boy, not sure what had just happened, and after a long moment croaked, "Bring me Brigman."

Without a word, the boy took off between the tents, kicking up dust with his bare heels.

It seemed to Roran that he sat waiting for over an hour. The mare's uncontrollable panting matched the rushing of blood in his ears. When he looked at the ground, it appeared as if it were still moving, receding tunnel-like toward a point infinitely far away. Somewhere, spurs clinked. A dozen or so warriors gathered nearby, leaning on spears and shields, their faces open displays of curiosity.

From across the camp, a broad-shouldered man in a blue tunic limped toward Roran, using a broken spear as a staff. He had a large, full beard, though his upper lip was shaved and it glittered with perspiration—whether from pain or heat Roran could not tell.

"You're Stronghammer?" he said.

Roran grunted an affirmative. He released his cramped grip on the saddle, reached inside his tunic, and handed Brigman the battered rectangle of parchment that contained his orders from Nasuada.

Brigman broke the wax seal with his thumbnail. He studied the parchment, then lowered it and gazed at Roran with a flat expression.

"We've been expecting you," he said. "One of Nasuada's pet spell-casters contacted me four days ago and said you had departed, but I didn't think you would arrive so soon."

"It wasn't easy," said Roran.

Brigman's bare upper lip curled. "No, I'm sure it wasn't . . . sir." He handed the parchment back. "The men are yours to command, Stronghammer. We were about to launch an attack on the western gate. Perhaps you would care to lead the charge?" The question was as pointed as a dagger.

The world seemed to tilt around Roran, and he gripped the saddle tighter. He was too tired to bandy words with anyone and do it well, and he knew it.

"Order them to stand down for the day," he said.

"Have you lost your wits? How else do you expect us to capture the city? It took us all morning to prepare the attack, and I'm not going to sit here twiddling my thumbs while you catch up on your sleep. Nasuada expects us to end the siege within a few days, and by Angvard, I'll see it done!"

In a voice pitched so low that only Brigman could hear, Roran growled, "You'll tell the men to stand down, or I'll have you strung up by your ankles and whipped for breaking orders. I'm not about to approve any sort of attack until I've had a chance to rest and look at the situation."

"You're a fool, you are. That would—"

"If you can't hold your tongue and do your duty, I'll thrash you myself—right here and now."

Brigman's nostrils flared. "In your state? You wouldn't stand a chance."

"You're wrong," said Roran. And he meant it. He was not sure how he might beat Brigman right then, but he knew in the deepest fibers of his being that he could.

Brigman seemed to struggle with himself. "Fine," he spat. "It wouldn't be good for the men to see us sprawling in the dirt anyway. We'll stay where we are, if that's what you want, but I won't be held accountable for the waste of time. Be it on your head, not mine."

"As it always is," said Roran, his throat tight with pain as he swung down from the mare. "Just as you're responsible for the mess you've made of this siege."

Brigman's brow darkened, and Roran saw the man's dislike of him curdle and turn to hate. He wished that he had chosen a more diplomatic response.

"Your tent is this way."

It was still morning when Roran woke.

A soft light diffused through the tent, lifting his spirits. For a moment, he thought he had only fallen asleep for a few minutes. Then he realized he felt too bright and alert for that to be the case.

He cursed quietly to himself, angry that he had allowed an entire day to slip through his fingers.

A thin blanket covered him, mostly unneeded in the balmy southern weather, especially since he was wearing his boots and clothes underneath. He pulled it off, then tried to sit upright.

A choked groan escaped him as his entire body seemed to stretch and tear. He fell back and lay gasping at the fabric above. The initial shock soon subsided, but it left behind a multitude of throbbing aches—some worse than others.

It took him several minutes to gather his strength. With a massive effort, he rolled onto his side and swung his legs over the edge of the cot. He stopped to catch his breath before attempting the seemingly impossible task of standing.

Once he was on his feet, he smiled sourly. It was going to be an interesting day.

The others were already up and waiting for him when he made

his way out of the tent. They looked worn and haggard; their movements were as stiff as his own. After exchanging greetings, Roran motioned toward the bandage on Delwin's forearm, where a tavern keeper had cut him with a paring knife. "Has the pain gone down?"

Delwin shrugged. "It's not so bad. I can fight if need be."

"Good."

"What do you intend to do first?" Carn asked.

Roran eyed the rising sun, calculating how much time remained until noon. "Take a walk," he said.

Starting from the center of the camp, Roran led his companions up and down each row of tents, inspecting the condition of the troops as well as the state of their equipment. Occasionally, he stopped to question a warrior before moving on. For the most part, the men were tired and disheartened, although he noticed their mood seemed to improve when they caught sight of him.

Roran's tour ended at the southern edge of the camp, as he had planned. There he and the others stopped to gaze at the imposing edifice that was Aroughs.

The city had been built in two tiers. The first was low and spread out and contained the majority of buildings, while the second, smaller tier occupied the top of a long, gentle rise, which was the tallest point for miles around. A wall encircled both levels of the city. Five gates were visible within the outer wall: two of them opened to roads that entered the city—one from the north and one from the east—and the other three sat astride canals that flowed southward, into the city. On the other side of Aroughs lay the restless sea, where the canals presumably emptied.

At least they don't have a moat, he thought.

The north-facing gate was scratched and scarred from a battering ram, and the ground in front of it was torn up with what Roran recognized as the tracks of battle. Three catapults, four ballistae of the sort he had knowledge of from his time on the *Dragon Wing*, and two ramshackle siege towers were arrayed before the outer wall.

A handful of men hunkered next to the machines of war, smoking pipes and playing dice on patches of leather. The machines appeared pitifully inadequate compared with the monolithic mass of the city.

The low, flat land surrounding Aroughs sloped downward toward the sea. Hundreds of farms dotted the green plain, each marked by a wooden fence and at least one thatched hut. Sumptuous estates stood here and there: sprawling stone manors protected by their own high walls and, Roran assumed, by their own guards. No doubt they belonged to the nobles of Aroughs, and perhaps certain well-off merchants.

"What do you think?" he asked Carn.

The magician shook his head, his drooping eyes even more mournful than usual. "We might as well lay siege to a mountain for all the good it'll do."

"Indeed," observed Brigman, walking up to them.

Roran kept his own observations to himself; he did not want the others to know how discouraged he was. *Nasuada is mad if she believes we can capture Aroughs with only eight hundred men. If I had eight thousand, and Eragon and Saphira to boot, then I might be sure of it. But not like this. . . .*

Yet he knew he had to find a way, for Katrina's sake, if nothing else.

Without looking at him, Roran said to Brigman, "Tell me about Aroughs."

Brigman twisted his spear several times, grinding the butt of it into the ground, before he replied: "Galbatorix had foresight; he saw to it that the city was fully stocked with food before we cut off the roads between here and the rest of the Empire. Water, as you can see, they have no shortage of. Even if we diverted the canals, they would still have several springs and wells inside the city. They could conceivably hold out until winter, if not longer, although I'd wager they'd be right sick of eating turnips before all was said and done. Also, Galbatorix garrisoned Aroughs with a fair number of soldiers—more than twice what we have—in addition to their usual contingent."

"How do you know this?"

"An informant. However, he had no experience with military strategy, and he provided us with an overly confident assessment of Aroughs's weaknesses."

"Ah."

"He also promised us that he would be able to let a small force of men into the city under the cover of dark."

"And?"

"We waited, but he never appeared, and we saw his head mounted over the parapet the following morning. It's still there, by the eastern gate."

"So it is. Are there other gates besides these five?"

"Aye, three more. By the docks, there's a water gate wide enough for all three streams to run out at once, and next to it a dry gate for men and horses. Then there's another dry gate over at that end"—he pointed toward the western side of the city—"same as the others."

"Can any of them be breached?"

"Not quickly. By the shore, we haven't room to maneuver properly or withdraw out of range of the soldiers' stones and arrows. That leaves us with these gates, and the western one as well. The lay of the land is much the same all around the city, except for the shore, so I chose to concentrate our attack on the nearest gate."

"What are they made of?"

"Iron and oak. They'll stand for hundreds of years unless we knock them down."

"Are they protected by any spells?"

"I wouldn't know, seeing as how Nasuada didn't see fit to send one of her magicians with us. Halstead has—"

"Halstead?"

"Lord Halstead, ruler of Aroughs. You must have heard of him."

"No."

A brief pause followed, wherein Roran could sense Brigman's contempt for him growing. Then the man continued, "Halstead has a conjurer of his own: a mean, sallow-looking creature we've seen atop the walls, muttering into his beard and trying to strike us down with his spells. He seems to be singularly incompetent, because he hasn't had much luck, save for two of the men I had on the battering ram, whom he managed to set on fire."

Roran exchanged glances with Carn—the magician appeared even more worried than before—but he decided it would be better to discuss the matter in private.

"Would it be easier to break through the gates on the canals?" he asked.

"Where would you stand? Look at how they're recessed within the wall, without so much as a step for purchase. What's more, there are slits and trapdoors in the roof of the entryway, so they can pour boiling oil, drop boulders, or fire crossbows at anyone foolish enough to venture in there."

"The gates can't be solid all the way down, or they would block the water."

"You're right about that. Below the surface is a latticework of wood and metal with holes large enough that they don't impede the flow overly much."

"I see. Are the gates kept lowered into the water most of the time, even when Aroughs isn't under siege?"

"At night for certain, but I believe they were left open during the daylight hours."

"Mmh. And what of the walls?"

Brigman shifted his weight. "Granite, polished smooth, and fit so closely together, you can't even slide a knife blade between the blocks. Dwarf work, I'd guess, from before the fall of the Riders. I'd also guess that the walls are filled with packed rubble, but I can't say for sure, since we haven't cracked the outer sheathing yet. They extend at least twelve feet below ground and probably more, which means we can't tunnel under them or weaken them with sapping."

Stepping forward, Brigman pointed at the manors to the north and west. "Most of the nobles have retreated into Aroughs, but they left men behind to protect their property. They've given us some trouble, attacking our scouts, stealing our horses, that sort of thing. We captured two of the estates early on"—he indicated a pair of burnt-out husks a few miles away—"but holding them was more trouble than it was worth, so we sacked them and put them to the torch. Unfortunately, we don't have enough men to secure the rest."

Baldor spoke then. "Why do the canals feed into Aroughs? It doesn't look as if they're used for watering crops."

"You don't need to water here, lad, any more than a northman needs to cart in snow during the winter. Staying dry is more a problem than not."

"Then what are they used for?" Roran inquired. "And where do they come from? You can't expect me to believe the water is drawn from the Jiet River, so many leagues away."

"Hardly," scoffed Brigman. "There are lakes in the marshes north of us. It's brackish, unwholesome water, but the people here are accustomed to it. A single channel carries it from the marshes to a point about three miles away. There the channel divides into the three canals you see here, and they run over a series of falls, which power the mills that grind flour for the city. The peasants cart their grain to the mills at harvesttime, and then the sacks of flour are loaded onto barges and floated down to Aroughs. It's also a handy way of moving other goods, like timber and wine, from the manor houses to the city."

Roran rubbed the back of his neck as he continued to examine Aroughs. What Brigman had told him intrigued him, but he was not sure how it could help. "Is there anything else of significance in the surrounding countryside?" he asked.

"Only a slate mine farther south along the coast."

He grunted, still thinking. "I want to visit the mills," he said. "But first I want to hear a full account of your time here, and I want to know how well provisioned we are with everything from arrows to biscuits."

"If you'll follow me . . . Stronghammer."

The next hour Roran spent in conference with Brigman and two of his lieutenants, listening and asking questions as they recounted each of the assaults they had launched against the city walls, as well as cataloging the stocks of supplies left to the warriors under his command.

At least we're not short of weapons, Roran thought as he counted the number of dead. Yet even if Nasuada had not set a time limit upon his mission, the men and horses did not have enough food to stay camped before Aroughs for more than another week.

Many of the facts and figures that Brigman and his lackeys related came from writing on scrolls of parchment. Roran strove to conceal the fact that he could not decipher the rows of angular black marks by insisting that the men read everything to him, but it irritated him that he was at the mercy of others. *Nasuada was right,* he realized. *I have to learn to read, else I cannot tell if someone is lying to me when they say that a piece of parchment says one thing or another. . . . Maybe Carn can teach me on our return to the Varden.*

The more Roran learned about Aroughs, the more he began to sympathize with Brigman's plight; capturing the city was a daunting task with no obvious solution. Despite his dislike for the man, Roran thought that the captain had done as well as could be expected under the circumstances. He had failed, Roran believed, not because he was an incompetent commander, but because he lacked the two qualities that had granted Roran victory time and time again: daring and imagination.

Upon finishing his review, Roran and his five companions rode with Brigman to inspect Aroughs's walls and gates from a closer, but still safe, distance. Sitting in a saddle again was incredibly painful for Roran, but he bore it without complaint.

As their steeds clattered onto the stone-paved road next to the camp and began to trot toward the city, Roran noticed that, on occasion, the horses' hooves produced a peculiar noise when they struck the ground. He remembered hearing a similar sound, and being bothered by it, during their final day of traveling.

Looking down, he saw that the flat stones that formed the surface of the road seemed to be set within tarnished silver, the veins of which formed an irregular, cobweb-like pattern.

Roran called out to Brigman and asked him about it, whereupon Brigman shouted, "The dirt here makes for poor mortar, so instead they use lead to hold the stones in place!"

Roran's initial reaction was disbelief, but Brigman appeared serious. He found it astonishing that any metal could be so common that people would squander it on building a road.

So they trotted down the lane of stone and lead toward the gleaming city beyond.

They studied Aroughs's defenses with great attentiveness. But their increased proximity revealed nothing new and only served to reinforce Roran's impression that the city was nigh on impregnable.

He guided his horse over to Carn's. The magician was staring at Aroughs with a glazed expression, his lips moving silently, as if he were talking to himself. Roran waited until he stopped, then quietly asked, "Are there any spells on the gates?"

"I think so," Carn replied, equally subdued, "but I'm not sure how many or what their intended purpose is. I'll need more time to tease out the answers."

"Why is it so difficult?"

"It's not, really. Most spells are easy to detect, unless someone has made an effort to hide them, and even then, the magic usually leaves certain telltale traces if you know what to look for. My concern is that one or more of the spells might be traps set to prevent people from meddling with the gates' enchantments. If that's so, and I approach them directly, I'll be sure to trigger them, and then who knows what will happen? I might dissolve into a puddle before your very eyes, which is a fate I would rather avoid, if I have my way."

"Do you want to stay here while we continue on?"

Carn shook his head. "I don't think it would be wise to leave you unguarded while we're away from camp. I'll return after sundown and see what I can do then. Besides, it would help if I were closer to the gates, and I don't dare go any nearer now, when I'm in plain sight of the sentinels."

"As you wish."

When Roran was satisfied they had learned everything they could by looking at the city, he had Brigman lead them to the nearest set of mills.

They were much as Brigman had described. The water in the canal flowed over three consecutive twenty-foot falls. At the base of each fall was a waterwheel, edged with buckets. The water splashed into the buckets, driving the machine round and round. The wheels were connected by thick axles to three identical buildings that stood stacked one above the other along the terraced bank and which contained the massive grindstones needed to produce the flour for Aroughs's population. Though the wheels were moving, Roran could tell they were disengaged from the complex arrangement of gears hidden inside the buildings, for he did not hear the rumble of the grindstones turning in their places.

He dismounted by the lowest mill and walked up the path between the buildings, eyeing the sluice gates that were above the falls and that controlled the amount of water released into them. The gates were open, but a deep pool of water still lay beneath each of the three slowly spinning wheels.

He stopped halfway up the hill and planted his feet on the edge of the soft, grassy bank, crossed his arms, and tucked his chin against his chest while he pondered how he could possibly capture Aroughs. That there was a trick or a strategy that would allow him to crack open the city like a ripe gourd, he was confident, but the solution eluded him.

He thought until he was tired of thinking, and then he gave himself over to the creaking of the turning axles and the splashing of the falling water.

Soothing as those sounds were, a thorn of unease still rankled him, for the place reminded him of Dempton's mill in Therinsford, where he had gone to work the day the Ra'zac had burned down his home and tortured his father, mortally wounding him.

Roran tried to ignore the memory, but it stayed with him, twisting in his gut.

If only I had waited another few hours to leave, I could have saved him. Then the more practical part of Roran replied: *Yes, and the Ra'zac would have killed me before I could have even raised a hand. Without Eragon to protect me, I would have been as helpless as a newborn babe.*

With a quiet step, Baldor joined him by the edge of the canal. "The others are wondering: have you decided on a plan?" he asked.

"I have ideas, but no plan. What of you?"

Baldor crossed his arms as well. "We could wait for Nasuada to send Eragon and Saphira to our aid."

"Bah."

For a while, they watched the never-ending motion of the water below them. Then Baldor said, "What if you just asked them to surrender? Maybe they'll be so frightened when they hear your name, they'll throw open the gates, fall at your feet, and beg for mercy."

Roran chuckled briefly. "I doubt word of me has reached all the way to Aroughs. Still . . ." He ran his fingers through his beard. "It might be worth a try, to put them off balance if nothing else."

"Even if we gain entrance to the city, can we hold it with so few men?"

"Maybe, maybe not."

A pause grew between them; then Baldor said, "How far we have come."

"Aye."

Again, the only sound was that of the water and of the turning wheels. Finally, Baldor said, "The snowmelt must not be as great here as it is at home. Otherwise, the wheels would be half under-water come springtime."

Roran shook his head. "It doesn't matter how much snow or rain they get. The sluice gates can be used to limit the amount of water that runs over the wheels, so they don't turn too fast."

"But once the water rises to the top of the gates?"

"Hopefully, the day's grinding is finished by then, but in any case, you uncouple the gears, raise the gates, and . . ." Roran trailed off as a series of images flashed through his mind, and his whole body flushed with warmth, as if he had drunk an entire tankard of mead in a single gulp.

Could I? he thought wildly. *Would it really work, or . . . It doesn't matter; we have to try. What else can we do?*

He strode out to the center of the berm that held back the middlemost pond and grasped the spokes that stuck out from the tall wooden screw used to raise and lower the sluice gate. The screw was stiff and hard to move, even though he set his shoulder against it and pushed with all his weight.

"Help me," he said to Baldor, who had remained on the bank, watching with puzzled interest.

Baldor carefully made his way to where Roran stood. Together they managed to close the sluice gate. Then, refusing to answer any questions, Roran insisted that they do the same with both the uppermost and the lowermost gates.

When all three were firmly shut, Roran walked back to Carn, Brigman, and the others and motioned for them to climb off their horses and gather around him. He tapped the head of his hammer while he waited, suddenly feeling unreasonably impatient.

"Well?" Brigman demanded once they were in place.

Roran looked each of them in the eyes, to make sure that he had their undivided attention, then he said, "Right, this is what we're going to do—" And he began to talk, quickly and intensely, for a full half hour, explaining everything that had occurred to him in that one, revelatory instant. As he spoke, Mandel began to grin, and though they remained more serious, Baldor, Delwin, and Hamund also appeared excited by the audacious nature of the scheme he outlined.

Their response gratified Roran. He had done much to earn their trust, and he was pleased to know that he could still count on their support. His only fear was that he might let them down; of all the fates he could imagine, only losing Katrina seemed worse.

Carn, on the other hand, appeared somewhat doubtful. This Roran had expected, but the magician's doubt was slight compared with Brigman's incredulity.

"You're mad!" he exclaimed once Roran had finished. "It'll never succeed."

"You take that back!" said Mandel, and jumped forward, his fists clenched. "Why, Roran's won more battles than you've ever fought in, and he did it without all the warriors you've had to order around!"

Brigman snarled, his bare upper lip curling like a snake. "You little whelp! I'll teach you a lesson in respect you'll never forget."

Roran pushed Mandel back before the younger man could attack Brigman. "Oi!" growled Roran. "Behave yourself." With a surly look, Mandel ceased resisting, but he continued to glower at Brigman, who sneered at him in return.

"It's an outlandish plan, to be sure," said Delwin, "but then, your outlandish plans have served us well in the past." The other men from Carvahall made sounds of agreement.

Carn nodded and said, "Maybe it will work and maybe it won't. I don't know. In any event, it's certain to catch our enemies by surprise, and I have to admit, I'm rather curious to see what will happen. Nothing like this has ever been tried before."

Roran smiled slightly. Addressing Brigman, he said, "To continue as before, now *that* would be mad. We have only two and a half days to seize Aroughs. Ordinary methods won't suffice, so we must hazard the *extra*ordinary."

"That may be," muttered Brigman, "but this is a ridiculous

venture that will kill many a good man, and for no reason other than to demonstrate your supposed cleverness."

His smile widening, Roran moved toward Brigman until only a few inches separated them. "You don't have to agree with me, Brigman; you only have to do what you're told. Now, will you follow my orders or not?"

The air between them grew warm from their breath and from the heat radiating off their skin. Brigman gritted his teeth and twisted his spear even more vigorously than before, but then his gaze wavered and he backed away. "Blast you," he said. "I'll be your dog for the while, Stronghammer, but there'll be a reckoning on this soon enough, just you watch, and then you'll have to answer for your decisions."

As long as we capture Aroughs, thought Roran, *I don't care*. "Mount up!" he shouted. "We have work to do, and little time to do it in! Hurry, hurry, hurry!"

✦ ✦ ✦

137

DRAS-LEONA

The sun was climbing into the sky, as was Saphira, when from his place on her back, Eragon spotted Helgrind on the edge of the northern horizon. He felt a surge of loathing as he beheld the distant spike of rock, which rose from the surrounding landscape like a single jagged tooth. So many of his most unpleasant memories were associated with Helgrind, he wished he could destroy it and see its bare gray spires fall crashing to the ground. Saphira was more indifferent to the dark tower of stone, but he could tell that she too disliked being near it.

By the time evening arrived, Helgrind lay behind them, while Dras-Leona lay before them, next to Leona Lake, where dozens of ships and boats bobbed at anchor. The low, broad city was as densely built and inhospitable as Eragon remembered, with its narrow, crooked streets, the filthy hovels packed close together against the yellow mud wall that ringed the center of the city, and behind the wall, the towering shape of Dras-Leona's immense cathedral, black and barbed, where the priests of Helgrind conducted their gruesome rituals.

A stream of refugees trailed along the road to the north—people fleeing the soon-to-be-besieged city for Teirm or Urû'baen, where they might find at least temporary safety from the Varden's inexorable advance.

Dras-Leona seemed as foul and evil to Eragon as when he had first visited it, and it aroused in him a lust for destruction such as he had not felt at either Feinster or Belatona. Here he wanted to lay waste with fire and sword; to lash out with all of the terrible, unnatural energies that were at his disposal; and to indulge in every savage urge and leave behind him nothing but a pit of smoking, blood-soaked ashes. For the poor and the crippled and the enslaved who lived within the confines of Dras-Leona, he had some sympathy. But he was wholly convinced of the city's corruption and believed that the best thing would be to raze it and rebuild it without the taint of perversity the religion of Helgrind had infected it with.

As he fantasized about tearing down the cathedral with Saphira's help, it occurred to him to wonder if the religion of the priests who practiced self-mutilation had a name. His study of the ancient language had taught him to appreciate the importance of names—names were power, names were *understanding*—and until he knew the name of the religion, he would not be able to fully apprehend its true nature.

In the waning light, the Varden settled on a series of cultivated fields just southeast of Dras-Leona, where the land rose up to a slight plateau, which would provide them with a modicum of protection should the enemy charge their position. The men were weary from marching, but Nasuada put them to work fortifying the camp, as well as assembling the mighty engines of war they had brought with them all the long way from Surda.

Eragon threw himself into the work with a will. First, he joined a team of men who were flattening the fields of wheat and barley, using planks with long loops of rope attached. It would have been faster to scythe the grain, either with steel or magic, but the stubble that remained would be dangerous and uncomfortable to walk over, much less to sleep upon. As it was, the compacted stalks formed a soft, springy surface as fine as any mattress, and one far preferable to the bare ground they were accustomed to.

Eragon labored alongside the other men for almost an hour, at which point they had cleared enough space for the tents of the Varden.

Then he helped in the construction of a siege tower. His greater-than-normal strength allowed him to shift beams that otherwise would have taken several warriors to move; thus, he was able to speed the process. A few of the dwarves who were still with the Varden oversaw the raising of the tower, for the engines were of their design.

Saphira helped as well. With her teeth and claws, she gouged deep trenches in the ground and piled the removed earth into embankments around the camp, accomplishing more in a few minutes than a hundred men could have in a whole day. And, with the fire from her maw and mighty sweeps of her tail, she leveled trees, fences, walls, houses, and everything else around the Varden that might give their foes cover. In all, she presented a picture of fearsome devastation sufficient to inspire trepidation in even the bravest of souls.

It was late at night when the Varden finally finished their preparations and Nasuada ordered the men, dwarves, and Urgals to bed.

Retiring to his tent, Eragon meditated until his mind was clear, as had become his habit. Instead of practicing his penmanship afterward, he spent the next few hours reviewing the spells he thought he might need the following day, as well as inventing new ones to address the specific challenges Dras-Leona presented.

When he felt ready for the battle to come, he abandoned himself to his waking dreams, which were more varied and energetic than usual, for despite his meditation, the prospect of the approaching action stirred his blood and would not allow him to relax. As always, the waiting and the uncertainty were the most difficult parts for him to bear, and he wished he were already in the midst of the fray, where he would have no time to worry about what might happen.

Saphira was equally restless. From her, he caught snatches of dreams that involved biting and tearing, and he could tell that she was looking forward to the fierce pleasure of battle. Her mood influenced his to a certain degree, but not enough to make him entirely forget his apprehension.

All too soon, morning arrived, and the Varden assembled before the exposed outskirts of Dras-Leona. The army was an imposing sight, but Eragon's admiration was tempered by his observation of the warriors' notched swords, dented helms, and battered shields, as well as the poorly repaired rents in their padded tunics and mail hauberks. If they succeeded in capturing Dras-Leona, they would be able to replace some of their equipment—as they had at Belatona, and before that, Feinster—but there was no replacing the men who bore them.

The longer this drags on, he said to Saphira, *the easier it will be for Galbatorix to defeat us when we arrive at Urû'baen.*

Then we must not delay, she replied.

Eragon sat astride her, next to Nasuada, who was garbed in full armor and mounted upon her fiery black charger, Battle-storm. Arrayed around them were his twelve elven guards, as well as an equal number of Nasuada's guards, the Nighthawks, increased from her normal allotment of six for the duration of the battle. The elves were on foot—for they refused to ride any steeds but those they had raised and trained themselves—while all of the Nighthawks were mounted, including the Urgals. Ten yards to the right were King Orrin and his hand-picked retinue of warriors, each of whom had a colorful plume attached to the crest of his helm. Narheim, the commander of the dwarves, and Garzhvog were both with their respective troops.

After exchanging nods, Nasuada and King Orrin spurred their mounts forward and trotted away from the main body of the Varden, toward the city. With his left hand, Eragon clutched the neck spike in front of him as Saphira followed.

Nasuada and King Orrin drew to a halt before they passed among the ramshackle buildings. At their signal, two heralds—one carrying the Varden's standard, the other Surda's—rode forth up the narrow street that ran through the maze of hovels to Dras-Leona's southern gate.

Eragon frowned as he watched the heralds advance. The city seemed unnaturally empty and quiet. No one was visible in the whole of Dras-Leona, not even upon the battlements of the thick yellow wall, where hundreds of Galbatorix's soldiers ought to be stationed.

The air smells wrong, said Saphira, and she growled ever so slightly, drawing Nasuada's attention.

At the base of the wall, the Varden's herald called forth in a voice that carried all the way back to Eragon and Saphira: "Hail! In the name of Lady Nasuada of the Varden and King Orrin of Surda, as well as all free peoples of Alagaësia, we bid you open your gates so we may deliver a message of import unto your lord and master, Marcus Tábor. By it, he may hope to profit greatly, as may every man, woman, and child within Dras-Leona."

From behind the wall, a man who could not be seen replied: "These gates shall not open. State your message where you stand."

"Speak you for Lord Tábor?"

"I do."

"Then we charge you to remind him that discussions of statesmanship are more properly pursued in the privacy of one's own chambers rather than in the open, where any might hear."

"I take no orders from you, lackey! Deliver your message—and quickly, too!—ere I lose patience and fill you with arrows."

Eragon was impressed; the herald did not appear flustered or cowed by the threat but continued without hesitation. "As you wish. Our liegelords offer peace and friendship to Lord Tábor and all the people of Dras-Leona. We have no argument with you, only with Galbatorix, and we would not fight you if we had the choice. Have we not a common cause? Many of us once lived in the Empire, and we left only because Galbatorix's cruel reign drove us from our lands. We are your kin, in blood and in spirit. Join forces with us, and we may yet free ourselves of the usurper who now sits in Urû'baen.

"Should you accept our offer, our liegelords do guarantee the safety of Lord Tábor and his family, as well as whoever else may now be in the service of the Empire, although none will be allowed to maintain their position if they have given oaths that cannot be broken. And if your oaths will not let you aid us, then at least do not hinder us. Raise your gates and lay down your swords, and we promise you will come to no harm. But try to bar us, and we shall sweep you aside like so much chaff, for none can withstand the might of our army, nor that of Eragon Shadeslayer and the dragon Saphira."

At the sound of her name, Saphira raised her head and loosed a terrifying roar.

Above the gate, Eragon saw a tall, cloaked figure climb onto the battlements and stand between two merlons, staring over the heralds toward Saphira. Eragon squinted, but he could not make out the man's face. Four other black-robed people joined the man, and those Eragon knew for priests of Helgrind by their truncated forms: one was missing a forearm, two were missing a leg each, and the last of their company was missing an arm *and* both legs, and was carried by his or her companions on a small padded litter.

The cloaked man threw back his head and uttered a peal of laughter that crashed and boomed with thunderous force. Below him, the heralds struggled to control their mounts as the horses reared and tried to bolt.

Eragon's stomach sank, and he gripped the hilt of Brisingr, ready to draw it at a moment's notice.

"None can withstand your might?" said the man, his voice echoing off the buildings. "You have an overly high opinion of yourselves, I think." And with a gigantic bellow, the glittering red mass of Thorn leaped from the streets below onto the roof of a house, piercing the wooden shingles with his talons. The dragon spread his huge, claw-tipped wings, opened his crimson maw, and raked the sky with a sheet of rippling flame.

In a mocking voice, Murtagh—for it *was* Murtagh, Eragon realized—added, "Dash yourselves against the walls all you want; you will never take Dras-Leona, not so long as Thorn and I are here to defend it. Send your finest warriors and magicians to fight us, and they will die, each and every one. That I promise. There isn't a man among you who can best us. Not even you . . . *Brother*. Run back to your hiding places before it is too late, and pray that Galbatorix does not venture forth to deal with you himself. Otherwise, death and sorrow will be your only reward."

A TOSS OF THE BONES

"**S**ir, sir! The gate's opening!"

Roran looked up from the map he was studying as one of the camp sentinels burst into the tent, red-faced and panting.

"Which gate?" Roran asked, a deadly calm settling over him. "Be precise." He put aside the rod he had been using to measure distances.

"The one closest to us, sir . . . on the road, not the canal."

Pulling his hammer out from under his belt, Roran left the tent and ran through the camp to its southern edge. There he trained his gaze on Aroughs. To his dismay, he saw several hundred horsemen pouring out of the city, their brightly colored pennants snapping in the wind as they assembled in a broad formation before the black maw of the open gateway.

They'll cut us to pieces, Roran thought, despairing. Only a hundred fifty or so of his men remained in the camp, and many were wounded and unable to fight. All the rest were at the mills he had visited the previous day, or at the slate mine farther down the coast, or along the banks of the westernmost canal, searching for the barges that were needed if his plan was to succeed. None of the warriors could be recalled in time to fend off the horsemen.

When he sent the men on their missions, Roran had been aware that he was leaving the camp vulnerable to a counterattack. However, he had hoped that the city folk would be too cowed by the recent assaults on their walls to attempt anything so daring— and that the warriors he had kept with him would be sufficient to convince any distant observers that the main body of his force was still stationed among the tents.

The first of those assumptions, it seemed, had most definitely proven to be a mistake. Whether the defenders of Aroughs were aware of his ruse, he was not entirely sure, but he thought it likely, given the rather limited number of horsemen gathering in front of the city. If the soldiers or their commanders had anticipated facing the full strength of Roran's company, he would have expected them to field twice as many troops. In either event, he still had to figure out a way to stave off their attack and save his men from being slaughtered.

Baldor, Carn, and Brigman ran up, weapons in hand. As Carn hastily donned a mail shirt, Baldor said, "What do we do?"

"There's nothing we *can* do," said Brigman. "You've doomed this whole expedition with your foolishness, Stronghammer. We have to flee—now—before those cursed riders are upon us."

Roran spat on the ground. "Retreat? We'll not retreat. The men can't escape on foot, and even if they could, I won't abandon our wounded."

"Don't you understand? We've lost here. If we stay, we'll be killed—or worse, taken prisoner!"

"Leave it, Brigman! I'm not about to turn tail and run!"

"Why not? So you don't have to admit you failed? Because you hope to salvage something of your honor in one final, pointless battle? Is that it? Can't you see that you'll only be causing the Varden even greater harm?"

By the base of the city, the horsemen raised their swords and spears over their heads and—with a chorus of whoops and shouts that were audible even over the distance—dug their spurs into their steeds and began to thunder across the sloping plain toward the Varden's encampment.

Brigman resumed his tirade: "I won't let you squander our lives merely to assuage your pride. Stay if you must, but—"

"Quiet!" Roran bellowed. "Keep your muzzle shut, or I'll shut it for you! Baldor, watch him. If he does anything you don't like, let him feel the point of your sword." Brigman swelled with anger, but he held his tongue as Baldor raised his sword and aimed it at Brigman's breast.

Roran guessed that he had maybe five minutes to decide upon a course of action. Five minutes in which so much hung in the balance.

He tried to imagine how they could kill or maim enough of the horsemen to drive them away, but almost immediately he discounted the possibility. There was nowhere to herd the onrushing cavalry where his men might have the advantage. The land was too flat, too empty, for any such maneuvers.

We can't win if we fight, so— What if we scare them? But how? Fire? Fire might prove as deadly to friend as to foe. Besides, the damp grass would only smolder. *Smoke? No, that's of no help.*

He glanced over at Carn. "Can you conjure up an image of Saphira and have her roar and breathe fire, as if she were really here?"

The spellcaster's thin cheeks drained of color. He shook his head, his expression panicky. "Maybe. I don't know, I've never tried before. I'd be creating an image of her from memory. It might not even look like a living creature." He nodded toward the line of galloping horsemen. "They'd know something was wrong."

Roran dug his nails into his palm. Four minutes remained, if that.

"It might be worth a try," he muttered. "We just need to distract them, confuse them. . . ." He glanced at the sky, hoping to see a curtain of rain sweeping toward the camp, but alas, a pair of attenuated clouds drifting high above was the only formation visible. *Confusion, uncertainty, doubt . . . What is it people fear? The unknown, the things they don't understand, that's what.*

In an instant, Roran thought of a half-dozen schemes to undermine the confidence of their foes, each more outlandish than the last, until he struck upon an idea that was so simple and so daring, it seemed perfect. Besides, unlike the others, it appealed to his ego, for it required the participation of only one other person: Carn.

"Order the men to hide in their tents!" he shouted, already

beginning to move. "And tell them to keep quiet; I don't want to hear so much as a peep from them unless we're attacked!"

Going to the nearest tent, which was empty, Roran jammed his hammer back under his belt and grabbed a dirty woolen blanket from one of the piles of bedding on the ground. Then he ran to a cookfire and scooped up a wide, stumplike section of log the warriors had been using as a stool.

With the log under one arm and the blanket thrown over the opposite shoulder, Roran sprinted out of the camp toward a slight mound perhaps a hundred feet in front of the tents. "Someone get me a set of knucklebones and a horn of mead!" he called. "And fetch me the table my maps are on. Now, blast it, now!"

Behind him, he heard a tumult of footsteps and jangling equipment as the men rushed to conceal themselves inside their tents. An eerie silence fell over the camp a few seconds later, save for the noise created by the men collecting the items he had requested.

Roran did not waste time looking back. At the crest of the mound, he set the log upright on its thicker end and twisted it back and forth several times to ensure that it would not wobble beneath him. When he was satisfied it was stable, he sat on it and looked out over the sloping field toward the charging horsemen.

Three minutes or less remained until they would arrive. Through the wood beneath him, he could feel the drumming of the horses' hooves—the sensation growing stronger every second.

"Where are the knucklebones and mead?!" he shouted without taking his eyes off the cavalry.

He smoothed his beard with a quick pass of his hand and tugged on the hem of his tunic. Fear made him wish that he were wearing his mail hauberk, but the colder, more cunning part of his mind reasoned that it would cause his enemies even greater apprehension to see him sitting there with no armor, as if he were totally at his ease. The same part of his mind also convinced him to leave his hammer tucked in his belt, so it would appear he felt safe in the presence of the soldiers.

"Sorry," Carn said breathlessly as he ran up to Roran, along with a man who was carrying the small folding table from Roran's tent. They placed the table before him and spread the blanket over it, whereupon Carn handed Roran a horn half-full of mead, as well as a leather cup containing the usual five knucklebones.

"Go on, get out of here," he said. Carn turned to leave, but Roran caught him by the arm. "Can you make the air shimmer on either side of me, as it does above a fire on a cold winter's day?"

Carn's eyes narrowed. "Possibly, but what good—"

"Just do it if you can. Now go, hide yourself!"

As the lanky magician sprinted back toward the camp, Roran shook the knucklebones in the cup, then poured them out onto the table and began to play by himself, tossing the bones into the air—first one, then two, then three, and so forth—and catching them on the back of his hand. His father, Garrow, had often amused himself in a like manner while smoking his pipe and sitting in a rickety old chair on the porch of their house during the long summer evenings of Palancar Valley. Sometimes Roran had played with him, and when he did, he usually lost, but mostly Garrow had preferred to compete against himself.

149

Though his heart was thumping hard and fast and his palms were slick with sweat, Roran strove to maintain a calm demeanor. If his gambit was to have the slightest chance of success, he had to comport himself with an air of unbreakable confidence, regardless of his actual emotions.

He kept his gaze focused on the knucklebones and refused to look up even as the horsemen drew closer and closer. The sound of the galloping animals swelled until he became convinced that they were going to ride right over him.

What a strange way to die, he thought, and smiled grimly. Then he thought of Katrina and of their unborn child, and he took comfort in the knowledge that, should he die, his bloodline would continue. It was not immortality such as Eragon possessed, but it was an immortality of a sort, and it would have to suffice.

At the last moment, when the cavalry was only a few yards away from the table, someone shouted, "Whoa! Whoa there! Rein in your horses. I say, rein in your horses!" And, with a clatter of buckles and creaking leather, the champing line of animals reluctantly slowed to a halt.

And still, Roran kept his eyes angled downward.

He sipped the pungent mead, then tossed the bones again and caught two of them on the back of his hand, where they lay rocking on the ridges of his tendons.

The aroma of freshly overturned soil wafted over him, warm and comforting, along with the distinctly less pleasant smell of lathered horseflesh.

"Ho there, my fine fellow!" said the same man who had ordered the soldiers to halt. "Ho there, I say! Who are you to sit here this splendid morning, drinking and enjoying a merry game of chance, as if you hadn't a care in the world? Do we not merit the courtesy of being met with drawn swords? Who are you, I say?"

Slowly, as if he had just noticed the presence of the soldiers and considered it to be of little importance, Roran raised his gaze from the table to regard a small bearded man with a flamboyantly plumed helm who sat before him on an enormous black war-horse, which was heaving like a pair of bellows.

"I'm nobody's *fine fellow,* and certainly not yours," Roran said, making no effort to conceal his dislike at being addressed in such a familiar manner. "Who are you, I might ask, to interrupt my game so rudely?"

The long, striped feathers mounted atop the man's helm bobbed and fluttered as he looked Roran over, as if Roran were an unfamiliar creature he had encountered while hunting. "Tharos the Quick is my name, Captain of the Guard. Rude as you are, I must tell you, it would grieve me mightily to kill a man as bold as yourself without knowing his name." As if to emphasize his words, Tharos lowered the spear he held until it was pointing at Roran.

Three rows of riders were clustered close behind Tharos. Among their numbers, Roran spied a slim, hook-nosed man with the emaciated face and arms—which were bare to the shoulders—that Roran had come to associate with the spellcasters of the Varden. Very suddenly, he found himself hoping that Carn had succeeded in making the air shimmer. However, he dared not turn his head to look.

"Stronghammer is my name," he said. With a single deft movement, he gathered up the knucklebones, tossed them skyward, and caught three on his hand. "Roran Stronghammer, and Eragon Shadeslayer is my cousin. You might have heard mention of him, if not of me."

A rustle of unease spread among the line of horsemen, and Roran thought he saw Tharos's eyes widen for an instant. "An impressive claim, that, but how can we be sure of its veracity? Any man might say he is another if it served his purpose."

Roran drew his hammer and slammed it down on the table with a muffled *thump*. Then, ignoring the soldiers, he resumed his game. He uttered a noise of disgust as two of the bones fell from the back of his hand, costing him the round.

"Ah," said Tharos, and coughed, clearing his throat. "You have a most illustrious reputation, Stronghammer, although some argue that it has been exaggerated beyond all reason. Is it true, for example, that you single-handedly felled nigh on three hundred men in the village of Deldarad in Surda?"

"I never learned what the place was called, but if Deldarad it was, then yes, I slew many a soldier there. It was only a hundred ninety-three, however, and I was well guarded by my own men while I fought."

"Only a hundred ninety-three?" Tharos said in a wondering tone. "You are too modest, Stronghammer. Such a feat might earn a man a place in many a song and story."

Roran shrugged and lifted the horn to his mouth, feigning the action of swallowing, for he could not afford to have his mind clouded by the potent dwarf brew. "I fight to win, not to lose. . . . Let me offer you a drink, as one warrior to another," he said, and extended the horn toward Tharos.

The short warrior hesitated, and his eyes darted toward the spellcaster behind him for a second. Then he wet his lips and said, "Perhaps I will at that." Dismounting his charger, Tharos handed his spear to one of the other soldiers, pulled off his gauntlets, and walked over to the table, where he cautiously accepted the horn from Roran.

Tharos sniffed at the mead, then downed a hearty quaff. The feathers on his helm quivered as he grimaced.

"It's not to your liking?" Roran asked, amused.

"I confess, these mountain drinks are too harsh for my tongue," Tharos said, returning the horn to Roran. "I much prefer the wines of our fields; they are warm and mellow and less likely to strip a man of his senses."

"'Tis sweet as mother's milk to me," Roran lied. "I drink it morning, noon, and night."

Donning his gloves once again, Tharos returned to the side of his horse, hauled himself into the saddle, and took back his spear from the soldier who had been holding it for him. He directed another glance toward the hook-nosed spellcaster behind him, whose complexion, Roran noticed, had acquired a deathly cast in the brief span since Tharos had set foot on the ground. Tharos must have noticed the change in his magician as well, for his own expression became strained.

"My thanks for your hospitality, Roran Stronghammer," he said, raising his voice so that his entire troop could hear. "Mayhap I will soon have the honor of entertaining you within the walls of Aroughs. If so, I promise to serve you the finest wines from my family's estate, and perhaps with them I will be able to wean you off such barbaric milk as you have there. I think you will find our wine has much to recommend it. We let it age in oaken casks for months or sometimes even years. It would be a pity if all that work were wasted and the casks were knocked open and the wine were allowed to run out into the streets and paint them red with the blood of our grapes."

"That would indeed be a shame," Roran replied, "but sometimes you cannot avoid spilling a bit of wine when cleaning your table." Holding the horn out to one side, he tipped it over and poured what little mead remained onto the grass below.

Tharos was utterly still for a moment—even the feathers on his helm were motionless—then, with an angry snarl, he yanked his horse around and shouted at his men, "Form up! Form up, I say. . . . Yah!" And with that final yell, he spurred his horse away from Roran, and the rest of the soldiers followed, urging their steeds to a gallop as they retraced their steps to Aroughs.

Roran maintained his pretense of arrogance and indifference until the soldiers were well away, then he slowly released his breath and rested his elbows on his knees. His hands were trembling slightly.

It worked, he thought, amazed.

He heard men running toward him from the camp, and he looked over his shoulder to see Baldor and Carn approaching, accompanied by at least fifty of the warriors who had been hiding within the tents.

"You did it!" exclaimed Baldor as they drew near. "You did it! I can't believe it!" He laughed and slapped Roran on the shoulder hard enough to knock him against the table.

The other men crowded around him, also laughing, as well as praising him with extravagant phrases, boasting that under his leadership they would capture Aroughs without so much as a single casualty, and belittling the courage and character of the city's inhabitants. Someone shoved a warm, half-full wineskin into his hand, which he stared at with unexpected loathing, then passed to the man directly to his left.

"Did you cast any spells?" he asked Carn, his words barely audible over the hubbub of the celebrations.

"What?" Carn leaned closer, and Roran repeated his question,

153

whereupon the magician smiled and nodded vigorously. "Aye. I managed to make the air shimmer as you wanted."

"And did you attack their enchanter? When they left, he looked as if he was about to faint."

Carn's smile broadened. "It was his own doing. He kept trying to break the illusion he thought I had created—to pierce the veil of shimmering air so he could see what lay behind—but there was nothing to break, nothing to pierce, so he expended all his strength in vain."

Then Roran chuckled, and his chuckle grew into a long, full-bodied laugh that rose above the excited clamor and rolled out over the fields in the direction of Aroughs.

For several minutes, he allowed himself to bask in the admiration of his men, until he heard a loud warning cry from one of the sentries stationed at the edge of the camp.

"Move aside! Let me see!" said Roran, and sprang to his feet. The warriors complied, and he beheld a lone man off to the west—whom he recognized as one of the party he had sent to search the banks of the canals—riding hard over the fields, heading toward the camp. "Have him come here," instructed Roran, and a lanky, red-haired swordsman ran off to intercept the rider.

While they waited for the man to arrive, Roran picked up the knucklebones and dropped them, one by one, into the leather cup. The bones made a satisfying clatter as they landed.

As soon as the warrior was within hailing distance, Roran called out, "Ho there! Is all well? Were you attacked?"

To Roran's annoyance, the man remained silent until he was only a few yards away, whereupon he jumped off his mount and presented himself before Roran, standing as stiff and straight as a sun-starved pine, and, in a loud voice, exclaimed, "Captain, sir!" Upon closer inspection, Roran realized that the man was actually more of a boy—that, in fact, he was the same scraggly youth who had grabbed his reins when he had first ridden into the camp. The realization did nothing to sate Roran's frustrated curiosity, though.

"Well, what is it? I haven't got all day."

"Sir! Hamund sent me to tell you that we found all the barges we need and that he's building the sleds to transport them across to the other canal."

Roran nodded. "Good. Does he need any more help to get them there in time?"

"Sir, no sir!"

"And is that all?"

"Sir, yes sir!"

"You don't have to keep calling me *sir*. Once is enough. Understood?"

"Sir, yes— Uh, yes s— Uh, I mean, yes, of course."

Roran suppressed a smile. "You've done well. Get yourself something to eat and then ride out to the mine and report back to me. I want to know what they've accomplished so far."

"Yes si— Sorry, sir— That is, I didn't . . . I'll be going at once, Captain." Two spots of crimson appeared on the youth's cheeks as he stammered. He ducked his head in a quick bow, then hurried back to his steed and trotted off toward the tents.

The visit left Roran in a more serious mood, for it reminded him that, as fortunate as they were to have won a reprieve from the soldiers' blades, there was much that still needed doing, and any of the tasks that lay before them might cost them the siege if handled badly.

To the warriors at large, he said, "Back to the camp with the lot of you! I want two rows of trenches dug around the tents by nightfall; those yellow-bellied soldiers might change their minds and decide to attack anyway, and I want to be prepared." A few of the men groaned at the mention of digging trenches, but the rest appeared to accept the order with good humor.

In a low voice, Carn said, "You don't want to tire them out too much before tomorrow."

"I know," Roran replied, also in a soft tone. "But the camp needs fortifying, and it'll help keep them from brooding. Besides, no matter how worn out they may be tomorrow, battle will give them new strength. It always does."

The day passed quickly for Roran when he was concentrating on some immediate problem or occupied with intense physical exertion, and slowly whenever his mind was free to ponder their situation. His men worked valiantly—by saving them from the soldiers, he had won their loyalty and devotion in a way that words never could—but it seemed ever more obvious to him that, despite their efforts, they would not be able to finish the preparations in the brief span of hours that remained.

All through the late morning, afternoon, and early evening, a sense of sick hopelessness grew within Roran, and he cursed himself for deciding upon such a complicated and ambitious plan.

I should have known from the start that we didn't have the time for this, he thought. But it was too late to try some other scheme. The only option left was to strive their utmost and hope that, somehow, it would be enough to wrest victory from the mistakes of his incompetence.

When dusk arrived, a faint spark of optimism leavened his pessimism, for all of a sudden, the preparations began to come together with unexpected speed. And a few hours later, when it was fully dark and the stars shone bright overhead, he found himself standing by the mills along with almost seven hundred of his men, having completed all of the arrangements needed if they were to capture Aroughs before the end of the following day.

Roran uttered a short laugh of relief, pride, and incredulousness as he gazed upon the object of their toils.

Then he congratulated the warriors around him and bade them return to their tents. "Rest now, while you can. We attack at dawn!"

And the men cheered, despite their evident exhaustion.

MY FRIEND, MY ENEMY

That night, Roran's sleep was shallow and troubled. It was impossible for him to entirely relax, knowing the importance of the upcoming battle and that he might very well be wounded during the fighting, as he often had been before. Those two thoughts caused a line of vibrating tension to form between his head and the base of his spine, a line that pulled him out of his dark, weird dreams at regular intervals.

As a result, he woke easily when a soft, dull *thud* sounded outside his tent.

He opened his eyes and stared at the panel of fabric above his head. The interior of the tent was barely visible, and only because of the faint line of orange torchlight that seeped through the gap between the flaps at the entrance. The air felt cold and dead against his skin, as if he were buried in a cave deep underground. Whatever the time, it was late, very late. Even the animals of the night would have returned to their lairs and gone to sleep. No one ought to be up, save the sentinels, and the sentinels were stationed nowhere near his tent.

Roran kept his breathing as slow and shallow as he could while he listened for any other noises. The loudest thing he heard was the beating of his own heart, which grew stronger and faster as the line of tension within him thrummed like a plucked lute string.

A minute passed.

Then another.

Then, just when he began to think there was no cause for alarm and the hammering in his veins began to slow, a shadow fell across the front of the tent, blocking the light from the torches beyond.

Roran's pulse tripled, his heart pounding as hard as if he were running up the side of a mountain. Whoever was there could not have come to rouse him for the assault on Aroughs, nor to bring him some piece of intelligence, for they would not have hesitated to call his name and barge inside.

A black-gloved hand—only a shade darker than the surrounding murk—slid between the entrance flaps and groped for the tie that held them closed.

Roran opened his mouth to raise the alarm, then changed his mind. It would be foolish to waste the advantage of surprise. Besides, if the intruder knew he had been spotted, he might panic, and panic could make him even more dangerous.

With his right hand, Roran carefully pulled his dagger from under the rolled-up cloak he used as a pillow and hid the weapon by his knee, beneath a fold in the blanket. At the same time, he grasped the edge of the blankets with his other hand.

A rim of golden light outlined the shape of the intruder as he slipped into the tent. Roran saw that the man was wearing a padded leather jerkin, but no plate or mail armor. Then the flap fell shut, and darkness enveloped them again.

The faceless figure crept toward where Roran lay.

Roran felt as if he was going to pass out from lack of air as he continued to restrict his breathing so that it would appear he was still asleep.

When the intruder was halfway to the cot, Roran tore his blankets off, threw them over the man, and, with a wild yell, leaped toward him, drawing back the dagger to stab him in the gut.

"Wait!" cried the man. Surprised, Roran stayed his hand, and the two of them crashed to the ground together. "Friend! I'm a friend!"

A half second later, Roran gasped as he felt two hard blows to his left kidney. The pain nearly incapacitated him, but he forced himself to roll away from the man, trying to put some distance between them.

Roran pushed himself to his feet, then he again charged at his attacker, who was still struggling to free himself from the blanket.

"Wait, I'm your friend!" cried the man, but Roran was not about to trust him a second time. It was well he did not, for as he slashed at the intruder, the man trapped Roran's right arm and dagger with a twirl of the blankets, then slashed at Roran with a knife he had produced from his jerkin. There was a faint tugging sensation across Roran's chest, but it was so slight, he paid it no mind.

Roran bellowed and yanked on the blanket as hard as he could, pulling the man off his feet and throwing him against one side of the tent, which collapsed on top of them, trapping them under the heavy wool. Roran shook the twisted blanket off his arm, then crawled toward the man, feeling his way through the darkness.

The hard sole of a boot struck Roran's left hand, and the tips of his fingers went numb.

Lunging forward, Roran caught the man by an ankle as he was trying to turn to face him head-on. The man kicked like a rabbit and broke Roran's grip, but Roran grabbed his ankle again and squeezed it through the thin leather, digging his fingers into the tendon at the back of the heel until the man roared in pain.

Before he could recover, Roran clawed his way up the man's body and pinned his knife hand to the ground. Roran tried to drive his dagger into the man's side, but he was too slow; his opponent found his wrist and seized it with a grip of iron.

"Who are you?" Roran growled.

"I'm your friend," the man said, his breath warm in Roran's face. It smelled like wine and mulled cider. Then he kneed Roran in the ribs three times in quick succession.

Roran bashed his forehead against the assassin's nose, breaking it with a loud *snap*. The man snarled and thrashed underneath him, but Roran refused to let him go.

"You're . . . no friend of mine," said Roran, grunting as he bore down on his right arm and slowly pushed the dagger toward the man's side. As they strained against one another, Roran was vaguely aware of people shouting outside the fallen tent.

At last the man's arm buckled, and with sudden ease, the dagger plunged through his jerkin and into the softness of living flesh. The man convulsed. Fast as he could, Roran stabbed him several more times, then buried the dagger in his chest.

Through the hilt of the dagger, Roran felt the birdlike flutters of the man's heart as it cut itself to pieces on the razor-sharp blade. Twice more the man shuddered and jerked, then ceased resisting and simply lay there, panting.

Roran continued to hold him as the life drained out of him, their embrace as intimate as any lovers'. Though the man had tried to kill him, and though Roran knew nothing about him besides that fact, he could not help but feel a sense of terrible closeness to him. Here was another human being—another living, thinking creature— whose life was ending because of what he had done.

"Who are you?" he whispered. "Who sent you?"

"I . . . I almost killed you," said the man, sounding perversely satisfied. Then he uttered a long, hollow sigh, his body went limp, and he was no more.

Roran let his head fall forward against the man's chest and gasped for air, shaking from head to toe as the shock of the attack racked his limbs.

People began to pull at the fabric resting on top of him. "Get it off me!" Roran shouted, and lashed out with his left arm, unable to bear any longer the oppressive weight of the wool, and the darkness, and the cramped space, and the stifling air.

A rent appeared in the panel above him as someone cut through the wool. Warm, flickering torchlight poured through the opening.

Frantic to escape his confinement, Roran lurched to his feet, grabbed at the edges of the slit, and dragged himself out of the collapsed tent. He staggered into the light, wearing nothing but his breeches, and looked round in confusion.

Baldor was standing there, as were Carn, Delwin, Mandel, and ten other warriors, all of whom held swords and axes at the ready. None of the men were fully dressed, save for two, whom Roran recognized as sentinels posted on the night watch.

"Gods," someone exclaimed, and Roran turned to see one of

the warriors peeling back the side of the ruined tent to expose the corpse of the assassin.

The dead man was of an unimposing size, with long, shaggy hair gathered in a ponytail and a leather patch mounted over his left eye. His nose was crooked and squashed flat—broken by Roran—and a mask of blood covered the lower part of his shaved face. More blood caked his chest and side and the ground beneath him. It appeared almost too much to have come from a single person.

"Roran," said Baldor. Roran continued to stare at the assassin, unable to tear his gaze away. "Roran," Baldor said again, but louder. "Roran, listen to me. Are you hurt? What happened? . . . Roran!"

The concern in Baldor's voice finally caught Roran's attention. "What?" he asked.

"Roran, are you hurt?!"

Why would he think that? Puzzled, Roran looked down at himself. The hair on his torso was matted with gore from top to bottom, while streaks of blood covered his arms and stained the upper part of his breeches.

"I'm fine," he said, though he had difficulty forming the words. "Has anyone else been attacked?"

In response, Delwin and Hamund moved apart, revealing a slumped body. It was the youth who had been running messages for him earlier.

"Ah!" groaned Roran, and sorrow filled him. "What was he doing wandering about?"

One of the warriors stepped forward. "I shared a tent with him, Captain. He always had to step out to relieve himself at night, 'cause he drank so much tea before turning in. His mother told him it would keep him from getting sick. . . . He was a good sort, Captain. He didn't deserve to be cut down from behind by some sneaking coward."

"No, he didn't," Roran murmured. *If he hadn't been there, I would be dead now.* He motioned toward the assassin. "Are there any more of these killers on the loose?"

The men stirred, glancing at each other; then Baldor said, "I don't think so."

"Have you checked?"

"No."

"Well then check! But try not to wake up everyone else; they need their sleep. And see to it that guards are stationed at the tents of all the commanders from now on." . . . *Should have thought of that before.*

Roran stayed where he was, feeling dull and stupid as Baldor issued a series of quick orders, and everyone but Carn, Delwin, and Hamund dispersed. Four of the warriors picked up the crumpled remains of the boy and carried him away to bury, while the rest set out to search the camp.

Going over to the assassin, Hamund nudged the man's knife with the tip of his boot. "You must have scared those soldiers more than we thought this morning."

"Must have."

Roran shivered. He was cold all over, especially his hands and feet, which were like ice. Carn noticed and fetched him a blanket. "Here," said Carn, and wrapped it around Roran's shoulders. "Come sit by one of the watchfires. I'll have some water heated so you can clean yourself. All right?"

Roran nodded, not trusting his tongue to work.

Carn started to lead him away, but before they had gone more than a few feet, the magician abruptly halted, forcing Roran to stop as well. "Delwin, Hamund," said Carn, "bring me a cot, something to sit on, a jug of mead, and several bandages as fast as you can. *Now*, if you please."

Startled, the two men sprang into action.

"Why?" asked Roran, confused. "What's wrong?"

His expression grim, Carn pointed at Roran's chest. "If you're not wounded, then what's *that*, pray tell?"

Roran looked where Carn was pointing and saw, hidden amid the hair and the gore on his breast, a long, deep cut that started in the middle of his right chest muscle, ran across his sternum, and ended just below his left nipple. At its widest, the gash hung open over a quarter of an inch, and it resembled nothing so much as a lipless mouth stretched wide in a huge, ghastly grin. The most disturbing feature of the cut, however, was the complete lack of blood; not so much as a single drop oozed out of the incision. Roran could clearly see the thin layer of yellow fat underneath his skin and, below it, the dark red muscle of his chest, which was the same color as a slice of raw venison.

Accustomed as he was to the horrific damage that swords, spears, and other weapons could wreak on flesh and bone, Roran still found the sight unnerving. He had suffered numerous injuries in the course of fighting the Empire—most notably when one of the Ra'zac had bitten his right shoulder during their capture of Katrina in Carvahall—but never before had he received such a large or uncanny wound.

"Does it hurt?" Carn asked.

Roran shook his head without looking up. "No." His throat tightened, and his heart—which was still racing from the fight—redoubled in speed, pounding so fast that one beat could not be distinguished from the next. *Was the knife poisoned?* he wondered.

"Roran, you have to relax," said Carn. "I think I can heal you, but you're only going to make this more difficult if you pass out." Taking him by the shoulder, he guided Roran back to the cot that Hamund had just dragged out of a tent, and Roran obediently sat.

"How am I supposed to relax?" he asked with a short, brittle laugh.

"Breathe deeply and imagine you're sinking into the ground each time you exhale. Trust me; it'll work."

Roran did as he was told, but the moment he released his third breath, his knotted muscles began to unclench and blood sprayed from the cut, splashing Carn on the face. The magician recoiled and uttered an oath. Fresh blood spilled down Roran's stomach, hot against his bare skin.

"*Now* it hurts," he said, gritting his teeth.

"Oi!" shouted Carn, and waved at Delwin, who was running toward them, his arms full of bandages and other items. As the villager deposited the mound of objects on one end of the cot, Carn grabbed a wad of lint and pressed it against Roran's wound, stopping the bleeding for the moment. "Lie down," he ordered.

Roran complied, and Hamund brought over a stool for Carn, who seated himself, keeping pressure on the lint the whole while. Extending his free hand, Carn snapped his fingers and said, "Open the mead and give it to me."

Once Delwin passed him the jug, Carn looked directly at Roran and said, "I have to clean out the cut before I can seal it with magic. Do you understand?"

Roran nodded. "Give me something to bite."

He heard the sound of buckles and straps being undone, then either Delwin or Hamund placed a thick sword belt between his teeth, and he clamped down on it with all his strength. "Do it!" he said as best he could past the obstruction in his mouth.

Before Roran had time to react, Carn plucked the lint off his chest and, in the same motion, poured mead across his wound, washing the hair, gore, and other accumulated filth out of the incision. As the mead struck, Roran uttered a strangled groan and arched his back, scrabbling at the sides of the cot.

"There, all done," said Carn, and put aside the jug.

Roran stared up at the stars, every muscle in his body quivering, and tried to ignore the pain as Carn placed his hands over the wound and began to murmur phrases in the ancient language.

After a few seconds, although it seemed more like minutes to Roran, he felt an almost unbearable itch deep within his chest as Carn repaired the damage the assassin's knife had caused. The itch crawled upward, toward the surface of his skin, and where it passed, the pain vanished. Still, the sensation was so unpleasant, it made him want to scratch at himself until he tore his flesh.

When it was over, Carn sighed and slumped over, holding his head in his hands.

Forcing his rebellious limbs to do as he wished, Roran swung his legs over the edge of the cot and sat upright. He ran a hand over his chest. Aside from the hair, it was perfectly smooth. Whole. Unblemished. Exactly as it had been before the one-eyed man had snuck into his tent.

Magic.

Off to the side, Delwin and Hamund stood staring. They appeared a bit wide-eyed, though he doubted anyone else would have noticed.

"Take yourselves to bed," he said, and waved. "We'll be leaving in a few hours, and I need you to be alert."

"Are you sure you'll be all right?" Delwin asked.

"Yes, yes," he lied. "Thank you for your help, but go now. How am I supposed to rest with the two of you hovering over me like mother hens?"

After they had departed, Roran rubbed his face and then sat looking at his trembling, bloodstained hands. He felt wrung out. Empty. As if he had done an entire week's worth of work in just a few minutes.

165

"Will you still be able to fight?" he asked Carn.

The magician shrugged. "Not so well as before. . . . It was a price that had to be paid, though. We can't go into battle without you to lead us."

Roran did not bother to argue. "You should get some rest. Dawn isn't far off."

"What of you?"

"I'm going to wash, find a tunic, and then check with Baldor and see if he's ferreted out any more of Galbatorix's killers."

"Aren't you going to lie down?"

"No." Without meaning to, he scratched at his chest. He stopped himself when he realized what he was doing. "I couldn't sleep before, and now . . ."

"I understand." Carn slowly rose from the stool. "I'll be in my tent if you need me."

Roran watched him stumble heavy-footed into the darkness. When he was no longer visible, Roran closed his eyes and thought of Katrina, in an attempt to calm himself. Summoning what little remained of his strength, he went over to his collapsed tent and dug through it until he located his clothes, weapons, armor, and a waterskin. The whole while, he studiously avoided looking at the body of the assassin, though he sometimes caught a glimpse as he moved about the pool of tangled cloth.

Finally, Roran knelt and, with eyes averted, yanked his dagger out of the corpse. The blade came free with the slithery sound of metal scraping against bone. He gave the dagger a hard shake, to remove any loose blood, and heard the splatter of several droplets striking the ground.

In the cold silence of the night, Roran slowly prepared himself for battle. Then he sought out Baldor—who assured him that no one else had gotten past the sentinels—and walked the perimeter of the camp, reviewing every aspect of their upcoming assault on Aroughs. Afterward, he found half a cold chicken left uneaten from dinner and sat gnawing on it and gazing at the stars.

Yet, no matter what he did, his mind returned again and again to the sight of the young man lying dead outside his tent. *Who is it who decides that one man should live and another should die? My life wasn't worth any more than his, but he's the one who's buried, while I get to enjoy at least a few more hours above the ground. Is it chance, random and cruel, or is there some purpose or pattern to all this, even if it lies beyond our ken?*

A FLOUR MADE OF FLAME

"How do you like having a sister?" Roran asked Baldor as they rode side by side toward the nearest set of mills in the gray half-light that precedes dawn.

"There's not much to like, is there? I mean, there's not much *of* her yet, if you take my meaning. She's as small as a kitten." Baldor tugged on his reins as his horse tried to veer toward a patch of particularly lush grass next to the trail. "It's strange to have another sibling—brother *or* sister—after so long."

Roran nodded. Twisting in the saddle, he glanced back over his shoulder, checking to make sure that the column of six hundred and fifty men who were following them on foot were keeping pace. At the mills, Roran dismounted and tethered his horse to a hitching post before the lowest of the three buildings. One warrior stayed behind to escort the animals back to camp.

Roran walked over to the canal and descended the wooden steps set within the muddy bank, which brought him to the edge of the water. Then he stepped out onto the rearmost of the four barges that were floating together in a line.

The barges were more like crude rafts than the flat-bottomed boats the villagers had ridden down the coast from Narda to Teirm, for which Roran was grateful, because it meant that they did not have pointed prows. This had made it relatively easy to fasten the four barges end to end with boards, nails, and ropes, thus creating a single rigid structure almost five hundred feet long.

The slabs of cut slate that the men had, at Roran's direction, hauled in wagons from the mine lay piled at the front of the lead barge, as well as along the sides of both the first and second barges.

On top of the slate, they had heaped sacks of flour—which they had found stored within the mills—until they had built a wall level with their waists. Where the slate ended on the second barge, the wall continued on, composed entirely of the sacks: two deep and five high.

The immense weight of the slate and the densely packed flour, combined with that of the barges themselves, served to transform the entire floating structure into a massive, waterborne battering ram, which Roran hoped would be capable of plowing through the gate at the far end of the canal as if it were made of so many rotted sticks. Even if the gate was enchanted—though Carn did not believe it was—Roran didn't think any one magician, save Galbatorix, would be strong enough to negate the forward momentum of the barges once they began to move downstream.

Also, the mounds of stone and flour would provide a measure of protection from spears, arrows, and other projectiles.

Roran carefully made his way across the shifting decks to the head of the barges. He wedged his spear and his shield against a pile of slate, then turned to watch as the warriors filed into the corridor between the walls.

Every man who boarded pushed the heavily laden barges deeper and deeper into the water, until they rode only a few inches above the surface.

Carn, Baldor, Hamund, Delwin, and Mandel joined Roran where he stood. They had all, by unspoken consent, elected to take for themselves the most dangerous position on the floating ram. If the Varden were to force their way into Aroughs, it would require a high degree of luck and skill, and none of them were willing to trust the attempt to anyone else.

Toward the rear of the barges, Roran glimpsed Brigman standing among the men he had once commanded. After Brigman's near insubordination the previous day, Roran had stripped him of all remaining authority and confined him to his tent. However, Brigman had begged to be allowed to join the final attack on Aroughs, and

Roran had reluctantly agreed; Brigman was handy with a blade, and every sword would make a difference in the upcoming fight.

Roran still wondered if he had made the right decision. He was fairly confident that the men were now loyal to him, not to Brigman, but Brigman had been their captain for many months, and such bonds were not easily forgotten. Even if Brigman did not try to cause trouble in the ranks, he had proved willing and able to ignore orders, at least when they came from Roran.

If he gives me any reason to distrust him, I'll strike him down on the spot, Roran thought. But the resolution was a futile one. If Brigman did turn on him, it would most likely be in the midst of such confusion that Roran would not even notice until it was too late.

When all but six of the men were packed onto the barges, Roran cupped his hands around his mouth and shouted, "Pry them loose!"

Two men stood upon the berm at the very top of the hill—the berm that slowed and held back the flow of water down the canal from the marshes to the north. Twenty feet below them lay the first waterwheel and the pool beneath it. At the front of that pool was the second berm, whereon stood two more men. Another twenty feet below them was the second waterwheel and the second deep, still pool. At the far end of the pool was the final berm and the final pair of men. And at the base of the final berm was the third and last waterwheel. From it, the current then flowed smoothly over the land until it arrived at Aroughs.

Built into the berms were the three sluice gates Roran had insisted upon closing, with Baldor's help, during his first visit to the mills. Over the course of the past two days, teams of men wielding shovels and pickaxes had dived under the rising water and cut away at the berms from the backsides until the layers of packed earth were nearly ready to give way. Then they had driven long, stout beams into the dirt on either side of the sluice gates.

The men on the middle and topmost berms now grasped those beams—which protruded several feet from the embankments—and began to work them back and forth with a steady rhythm. In accordance with their plan, the duo stationed on the lowest berm waited several moments before they, too, joined in the effort.

Roran gripped a flour sack as he watched. If their timing was off by even a few seconds, disaster would ensue.

For almost a minute, nothing happened.

Then, with an ominous rumble, the topmost sluice gate was pried free. The berm bulged outward, the earth cracking and crumbling, and a huge tongue of muddy water poured over the waterwheel below, spinning it faster than it was ever intended to turn.

As the berm collapsed, the men standing on top of it jumped to shore, landing with only inches to spare.

Spray shot up thirty feet or more as the tongue of water plunged into the smooth black pool underneath the waterwheel. The impact sent a frothing wave several feet high rushing toward the next berm.

Seeing it coming, the middlemost pair of warriors abandoned their posts, also leaping for the safety of solid ground.

It was well they did. When the wave struck, needle-thin jets erupted around the frame of the next sluice gate, which then flew out of its setting as if a dragon had kicked it, and the churning contents of the pool swept away what remained of the berm.

The raging torrent crashed against the second waterwheel with even more force than it had the previous one. The timbers groaned and creaked under the onslaught, and for the first time, it occurred to Roran that one or more of the wheels might break loose. If that happened, it would pose a serious danger to his men, as well as to the barges, and could very well end the attack on Aroughs before it had even begun.

"Cut us loose!" he shouted.

One of the men chopped through the rope that tethered them to the bank, while others bent to pick up ten-foot-long poles, which they stuck into the canal and pushed on with all their might.

The heavily laden barges inched forward, gaining speed far slower than Roran would have liked.

Even as the avalanche of water bore down upon them, the two

men standing on the lowest berm continued to pull on the beams embedded within the weakened rampart. Less than a second before the avalanche washed over them, the berm shuddered and sagged, and the men threw themselves off of it.

The water punched a hole in the earthen dam as easily as if it were made of sodden bread and slammed into the final waterwheel. Wood shattered—the sound as loud and sharp as breaking ice—and the wheel canted outward several degrees, but to Roran's relief, it held. Then, with a thunderous roar, the pillar of water dashed itself against the base of the terraced hill with an explosion of mist.

A gust of cold wind slapped Roran in the face, more than two hundred yards downstream.

"Faster!" he shouted to the men poling the barge, as a turbulent mass of water emerged from within the folds of mist and hurtled down the canal.

The flood overtook them with incredible speed. When it collided with the back of the four conjoined barges, the entire craft jolted forward, throwing Roran and the warriors toward the stern and knocking a number of them off their feet. Some sacks of flour dropped into the canal or rolled inward, against the men.

As the surging water lifted the rearmost barge several feet above the rest, the nearly five-hundred-foot-long vessel began to slue sideways. If the trend continued, Roran knew they would soon become wedged between the banks of the canal, and that, moments later, the force of the current would tear the barges apart.

"Keep us straight!" he bellowed, pushing himself off the sacks of flour he had fallen on. "Don't let us turn!"

At the sound of his voice, the warriors scrambled to push the lumbering vessel away from the sloping banks and toward the center of the canal. Springing atop the piles of slate at the prow, Roran shouted directions, and together they successfully steered the barges down the curving channel.

"We did it!" Baldor exclaimed, a stupid grin on his face.

"Don't crow yet," Roran warned. "We still have a ways to go."

The eastern sky had turned straw yellow by the time they were level with their camp, a mile from Aroughs. At the speed they were moving, they would reach the city before the sun peeked over the horizon, and the gray shadows that covered the land would help shroud them from the lookouts stationed on the walls and towers.

Although the leading edge of the water had already outstripped them, the barges were still gathering speed, as the city lay below the mills and there was not a single hill or hummock between to slow their progress.

"Listen," said Roran, cupping his hands around his mouth and raising his voice so that all the men could hear. "We may fall into the water when we hit the outer gate, so be prepared to swim. Until we can get onto dry land, we'll make easy targets. Once we're ashore, we have but one goal: to make our way up to the inner wall before they think to close the gates there, because if they do, we'll never capture Aroughs. If we can get past that second wall, it should be a simple matter to find Lord Halstead and force his surrender. Failing that, we'll secure the fortifications at the center of the city, then move outward, street by street, until all of Aroughs is under our control.

"Remember, we'll be outnumbered by more than two to one, so stay close to your shield mate and be on your guard at all times. Don't wander off by yourself, and don't let yourself be separated from the rest of the group. The soldiers know the streets better than we do, and they'll ambush you when you least expect it. If you do end up alone, head for the center, because that's where we'll be.

"Today we strike a mighty blow for the Varden. Today we win honor and glory such as most men dream about. Today . . . today we grave our mark onto the face of history. What we accomplish in the next few hours, the bards will sing about for a hundred years to come. Think of your friends. Think of your families, of your parents, your wives, your children. Fight well, for we fight for them. We fight for freedom!"

The men roared in response.

Roran let them work themselves into a frenzy; then he lifted a hand and said, "Shields!" And, as one, the men crouched and lifted their shields, covering themselves and their companions so that it looked as if the middle of the makeshift battering ram were clad in scale armor made to fit the limb of a giant.

Satisfied, Roran hopped down from the pile of slate and looked at Carn, Baldor, and the four other men who had traveled with him from Belatona. The youngest, Mandel, appeared apprehensive, but Roran knew his nerves would hold.

"Ready?" he asked, and they each answered in the affirmative.

Then Roran laughed, and when Baldor pressed him for an explanation, he said, "If only my father could see me now!"

And Baldor laughed as well.

Roran kept a keen eye on the main swell of the water. Once it entered the city, the soldiers might notice that something was amiss and raise the alarm. He wanted them to raise the alarm, but not for that reason, and so, when it appeared the swell was about five minutes away from Aroughs, he motioned to Carn and said, "Send the signal."

The magician nodded and hunched over, his lips moving as they formed the strange shapes of the ancient language. After a few moments, he straightened and said, "It is done."

Roran looked off to the west. There, on the field before Aroughs, stood the Varden's catapults, ballistae, and siege towers. The siege towers remained motionless, but the other engines of war stirred into action, casting their darts and stones in high, arcing paths toward the pristine white walls of the city. And he knew that fifty of his men on the far side of the city were even then blowing trumpets, yelling war cries, firing flaming arrows, and doing everything they could to draw the attention of the defending soldiers and make it appear as if a far larger force were attempting to storm the city.

A deep calm settled over Roran.

Battle was about to be joined.

Men were about to die.

He might be one of them.

Knowing this gave him a clarity of thought, and every trace of exhaustion vanished, along with the faint tremor that had plagued him since the attempt on his life just hours before. Nothing was so invigorating as fighting—not food, not laughter, not working with his hands, not even love—and though he hated it, he could not deny the power of its attraction. He had never wanted to be a warrior, but a warrior he had become, and he was determined to best all who came before him.

Squatting, Roran peered between two sharp-edged slabs of slate at the rapidly approaching gate that barred their path. To the surface of the water and somewhat below, for the water had risen, the gate was made of solid oak planks, stained dark with age and moisture. Beneath the surface, he knew there was a grid of iron and wood, much like a portcullis, through which the water was free to pass. The upper part would be the most difficult to breach, but he guessed that long periods of immersion had weakened the grid below, and if part of it could be torn away, breaking through the oak boards above would be far easier. Thus, he had ordered two stout logs attached to the underside of the lead barge. Since these were submerged, they would strike the lower half of the gate even as the prow rammed into the upper.

It was a clever plan, but he had no idea if it would really work.

"Steady," he whispered more to himself than anyone else as the gate drew near.

A few of the warriors near the rear of the craft continued to steer the barges with their poles, but the rest remained hidden beneath the lapped carapace of shields.

The mouth of the archway that led to the gate loomed large before them, like the entrance to a cave. As the tip of the vessel slid underneath the shadowed archway, Roran saw the face of a soldier, as round and white as a full moon, appear over the edge of the wall, more than thirty feet above, and peer down at the barges with an expression of horrified astonishment.

The barges were moving so fast by then, Roran only had time to utter a single pungent curse before the current swept them into the cool darkness of the passageway, and the vaulted ceiling cut off his view of the soldier.

The barges struck the gate.

The force of the impact threw Roran forward against the wall of slate he squatted behind. His head bounced off the stone, and though he wore a helm and arming cap, his ears rang. The deck shuddered and reared, and even through the noise in his ears, he heard wood cracking and breaking, and the shriek of twisting metal.

One of the slate slabs slipped backward and fell onto him, bruising his arms and shoulders. He grabbed the slab by the edges and, with a burst of furious strength, threw it overboard, where it shattered against the side of the passageway.

In the gloom that surrounded them, it was difficult to see what was happening; all was shifting confusion and echoing clamor. Water poured over his feet, and he realized that the barge was awash, though whether it would sink, he could not tell.

"Give me an ax!" he shouted, holding a hand out behind him. "An ax, give me an ax!"

He staggered as the barge lurched forward half a foot, nearly knocking him over. The gate had caved inward somewhat, but it was still holding firm. In time, the continued pressure of the water might push the barge through the gate, but he could not wait for nature to take its course.

As someone pressed the smooth haft of an ax into his outstretched hand, six glowing rectangles appeared in the ceiling as covers were drawn back from murder holes. The rectangles flickered, and crossbow bolts hissed down upon the barges, adding loud *thumps* to the tumult wherever they struck wood.

Somewhere a man screamed.

"Carn!" shouted Roran. "Do something!"

Leaving the magician to his devices, Roran started to crawl up the heaving deck and over the piles of slate toward the prow of the barge. And the barge lurched forward several more inches. Another deafening groan emanated from the center of the gate, and light shone through cracks in the oaken planks.

A quarrel skipped off the slate next to Roran's right hand, leaving a smear of iron on the stone.

He redoubled his speed.

Just as he reached the very front of the barge, a piercing, grating, tearing sound forced him to clap his hands over his ears and pull back.

A heavy wave washed over him, blinding him for a moment. Blinking to clear his vision, he saw that part of the gate had collapsed into the canal; there was now enough space for the barge to gain access to the city. Above the prow of the vessel, however, jagged spars of wood stuck out from the remnants of the gate at the same height as a man's chest, neck, or head.

Without hesitation, Roran rolled backward and dropped behind the breastwork of slate. "Heads down!" he roared, covering himself with his shield.

The barges glided forward, out of the hail of deadly crossbow bolts and into an enormous stone room lit by torches mounted on the walls.

At the far end of the room, the water in the canal flowed through another lowered gate, this one a portcullis from top to bottom. Through the latticework of wood and metal, Roran could see buildings within the city proper.

Extending from both sides of the room were stone quays for loading and unloading cargo. Pulleys, ropes, and empty nets hung from the ceiling, and a crane was mounted upon a high stone platform in the middle of each artificial shore. At the front of the room and at the back, stairs and walkways protruding from the mold-covered walls would allow a person to cross over the water without getting wet. The rear walkway also granted access to the guardrooms above the tunnel the barges had entered through, as well as, Roran assumed, to the upper part of the city's defenses, such as the parapet where he had seen the soldier.

Frustration welled up inside of Roran as he beheld the lowered gate. He had hoped to be able to sail straight into the main body of the city and avoid getting trapped on the water by the guards.

Well, it can't be helped now, he thought.

Behind them, crimson-clad soldiers poured out of the guardrooms onto the walkway, where they knelt and began to crank on their crossbows, readying them for another volley.

"Over!" Roran shouted, waving his arm toward the docks on the left. The warriors grabbed their poles once more and pushed the interlocked barges toward the edge of the canal. The dozens and dozens of bolts that protruded from their shields gave the company the appearance of a hedgehog.

As the barge neared the docks, twenty of the defending soldiers drew their swords and ran down the stairs off the walkway to intercept the Varden before they could land.

"Hurry!" he shouted.

A bolt buried itself in his shield, the diamond-shaped tip boring through the inch-and-a-half-thick wood to protrude over his forearm. He stumbled and caught himself, knowing that he had only moments before more archers fired on him.

Then Roran jumped for the dock, arms spread wide for balance. He landed heavily, one knee striking the floor, and only just had time to pull his hammer from his belt before the soldiers were upon him.

It was with a sense of relief and savage joy that Roran met them. He was sick of plotting and planning and worrying about what might be. Here at last were honest foes—not creeping assassins—that he could fight and kill.

The encounter was short, fierce, and bloody. Roran slew or

incapacitated three of the soldiers within the first few seconds. Then Baldor, Delwin, Hamund, Mandel, and others joined him to force the soldiers away from the water.

Roran was no swordsman, so he made no attempt to fence with his opponents. Instead, he let them hit his shield all they wanted, while he used his hammer to break their bones in return. Occasionally, he had to parry a cut or a stab, but he tried to avoid exchanging more than a few blows with any one person, because he knew his lack of experience would soon prove fatal. The most useful trick of fighting, he had discovered, was not some fancy twirl of the sword or some complicated feint that took years to master, but rather seizing the initiative and doing whatever his enemy least expected.

Breaking free of the brawl, Roran sprinted toward the stairs that led to the walkway where the archers knelt, firing at the men scrambling off the barges.

Roran bounded up the stairs three at a time and, swinging his hammer, caught the first archer full in the face. The next soldier in line had already fired his crossbow, so he dropped it and reached for the hilt of his short sword, retreating backward as he did.

The soldier only managed to pull his blade partway out of its sheath before Roran struck him in the chest, breaking his ribs.

One of the things Roran liked about fighting with a hammer was that he did not have to pay much attention to what kind of armor his opponents were wearing. A hammer, like any blunt weapon, inflicted injuries by the strength of its impact, not by the cutting or piercing of flesh. The simplicity of the approach appealed to him.

The third soldier on the walkway managed to shoot a bolt at him before he took another step. This time the shaft of the quarrel made it halfway through his shield and almost poked him in the chest. Keeping the deadly point well away from his body, Roran charged the man and swung at his shoulder. The soldier used his crossbow to block the attack, so Roran immediately followed with a backhand blow of his shield, which knocked the soldier screaming and flailing over the railing of the walkway.

The maneuver left Roran wholly exposed, however, and as he returned his attention to the five soldiers who remained on the walkway, he saw three of them aiming straight at his heart.

The soldiers fired.

Just before the bolts tore through him, they veered to the right and skittered across the blackened walls, like giant angry wasps.

Roran knew it was Carn who had saved him, and he resolved to find some way to thank the magician once they were no longer in mortal danger.

He charged the remaining soldiers and dispatched them with a furious volley of strikes, as if they were so many bent nails he was hammering down. Then he broke off the crossbow bolt that was sticking through his shield and turned to see how the battle below was progressing.

The last soldier on the docks crumpled to the blood-streaked floor at that very moment, and his head rolled away from his body and dropped into the canal, where it sank beneath a plume of bubbles.

Roughly two-thirds of the Varden had disembarked and were gathering in orderly ranks along the edge of the water.

Roran opened his mouth, intending to order them to move back from the canal—so that the men still on the barges had more room to get off—when the doors set into the left wall burst open and a horde of soldiers poured into the room.

Blast it! Where are they coming from? And how many are there?

Just as Roran started toward the stairs to help his men fend off the newcomers, Carn—who still stood at the head of the listing barges—raised his arms, pointed at the onrushing soldiers, and shouted a series of harsh, twisted words in the ancient language.

At his eldritch command, two sacks of flour and a single slab of slate flew off the barges and into the ranks of closely packed soldiers, cutting down over a dozen. The sacks burst open after the third or fourth impact, and clouds of ivory flour billowed out over the soldiers, blinding and choking them.

A second later, there was a flare of light next to the wall behind the soldiers, and a huge roiling fireball, orange and sooty, raced through the clouds of flour, devouring the fine powder with rapacious greed and producing a sound like a hundred flags flapping in a high wind.

Roran ducked behind his shield and felt searing heat against his legs and the bare skin of his cheeks as the fireball burned itself out only yards away from the walkway, glowing motes becoming ash that drifted downward: a black, charnel rain fitting only for a funeral.

Once the sullen glare had faded, he cautiously raised his head. A tendril of hot, foul-smelling smoke tickled his nostrils and stung his eyes, and with a start, he realized that his beard was on fire. He cursed and dropped his hammer and batted at the tiny grasping flames until he had extinguished them.

"Oi!" he shouted down at Carn. "You singed my beard! Be more careful, or I'll have your head on a pike!"

Most of the soldiers lay curled on the ground, cupping their burned faces. Others were thrashing about with their clothes on fire or were flailing blindly in circles with their weapons, in an attempt to fend off any attacks by the Varden. Roran's own men appeared to have escaped with only minor burns—most had been standing outside the radius of the fireball—although the unexpected conflagration had left them disoriented and unsteady.

"Stop gaping like fools and get after those groping rascals before they regain their senses!" he ordered, banging his hammer against the railing to ensure that he had their attention.

The Varden heavily outnumbered the soldiers, and by the time Roran reached the bottom of the stairs, they had already put to death fully three-quarters of the defending force.

Leaving the disposal of the few remaining soldiers to his more-than-able warriors, Roran made his way toward the large double doors to the left of the canal—doors wide enough for two wagons to drive through abreast. As he did, he came upon Carn, who was sitting at the base of the crane's platform, eating out of a leather pouch he always carried. The pouch, Roran knew, contained a mixture of lard, honey, powdered beef liver, lamb's heart, and berries. The one time Carn had given him a piece, he had gagged—but even a few bites could keep a man on his feet for a whole day's worth of hard work.

To Roran's concern, the magician looked utterly exhausted. "Can you continue?" Roran asked, pausing by him.

Carn nodded. "I just need a moment. . . . The bolts in the tunnel, and then the sacks of flour and the piece of slate . . ." He pushed another morsel of food in his mouth. "It was a bit much all at once."

Reassured, Roran started to move away, but Carn caught him by the arm. "I didn't do it," he said, and his eyes crinkled with amusement. "Singe your beard, that is. The torches must have started the fire."

Roran grunted, and continued on to the doors. "Form up!" he shouted, and slapped his shield with the flat of his hammer. "Baldor, Delwin, you take the lead with me. The rest of you, line up behind us. Shields out, swords drawn, arrows nocked. Halstead probably doesn't know yet that we're in the city, so don't let anyone escape who could warn him. . . . Ready, then? Right, with me!"

Together he and Baldor—whose cheeks and nose were red from the explosion—unbarred the doors and threw them open, revealing the interior of Aroughs.

181

DUST AND ASHES

Dozens of large plaster-sided buildings stood clustered around the portal in the city's outer wall, where the canal entered Aroughs. All of the buildings—cold and forbidding with the empty stare of their black windows—appeared to be warehouses or storage facilities, which, coupled with the early-morning hour, meant it was unlikely that anyone had noticed the Varden's clash with the guards.

Roran had no intention of staying around to find out for sure.

Hazy rays of newborn light streaked horizontally across the city, gilding the tops of the towers, the battlements, the cupolas, and the slanted roofs. The streets and alleyways were cloaked in shadows the color of tarnished silver, and the water in its stone-lined channel was dark and dismal and laced with streaks of blood. High above gleamed a lone wandering star, a furtive spark in the brightening blue mantle, where the sun's growing radiance had obscured all of the other nighttime jewels.

Forward the Varden trotted, their leather boots scuffing against the cobblestone street.

Off in the distance, a cock crowed.

Roran led them through the warren of buildings toward the inner wall of the city, but not always choosing the most obvious or direct route, so as to reduce their chances of encountering someone in the streets. The lanes they followed were narrow and murky, and sometimes he had difficulty seeing where he was placing his feet.

Filth clotted the gutters of the streets. The stench filled him with loathing and made him wish for the open fields he was used to.

How can anyone bear to live in such conditions? he wondered. *Even pigs won't wallow in their own dirt.*

Away from the curtain wall, the buildings changed to houses and shops: tall, crossbeamed, with whitewashed walls and wrought-iron fixtures upon the doors. Behind the shuttered windows, Roran sometimes heard the sound of voices, or the clatter of dishes, or the scrape of a chair being pulled across a wooden floor.

We're running out of time, he thought. Another few minutes and the streets would be teeming with the denizens of Aroughs.

As if to fulfill his prediction, two men stepped out of an alleyway in front of the column of warriors. Both of the city dwellers carried yokes on their shoulders with buckets of fresh milk hanging off the ends.

The men stopped with surprise as they saw the Varden, the milk sloshing out of the buckets. Their eyes widened, and their mouths fell open in preparation of some exclamation.

Roran halted, as did the troop behind him. "If you scream, we'll kill you," he said in a soft, friendly voice.

The men shivered and inched away.

Roran stepped forward. "If you run, we'll kill you." Without taking his eyes off the two frightened men, he uttered Carn's name and, when the magician arrived at his side, he said, "Put them to sleep for me, if you would."

The magician quickly recited a phrase in the ancient language, ending with a word that sounded to Roran something like *slytha*. The two men collapsed bonelessly to the ground, their buckets tipping over as they struck the cobblestones. Milk sheeted down the lane, forming a delicate web of white veins as it settled into the grooves between the stones of the street.

"Pull them off to the side," Roran said, "where they can't be seen."

As soon as his warriors had dragged the two unconscious men out of the way, he ordered the Varden forward once more, resuming their hurried march toward the inner wall.

Before they had gone more than a hundred feet, however, they turned a corner and ran headlong into a group of four soldiers.

This time Roran showed no mercy. He sprinted across the space that separated them and, while the soldiers were still trying to gather their wits, he buried the flat blade of his hammer into the base of the lead soldier's neck. Likewise, Baldor cut down one of the other soldiers, swinging his sword with a strength few men could match, a strength born of years spent working at his father's forge.

The last two soldiers squawked with alarm, turned, and ran.

An arrow shot past Roran's shoulder from somewhere behind him and took one soldier in the back, knocking him to the ground. A moment later, Carn barked, "Jierda!" The neck of the final soldier broke with an audible *snap*, and he tumbled forward to lie motionless in the center of the street.

The soldier with the arrow in him began to scream: "The Varden are here! The Varden are here! Sound the alarm, the—"

184 Drawing his dagger, Roran ran over to the man and cut his throat. He wiped the blade clean on the man's tunic, then stood and said, "Move out, now!"

As one, the Varden charged up the streets toward the inner wall of Aroughs.

When they were only a hundred feet away, Roran stopped in an alley behind a house and raised a hand, signaling his men to wait. Then he crept along the side of the house and peered around the corner at the portcullis set within the tall granite wall.

The gate was closed.

To the left of the gate, however, a small sally port stood wide open. Even as he watched, a soldier ran out through it and headed off toward the western edge of the city.

Roran cursed to himself as he stared at the sally port. He was not about to give up, not when they had made it this far, but their position was growing ever more precarious, and he had no doubt that they had only a few more minutes before curfew lifted and their presence became widely known.

He withdrew behind the side of the house and bowed his head as he thought furiously.

"Mandel," he said, and snapped his fingers. "Delwin, Carn, and you three." He pointed at a trio of fierce-looking warriors—older men who, by their very age, he knew must have a knack for winning battles. "Come with me. Baldor, you're in charge of the rest. If we don't make it back, get yourselves to safety. That's an order."

Baldor nodded, his expression grim.

With the six warriors he had selected, Roran circled the main thoroughfare that led to the gate until they reached the rubbish-strewn base of the outward-slanting wall, perhaps fifty feet from the portcullis and the open sally port.

A soldier was stationed on each of the two gate towers, but at the moment, neither was visible, and unless they stuck their heads over the edges of the battlements, they would not be able to see Roran and his companions approaching.

In a whisper, Roran said, "Once we're through the door, you, you, and you"—he motioned at Carn, Delwin, and one of the other warriors—"make for the guardhouse on the other side fast as you can. We'll take the near one. Do what you have to, but *get that gate open*. There may be only one wheel to turn, or we may have to work together to raise it, so don't think you can go and die on me. Ready? . . . *Now!*"

185

Running as quietly as he could, Roran dashed along the wall and, with a quick turn, darted into the sally port.

Before him was a twenty-foot-long chamber that opened to a large square with a tiered fountain in the center. Men in fine clothes were hurrying back and forth across the square, many of them clutching scrolls.

Ignoring them, Roran turned to a closed door, which he unlatched by hand, restraining the urge to kick it open. Through the door was a dingy guardroom with a spiral staircase built into one wall.

He raced up the stairs and, after a single revolution, found himself in a low-ceilinged room, where five soldiers were smoking and playing dice at a table set next to a huge windlass wrapped with chains as thick as his arm.

"Greetings!" said Roran in a deep, commanding voice. "I have a most important message for you."

The soldiers hesitated, then sprang to their feet, pushing back the benches they were sitting on. The wooden legs screeched as they dragged over the floor.

They were too late. Brief though it was, their indecision was all Roran needed to cross the distance between them before the soldiers could draw their weapons.

Roran bellowed as he waded into their midst, lashing out left and right with his hammer and driving the five men back into a corner. Then Mandel and the two other warriors were at his side, swords flashing. Together they made short work of the guards.

When he stood over the twitching body of the last soldier, Roran spat on the ground and said, "Don't trust strangers."

The fighting had polluted the room with a collection of horrific odors, which seemed to press against Roran like a thick, heavy blanket made of the most unpleasant substance he could imagine. He was barely able to breathe without being sick, so he covered his nose and mouth with the sleeve of his tunic, trying to filter out some of the smells.

The four of them went to the windlass, being careful not to slip on the pools of blood, and studied it for a moment as they figured out its workings.

Roran spun around, raising his hammer as he heard a clink of metal and then the loud creak of a wooden trapdoor being pulled open, followed by a clatter of footsteps as a soldier descended the winding staircase from the gate tower above.

"Taurin, what in the blazes is going—" The soldier's voice died in his throat and he stopped partway down the stairs as he caught sight of Roran and his companions, as well as the mangled bodies in the corner.

A warrior to Roran's right threw a spear at the soldier, but the soldier ducked and the spear struck the wall above him. The soldier cursed and scrambled back up the stairs on all fours, vanishing behind a curve of the wall.

A moment later, the trapdoor slammed shut with an echoing *boom*, and then they heard the soldier wind a horn and shout frantic warnings to the people in the square.

Roran scowled and returned to the windlass. "Leave him," he said, shoving his hammer under his belt. He leaned against the spoked wheel used to raise and lower the portcullis and pushed as hard as he could, straining every muscle. The other men added their strength to his, and slowly, ever so slowly, the wheel began to turn, the ratchet on the side of the windlass clicking loudly as the huge wooden catch slid over the teeth below.

The effort needed to turn the wheel became substantially easier a few seconds later, a fact that Roran attributed to the team he had sent to infiltrate the other guardhouse.

They did not bother to raise the portcullis all the way; after a half minute of grunting and sweating, the fierce war cries of the Varden reached their ears as the men waiting outside charged through the gate and into the square.

Roran released the wheel, then pulled out his hammer again and made for the stairs with the others in tow.

Outside the guardhouse, he spotted Carn and Delwin just as they emerged from the structure on the other side of the gate. Neither appeared injured, but Roran noticed that the older warrior who had accompanied them was now absent.

While they waited for Roran's group to rejoin them, Baldor and the rest of the Varden organized themselves into a solid block of men at the edge of the square. They stood five ranks deep, shoulder to shoulder with their shields overlapping.

As he trotted over to them, Roran saw a large contingent of soldiers emerge from among the buildings at the far side of the square. There they assumed a defensive formation, angling their spears and pikes outward, so they resembled a long, low pincushion stuck full of needles. He estimated that about one hundred fifty soldiers were present—a number that his warriors could certainly overcome, but at a cost of both time and men.

His mood grew even more grim as the same hook-nosed magician whom he had seen on the previous day stepped out in front of the rows of soldiers and spread his arms above his head, a nimbus of black lighting crackling around each of his hands. Roran had learned enough about magic from Eragon to know that the lightning was probably more for show than anything else, but show or not, he had no doubt that the enemy spellcaster was enormously dangerous.

Carn arrived at the head of the warriors seconds after Roran. Together they and Baldor gazed at the magician and the ridge of soldiers assembled in opposition.

"Can you kill him?" Roran asked quietly, so the men behind him could not hear.

"I'll have to try, now won't I?" replied Carn. He wiped his mouth with the back of his hand. Perspiration beaded his face.

"If you want, we can rush him. He can't kill us all before we wear down his wards and put a blade through his heart."

"You don't know that. . . . No, this is my responsibility, and I have to deal with it."

"Is there anything we can do to help?"

Carn uttered a nervous laugh. "You could shoot some arrows at him. Blocking them might weaken him enough that he'll make a mistake. But whatever you do, don't get between us. . . . It won't be safe, for you or for me."

Roran transferred his hammer to his left hand, then placed his right on Carn's shoulder. "You'll be fine. Remember, he's not that clever. You tricked him before, and you can trick him again."

"I know."

"Good luck," said Roran.

Carn nodded once, then walked toward the fountain in the center of the square. The light from the sun had reached the plume of dancing water, which glittered like handfuls of diamonds tossed into the air.

The hook-nosed magician also walked toward the fountain, matching his steps to Carn's until they stood only twenty feet apart, whereupon they both stopped.

From where Roran was standing, Carn and his opponent appeared to be talking to each other, but they were too far away for him to make out what they said. Then both of the spellcasters went rigid, as if someone had jabbed them with poniards.

That was what Roran had been waiting for: a sign that they were dueling with their minds, too busy to pay attention to their surroundings.

"Archers!" he barked. "Go there and there," and he pointed at either side of the square. "Put as many arrows into that traitorous dog as you can, but don't you dare hit Carn or I'll have you fed alive to Saphira."

The soldiers shifted uneasily as the two groups of archers advanced partway across the square, but none of Galbatorix's crimson-clad troops broke formation or moved to engage the Varden.

They must have a great deal of confidence in that pet viper of theirs, Roran thought, concerned.

Dozens of brown, goose-feather-fletched arrows arched spinning and whistling toward the enemy magician, and for a moment, Roran hoped that they might be able to kill him. Five feet from the hook-nosed man, however, every single shaft shattered and dropped to the ground, as if they had run headlong into a wall of stone.

Roran bounced on his heels, too tense to stand still. He hated having to wait, doing nothing, while his friend was in danger. Moreover, every passing moment gave Lord Halstead more of an opportunity to figure out what was happening and devise an effective response. If Roran's men were to avoid being crushed by the Empire's superior forces, they had to keep their enemies off balance, unsure of where to turn or what to do.

"On your toes!" he said, turning to the warriors. "Let's see if we

189

can do some good while Carn is fighting to save our necks. We're going to flank those soldiers. Half of you come with me; the rest follow Delwin here. They can't block off every single street, so Delwin, you and your men work your way past the soldiers, then loop back around and attack them from behind. We'll keep them busy on this front, so they won't put up much resistance. If any of the soldiers try to run, let them. It would take too long to kill them all anyway. Got it? . . . Go, go, go!"

The men quickly separated into two groups. Leading his, Roran ran up the right-hand edge of the square, while Delwin did the same on the left.

When both bands of men were almost level with the fountain, Roran saw the enemy magician look toward him. It was the merest flicker of a glance, sidelong and fleeting, but the distraction, whether intended or not, seemed to have an immediate effect on his duel with Carn. As the hook-nosed man returned his gaze to Carn, the snarl upon his face deepened into a painful rictus, and veins began to bulge on his knotted brow and on his corded neck, and his whole head flushed a dark, angry red, as if it were so swollen with blood that it might burst asunder.

"No!" howled the man, and then he shouted something in the ancient language that Roran could not understand.

A fraction of a second later, Carn shouted something as well and, for a moment, their two voices overlapped with such a dire mixture of terror, desolation, hate, and fury that Roran knew deep in his bones that the duel had somehow gone horribly wrong.

Carn vanished amid a blaze of blue light. Then a white, dome-like shell flashed outward from where he had been standing and expanded across the square in less time than it took Roran to blink.

The world went black. An unbearable heat pressed against Roran, and everything turned and twisted around him as he tumbled through a formless space.

His hammer was wrenched out of his hand, and pain erupted

in the side of his right knee. Then a hard object smashed into his mouth, and he felt a tooth pop loose, filling his mouth with blood.

When he finally came to rest, he remained where he was, lying on his belly, too stunned to move. His senses gradually returned, and he saw the smooth, gray-green surface of a paving stone underneath his nose, and he smelled the lead mortar that surrounded the stone, and all throughout his body he became aware of aches and bruises clamoring for his attention. The only sound he could hear was that of his pounding heart.

Some of the blood in his mouth and throat went into his lungs as he started to breathe again. Desperate for air, he coughed and sat upright, spitting out gobs of black phlegm. He saw the tooth, one of his incisors, fly out and bounce against the paving stone, startling white against the splotches of spewed blood. He caught it and examined it; the end of the incisor was chipped, but the root appeared intact, so he licked the tooth clean then pushed it back into the hole in his gums, wincing as he poked the sore flesh.

Levering himself off the ground, he got to his feet. He had been thrown against the doorstep of one of the houses that bordered the square. His men were scattered about him, arms and legs askew, helmets lost, swords torn away.

Again Roran was grateful that he carried a hammer, for several of the Varden had managed to stab themselves or their shield mates during the tumult.

Hammer? Where is my hammer? he belatedly thought. He cast about the ground until he spotted the handle of his weapon protruding from beneath the legs of a nearby warrior. He pulled it free, then turned to look at the square.

Soldiers and Varden alike had been tossed sprawling. Nothing remained of the fountain except for a low pile of rubble from which water spurted at erratic intervals. Next to it, where Carn had been, lay a blackened, withered corpse, its smoking limbs clenched tight, like those of a dead spider, the whole thing so charred and pitted and burned away that it was barely recognizable as anything that had once been alive or human. Inexplicably, the hook-nosed magician still stood in the same place, though the explosion had robbed him of his outer clothes, leaving him wearing nothing but his breeches.

Uncontrollable anger gripped Roran, and without a thought for his own preservation, he staggered toward the center of the square, determined to kill the magician once and for all.

The bare-chested conjurer held his ground even as Roran drew near. Raising his hammer, Roran broke out into a shambling run and shouted a war cry that he could hear but dimly.

And yet the magician made no move to defend himself.

In fact, Roran realized that the spellcaster had not stirred so much as an inch since the explosion. It was as if he were a statue of a man and not the thing itself.

The spellcaster's seeming indifference to Roran's approach tempted Roran to ignore the man's unusual behavior—or lack of behavior, as it was—and simply bash him over the head before he recovered from whatever strange stupor ailed him. However, Roran's wariness cooled his lust for vengeance and caused him to slow to a stop not five feet from the magician.

He was glad he did.

While the magician had appeared normal from a distance, up close, Roran saw that his skin was loose and wrinkled like that of a man thrice his age, and that it had acquired a coarse, leathery texture. The color of his skin had darkened as well, and was continuing to darken, moment by moment, as if his entire body had been bitten by frost.

The man's chest was heaving and his eyeballs were rolling in their sockets, showing white, but other than that, he seemed incapable of movement.

As Roran watched, the man's arms, neck, and chest shriveled, and his bones appeared in sharp relief—from the bowlike curve of his collarbones to the hollow saddle of his hips, where his stomach hung like an empty waterskin. His lips puckered and drew back farther than they were intended to over his yellow teeth, baring them in a grisly snarl, while his eyeballs deflated as if they were engorged ticks being squished empty of blood, and the surrounding flesh sank inward.

The man's breathing—a panicked, high-pitched sawing—faltered then, but still did not entirely cease.

Horrified, Roran stepped backward. He felt something slick beneath his boots and looked down to see that he was standing in a spreading puddle of water. At first he thought it was from the broken fountain, but then he realized that the water was flowing outward from the feet of the paralyzed magician.

Roran cursed, revulsion filling him, and jumped to a dry patch of ground. Seeing the water, he understood what it was Carn had done, and his already profound sense of horror increased. Carn, it seemed, had cast a spell that was drawing every single drop of moisture from the magician's body.

Over the span of only another few seconds, the spell reduced the man to no more than a knobby skeleton wrapped in a shell of hard black skin, mummifying him the same as if he had been left in the Hadarac Desert, exposed to a hundred years of wind and sun and shifting sands. Although he was most certainly dead by then, he did not fall, as Carn's magic held him upright: a ghastly, grinning specter that was the equal of the most terrible things Roran had ever seen in his nightmares or on the battlefield—both being much the same.

Then the surface of the man's desiccated body blurred as it dissolved into a fine gray dust, which sifted downward in gauzy curtains and lay floating atop the water below, like ashes from a forest fire. Muscle and bone soon followed, then the stony organs, and then the last parts of the hook-nosed magician crumbled away, leaving behind only a small, conical mound of powder rising out of the pool of water that had once sustained its life.

Roran looked over at Carn's corpse, then looked away just as quickly, unable to bear the sight. *At least you had your revenge on him*. Then he put aside thoughts of his slain friend, for they were too painful to dwell on, and instead concentrated upon the most immediate problem at hand: the soldiers at the southern end of the square, who were slowly picking themselves up off the ground.

Roran saw the Varden doing much the same. "Oi!" he shouted. "With me! We'll never have a better chance than now." He pointed at some of his men who were obviously wounded. "Help them up and put them in the center of the formation. No one gets left behind. No one!" His lips and mouth throbbed as he spoke, and his head ached as if he had been up all night drinking.

The Varden rallied at the sound of his voice and hurried to join him. As the men gathered into a broad column behind him, Roran took his place in the foremost rank of warriors, between Baldor and Delwin, both of whom bore bloody scrapes from the explosion.

"Carn is dead?" Baldor asked.

Roran nodded and lifted his shield, as did the other men, so that they formed a solid, outward-facing wall.

"Then we better hope Halstead doesn't have another magician hidden away somewhere," Delwin muttered.

When the Varden were all in place, Roran shouted, "Forward march!" and the warriors tramped across the remainder of the courtyard.

Whether because their leadership was less effective than the Varden's or because the blast had dealt them a more severe blow, the Empire soldiers had failed to recover as quickly and so were still disorganized when the Varden drove into their midst.

Roran grunted and staggered back a step as a spear embedded itself in his shield, numbing his arm and dragging it down through sheer weight. Reaching around, he swept his hammer across the face of the shield. It bounced off the haft of the spear, which refused to budge.

A soldier in front of him, perhaps the very one who had thrown the spear, seized the opportunity to run at him and swing his sword at Roran's neck. Roran started to lift his shield, along with the spear lodged in it, but it was too heavy and cumbersome for him to protect himself with. So he used his hammer instead, lashing out at the descending sword.

On edge, however, the blade was almost impossible for him to see, and he timed his parry badly and missed the sword with his hammer. He would have died then, except that his knuckles clipped the flat of the blade, deflecting it several inches to the side.

A line of fire cut through Roran's right shoulder. Jagged bolts of lightning shot down his side, and his vision flashed bright yellow. His right knee buckled and he fell forward.

Stone underneath him. Feet and legs around him, hemming him in so he could not roll away to safety. His whole body sluggish and unresponsive, as if he were trapped in honey.

Too slow, too slow, he thought as he struggled to free his arm from the shield and get his feet back under him. If he stayed on the ground, he would be either stabbed or trampled. *Too slow!*

Then he saw the soldier collapse in front of him, clutching at his belly, and a second later, someone pulled Roran up by the collar of his hauberk and held him upright while he regained his footing. It was Baldor.

Twisting his neck, Roran looked at where the soldier had struck him. Five links in his mail shirt had split open, but other than that, the armor had held. Despite the blood oozing out of the rent, and the pain that racked his neck and arm, he did not think the wound was life-threatening, nor was he about to stop and find out. His right arm still worked—at least enough to continue fighting—and that was all he cared about at the moment.

Someone passed him a replacement shield. He grimly shouldered it and pressed onward with his men, forcing the soldiers to retreat along the wide street that led from the square.

The soldiers soon broke and ran in the face of the Varden's overwhelming strength, fleeing down the myriad side streets and alleys that branched off the thoroughfare.

Roran paused then and sent fifty of his men back to close the portcullis and sally port and to guard them against any foes who might seek to follow the Varden into the heart of Aroughs. Most of the soldiers in the city would be stationed close to the outer wall to repel besiegers, and Roran had no desire to face them in open battle. To do so would be suicidal, given the size of Halstead's forces.

The Varden met little resistance thereafter as they progressed through the inner city to the large, well-appointed palace where Lord Halstead ruled.

A spacious courtyard with an artificial pond—wherein swam geese and white swans—lay before the palace, which towered several stories above the rest of Aroughs. The palace was a beautiful, ornate structure of open arches, colonnades, and wide balconies intended for dancing and parties. Unlike the castle in the heart of Belatona, it had obviously been built with pleasure in mind, not defense.

They must have assumed no one could get past their walls, thought Roran.

Several dozen guards and soldiers in the courtyard charged haphazardly at the Varden when they caught sight of them, shouting war cries the whole while.

"Stay in formation!" Roran ordered as the men rushed toward them.

For a minute or two, the sound of clashing arms filled the courtyard. The geese and the swans honked with alarm at the commotion and beat the water with their wings, but none of them dared leave the confines of their pond.

It did not take long for the Varden to rout the soldiers and guards. Then they stormed the entryway of the palace, which was so richly decorated with paintings on the walls and ceilings—as well as gilt moldings, carved furniture, and a patterned floor—that Roran found it difficult to take in all at once. The wealth required to build and maintain such an edifice was more than he could comprehend. The entire farm where he had grown up had not been equal the worth of a single chair in that grand hall.

Through an open doorway, he saw three servingwomen running down another long corridor as fast as their skirts would allow.

"Don't let them get away!" he exclaimed.

Five swordsmen broke off from the main body of the Varden and dashed after the women, catching them before they reached the end of the passageway. The women uttered piercing screams and struggled ferociously, clawing at their captors, as the men dragged them back to where Roran was waiting.

"Enough!" shouted Roran when they were in front of him, and the women ceased fighting, although they continued to whimper and moan. The oldest of the three, a stout matron who had her silver hair pulled back in an untidy bun and who carried a ring of keys at her waist, appeared the most reasonable, so Roran asked her, "Where is Lord Halstead?"

The woman stiffened and lifted her chin. "Do with me what you will, sir, but I'll not betray my master."

Roran moved toward her until they were only a foot apart. "Listen to me, and listen well," he growled. "Aroughs has fallen, and you and everyone else in this city are at my mercy. Nothing you can do will change that. Tell me where Halstead is, and we'll let you and your companions go. You can't save him from his doom, but you can save yourselves." His torn lips were so swollen, he was barely able to make himself understood, and with every word, flecks of blood flew from his mouth.

"My own fate doesn't matter, sir," said the woman, her expression as determined as any warrior's.

Roran cursed and slapped his hammer against his shield, producing a harsh crash that echoed loudly in the cavernous hall. The women flinched at the sound. "Have you taken leave of your senses? Is Halstead worth your life? Is the Empire? Is Galbatorix?"

"I don't know about Galbatorix or the Empire, sir, but Halstead has always been kind enough to us serving folk, and I'll not see him strung up by the likes of you. Filthy, ungrateful *muck*, that's what you are."

"Is that so?" He stared at her fiercely. "How long do you think you can hold your tongue if I decide to let my men wring the truth out of you?"

"You'll never make me talk," she declared, and he believed her.

"What about them?" He nodded toward the other women, the youngest of whom could not have been more than seventeen. "Are you willing to let them be cut into pieces just to save your master?"

The woman sniffed disdainfully, then said, "Lord Halstead is in the east wing of the palace. Take the corridor over there, go through the Yellow Room and Lady Galiana's flower garden, and you'll find him sure as rain."

Roran listened with suspicion. Her capitulation seemed too quick and too easy given her earlier resistance. Also, while she spoke, he noticed that the other two women reacted with surprise and some other emotion he could not identify. *Confusion?* he wondered. In any event, they did not react the way he would have expected if the silver-haired woman had just delivered their lord into the arms of their enemies. They were too quiet, too subdued, as if they were hiding something.

Of the two, the girl was the less skilled at masking her feelings, so Roran turned on her with all the savagery he could muster. "You there, she's lying, isn't she? Where is Halstead? *Tell me!*"

The girl opened her mouth and shook her head, speechless. She tried to back away from him, but one of the warriors held her in place.

Roran stomped over to her, jammed his shield flat against her chest, knocking the air out of her, and leaned his weight against it, pinning her between him and the man behind her. Lifting his hammer, Roran touched it to the side of her cheek. "You're rather pretty, but you'll have a hard time finding anyone but old men to court you if I knock out your front teeth. I lost a tooth myself today, but I managed to put it back in. See?" And he spread his lips in what he was sure was a gruesome approximation of a smile. "I'll keep your teeth, though, so you won't be able to do the same. They'll make a fine trophy, eh?" And he made a threatening motion with the hammer.

The girl cringed and cried, "No! Please, sir, I don't know. Please! He was in his quarters, meeting with his captains, but then he and Lady Galiana were going to go to the tunnel to the docks, and—"

"Thara, you fool!" exclaimed the matron.

"There's a ship waiting for them, there is, and I don't know where he is now, but please don't hit me, I don't know anything else, sir, and—"

"His quarters," barked Roran. "Where are they?"

Sobbing, the girl told him.

"Let them go," he said when she finished, and the three women darted out of the entryway, the hard heels of their shoes clattering against the polished floor.

Roran led the Varden through the enormous building in accordance with the girl's instructions. Scores of half-dressed men and women crossed their paths, but none paused to fight. The palace rang with shouts and screams to the point where he wanted to plug his ears with his fingers.

Partway to their destination, they came upon an atrium with a statue of a huge black dragon in the middle. Roran wondered if it was supposed to be Galbatorix's dragon, Shruikan. As they trooped past the statue, Roran heard a *twang,* and then something struck him in the back.

He fell against a stone bench next to the path and clutched at it. *Pain.*

Agonizing, thought-destroying pain, the likes of which he had never experienced before. Pain so intense, he would have cut off his own hand to make it stop. It felt as if a red-hot poker were being pressed into his back.

He could not move. . . .

He could not breathe. . . .

Even the smallest shift in position caused him unbearable torment.

Shadows fell across him, and he heard Baldor and Delwin shouting, then Brigman, of all people, was saying something as well, although Roran could not make sense of it.

The pain suddenly increased tenfold, and he bellowed, which only made it worse. With a supreme effort of will, he forced himself to remain absolutely still. Tears ran from the corners of his clenched eyes.

Then Brigman was talking to him. "Roran, you have an arrow in your back. We tried to catch the archer, but he escaped."

"Hurts . . . ," Roran gasped.

"That's because the arrow hit one of your ribs. It would have gone right through you, otherwise. You're lucky it wasn't an inch higher or lower and that it missed your spine and your shoulder blade."

"Pull it out," he said between gritted teeth.

"We can't; the arrow has a barbed head. And we can't push it through to the other side. It has to be cut out. I have some experience with this, Roran. If you trust me to wield the knife, I can do it here and now. Or, if you prefer, we can wait until we find you a healer. There must be one or two somewhere in the palace."

Though he hated to put himself in Brigman's power, Roran could bear the pain no longer, so he said, "Do it here. . . . Baldor . . ."

"Yes, Roran?"

"Take fifty men and find Halstead. Whatever happens, he can't escape. Delwin . . . stay with me."

A brief discussion ensued between Baldor, Delwin, and Brigman, of which Roran heard but a few scattered words. Then a large portion of the Varden departed the atrium, which was noticeably quieter afterward.

At Brigman's insistence, a team of warriors fetched chairs from a nearby room, broke them into pieces, and built a fire on the gravel-lined path next to the statue. Into the fire was placed the tip of a dagger, which Roran knew Brigman would use to cauterize the wound in his back after removing the arrow, lest he bleed to death.

As he lay on the bench, stiff and trembling, Roran focused on controlling his breathing, taking slow, shallow breaths to minimize the pain. Difficult as it was, he purged his mind of all other thoughts. What had been and what might be did not matter, only the steady inflow and outflow of air through his nostrils.

He almost passed out when four men lifted him from the bench and lowered him facedown to the ground. Someone stuffed a leather glove into his mouth, aggravating the ache from his torn lips, while at the same time, rough hands grasped each of his legs and arms, stretching them out to their fullest extent and pinning them in place.

Roran glanced backward to see Brigman kneeling over him, holding a curved hunting knife in one hand. The knife began to descend, and Roran closed his eyes again and bit down hard on the glove.

He breathed in.

He breathed out.

And then time and memory ceased for him.

Interregnum

Roran sat hunched over the edge of the table, toying with a jewel-encrusted goblet that he stared at without interest.

Night had fallen, and the only light in the lavish bed-chamber came from the two candles on the desk and the small fire glowing on the hearth by the empty four-poster bed. All was quiet, save for an occasional crackle of burning wood.

A faint salty breeze wafted through the windows, parting the thin white curtains. He turned his face to catch the draft, welcoming the touch of cool air against his fevered skin.

Through the windows, he could see Aroughs laid out before him. Watchfires dotted the streets at intersections here and there, but otherwise the city was dark and motionless—unusually so, for everyone who could was hiding in their homes.

When the breeze ceased, he took another sip from the goblet, pouring the wine directly down his throat to avoid having to swallow. A drop fell onto the split in his lower lip, and he tensed and sucked in his breath while he waited for the spike of pain to vanish.

He set the goblet on the desk, next to the plate of bread and lamb and the half-empty bottle of wine, then glanced at the mirror propped upright between the two candles. It still reflected nothing but his own haggard face, bruised, bloodied, and missing a goodly portion of his beard on the right-hand side.

He looked away. She would contact him when she did. In the meantime he would wait. It was all he could do; he hurt too much to sleep.

He picked up the goblet again and rolled it between his fingers.

Time passed.

* * *

Late that night, the mirror shimmered like a rippling pool of quicksilver, causing Roran to blink and gaze at it through bleary, half-closed eyes.

The teardrop shape of Nasuada's face took form before him, her expression as serious as ever. "Roran," she said by way of greeting, her voice clear and strong.

"Lady Nasuada." He straightened off the table as far as he dared, which was only a few inches.

"Have you been captured?"

"No."

"Then I take it that Carn is either dead or wounded."

"He died while fighting another magician."

"I'm sorry to hear it. . . . He seemed a decent man, and we can ill afford to lose any of our spellcasters." She paused for a moment. "And what of Aroughs?"

"The city is ours."

Nasuada's eyebrows rose. "Truly? I am most impressed. Tell me, how went the battle? Did everything go according to plan?"

Opening his jaw as little as he could, so as to minimize the discomfort of talking, Roran mumbled his way through an account of the past several days, from his arrival at Aroughs to the one-eyed man who had attacked him in his tent to the breaking of the dams at the mills to how the Varden had fought their way through Aroughs to the palace of Lord Halstead, including Carn's duel with the enemy magician.

Then Roran related how he had been shot in the back, and how Brigman had cut the arrow out of him. "I'm lucky he was there; he did a good job of it. If not for him, I would have been next to useless until we found a healer." He cringed inwardly as, for a second, the memory of his wounds being cauterized jumped to the forefront of his mind, and he again felt the touch of hot metal against his flesh.

"I hope you did find a healer to look at you."

"Aye, later, but he was no spellcaster."

Nasuada leaned back in her chair and studied him for a while. "I'm astonished you still have the strength to talk to me. The people of Carvahall are indeed made of stern stuff."

"Afterward, we secured the palace, as well as the rest of Aroughs, although there are still a few places where our grip is weak. It was fairly easy to convince the soldiers to surrender once they realized we had slipped behind their lines and captured the center of the city."

"And what of Lord Halstead? Did you capture him as well?"

"He was attempting to escape the palace when some of my men chanced upon him. Halstead had only a small number of guards with him, not enough to fight off our warriors, so he and his retainers fled into a wine cellar and barricaded themselves inside. . . ." Roran rubbed his thumb over a ruby set in the goblet before him. "They wouldn't surrender, and I didn't dare storm the room; it would have been too costly. So . . . I ordered the men to fetch pots of oil from the kitchens, light them on fire, and throw them against the door."

"Were you trying to smoke them out?" Nasuada asked.

He nodded slowly. "A few of the soldiers ran out once the door burned down, but Halstead waited too long. We found him on the floor, suffocated."

"That is unfortunate."

"Also . . . his daughter, Lady Galiana." In his mind, he could still see her: tiny, delicate, garbed in a beautiful lavender dress covered with frills and ribbons.

Nasuada frowned. "Who succeeds Halstead as the earl of Fenmark?"

"Tharos the Quick."

"The same who led the charge against you yesterday?"

"The same."

It had been midafternoon when his men had brought Tharos before him. The small, bearded man had appeared dazed, though uninjured, and he had been missing his helm with its flamboyant plumes. To him, Roran—who was lying belly-down on a padded couch to save his back—had said, "I believe you owe me a bottle of wine."

"How have you done this?!" Tharos had demanded in response, the sound of despair ringing in his voice. "The city was impregnable. None but a dragon could have broken our walls. And yet look what you wrought. You are something other than human, something other than . . ." And he had fallen silent, unable to speak any longer.

"How did he react to the deaths of his father and sister?" Nasuada asked.

Roran leaned his head against his hand. His brow was slick with sweat, so he wiped it dry with his sleeve. He shivered. Despite the perspiration, he felt cold all over, especially in his hands and feet. "He didn't seem to much care about his father. His sister, though . . ." Roran winced as he remembered the torrent of abuse Tharos had directed at him after learning that Galiana was dead.

"If ever I get the chance, I'll kill you for this," Tharos had said. "I swear it."

"You had best move quickly, then," Roran had retorted. "Another has already claimed my life, and if anyone is going to kill me, my guess is that it'll be her."

". . . Roran? . . . Roran!"

With a faint sense of surprise, he realized that Nasuada was calling his name. He looked at her again, framed in the mirror like a portrait, and struggled to find his tongue. At last he said, "Tharos isn't really the earl of Fenmark. He's the youngest of Halstead's seven sons, but all of his brothers have fled or are hiding. So, for the time being, Tharos is the only one left to claim the title. He makes a good envoy between us and the elders of the city. Without Carn, though, there's no way for me to tell who is sworn to Galbatorix and who isn't. Most of the lords and ladies are, I assume, and the soldiers, of course, but it's impossible to know who else."

Nasuada pursed her lips. "I see. . . . Dauth is the closest city to you. I'll ask Lady Alarice—whom I believe you've met—to send someone to Aroughs who is skilled in the art of reading minds. Most nobles keep one such person in their retinue, so it should be easy enough for Alarice to fulfill our request. However, when we marched for the Burning Plains, King Orrin brought with him every spellcaster of note from Surda, which means that whoever Alarice sends will most likely have no other skill with magic besides the ability to hear others' thoughts. And without the proper spells, it will be difficult to prevent those who are loyal to Galbatorix from opposing us at every turn."

While she spoke, Roran allowed his gaze to drift across the desk until it came to rest on the dark bottle of wine. *I wonder if Tharos poisoned it?* The thought failed to alarm him.

Then Nasuada was speaking to him again: ". . . hope that you have kept tight rein over your men and not let them run wild in Aroughs, burning, plundering, and taking liberties with its people?"

Roran was so tired, he found it difficult to marshal a coherent response, but at last he managed to say, "There are too few of us for the men to make mischief. They know as well as I do that the soldiers could retake the city if we gave them even the slightest opportunity."

"A mixed blessing, I suppose. . . . How many casualties did you suffer during the attack?"

"Forty-two."

For a while, silence lay between them. Then Nasuada said, "Did Carn have any family?"

Roran shrugged, a slight inward motion of his left shoulder. "I don't know. He was from somewhere in the north, I think, but neither of us really talked about our lives before . . . before all of this. . . . It never seemed that important."

A sudden itch in Roran's throat forced him to cough again and again, and he curled over the table until his forehead touched the wood, grimacing as waves of pain assailed him from his back, his shoulder, and his mangled mouth. His convulsions were so violent, the wine in the goblet slopped over the rim and spilled onto his hand and wrist.

As he slowly recovered, Nasuada said, "Roran, you have to summon a healer to examine you. You're unwell, and you ought to be in bed."

"No." He wiped the spittle from the corner of his mouth, then looked up at her. "They've done all they can, and I'm no child to be fussed over."

Nasuada hesitated, then dipped her head. "As you wish."

"Now what happens?" he asked. "Am I finished here?"

"It was my intention to have you return as soon as we captured Aroughs—however that was accomplished—but you're in no condition to ride all the way to Dras-Leona. You'll have to wait until—"

"I won't wait," Roran growled. He grabbed the mirror and pulled it toward him until it was only a few inches from his face. "Don't you coddle me, Nasuada. I can ride, and I can ride fast. The only reason I came here is because Aroughs was a threat to the Varden. That threat is gone now—I removed it—and I'm not about to stay here, injuries or no injuries, while my wife and unborn child sit camped less than a mile away from Murtagh and his dragon!"

Nasuada's voice hardened for a moment. "You went to Aroughs because *I* sent you." Then, in a more relaxed tone, she said, "However, your point is well taken. You may return at once, if you are able. There's no reason for you to ride night and day, as you did during the journey there, but neither should you dawdle. Be sensible about it. I don't want to have to explain to Katrina that you killed yourself traveling. . . . Whom do you think I should select as your replacement when you leave Aroughs?"

"Captain Brigman."

"Brigman? Why? Didn't you have some difficulties with him?"

"He helped keep the men in line after I was shot. My head wasn't very clear at the time—"

"I imagine not."

"—and he saw to it that they didn't panic or lose their nerve.

Also, he led them on my behalf while I was stuck in this miserable music box of a castle. He was the only one who had the experience for it. Without him, we wouldn't have been able to extend our control over the whole of Aroughs. The men like him, and he's skilled at planning and organizing. He'll do well at governing the city."

"Brigman it is, then." Nasuada looked away from the mirror and murmured something to a person he could not see. Turning back to him, she said, "I must admit, I never thought you would actually capture Aroughs. It seemed impossible that anyone could breach the city's defenses in so little time, with so few men, and without the aid of either a dragon or Rider."

"Then why send me here?"

"Because I had to try *something* before letting Eragon and Saphira fly so far away, and because you have made a habit of confounding expectations and prevailing where others would have faltered or given up. If the impossible *were* to happen, it seemed most likely that it would occur under your watch, as indeed it did."

Roran snorted softly. *And how long can I keep tempting fate before I end up dead like Carn?*

"Sneer if you want, but you cannot deny your own success. You have won a great victory for us today, Stronghammer. Or rather, Captain Stronghammer, I ought to say. You have more than earned the right to that title. I am immensely grateful for what you have done. By capturing Aroughs, you have freed us from the prospect of fighting a war on two fronts, which would have almost certainly meant our destruction. All of the Varden are in your debt, and I promise you, the sacrifices you and your men have made will not be forgotten."

Roran tried to say something, failed, tried again, and failed a second time before he finally managed to say: "I . . . I will be sure to let the men know how you feel. It will mean a lot to them."

"Please do. And now I must bid you farewell. It is late, you are sick, and I have kept you far too long as it is."

"Wait . . ." He reached toward her and struck the tips of his fingers against the mirror. "Wait. You haven't told me: How goes the siege of Dras-Leona?"

She stared at him, her expression flat. "Badly. And it shows no signs of improving. We could use you here, Stronghammer. If we don't find a way to bring this situation to an end, and soon, everything we have fought for will be lost."

✦ ✦ ✦

THARDSVERGÛNDNZMAL

"You're fine," said Eragon, exasperated. "Stop worrying. There's nothing you can do about it anyway."

Saphira growled and continued to study her image in the lake. She turned her head from side to side, then exhaled heavily, releasing a cloud of smoke that drifted out over the water like a small, lost thundercloud.

Are you sure? she asked, and looked toward him. *What if it doesn't grow back?*

"Dragons grow new scales all the time. You know that."

Yes, but I've never lost one before!

He did not bother to hide his smile; he knew she would sense his amusement. "You shouldn't be so upset. It wasn't very big." Reaching out, he traced the diamond-shaped hole on the left side of her snout, where the object of her consternation had so recently been ensconced. The gap in her sparkling armor was no larger than the end of his thumb and about an inch deep. At the bottom of it, her leathery blue hide was visible.

Curious, he touched her skin with the tip of his index finger. It felt warm and smooth, like the belly of a calf.

Saphira snorted and pulled her head away from him. *Stop that; it tickles.*

He chuckled and kicked at the water by the base of the rock he was sitting on, enjoying the sensation against the bottom of his bare feet.

It may not have been very big, she said, *but everyone will notice that it's missing. How could they not? One might as well overlook a bare patch of earth on the crest of a snow-covered mountain.* And her eyes rolled forward as she tried to peer down her long snout at the small, dark hole above her nostril.

Eragon laughed and splashed a handful of water at her. Then, to soothe her injured pride, he said, "No one will notice, Saphira. Trust me. Besides, even if they do, they'll take it for a battle wound and consider you all the more fearsome because of it."

You think so? She returned to examining herself in the lake. The water and her scales reflected off each other in a dazzling array of rainbow-hued flecks. *What if a soldier stabs me there? The blade would go right through me. Perhaps I should ask the dwarves to make a metal plate to cover the area until the scale regrows.*

"That would look exceedingly ridiculous."

It would?

"Mm-hmm." He nodded, on the verge of laughing again.

She sniffed. *There's no need to make fun of me. How would you like it if the fur on your head started falling out, or you lost one of those silly little nubs you call teeth? I would end up having to comfort you, no doubt.*

"No doubt," he agreed easily. "But then, teeth don't grow back." He pushed himself off the rock and made his way up the shore to where he had left his boots, stepping carefully to avoid hurting his feet on the stones and branches that littered the water's edge. Saphira followed him, the soft earth squishing between her talons.

You could cast a spell to protect just that spot, she said as he pulled on his boots.

"I could. Do you want me to?"

I do.

He worked out the enchantment in his head while he laced up his boots, then placed the palm of his right hand over the pit in her snout and murmured the necessary words in the ancient language. A faint azure glow emanated from underneath his hand as he bound the ward to her body.

"There," he said when he finished. "Now you have nothing to worry about."

Except that I'm still missing a scale.

He gave her a push on the jaw. "Come on, you. Let's go back to camp."

Together they left the lake and climbed the steep, crumbling bank behind them, Eragon using the exposed tree roots as handholds.

At the top of the rise, they had an unobstructed view of the Varden's camp a half mile to the east, as well as, somewhat north of the camp, the sprawling mess of Dras-Leona. The only signs of life within the city were the tendrils of smoke that rose from the chimneys of many a house. As always, Thorn lay draped across the battlements above the southern gate, basking in the bright afternoon light. The red dragon looked asleep, but Eragon knew from experience that he was keeping a close eye on the Varden, and the moment anyone began to approach the city, he would rouse himself and issue a warning to Murtagh and the others inside.

Eragon hopped onto Saphira's back, and she carried him to the camp at a leisurely pace.

When they arrived, he slid to the ground and took the lead as they moved between the tents. The camp was quiet, and everything about it felt slow and sleepy, from the low, drawling tones of the warriors' conversations to the pennants that hung motionless in the thick air. The only creatures who appeared immune to the general lethargy were the lean, half-feral dogs that ranged through the camp, constantly sniffing as they searched for discarded scraps of food. A number of the dogs bore scratches on their muzzles and flanks, the result of making the foolish, if understandable, mistake of thinking they could chase and torment a green-eyed werecat as they would any other cat. When it had happened, their yelps of pain had attracted the attention of the entire camp, and the men had laughed to see the dogs running away from the werecat with their tails between their legs.

Conscious of the many looks he and Saphira attracted, Eragon kept his chin high and his shoulders square and adopted a vigorous stride in an attempt to convey an impression of purpose and energy. The men needed to see that he was still full of confidence, and that he had not allowed the tedium of their present predicament to weigh him down.

If only Murtagh and Thorn would leave, thought Eragon. *They wouldn't have to be gone for more than a day for us to capture the city.*

So far, the siege of Dras-Leona had proven to be singularly uneventful. Nasuada refused to attack the city, for as she had said to Eragon, "You barely managed to best Murtagh the last time you met—do you forget how he stabbed you in the hip?—and he promised that he would be stronger still when you next crossed paths. Murtagh may be many things, but I am not inclined to believe he is a liar."

"Strength isn't everything when it comes to a fight between magicians," Eragon had pointed out.

"No, but it's not unimportant either. Also, he now has the support of the priests of Helgrind, more than a few of whom I suspect are magicians. I won't risk letting you face them and Murtagh head-on in battle, not even with Blödhgarm's spellcasters by your side. Until we can contrive to lure Murtagh and Thorn away, or trap them, or otherwise gain an advantage over them, we stay here, and we don't move against Dras-Leona."

Eragon had protested, arguing that it was impractical to stall their invasion, and that if he could not defeat Murtagh, what hope did she think he would have against Galbatorix? But Nasuada had remained unconvinced.

They—along with Arya, Blödhgarm, and all the spellcasters of Du Vrangr Gata—had planned and plotted and searched for ways to gain the advantage Nasuada had spoken of. But every strategy they considered was flawed because it required more time and resources than were at the Varden's disposal, or else because it ultimately failed to resolve the question of how to kill, capture, or drive off Murtagh and Thorn.

Nasuada had even gone to Elva and asked her if she would use her ability—which allowed her to sense other people's pain, as well as any pain they were about to suffer in the immediate future—to overcome Murtagh or to surreptitiously gain entrance to the city. The silver-browed girl had laughed at Nasuada and sent her away with gibes and insults, saying, "I owe no bond of allegiance to you or anyone else, Nasuada. Find some other child to win your battles for you; I'll not do it."

And so, the Varden waited.

As day inexorably followed day, Eragon had watched the men grow sullen and discontent, and Nasuada had become increasingly worried. An army, Eragon had learned, was a ravenous, insatiable beast that would soon die and separate into its constituent elements unless massive amounts of food were shoveled into its many thousands of stomachs upon a regular basis. When marching into new territory, obtaining supplies for an army was a simple matter of confiscating food and other essentials from the people they conquered, and stripping resources from the surrounding countryside. Like a plague of locusts, the Varden left a barren swath of land in their wake, a swath devoid of most everything needed to support life.

Once they stopped moving, they soon exhausted the stores of food close at hand and were forced to subsist entirely on provisions brought to them from Surda and the several cities they had captured. Generous as the inhabitants of Surda were, and rich as the vanquished cities were, the regular deliveries of goods were not enough to sustain the Varden for much longer.

Though Eragon knew the warriors were devoted to their cause, he had no doubt that, when faced with the prospect of a slow, agonizing death by starvation that would accomplish nothing besides giving Galbatorix the satisfaction of gloating over their defeat, most men would elect to flee to some distant corner of Alagaësia, where they could live out the rest of their lives in safety from the Empire.

That moment had not yet arrived, but it was fast approaching.

Fear of that fate, Eragon was sure, was what had been keeping Nasuada up at night, so that she appeared increasingly haggard each morning, the bags under her eyes like small, sad smiles.

The difficulties they had faced at Dras-Leona made Eragon grateful that Roran had avoided becoming similarly bogged down at Aroughs and heightened his admiration and appreciation for what his cousin had accomplished at the southern city. *He's a braver man than I.* Nasuada would disapprove, but Eragon was determined that once Roran returned—which, if all went well, would be in just a few days—Eragon would once again provide him with a full set of wards. Eragon had already lost too many members of his family to the Empire and Galbatorix, and he was not about to let the same doom befall Roran.

He paused to let a trio of arguing dwarves cross the path in front of him. The dwarves wore no helms or insignia, but he knew they were not of Dûrgrimst Ingeitum, for their plaited beards were trimmed with beads—a fashion he had never seen among the Ingeitum. Whatever the dwarves were quarreling about was a mystery to him—he could not understand more than a few words of their guttural language—but the topic was obviously of all-consuming importance, judging by their loud voices, unrestrained gestures, exaggerated expressions, and their failure to notice either him or Saphira standing in the path.

Eragon smiled as they passed; he found their preoccupation somewhat comical, despite their evident seriousness. Much to the relief of everyone in the Varden, the dwarves' army, led by their new king, Orik, had arrived at Dras-Leona two days before. That, and Roran's victory at Aroughs, had since become the main topics of conversation throughout the camp. The dwarves nearly doubled the size of the Varden's allied forces and would substantially increase the chances of the Varden reaching Urû'baen and Galbatorix if a favorable solution to the impasse with Murtagh and Thorn could be found.

As he and Saphira walked through the camp, Eragon caught sight of Katrina sitting outside her tent, knitting clothes for her child-to-be. She greeted him with a raised hand and by calling, "Cousin!"

He replied in kind, as had become their habit since her marriage.

After both he and Saphira enjoyed a leisurely lunch—which involved a fair amount of tearing and crunching on Saphira's part—they retired to the patch of soft, sunlit grass next to Eragon's tent. By order of Nasuada, the patch was always left open for Saphira's use, a dictate that the Varden observed with religious zeal.

There Saphira curled up to doze in the midday warmth, while Eragon fetched *Domia abr Wyrda* from his saddlebags, then climbed under the overhang of her left wing to nestle in the partially shaded hollow between the inner curve of her neck and her muscular foreleg. The light that shone through the folds of her wing, as well as that cast off in winking highlights from her scales, painted his skin a weird, purplish hue and covered the pages of the book with a smattering of glowing shapes that made it difficult to read the thin, angular runes. But he did not mind; the pleasure of sitting with Saphira more than made up for the inconvenience.

They sat together for an hour or two, until Saphira had digested her meal and Eragon was tired of deciphering the convoluted sentences of Heslant the Monk. Then, bored, they wandered through the camp, inspecting the defenses and occasionally exchanging words with the sentinels stationed along the perimeter.

Near the eastern edge of the camp, where the bulk of the dwarves were situated, they came across a dwarf who was squatting next to a bucket of water, his sleeves rolled up past his elbows, molding a fist-sized ball of dirt with his hands. By his feet was a puddle of mud and a stick that had been used to stir it.

The sight was so incongruous, several moments elapsed before Eragon realized that the dwarf was Orik.

"Derûndânn, Eragon . . . Saphira," said Orik without looking up.

"Derûndânn," said Eragon, repeating the traditional dwarvish greeting, and squatted on the other side of the puddle. He watched as Orik continued to refine the contours of the ball, smoothing and shaping it with the outer curve of his right thumb. Every so often, Orik reached down, grabbed a handful of dry dirt, and sprinkled it over the yellowish orb of earth, then gently brushed off the excess.

"I never thought to see the king of the dwarves crouched on the ground, playing in the mud like a child," Eragon said.

Orik huffed, blowing out his mustache. "And I never thought to have a dragon and a Rider staring at me while I made an Erôthknurl."

"And what is an Erôthknurl?"

"A thardsvergûndnzmal."

"A *thardsver*—?" Eragon gave up halfway through the word, unable to remember the whole of it, much less pronounce it. "And that is . . . ?"

"Something that appears to be other than what it actually is." Orik raised the ball of dirt. "Like this. This is a stone fashioned from earth. Or, rather, so it shall seem when I am done."

"A stone from earth. . . . Is it magic?"

"No, it is mine own skill. Nothing more."

When Orik failed to explain further, Eragon asked, "How is it done?"

"If you are patient, you will see." Then, after a while, Orik relented and said, "First, you must find some dirt."

"A hard task, that."

From under his bushy eyebrows, Orik gave him a look. "Some types of dirt are better than others. Sand, for example, will not work. The dirt must have particles of varying size, so that it will stick together properly. Also, it should have some clay in it, as this does. But most important, if I do this"—and he patted his hand against a bare strip of ground among the clumps of trampled grass—"there must be lots of dust in the dirt. See?" He held up his hand, showing Eragon the layer of fine powder that clung to his palm.

"Why is that important?"

"Ah," said Orik, and tapped the side of his nose, leaving behind a whitish smear. He resumed rubbing the sphere with his hands, turning it so that it would remain symmetrical. "Once you have good dirt, you wet it and you mix it like water and flour until you have a nice, thick mud." He nodded at the pool by his feet. "From the mud, you form a ball, like so, eh? Then you squeeze it and wring out every drop you can. Then you make the ball perfectly round. When it begins to feel sticky, you do as I am doing: you pour dirt over it, to draw out more moisture from the interior. This you continue until the ball is dry enough to hold its shape, but not so dry that it cracks.

"Mine Erôthknurl is almost to that point. When it gets there, I shall bear it to mine tent and leave it in the sun for a goodly while. The light and the warmth will draw out even more moisture from the center; then I shall again pour dirt over it and again clean it off. After three or four times, the outside of mine Erôthknurl should be as hard as the hide of a Nagra."

"All that just to have a ball of dry mud?" said Eragon, puzzled. Saphira shared his sentiment.

Orik scooped up another handful of dirt. "No, because that's not the end of it. Next is when the dust becomes of use. I take it, and I smear the outside of the Erôthknurl with it, which forms a thin, smooth shell. Then I will let the ball rest and wait for more moisture to seep to the surface, then dust, then wait, then dust, then wait, and so on."

"And how long will that take?"

"Until the dust no longer adheres to the Erôthknurl. The shell it forms is what gives an Erôthknurl its beauty. Over the course of a day, it will acquire a brilliant sheen, as if it were made of polished marble. With no buffing, no grinding, no magic—with only your heart, head, and hands—you will have made a stone out of common earth . . . a fragile stone, it is true, but a stone nevertheless."

Despite Orik's insistence, Eragon still found it hard to believe that the mud at his feet could be transformed into anything like what Orik had described without the use of magic.

Why are you making one, though, Orik dwarf king? Saphira asked. *You must have many responsibilities now that you are ruler of your people.*

Orik grunted. "I have nothing I must needs do at the moment. My men are ready for battle, but there is no battle for us to fight, and it would be bad for them if I were to fuss over them like a mother hen. Nor do I want to sit alone in my tent, watching mine beard grow. . . . Thus the Erôthknurl."

He fell silent then, but it seemed to Eragon that something was bothering Orik, so Eragon held his tongue and waited to see if Orik would say anything else. After a minute, Orik cleared his throat and said, "Used to be, I could drink and play dice with the others of mine clan, and it mattered not that I was Hrothgar's adopted heir. We could still talk and laugh together without it feeling uncomfortable. I asked for no favors, nor did I show any. But now it is different. My friends cannot forget that I am their king, and I cannot ignore how their behavior has changed toward me."

"That is only to be expected," Eragon pointed out. He empathized with Orik's plight, for he had experienced much the same thing since becoming a Rider.

"Perhaps. But knowing it makes it no easier to bear." Orik made an exasperated sound. "Ach, life is a strange, cruel journey sometimes. . . . I admired Hrothgar as a king, but it often seemed to me that he was short with those he dealt with when he had no reason to be. Now I understand better why he was the way he was." Orik cupped the ball of dirt with both hands and gazed at it, his brow knotted in a scowl. "When you met with Grimstborith Gannel in Tarnag, did he explain to you the significance of the Erôthknurln?"

"He never mentioned it."

"I suppose there were other matters that needed talking about. . . . Still, as one of the Ingeitum, and as an adopted knurla, you should know the import and symbology of the Erôthknurln. It is not just a way to focus the mind, pass the time, and create an interesting keepsake. No. The act of making a stone out of earth is a sacred one. By it, we reaffirm our faith in Helzvog's power and offer tribute to him. One should approach the task with reverence and purpose. Crafting an Erôthknurl is a form of worship, and the gods do not look kindly on those who perform the rites in a frivolous manner. . . . From stone, flesh; from flesh, earth; and from earth, stone again. The wheel turns and we see but a glimpse of the entirety."

Only then did Eragon appreciate the depth of Orik's disquiet. "You ought to have Hvedra with you," he said. "She would keep you company and prevent you from becoming so grim. I've never seen you as happy as when you were with her at Bregan Hold."

The lines around Orik's downcast eyes deepened as he smiled. "Aye. . . . But she is the grimstcarvlorss of the Ingeitum, and she cannot abandon her duties just to comfort me. Besides, I could not rest easy if she were within a hundred leagues of Murtagh and Thorn or, worse, Galbatorix and his accursed black dragon."

In an attempt to cheer Orik up, Eragon said, "You remind me of the answer to a riddle: a dwarf king sitting on the ground, making a stone out of dirt. I'm not sure how the riddle itself would go, but perhaps, something along the lines of:

> *Strong and stout,*
> *Thirteen stars upon his brow,*
> *Living stone sat shaping dead earth into dead stone.*

"It doesn't rhyme, but then, you can't expect me to compose proper verse on the spur of the moment. I would imagine that a riddle like that would be quite a head-scratcher for most people."

"Humph," said Orik. "Not for a dwarf. Even our children could solve it quick as you please."

A dragon too, said Saphira.

"I suppose you're right," said Eragon.

Then he asked Orik about everything that had happened among the dwarves after he and Saphira had left Tronjheim for their second trip to the forest of the elves. Eragon had not had an opportunity to talk with Orik for any great length of time since the dwarves had arrived at Dras-Leona, and he was eager to hear how his friend had gotten along since assuming the throne.

Orik did not seem to mind explaining the intricacies of the dwarves' politics. Indeed, as he spoke, his expression brightened and he became increasingly animated. He spent nearly an hour recounting the bickering and maneuvering that had gone on between the dwarf clans prior to assembling their army and marching to join the Varden. The clans were a fractious lot, as Eragon well knew, and even as king, Orik had difficulty commanding their obedience.

"It's like trying to herd a flock of geese," said Orik. "They're always trying to go off on their own, they make an obnoxious noise, and they'll bite your hand first chance they get."

During the course of Orik's narration, Eragon thought to ask about Vermûnd. He had often wondered what had become of the dwarf chief who had plotted to assassinate him. He liked to know where his enemies were, especially one as dangerous as Vermûnd.

"He returned to his home village of Feldarast," Orik said. "There, by all accounts, he sits and drinks and rages about what is and what might have been. But none now listen to him. The knurlan of Az Sweldn rak Anhûin are proud and stubborn. In most cases, they would remain loyal to Vermûnd regardless of what the other clans might do or say, but attempting to kill a guest is an unforgivable offense. And not all of Az Sweldn rak Anhûin hate you like Vermûnd does. I cannot believe that they will agree to remain cut off from the rest of their kind just to protect a grimstborith who has lost every scrap of his honor. It may take years, but eventually they will turn against him. Already I have heard that many of the clan shun Vermûnd, even as they themselves are shunned."

"What do you think will happen to him?"

"He will accept the inevitable and step down, or else one day someone will slip poison into his mead, or perhaps a dagger between his ribs. Either way, he is no longer a threat to you as the leader of Az Sweldn rak Anhûin."

They continued to talk until Orik had finished the first few stages of shaping his Erôthknurl and was ready to take the ball of dirt and set it to rest upon a piece of cloth by his tent to dry. As Orik rose to his feet and gathered up his bucket and stick, he said, "I appreciate you being so kind as to listen to me, Eragon. And you as well, Saphira. Strange as it may seem, you are the only ones besides Hvedra to whom I can talk freely. Everyone else . . ." He shrugged. "Bah."

Eragon got to his feet as well. "You're our friend, Orik, whether you are king of the dwarves or not. We're always happy to talk with you. And you know, you don't have to worry about us telling others what you've said."

"Aye, I know that, Eragon." Orik squinted up at him. "You participate in the goings-on of the world, and yet you haven't gotten caught up in all the petty scheming around you."

"It doesn't interest me. Besides, there are more important things to deal with at the moment."

"That's good. A Rider should stand apart from everyone else. Otherwise, how can you judge things for yourself? I never used to appreciate the Riders' independence, but now I do, if only for selfish reasons."

"I don't stand entirely apart," said Eragon. "I'm sworn both to you and to Nasuada."

Orik inclined his head. "True enough. But you are not fully part of the Varden—or the Ingeitum either, for that matter. Whatever the case may be, I'm glad I can trust you."

A smile crept across Eragon's face. "As am I."

"After all, we're foster brothers, aren't we? And brothers ought to watch each other's backs."

That they should, thought Eragon, though he did not say it out loud. "Foster brothers," he agreed, and clapped Orik on the shoulder.

THE WAY OF KNOWING

Later that afternoon, when it seemed increasingly unlikely that the Empire would launch an attack from Dras-Leona in the few remaining hours of sunlight, Eragon and Saphira went to the sparring field at the rear of the Varden camp.

There Eragon met with Arya, as he had done every day since arriving at the city. He asked after her, and she answered briefly—she had been stuck in a tiresome conference with Nasuada and King Orrin since before dawn. Then Eragon drew his sword and Arya hers, and they took up positions opposite each other. For a change, they had agreed beforehand to use shields; it was closer to the reality of actual combat, and it introduced a welcome element of variety into their duels.

They circled each other with short, smooth steps, moving like dancers over the uneven ground, feeling their way with their feet and never looking down, never looking away from one another.

This was Eragon's favorite part of their fights. There was something profoundly intimate about staring into Arya's eyes, without blinking, without wavering, and having her stare back at him with the same degree of focus and intensity. It could be disconcerting, but he enjoyed the sense of connection it created between them.

Arya initiated the first attack, and within the span of a second, Eragon found himself standing hunched over at an awkward angle, her blade pressed against the left side of his neck, tugging painfully at his skin. Eragon remained frozen until Arya saw fit to release the pressure and allow him to stand upright.

"That was sloppy," she said.

"How is it you keep besting me?" he growled, far from pleased.

"Because," she replied, and feinted toward his right shoulder, causing him to raise his shield and leap backward in alarm, "I've had over a hundred years of practice. It would be odd if I *weren't* better than you, now wouldn't it? You should be proud that you've managed to mark me at all. Few can."

Brisingr whistled through the air as Eragon struck at her lead thigh. A loud *clang* resounded as she stopped the blow with her shield. She countered with a clever twisting stab that caught him on his sword wrist and sent icy needles shooting up his arm and shoulder to the base of his skull.

Wincing, he disengaged, seeking a temporary reprieve. One of the challenges of fighting elves was that because of their speed and strength, they could lunge forward and engage an enemy at distances far greater than any human could. Therefore, to be safe from Arya, he had to move nearly a hundred feet away from her.

Before he could put much distance between them, Arya sprang after him, taking two flying steps, her hair streaming behind her. Eragon swung at her while she was still airborne, but she turned so that his sword passed along the length of her body, without touching it. Then she slipped the edge of her shield underneath his and yanked it away, leaving his chest completely exposed. Fast as could be, she brought her sword up and again pressed it against his neck, this time underneath his chin.

She held him in that position, her large, wide-set eyes only inches away from his. There was a ferocity and intentness to her expression that he was uncertain how to interpret, but it gave him pause.

A shadow seemed to flit across Arya's face then, and she lowered her sword and stepped away.

Eragon rubbed his throat. "If you know so much about swordsmanship," he said, "then why can't you teach me to be better?"

Her emerald eyes burned with even greater force. "I'm trying," she said, "but the problem is not here." She tapped her sword against his right arm. "The problem is here." She tapped his helm, metal clinking against metal. "And I don't know how else to teach you what you need to learn except by showing you your mistakes over and over again until you stop making them." She rapped his helm once more. "Even if it means I have to beat you black-and-blue in order to do it."

That she continued to defeat him with such regularity hurt his pride far more than he was willing to admit, even to Saphira, and it made him doubt whether he would ever be able to triumph over Galbatorix, Murtagh, or any other truly formidable opponent, should he be so unfortunate as to face them in single combat without the help of Saphira or his magic.

Wheeling away from Arya, Eragon stomped over to a spot some ten yards distant.

"Well?" he said through clenched teeth. "Get on with it, then." And he settled into a low crouch as he readied himself for another onslaught.

Arya narrowed her eyes to slits, which gave her angled face an evil look. "Very well."

They rushed at each other, both shouting war cries, and the field echoed with the sounds of their furious clash. Match after match they fought, until they were tired, sweaty, and coated with dust, and Eragon was striped with many painful welts. And still they continued to dash themselves against one another with a grim-faced determination that had hitherto been absent from their duels. Neither of them asked to end their brutal, bruising contest, and neither of them offered to.

Saphira watched from the side of the field, where she lay sprawled across the springy mat of grass. For the most part, she kept her thoughts to herself, so as to avoid distracting Eragon, but every now and then she made a short observation about his technique or Arya's, observations that Eragon invariably found helpful. Also, he suspected that she had intervened on more than one occasion to save him from a particularly dangerous blow, for at times his arms and legs seemed to move slightly faster than they should have, or even slightly before he intended to move them himself, and when that happened, he felt a tickle in the back of his mind that he knew meant Saphira was meddling with some part of his consciousness.

At last he asked her to stop. *I have to be able to do this myself, Saphira,* he said. *You can't help me every time I need it.*

I can try.

I know. I feel the same way about you. But this is my mountain to climb, not yours.

The edge of her lip twitched. *Why climb when you can fly? You'll never get anywhere on those short little legs of yours.*

That's not true and you know it. Besides, if I were flying, it would be on borrowed wings, and I would gain nothing by it other than the cheap thrill of an unearned victory.

Victory is victory and dead is dead, however it is achieved.

Saphira . . . , he said warningly.

Little one.

Still, to his relief, she left him to his own devices after that, though she continued to watch him with unceasing vigilance.

Along with Saphira, the elves assigned to guard her and Eragon had gathered along the edge of the field. Their presence made Eragon uncomfortable—he disliked having anyone other than Saphira or Arya witness his failures—but he knew the elves would never agree to withdraw to the tents. In any event, they did serve one useful purpose aside from protecting him and Saphira: keeping the other warriors on the field from wandering over to gawk at a Rider and an elf going at it hammer and tongs. Not that Blödhgarm's spellcasters did anything specific to discourage onlookers, but their very aspect was intimidating enough to ward off casual spectators.

The longer he fought with Arya, the more frustrated Eragon became. He won two of their matches—barely, frantically, with desperate ploys that succeeded more by luck than skill, and that he never would have attempted in a real duel unless he no longer cared for his own safety—but except for those isolated victories, Arya continued to beat him with depressing ease.

Eventually, Eragon's anger and frustration boiled over, and all sense of proportion deserted him. Inspired by the methods that had granted him his few successes, Eragon lifted his right arm and prepared to *throw* Brisingr at Arya, even as he might a battle-ax.

Just at that moment, another mind touched Eragon's, a mind that Eragon instantly knew belonged to neither Arya nor Saphira, nor any of the other elves, for it was unmistakably male, and it was unmistakably dragon. Eragon recoiled from the contact, racing to order his thoughts so as to ward off what he feared was an attack by Thorn. But before he could, an immense voice echoed through the shadowed byways of his consciousness, like the sound of a mountain shifting under its own weight:

Enough, said Glaedr.

Eragon stiffened and stumbled forward a half step, rising onto the balls of his feet, as he stopped himself from throwing Brisingr. He saw or sensed Arya, Saphira, and Blödhgarm's spellcasters react as well, stirring with surprise, and he knew that they too had heard Glaedr.

The dragon's mind felt much the same as before—old and unfathomable and torn with grief. But for the first time since Oromis's death at Gil'ead, Glaedr seemed possessed of an urge to do something other than sink ever deeper into the all-enveloping morass of his private torments.

Glaedr-elda! Eragon and Saphira said at the same time.

How are you—

Are you all right—

Did you—

Others spoke as well—Arya; Blödhgarm; two more of the elves, whom Eragon could not identify—and their mass of conflicting words clattered together in an incomprehensible discord.

Enough, Glaedr repeated, sounding both weary and exasperated. *Do you wish to attract unwanted attention?*

At once everyone fell silent as they waited to hear what the golden dragon would say next. Excited, Eragon exchanged glances with Arya.

Glaedr did not speak immediately, but watched them for another few minutes, his presence weighing heavily against Eragon's consciousness, even as Eragon was sure it did with the others.

Then, in his sonorous, magisterial voice, Glaedr said, *This has gone on long enough. . . . Eragon, you should not spend so much time sparring. It is distracting you from more important matters. The sword in Galbatorix's hand is not what you need fear the most, nor the sword in his mouth, but rather the sword in his mind. His greatest talent lies in his ability to worm his way into the smallest parts of your being and force you to obey his will. Instead of these bouts with Arya, you should concentrate on improving your mastery over your thoughts; they are still woefully undisciplined. . . . Why, then, do you still persist with this futile endeavor?*

A host of answers leaped to the forefront of Eragon's mind: that he enjoyed crossing blades with Arya, despite the aggravation it caused him; that he wanted to be the very best sword fighter he could—the very best in the world, if possible; that the exercise helped calm his nerves and shape his body; and many more reasons besides. He tried to suppress the welter of thoughts, both to preserve some measure of privacy and to avoid inundating Glaedr with unwanted information, thus confirming the dragon's opinion about his lack of discipline. He did not entirely succeed, however, and a faint air of disappointment emanated from Glaedr.

Eragon chose his strongest arguments. *If I can hold Galbatorix off with my mind—even if I can't beat him—if I can just hold him off, then this may still be decided by the sword. In any case, the king isn't the only enemy we should be worried about: there's Murtagh, for one, and who knows what other kinds of men or creatures Galbatorix has in his service? I wasn't able to defeat Durza by myself, nor Varaug, nor even Murtagh. Always I've had help. But I can't rely on Arya or Saphira or Blödhgarm to rescue me every time I get into trouble. I have to be better with a blade, and yet I can't seem to make any progress, no matter how hard I try.*

Varaug? Glaedr queried. *I have not heard that name before.*

It fell to Eragon, then, to tell Glaedr about the capture of Feinster and how he and Arya had killed the newly born Shade even as Oromis and Glaedr had met their deaths—differing kinds of deaths, but both still mortal ends—while battling in the skies over Gil'ead. Eragon also summarized the Varden's activities thereafter, for he realized that Glaedr had kept himself so isolated, he had little knowledge of them. The account took Eragon several minutes to deliver, during which time he and the elves stood frozen on the field, staring past each other with unseeing eyes, their attention turned inward as they concentrated on the rapid exchange of thoughts, images, and feelings.

Another long silence followed as Glaedr digested what he had learned. When he again deigned to speak, it was with a tinge of amusement: *You are overly ambitious if your goal is to be able to kill Shades with impunity. Even the oldest and wisest of the Riders would have hesitated to attack a Shade alone. You have already survived encounters with two of them, which is two more than most. Be grateful you have been so lucky and leave it at that. Trying to outmatch a Shade is like trying to fly higher than the sun.*

Yes, replied Eragon, *but our foes are as strong as Shades or even stronger, and Galbatorix may create more of them just to slow our progress. He uses them carelessly, without heed for the destruction they could cause throughout the land.*

Ebrithil, said Arya, *he is right. Our enemies are deadly in the extreme . . . as you well know—*this she added in a gentle tone—*and Eragon is not at the level he needs to be. To prepare for what lies before us, he has to attain mastery. I have done my best to teach him, but mastery ultimately must come from within, not without.*

Her defense of him warmed Eragon's heart.

As before, Glaedr was slow to respond. *Nor has Eragon mastered his thoughts, as he must also do. Neither of these abilities, mental or physical, is of much use alone, but of the two, the mental is more important. One can win a battle against both a spellcaster and a swordsman with the mind alone. Your mind and your body ought to be in balance, but if you must choose which of them to train, you should choose your mind. Arya . . . Blödhgarm . . . Yaela . . . you know this is true. Why have none of you taken it upon yourselves to continue Eragon's instruction in this area?*

Arya cast her eyes at the ground, somewhat like a chastised child, while the fur on Blödhgarm's shoulders rippled and stood on end, and he pulled back his lips to reveal the tips of his sharp white fangs.

It was Blödhgarm who finally dared reply. Speaking wholly in the ancient language, the first to do so, he said, *Arya is here as the ambassador of our people. I and my band are here to protect the lives of Saphira Brightscales and Eragon Shadeslayer, and it has been a difficult and time-consuming task. We have all tried to help Eragon, but it is not our place to train a Rider, nor would we presume to attempt it when one of his rightful masters was still alive and present . . . even if that master was neglecting his duty.*

Dark clouds of anger gathered within Glaedr, like massive thunderheads building on the horizon. Eragon distanced himself from Glaedr's consciousness, wary of the dragon's wrath. Glaedr was no longer capable of physically harming anyone, but he was still incredibly dangerous, and should he lose control and lash out with his mind, none of them would be able to withstand his might.

Blödhgarm's rudeness and insensitivity initially shocked Eragon— he had never heard an elf speak to a dragon like that before—but after a moment's reflection, Eragon realized that Blödhgarm must have done it to draw Glaedr out and prevent him from retreating into his shell of misery. Eragon admired the elf's courage, but he wondered whether insulting Glaedr was really the best approach. It certainly wasn't the *safest* plan.

The billowing thunderheads swelled in size, illuminated by brief, lightning-like flashes, as Glaedr's mind jumped from one thought to another. *You have overstepped your bounds, elf,* he growled, also in the ancient language. *My actions are not for you to question. You cannot even begin to comprehend what I have lost. If it were not for Eragon and Saphira and my duty to them, I would have gone mad long ago. So do not accuse me of negligence, Blödhgarm, son of Ildrid, unless you wish to test yourself against the last of the high Old Ones.*

Baring his teeth even more, Blödhgarm hissed. In spite of that, Eragon detected a hint of satisfaction in the elf's visage. To Eragon's dismay, Blödhgarm pressed on, saying, *Then do not blame us for failing to fulfill what are your responsibilities, not ours, Old One. Our whole race mourns your loss, but you cannot expect us to make allowances for your self-pity when we are at war with the most deadly enemy in our history—the same enemy who exterminated nearly every one of your kind, and who also killed your Rider.*

Glaedr's fury was volcanic. Black and terrible, it battered against Eragon with such force, he felt as if the fabric of his being might split asunder, like a sail caught in the wind. On the other side of the field, he saw men drop their weapons and clutch at their heads, grimacing with pain.

My self-pity? said Glaedr, forcing out each word, and each word sounding like a pronouncement of doom. In the recesses of the dragon's mind, Eragon sensed something unpleasant taking shape that, if allowed to reach fruition, might be the cause of much sorrow and regret.

Then Saphira spoke, and her mental voice cut through Glaedr's churning emotions like a knife through water. *Master,* she said, *I have been worried about you. It is good to know that you are well and strong again. None of us are your equal, and we have need of your help. Without you, we cannot hope to defeat the Empire.*

Glaedr rumbled ominously, but he did not ignore, interrupt, or insult her. Indeed, her praise seemed to please him, even if only a little. After all, as Eragon reflected, if there was one thing dragons were susceptible to, it was flattery, as Saphira was well aware.

Without pausing to allow Glaedr to respond, Saphira said, *Since you no longer have use of your wings, let me offer my own as a replacement. The air is calm, the sky is clear, and it would be a joy to fly high above the ground, higher than even the eagles dare soar. After so long trapped within your heart of hearts, you must yearn to leave all this behind and feel the currents of air rising beneath you once more.*

The black storm within Glaedr abated somewhat, although it remained vast and threatening, teetering on the edge of renewed violence. *That . . . would be pleasant.*

Then we shall fly together soon. But, Master?

Yes, youngling?

There is something I wish to ask of you first.

Then ask it.

Will you help Eragon with his swordsmanship? Can you help him? He isn't as skilled as he needs to be, and I don't want to lose my Rider. Saphira remained dignified throughout, but there was a note of pleading in her voice that caused Eragon's throat to tighten.

The thunderheads collapsed inward on themselves, leaving behind a bare gray landscape that seemed inexpressibly sad to Eragon. Glaedr paused. Strange, half-seen shapes moved slowly along the edge of the landscape—hulking monoliths that Eragon had no desire to meet up close.

Very well, Glaedr said at long last. *I will do what I can for your Rider, but after we are done on this field, he must let me teach him as I see fit.*

Agreed, said Saphira. Eragon saw Arya and the other elves relax, as if they had been holding their breath.

Eragon withdrew from the others for a moment as Trianna and several other magicians who served in the Varden contacted him, each demanding to know what they had just felt tearing at their minds and what had so upset the men and animals in the camp. Trianna overrode the others, saying, *Are we under attack, Shadeslayer? Is it Thorn? Is it Shruikan?!* Her panic was so strong, it made Eragon want to throw down his sword and shield and run for safety.

No, everything is fine, he said as evenly as he could. Glaedr's existence was still a secret to most of the Varden, including Trianna and the magicians who answered to her. Eragon wanted to keep it that way, lest word of the golden dragon should reach the Empire's spies. Lying while in communication with another person's mind was difficult in the extreme—since it was nearly impossible to avoid thinking about whatever it was you wanted to keep hidden—so Eragon kept the conversation as short as he could. *The elves and I were practicing magic. I'll explain it later, but there's no need to be worried.*

He could tell that his reassurances did not entirely convince them, but they dared not press him for a more detailed explanation and bade him farewell before walling off their minds from his inner eye.

Arya must have noticed a change in his bearing, for she walked over to him and, in a low murmur, asked, "Is everything all right?"

"Fine," Eragon replied in a similar undertone. He nodded toward the men who were picking up their weapons. "I had to answer a few questions."

"Ah. You didn't tell them who—"

"Of course not."

Take up your positions as before, Glaedr rumbled, and Eragon and Arya separated and paced off twenty feet in either direction.

Knowing that it might be a mistake but unable to restrain himself, Eragon said, *Master, can you really teach me what I need to know before we reach Urû'baen? So little time is left to us, I—*

I can teach you right now, if you will listen to me, said Glaedr. *But you will have to listen harder than ever before.*

I am listening, Master. Still, Eragon could not help wondering how much the dragon really knew about sword fighting. Glaedr would have learned a great deal from Oromis, even as Saphira had learned from Eragon, but despite those shared experiences, Glaedr had never held a sword himself—how could he have? Glaedr instructing Eragon on fencing would be like Eragon instructing a dragon on how to navigate the thermals rising off the side of a mountain;

Eragon could do it, but he would not be able to explain it as well as Saphira, for his knowledge was secondhand, and no amount of abstract contemplation could overcome that disadvantage.

Eragon kept his doubts to himself, but something of them must have seeped past his barriers to Glaedr, because the dragon made an amused sound—or rather, he imitated one within his mind, the habits of the body being hard to forget—and said, *All great fighting is the same, Eragon, even as all great warriors are the same. Past a certain point, it does not matter whether you wield a sword, a claw, a tooth, or a tail. It is true, you must be capable with your weapon, but anyone with the time and the inclination can acquire technical proficiency. To achieve greatness, though, that requires artistry. That requires imagination and thoughtfulness, and it is those qualities that the best warriors share, even if, on the surface, they appear completely different.*

Glaedr fell silent for a moment, then said, *Now, what was it I told you before?*

Eragon did not have to even stop to consider. *That I had to learn to see what I was looking at. And I've tried, Master. I have.*

But still you do not see. Look at Arya. Why has she been able to beat you again and again? Because she understands you, Eragon. She knows who you are and how you think, and that is what allows her to defeat you so consistently. Why is it Murtagh was able to trounce you on the Burning Plains, even though he was nowhere near as fast or strong as you?

Because I was tired and—

And how is it he succeeded in wounding you in the hip when last you met, and yet you were only able to give him a scratch on the cheek? I will tell you, Eragon. It was not because you were tired and he was not. No, it was because he understands you, Eragon, but you do not understand him. Murtagh knows more than you, and thus he has power over you, as does Arya.

And still Glaedr spoke: *Look at her, Eragon. Look at her well. She sees you for who you are, but do you see her in return? Do you see her clearly enough to defeat her in battle?*

Eragon locked eyes with Arya and found within them a combination of determination and defensiveness, as if she was challenging him to attempt to pry open her secrets, but she was also afraid of what would happen if he did. Doubt welled up inside Eragon. Did he really know her as well as he thought? Or had he deceived himself into mistaking the outer for the inner?

You have allowed yourself to become angrier than you should, said Glaedr softly. *Anger has its place, but it will not help you here. The way of the warrior is the way of knowing. If that knowledge requires you to use anger, then you use anger, but you cannot wrest forth knowledge by losing your temper. Pain and frustration will be your only reward if you try.*

Instead, you must strive to be calm, even if a hundred ravening enemies are snapping at your heels. Empty your mind and allow it to become like a tranquil pool that reflects everything around it and yet remains untouched by its surroundings. Understanding will come to you in that emptiness, when you are free of irrational fears about victory and defeat, life and death.

You cannot predict every eventuality, and you cannot guarantee success every time you face an enemy, but by seeing all and discounting nothing, you may adapt without hesitation to any change. The warrior who can adapt the easiest to the unexpected is the warrior who will live the longest.

So, look at Arya, see what you are looking at, and then take the action you deem most appropriate. And once you are in motion, do not allow your thoughts to distract you. Think without thinking, so that you act as if out of instinct and not reason. Go now, and try.

Eragon took a minute to collect himself and consider everything he knew about Arya: her likes and dislikes, her habits and mannerisms, the important events of her life, what she feared and what she hoped for, and most importantly, her underlying temperament—that which dictated her approach to life ... and to fighting. All that he considered, and from it he attempted to divine the essence of her personality. It was a daunting task, especially since he made an effort to view her not as he usually did—as a beautiful woman he admired and longed for—but as the person she actually was, whole and complete and separate from his own needs and wants.

He drew what conclusions he could within such a brief span of time, although he worried that his observations were childish and overly simplistic. Then he set aside his uncertainty, stepped forward, and raised his sword and shield.

He knew that Arya would be expecting him to try something different, so he opened their duel as he had twice before: shuffling in a diagonal toward her right shoulder, as if to circumvent her shield and attack her flank where it was unguarded. The ruse would not fool her, but it would keep her guessing as to what he was actually up to, and the longer he could maintain that uncertainty, the better.

A small, rough rock turned under the ball of his right foot. He shifted his weight to the side so as to keep his balance.

The motion caused a nearly indiscernible hitch in his otherwise smooth stride, but Arya spotted the irregularity and leaped at him, a clarion yell ringing from her lips.

Their swords glanced off one another, once, twice, and then Eragon turned and—possessed of a sudden and deep-seated conviction that Arya was going to strike next at his head—he stabbed at her chest, fast as he could, aiming for a spot near her breastbone that she would have to leave open if she swung at his helm.

His intuition was right, but his reckoning was off.

He stabbed so quickly, Arya did not have an opportunity to move her arm out of the way, and the hilt of her sword deflected Brisingr's dark blue tip and sent it sailing harmlessly past her cheek.

An instant later, the world tilted around Eragon and bursts of red and orange sparks appeared scattered across his field of vision. He staggered and dropped to one knee, supporting himself with both hands on the ground. A dull roaring filled his ears.

The sound gradually subsided, at which point Glaedr said, *Do not try to move quickly, Eragon. Do not try to move slowly. Only move at the correct moment and your blow will appear neither fast nor slow but effortless. Timing is everything in battle. You must pay close attention to the patterns and rhythms of your opponents' bodies: where they are strong, where they are weak, where stiff and where flexible. Match those rhythms when it serves your purpose and confuse them when it does not, and you will be able to shape the flow of the battle as it pleases you. This you should understand thoroughly. Fix it in your mind and think on it more later. . . . Now try again!*

Glaring at Arya, Eragon got back to his feet, shook his head to clear it, and, for what seemed the hundredth time, assumed an on-guard position. His welts and bruises flared with renewed pain, making him feel like an arthritic old man.

Arya tossed back her hair and smiled at him, baring her strong white teeth.

The gesture had no effect on him. He was focused on the task at hand and was not about to allow himself to fall for the same trick twice.

Even before the smile began to fade from her lips, he was sprinting forward, Brisingr held low and to the side while he led with his shield. As he hoped, the position of his sword tempted Arya into a rash, preemptive strike: a slashing blow that would have taken him in the collarbone if it had landed.

Eragon ducked underneath the blow, letting it bounce off his shield, and brought Brisingr up and around, as if to cut her across the legs and hips. She blocked him with her shield, then shoved him away, knocking the air from his lungs.

A brief lull followed as they circled each other, both searching for an opening to exploit. The air between them was fraught with tension as he studied her and she him, their movements quick and jerky, almost birdlike, from the overabundance of energy coursing through their veins.

The strain broke like a glass rod snapping in two.

He struck at her and she parried, their blades moving with such speed, they were nearly invisible. As they exchanged blows, Eragon kept his eyes riveted on hers, but he also strove—as Glaedr had advised—to observe the rhythms and patterns of her body, while also remembering who she was and how she was likely to act and react. He wanted to win so badly, he felt as if he might burst if he didn't.

And yet, despite all his efforts, Arya caught him by surprise with a reverse pommel strike to his ribs.

Eragon stopped and swore an oath.

That was better, said Glaedr. *Much better. Your timing was almost perfect.*

But not quite.

No, not quite. You are still too angry, and your mind is still too cluttered. Keep hold of the things you need to remember, but don't let them distract you from what is happening. Find a place of calm within yourself, and let the concerns of the world wash over you without sweeping you away with them. You should feel as you did when Oromis had you listen to the thoughts of the creatures in the forest. Then you were aware of everything that was going on around you, yet you were not fixated on any one detail. Do not look at Arya's eyes alone. Your focus is too narrow, too detailed.

But Brom told me—

There are many ways of using the eyes. Brom had his, but it was not the most flexible of styles, nor the most appropriate for large battles. He spent most of his life fighting one on one, or in small groups, and his habits reflected that. Better to see widely than to see too closely and allow some feature of place or situation to catch you unawares. Do you understand?

Yes, Master.

Then once more, and this time, allow yourself to relax and broaden your perception.

Eragon again reviewed his knowledge of Arya. When he had decided on a plan, he closed his eyes, slowed his breathing, and sank deep within himself. His fears and anxieties gradually drained out of him, leaving behind a profound emptiness that dulled the pain of his injuries and gave him a sense of unusual clarity. Though he did not lose interest in winning, the prospect of defeat no longer troubled him. What would be would be, and he would not struggle unnecessarily against the decrees of fate.

"Ready?" asked Arya when he opened his eyes again.

"Ready."

They took up their starting positions, then stayed there, motionless, each of them waiting for the other to attack first. The sun was to Eragon's right, which meant that if he could maneuver Arya in the opposite direction, the light would be in her eyes. He had tried before, without success, but now he thought of a way he might be able to manage it.

He knew that Arya was confident she could beat him. He was sure she did not disregard his abilities, but however conscious she was of his skill and his desire to improve, she had won the overwhelming majority of their matches. Those experiences had shown her that he would be easy to defeat, even if, intellectually, she might know better. Her confidence, therefore, was also her weakness.

She thinks she's better than me with a sword, he said to himself. *And maybe she is, but I can use her expectations against her. They'll be her undoing, if anything is.*

He sidled forward a few feet and smiled at Arya even as she had smiled at him. Her face stayed impressively blank. A moment later, she charged him, as if she was going to tackle him and drive him to the ground.

He sprang backward, edging to the right, so as to begin guiding her in the direction he wanted.

Arya stopped short several yards away from him and remained as still as a wild animal caught in a clearing. Then she traced a half circle in front of her with her sword while she stared at him. He suspected that having Glaedr watching them made her all the more determined to give a good showing of herself.

She shocked him then by uttering a soft, catlike growl. Like her smile before, the growl was a weapon for unsettling him. And it worked, but only partly, for he had come to expect such gestures, if not that particular one.

Arya crossed the intervening distance with a single bound and began swinging at him with heavy, looping blows that he blocked with his shield. He let her attack without opposition, as if her blows were too strong for him to do anything more than defend himself. With every loud, painful jolt to his arm and shoulder, he retreated farther to the right, stumbling now and then to increase the impression of being driven back.

And still he remained calm and composed—empty.

He knew that the opportune moment was going to arrive even before it did, and once it had, he acted without thought or hesitation, without attempting to be fast or slow, seeking only to fulfill the potential of that single, perfect instant.

As Arya's sword descended toward him in a flashing arc, he pivoted to the right, sidestepping the blade while also putting the sun squarely at his back.

The tip of her sword buried itself in the ground with a solid *thunk*.

Arya turned her head, so as to keep him in sight, and made the mistake of looking directly into the sun. She squinted, and her pupils contracted to small, dark spots.

While she was blinded, Eragon stabbed Brisingr underneath her left arm, poking her in the ribs. He could have struck her on the nape of her neck—and he would have if they had really been fighting—but he refrained, for even with a dulled sword, such a blow could kill.

Arya let out a sharp cry as Brisingr made contact, and she fell back several steps. She stood with her arm pressed against her side and her brow furrowed with pain and stared at him with an odd expression.

Excellent! Glaedr crowed. *And again!*

Eragon felt a momentary glow of satisfaction; then he released his hold on the emotion and returned to his previous state of detached watchfulness.

When Arya's face cleared and she lowered her arm, she and Eragon carefully edged around each other until neither had the sun in their eyes, at which point they began anew. Eragon quickly noticed that Arya was treating him with greater caution than before. Most times, that would have pleased him and inspired him to attack more aggressively, but he resisted the urge, for it now seemed obvious to him that she was doing it on purpose. If he swallowed her bait, he would soon find himself at her mercy, as he had so often before.

The duel lasted for only a few seconds, though it was still long enough for them to exchange a flurry of blows. Shields cracked, chunks of torn sod flew over the ground, and sword rang against sword as they flowed from one stance to another, their bodies twisting through the air like twin columns of smoke.

In the end, the result was the same as before. Eragon slipped past Arya's guard with an adroit bit of footwork and a flick of his wrist, which resulted in him slashing Arya across her chest, from shoulder to sternum.

The blow staggered Arya and she collapsed to one knee, where she remained, scowling and breathing heavily through pinched nostrils. Her cheeks grew unusually pale, save for a crimson blotch that appeared high on each side.

Again! ordered Glaedr.

Eragon and Arya complied without question. With his two victories, Eragon's weariness had diminished, though he could tell that the opposite was true for Arya.

The next match had no clear winner; Arya rallied and managed to foil all of Eragon's tricks and traps, even as he did hers. On and on they fought, until at last they were both so tired, neither was able to continue, and they stood leaning on swords that were too heavy to lift, panting, sweat dripping from their faces.

Again, said Glaedr in a low voice.

Eragon grimaced as he yanked Brisingr out of the ground. The more exhausted he became, the harder it was to keep his mind uncluttered and to ignore the complaints of his aching body. Also, he found it increasingly difficult to maintain an even temper and avoid falling prey to the foul mood that usually beset him when he needed rest. Learning to deal with that challenge, he supposed, was part of what Glaedr was trying to teach him.

His shoulders were burning too much for him to hold his sword and shield in front of him. Instead, Eragon let them hang by his waist and hoped he could lift them fast enough when needed. Arya did the same.

They shuffled toward each other in a crude imitation of their earlier grace.

Eragon was utterly spent, and yet he refused to give up. In a way that he did not entirely understand, their sparring seemed to have become something more than just a test of arms; it had become a test of who he was: of his character, of his strength, and of his resilience. Nor was it Glaedr who was testing him, or so he felt, but rather Arya. It was as if she wanted something from him, as if she wanted him to prove . . . what, he knew not, but he was determined to acquit himself as well as he could. However long she was willing to keep sparring, so too was he, no matter how much it hurt.

A drop of sweat rolled into his left eye. He blinked, and Arya lunged at him, shouting.

Once more they engaged in their deadly dance, and once more they fought to a standstill. Fatigue made them clumsy, yet they moved together with a rough harmony that prevented either from gaining victory.

Eventually, they ended up standing face to face, their swords locked at the hilts, pushing at each other with what little remained of their strength.

Then, as they stood there, struggling back and forth without avail, Eragon said in a low, fierce voice, "I . . . see . . . you."

A bright spark appeared in Arya's eyes, then vanished just as quickly.

242

A HEART-TO-HEART

Glaedr had them fight twice more. Each duel was shorter than the last, and each resulted in a draw, which frustrated the golden dragon more than it did Eragon or Arya.

Glaedr would have kept them sparring until it became abundantly clear who was the better warrior, but by the end of the last duel, they were both so tired that they dropped to the ground and lay side by side, heaving for air, and even Glaedr had to admit that it would be counterproductive, if not downright harmful, for them to continue.

Once they had recovered enough to stand and walk, Glaedr summoned them to Eragon's tent.

First, with energy from Saphira, they healed their more painful injuries. Then they returned their ruined shields to the Varden's weapon master, Fredric, who provided them with replacements, although only after lecturing them on how they ought to take better care of their equipment.

When they arrived at the tent, they found Nasuada waiting for them, along with her usual accompaniment of guards. "It's about time," she said in a tart voice. "If the two of you are done trying to batter each other to pieces, we need to talk." Without another word, she ducked inside.

Blödhgarm and his fellow spellcasters arranged themselves in a large circle around the tent, which Eragon could tell made Nasuada's guards uneasy.

Eragon and Arya followed Nasuada into the tent; then Saphira surprised them by pushing the front of her head past the entrance flaps and promptly filling the cramped space with the smell of smoke and burnt meat.

The sudden appearance of Saphira's scaly snout took Nasuada aback, but she quickly recovered. Addressing herself to Eragon, she said, "That was Glaedr I felt, wasn't it?"

He glanced toward the front of the tent, hoping that her guards were too far away to hear, then nodded. "It was."

"Ah, I knew it!" she exclaimed, sounding satisfied. Then her expression became uncertain. "May I speak with him? Is it . . . allowed, or will he only communicate with an elf or a Rider?"

Eragon hesitated and looked to Arya for guidance. "I don't know," he said. "He still hasn't entirely recovered. He may not want to—"

I will speak with you, Nasuada, daughter of Ajihad, Glaedr said, his voice echoing in their heads. *Ask of me what you will, then leave us to our work; there is much that still needs to be done in order to prepare Eragon for the challenges ahead.*

Eragon had never seen Nasuada look awestruck before, but now she did. *"Where?"* she mouthed, and spread her hands.

He pointed at a patch of dirt by his bed.

Nasuada raised her eyebrows; then she nodded, and drawing herself up, she formally greeted Glaedr. An exchange of pleasantries followed, during the course of which Nasuada inquired after Glaedr's health and asked if there was anything the Varden could provide him with. In response to the first question—which had made Eragon nervous—Glaedr politely explained that his health was just fine, thank you; and as far as the second matter went, he needed nothing from the Varden, though he appreciated her concern. *I no longer eat,* he said; *I no longer drink; and I no longer sleep as you would understand it. My only pleasure now, my only indulgence, lies in contemplating how I might bring about Galbatorix's downfall.*

"That," said Nasuada, "I can understand, for I feel much the same."

Then she asked Glaedr if he had any advice as to how the Varden could capture Dras-Leona without it costing them an unacceptable amount of men and materiel, as well as, in her words, "handing over Eragon and Saphira to the Empire, like so many trussed-up chickens."

She spent some time explaining the situation to Glaedr in greater specificity, whereupon, after due consideration, he said, *I have no easy solution for you, Nasuada. I will continue to think on it, but at the moment, I cannot see a way clear for the Varden. If Murtagh and Thorn were by themselves, I might easily overcome their minds. However, Galbatorix has given them too many Eldunarí for me to do that. Even with Eragon, Saphira, and the elves to help, victory would be no sure thing.*

Visibly disappointed, Nasuada was silent for a brief while; then she pressed her hands flat against the front of her dress and thanked Glaedr for his time. She bade them farewell and took her leave, stepping carefully around Saphira's head so as not to touch her.

Eragon relaxed somewhat as he sat on his cot, while Arya seated herself on a short, three-legged stool. He wiped his palms on the knees of his trousers—for his hands felt sticky, as did the rest of him—then offered Arya a drink from his waterskin, which she gratefully accepted. When she was finished, he gulped down several mouthfuls himself. Their sparring had left him ravenous. The water stifled the growls and rumbles coming from his stomach, but he hoped that Glaedr would not detain them for much longer. The sun had nearly set, and he wanted to get a hot meal from the Varden's cooks before they damped their fires and turned in for the night. Otherwise, he knew he would end up gnawing on stale bread, dried strips of meat, moldy sheep cheese, and if he was lucky, a raw onion or two—hardly an appealing prospect.

Once they were both settled, Glaedr began to speak, lecturing Eragon on the principles of mental combat. These Eragon was already familiar with, but he listened closely, and when the golden dragon told him to do something, he followed Glaedr's instructions without question or complaint.

They soon progressed beyond maxims to applied practice. Glaedr

245

started by testing Eragon's defenses with attacks of ever-increasing strength, which then led to them engaging in all-out battles where they each struggled to obtain dominance, even if for only a moment, over the other's thoughts.

While they fought, Eragon lay on his back with his eyes closed, all of his energies concentrated inward on the tempest that raged between him and Glaedr. His earlier exertions had left him weak and thick-headed—whereas the golden dragon was fresh and well rested, in addition to being immensely powerful—and that made it difficult for Eragon to do much more than foil Glaedr's attacks. Nevertheless, he managed to hold his own reasonably well, knowing that, in a real fight, the winner would have undoubtedly been Glaedr.

Fortunately, Glaedr made some allowances for Eragon's condition, although, as he said, *You must be ready to defend your innermost self at any given moment, even when you are sleeping. It may very well be that you will end up facing Galbatorix or Murtagh when you are as exhausted as you are now.*

After two more bouts, Glaedr withdrew to the role of a—very vocal—spectator, while he had Arya take his place as Eragon's antagonist. She was just as tired as Eragon, but he quickly found that, when it came to a wizard's duel, she was more than his equal. It did not surprise him. The one time before they had clashed in their minds, she had almost killed him, and that was when she was still drugged from her captivity in Gil'ead. Glaedr's thoughts were disciplined and focused, but even he could not match the ironbound control Arya exerted over her consciousness.

Her self-mastery was a trait Eragon had noticed was common among the elves. Foremost in that regard had been Oromis, who, it seemed to Eragon, had been in such perfect command of himself, never the slightest doubt or worry had bothered him. Eragon considered the elves' restraint an innate characteristic of their race, as well as a natural outcome of their rigorous upbringing, education, and use of the ancient language. Speaking and thinking in a language that prevented one from lying—and every word of which contained the potential to unlock a spell—discouraged carelessness in thought or speech and fostered an aversion to allowing one's emotions to sweep one away. As a rule, then, elves possessed far more self-control than the members of other races.

He and Arya wrestled with their minds for a few minutes—he seeking to escape her all-encompassing grip, she seeking to pin and hold him so that she could impose her will on his thoughts. She caught him several times, but he always wiggled free after a second or two, though he knew, had she meant him harm, it would have been too late to save himself.

And the whole time their minds were touching, Eragon was aware of the wild strains of music that wafted through the dark spaces of Arya's consciousness. They lured him away from his own body and threatened to snare him in a web of strange and eerie melodies that had no counterparts among earthly songs. He would have happily succumbed to the bewitchment of the music had it not been for the distraction of Arya's attacks and the knowledge that humans did not often fare well if they became too fascinated with the workings of an elf's mind. He might escape unscathed. He was a Rider, after all. He was different. But it was a risk he was not willing to take, not so long as he valued his sanity. He had heard that delving into Blödhgarm's mind had reduced Nasuada's guard Garven to a slack-jawed dreamer.

So he resisted the temptation, hard as it was.

Then Glaedr had Saphira join the fray, sometimes in opposition to Eragon and sometimes in support of him, for as the elder dragon said, *You must be as skilled in this as Eragon, Brightscales.* The addition of Saphira substantially altered the outcome of their mental struggles. Together she and Eragon were able to fend off Arya with regularity, if not ease. Their combined might even allowed them to subdue Arya on two separate occasions. When Saphira was allied with Arya, however, the two of them so outstripped Eragon that he gave up any attempt at offense and, instead, retreated deep inside himself, curling into a tight ball like a wounded animal while he recited scraps of verse and waited for the waves of mental energy they hurled at him to subside.

Lastly, Glaedr had them pair off—he with Arya, and Eragon with Saphira—and they fought a duel like that, as if they were two sets of Riders and dragons met in combat. For the first few strenuous minutes, they were fairly matched, but in the end, Glaedr's strength, experience, and cunning combined with Arya's rigorous proficiency proved too much for Eragon and Saphira to overcome, and they had no choice but to concede defeat.

Afterward, Eragon sensed discontent emanating from Glaedr. Stung by it, he said, *We'll do better tomorrow, Master.*

Glaedr's mood darkened further. Even he seemed weary from their practice. *You did well enough, youngling. I could not have asked any more from either of you had you been placed under my wing as apprentices in Vroengard. However, it is impossible for you to learn what you need to learn in a matter of days or weeks. Time gushes between our teeth like water, and soon it will all be gone. It takes years to master the art of fighting with your mind: years and decades and centuries, and even then, there is still more to learn, more to discover—about yourself, about your enemies, and about the very underpinnings of the world.* With an angry growl, he fell silent.

Then we will learn what we can and let fate decide the rest, said Eragon. *Besides, Galbatorix may have had a hundred years to train his mind, but it has also been over a hundred years since you last taught him. He's sure to have forgotten something in the interim. With you helping us, I know we can beat him.*

Glaedr snorted. *Your tongue grows ever smoother, Eragon Shadeslayer.* Nevertheless, he sounded pleased. He admonished them to eat and rest, and then he withdrew from their minds and said no more.

Eragon was sure that the golden dragon was still watching them, but Eragon could no longer feel his presence, and an unexpected sense of emptiness settled over him.

A chill crept through his limbs, and he shivered.

He, Saphira, and Arya sat in the darkening tent, none of them willing to speak. Then, rousing himself, Eragon said, "He seems better." His voice creaked from disuse, and he again reached for the waterskin.

"This is good for him," said Arya. "*You* are good for him. Without something to give him purpose, his grief would have killed him. That he has survived at all is . . . impressive. I admire him for it. Few beings—human, elf, or dragon—could continue to function rationally after such a loss."

"Brom did."

"He was equally remarkable."

If we kill Galbatorix and Shruikan, how do you think Glaedr will react? Saphira asked. *Will he keep going, or will he just . . . stop?*

Arya's pupils reflected a shimmer of light as she looked past Eragon toward Saphira. "Only time will tell. I hope not, but if we are triumphant in Urû'baen, it may very well be that Glaedr will find he is no longer able to continue on his own, without Oromis."

"We can't just let him give up!"

I agree.

"It is not our place to stop him if he decides to enter the void," Arya said sternly. "The choice is his to make, and his alone."

"Yes, but we can reason with him and try to help him see that life is still worth living."

She was still for a while, her face solemn; then she said, "I do not want him to die. No elf does. However, if every waking moment is a torment to him, then won't it be better for him to seek release?"

Neither Eragon nor Saphira had an answer for her.

The three of them continued to discuss the day's events for a short while longer; then Saphira pulled her head out of the tent and went to sit on the neighboring patch of grass. *I feel like a fox with her head stuck down a rabbit hole,* she complained. *It makes my scales itch, not being able to see if someone is creeping up on me.*

Eragon expected Arya to leave as well, but to his surprise, she stayed, seemingly content to sit and talk with him about this and that. He was only too eager to comply. His earlier hunger had vanished during his bouts of mental combat with her, Saphira, and Glaedr, and in any case, he was more than willing to forgo a hot meal in exchange for the pleasure of her company.

Night closed in around them, and the camp grew ever quieter as their conversation meandered from one topic to another. Eragon felt giddy from exhaustion and excitement—almost as if he had drunk too much mead—and he noticed that Arya also seemed more at ease than normal. They talked of many things: of Glaedr and of their sparring; of the siege of Dras-Leona and what might be done about it; and of other, less important matters, such as the crane Arya had seen hunting among the rushes by the edge of the lake, and the scale Saphira had lost from her nose, and how the season was turning and the days were again growing colder. But always they returned to the one topic that was ever present in their thoughts, and that was Galbatorix and what awaited them in Urû'baen.

While they speculated, as they had so many times before, about the types of magical traps Galbatorix might have set for them and how best to avoid them, Eragon thought of Saphira's question about Glaedr, and he said, "Arya?"

"Yes?" She drew the word out, her voice rising and falling with a faint lilt.

"What do you want to do once this is all over?" *If we're still alive, that is.*

"What do *you* want to do?"

He fingered Brisingr's pommel as he considered the question. "I don't know. I haven't let myself think much past Urû'baen. . . . It would depend on what she wants, but I suppose Saphira and I might return to Palancar Valley. I could build a hall on one of the foothills of the mountains. We might not spend much time there, but at least we would have a home to return to when we weren't flying from one part of Alagaësia to another." He half smiled. "I'm sure there will be plenty to keep us busy, even if Galbatorix is dead. . . . But you still haven't answered my question: what will *you* do if we win? You must have some idea. You've had longer to think about it than I have."

Arya drew one leg up onto the stool, wrapped her arms around it, and rested her chin on her knee. In the dim half-light of the tent, her face appeared to float against a featureless black background, like an apparition conjured out of the night.

"I have spent more time among humans and dwarves than I have among the älfakyn," she said, using the elves' name in the ancient language. "I have grown used to it, and I would not want to return to live in Ellesméra. Too little happens there; centuries can slip by without notice while you sit and stare at the stars. No, I think I will continue to serve my mother as her ambassador. The reason I first left Du Weldenvarden was because I wanted to help right the balance of the world. As you said, there will still be much that needs doing if we manage to topple Galbatorix, much that needs putting right, and I would be a part of it."

"Ah." It was not exactly what he had hoped she might say, but at least it presented the possibility that they would not entirely lose contact after Urû'baen, and that he would still be able to see her now and then.

If Arya noticed his discontent, she gave no sign of it.

They talked for another few minutes, then Arya made her excuses and rose to leave.

As she stepped past him, Eragon reached toward her, as if to stop her, then quickly drew back his hand. "Wait," he said softly, unsure of what he hoped for, but hoping nevertheless. The beat of his heart increased, pounding in his ears, and his cheeks grew warm.

Arya paused with her back to him by the entrance of the tent. "Good night, Eragon," she said. Then she slipped out between the entrance flaps and vanished into the night, leaving him to sit alone in the dark.

251

DISCOVERY

The next three days passed quickly for Eragon, if not for the rest of the Varden, who remained mired in lethargy. The stand-off with Dras-Leona continued unabated, although there was some excitement when Thorn altered his customary location from above the front gates to a section of the rampart several hundred feet to the right. After much discussion—and after consulting extensively with Saphira—Nasuada and her advisers concluded that Thorn had relocated for no other reason than comfort; the other section of rampart was somewhat flatter and longer. Aside from that, the siege lumbered on without change.

Meanwhile, Eragon spent the mornings and evenings studying with Glaedr and the afternoons sparring with Arya and several other elves. His matches with the elves were not as long or strenuous as his previous one with Arya—for it would have been foolish to push himself that hard every day—but his sessions with Glaedr were as intense as ever. The ancient dragon never flagged in his efforts to improve Eragon's skills and knowledge, and he made no allowances for mistakes or exhaustion.

Eragon was pleased to find that he was finally able to hold his own when dueling with the elves. But it was mentally taxing, for if his concentration lapsed for even a moment, he would end up with a sword jabbed in his ribs or pressed against his throat.

With his lessons from Glaedr, he made what would have been considered exemplary progress under normal circumstances, but given the situation, both he and Glaedr were frustrated with the pace of his learning.

On the second day, during his morning lesson with Glaedr,

Eragon thought to say, *Master, when I first arrived at the Varden in Farthen Dûr, the Twins tested me—they tested my knowledge of the ancient language, and of magic in general.*

You told this to Oromis. Why repeat it to me now?

Because, it occurred to me . . . the Twins asked me to summon the true form of a silver ring. At the time, I didn't know how. Arya explained it to me later: how, with the ancient language, you can conjure up the essence of any thing or creature. Yet Oromis never spoke of it, and I was wondering . . . why not?

Glaedr seemed to sigh. *Summoning the true form of an object is a difficult kind of magic. In order for it to work, you must understand everything of importance about the object in question—even as you must in order to guess the true name of a person or animal. Furthermore, it's of little practical value. And it's dangerous. Very dangerous. The spell cannot be structured as a continuing process that you can end at any time. Either you succeed in summoning the true form of an object . . . or you fail and die. There was no reason for Oromis to have you try anything so risky, nor were you advanced enough in your studies to even discuss the topic.*

Eragon shuddered inwardly as he realized just how angry Arya must have been with the Twins to summon the true form of the ring they held. Then he said, *I would like to try it now.*

Eragon felt the full force of Glaedr's attention focused on him. *Why?*

I need to know if I have that level of understanding, even if only for one small thing.

Again: why?

Unable to explain with words, Eragon poured his jumble of thoughts and feelings into Glaedr's consciousness. When he finished, Glaedr was silent for a while, digesting the flow of information. *Am I right to say,* began the dragon, *that you equate this with defeating Galbatorix? You believe that if you can do this and live, then you might be able to defeat the king?*

Yes, said Eragon, relieved. He had been unable to articulate his motivation as clearly as the dragon, but that was exactly it.

And are you determined to try this?

Yes, Master.

It may kill you, Glaedr reminded him.

I know.

Eragon! exclaimed Saphira, her thoughts faint in his mind. She was flying high above the camp, watching for possible danger while he studied with Glaedr. *It's far too dangerous. I won't allow it.*

I have to do this, he replied quietly.

To Saphira, but also to Eragon, Glaedr said, *If he insists, then it is best he tries where I can watch. If his knowledge fails him, I may be able to supply the needed information and save him.*

Saphira growled—an angry, ripping sound that filled Eragon's mind—and then, from outside the tent, Eragon heard a fearsome rush of air and startled cries from men and elves as she dove to the ground. She landed with such force, the tent and everything in it shook.

A few seconds later, she stuck her head into the tent and glared at Eragon. She was panting, and the wind from her nostrils ruffled his hair and made his eyes water from the odor of burnt meat. *You're as thick-headed as a Kull,* she said.

No more than you.

Her lip curled in a hint of a snarl. *Why are we waiting? If you must do this, let us be done with it!*

What will you choose to summon? asked Glaedr. *It must be something you are intimately familiar with.*

Eragon let his gaze drift over the interior of the tent, then down to the sapphire ring he wore on his right hand. *Aren . . .* He had rarely taken the ring off since Ajihad had given it to him from Brom. It had become a part of his body as surely as his arms or legs. During the hours he had spent looking at it, he had memorized every curve and facet, and if he closed his eyes, he could call up an image that was a perfect reproduction of the actual object. But for all that, there was much he did *not* know about the ring—its history, how the elves had made it, and, ultimately, what spells might or might not be woven into its fabric.

No . . . not Aren.

Then his gaze slid from the ring to the pommel of Brisingr, where the sword stood leaning against the corner of his cot. "Brisingr," he murmured.

A muffled *whump* emanated from the blade, and the sword rose a half inch out of its scabbard, as if pushed from beneath, and small tongues of flame leaped up from the mouth of the sheath, licking the underside of the hilt. The flames vanished and the sword slid back into the scabbard as Eragon quickly ended the unintentional spell.

Brisingr, he thought, utterly certain of his choice. It had been Rhunön's skill that had crafted the sword, but it was he who had wielded the tools, and he had been joined with the elf smith's mind throughout the process. If there was any one object in the world he understood through and through, it was his sword.

Are you sure? asked Glaedr.

Eragon nodded, then caught himself as he remembered the golden dragon could not see him. *Yes, Master. . . . A question, though: is* Brisingr *the true name of the sword, and if not, do I need its true name for the spell to work?*

Brisingr is the name of fire, as you well know. The true name of your sword is undoubtedly something far more complicated, although it might very well include brisingr *within its description. If you wish, you could refer to the sword by its true name, but you could just as easily call it* Sword *and achieve the same result, so long as you maintain the proper knowledge at the forefront of your mind. The name is merely a label for the knowledge, and you do not need the label in order to make use of the knowledge. It is a subtle distinction, but an important one. Do you understand?*

I do.

Then proceed as you will.

Eragon took a moment to collect himself. Then he found the nub in the back of his mind and reached through it to tap his body's store of energy. Channeling that energy into the word he spoke, while also thinking about everything he knew of the sword, he said clearly and distinctly:

"Brisingr!"

Eragon felt his strength ebb precipitously. Alarmed, he tried to speak, tried to move, but the spell bound him in place. He could not even blink or breathe.

Unlike before, the sheathed sword did not burst into flame; it wavered, like a reflection in water. Then, in the air next to the weapon, a transparent apparition appeared: a perfect, glowing likeness of Brisingr free of its sheath. As well made as was the sword itself—and Eragon had never found so much as a single flaw—the duplicate floating before him was even more refined. It was as if he was seeing the *idea* of the sword, an idea that not even Rhunön, with all her experience working metal, could hope to capture.

As soon as the manifestation became visible, Eragon was again able to breathe and move. He maintained the spell for several seconds, so he could marvel at the beauty of the summoning, and then he let the spell slip free of his grasp and the ghostly sword slowly faded into oblivion.

In its absence, the inside of the tent seemed unexpectedly dark.

Only then did Eragon again become aware of Saphira and Glaedr pressing against his consciousness, watching with steadfast attentiveness every thought that flickered through his mind. Both of the dragons were as tense as Eragon had ever felt them. If he were to poke Saphira, he guessed she would be so startled, she would twist herself in circles.

And if I were to poke you, nothing would be left but a smear, she commented.

Eragon smiled and lowered himself onto the cot, tired.

In his mind, Eragon heard a sound like wind rushing across a lonely plain as Glaedr relaxed. *You did well, Shadeslayer.* Glaedr's praise surprised Eragon; the old dragon had given out few enough compliments since he had begun teaching Eragon. *But let us not try it again.*

Eragon shivered and rubbed his arms, trying to dispel the cold that had crept into his limbs. *Agreed, Master.* It was not an experience he was eager to replicate. Still, he felt a deep sense of satisfaction. He had proven without a doubt that there was at least one thing in Alagaësia that he could do as well as anyone possibly could.

And that gave him hope.

On the morning of the third day, Roran arrived back at the Varden, along with his companions: tired, wounded, and travel-worn. Roran's return stirred the Varden from their torpor for a few hours— he and the others with him were given a hero's welcome—but an air of boredom soon settled over the majority of the Varden again.

Eragon was relieved to see Roran. He had known his cousin was safe, as he had scryed him several times while he was gone. Nevertheless, seeing him in person freed Eragon of an anxiety that, until that very moment, he had not realized he was carrying. Roran was the only family he had left—Murtagh did not count, as far as Eragon was concerned—and Eragon could not bear the thought of losing him.

Now, seeing Roran up close, Eragon was shocked by his appearance. He had expected Roran and the others to be exhausted, but Roran seemed far more haggard than his companions; he looked as if he had aged five years over the course of the trip. His eyes were red and dark-ringed, his brow was lined, and he moved stiffly, as if every inch of his body was covered in bruises. And then there was his beard, which had been burned half off and which now had a mottled, mangy appearance.

The five men—one less than their original number—went first to visit the healers of Du Vrangr Gata, where the spellcasters attended to their wounds. Then they presented themselves to Nasuada in her pavilion. After commending them for their bravery, Nasuada dismissed all of the men except Roran, whom she asked to deliver a detailed account of his journey to and from Aroughs, as well as the capture of the city itself. The telling took some time, but both Nasuada and Eragon—who was standing by her right hand—listened with rapt and sometimes horrified attention while Roran spoke. When he finished, Nasuada surprised both him and Eragon by announcing that she was placing Roran in charge of one of the Varden's battalions.

Eragon expected the news to please Roran. Instead, he saw the lines in his cousin's face deepen and his brows draw together in a frown. Roran made no objection or complaint, however, but bowed and said in his rough voice, "As you wish, Lady Nasuada."

Later, Eragon walked Roran to his tent, where Katrina was waiting for them. She greeted Roran with such an obvious display of emotion that Eragon averted his eyes, embarrassed.

With Saphira, the three of them dined together, but Eragon and Saphira excused themselves as soon as they could, for it was obvious that Roran had no energy for company and Katrina wished to have him for herself.

As he and Saphira wandered through the camp in the deepening dusk, Eragon heard someone behind him shout, "Eragon! Eragon! Wait a moment!"

He turned to see the thin, gangly figure of the scholar Jeod running toward him, strands of hair flying around his lean face. In his left hand, Jeod clutched a ragged scrap of parchment.

"What is it?" Eragon asked, worried.

"This!" exclaimed Jeod, his eyes gleaming. He held up the parchment and shook it. "I've done it again, Eragon! I've found a way!" In the fading light, the scar on his scalp and temple appeared startlingly pale against his tanned skin.

"You've done *what* again? You've found *what* way? Slow down; you're not making sense!"

Jeod glanced around furtively, then he leaned close to Eragon and whispered, "All my reading and searching has paid off. I've discovered a hidden tunnel that leads straight into Dras-Leona!"

DECISIONS

"Explain it to me again," said Nasuada.

Eragon shifted his weight, impatient, but he held his tongue.

From the piles of scrolls and books in front of him, Jeod picked up a slim volume bound in red leather and began his narrative for the third time: "Some five hundred years ago, as best I can tell—"

Jörmundur interrupted him with a motion of his hand. "Leave out your qualifiers. We know this is speculation."

Jeod began again: "Some five hundred years ago, Queen Forna sent Erst Graybeard to Dras-Leona, or rather what was to *become* Dras-Leona."

"And why did she send him?" asked Nasuada while she toyed with the fringe of her sleeve.

"The dwarves were in the midst of a clan war, and Forna hoped that she could secure the support of our race by helping King Radgar with the planning and construction of the fortifications for the city, even as the dwarves engineered the defenses for Aroughs."

Nasuada rolled a strand of cloth between her fingers. "And then Dolgrath Halfstave killed Forna. . . ."

"Aye. And Erst Graybeard had no choice but to return to the Beor Mountains as fast as he could, to defend his clan from Halfstave's predations. But"—Jeod held up a finger, then opened the red book—"before he left, it seems Erst did start on his work. King Radgar's chief adviser, Lord Yardley, wrote in his memoirs that Erst had begun to draw up plans for the sewer system underneath the center of the city, since that would affect how the fortifications would be built."

From his place at the far end of the table that filled the middle of Nasuada's pavilion, Orik nodded and said, "That's true enough. You have to work out where and how the weight is distributed and determine what's appropriate for the kind of earth you're dealing with. Otherwise, you're liable to have cave-ins."

Jeod continued: "Of course, Dras-Leona *doesn't* have underground sewers, so I assumed that nothing like Erst's plans were ever put into effect. However, a few pages later, Yardley says . . ." Peering down his nose at the book, Jeod read, ". . . *and in a most lamentable turn of events, the reavers burned many a house and made off with many a family treasure. The soldiers were slow to respond, for they had been put to work underground, laboring like common peasants.*"

Jeod lowered the book. "Now, what were they excavating? I was unable to find any further mention of subterranean activities in or around Dras-Leona, until—" Putting down the red volume, he selected another book, this one a massive, wood-paneled tome nearly a foot thick. "I happened to be perusing *The Acts of Taradas and Other Mysteries of Occult Phenomena as Recorded Throughout the Ages of Men, Dwarves, and the Most Ancient Elves* when—"

"It is a work filled with mistakes," said Arya. She stood by the left side of the table, leaning on both hands over a map of the city. "The author knew little of my people, and what he did not know, he invented."

"That may be," said Jeod, "but he knew a great deal about humans, and it is humans we are interested in." Jeod opened the book close to the middle and gently lowered the upper half to the table, so it lay flat. "During his investigations, Othman spent some time in this region. He mainly studied Helgrind and the strange happenings associated with it, but he also had this to say about Dras-Leona: *The people of the city also often complain of peculiar sounds and odors wafting up from under their streets and floors, especially at night, which they attribute to ghosts and spirits and other uncanny creatures, but if they are spirits, they are unlike any I have heard of before, as spirits elsewhere seem to avoid enclosed spaces.*"

Jeod closed the book. "Fortunately, Othman was nothing if not thorough, and he marked the locations of the sounds on a map of Dras-Leona, where, as you can see, they form a nearly straight line through the old part of the city."

"And you think this indicates the presence of a tunnel," said Nasuada. It was a statement, not a question.

"I do," said Jeod, bobbing his head.

Sitting next to Nasuada, King Orrin, who had said little, spoke. "Nothing you have shown us so far, Goodman Jeod, has yet to prove that this is actually a tunnel. If there is a space under the city, it might very well be a cellar or a catacomb or some other chamber that only leads to the building above. Even if it *is* a tunnel, we do not know if it exits anywhere outside of Dras-Leona, nor, assuming its existence, where it would lead. To the heart of the palace, perhaps? What's more, by your own account, it's likely the construction of this hypothetical tunnel was never completed in the first place."

"It seems unlikely it could be anything *but* a tunnel, given its shape, Your Majesty," said Jeod. "No cellar or catacomb would be so narrow or long. As for whether it was completed . . . we know it was never used for its intended purpose, but we also know that it lasted at least up until Othman's time, which means the tunnel or passageway or what-have-you must have been finished to *some* degree, otherwise the seep of water would have destroyed it long ago."

"What of the exit, then—or the entrance, if you will?" asked the king.

Jeod scrabbled among the piles of scrolls for a few moments before pulling out another map of Dras-Leona, this one showing a portion of the surrounding landscape. "That I can't be sure about, but if it does lead out of the city, then it would exit somewhere around here—" He placed his index finger on a spot close to the eastern side of the city. Most of the buildings outside the walls that protected the heart of Dras-Leona were located on the western side of the city, next to the lake. This meant that the location Jeod was pointing at, though empty land, was closer to the center of Dras-Leona than one could get from any other direction without encountering buildings. "But it's impossible to tell without going there to look for it in person."

Eragon frowned. He had thought Jeod's discovery would be more certain.

"You are to be congratulated on your research, Goodman Jeod," said Nasuada. "You may have once again performed a great service for the Varden." She rose from her high-backed chair and walked over to look at the map. The hem of her dress rustled as it dragged across the ground. "If we send a scout to investigate, we risk alerting the Empire to our interest in that area. Assuming the tunnel exists, it would be of little value to us then; Murtagh and Thorn would be expecting us on the other end." She looked at Jeod. "How wide do you think this tunnel would be? How many men could fit in it?"

"I couldn't say. It might be——"

Orik cleared his throat, then said, "The earth here is soft and claylike, with a fair bit of silt layered throughout it—horrible for tunneling. If Erst had any sense, he wouldn't have planned to have one large channel carry away the city's waste; he would have laid down several smaller passageways, to reduce the likelihood of a cave-in. I'd guess that none of them would be wider than a yard or so."

"Too narrow for more than a single man to pass through at a time," said Jeod.

"Too narrow for more than a single knurla," added Orik.

Nasuada returned to her seat and stared at the map with unfocused eyes, as if she were gazing at something far away.

After a few moments of silence, Eragon said, "I could search for the tunnel. I know how to hide myself with magic; the sentries would never see me."

"Perhaps," murmured Nasuada. "But I still don't like the idea of having you or anyone else running about. The likelihood of the Empire noticing is too high. What if Murtagh is watching? Could you fool him? Do you even know what he is capable of now?" She shook her head. "No, we must act as if the tunnel exists and make our decisions accordingly. If events prove otherwise, it won't have cost us anything, but if the tunnel *is* there . . . it should allow us to capture Dras-Leona once and for all."

"What have you in mind?" asked King Orrin in a tone of caution.

"Something bold; something . . . *unexpected*."

Eragon snorted softly. "Perhaps you should consult Roran, then."

"I have no need of Roran's help in devising my plans, Eragon."

Nasuada fell silent again, and everyone in the pavilion, including Eragon, waited to see what she would come up with. At last she stirred and said, "This: we send a small team of warriors to open the gates from the inside."

"And how is anyone supposed to manage that?" demanded Orik. "It would be tricky enough if all they had to face were the hundreds of soldiers stationed in the area, but in case you have forgotten, there's also a giant, fire-breathing lizard lounging close by, and *he's* sure to take an interest in anyone foolish enough to pry open the gates. And that's not even taking Murtagh into account."

Before the discussion could devolve, Eragon said, "I can do it."

The words had an immediate, chilling effect on the conversation.

Eragon expected Nasuada to reject his suggestion out of hand, but she surprised him by considering it. Then she surprised him further when she said, "Very well."

All the arguments Eragon had built up fell away as he stared at Nasuada with astonishment. She had obviously followed the same chain of reasoning as he had.

The tent erupted in a confusion of overlapping voices as everyone began to speak at once. Arya won out over the din: "Nasuada, you cannot allow Eragon to endanger himself so. It would be unconscionable. Send some of Blödhgarm's spellcasters instead; I know they would agree to help, and they are as mighty warriors as any you can find, including Eragon."

Nasuada shook her head. "None of Galbatorix's men would dare kill Eragon—not Murtagh, not the king's pet magicians, not even the lowest of soldiers. We should use that to our advantage. Besides, Eragon is our strongest spellcaster, and it may require a great deal of strength to force open the gates. Of all of us, he has the best chance of success."

"What if he is captured, though? He can't hold his own against Murtagh. You know that!"

"We'll distract Murtagh and Thorn, and that will give Eragon the opportunity he needs."

Arya lifted her chin. "How? How will you distract them?"

"We'll make as though to attack Dras-Leona from the south. Saphira will fly around the city, setting buildings on fire and killing soldiers on the walls. Thorn and Murtagh will have no choice but to give chase, especially since it will appear as if Eragon is riding Saphira the whole time. Blödhgarm and his fellow spellcasters can conjure up a facsimile of Eragon, as they did before. As long as Murtagh doesn't get too close, he'll never discover our subterfuge."

"You are determined in this?"

"I am."

Arya's face hardened. "Then I will accompany Eragon."

Relief seeped through Eragon. He had hoped she would go with him, but he had been uncertain whether to ask, for fear she would refuse.

Nasuada sighed. "You are Islanzadí's daughter. I would not like to place you in such danger. If you were to die . . . Remember how your mother reacted when she thought Durza had killed you. We cannot afford to lose the help of your people."

"My mother—" Arya clamped her lips shut, cutting herself off, then began anew: "I can assure you, Lady Nasuada, Queen Islanzadí shall not abandon the Varden, whatever may happen to me. Of that, you need have no concern. I *will* accompany Eragon, as will two of Blödhgarm's spellcasters."

Nasuada shook her head. "No, you can only take one. Murtagh is familiar with the number of elves who have been protecting Eragon. If he notices that two or more are missing, he may suspect a trap of some sort. In any event, Saphira will need as much help as she can get if she's to keep out of Murtagh's grasp."

"Three people are not enough to attempt such a mission," insisted Arya. "We would be unable to ensure Eragon's safety, much less open the gates."

"Then one of Du Vrangr Gata can go with you as well."

A hint of derision colored Arya's expression. "None of your spellcasters are strong or skilled enough. We'll be outnumbered a hundred to one, or worse. Both ordinary swordsmen and trained magicians will be arrayed against us. Only elves or Riders—"

"Or Shades," Orik rumbled.

"Or Shades," Arya conceded, though Eragon could tell she was irritated. "Only those could hope to prevail against such odds. And even then it is no sure thing. Let us take two of Blödhgarm's spellcasters. No one else is fit for the task, not among the Varden."

"Oh, and what am I, chopped liver?"

Everyone turned to look, surprised, as Angela stepped forward from a corner at the back of the tent. Eragon had not even suspected she was there.

"What a strange expression," said the herbalist. "Who would compare themselves to chopped liver in the first place? If you *have* to choose an organ, why not pick a gallbladder or a thymus gland instead? Much more interesting than a liver. Or what about chopped t—" She smiled. "Well, I suppose that's not important." She stopped in front of Arya and looked up at her. "Will you object if *I* accompany you, Älfa? I'm not a member of the Varden, not strictly speaking, but I'm still willing to round out this quartet of yours."

Much to Eragon's surprise, Arya bowed her head and said, "Of course, wise one. I meant no offense. It would be an honor to have you with us."

"Good!" exclaimed Angela. "That is, assuming *you* don't mind," she said, directing her words to Nasuada.

Appearing somewhat bemused, Nasuada shook her head. "If you are willing, and neither Eragon nor Arya objects, then I can think of no reason why you shouldn't go. I can't imagine why you'd want to, though."

Angela tossed her curls. "Do you expect me to explain every decision I make? . . . Oh, very well, if it'll satisfy your curiosity, let's say I have a grudge against the priests of Helgrind, and I'd like the chance to do them some mischief. And besides, if Murtagh puts in an appearance, I have a trick or two up my sleeve that might give him a bit of a turn."

"We should ask Elva to go with us as well," said Eragon. "If anyone can help us avoid danger . . ."

Nasuada frowned. "Last we spoke, she made her position clear enough. I'll not go bowing and scraping to her in an attempt to convince her otherwise."

"I'll talk with her," said Eragon. "I'm the one she's angry with, and I'm the one who should ask her."

Nasuada plucked at the fringe of her golden dress. She rolled several strands between her fingers, then abruptly said, "Do as you wish. I dislike the thought of sending a child—even one as gifted as Elva—into battle. However, I suppose she is more than capable of protecting herself."

"As long as the pain of those around her doesn't overwhelm her," said Angela. "The last few battles have left her curled in a ball, barely able to move or breathe."

Nasuada stilled her fingers and peered at Eragon with a serious expression. "She's unpredictable. If she does choose to go along, be careful of her, Eragon."

"I will," he promised.

Then Nasuada began to discuss questions of logistics with Orrin and Orik, and Eragon withdrew somewhat from the conversation, for he had little to contribute.

In the privacy of his mind, he reached out to Saphira, who had been listening, through him, to the goings-on. *Well?* he asked. *What do you think? You've been awfully quiet. I thought for sure you would say something when Nasuada proposed sneaking into Dras-Leona.*

I said nothing because I had nothing to say. It is a good plan.

You agree with her?!

We are no longer awkward younglings, Eragon. Our enemies may be fearsome, but so are we. It is time we remind them of that.

Does it bother you that we'll be apart?

Of course it bothers me, she growled. *Wherever you go, enemies flock to you like flies to flesh. However, you are not as helpless as you once were.* And she almost seemed to purr.

Me, helpless? he said with mock outrage.

Only a little bit. But your bite is more dangerous than before.

So is yours.

Mmm. . . . I go to hunt. A wing-breaking storm is building, and I'll not have a chance to eat again until after we attack.

Fly safely, he said.

As he felt her presence receding from him, Eragon returned his attention to the conversation within the tent, for he knew his life, and that of Saphira, would depend on the decisions Nasuada, Orik, and Orrin would make.

267

UNDER HILL AND STONE

E ragon rolled his shoulders, trying to get his mail hauberk to rest comfortably under the tunic he wore to hide the armor.

Darkness lay all around them, heavy and oppressive. A thick layer of clouds obscured the moon and the stars. Without the red werelight Angela held in the palm of her hand, even Eragon and the elves would have been unable to see.

The air was humid, and once or twice, Eragon felt a few cold drops of rain strike his cheeks.

Elva had laughed and refused when he had asked for her help. He had argued with her long and hard, but to no avail. Saphira had even intervened, flying down to the tent where the witch-child was staying and placing her massive head just feet away from the girl, forcing her to look into one of Saphira's brilliant, unblinking eyes.

Elva had not had the temerity to laugh then, but she remained obdurate in her refusal. Her stubbornness frustrated Eragon. Still, he could not help but admire her strength of character; to say no to both a Rider and a dragon was no small thing. Then again, she had endured an incredible amount of pain in her short life, and the experience had hardened her to a degree rarely seen even in the most jaded of warriors.

Beside him, Arya fastened a long cloak around her neck. Eragon wore one as well, as did Angela and the black-haired elf Wyrden, whom Blödhgarm had chosen to accompany them. The cloaks were needed to protect them against the night chill, as well as to conceal their weapons from anyone they might encounter in the city, if they got that far.

Nasuada, Jörmundur, and Saphira had accompanied them to the

edge of the camp, where they now stood. Among the tents, the men of the Varden, dwarves, and Urgals were busy preparing to march forth.

"Don't forget," said Nasuada, her breath steaming in front of her, "if you can't reach the gates by dawn, find somewhere to wait until tomorrow morning, and we'll try again then."

"We may not have the luxury of waiting," said Arya.

Nasuada rubbed her arms and nodded. She appeared unusually worried. "I know. Either way, we'll be ready to attack as soon as you contact us, no matter the time of day. Your safety is more important than capturing Dras-Leona. Remember that." Her gaze drifted toward Eragon as she spoke.

"We should be off," said Wyrden. "The night grows old."

Eragon pressed his forehead against Saphira for a moment. *Good hunting*, she said softly.

And you as well.

They reluctantly parted, and Eragon joined Arya and Wyrden as they followed Angela away from the camp, heading toward the eastern edge of the city. Nasuada and Jörmundur murmured well-wishes and farewells as they strode past, and then all was quiet, save the sounds of their breathing and of their boots on the ground.

Angela dimmed the light in her palm until it was barely bright enough for Eragon to see his feet. He had to strain his eyes to spot rocks and branches that lay in the way.

They walked in silence for nearly an hour, at which point the herbalist stopped and whispered, "We're here, as best I can tell. I'm fairly good at reckoning distances, but we might be off by more than a thousand feet. It's hard to be certain of anything in this gloom."

Off to their left, a half-dozen pinpricks of light floated above the horizon, the only evidence that they were anywhere near Dras-Leona. The lights seemed close enough to pluck from the air.

He and the two women gathered around Wyrden as the elf knelt and pulled the glove off his right hand. Placing his palm against the bare earth, Wyrden began to croon the spell he had learned from the dwarven magician whom—ere they left on their mission—Orik had sent to instruct them in the ways of detecting underground chambers.

While the elf sang, Eragon stared into the surrounding blackness, listening and watching for enemies. The fall of raindrops on his face increased. He hoped the weather would improve before battle was joined, if battle was to be joined.

An owl hooted somewhere, and he reached for Brisingr, only to stop himself and clench his fist. *Barzûl*, he said to himself, using Orik's favorite curse. He was more nervous than he ought to be. The knowledge that he might be about to fight Murtagh and Thorn again—singly or together—had put him on edge.

I'll be sure to lose if I keep on like this, he thought. So he slowed his breathing and initiated the first of the mental exercises Glaedr had taught him for establishing control over his emotions.

The old dragon had not been enthusiastic about the mission when Eragon told him about it, but neither had he opposed it. After discussing various contingencies, Glaedr had said: *Beware of the shadows, Eragon. Strange things lurk in dark places*, which, Eragon thought, was hardly an encouraging statement.

He wiped the accumulated moisture off his face, keeping his other hand close to the hilt of his sword. The leather of his glove was warm and smooth against his skin.

Lowering his hand, he hooked his thumb under his sword belt, the belt of Beloth the Wise, conscious of the weight of the twelve flawless diamonds concealed within. That morning, he had gone to the livestock pens, and as the cooks killed the birds and sheep for the army's breakfast, he had transferred the animals' dying energy into the gems. He hated doing so; when he reached out with his mind to an animal—if it still had its head attached—the animal's fear and pain became his own, and as it slipped into the void, he felt as if he himself were dying. It was a horrible, panic-inducing experience. Whenever he could, he had whispered words in the ancient language to the animals in an attempt to comfort them. Sometimes it worked, sometimes not. Though the creatures would have died in any case, and though he needed the energy, he hated the practice, for it made him feel as if *he* were responsible for their deaths. It made him feel unclean.

Now he fancied that the belt was slightly heavier than before, laden as it was with the energy from so many animals. Even if the diamonds within had been worthless, Eragon would have regarded the belt as valuable beyond gold, on account of the dozens of lives that had gone into filling it.

As Wyrden ceased singing, Arya asked, "Have you found it?"

"This way," said Wyrden, standing.

Relief and trepidation swept through Eragon. *Jeod was right!*

Wyrden led them over a road and a series of small hills, then down into a shallow wash hidden within the folds of the land. "The mouth of the tunnel should be somewhere here," said the elf, and gestured at the western bank of the depression.

The herbalist increased the brightness of her werelight enough for them to search by; then Eragon, Arya, and Wyrden began to comb through the brush along the side of the bank, poking at the ground with sticks. Twice Eragon barked his shins against the stumps of fallen birch trees, causing him to suck in his breath with pain. He wished he was wearing bracers, but he had left them behind, along with his shield, because they would have attracted too much attention in the city.

For twenty minutes, they searched, ranging up and down the bank as they worked their way out from their starting point. At last Eragon heard a ring of metal, and then Arya softly called, "Here."

He and the others hurried toward her, where she stood by a small, overgrown hollow in the side of the bank. Arya drew aside the brush to reveal a stone-lined tunnel five feet tall and three feet wide. A rusting iron grate covered the gaping hole.

"Look," said Arya, and she pointed at the ground.

Eragon looked, and he saw a path leading out of the tunnel. Even by the weird red illumination of the herbalist's werelight, Eragon could tell that the trail had been worn into place by the passage of tramping feet. One or more people must have been using the tunnel to surreptitiously enter and exit Dras-Leona.

"We should proceed with caution," whispered Wyrden.

Angela made a faint noise in her throat. "How else were you planning to proceed? With blaring trumpets and shouting heralds? Really."

The elf refrained from answering, but he appeared distinctly uncomfortable.

Arya and Wyrden pulled off the grating and cautiously moved into the tunnel. Both conjured werelights of their own. The flameless orbs floated over their heads like small red suns, though they emitted no more light than a handful of coals.

Eragon hung back and said to Angela, "Why do the elves treat you so respectfully? They seem almost afraid of you."

"Am I not deserving of respect?"

He hesitated. "One of these days, you know, you're going to have to tell me about yourself."

"What makes you think that?" And she pushed past him to enter the tunnel, her cloak flapping like the wings of a Lethrblaka.

Shaking his head, Eragon followed.

The short herbalist did not have to bend much in order to avoid bumping into the ceiling, but Eragon had to hunch like an old man with rheumatism, as did the two elves. For the most part, the tunnel was empty. A fine layer of caked dirt covered the floor. A few sticks and rocks, and even a discarded snakeskin, were scattered near the mouth of the tunnel. The passageway smelled like damp straw and moth wings.

Eragon and the others walked as quietly as they could, but the tunnel magnified sounds. Every bump and scrape echoed, filling the air with a multitude of overlapping whispers that seemed to murmur and sigh with a life of their own. The whispers made Eragon feel as if they were surrounded by a host of disembodied spirits who were commenting on their every move.

So much for sneaking up on anyone, he thought as he scuffed his boot against a rock, which bounced against the side of the tunnel with a loud *clack* that multiplied a hundredfold as it spread through the tunnel.

"Sorry," he mouthed as everyone looked at him.

A wry smile touched his lips. *At least we know what causes the strange sounds underneath Dras-Leona.* He would have to tell Jeod on their return.

When they had gone a fair ways down the tunnel, Eragon paused and looked back at the entrance, which was already lost in darkness. The gloom seemed almost palpable, like a heavy cloth draped over the world. Combined with the close-set walls and low ceiling, it left him feeling cramped and constricted. Normally, he did not mind being in enclosed places, but the tunnel reminded him of the warren of rough-hewn passageways within Helgrind where he and Roran had fought the Ra'zac—hardly a pleasant memory.

He took a deep breath, then released it.

Just as he was about to continue forward, he caught a glimpse of two large eyes gleaming in the shadows, like a pair of copper-colored moonstones. He grabbed Brisingr and had already drawn the sword several inches from its scabbard when Solembum appeared out of the murk, padding along on silent paws.

The werecat stopped at the edge of the light. He twitched his black-tipped ears, and his jaws parted in what seemed to be an expression of amusement.

Eragon relaxed and acknowledged the werecat's presence with a dip of his head. *I should have guessed.* Wherever Angela went, Solembum invariably followed. Again Eragon wondered about the herbalist's past: *How did she ever win his loyalty?*

As the rest of the party grew distant, the shadows crept over Solembum once more, hiding him from Eragon's sight.

Comforted by the knowledge that the werecat was watching his back, Eragon hurried to catch up.

Before the group left the camp, Nasuada had briefed them on

the exact number of soldiers in the city, as well as where they were stationed and their duties and habits. She had also given them details about Murtagh's sleeping quarters, what he ate, and even his mood the previous evening. Her information had been remarkably precise. When questioned, she had smiled and explained that, since the Varden had arrived, the werecats had been spying for her within Dras-Leona. Once Eragon and his companions emerged within the city, the werecats would escort them to the southern gates but would not reveal their own presence to the Empire if at all possible, else they would no longer be able to supply Nasuada with intelligence as effectively. After all, who would suspect that the unusually large cat lounging nearby was actually an enemy spy?

It occurred to Eragon then, as he reviewed Nasuada's briefing, that one of Murtagh's greatest weaknesses was that he still had to sleep. *If we don't capture or kill him today, the next time we meet, it might help us to find a way to wake him in the middle of the night—and for more nights than one, if we could manage it. Three or four days without proper sleep and he'd be in no fit shape to fight.*

On and on they went through the tunnel, which ran straight as an arrow, never bending, never turning. Eragon thought he detected a slight upward slant to the floor—which would make sense, as it was designed to channel waste out of the city—but he was not entirely sure.

After a while, the dirt beneath their feet began to soften and stick to their boots, like wet clay. Water dripped from the ceiling, sometimes landing on the nape of Eragon's neck and rolling down his spine, like the touch of a cold finger. He slipped once on a patch of mud and, when he put out a hand for balance, found the wall covered in slime.

An indeterminate amount of time passed. They might have spent an hour in the tunnel. They might have spent ten. Or maybe it was only a few minutes. Whatever the case, Eragon's neck and shoulders hurt from standing half bent over, and he grew tired of staring at what seemed to be the same twenty feet of rose-hued stone.

At last he noticed the echoes were waning and ever more of a delay was appearing between each repetition of the sounds. Soon afterward, the tunnel disgorged them into a large rectangular chamber with a ridged, half-dome ceiling over fifteen feet high at its apex. The chamber was empty, except for a rotting barrel in one corner. Across from them, three identical archways opened to three identical rooms, small and dark. Where those led, Eragon could not see.

The group stopped, and Eragon slowly straightened his back, wincing as his sore muscles stretched.

"This would not have been part of Erst Graybeard's plans," said Arya.

"Which path should we pick?" asked Wyrden.

"Isn't it obvious?" asked the herbalist. "The left one. It's always the left one." And she strode toward that selfsame arch even as she spoke.

Eragon could not help himself. "Left according to which direction? If you were starting from the other side, left—"

"Left would be right and right would be left, yes, yes," said the herbalist. Her eyes narrowed. "Sometimes you're too clever for your own good, Shadeslayer. . . . Very well, we'll try it your way. But don't say I didn't warn you if we end up wandering around here for days on end."

Eragon would actually have preferred to take the center archway, as it seemed the most likely to lead them up to the streets, but he did not want to get into an argument with the herbalist. *Either way, we'll find stairs soon enough,* he thought. *There can't be that many chambers under Dras-Leona.*

Holding her werelight aloft, Angela took the lead. Wyrden and Arya followed while Eragon brought up the rear.

The room through the rightmost archway was larger than it had first appeared, for it extended to the side for twenty feet, then turned and continued for another few yards, whereupon it ended at a corridor studded with empty sconces. Down the corridor was another small room lined with three arches, each of which led to rooms with even more archways, and so on.

Who built these and why? Eragon wondered, bewildered. All the rooms they saw were deserted and empty of furnishings. The only things they found within were a two-legged stool that fell apart when he nudged it with the tip of his boot and a pile of broken pottery lying in a corner beneath a veil of spiderwebs.

Angela never hesitated or seemed confused about which direction to go, for without fail, she chose the path to the right. Eragon would have objected, except that he could think of no better alternative to her method.

The herbalist stopped when they arrived at a circular room with seven equally spaced archways placed along the walls. Seven corridors, including the one they had just traversed, stretched out from the archways.

"Mark where we came from, or we'll get completely turned around," said Arya.

Eragon went to the corridor and, with the tip of Brisingr's crossguard, scratched a line on the stone wall. As he did, he peered into the darkness, searching for a glimpse of Solembum, but he saw not so much as a whisker. Eragon hoped the werecat had not gotten lost somewhere in the maze of rooms. He almost reached out with his mind to find him, but resisted the urge; if anyone else felt him groping around, it might alert the Empire to their location.

"Ah!" exclaimed Angela, and the shadows around Eragon shifted as the herbalist stood on tiptoe and raised her werelight as high as she could.

Eragon hurried to the center of the room, where she stood with Arya and Wyrden. "What is it?" he whispered.

"The ceiling, Eragon," murmured Arya. "Look at the ceiling."

He did as he was told, but saw only blocks of ancient, mold-covered stones crazed with so many cracks, it seemed amazing the ceiling had not collapsed long ago.

Then his vision shifted and he gasped.

The lines were not cracks but rather deeply carved runes—rows of them. They were neat and small, with sharp angles and straight stems. Mold and the passage of centuries had obscured parts of the text, but most of it remained legible.

Eragon struggled with the runes for a short while, but he recognized only a few of the words, and those were spelled differently than he was used to. "What does it say?" he asked. "Is it Dwarvish?"

"No," said Wyrden. "It is the language of your people, but as it was spoken and written long ago, and of a very particular dialect: that of the zealot Tosk."

The name struck a chord in Eragon. "When Roran and I rescued Katrina, we heard the priests of Helgrind mention a book of Tosk."

Wyrden nodded. "It serves as the foundation of their faith. Tosk was not the first to offer up prayers to Helgrind, but he was the first to codify his beliefs and practices, and many others have imitated him since. Those who worship Helgrind regard him as a prophet of the divine. And *this*"—the elf cast his arms out wide—"is a history of Tosk, from his birth to his death: a true history, such as his disciples have never shared with those outside their sect."

"We could learn much from this," said Angela, never taking her eyes off the ceiling. "If only we had the time . . ." Eragon was surprised to see her so enthralled.

Arya glanced at the seven corridors. "A moment, then, but read quickly."

While Angela and Wyrden perused the runes with avid intensity, Arya walked over to one of the archways and, in an undertone, began to chant a spell for finding and locating. When she finished, she waited a moment with her head cocked, then moved on to the next archway.

Eragon stared at the runes a bit longer. Then he returned to the mouth of the corridor that had brought them to the room and leaned against a wall while he waited. The cold of the stones seeped into his shoulder.

Arya stopped in front of the fourth archway. The now-familiar cadence of her recitation rose and fell like a soft sigh of wind.

Again, nothing.

A faint tickling on the back of his right hand caused Eragon to look down. A huge, wingless cricket clung to his glove. The insect was hideous: black and bulbous, with barbed legs and a massive, skull-like head. Its carapace gleamed like oil.

Eragon shuddered, his skin crawling, and shook his arm, flinging the cricket into the darkness.

It landed with an audible *thump*.

The fifth corridor proved no more fruitful for Arya than the preceding four. She bypassed the opening where Eragon stood and stationed herself in front of the seventh archway.

Before she could cast her spell, a guttural yowl echoed down the corridors, seemingly from all directions at once; then there was a hiss and a spat and a screech that made every hair on Eragon's body stand on end.

Angela whirled around. "Solembum!"

As one, the four of them drew their blades.

Eragon backed into the center of the room, his gaze darting from one archway to the next. His gedwëy ignasia itched and tingled like a fleabite—a useless warning, for it did not tell him where or what the danger was.

"This way," said Arya, moving toward the seventh archway.

The herbalist refused to budge. "No!" she whispered vehemently. "We have to help him." Eragon noticed that she held a short sword with a strange colorless blade that flashed gemlike in the light.

Arya scowled. "If Murtagh learns we're here, we'll—"

It happened so quickly and silently, Eragon would never have noticed had he not been looking in the right direction: a half-dozen doors hidden within the walls of three different corridors swung open, and thirty or so black-garbed men ran out toward them, swords in hand.

"Letta!" shouted Wyrden, and the men in one group collided with each other as if those in front had run headlong into a wall.

Then the rest of the attackers fell upon them, and there was no time for magic. Eragon easily parried a stab, and with a looping backhanded stroke, sliced off the attacker's head. Like all the others, the man wore a kerchief tied over his face, so only his eyes were exposed, and the kerchief fluttered as the head fell spinning toward the floor.

Eragon was relieved when he felt Brisingr sink into flesh and blood. For a moment, he had feared that their opponents were protected by spells or armor—or, worse, that they were something other than human.

He skewered another man through the ribs and had just turned to deal with two more of his attackers when a sword that should not have been there arced through the air toward his throat. His wards saved him from certain death, yet with the blade an inch away from his neck, Eragon could not help but stumble back.

To his astonishment, the man he had stabbed was still standing, blood streaming down his side, seemingly oblivious to the hole Eragon had poked through him.

Dread settled over Eragon. "They can't feel pain," he shouted, even as he frantically blocked swords from three different directions. If anyone heard him, they failed to respond.

He wasted no more time talking, but concentrated on fighting the men in front of him, trusting his companions to protect his back.

Eragon lunged and parried and dodged, whipping Brisingr through the air as if it weighed no more than a switch. Ordinarily, he could have killed any of the men in an instant, but the fact that they were impervious to pain meant that he had to either behead them, stab them through the heart, or cut them and hold them off until loss of blood rendered them unconscious. Otherwise, the attackers kept trying to kill him, regardless of their injuries. The number of men made it difficult to evade all of their blows and strike back in return. He could have stopped defending himself and just let his wards protect him, but that would tire him just as quickly as swinging Brisingr. And since he could not predict exactly when his wards would fail—as they must at a certain point, else they would kill him—and he knew he might need them later on, he fought just as carefully and cautiously as if he were facing men whose swords could kill or maim with a single stroke.

More black-garbed warriors streamed out of the hidden doorways within the corridors. They crowded around Eragon, pushing him back through sheer weight of numbers. Hands clung to his legs and arms, threatening to immobilize him.

"Kverst," he growled under his breath, uttering one of the twelve death words Oromis had taught him. As he had suspected, his spell had no effect: the men were warded against direct magical attacks. He quickly readied a spell Murtagh had once used on him: "Thrysta vindr!" It was a roundabout way of striking at the men, as he was not actually hitting them but rather pushing the air against them. In any case, it worked.

A howl of wind filled the chamber, clawing at Eragon's hair and cloak and sending the men closest to him flying back into their compatriots, clearing a space of ten feet in front of him. His strength decreased commensurately, but not enough to incapacitate him.

He turned to see how the others were doing. He had not been the first to find a way to circumvent the men's wards; bolts of lightning extended from Wyrden's right arm and wrapped themselves around any warrior unfortunate enough to pass in front of him. The glowing cables of energy appeared almost liquid as they writhed around their victims.

Still more men were forcing their way into the room, however.

"This way!" cried Arya, and sprang toward the seventh corridor—the one she had failed to examine before the ambush.

Wyrden followed, as did Eragon. Angela brought up the rear, limping and clutching at a bloody cut on her shoulder. Behind them, the black-garbed men hesitated, milling in the chamber for a moment. Then, with a mighty roar, they gave chase.

As he sprinted down the corridor, Eragon strove to compose a variation of his earlier spell that would allow him to kill the men instead of just knocking them away. He quickly devised one and held it in readiness to use as soon as he could see a fair number of the attackers.

Who are they? he wondered. *How many of them are there?*

Up ahead, he glimpsed an opening through which shone a faint purplish light. He just had time to feel apprehensive about its source before the herbalist uttered a loud cry, and there was a dull orange flash and a teeth-jarring *thud*, and the smell of sulfur filled the air.

Eragon whirled around to see five men dragging the herbalist through a doorway that had opened in the side of the corridor. "No!" yelled Eragon, but before he could stop it, the door swung shut as silently as it had opened, and the wall appeared perfectly solid once more.

"Brisingr!" he shouted, and his sword erupted in flame. He placed the tip against the wall and attempted to push it through the stone, intending to cut open the door. The stone was thick, though, and slow to melt, and he soon realized it would take far more energy than he was willing to sacrifice.

Then Arya appeared beside him, and she placed a hand where the door was and murmured, "Ládrin." *Open.* The door remained stubbornly closed, but Eragon was embarrassed he had not thought to try that first.

Their pursuers were so close by now that he and Arya had no choice but to turn and face them. Eragon wanted to cast the spell he had invented, but the corridor was only wide enough for two men to approach at a time; he would not be able to kill the rest, as they were hidden from sight. Better to keep the spell a secret, he decided, and save it for when he could wipe out most of the warriors at once.

He and Arya beheaded the two lead men, then attacked the next pair of warriors as they stepped over the bodies. In quick succession, they killed six more men, but there seemed to be no end of them.

"Through here!" shouted Wyrden.

"Stenr slauta!" exclaimed Arya, and all along the corridor—up to a few yards from where she stood—the stones in the walls exploded into the passageway. The hail of sharp fragments caused the black-clad men to cower and falter, and more than one fell to the floor, crippled.

Together Eragon and Arya turned to follow Wyrden, who was running toward the opening at the end of the corridor. The elf was only thirty feet away from it.

Then ten . . .

Then five . . .

And then a thicket of amethyst spikes shot out of holes in the floor and the ceiling, catching Wyrden between them. The elf seemed to float in the middle of the corridor, the spikes less than an inch away from his skin as his wards repelled the crystal thorns. Then a crackling discharge of energy ran the length of each spike and the needle-sharp tips flared painfully bright, and with an unpleasant *crunch*, they slid home.

Wyrden screamed and thrashed, and then his werelight went out and he moved no more.

Eragon stared with disbelief as he stumbled to a stop before the spikes. For all his experience in battle, he had never before been present at the death of an elf. Wyrden and Blödhgarm and the rest of their cohort were so accomplished, Eragon had believed that the only way they were likely to die was while fighting either Galbatorix or Murtagh.

Arya appeared equally stunned. She rallied quickly, however. "Eragon," she said in an urgent voice, "cut us a path with Brisingr."

He understood. His sword, unlike hers, would be impervious to whatever evil magic the spikes contained.

He drew back his arm and swung as hard as he could. A half-dozen of the spikes shattered beneath Brisingr's adamantine edge. The amethyst emitted a bell-like tone as it broke, and when the shards struck the ground, they tinkled like ice.

Eragon kept to the right of the corridor, making sure not to hit the blood-streaked spikes that held up Wyrden's body. Again and again he swung, hacking his way through the glittering thicket. With every blow, he sent pieces of amethyst flying through the air. One sliced his left cheek, and he winced, surprised and concerned that his wards had failed.

The jagged remnants of the broken spikes forced him to move carefully. The stumps below could easily pierce his boots, while the ones above threatened to cut him about the head and neck. Still, he managed to navigate to the far side of the thicket with only a small gash on his right calf, which stung whenever he put his weight on the leg.

The black-clad warriors nearly caught up with them as he helped Arya past the last few rows of spikes. Once she was free, they rushed through the opening and into the purplish light, Eragon with every intention of then turning around and confronting their attackers head-on and killing every last one of them in retaliation for Wyrden's death.

On the other side of the opening was a dark, heavily built chamber that reminded Eragon of the caves under Tronjheim. A huge circular pattern of inlaid stone—marble and chalcedony and polished hematite—occupied the center of the floor. Around the edge of the patterned disk stood rough, fist-sized chunks of amethyst set within silver collars. Each piece of the purple rock glowed softly—the source of the light they had seen from the corridor. Across the disk, against the far wall, was a large black altar draped with a gold and crimson cloth. Pillars and candelabra flanked the altar, with a closed door on each side.

All this Eragon saw as he barreled into the room, in the brief instant before he realized that his momentum was going to carry him through the ring of amethysts and onto the disk. He tried to stop himself, tried to turn aside, but he was moving too fast.

Desperate, he did the one thing he could: he jumped toward the altar, hoping he could clear the disk in a single bound.

As he sailed over the nearest of the amethyst stones, his last feeling was regret, and his last thought was of Saphira.

TO FEED A GOD

The first thing Eragon noticed was the difference in the colors. The stone blocks in the ceiling appeared richer than before. Details that had been obscure now seemed sharp and vivid, while others that had been prominent were subdued. Below him, the sumptuous nature of the patterned disk was even more apparent.

It took him a moment to understand the reason for the change: Arya's red werelight no longer illuminated the chamber. Instead, what light there was came from the muted glow of the crystals and the lit candles in the candelabra.

Only then did he realize that something was crammed into his mouth, stretching his jaw painfully wide, and that he was hanging by his wrists from a chain mounted in the ceiling. He tried to move and found that his ankles were shackled and secured to a metal loop in the floor.

As he twisted in place, he saw Arya next to him, trussed and suspended in the same manner. Like him, she was gagged with a ball of cloth in her mouth and a rag tied around her head to hold it in place.

She was already awake and watching him, and he saw she was relieved at his return to consciousness.

Why hasn't she escaped already? he wondered. Then: *What happened?* His thoughts felt thick and slow, as if he were drunk with exhaustion.

He looked down and saw that he had been stripped of his weapons and armor; he was clad only in his leggings. The belt of Beloth the Wise was gone, as was the necklace the dwarves had given him that prevented anyone from scrying him.

Looking up, he saw that the elf ring Aren was missing from his hand.

A touch of panic gripped him. Then he reassured himself with the knowledge that he was not helpless, not so long as he could work magic. Because of the cloth in his mouth, he would have to cast a spell without uttering it aloud, which was somewhat more dangerous than the normal method—for if his thoughts strayed during the process, he might accidentally select the wrong words—but not so dangerous as casting a spell without any use of the ancient language at all, which was perilous indeed. In any event, it would take only a small amount of energy for him to free himself, and he was confident he could do it without too much trouble.

He closed his eyes and gathered his resources in preparation. As he did, he heard Arya rattling her chain and making muffled noises.

Glancing over, he saw her shaking her head at him. He raised his eyebrows in a wordless inquiry: *what is it?* But she was unable to do anything more than grunt and continue to shake her head.

Frustrated, Eragon cautiously pushed out his mind toward her—alert for the slightest hint of intrusion from anyone else—but to his alarm, he felt only a soft, indistinct pressure surrounding him, as if bales of wool were packed around his mind.

Panic began to well up inside of him again, despite his efforts to control it.

He was not drugged. Of that, he was sure. But he did not know what else besides a drug could prevent him from touching Arya's mind. If it was magic, it was magic unlike any he was familiar with.

He and Arya stared at each other for a moment; then a stir of motion drew Eragon's eye upward and he saw lines of blood running down her forearms from where the manacles around her wrists had scraped away the skin.

Rage engulfed him. He grabbed the chain above him and yanked on it as hard as he could. The links held, but he refused to give up. In a frenzy of anger, he pulled on it again and again, without regard for the harm he was causing himself.

At last he stopped and hung limply while hot blood dripped from his wrists onto the back of his neck and shoulders.

Determined to escape, he delved into the flow of energy within his body and, directing the spell at his shackles, he mentally shouted, *Kverst malmr du huildrs edtha, mar fröma né thön eka threyja!*

He screamed into his gag as every nerve in his body seared with pain. Unable to maintain his concentration, he lost his grip on the spell, and the enchantment ended.

The pain vanished at once, but it left him devoid of breath, with his heart pounding as heavily as if he had just jumped off a cliff. The experience was similar to the seizures he had suffered before the dragons healed the scar on his back during the Agaetí Blödhren.

As he slowly recovered, he saw Arya gazing at him with a concerned expression. *She must have tried a spell herself.* Then: *How could this have happened?* The two of them bound and helpless, Wyrden dead, the herbalist captured or slain, and Solembum most likely lying hurt somewhere in the underground maze, if the black-clad warriors had not already killed the werecat. Eragon could not understand it. He, Arya, Wyrden, and Angela had been as capable and dangerous a group as any in Alagaësia. And yet they had failed, and he and Arya were at the mercy of their enemies.

If we can't escape . . . He shied away from the thought; it did not bear dwelling on. More than anything, he wished he could contact Saphira, if only to be assured that she was still safe and to take comfort in her companionship. Though Arya was with him, he felt incredibly alone, and that unnerved him most of all.

Despite the agony in his wrists, he resumed pulling on the chain, convinced that if he just kept at it long enough, he could work it loose from the ceiling. He tried twisting it, thinking it would be easier to break that way, but the fetters around his ankles kept him from turning very far to either side.

The sores on his wrist eventually forced him to stop. They burned like fire, and he was afraid he might end up cutting into muscle if he continued. Also, he worried he might lose too much blood, as the sores were already bleeding heavily, and he did not know how long he and Arya would have to hang there, waiting.

It was impossible to tell what time it was, but he guessed that they had been captives for only a few hours at the most, given that he did not feel the need to eat, drink, or relieve himself. That would change, though, and then their discomfort would only increase.

The pain in Eragon's wrists made every minute seem unbearably long. Occasionally, he and Arya would stare at each other and try to communicate, but their efforts always failed. Twice his sores crusted over enough that he risked yanking on the chain again, but to no avail. For the most part, he and Arya *endured*.

Then, when Eragon had begun to wonder if anyone was ever going to come, he heard the *clang* of iron bells from somewhere in the tunnels and passageways, and the doors on either side of the black altar swung open on silent hinges. Eragon's muscles tensed in anticipation. He fixed his eyes on the openings, as did Arya.

A seemingly endless minute passed.

With a brash, jarring toll, the bells sounded again, filling the chamber with a swarm of angry echoes. Through the doorways marched three novitiates: young men garbed in golden cloth, each carrying a metal frame hung with bells. Behind them followed twenty-four men and women, not one of whom possessed a full set of limbs. Unlike their predecessors, the cripples wore robes of dark leather, tailored to match their individual infirmities. And last of all, six oiled slaves carried in a bier, upon which, propped upright, rested an armless, legless, toothless, seemingly sexless figure: the High Priest of Helgrind. From its head rose a three-foot-high crest, which only made the creature appear even more misshapen.

The priests and novitiates positioned themselves around the edge of the patterned disk on the floor, while the slaves gently lowered the bier onto the altar at the head of the room. Then the three perfect, handsome young men shook the bells once more, creating a discordant crash, and the leather-clad priests chanted a short phrase so quickly that Eragon was not sure what they said, though it had the sound of ritual. Amongst the crush of words, he caught the names of the three peaks of Helgrind: Gorm, Ilda, and Fell Angvara.

The High Priest gazed at him and Arya with eyes like chips of obsidian. "Welcome to the halls of Tosk," it said, and its withered mouth distorted the words. "Twice now you have invaded our inner sanctums, Dragon Rider. You shall not have the opportunity to do so again. . . . Galbatorix would have us spare your lives and send you to Urû'baen. He believes he can force you to serve him. He dreams of resurrecting the Riders and restoring the race of dragons. I say his dreams are folly. You are too dangerous, and we do not want to see the dragons resurgent. It is commonly believed that we worship Helgrind. That is a lie we tell others to conceal the true nature of our religion. It is not Helgrind that we revere—it is the Old Ones who made their lair within and to whom we sacrificed our flesh and blood. The Ra'zac are our gods, Dragon Rider—the Ra'zac and the Lethrblaka."

Dread crept through Eragon like a sickness.

The High Priest spat at him, and spittle drooled from its slack lower lip. "There is no torture horrible enough for your crime, Rider. You killed our gods, you and that accursed dragon of yours. For that, you must die."

Eragon struggled against his bonds and tried to shout through his gag. If he could talk, he could stall for time by telling them what the Ra'zac's last words had been, perhaps, or by threatening them with Saphira's vengeance. But their captors showed no inclination to remove his gag.

In a hideous gesture, the High Priest smiled, showing its gray gums. "You will never escape, Rider. The crystals here were enchanted to trap any who might try to desecrate our temple or steal our treasures, even one such as you. Nor is there anyone to rescue you. Two of your companions are dead—yes, even that meddlesome witch—and Murtagh knows nothing of your presence here. Today is the day of your doom, Eragon *Shadeslayer*." Then the High Priest tilted back its head and uttered a gruesome, gurgling whistle.

From the dark doorway to the left of the altar, there appeared four bare-chested slaves. On their shoulders, they bore a platform with two large, shallow, cuplike protrusions in the middle. Within the protrusions lay a pair of oval objects, each about a foot and a half long and half a foot thick. The objects were blue black and pitted like sandstone.

Time seemed to slow for Eragon. *They can't be . . . ,* he thought. Saphira's egg had been smooth, however, and veined like marble. Whatever these objects were, they were not dragon eggs. The alternatives frightened him even more.

"Since you killed the Old Ones," said the High Priest, "it is only fitting that you provide the food for their rebirth. You do not deserve such a great honor, but it will please the Old Ones, and in all things we strive to satisfy their desires. We are their faithful servants, and they our masters cruel and implacable: the three-faced god—the hunters of men, the eaters of flesh, and the drinkers of blood. To them, we offer up our bodies in hope of revelation into the mysteries of this life and in hope of absolution for our transgressions. As Tosk wrote, so shall it be."

In unison, the leather-clad priests repeated: "As Tosk wrote, so shall it be."

The High Priest nodded. "The Old Ones have always nested on Helgrind, but in the time of my grandfather's father, Galbatorix stole their eggs and killed their young, and he forced them to swear fealty to him lest he eradicate their line entirely. He hollowed out the caves and tunnels they have used ever since, and to us, to their devoted acolytes, he gave charge of their eggs—to watch and to hold and to care for until they were needed. This we have done, and none may fault us for our service.

"But we pray that someday Galbatorix shall be overthrown, for none should bind the Old Ones to their will. It is an abomination." The deformed creature licked its lips, and to his disgust, Eragon saw that part of its tongue was missing: carved away by a knife. "You, too, we wish gone, Rider. The dragons were the Old Ones' greatest enemies. Without them, and without Galbatorix, there would be no one to stop the Old Ones from feasting where and how they will."

As the High Priest spoke, the four slaves bearing the platform walked forth and carefully lowered it from their shoulders onto the patterned disk, setting it down several paces in front of Eragon and Arya. Once they finished, they bowed their heads and retreated through the doorway from which they had come.

"Who could ask for anything more than to feed a god with the marrow of their bones?" asked the High Priest. "Rejoice, both of you, for today you receive the blessing of the Old Ones, and by your sacrifice, the record of your sins shall be washed clean and you shall enter the afterlife as pure as a newly born child."

Then the High Priest and its followers raised their faces toward the ceiling and began to intone a strange, oddly accented song that Eragon had trouble understanding. He wondered if it was in the dialect of Tosk. At times, he heard what he thought were words in the ancient language—mangled and misused, but still the ancient language.

When the grotesque congregation finished, ending with another chorus of "As Tosk wrote, so shall it be," the three novitiates shook the bells in an ecstasy of religious fervor, and the resulting clamor seemed loud enough to bring down the ceiling.

Still shaking the bells, the novitiates filed out of the room. The four-and-twenty lesser priests departed next, and then, bringing up the rear of the procession, their limbless master, transported upon its bier by the six oiled slaves.

The door closed behind them with an ominous *boom*, and Eragon heard a heavy bar fall into place on the other side.

He turned to look at Arya. The expression in her eyes was that of despair, and he knew she had no more idea of how to escape than he did.

He gazed upward again and pulled on the chain that held him, using as much of his strength as he dared. The sores on his wrists again tore open, and they sprinkled him with drops of blood.

In front of them, the leftmost egg began to rock back and forth ever so slightly, and from it came a faint tapping, like the rapping of a tiny hammer.

A profound sense of horror suffused Eragon. Of all the ways he could imagine dying, being eaten alive by a Ra'zac was by far the worst. He yanked on the chain with renewed determination, biting his gag to help him withstand the agony in his arms. The resulting pain caused his vision to flicker.

Next to him, Arya thrashed and twisted as well, both of them fighting in deadly silence to free themselves.

And still the *tap-tap-tap*ping continued on the blue-black shell.

It's no use, Eragon realized. The chain would not give. As soon as he accepted the fact, it became obvious that it would be impossible to avoid being hurt far worse than he already was. The only question was whether his injuries would be forced upon him or whether they would be of his own choosing. *If nothing else, I have to save Arya.*

He studied the iron bands around his wrists. *If I can break my thumbs, I might be able to pull my hands out. Then at least I could fight. Maybe I could grab a piece of the Ra'zac's shell and use it as a knife.* With something to cut, he could free his legs as well, though the thought was so terrifying, he ignored it for the time being. *All I would have to do is crawl out of the circle of stones.* He would be able to use magic then, and he could stop the pain and the bleeding. What he was considering would only take a few minutes, but he knew they would be the longest minutes of his life.

He drew in a breath in preparation. *Left hand first.*

Before he could start, Arya screamed.

He spun toward her and uttered a wordless exclamation as he saw the mangled fingers of her right hand. Her skin was pushed up like a glove toward her nails, and the white of bone showed amid crimson muscle. Arya sagged and appeared to lose consciousness for a moment; then she recovered and pulled on her arm once more. Eragon cried out with her as her hand slid through the metal cuff, tearing off skin and flesh. Her arm fell to her side, hiding the hand from his sight, though he could see the blood splattering on the floor by her feet.

Tears blurred his eyes, and he shouted her name into his gag, but she seemed not to hear him.

As she braced herself to repeat the process, the door to the right of the altar opened, and one of the golden-robed novitiates slipped into the chamber. Seeing him, Arya hesitated, though Eragon knew she would pull her other hand out of the manacle at the slightest hint of danger.

The young man looked askance at Arya, then cautiously made his way to the center of the patterned disk, casting apprehensive glances at the egg that was rocking back and forth. The youth was slight, with large eyes and delicate features; it seemed obvious to Eragon that he had been chosen for his position because of his appearance.

"Here," whispered the youth. "I brought these." From within his robes, he produced a file, a chisel, and a wooden mallet. "If I help, you have to take me with you. I can't stand it here any longer. I hate it. It's horrible! Promise you'll take me with you!"

Even before he finished speaking, Eragon was nodding his assent. As the young man started toward him, though, Eragon growled and motioned with his head in Arya's direction. It took a few seconds before the novitiate understood.

"Oh, yes," murmured the young man, and went over to Arya instead. Eragon ground his teeth through the gag in anger over the youth's slowness.

The harsh scrape of the file soon drowned out the tapping from within the wobbling egg.

Eragon watched as best he could while their would-be rescuer sawed on a section of chain above Arya's left hand. *Keep the file on the same link, you fool!* Eragon raged. The novitiate looked as if he had never used a file before, and Eragon doubted that the youth had the strength or endurance to cut through even a small amount of metal.

Arya hung limply while the novitiate worked, her long hair covering her face. She trembled at regular intervals, and the fall of blood from her ruined hand continued unabated.

To Eragon's dismay, the file did not seem to be leaving a mark on the chain. Whatever magics protected the metal, they were too strong for something as simple as a file to overcome.

The novitiate huffed, appearing petulant at his lack of progress. He paused and wiped his brow, then, frowning, attacked the chain once again, elbows flailing, chest heaving, the sleeves of his robe flapping wildly.

Don't you realize it's not going to work? thought Eragon. *Try the chisel on the shackles around her ankles instead.*

The young man continued as he was.

A sharp *crack* echoed through the chamber, and Eragon saw a thin fissure appear at the top of the dark, pitted egg. The fissure lengthened, and a web of hairline fractures spread outward from it.

Then the second egg began to wobble as well, and from it came another *tap-tap-tap*ping, which joined with the first to form a maddening rhythm.

The novitiate went pale, then dropped the file and backed away from Arya, shaking his head. "I'm sorry. . . . I'm sorry. It's too late." His face crumpled, and tears rolled from his eyes. "I'm sorry."

Eragon's alarm increased as the young man pulled a dagger from within his robes. "There's nothing else I can do," he said, almost as if he were speaking to himself. "Nothing else . . ." He sniffed and moved toward Eragon. "It's for the best."

As the young man stepped forward, Eragon wrenched at his bonds, trying to pull one of his hands out of the manacles. The iron cuffs were too tight, however, and all he succeeded in doing was scraping more of the skin off his wrists.

"I'm sorry," whispered the young man as he stopped in front of Eragon and drew back the dagger.

No! Eragon shouted in his mind.

A chunk of glittering amethyst hurtled out of the tunnel that had brought Eragon and Arya to the chamber. It struck the novitiate in the back of the head, and he fell against Eragon. Eragon flinched as he felt the edge of the dagger slide across his ribs. Then the young man tumbled to the floor and lay there, unconscious.

From within the depths of the tunnel emerged a small, limping figure. Eragon stared, and as the figure moved into the light, he saw that it was none other than Solembum.

Relief swept through Eragon.

The werecat was in his human form, and he was naked except for a ragged loincloth that looked as if it had been torn from the clothes of their attackers. His spiky black hair stood nearly on end, and a feral snarl disfigured his lips. Several cuts covered his forearms, his left ear hung drooping from the side of his head, and a strip of skin was missing from his scalp. He carried a blood-smeared knife.

And following a few paces behind the werecat was the herbalist, Angela.

INFIDELS ON THE LOOSE

"**W**hat an idiot," proclaimed Angela as she hurried to the edge of the patterned disk on the floor. She was bleeding from a number of cuts and scratches, and her clothes were stained with even more blood, which Eragon suspected was not her own. Otherwise, she appeared unharmed. "All he had to do was—*this*!"

And she swung her sword with its transparent blade up and over her head, and brought the pommel down against one of the amethysts that ringed the disk. The crystal shattered with an odd *snap*, like a shock of static, and the light it emitted flickered and went out. The other crystals maintained their radiance.

Without pause, Angela stepped to the next piece of amethyst and broke it as well, then the one after it, and so on.

Never in his life had Eragon been so grateful to see anyone.

He alternated between watching the herbalist and watching the cracks widening at the top of the first egg. The Ra'zac had almost pecked its way out, a fact it seemed to be aware of, for it was squeaking and tapping with increased vigor. Between the pieces of shell, Eragon saw a thick white membrane and the beaked head of the Ra'zac pushing blindly against it, horrible and monstrous.

Hurry, hurry, Eragon thought as a fragment as large as his hand fell from the egg and clattered against the floor, like a plate made of fired clay.

The membrane tore, and the young Ra'zac stuck its head out of the egg, revealing its barbed purple tongue as it uttered a triumphant screech. Slime dripped from its carapace, and a fungus-like smell pervaded the chamber.

Eragon tugged at his bonds once more, futile as it was.

The Ra'zac screeched again, then struggled to extricate itself from the remainder of the egg. It pulled one clawed arm free, but in the process it unbalanced the egg, which tipped to one side, spilling a thick, yellowish fluid across the patterned disk. The grotesque hatchling lay on its side for a moment, stunned. Then it stirred and got to its feet, where it stood, swaying and uncertain, clicking to itself like an agitated insect.

Eragon stared, appalled and terrified, but also fascinated.

The Ra'zac had a deep, ridged chest that made it look as if its ribs were on the outside of its body, not the inside. The creature's limbs were thin and knobby, like sticks, and its waist was narrower than any human's. Each leg had an extra backward-bending joint, something that Eragon had never seen before, but which accounted for the Ra'zac's unsettling gait. Its carapace appeared soft and malleable, unlike those of the more mature Ra'zac Eragon had encountered. No doubt it would harden in time.

The Ra'zac tilted its head—its huge, protruding, pupil-less eyes catching the light—and it chittered as if it had just discovered something exciting. Then it took a tentative step toward Arya . . . and another . . . and then another, its beak parting as it strained toward the pool of blood by her feet.

Eragon shouted into his gag, hoping to distract the creature, but other than a quick glance, it ignored him.

"*Now!*" exclaimed Angela, and she broke the last of the crystals.

Even as the shards of amethyst skittered across the floor, Solembum leaped toward the Ra'zac. The werecat's form blurred in midair—head shrinking, legs shortening, fur sprouting—and he landed on all fours, his body once more that of an animal.

The Ra'zac hissed and clawed at Solembum, but the werecat dodged the blow and, faster than the eye could follow, slapped the Ra'zac's head with one of his large, heavy paws.

The Ra'zac's neck broke with a *crack*, and the creature flew across the room and landed in a twisted heap, where it lay twitching for several seconds.

Solembum hissed, his one uninjured ear pressed flat against his skull; then he wriggled out of the loincloth that was still tied around his hips and went over to sit and wait by the other egg.

"What *have* you done to yourself?" said Angela as she hurried over to Arya. Arya wearily lifted her head, but she made no attempt to answer.

With three swift strokes of her colorless blade, the herbalist sliced through Arya's remaining cuffs, as if the tempered metal were no harder than cheese.

Arya fell to her knees and doubled over, pressing her injured hand against her stomach. With her other hand, she tore at her gag.

The burning in Eragon's shoulders eased when Angela cut him free and he was finally able to lower his arms. He pulled the cloth out of his mouth and, in a hoarse voice, said, "We thought you were dead."

"They'll have to try harder than that if they want to kill me. Bunglers, the lot of them."

Still doubled over, Arya began to chant spells of binding and healing. Her words were soft and strained, but she never faltered or misspoke.

While she worked to repair the damage to her hand, Eragon healed the cut on his ribs as well as the sores on his wrists. Then he motioned at Solembum and said, "Move."

The werecat flicked his tail but did as Eragon asked.

Lifting his right hand, Eragon said, "Brisingr!"

A pillar of blue flame erupted around the second egg. The creature inside screamed: a terrible, unearthly sound, more like the screech of tearing metal than the cry of person or beast.

Narrowing his eyes against the heat, Eragon watched with satisfaction as the egg burned. *And let that be the last of them*, he thought. When the screaming ceased, he extinguished the flame, and it went out from the bottom up. The silence afterward was unexpectedly complete, for Arya had finished her incantations and all was still.

Angela was the first to stir. She went to Solembum and stood over him, murmuring in the ancient language as she mended his ear and other wounds.

Eragon knelt by Arya and put a hand on her shoulder. She looked up at him, then uncurled her body enough to show him her hand. The skin along the lower third of her thumb, as well as along the outer edge of her palm and across the back of her hand, was shiny and bright red. However, the muscles underneath appeared sound.

"Why didn't you finish healing it?" he asked. "If you're too tired, I can—"

She shook her head. "I damaged several nerves . . . and I can't seem to repair them. I need Blödhgarm's help; he is more skilled than I at manipulating flesh."

"Can you fight?"

"If I'm careful."

He tightened his grip on her shoulder for a moment. "What you did—"

"I only did what was logical."

"Most people wouldn't have had the strength. . . . I tried, but my hand was too big. See?" And he held up his hand against hers.

She nodded, then grasped his arm and slowly got to her feet. Eragon rose with her, providing her with a steady support.

"We have to find our weapons," he said, "as well as my ring, my belt, and the necklace the dwarves gave me."

Angela frowned. "Why your belt? Is it enchanted?"

When Eragon hesitated, unsure whether to tell her the truth, Arya said, "You would not know the name of its maker, wise one, but during your travels, you must surely have heard tell of the belt of the twelve stars."

The herbalist's eyes widened. "*That* belt?! But I thought it was lost over four centuries ago, destroyed during the—"

"We recovered it," said Arya flatly.

Eragon could see that the herbalist longed to ask more questions, but she merely said, "I see. . . . We can't waste time searching every room in this warren, though. Once the priests realize you've escaped, we'll have the whole pack of them nipping at our heels."

Eragon motioned toward the novitiate on the floor and said, "Maybe he can tell us where they took our things."

Dropping into a squat, the herbalist placed two fingers against the youth's jugular vein, feeling his pulse. Then she slapped his cheeks and peeled back his eyelids.

The novitiate remained slack and motionless.

His lack of response seemed to annoy the herbalist. "One moment," she said, closing her eyes. A slight frown creased her brow. For a while, she was still; then she sprang upward with sudden speed. "What a self-absorbed little wretch! No wonder his parents sent him to join the priests. I'm surprised they put up with him as long as they did."

"Does he know anything of use?" asked Eragon.

"Only the path to the surface." She pointed toward the door to the left of the altar, the same door through which the priests had entered and departed. "It's amazing that he tried to free you; I suspect it's the first time in his life he's ever done anything of his own accord."

"We have to bring him with us." Eragon hated to say it, but duty compelled him. "I promised we would if he helped us."

"He tried to kill you!"

"I gave my word."

Angela sighed and rolled her eyes. To Arya, she said, "I don't suppose you can convince him otherwise?"

Arya shook her head, then hoisted the young man onto her shoulder without apparent effort. "I'll carry him," she said.

"In that case," the herbalist said to Eragon, "you had best have this, since it seems you and I are to do most of the fighting." She handed him her short sword, then drew a poniard with a jeweled hilt from within the folds of her dress.

"What is it made of?" Eragon asked as he peered through the transparent blade of the sword, noticing how it caught and reflected the light. The substance reminded him of diamond, but he could not imagine that anyone would make a weapon out of a gemstone; the amount of energy required to keep the stone from breaking with every blow would soon exhaust any normal magician.

"Neither stone nor metal," said the herbalist. "A word of caution, though. You must take great care when handling it. Never touch the edge or allow anything you cherish to come near it, else you will regret it. Likewise, never lean the sword against something you might need—your leg, for example."

Wary, Eragon held the sword farther away from his body. "Why?"

"Because," said the herbalist with evident relish, "*this* is the sharpest blade in all of existence. No other sword or knife or ax can match the keenness of its edge, not even Brisingr. It is the ultimate embodiment of an incision-making instrument. *This*"—she paused for emphasis—"is the archetype of an inclined plane. . . . You'll not find its equal anywhere. It can cut through anything not protected by magic, and many things that are. Try it if you don't believe me."

Eragon looked around for something to test the sword against. In the end, he strode over to the altar and swung the blade at one corner of the stone slab.

"Not so quickly!" cried Angela.

The transparent blade passed through four inches of stone as if the granite were no harder than custard, then continued down toward his feet. Eragon yelped and jumped back, barely managing to stop his arm before he cut himself.

The corner of the altar bounced off the step below and then tumbled clacking toward the middle of the room.

The blade of the sword, Eragon realized, might very well be diamond after all. It would not need as much protection as he had assumed, since it would rarely meet with any substantial resistance.

"Here," said Angela. "You had better have this as well." She unbuckled the sword's scabbard and gave it to him. "It's one of the few things you *can't* cut with that blade."

It took Eragon a moment to find his voice after so nearly lopping off his toes. "Does the sword have a name?"

Angela laughed. "Of course. In the ancient language, its name is Albitr, which means exactly what you think. But I prefer to call it Tinkledeath."

"Tinkledeath!"

"Yes. Because of the sound the blade makes when you tap it." She demonstrated with the tip of a fingernail and smiled at the resulting high-pitched note that pierced the darkened chamber like a ray of sunshine. "Now then, shall we be off?"

Eragon checked to make sure they were not forgetting anything; then he nodded, strode to the left-hand door, and opened it as quietly as he could.

Through the doorway was a long, broad hallway lit by torches. And standing guard in two smart rows, one along each side of the hallway, were twenty of the black-garbed warriors who had ambushed them earlier.

They looked at Eragon and reached for their weapons.

A curse ran through Eragon's mind, and he sprang forward, intending to attack before the warriors could draw their swords and organize themselves into an effective group. He had only covered a few feet, however, when a flicker of movement appeared next to each man: a soft, shadowy blur, like the motion of a windblown pennant seen at the edge of his vision.

Without so much as a single cry, the twenty men stiffened and fell to the floor, dead, every last one of them.

Alarmed, Eragon slowed to a stop before he ran into the bodies. Each of the men had been stabbed through an eye, as neat as could be.

He turned to ask Arya and Angela if they knew what had happened, but the words died in his throat as he beheld the herbalist.

She stood braced against a wall, leaning on her knees and panting heavily. Her skin had gone deathly white, and her hands were shaking. Blood dripped from her poniard.

Awe and fear filled Eragon. Whatever the herbalist had done, it was beyond his understanding.

"Wise one," said Arya, and she too sounded uncertain, "how did you manage to do this?"

The herbalist chuckled between breaths, then said, "I used a trick . . . I learned from my master . . . Tenga . . . ages ago. May a thousand spiders bite his ears and knobbly bits."

"Yes, but *how* did you do it?" insisted Eragon. *A trick like that might be useful in Urû'baen.*

The herbalist chuckled again. "What is time but motion? And what is motion but heat? And are not heat and energy but different names for the same thing?" She pushed herself off the wall, walked over to Eragon, and patted him on the cheek. "When you understand the implications of that, you'll understand how and what I did. . . . I won't be able to use the spell again today, not without hurting myself, so don't expect me to kill everyone the next time we run into a batch of men."

With some difficulty, Eragon swallowed his curiosity and nodded.

He stripped a tunic and a padded jerkin off one of the fallen men, and after donning the clothes, he led the way down the hall and through the archway at the far end.

They encountered no one else in the complex of rooms and corridors thereafter, nor did they find any sign of their stolen possessions. Although Eragon was glad to avoid notice, the absence of even servants worried him. He hoped that he and his companions had not triggered alarms that had warned the priests of their escape.

Unlike the abandoned chambers they had seen before the ambush, those they passed through now were filled with tapestries, furniture, and strange devices made of brass and crystal, the purpose of which Eragon could not fathom. More than once, a desk or a bookcase tempted him to pause and inspect its contents, but he always resisted the urge. They did not have time to read musty old papers, no matter how intriguing.

Angela chose the path they took whenever there was more than one option, but Eragon remained in the lead, clutching the wire-wrapped hilt of Tinkledeath with a grip so hard, his hand began to cramp.

Soon enough, they arrived at a passageway ending in a flight of stone steps that narrowed as it rose. Two novitiates stood by the stairs, one on either side, each holding a rack of bells such as Eragon had seen earlier.

He ran at the two young men and managed to stab one novitiate through the neck before he could shout or ring his bells. The other, however, had time to do both before Solembum leaped on him and bore him to the ground, tearing at his face, and the whole of the passageway rang with the clamor.

"Hurry!" Eragon cried as he bounded up the stairs.

At the top of the steps was a freestanding wall some ten feet wide, covered with ornate scrollwork and carvings that seemed vaguely familiar to Eragon. He dodged around the wall and came out into a beam of rose-tinted light of such intensity that he faltered, confused. He lifted Tinkledeath's scabbard to shade his eyes.

Not five feet in front of him, the High Priest sat on its bier, blood dripping from a cut on its shoulder. Another of the priests— a woman missing both her hands—sat kneeling by the side of the bier, catching the fall of blood in a golden chalice that she held clamped between her forearms. Both she and the High Priest stared at Eragon with astonishment.

Then Eragon looked past them and saw, as if in a series of lightning flashes: Massive ribbed columns rising toward a vaulted ceiling that vanished into shadow. Stained-glass windows set within towering walls—the windows on the left burning with light from the rising sun; those on the right dull and flat, lifeless. Pale statues standing between the windows. Rows of granite pews, dappled with different colors, extending all the way to the far-off entrance to the nave. And, filling the first four rows, a flock of leather-garbed priests, their faces upturned and their mouths opened in song, like so many hatchlings begging for food.

He was, Eragon belatedly realized, standing in the great cathedral of Dras-Leona, on the other side of the altar he had once knelt before in reverence, long ago.

The handless woman dropped the chalice and stood, throwing her arms out wide as she shielded the High Priest with her body. Behind her, Eragon glimpsed the blue of Brisingr's sheath lying near the leading edge of the bier, and he thought he saw Aren next to it.

Before he could chase after his sword, two guards rushed toward him from either side of the altar, slashing at him with engraved, red-tasseled pikes. He sidestepped the first guard and sliced the shaft of the man's pike in half, sending the blade flying through the air. Then Eragon sliced the man himself in half; Tinkledeath passed through his flesh and bones with shocking ease.

Eragon dispatched the second guard just as quickly and turned to face a pair approaching from behind. The herbalist joined him, brandishing her poniard, and somewhere off to his left, Solembum growled. Arya hung back from the fighting, still carrying the young man.

The spilled blood from the chalice had coated the floor around the altar. The guards slipped in the puddle and the rear man fell and knocked his companion off his feet. Eragon shuffled toward them— never lifting his feet off the floor so as to avoid losing his balance— and before the guards could react, he slew them both, taking care to control the herbalist's enchanted blade as it effortlessly cut through the two men.

As he did, Eragon was aware that the High Priest was screaming, as if at a great distance, "Kill the infidels! Kill them! Don't let the blasphemers escape! They must be punished for their crimes against the Old Ones!"

The congregation of priests began to howl and stamp their feet, and Eragon felt their minds clawing at his, like a pack of wolves tearing at a weakened deer. He retreated deep within himself, warding off the attacks with techniques he had been practicing under Glaedr's tutelage. It was difficult to defend himself from so many foes, however, and he feared that he would not be able to maintain his barriers for long. His one advantage was that the panicked, disorganized priests attacked him as individuals, not as a unit; their combined might would have overwhelmed him.

Then Arya's consciousness was pressing against his—a familiar, comforting presence amid the clutch of enemies scrabbling against his inner self. Relieved, he opened himself to her, and they joined their minds, even as he and Saphira would do, and for a time their identities merged and he lost the ability to determine where many of their shared thoughts and feelings came from.

Together they stabbed with their minds at one of the priests. The man struggled to evade their grasp, like a fish wriggling through their fingers, but they tightened their grip and refused to let him escape. He was reciting a stilted, oddly worded phrase in an attempt to keep them out of his consciousness; Eragon assumed it was a scrap of scripture from the Book of Tosk.

The priest lacked discipline, however, and his concentration soon wavered as he thought, *The infidels are too close to Master. We have to kill them before— Wait! No! No . . . !*

Eragon and Arya seized upon the priest's weakness and quickly subjugated the man's thoughts to their will. Once they were certain he could not retaliate against them with mind or body, Arya cast a spell that, from examining the priest's memories, she knew could slip past his wards.

In the third row of pews, a man screamed and burst into flame, green fire pouring from his ears, mouth, and eyes. The flames ignited the clothes of several priests close to him, and the burning men and women began to thrash and run about wildly, further disrupting the attacks against Eragon. The rippling flames sounded like branches snapping in a storm.

The herbalist ran down from the altar and moved among the priests, stabbing here and there. Solembum followed close at her heels, finishing off those she felled.

After that, it was easy for Eragon and Arya to invade and seize control of their enemies' minds. Continuing to work together, they killed four more priests, at which point the rest of the congregation broke and scattered. Some fled through the vestibule that Eragon remembered led to the priory next to the cathedral, while others crouched behind the pews and wrapped their arms around their heads.

Six of the priests, however, neither fled nor hid, but rather charged Eragon, brandishing curved knives with what hands they still possessed. Eragon cut at the first priest before she could strike at him. To his annoyance, the woman was protected by a ward that stopped Tinkledeath half a foot from her neck, causing the sword to turn in his hand and a shock to run up his arm. With his left hand, Eragon swung at the woman. For whatever reason, the spell did not stop his fist, and he felt the bones in her chest give way as he knocked her sprawling into the people behind her.

The remaining priests extricated themselves and resumed their charge. Stepping forward, Eragon blocked a clumsy slash from the foremost priest; then—with a shout of "Ha!"—he drove his fist into the man's gut and sent him flying into a pew, which the priest struck with a nasty crack.

Eragon killed the next man in a similar manner. A green and yellow dart buried itself in the throat of the priest to his right, and there was a tawny blur as Solembum leaped past him and tackled another of the group.

That left but one of Tosk's followers standing before him. With her free hand, Arya grabbed the woman by the front of her leather robes and threw her screaming thirty feet over the pews.

Four novitiates had lifted up the High Priest's bier and were carrying it at a quick trot along the east side of the cathedral as they headed toward the front entrance of the building.

Seeing them escaping, Eragon uttered a roar and bounded onto the altar, knocking a plate and goblet to the floor. From there, he jumped out over the bodies of the fallen priests. He landed lightly in the aisle and sprinted to the end of the cathedral, heading off the novitiates.

The four young men stopped when they saw Eragon arrive at the doors. "Turn around!" shrieked the High Priest. "Turn around!" Its servants obeyed, only to be confronted by Arya standing behind them, one of their own slung over her right shoulder.

The novitiates yelped and turned sideways, darting between two rows of pews. Before they had gone more than a few feet, Solembum stepped around the end of the pews and began to pad toward them. The werecat's ears were pressed flat against his skull, and the constant low rumble of his growl made Eragon's neck prickle. Close behind him came Angela, striding down the cathedral from the altar, her poniard in one hand and a green and yellow dart in the other.

Eragon wondered how many weapons she had about herself.

To their credit, the novitiates did not lose their courage or abandon their master. Instead, the four shouted and ran even faster at Solembum, presumably because the werecat was the smallest and the closest of their opponents, and because they believed he would be the easiest to overcome.

They were mistaken.

In a single lithe movement, Solembum crouched, jumped from the floor to the top of a pew. Then, without stopping, he leaped toward one of the two lead novitiates.

As the werecat sailed through the air, the High Priest shouted something in the ancient language—Eragon did not recognize the word, but the sound of it was unmistakably that of the elves' native language. Whatever the spell was, it seemed to have no effect on Solembum, although Eragon saw Angela stumble as if she had been struck.

Solembum collided with the novitiate at whom he had flung

himself, and the young man tumbled to the floor, screaming as Solembum mauled him. The rest of the novitiates tripped over their companion's body, and the lot of them fell in a tangled heap, spilling the High Priest off its bier and onto one of the pews, where the creature lay squirming like a maggot.

Eragon caught up with them a second later, and with three swift strokes, he slew all of the novitiates, save the one whose neck Solembum held clamped between his jaws.

Once Eragon was sure the men were dead, he turned to strike down the High Priest once and for all. As he started toward the limbless figure, another mind invaded his, probing and grasping at the most intimate parts of his self, seeking to control his thoughts. The vicious attack forced Eragon to stop and concentrate on defending himself from the intruder.

Out of the corner of his eye, he saw that Arya and Solembum also appeared immobilized. The herbalist was the sole exception. She paused for a moment when the attack commenced, but then she continued to walk with slow, shuffling steps toward Eragon.

The High Priest stared at Eragon, its deep-set, dark-ringed eyes burning with hate and fury. If the creature had had arms and legs, Eragon was convinced that it would have tried to tear out his heart with its bare hands. As it was, the malevolence of its gaze was so intense, Eragon half expected the priest to wiggle off the pew and start biting at his ankles.

The assault on his mind intensified as Angela drew near. The High Priest—for it *had* to be the High Priest who was responsible— was far more skilled than any of its underlings. To engage in mental combat with four different people at once, and to present a credible threat to each of the four, was a remarkable feat, especially when the enemies were an elf, a Dragon Rider, a witch, and a werecat. The High Priest had one of the most formidable minds Eragon had ever encountered; if not for the help of his companions, Eragon suspected that he would have succumbed to the creature's onslaughts.

The priest did things the likes of which Eragon had never experienced before, such as binding Eragon's stray thoughts to Arya's and Solembum's, wrapping them into a knot of such confusion that for brief moments Eragon lost track of his own identity.

At last Angela turned in to the space between the pews. She picked her way around Solembum—who crouched next to the novitiate he had killed, every hair on his body standing on end—and then carefully made her way over the corpses of the three novitiates Eragon had slain.

As she approached, the High Priest began to thrash like a hooked fish in an attempt to push itself farther up the pew. At the same time, the pressure on Eragon's mind lessened, although not enough for him to risk moving.

The herbalist stopped when she reached the High Priest, and the High Priest surprised Eragon by giving up its struggle and lying panting on the seat of the bench. For a minute, the hollow-eyed creature and the short, stern-faced woman glared at each other, an invisible battle of wills taking place between them.

Then the High Priest flinched, and a smile appeared on Angela's lips. She dropped her poniard and, from within her dress, drew forth a tiny dagger with a blade the color of a ruddy sunset. Leaning over the High Priest, she whispered, ever so faintly, "You ought to know my name, tongueless one. If you had, you never would have dared oppose us. Here, let me tell it to you. . . ."

Her voice dropped even lower then, too low for Eragon to hear, but as she spoke, the High Priest blanched, and its puckered mouth opened, forming a round black oval, and an unearthly howl emanated from its throat, and the whole of the cathedral rang with the creature's baying.

"Oh, be quiet!" exclaimed the herbalist, and she buried her sunset-colored dagger in the center of the High Priest's chest.

The blade flashed white-hot and vanished with a sound like a far-off thunderclap. The area around the wound glowed like burning wood; then skin and flesh began to disintegrate into a fine, dark soot that poured into the High Priest's chest. With a choked gargle, the creature's howl ceased as abruptly as it had begun.

The spell quickly devoured the rest of the High Priest, reducing its body to a pile of black powder, the shape of which matched the outline of the priest's head and torso.

"And good riddance," said Angela with a firm nod.

THE TOLLING OF THE BELL

Eragon shook himself as if waking from a bad dream.

Now that he no longer had to fight off the High Priest, he gradually became aware that the priory bell was tolling—a loud, insistent sound that reminded him of when the Ra'zac had chased him from the cathedral during his first visit to Dras-Leona, with Brom.

Murtagh and Thorn will be here soon, he thought. *We have to leave before then.*

He sheathed Tinkledeath and handed it to Angela. "Here," he said, "I think you'll want this." Then he pulled the corpses of the novitiates aside until he uncovered Brisingr. As his hand closed around the hilt, a sense of relief swept through him. Though the herbalist's sword was a good and dangerous blade, it was not *his* weapon. Without Brisingr, he felt exposed, vulnerable—the same as he did whenever he and Saphira were apart.

It took him another few moments of searching to find his ring, which had rolled under one of the pews, and his necklace, which was wrapped around one of the handles of the bier. Among the pile of bodies, he also discovered Arya's sword, which she was pleased to recover. But of his belt, the belt of Beloth the Wise, there was no sign.

Eragon looked under all the nearby pews, and he even ran back to the altar and inspected the area around it.

"It's not here," he finally said, despairing. He turned toward the freestanding wall that hid the entrance to the underground chambers. "They must have left it in the tunnels." He cast his gaze in the direction of the priory. "Or maybe . . ." He hesitated, torn between the two options.

Muttering the words under his breath, he cast a spell designed to find and lead him to the belt, but the only result he received was an image of smooth gray emptiness. As he had feared, there were wards around the belt that protected it from magical observation or interference, just as similar wards protected Brisingr.

Eragon scowled and took a half step toward the freestanding wall. The bell tolled louder than ever.

"Eragon," called Arya from the other end of the cathedral, shifting the unconscious novitiate from one shoulder to the other. "We have to go."

"But—"

"Oromis would understand. It's not your fault."

"But—"

"Leave it! The belt has been lost before. We will find it again. But for now, we must fly. Hurry!"

Eragon cursed, spun around, and ran to join Arya, Angela, and Solembum at the front of the cathedral. *Of all the things to lose . . .* It seemed almost sacrilegious to abandon the belt when so many creatures had died to fill it with energy. Besides, he had a horrible feeling that he might have need of that energy before the day was out.

Even as he and the herbalist pushed open the heavy doors that led out of the cathedral, Eragon sent his mind questing for Saphira, who he knew would be circling high above the city, waiting for him to contact her. The time for discretion had long since passed, and Eragon no longer cared if Murtagh or some other magician sensed his presence.

He soon felt the familiar touch of Saphira's consciousness. As their thoughts melded together once again, a certain tightness in Eragon's chest vanished.

What took you so long? exclaimed Saphira. He could taste her worry, and he knew she had been considering descending upon Dras-Leona and tearing it to pieces in search of him.

He poured his memories into her, sharing everything that had happened to him since they parted. The process took a few seconds, by which time he, Arya, Angela, and the werecat had exited the cathedral and were running down the front steps.

Without pausing to give Saphira an opportunity to make sense of his jumbled recollections, Eragon said, *We need a distraction—now!*

She acknowledged his statement, and he could feel her tip into a steep dive.

Also, tell Nasuada to start her attack. We'll be at the south gate in a few minutes. If the Varden aren't there when we open it, I don't know how we're going to escape.

✦ ✦ ✦

BLACK-SHRIKE-THORN-CAVE

The cool, moist, morning-air-off-water whistled past Saphira's head as she dove toward the rat-nest-city half lit by the rising sun. The low rays of light made the smelly-wood-eggshell-buildings stand out in high relief, their western sides black with shadow.

The wolf-elf-in-Eragon's-shape who was riding on her back shouted something at her, but the hungry wind tore at his words, and she could not make out his meaning. He began to ask her questions with his song-filled-mind, but she did not wait to let him finish. Instead, she told him of Eragon's plight and asked him to alert Nasuada that now was the time for action.

How the shadow-of-Eragon that Blödhgarm wore was supposed to fool anyone, Saphira could not understand. He did not smell like her partner-of-heart-and-mind, nor did his thoughts feel like Eragon's. Still, the two-legs seemed impressed by the apparition, and it was two-legs they were trying to fool.

On the left side of the rat-nest-city, the glittering shape of Thorn lay stretched out along the battlements above the southern gate. He lifted his crimson head, and she could tell that he had spotted her hurtling toward the break-bone-ground, as she had expected. Her feelings toward Thorn were too complicated to sum up in a few brief impressions. Every time she thought of him, she became confused and uncertain, something she was unaccustomed to.

Nevertheless, she was not about to let the upstart whelp best her in battle.

As the dark chimneys and sharp-edged roofs grew larger, she spread her wings a bit more, feeling the increased strain in her chest, shoulders, and wing muscles as she began to slow their descent. When she was only a few hundred feet above the closely packed swell of buildings, she swooped upward and allowed her wings to snap out to their full extent. The effort required to stop her fall was immense; for a moment, it felt as if the wind might tear her wings free of their sockets.

She shifted her tail to maintain balance, then wheeled over the city until she located the black-shrike-thorn-cave where the blood-mad-priests worshipped. Tucking in her wings again, she dropped the last number of feet and, with a thunderous crash, landed on the middle of the cathedral's roof.

She dug her claws into the tiles of the roof to stop herself from sliding off into the street below. Then she threw back her head and roared as loudly as she could, challenging the world and everything in it.

There was a bell clanging in the tower of the building next to the black-shrike-thorn-cave. She found the noise irritating, so she twisted her neck and loosed a jet of blue and yellow flame at it. The tower did not catch fire, as it was stone, but the rope and beams supporting the bell ignited, and a few seconds later, the bell fell crashing into the interior of the tower.

That pleased her, as did the two-legs-round-ears who ran screaming from the area. She was a dragon, after all. It was only right that they should fear her.

One of the two-legs paused by the edge of the square in front of the black-shrike-thorn-cave, and she heard him shout a spell at her, his voice like the squeaking of a frightened mouse. Whatever the spell was, Eragon's wards shielded her from it—at least she assumed they did, for she noticed no difference in how she felt or in the appearance of the world around her.

The wolf-elf-in-Eragon's-shape killed the magician for her. She could feel how Blödhgarm grasped hold of the spellcaster's mind and wrestled the two-legs-round-ears' thoughts into submission, whereupon Blödhgarm uttered a single word in the ancient-elf-magic-language, and the two-legs-round-ears fell to the ground, blood seeping from his open mouth.

Then the wolf-elf tapped her on the shoulder and said, "Ready yourself, Brightscales. Here they come."

She saw Thorn rising above the edge of the rooftops, Eragon-half-brother-Murtagh a small, dark figure on his back. In the light of the morning sun, Thorn shone and sparkled almost as brilliantly as she herself did. Her scales were cleaner than his, though, as she had taken special care when grooming earlier. She could not imagine going into battle looking anything but her best. Her enemies should not only fear her, but admire her.

She knew it was vanity on her part, but she did not care. No other race could match the grandeur of the dragons. Also, she was the last female of her kind, and she wanted those who saw her to marvel at her appearance and to remember her well, so if dragons were to vanish forevermore, two-legs would continue to speak of them with the proper respect, awe, and wonder.

As Thorn climbed a thousand or more feet above the rat-nest-city, Saphira spared a quick glance around to make sure that partner-of-her-heart-and-mind-Eragon was nowhere near the black-shrike-thorn-cave. She did not want to hurt him by accident in the fight that was about to take place. He was a fierce hunter, but he was small and easily squished.

She was still working to unravel the dark-echoing-painful-memories Eragon had shared with her, but she understood enough of them to know that events had once again proved what she had long believed: that whenever she and her partner-of-heart-and-mind were apart, he ended up in trouble of one form or another. Eragon, she knew, would disagree, but his latest misadventure had done nothing to convince her otherwise, and she felt a perverse satisfaction in having been right.

Once Thorn reached an appropriate height, he twisted round and dove toward her, flames shooting from his open maw.

The fire she did not fear—Eragon's wards would shield her from it—but Thorn's massive weight and strength would allow him to quickly exhaust any spells designed to shield her from physical danger. To protect herself, she ducked and pressed her body flat against the cathedral, even as she twisted her neck and snapped at Thorn's pale underbelly.

A swirling wall of flames engulfed her, rumbling and roaring like a giant waterfall. The flames were so bright, she instinctively closed her inner eyelids, the same as she would when underwater, and then the light was no longer blinding.

The flames soon cleared, and as Thorn rushed past overhead, the tip of his thick, rib-bruising tail traced a line across the membrane of her right wing. The scratch bled, but not profusely, and she did not think it would cause her much difficulty while flying, painful though it was.

Thorn dove at her again and again, trying to bait her into taking to the air. She refused to budge, however, and after a few more passes, he tired of harrying her and landed on the other end of the black-shrike-thorn-cave, his huge wings outstretched for balance.

The entire building shook as Thorn dropped to all fours, and many of the gem-glass-picture-windows in the walls below shattered and fell tinkling to the ground. Thorn was bigger than her now, as a result of the egg-breaker-Galbatorix's meddling, but she was not intimidated. She had more experience than Thorn, and besides, she had trained with Glaedr, who had been larger than both she and Thorn combined. Also, Thorn dared not kill her . . . nor did she think he wanted to.

The red dragon snarled and stepped forward, the tips of his claws scraping against the tiles on the roof. She snarled in return and retreated several feet, until she could feel her tail pressing against the base of the spires that rose up like a wall at the front of the black-shrike-thorn-cave.

The tip of Thorn's tail twitched, and she knew he was about to pounce.

She drew in her breath and bathed him in a torrent of flickering flames. Her task now was to keep Thorn and Murtagh from realizing that it was not Eragon who was sitting on her. To that end, she could either stay far enough away from Thorn that Murtagh would be unable to read the thoughts of the wolf-elf-in-Eragon's-shape, or she could attack often and ferociously enough that Murtagh would not have the opportunity—which would be difficult, as Murtagh was used to fighting from Thorn's back even while Thorn turned and twisted through the air. Still, they were close to the ground, and that would help her, for she preferred to attack. Always to attack.

"Is that the best you can do?" Murtagh shouted with a magically enhanced voice from within the ever-shifting cocoon of fire.

Even as the last of the flames died in her mouth, Saphira leaped toward Thorn. She struck him full in the chest, and their necks intertwined, heads slapping against one another as they each tried to fix their teeth around the other's throat. The force of the impact pushed Thorn backward off the black-shrike-thorn-cave, and he flailed his wings, buffeting Saphira as both he and she fell toward the ground.

They landed with a crash that split paving stones and jarred the nearby houses. Something cracked in Thorn's left wing-shoulder, and his back arched unnaturally as Murtagh's wards kept the dragon from crushing him flat.

Saphira could hear Murtagh cursing from underneath Thorn, and she decided that it would be best to move away before the angry two-legs-round-ears started casting spells.

She jumped up, kicking Thorn in the belly as she did so, and alit on the peak of the house behind the red dragon. The building was too weak to support her, so she took flight again and, just for good measure, set the row of buildings on fire.

Let them deal with that, she thought, satisfied, as the flames gnawed hungrily at the wooden structures.

Returning to the black-shrike-thorn-cave, she slipped her claws under the tiles and began to tear open the roof, ripping it apart the same as she had ripped apart the roof of the castle in Durza-Gil'ead.

Only now she was bigger. Now she was stronger. And the blocks of stone seemed to weigh no more than pebbles did to Eragon. The blood-mad-priests who worshipped within had hurt the partner-of-her-heart-and-mind, had hurt dragon-blood-elf-Arya, young-face-old-mind-Angela, and the werecat Solembum—he of the many names—and they had killed Wyrden. For that, Saphira was determined to destroy the black-shrike-thorn-cave in revenge.

Within seconds, she opened a gaping hole in the ceiling of the building. She filled the interior with a burst of flame, then hooked her claws into the ends of the brass pipes of the wind organ and pulled them free of the rear wall of the cathedral. They fell clanging and crashing onto the pews below.

Thorn roared, and then he sprang up from the street into the air above the black-shrike-thorn-cave and hung there, flapping heavily to maintain his position. He appeared as a featureless black silhouette against the wall of flames rising from the houses behind him, save for his translucent wings, which glowed orange and crimson.

He lunged toward her, reaching out with his serrated claws.

Saphira waited until the last possible moment; then she leaped to the side, off the black-shrike-thorn-cave, and Thorn rammed headfirst into the base of the cathedral's central spire. The tall-hole-ridden-stone-spike shuddered under the impact, and the very top of it—an ornate golden rod—toppled over and plunged more than four hundred feet to the square below.

Roaring with frustration, Thorn struggled to right himself. His hindquarters slid into the opening Saphira had torn in the roof, and he scrabbled against the tiles as he tried to claw his way back out.

While he did, Saphira flew to the front of the black-shrike-thorn-cave and positioned herself on the opposite side of the spire Thorn had collided with.

She gathered her strength, then batted the spire with her right forepaw.

Statues and carved decorations shattered underneath her foot; clouds of dust clogged her nostrils; and bits of stone and mortar rained down upon the square. The spire held, though, so she struck it again.

Thorn's bellowing took on a frantic note as he realized what she was doing, and he strove even harder to pull himself free.

On Saphira's third blow, the tall-stone-spike cracked at the base and, with agonizing slowness, collapsed backward, falling toward the roof. Thorn only had time to utter a furious snarl, and then the tower of rubble landed on top of him, knocking him down into the shell of the ruined building and burying him under piles of rubble.

The sound of the spire smashing to pieces echoed across the whole of the rat-nest-city, like a clap of rolling thunder.

Saphira snarled in response, this time with a sense of savage victory. Thorn would dig himself out soon enough, but until then, he was at her mercy.

Tilting her wings, she circled the black-shrike-thorn-cave. As she passed along the sides of the building, she swung at the fluted buttresses that supported the walls, demolishing them one at a time. The blocks of stone tumbled to the ground, creating an unpleasant din.

321

When she had removed all the buttressess, the unsupported walls began to sway and bulge outward. Thorn's efforts to extricate himself only worsened the situation, and after a few seconds, the walls gave way. The entire structure collapsed with an avalanche-like rumble, and a huge plume of dust billowed upward.

Saphira crowed with triumph; then she landed on her hind legs next to the mound of debris and proceeded to paint the blocks of stone with the hottest stream of fire she could summon forth. Flames were easy to deflect with magic, but deflecting actual heat required greater effort and energy. By forcing Murtagh to expend even more of his strength to keep Thorn and himself from being cooked alive, as well as whatever energy he was using to avoid being squished, she hoped to deplete his reserves enough that Eragon and the two-legs-pointed-ears might have a chance of defeating him.

While she breathed fire, the wolf-elf on her back chanted spells, though what they were for she did not know, nor did she particularly care. She trusted the two-legs. Whatever he was doing, she was sure it would help.

Saphira skittered backward as the blocks in the center of the mound exploded outward and, with a roar, Thorn lurched free of the rubble. His wings were crumpled like those of a stepped-on butterfly, and he was bleeding from several gashes along his legs and back.

He glared at her and snarled, his ruby eyes dark with battle rage. For the first time, she had truly angered him, and she could see that he was eager to tear at her flesh and taste her blood.

Good, she thought. Maybe he was not quite such a beaten-frightened-cur as she had assumed.

Murtagh reached into a pouch on his belt and removed a small round object. From experience, Saphira knew that it was enchanted and he would use it to heal Thorn's injuries.

Without waiting, she took flight, trying to gain as much altitude as possible before Thorn was able to set off in pursuit. She glanced down after a few wing beats and saw him rising toward her at a furious speed, a large-red-sharp-claw-sparrowhawk.

She twisted in the air and was just about to dive at him when, in the depths of her mind, she heard Eragon shout:

Saphira!

Alarmed, she continued to twist until she was aimed at the southern arch-gate of the city, where she had sensed Eragon's presence. She pulled in her wings as close as she dared and dropped in a steep angle toward the arch.

Thorn lunged at her as she plummeted past, and she knew without looking that he was following close behind.

And so the two of them raced toward the thin wall of the rat-nest-city, and the cool morning-air-off-water howled like a wounded wolf in Saphira's ears.

◆　◆　◆

HAMMER AND HELM

*A*t last! thought Roran as the Varden's horns sounded the advance.

He glanced at Dras-Leona and caught a glimpse of Saphira diving toward the dark mass of buildings, her scales blazing in the light of the rising sun. Below, Thorn stirred, like some great cat that had been sunning itself on a fence, and took off in pursuit.

A surge of energy coursed through Roran. The time for battle had finally arrived, and he was eager to be done with it. He spared a quick thought of concern for Eragon, then pushed himself off the log where he was sitting and trotted over to join the rest of the men as they gathered in a wide rectangular formation.

Roran glanced up and down the ranks, checking that the troops were ready. They had been waiting for most of the night, and the men were tired, but he knew that fear and excitement would soon clear their minds. Roran was tired as well, but he paid it no mind; he could sleep when the battle was over. Until then, his main concern was keeping his men and himself alive.

He did wish he had time for a cup of hot tea, though, to help settle his stomach. He had eaten something bad for dinner and had been racked with cramps and nausea ever since. Still, the discomfort was not enough to prevent him from fighting. Or so he hoped.

Satisfied with the state of his men, Roran pulled on his helm, pushing it down over his quilted arming cap. Then he drew his hammer and slipped his left arm through the straps on his shield.

"At your command," said Horst, walking up to him.

Roran nodded. He had chosen the smith as his second in command, a decision that Nasuada had accepted without dissent. Other than Eragon, there was no one Roran would rather have by his side. It was selfish of him, he knew—Horst had a newborn child, and the Varden needed his metalworking skills—but Roran could not think of anyone else as well suited for the job. Horst had not seemed especially pleased by the promotion, but neither had he seemed upset. Instead, he had gone about organizing Roran's battalion with the calm assurance and competency that Roran knew he possessed.

The horns sounded again, and Roran lifted his hammer over his head. "Forward!" he shouted.

He took the lead as the many hundreds of men started off, accompanied on either side by the Varden's four other battalions.

As the warriors trotted across the open fields that separated them from Dras-Leona, cries of alarm rang out in the city. Bells and horns sounded a moment later, and soon the whole city was filled with an angry clamor as the defenders roused themselves. Adding to the commotion were the most terrible roars and crashes from the center of the city, where the two dragons were fighting. Occasionally, Roran saw one or another of them appear above the tops of the buildings, the dragon's hide bright and sparkling, but for the most part, the two giants remained hidden from sight.

The maze of ramshackle buildings that surrounded the city walls quickly drew near. The narrow, gloomy streets looked ominous and foreboding to Roran. It would be easy for the Empire's soldiers—or even the citizens of Dras-Leona—to ambush them within the twisting passageways. Fighting in such close quarters would be even more brutal, confusing, and messy than normal. If it came to that, Roran knew that few of his men would escape unscathed.

As he moved into the shadows beneath the eaves of the first line of hovels, a hard knot of unease settled in Roran's gut, exacerbating his queasiness. He licked his lips, feeling sick.

Eragon had better open that gate, he thought. *If not . . . we'll be stuck out here like so many lambs penned up for slaughter.*

❖ ❖ ❖

AND THE WALLS FELL . . .

The sound of crashing masonry caused Eragon to pause and look back.

Between the peaks of two distant houses, he saw an empty space where the barbed spire of the cathedral used to be. In its place, a column of dust billowed toward the clouds above, like a pillar of white smoke.

Eragon smiled to himself, proud of Saphira. When it came to spreading chaos and destruction, dragons were without equal. *Go on*, he thought. *Smash it to pieces! Bury their holy places under a thousand feet of stone!*

Then he resumed trotting down the dark, winding cobblestone street, along with Arya, Angela, and Solembum. There were a number of people already in the streets: merchants going to open their shops, night watchmen on their way to bed, drunk noblemen just emerging from their revels, vagrants sleeping in doorways, as well as soldiers running pell-mell toward the city walls.

All of the people, even those who were running, kept looking in the direction of the cathedral as the noise of the two dragons fighting rumbled through the city. Everyone—from the sore-ridden beggars to the hardened soldiers to the richly dressed nobles—appeared terrified, and none of them gave Eragon or his companions so much as a second glance.

It helped, Eragon supposed, that he and Arya could pass for ordinary humans on brief inspection.

At Eragon's insistence, Arya had deposited the unconscious novitiate in an alleyway a fair distance from the cathedral. "I promised we'd take him with us," Eragon had explained, "but I never said how far. He can find his own way from here." Arya had acquiesced and seemed relieved to be rid of the novitiate's weight.

As the four of them hurried down the street, a strange sense of familiarity came over Eragon. His last visit to Dras-Leona had ended in much the same way: with him running between the dirty, close-set buildings, hoping to reach one of the city's gates before the Empire found him. Only this time he had more to fear than just the Ra'zac.

He glanced toward the cathedral again. All Saphira had to do was keep Murtagh and Thorn busy for another few minutes, and then it would be too late for either of them to stop the Varden. However, minutes could be like hours during a battle, and Eragon was acutely aware of how fast the balance of power could change.

Hold fast! he thought, though he did not send his words to Saphira, lest he distract her or give away his position. *Just a little longer!*

The streets grew ever narrower as they approached the city wall, and the overhanging buildings—houses mostly—blocked out everything but a thin strip of the azure sky. Sewage lay stagnant in the gutters along the edges of the buildings; Eragon and Arya used their sleeves to mask their noses and mouths. The stench seemed not to affect the herbalist, although Solembum growled and whipped his tail in annoyance.

A flicker of movement on the roof of a nearby building caught Eragon's attention, but whatever caused it had vanished by the time he looked. He continued to gaze upward and, after a few moments, began to pick out certain odd sights: a patch of white against the soot-coated bricks of a chimney; strange pointed shapes outlined against the morning sky; a small oval spot, the size of a coin, that gleamed firelike in the shadows.

With a shock, he realized that the rooftops were lined with dozens of werecats, all in their animal form. The werecats ran from building to building, watching silently from above as Eragon and his companions threaded their way through the dim maze of the city.

Eragon knew that the elusive shapeshifters would not deign to help except in the most desperate of circumstances—they wished to keep their involvement with the Varden a secret from Galbatorix for as long as possible—but he found it heartening to have them so close.

The street ended at an intersection of five other lanes. Eragon consulted with Arya and the herbalist; then they decided to take the path opposite theirs and continue in the same direction.

A hundred feet ahead, the street they had chosen took a sharp turn and opened onto the square that lay before Dras-Leona's southern gate.

Eragon stopped.

Hundreds of soldiers stood gathered before the gate. The men milled about in seeming confusion as they donned weapons and armor, and their commanders bellowed orders at them. The golden thread stitched onto the soldiers' crimson tunics glittered as they rushed to and fro.

The presence of the soldiers dismayed Eragon, but he was even more dismayed to see that the city's defenders had piled a huge mound of rubble against the inside of the gates, to keep the Varden from battering them in.

Eragon swore. The mound was so large, it would take a team of fifty men several days to clear it away. Saphira could dig the gates free in a few minutes, but Murtagh and Thorn would never give her the opportunity.

We need another distraction, he thought. What that distraction should be, however, eluded him. *Saphira!* he cried, casting his thoughts out toward her. She heard him, of that he was sure, but he had no time to explain the situation to her, for at that very moment, one of the soldiers stopped and pointed at Eragon and his companions.

"Rebels!"

Eragon tore Brisingr from its scabbard and sprang forward before the rest of the soldiers could heed the man's warning. He had no other choice. To retreat would be to abandon the Varden to the mercies of the Empire. Besides, he could not leave Saphira to deal with both the wall *and* the soldiers by herself.

He shouted as he leaped, as did Arya, who joined him in his mad charge. Together they cut their way into the midst of the surprised soldiers. For a few brief moments, the men were so bewildered, several did not seem to realize Eragon was their foe until he had stabbed them.

Flights of arrows arced down into the square from the bowmen stationed on the parapet. A handful of the shafts bounced off Eragon's wards. The rest killed or injured the Empire's own men.

Fast as he was, Eragon could not block all of the swords and spears and daggers poking at him. He could feel his strength ebbing at an alarming rate as his magic repelled the attacks. Unless he could win free of the press, the soldiers would end up exhausting him to the point where he could no longer fight.

With a ferocious war cry, he spun in a circle, holding Brisingr close to his waist as he scythed down all the soldiers standing within reach.

The iridescent blue blade cut through bone and flesh as if they were equally insubstantial. Blood trailed from the tip in long, twisting ribbons that slowly separated into glistening drops, like orbs of polished coral, while the men he cut doubled over, clutching at their bellies as they attempted to hold closed their wounds.

Every detail seemed bright and hard-edged, as if sculpted from glass. Eragon could make out individual hairs in the beard of the swordsman in front of him. He could count the drops of sweat that beaded the skin below the man's eyes, and he could have pointed to every stain, scuff, and tear in and on the swordsman's outfit.

The noise of combat was painfully loud to his sensitive ears, but Eragon felt a deep sense of calm. He was not immune to the fears that had troubled him before, but they did not waken quite so easily, and he fought better because of it.

He completed his spin and was just moving toward the swordsman when Saphira swooped past overhead. Her wings were pulled tight against her body, and they fluttered like leaves in a gale. As she passed by, a blast of wind tousled Eragon's hair and pressed him toward the ground.

An instant later, Thorn followed Saphira, teeth bared, flames boiling in his open maw. The two dragons hurtled a half mile beyond Dras-Leona's yellow mud wall; then they looped around and began to race back.

From outside the walls, Eragon heard a loud cheer. *The Varden must be almost to the gates.*

A patch of skin on his left forearm burned as if someone had poured hot fat on it. He hissed and shook his arm, but the feeling persisted. Then he saw a blotch of blood soaking through his tunic. He glanced back at Saphira. It had to be dragon blood, but he could not tell whose.

As the dragons approached, Eragon took advantage of the soldiers' momentary daze to kill three more. Then the rest of the men regained their wits, and the battle resumed in earnest.

A soldier with a battle-ax stepped in front of Eragon and started to swing at him. Halfway through the stroke, Arya dispatched the man with a slash from behind, nearly cutting him in twain.

With a quick nod, Eragon acknowledged her help. By unspoken agreement, they stood back to back and faced the soldiers together.

He could feel Arya panting as hard as he was. Though they were stronger and faster than most humans, there was a limit to their endurance, a limit to their resources. They had already killed dozens, but hundreds remained, and Eragon knew that reinforcements would soon arrive from elsewhere in Dras-Leona.

"What now?" he shouted, parrying a spear jabbed at his thigh.

"Magic!" Arya replied.

As Eragon fended off the soldiers' attacks, he began to recite every spell he could think of that might kill their enemies.

Another gust of wind ruffled his hair, and a cool shadow swept over him as Saphira circled above, dissipating her excess speed. She flared her wings and started to drop toward the battlements of the wall.

Before she could land, Thorn caught up with her. The red dragon dove, breathing a jet of flame over a hundred feet long. Saphira roared with frustration and veered away from the wall as she flapped quickly to gain altitude. The two dragons spiraled around each other as they climbed into the sky, biting and clawing with furious abandon.

Seeing Saphira in danger only reinforced Eragon's determination. He increased the speed with which he spoke, chanting the words of the ancient language as quickly as he could without mispronunciation. But no matter what he tried, neither his spells nor Arya's had any effect on the soldiers.

Then Murtagh's voice boomed out of the sky, like the voice of a cloud-scraping giant: "Those men are under *my* protection, Brother!"

Eragon looked up and saw Thorn plummeting toward the square. The red dragon's sudden change in direction had caught Saphira unawares. She still hung high above the city, a dark blue shape against the lighter blue of the sky.

They know, Eragon thought, and dread punctured his earlier calm.

He lowered his gaze and swept it over the throng. More and more soldiers were streaming out of the streets along either side of Dras-Leona's wall. The herbalist was backed up against one of the bordering houses, throwing glass vials with one hand and swinging Tinkledeath with the other. The vials released clouds of green vapor when they broke, and any soldiers caught in the miasma fell to the ground, clutching their throats and thrashing as little brown mushrooms sprang up on every inch of exposed skin. Behind Angela, upon a flat-topped garden wall, crouched Solembum. The werecat used his vantage point to claw at the soldiers' faces and pull off their helms, distracting them as they attempted to close with the herbalist. Both he and Angela looked beleaguered, and Eragon doubted they would be able to hold out much longer.

Nothing Eragon saw gave him hope. He turned his eyes back toward the immense bulk of Thorn even as the red dragon filled his wings with air and slowed his descent.

"We have to leave!" Arya shouted.

Eragon hesitated. It would be a simple matter to lift Arya, Angela, Solembum, and himself over the wall, to where the Varden would be waiting. But if they fled, the Varden would be no better off than before. Their army could not afford to wait any longer: after another few days, their supplies would run out and the men would begin to desert. Once that happened, Eragon knew they would never again succeed in uniting all the races against Galbatorix.

Thorn's body and wings blotted out the sky, casting the area in ruddy darkness and hiding Saphira from view. Globules of blood, each the size of Eragon's fist, dripped from Thorn's neck and legs, and more than one of the soldiers cried out in pain as the liquid scalded them.

"Eragon! Now!" shouted Arya. She grabbed his arm and pulled, but still he held his ground, unwilling to admit defeat.

Arya pulled harder, forcing Eragon to look down in order to stay on his feet. As he did, his eye fell on the third finger of his right hand, where he wore Aren.

He had hoped to save the energy contained within the ring for the day when he might finally confront Galbatorix. It was a meager amount compared with what the king had undoubtedly accumulated during his long years on the throne, but it was the greatest store of power Eragon possessed, and he knew he would not have the chance to gather its equal before the Varden reached Urû'baen, if indeed they did. Also, it was one of the few things Brom had left him. For both those reasons he was reluctant to use any of the energy.

Nevertheless, he could think of no alternative.

The pool of energy within Aren had always seemed enormous to Eragon; now he wondered if it would be enough for what he intended.

At the edge of his vision, he saw Thorn reaching toward him with talons as large as a man, and some small part of him screamed to run away before the monster above caught him and ate him alive.

Eragon drew in his breath, then he breached Aren's precious hoard and shouted, "Jierda!"

The torrent of energy that flowed through him was greater than any he had ever experienced; it was like an ice-cold river that burned and tingled with almost unbearable intensity. The sensation was both agonizing and ecstatic.

At his command, the huge pile of rubble blocking the gates erupted toward the sky in a solid pillar of earth and stone. The rubble struck Thorn in the side, shredding his wing and knocking the screeching dragon beyond the outskirts of Dras-Leona. Then the pillar spread outward, forming a loose canopy over the southern half of the city.

The launch of the rubble shook the square and drove everyone to the ground. Eragon landed on his hands and knees and remained there, staring upward as he maintained the spell.

When the energy in the ring was almost depleted, he whispered, "Gánga raehta." Like a dark thunderhead caught in a gale, the plume drifted to the right, in the direction of the docks and Leona Lake. Eragon continued to push the rubble away from the center of the city for as long as he could; then, as the last remnants of the energy coursed through him, he ended the spell.

With a deceptively soft sound, the cloud of debris collapsed inward. The heavier elements—the stones, the broken pieces of wood, and the clumps of dirt—fell straight down, pummeling the surface of the lake, while the smaller particles remained suspended in the air, forming a large brown smudge that slowly drifted farther west.

Where the rubble had been was now an empty crater. Broken paving stones edged the hollow, like a circle of shattered teeth. The gates to the city hung open, warped and splintered, damaged beyond repair.

Through the off-kilter gates, Eragon saw the Varden massed in the streets beyond. He released his breath and allowed his head to fall forward in exhaustion. *It worked*, he thought, dumbfounded. Then he slowly pushed himself upright, vaguely aware that the danger had not yet passed.

While the soldiers struggled to their feet, the Varden poured into Dras-Leona, shouting war cries and banging their swords on their shields. A few seconds later, Saphira landed among them, and what had been about to turn into a pitched battle became a rout as the soldiers scrambled to save themselves.

Eragon glimpsed Roran among the sea of men and dwarves but lost sight of him before he could catch his cousin's attention.

Arya . . . ? Eragon turned and was alarmed to find that she was not next to him. He broadened his search and soon spotted her halfway across the square, surrounded by twenty or so soldiers. The men were holding her arms and legs with grim tenacity as they tried to drag her away. Arya freed one of her hands and struck a man in the chin, breaking his neck, but another soldier took his place before she could swing again.

Eragon sprinted toward her. In his exhaustion, he let his sword arm swing too low, and the tip of Brisingr caught on the mail hauberk of a fallen soldier, tearing the hilt from his grip. The sword clattered to the ground, and Eragon hesitated, not sure if he should turn back, but then he saw two of the soldiers stabbing at Arya with daggers, and he redoubled his speed.

Just as he reached her, Arya shook off her attackers for a moment. The men lunged with outstretched hands, but before they could recapture her, Eragon struck one man in the side, driving his fist into the man's rib cage. A soldier with a pair of waxed mustachios stabbed at Eragon's chest. Eragon caught the blade with his bare hands, ripped it from the soldier's grip, broke the sword in two, and eviscerated the soldier with the stump of his own weapon. Within seconds, all the soldiers who had threatened Arya lay dead or dying. Those Eragon had not killed, Arya slew.

Afterward, Arya said, "I would have been able to defeat them on my own."

Eragon leaned over, resting his hands on his knees as he caught his breath. "I know. . . ." He nodded toward her right hand—the one she had injured pulling through the iron cuff—which she held curled against her leg. "Consider it my thanks."

"A grim sort of present." But she said it with a faint smile on her lips.

Most of the soldiers had fled the square; those who remained were backed against the houses, hemmed in by the Varden. Even as Eragon looked about, he saw scores of Galbatorix's men throw down their weapons and surrender.

Together he and Arya retrieved his sword, and then they walked to the yellow mud wall, where the ground was relatively clear of filth. Sitting against the wall, they watched the Varden march into the city.

Saphira soon joined them. She nuzzled Eragon, who smiled and scratched her snout. She hummed in response. *You did it*, she said.

We did it, he replied.

Up on her back, Blödhgarm loosened the straps that held his legs in Saphira's saddle, then slid down her side. For a moment, Eragon had the supremely disorienting experience of meeting himself. He immediately decided that he disliked how his hair curled at the temples.

Blödhgarm uttered an indistinct word in the ancient language; then his shape shimmered like a heat reflection and he was once again himself: tall, furred, yellow-eyed, long-eared, and sharp-toothed. He appeared neither elf nor human, but in his tense, hard-set expression, Eragon detected the stamp of sorrow and anger combined.

"Shadeslayer," he said, and bowed to both Arya and Eragon. "Saphira has told me of Wyrden's fate. I—"

Before he could finish his sentence, the ten remaining elves under Blödhgarm's command emerged from within the press of the Varden and hurried over, swords in hand.

"Shadeslayer!" they exclaimed. "Argetlam! Brightscales!"

Eragon greeted them tiredly and strove to answer their questions, even though he would rather have done nothing at all.

Then a roar cut through their conversation, and a shadow fell across them, and Eragon looked up to see Thorn—whole and sound once more—balancing on a column of air high above.

Eragon cursed and scrambled onto Saphira, drawing Brisingr, while Arya, Blödhgarm, and the other elves formed a protective circle around her. Their combined might was formidable, but whether it would be enough to fend off Murtagh, Eragon did not know.

As one, the Varden gazed upward. Brave they might be, but even the bravest might shrink before a dragon.

"Brother!" shouted Murtagh, his augmented voice so loud that Eragon covered his ears. "I'll have blood from you for the injuries you caused Thorn! Take Dras-Leona if you want. It means nothing to Galbatorix. But you've not seen the last of us, Eragon Shadeslayer, that I swear."

And then Thorn turned and flew north over Dras-Leona, and soon vanished within the veil of smoke that rose from the houses burning next to the ruined cathedral.

BY THE BANKS OF LAKE LEONA

Eragon strode through the darkened camp, his jaw set and his fists clenched.

He had spent the last few hours in conference with Nasuada, Orik, Arya, Garzhvog, King Orrin, and their various advisers, discussing the day's events and assessing the Varden's current situation. Near the end of the meeting, they had contacted Queen Islanzadí to inform her that the Varden had captured Dras-Leona, as well as to tell her of Wyrden's death.

Eragon had not enjoyed explaining to the queen how one of her oldest and most powerful spellcasters had died, nor had the queen been pleased to receive the news. Her initial reaction had been one of such sadness, it surprised him; he had not thought she knew Wyrden that well.

Talking with Islanzadí had left Eragon in a foul mood, for it had reinforced for him how random and unnecessary Wyrden's death had been. *If I had been in the lead, I would have been the one impaled on those spikes*, he thought as he continued his search through the camp. *Or it could have been Arya.*

Saphira knew what he was up to, but she had decided to return to the space by his tent where she normally slept, for as she said, *If I go tromping up and down the rows of tents, I'll keep the Varden awake, and they have earned their rest.* Their minds remained joined, though, and he knew if he needed her, she would be at his side within seconds.

To preserve his night vision, Eragon avoided going near the bonfires and torches that burned before many of the tents, but he made sure to inspect each pool of light for his prey.

As he hunted, it occurred to him that she might elude him

entirely. His feelings for her were far from friendly, and that would allow her to sense his location and avoid him, if she wanted. Yet he did not think she was a coward. Despite her youth, she was one of the hardest people he had met, human, elf, or dwarf.

At last he spotted Elva sitting in front of a small, nondescript tent, weaving a cat's cradle by the light of a dying fire. Next to her sat the girl's caretaker, Greta, a pair of long wooden knitting needles darting in her gnarled hands.

For a moment, Eragon stood and watched. The old woman appeared more content than he had ever seen her, and he found himself reluctant to disturb her repose.

Then Elva said, "Do not lose your nerve now, Eragon. Not when you have come so far." Her voice was curiously subdued, as if she had been crying, but when she looked up, her gaze was fierce and challenging.

Greta appeared startled when Eragon made his way into the light; she gathered up her yarn and needles and bowed, saying, "Greetings, Shadeslayer. May I offer you anything to eat or drink?"

"No, thank you." Eragon stopped before Elva and stared down at the small-framed girl. She stared back at him for a moment, then returned to weaving the loop of yarn between her fingers. Her violet eyes, he noted with a strange twist in his stomach, were the same color as the amethyst crystals the priests of Helgrind had used to kill Wyrden and imprison Arya and himself.

Eragon knelt and grabbed the tangle of yarn about the middle, stopping Elva's motion.

"I know what you intend to say," she stated.

"That may be," he growled, "but I'm still going to say it. You killed Wyrden—you killed him as surely as if you had stabbed him yourself. If you had come with us, you could have warned him about the trap. You could have warned all of us. I watched Wyrden die, and I watched Arya tear half her hand off, because of *you*. Because of your anger. Because of your stubbornness. Because of your pride. . . . Hate me if you will, but don't you dare make anyone else suffer for it. If you want the Varden to lose, then go join Galbatorix and be done with it. Well, is that what you want?"

Elva slowly shook her head.

"Then I don't ever want to hear that you've refused to help Nasuada for no other reason than spite, else there will be a reckoning between you and me, Elva Farseer, and it's not one you would win."

"You could never defeat me," she mumbled, her voice thick with emotion.

"You might be surprised. You have a valuable talent, Elva. The Varden needs your help, now more than ever. I don't know how we're going to defeat the king at Urû'baen, but if you stand with us— if you turn your skill against him—we might just have a chance."

Elva seemed to struggle with herself. Then she nodded, and Eragon saw that she was crying, tears overflowing from her eyes. He took no pleasure in her distress, but he felt a certain amount of satisfaction that his words had affected her so strongly.

"I'm sorry," she whispered.

He released the yarn and stood. "Your apologies cannot bring back Wyrden. Do better in the future, and perhaps you can atone for your mistake."

He nodded to the old woman Greta, who had remained silent throughout their exchange, and then he strode out of the light and back between the dark rows of tents.

You did well, said Saphira. *She will act differently from now on, I think.*

I hope so.

Upbraiding Elva had been an unusual experience for Eragon. He remembered when Brom and Garrow had chastised him for making mistakes, and to now find himself the one doing the chastising left him feeling . . . different . . . more mature.

And so the wheel turns, he thought.

He took his time walking through the camp, enjoying the cool breeze wafting off the lake hidden within the shadows.

After the capture of Dras-Leona, Nasuada had surprised everyone by insisting that the Varden not stay the night in the city. She had given no explanation for her decision, but Eragon suspected it was because the long delay at Dras-Leona had left her overeager to resume their journey to Urû'baen, and also because she had no desire to linger within the city, where any number of Galbatorix's agents might be lurking.

Once the Varden had secured the streets, Nasuada detailed a number of warriors to remain in the city, under the command of Martland Redbeard. Then the Varden had left Dras-Leona and marched north, following the shore of the neighboring lake. Along the way, a constant stream of messengers had ridden back and forth between the Varden and Dras-Leona as Martland and Nasuada conferred about the numerous issues attending the governance of the city.

Before the Varden had departed, Eragon, Saphira, and Blödhgarm's spellcasters had returned to the ruined cathedral, retrieved Wyrden's body, and searched for the belt of Beloth the Wise. It had taken only a few minutes for Saphira to pull aside the jumble of stone that blocked the entrance to the underground chambers and for Blödhgarm and the other elves to fetch Wyrden. But no matter how long they looked, and no matter what spells they used, they could not find the belt.

The elves had carried Wyrden on their shields out of the city, to a knoll next to a small creek. There they buried him while singing several aching laments in the ancient language—songs so sad that Eragon had wept without restraint and all the birds and animals within hearing had stopped and listened.

The silver-haired elf woman Yaela had knelt by the side of the grave, taken an acorn from the pouch on her belt, and planted it directly above Wyrden's chest. And then the twelve elves, Arya included, sang to the acorn, which took root and sprouted and grew twining upward, reaching and grasping toward the sky like a clutch of hands.

When the elves had finished, the leafy oak stood twenty feet high, with long strings of green flowers at the end of every branch.

Eragon had thought it was the nicest burial he had ever attended. He much preferred it to the dwarves' practice of entombing their dead in hard, cold stone deep below the ground, and he liked the idea of one's body providing food for a tree that might live for hundreds of years more. If he had to die, he decided that he would want an apple tree planted over him, so that his friends and family could eat the fruit born of his body.

The concept had amused him tremendously, albeit in a rather morbid manner.

Besides searching the cathedral and retrieving Wyrden's body, Eragon had also done one other thing of note in Dras-Leona after its capture. He had, with Nasuada's approval, declared every slave within the city a free person, and he had personally gone to the manors and auction houses and cut loose many of the men, women, and children chained therein. The act had given him a great deal of satisfaction, and he hoped it would improve the lives of the people he had released.

As he drew near his tent, he saw Arya waiting for him by the entrance. Eragon quickened his stride, but before he could greet her, someone called out: "Shadeslayer!"

Eragon turned and saw one of Nasuada's pages trotting toward them. "Shadeslayer," the boy repeated, somewhat out of breath, and bowed to Arya. "Lady Nasuada would like you to come to her tent an hour before dawn tomorrow morning, in order to confer with her. What shall I tell her, Lady Arya?"

"You may tell her I will be there when she wishes," Arya replied, inclining her head slightly.

The page bowed again, and then he spun around and ran off in the direction from which he had come.

"It's somewhat confusing, now that we've both killed a Shade," Eragon observed with a faint grin.

Arya smiled as well, the motion of her lips almost invisible in the darkness. "Would you rather I had let Varaug live?"

"No . . . no, not at all."

"I could have kept him as a slave, to do my bidding."

"Now you're teasing me," he said.

She made a soft sound of amusement.

"Perhaps I should call you Princess instead—Princess Arya." He said it again, enjoying the feel of the words in his mouth.

"You should not call me that," she said, more serious. "I am not a princess."

"Why not? Your mother is a queen. How can you not be a princess? Her title is *dröttning*, yours is *dröttningu*. One means 'queen,' and the other—"

"Does not mean 'princess,'" she said. "Not exactly. There is no true equivalent in this language."

"But if your mother were to die or step down from her throne, you would take her place as ruler of your people, wouldn't you?"

"It is not that simple."

Arya did not seem inclined to explain further, so Eragon said, "Would you like to go in?"

"I would," she said.

Eragon pulled open the entrance to his tent, and Arya ducked inside. After a quick glance at Saphira—who lay curled up nearby, breathing heavily as she drifted off to sleep—Eragon followed.

He went to the lantern that hung from the pole in the center of the tent and murmured, "Istalrí," not using *brisingr*, so as to avoid igniting his sword. The resulting flame filled the interior with a warm, steady light that made the sparsely furnished army tent seem almost cozy.

They sat, and Arya said, "I found this among Wyrden's belongings, and I thought we might enjoy it together." From the side pocket of her pants, she produced a carved wooden flask about the size of Eragon's hand. She handed it to him.

Eragon unstoppered the flask and sniffed at the mouth. He raised his eyebrows as he smelled the strong, sweet scent of liqueur.

"Is it faelnirv?" he asked, naming the drink the elves made from elderberries and, Narí had claimed, moonbeams.

Arya laughed, and her voice rang like well-tempered steel. "It is, but Wyrden added something else to it."

"Oh?"

"The leaves of a plant that grows in the eastern part of Du Weldenvarden, along the shores of Röna Lake."

He frowned. "Do I know the name of this plant?"

"Probably, but it's of no importance. Go on: drink. You'll like it; I promise."

And she laughed again, which gave him pause. He had never seen her like this before. She seemed fey and reckless, and with a jolt of surprise, he realized she was already rather tipsy.

Eragon hesitated, and he wondered if Glaedr was watching them. Then he lifted the flask to his lips and swallowed a mouthful of the faelnirv. The liqueur tasted different than he was accustomed to; it had a potent, musky flavor similar to the scent of a marten or a stoat.

Eragon grimaced and fought the urge to gag as the faelnirv burned a track down his throat. He took another, smaller sip and then passed the flask back to Arya, who drank as well.

The past day had been one of blood and horror. He had spent most of it fighting, killing, almost being killed himself, and he needed a release. . . . He needed to forget. The tension he felt was too deep-seated to ease with mental tricks alone. Something else was required. Something that came from outside of himself, even as the violence he had participated in had, for the most part, been external, not internal.

When Arya returned the flask to him, he downed a large quaff and then chuckled, unable to help himself.

Arya raised an eyebrow and regarded him with a thoughtful, if merry, expression. "What amuses you so?"

"This . . . Us . . . The fact that we're still alive, and *they*"— he waved his hand in the direction of Dras-Leona—"aren't. Life amuses me, life and death." A warm glow had already begun to form in his belly, and the tips of his ears had started to tingle.

"It is nice to be alive," said Arya.

They continued to pass the flask back and forth until it was empty, at which point Eragon fit the stopper back into the mouth of the container—a task that required several attempts, for his fingers felt thick and clumsy, and the cot seemed to tilt underneath him, like the deck of a ship at sea.

He gave the empty flask to Arya, and as she took it, he grasped her hand, her right hand, and turned it toward the light. The skin was once more smooth and unblemished. No sign of her injury remained. "Blödhgarm healed you?" said Eragon.

Arya nodded, and he released her. "Mostly. I have full use of my hand again." She demonstrated by opening and closing it several times. "But there is still a patch of skin by the base of my thumb where I have no feeling." She pointed with her left index finger.

Eragon reached out and lightly touched the area. "Here?"

"Here," she said, and moved his hand a bit to the right.

"And Blödhgarm wasn't able do anything about it?"

She shook her head. "He tried a half-dozen spells, but the nerves refuse to rejoin." She made a dismissive motion. "It's of no consequence. I can still wield a sword and I can still draw a bow. That is all that matters."

Eragon hesitated, then said, "You know . . . how grateful I am for what you did—what you tried to do. I'm only sorry it left you with a permanent mark. If I could have prevented it somehow . . ."

"Do not feel bad because of it. It's impossible to go through life unscathed. Nor should you want to. By the hurts we accumulate, we measure both our follies and our accomplishments."

"Angela said something similar about enemies—that if you didn't make them, you were a coward or worse."

Arya nodded. "There is some truth to that."

They continued to talk and laugh as the night wore on. Instead of weakening, the effects of the altered faelnirv continued to strengthen. A giddy haze settled over Eragon, and he noticed that the pockets of shadow in the tent looked as if they were swirling, and strange, flashing lights—like those he normally saw when he closed his eyes at night—floated across his field of vision. The tips of his ears were burning fever-hot, and the skin on his back itched and crawled, as if ants were marching over it. Also, certain sounds had acquired a peculiar intensity—the rhythmic chirping of the lakeside insects, for example, and the crackle of the torch outside his tent; they dominated his hearing to the point where he had difficulty singling out any other noise.

Have I been poisoned? he wondered.

"What is it?" asked Arya, noticing his alarm.

He wet his mouth, which had become incredibly, painfully dry, and told her what he was experiencing.

Arya laughed and leaned back, her eyes heavy and half-lidded. "That is as it should be. The sensations will wear off by dawn. Until then, relax and allow yourself to enjoy them."

Eragon struggled with himself for a moment as he debated whether to use a spell to clear his mind—if indeed he could—but then he decided to trust Arya and follow her advice.

As the world bent around him, it occurred to Eragon how dependent he was on his senses to determine what was real and what was not. He would have sworn that the flashing lights were there, though the rational part of his mind knew they were only faelnirv-induced apparitions.

He and Arya continued to talk, but their conversation became increasingly disjointed and incoherent. Nevertheless, Eragon was convinced that everything they said was of paramount importance, although he could not have explained why, nor could he remember what they had discussed only moments before.

Some time later, Eragon heard the low, throaty sound of a reed pipe being played somewhere in the camp. At first he thought he was imagining the lilting tones, but then he saw Arya cock her head and turn in the direction of the music, as if she too had noticed it.

Who was playing and why, Eragon could not tell. Nor did he care. It was as if the melody had sprung out of the blackness of the night itself, like a wind, lonely and forsaken.

He listened with his head tilted back and his eyelids nearly closed while fantastical images roiled within his mind, images that the faelnirv had induced but that the music shaped.

As it progressed, the melody grew ever more wild, and what had been plaintive became urgent, and the notes trilled up and down in a manner so fast, so insistent, so complicated, so *alarming* that Eragon began to fear for the safety of the musician. To play that quickly and that skillfully seemed unnatural, even for an elf.

Arya laughed as the music reached a particularly fevered pitch, and she leaped to her feet and struck a pose, lifting her arms over her head. She stamped her foot against the ground and clapped her hands—once, twice, three times—and then, much to Eragon's astonishment, she began to dance. Her movements were slow at first, almost languorous, but soon her pace increased until she matched the frenzied beat of the music.

The music soon peaked, then began to gradually subside as the piper restated and resolved the themes of the melody. But before the music ceased, a sudden itch made Eragon grab his right hand and scratch at the palm. At the same moment, he felt a twinge in the back of his mind as one of his wards flared to life, warning him of some danger.

A second later, a dragon roared overhead.

Cold fear stabbed through Eragon.

The roar did not belong to Saphira.

THE WORD OF A RIDER

Eragon grabbed Brisingr, and then he and Arya dashed from the tent.

Outside, Eragon staggered and fell to one knee as the ground seemed to pitch underneath him. He clutched at a tuft of grass, using it as an anchor while he waited for the dizziness to abate.

When he dared look up, he squinted. The light from the nearby torches was painfully bright; the flames swam before him like fish, as if detached from the oil-soaked rags that fed them.

Balance is gone, thought Eragon. *Can't trust my vision. Have to clear my mind. Have to—*

A patch of motion caught his eye, and he ducked. Saphira's tail swept over him, passing only inches above his head, then struck his tent and flattened it, breaking the wooden poles like so many dry twigs.

Saphira snarled, snapping at the empty air as she struggled to her feet. Then she paused, confused.

Little one, what—

A sound like a mighty wind interrupted her, and from out of the blackness of the sky, there emerged Thorn, red as blood and glittering like a million shifting stars. He landed close to Nasuada's pavilion, and the earth shook from the impact of his weight.

Eragon heard Nasuada's guards shouting; then Thorn swung his right forepaw across the ground, and half the shouts went silent.

From rigging strapped to the sides of the red dragon, several dozen soldiers leaped down and spread outward, stabbing into tents and cutting down the watchmen who ran at them.

Horns blared along the perimeter of the camp. At the same time, the sounds of combat erupted near their outer defenses, marking, Eragon thought, a secondary attack, from the north.

How many soldiers are there? he wondered. *Are we surrounded?* Panic blossomed within him so strongly that it almost overrode his sense of reason and sent him running blindly into the night. Only the knowledge that the faelnirv was responsible for his reaction held him in place.

He whispered a quick healing spell, hoping it might counteract the effects of the liqueur, but to no avail. Disappointed, he carefully stood, drew Brisingr, and joined Arya to stand shoulder to shoulder with her as five soldiers ran toward them. Eragon was not sure how he and Arya could fight them off. Not in their condition.

The men were less than twenty feet away when Saphira growled and slapped the ground with her tail, knocking the soldiers over. Eragon—who had sensed what Saphira was about to do—grabbed Arya, and she grabbed him, and by supporting each other, they were able to remain upright.

Then Blödhgarm and another elf, Laufin, sprinted out of the maze of tents and slew the five soldiers before they could regain their footing. The other elves followed close behind.

Another group of soldiers, this one over twenty strong, ran toward Eragon and Arya, almost as if the men knew where to find them.

The elves arranged themselves in a line in front of Eragon and Arya. But before the soldiers came within reach of the elves' swords, one of the tents burst open and Angela charged howling into the midst of the soldiers, catching them by surprise.

The herbalist was wearing a red nightgown, her curly hair was in disarray, and in each hand she wielded a wool comb. The combs were three feet long and had two rows of steel tines mounted at an angle on the ends. The tines were longer than Eragon's forearm and were sharpened to needle-like points—he knew that if you pricked yourself, you could catch blood poisoning from the unwashed wool they had been drawn through.

Two of the soldiers fell as Angela buried the wool combs in their sides, driving the tines right through their hauberks. The herbalist was more than a foot shorter than some of the men, but she showed no sign of fear as she bounded among them. To the contrary, she was the picture of ferocity, with her wild hair and her shouting and her dark-eyed expression.

The soldiers encircled Angela and closed in around her, hiding her from sight, and for a moment, Eragon feared they would overwhelm her.

Then, from elsewhere in the camp, he saw Solembum racing toward the knot of soldiers, the werecat's ears pressed flat against his skull. More werecats trailed him: twenty, thirty, forty—a whole pack, and all in their animal forms.

A cacophony of hisses, yowls, and screams filled the night as the werecats sprang upon the soldiers and pulled them to the ground, tearing at them with claws and teeth. The soldiers fought back as best they could, but they were no match for the large, shaggy cats.

The whole sequence, from Angela's appearance to the intervention of the werecats, transpired with such speed, Eragon barely had time to react. As the werecats swarmed the soldiers, he blinked and wet his parched mouth, feeling a sense of unreality about everything around him.

Then Saphira said, *Quick, onto my back,* and she crouched so he could climb onto her.

"Wait," said Arya, and put a hand on his arm. She murmured a few phrases in the ancient language. An instant later, the distortion of Eragon's senses vanished and he again found himself in full command of his body.

He gave Arya a grateful glance, then tossed Brisingr's scabbard onto the remains of his tent, scrambled up Saphira's right foreleg, and settled into his usual position at the base of her neck. Without a saddle, the sharp edges of her scales dug into the insides of his legs, a feeling he well remembered from their first flight together.

"We need the Dauthdaert," he shouted down to Arya.

She nodded and ran toward her own tent, which was several hundred feet away, on the eastern side of the camp.

Another consciousness, not Saphira's, pressed against Eragon's mind, and he drew in his thoughts to protect himself. Then he realized the being was Glaedr, and he allowed the golden dragon past his guard.

I will help, said Glaedr. Behind his words, Eragon sensed a terrible, seething anger directed at Thorn and Murtagh, an anger that seemed powerful enough to burn the world to cinders. *Join your minds with me, Eragon, Saphira. And you as well, Blödhgarm, and you, Laufin, and the rest of your kind. Let me see with your eyes, and let me listen with your ears, so that I can advise you as to what to do, and so that I can lend you my strength when needed.*

Saphira leaped forward, half flying, half gliding over the rows of tents toward the huge ruby mass of Thorn. The elves followed below, killing what soldiers they encountered.

Saphira had the advantage of height, as Thorn was still on the ground. She angled toward him—intending, Eragon knew, to alight on Thorn's back and fix her jaws upon his neck—but as he saw her coming, the red dragon snarled and twisted to face her, crouching like a smaller dog confronting a larger one.

Eragon just had time to notice that Thorn's saddle was empty, and then the dragon reared and batted at Saphira with one of his thick, muscular forelegs. His heavy paw swung through the air with a loud rushing sound. In the gloom, his claws appeared startlingly white.

Saphira veered to the side, contorting her body to avoid the blow. The ground and the sky tilted around Eragon, and he found himself looking up at the camp as the tip of Saphira's right wing tore apart someone's tent.

The force of the turn tugged on Eragon, pulling him away from Saphira. Her scales started to slip out from between his legs. He clenched his thighs and tightened his hold on the spike in front of

349

him, but Saphira's motion was too violent to withstand, and a second later, his grip gave way and he found himself tumbling through the air, without a clear idea of which direction was up and which was down.

Even as he fell, he made sure to maintain his grasp on Brisingr and to keep the blade well away from his body; wards or no wards, the sword could still injure him, due to Rhunön's spellwork.

Little one!

"Letta!" Eragon shouted, and with a jolt, he stopped dead in the air, no more than ten feet above the ground. While the world seemed to keep spinning for another few seconds, he glimpsed Saphira's sparkling outline as she circled around to retrieve him.

Thorn bellowed and sprayed the rows of tents between him and Eragon with a layer of white-hot flames that leaped up toward the sky. Screams of agony swiftly followed as the men within burned to death.

Eragon raised a hand to shield his face. His magic protected him from serious injury, but the heat was uncomfortable. *I'm fine. Don't turn back*, he said, not only to Saphira but also to Glaedr and the elves. *You have to stop them. I'll meet you by Nasuada's pavilion.*

Saphira's disapproval was palpable, but she altered her course to resume her attack on Thorn.

Eragon released his spell and dropped to the ground. He landed lightly on the balls of his feet, then set off at a run between the burning tents, many of which were already collapsing, sending up pillars of orange sparks.

The smoke and the stench of burnt wool made it hard for Eragon to breathe. He coughed, and his eyes began to water, blurring the lower part of his vision.

Several hundred feet ahead, Saphira and Thorn tussled, two giants in the night. Eragon felt a sense of primal fear. What was he doing running *toward* them, toward a pair of snapping, snarling creatures, each larger than a house—larger than two houses in

Thorn's case—and each with claws, fangs, spikes larger than his whole body? Even after the initial surge of fear subsided, a small amount of trepidation remained as he raced ahead.

He hoped Roran and Katrina were safe. Their tent was on the opposite side of the camp, but Thorn and the soldiers might turn in that direction at any moment.

"Eragon!"

Arya loped through the burning debris, carrying the Dauthdaert in her left hand. A faint green nimbus surrounded the barbed blade of the lance, although the glow was hard to see against the backdrop of flames. Trotting alongside her was Orik, who barreled through the tongues of fire as if they were no more dangerous than wisps of vapor. The dwarf was shirtless and helmetless. He held the ancient war hammer Volund in one hand and a small round shield in the other. Blood smeared both ends of the hammer.

Eragon greeted them with a raised hand and a cry, glad to have his friends with him. When she caught up, Arya offered him the lance, but Eragon shook his head. "Keep it!" he said. "We'll have a better chance of stopping Thorn if you use Niernen and I use Brisingr."

Arya nodded and tightened her grip on the lance. For the first time, Eragon wondered if, as an elf, she would be able to bring herself to kill a dragon. Then he put the thought aside. If there was one thing he knew about Arya, it was that she always did what was necessary, no matter how difficult.

Thorn clawed Saphira's ribs, and Eragon gasped as he felt her pain through their bond. From Blödhgarm's mind, he gathered that the elves were close to the dragons, busy fighting the soldiers. Not even they dared move any nearer to Saphira and Thorn, for fear of being crushed underfoot.

"Over there," said Orik, and pointed with his hammer toward a cluster of soldiers moving through the rows of destroyed tents.

"Leave them," said Arya. "We have to help Saphira."

Orik grunted. "Right, then, off we go."

The three of them dashed forward, but Eragon and Arya soon left Orik far behind. No dwarf could hope to keep up with them, not even one as strong and fit as Orik.

"Go on!" shouted Orik from behind. "I'll follow as fast as I can!"

As Eragon dodged scraps of burning fabric that were floating through the air, he spotted Nar Garzhvog amid a knot of ten soldiers. The horned Kull appeared grotesque by the ruddy light of the flames; his lips were drawn back from his fangs, and the shadows on his heavy brow ridge gave his face a crude, brutal look, as if his skull had been hacked out of a boulder with a dull chisel. Fighting barehanded, he grabbed a soldier and tore him limb from limb as easily as Eragon might tear apart a roast chicken.

A few paces later, the burning tents ended. On the other side of the flames, all was confusion.

Blödhgarm and two of his spellcasters stood facing four blackrobed men, who Eragon assumed were magicians of the Empire. Neither the men nor the elves stirred, though their faces displayed immense strain. Dozens of soldiers lay dead on the ground, but others still ran free, some bearing wounds so horrendous that Eragon knew at once the men were immune to pain.

He could not see the rest of the elves, but he could sense their presence on the other side of Nasuada's red pavilion, which stood in the center of the havoc.

Groups of werecats chased soldiers back and forth throughout the clearing around the pavilion. King Halfpaw and his mate, Shadowhunter, led two of the groups; Solembum led a third.

Close to the pavilion stood the herbalist, dueling with a large, burly man—she fighting with her wool combs, he with a mace in one hand and a flail in the other. The two seemed fairly matched, despite their differences in sex, weight, height, reach, and equipment.

To Eragon's surprise, Elva was there as well, sitting on the end of a barrel. The witch-child had her arms wrapped around her stomach and appeared deathly ill, but she too was participating in the battle, albeit in her own unique way. Clustered before her were a dozen soldiers, and Eragon saw that she was speaking rapidly to them, her small mouth moving in a blur. As she spoke, each man reacted differently: one stood fixed in place, seemingly unable to move; one cringed and covered his face with his hands; one knelt and stabbed himself in the chest with a long dagger; another flung down his weapons and ran off through the camp; and still another babbled like a fool. None lifted their swords against her, and none went on to attack anyone else.

And looming above the mayhem, like two living mountains, were Saphira and Thorn. They had moved off to the left of the pavilion and were circling each other, trampling row after row of tents. Tongues of flames flickered in the pits of their nostrils and in the gaps between their saber-like teeth.

Eragon hesitated. The welter of sounds and motions was hard to take in, and he was uncertain where he was needed most.

Murtagh? he asked Glaedr.

We've yet to find him, if he's even here. I can't feel his mind, but it's hard to know for sure with so many people and spells in one place. Through their link, Eragon could tell that the golden dragon was doing far more than just talking to him; Glaedr was listening simultaneously to the thoughts of Saphira and the elves, as well as helping Blödhgarm and his two companions in their mental struggle against the Empire's magicians.

Eragon was confident that they would be able to defeat the magicians, just as he was confident that Angela and Elva were perfectly capable of defending themselves from the rest of the soldiers. Saphira, however, was already wounded in several places, and she was hard-pressed to keep Thorn from attacking the rest of the camp.

Eragon glanced at the Dauthdaert in Arya's hand, then back at the massive shapes of the dragons. *We have to kill him*, Eragon thought, and his heart grew heavy. Then his eye fell on Elva, and a new idea took root in his mind. The girl's words were more powerful than any weapon; no one, not even Galbatorix, could withstand them. If she could but speak to Thorn, she could drive him away.

No! growled Glaedr. *You waste time, youngling. Go to your dragon—now! She needs your help. You must kill Thorn, not scare him into fleeing! He is broken, and there is nothing you can do to save him.*

Eragon looked at Arya, and she looked at him.

"Elva would be faster," he said.

"We have the Dauthdaert—"

"Too dangerous. Too difficult."

Arya hesitated, then nodded. Together they started toward Elva.

Before they reached her, Eragon heard a muffled scream. He turned and, to his horror, saw Murtagh striding out of the pavilion, dragging Nasuada by her wrists.

Nasuada's hair was disheveled. A nasty scratch marred one of her cheeks, and her yellow dressing gown was torn in several places. She kicked at Murtagh's knee, but her heel bounced off a ward, leaving Murtagh untouched. He pulled her closer with a cruel tug, then struck her on the temple with the pommel of Zar'roc, knocking her unconscious.

Eragon yelled and swerved toward them.

Murtagh gave him a brief look. Then he sheathed his sword, hoisted Nasuada onto a shoulder, and knelt on one knee, where he bowed his head, as if in prayer.

A spike of pain from Saphira distracted Eragon, and she cried, *Beware! He's escaped me!*

As Eragon leaped over a mound of corpses, he risked a quick glance upward and saw Thorn's glittering belly and velvet wings blotting out half the stars in the sky. The red dragon spun slightly as he drifted downward, like a large, weighted leaf.

Eragon dove to the side and rolled behind the pavilion, trying to put distance between himself and the dragon. A rock dug into his shoulder as he landed.

Without slowing, Thorn reached down with his right foreleg, which was as thick and knotted as a tree trunk, and closed his enormous paw around Murtagh and Nasuada. His claws sank into the earth, excavating a plug of dirt several feet deep as he picked up the two humans.

Then, with a triumphant roar and the bone-jarring *thuds* of flapping wings, Thorn arched upward and started to climb away from the camp.

From where she and Thorn had been grappling, Saphira took off in pursuit, streamers of blood unfurling from bites and claw marks along her limbs. She was faster than Thorn, but even if she caught him, Eragon could not imagine how she could rescue Nasuada without injuring her.

A breath of wind tugged at his hair as Arya sped past him. She ran up a pile of barrels and jumped, and her leap carried her high into the air, higher than any elf could jump without assistance. Reaching out, she grabbed hold of Thorn's tail and hung dangling from it like an ornament.

Eragon took a half step forward, as if to stop her, then cursed and growled, "Audr!"

The spell launched him into the sky, like an arrow from a bow. He reached out to Glaedr, and the old dragon fed him energy to sustain his ascension. Eragon burned the energy without heed, not caring the price, only wanting to reach Thorn before something horrible happened to Nasuada or Arya.

As he hurtled past Saphira, Eragon watched as Arya began to climb up Thorn's tail. She clung to the spikes along his spine with her right hand, using them like the rungs on a ladder. With her left, she plunged the Dauthdaert into Thorn, anchoring herself with the blade of the spear even as she pulled herself higher and higher up his heaving body. Thorn wriggled and twisted and snapped at her, like a horse irritated by a fly, but he could not reach her.

Then the blood-red dragon drew in his wings and legs, and with his precious cargo cradled close against his chest, he dove toward the ground, spinning round and round in a death spiral. The Dauthdaert tore loose from Thorn's flesh, and Arya stretched out at an angle to him as she held on to a spike with only her right hand—her weak hand, the hand she had injured in the catacombs under Dras-Leona.

Ere long, her fingers loosened and she fell away from Thorn, her arms and legs flung outward like the spokes of a wagon wheel. No doubt the result of a spell she had cast, her gyrations slowed and then ceased, as did her downward trajectory, until at last she floated upright in the night sky. Illuminated by the glow of the Dauthdaert, which she still held, she appeared to Eragon like a green firefly hovering in the darkness.

Thorn flared his wings and looped back toward her. Arya's head swiveled as she looked over at Saphira; then she rotated in the air to face Thorn.

A malefic light sprang into existence between Thorn's jaws an instant before an ever-expanding wall of flames billowed out of his maw and rolled over Arya, obscuring her form.

By then, Eragon was less than fifty feet away—close enough that the heat stung his cheeks.

The flames cleared to reveal Thorn turning away from Arya, doubling back on himself as quickly as his bulk would allow. As he did, he swung his tail, whipping it through the air faster than she could hope to evade.

"No!" shouted Eragon.

There was a *crack* as the tail struck Arya. It knocked her into the darkness, like a stone loosed from a sling, and the Dauthdaert separated from her and arced downward, its glow dwindling to a faint point that soon vanished altogether.

Iron bands seemed to tighten around Eragon's chest, squeezing the breath out of him. Thorn was pulling away, but Eragon might still be able to overtake the dragon if he drew even more energy from Glaedr. However, his connection with Glaedr was growing tenuous and Eragon could not hope to best Thorn and Murtagh alone and high above the ground, not when Murtagh had dozens or more Eldunarí at his disposal.

Eragon swore, cut off the spell that was propelling him through the air, and dove headfirst after Arya. The wind screamed in his ears and tore at his hair and clothes, and mashed the skin on his cheeks flat, and forced him to narrow his eyes to slits. An insect struck him on the neck; the impact stung as fiercely as if he had been hit by a pebble.

As he fell, Eragon searched with his mind for Arya's consciousness. He had just sensed a glimmer of awareness somewhere in the gloom below when Saphira shot out beneath him, her scales muted in the light of the stars. She turned upside down, and Eragon saw her reach out and catch a small, dark object with her forepaws.

A jolt of pain went through the mind Eragon had touched; then all thought ceased within it and he felt no more.

I have her, little one, said Saphira.

"Letta," Eragon said, and he slowed to a halt.

He looked for Thorn again, but saw only stars and blackness. To the east, he heard twice the indistinct sound of flapping wings, then all was silent.

Eragon looked toward the Varden's camp. Patches of fire glowed orange and sullen through layers of smoke. Hundreds of tents lay crumpled in the dirt, along with however many men had failed to escape before Saphira and Thorn trampled them. But those men were not the only victims of the attack. From his height, Eragon could not pick out the bodies, but he knew the soldiers had killed scores.

The taste of ashes filled Eragon's mouth. He was shaking; tears of rage and fear and frustration clouded his eyes. Arya was injured—perhaps dead. Nasuada was gone, captured, and soon she would be at the mercy of Galbatorix's most skilled torturers.

Hopelessness overcame Eragon.

How could they continue now? How could they possibly hope for victory without Nasuada to lead them?

CONCLAVE OF KINGS

Upon landing in the Varden's camp with Saphira, Eragon slid down her side and ran to the patch of grass where she had gently deposited Arya.

The elf lay facedown, limp and motionless. When Eragon rolled her over, her eyes flickered open. "Thorn . . . What of Thorn?" she whispered.

He escaped, said Saphira.

"And . . . Nasuada? Did you rescue her?"

Eragon looked down and shook his head.

Sorrow passed over Arya's face. She coughed and winced, then started to sit up. A thread of blood trickled from the corner of her mouth.

"Wait," said Eragon. "Don't move. I'll fetch Blödhgarm."

"There's no need." Grasping his shoulder, Arya pulled herself onto her feet, then gingerly rose to her full height. Her breath caught as her muscles stretched, and Eragon saw the pain she was trying to hide. "I'm only bruised, not broken. My wards protected me from the worst of Thorn's blow."

Eragon was doubtful, but he accepted her statement.

What now? asked Saphira, moving closer to them. The sharp, musky smell of her blood was thick in Eragon's nostrils.

Eragon looked around at the flames and destruction in the camp. Again he thought of Roran and Katrina and wondered if they had survived the attack. *What now indeed?*

Circumstances answered his question. First, a pair of wounded soldiers ran out of a bank of smoke and attacked him and Arya. By the time Eragon dispatched them, eight of the elves had converged upon their location.

After Eragon convinced them he was unharmed, the elves turned their attention to Saphira and insisted on healing the bites and scratches Thorn had given her, even though Eragon would have preferred to do it himself.

Knowing that the healing was going to require several minutes, Eragon left Saphira with the elves and hurried back through the rows of tents to the area near Nasuada's pavilion, where Blödhgarm and the two other elven spellcasters were still locked in mental combat with the last of the four enemy magicians.

The remaining magician was kneeling on the ground, his brow pressed against his knees and his arms wrapped around the nape of his neck. Instead of adding his thoughts to the invisible fray, Eragon strode over to the magician, tapped him on the shoulder, and shouted, "Ha!"

The magician quivered, startled, and the distraction allowed the elves to slip past his defenses. This Eragon knew because the man convulsed and then rolled over, the whites of his eyes showing, and a yellowish foam bubbled out of his mouth. Soon afterward, he ceased breathing.

With clipped sentences, Eragon explained to Blödhgarm and the two other elves what had happened to Arya and Nasuada. Blödhgarm's fur bristled, and his yellow eyes burned with anger. But his only comment was to say in the ancient language, "Dark times are upon us, Shadeslayer." Then he sent Yaela to find and retrieve the Dauthdaert from wherever it had fallen.

Together Eragon, Blödhgarm, and Uthinarë, the elf who had stayed with them, ranged through the camp, rounding up and killing the few soldiers who had escaped the teeth of the werecats and the blades of the men, dwarves, elves, and Urgals. They also used their magic to extinguish some of the larger blazes, snuffing them out as easily as the flame of a candle.

The whole while, an overwhelming sense of dread clutched at Eragon, pressing down on him like a pile of sodden fleeces and constricting his mind so that he found it difficult to think of anything other than death, defeat, and failure. He felt as if the world were crumbling around him—as if everything he and the Varden had striven to accomplish was unspooling rapidly, and there was nothing he could do to regain control. The sense of helplessness sapped his will to do anything other than sit in a corner and give in to misery. Still, he refused to satisfy the urge, for if he did, then he might as well be dead. So he kept moving, laboring alongside the elves in spite of his despair.

It did not improve his mood when Glaedr contacted him and said, *If you had listened to me, we might have stopped Thorn and saved Nasuada.*

And we might not have, said Eragon. He did not want to discuss the subject further but felt compelled to add: *You let your anger cloud your sight. Killing Thorn wasn't the only solution, nor should you have been so quick to destroy one of the only remaining members of your kind.*

Do not think to lecture me, youngling! snapped Glaedr. *You cannot begin to understand what I have lost.*

I understand better than most, Eragon replied, but Glaedr had already withdrawn from his mind, and Eragon did not think the dragon heard him.

Eragon had just put out one fire and was moving to the next when Roran hurried to him and grasped his arm. "Are you hurt?"

Relief swept through Eragon as he saw his cousin alive and well. "No," he said.

"And Saphira?"

"The elves have already mended her wounds. What of Katrina? Is she safe?"

Roran nodded, and his posture relaxed slightly, but his expression remained troubled. "Eragon," he said, drawing closer, "what's happened? What *is* happening? I saw Jörmundur running around like a chicken with its head cut off, and Nasuada's guards look grim as death, and I can't get anyone to talk to me. Are we still in danger? Is Galbatorix about to attack?"

Eragon glanced around, then drew Roran to the side, where no one else could hear. "You can't tell anyone. Not yet," he cautioned.

"You have my word."

With a few quick sentences, Eragon summarized the situation to Roran. By the time he finished, Roran's expression had grown bleak. "We can't let the Varden disband," he said.

"Of course not. That won't happen, but King Orrin may try to assume command, or—" Eragon fell silent as a group of warriors passed nearby. Then: "Stay with me, will you? I may need your help."

"My help? For what would you need *my* help?"

"The whole army admires you, Roran, even the Urgals. You're Stronghammer, the hero of Aroughs, and your opinion carries weight. That might prove important."

Roran was silent for a moment, then nodded. "I'll do what I can."

"For now, just keep watch for soldiers," said Eragon, and continued toward the fire that was his intended destination.

Half an hour later, as quiet and order had begun to settle over the camp again, a runner informed Eragon that Arya desired his immediate presence in King Orik's pavilion.

Eragon and Roran exchanged glances, then set out toward the northwestern quadrant of the camp, where the majority of the dwarves had pitched their tents.

"There is no choice," said Jörmundur. "Nasuada made her wishes perfectly clear. You, Eragon, must take her place and lead the Varden in her stead."

The faces ringing the interior of the tent were stern and unyielding. Dark shadows clung to the hollows of their temples and to the deep frown lines of the assorted two-legs, as Eragon knew Saphira would have called them. The only one not frowning was Saphira— her head was pushed through the entrance to the pavilion so that she could participate in the conclave—but her lips were pulled back slightly, as if she was about to snarl.

Also present were King Orrin, a purple cloak wrapped over his night robes; Arya, looking shaken but determined; King Orik, who had found a mail shirt to cover himself; the werecat king, Grimrr Halfpaw, a white linen bandage wrapped around a sword cut on his right shoulder; Nar Garzhvog, the Kull, stooping to avoid brushing his horns against the ceiling; and Roran, who stood by the wall of the tent listening to the proceedings, so far without comment.

No one else had been allowed into the pavilion. Not guards, not advisers, not servants, not even Blödhgarm or the other elves. Outside, a block of men, dwarves, and Urgals stood twelve deep before the entrance—their task to prevent anyone, no matter how powerful or dangerous, from interfering with the meeting. And woven about the tent were a number of hastily cast spells intended to prevent eavesdropping both mundane and magical.

362 "I never wanted this," said Eragon, staring down at the map of Alagaësia stretched out on the table in the center of the pavilion.

"None of us did," said King Orrin in a biting tone.

It had been wise of Arya, Eragon thought, to stage the meeting in Orik's pavilion. The dwarf king was known to be a staunch supporter of Nasuada and the Varden—as well as being Eragon's clan chief and foster brother—but no one could accuse him of aspiring to Nasuada's position, nor would the humans necessarily accept him as her replacement.

Still, by staging the meeting in Orik's pavilion, Arya had strengthened Eragon's case and undercut his critics, without appearing to endorse or attack either. She was, Eragon had to admit, far more accomplished at manipulating others than he. The only risk in what she had done was that it might cause others to think Orik was his master, but that was a risk Eragon was willing to accept in exchange for his friend's support.

"I never wanted this," he repeated, then lifted his gaze to meet the watchful eyes of those around him. "But now that it's happened, I swear on the graves of all we've lost that I'll do my best to live up to Nasuada's example and lead the Varden to victory against Galbatorix and the Empire." He strove to project an air of confidence, but the truth was, the enormity of the situation frightened him and he had no idea whether he was up to the task. Nasuada had been impressively capable, and it was intimidating to consider trying to do even half of what she had done.

"Very commendable, I'm sure," said King Orrin. "However, the Varden has always worked in concert with its allies—with the men of Surda; with our royal friend King Orik and the dwarves of the Beor Mountains; with the elves; and now, more recently, with the Urgals, as led by Nar Garzhvog, and with the werecats." He nodded toward Grimrr, who nodded briefly in return. "It would not do for the rank and file to see us disagreeing with one another in public. Would you not agree?"

"Of course."

"Of course," said King Orrin. "I take it, then, you will continue to consult with us on matters of importance, even as Nasuada did?" Eragon hesitated, but before he could reply, Orrin resumed speaking: "All of us"—he motioned toward the others in the tent—"have risked an enormous amount in this venture, and none of us would appreciate being dictated to. Nor would we submit to it. To be blunt, despite your many accomplishments, Eragon *Shadeslayer*, you are still young and inexperienced, and that inexperience might very well prove fatal. The rest of us have had the benefit of many years leading our respective forces, or watching others lead. We can help guide you onto the right path, and perhaps together we can still find a way to right this mess and overthrow Galbatorix."

Everything Orrin said was true, Eragon thought—he *was* still young and inexperienced, and he *did* need the others' advice—but he could not admit as much without appearing weak.

So, instead, he replied, "You may rest assured that I will consult with you when needed, but my decisions, as always, will remain my own."

"Forgive me, Shadeslayer, but I have difficulty believing that. Your familiarity with the elves"—Orrin eyed Arya—"is commonly known. What's more, you are an adopted member of the Ingeitum clan, and subject to the authority of their clan chief, who just so happens to be King Orik. Perhaps I am mistaken, but it seems doubtful that your decisions will be your own."

"First, you counsel me to listen to our allies. Now you don't. Is it perhaps that you would prefer I listen to you, and you alone?" Eragon's anger grew as he spoke.

"I would prefer that your choices be in the best interests of our people, and not those of another race!"

"They have been," growled Eragon. "And they will continue to be. I owe my allegiance to both the Varden and the Ingeitum clan, yes, but also to Saphira, and Nasuada, and my family as well. Many have claim on me, even as many have claim on you, *Your Majesty*. My foremost concern, however, is defeating Galbatorix and the Empire. It always has been, and if there is a conflict among my loyalties, *that* is what shall take precedence. Question my judgment, if you must, but do not question my motives. And I would thank you to refrain from implying that I'm a traitor to my kind!"

Orrin scowled, color rising in his cheeks, and he was about to utter a retort when a loud *bang* interrupted him as Orik struck his war hammer, Volund, against his shield.

"Enough of this nonsense!" exclaimed Orik, glowering. "You worry about a crack in the floor while the whole mountain is about to come down upon us!"

Orrin's scowl deepened, but he did not pursue the matter further. Instead, he picked up his goblet of wine from the table and sank back into the depths of his chair, where he stared at Eragon with a dark, smoldering gaze.

I think he hates you, said Saphira.

That, or he hates what I represent. Either way, I'm an obstacle to him. He'll bear watching.

"The question before us is simple," said Orik. "What should we do now that Nasuada is gone?" He placed Volund flat on the table and ran his gnarled hand over his head. "Mine opinion is that our situation is the same as it was this morning. Unless we admit defeat and sue for peace, we still have only one choice: march to Urû'baen fast as our feet will carry us. Nasuada herself was never going to fight Galbatorix. That will fall to you"—he motioned toward Eragon and Saphira—"and the elves. Nasuada brought us this far, and while she will be greatly missed, we do not need her to continue. Our path allows for little deviation. Even if she were present, I cannot see her doing anything else. To Urû'baen, we must go, and that's the end of it."

Grimrr toyed with a small black-bladed dagger, seemingly indifferent to the conversation.

"I agree," said Arya. "We have no other choice."

Above them, Garzhvog's massive head dipped, causing misshapen shadows to glide across the pavilion walls. "The dwarf speaks well. The Urgralgra will stay with the Varden as long as Firesword is war chief. With him and Flametongue to lead our charges, we will collect the debt of blood that the lack-horned betrayer, Galbatorix, still owes us."

Eragon shifted slightly, uncomfortable.

"That's all very well and good," said King Orrin, "but I've yet to hear how we are supposed to defeat Murtagh and Galbatorix when we get to Urû'baen."

"We have the Dauthdaert," Eragon pointed out, for Yaela had retrieved the spear, "and with it, we can—"

King Orrin waved one hand. "Yes, yes, the Dauthdaert. It didn't help you stop Thorn, and I can't imagine that Galbatorix will let you come anywhere near him or Shruikan with it. Either way, it doesn't change the fact that you're still no match for that black-hearted traitor. Blast it, Shadeslayer, you're not even a match for your own brother, and he's been a Rider for less time than you!"

Half brother, Eragon thought, but he held his tongue. He could find no way to rebut Orrin's points; they were valid, each and every one, and they left him feeling shamed.

The king continued: "We entered this war with the understanding that you would find a way of countering Galbatorix's unnatural strength. So Nasuada promised and assured us. And yet here we are, about to confront the most powerful magician in recorded history, and we're no closer to defeating him than when we began!"

"We went to war," Eragon said quietly, "because it was the first time since the Riders fell that we've had even the slightest chance of overthrowing Galbatorix. You know that."

"What chance?" sneered the king. "We're puppets, all of us, dancing according to Galbatorix's whims. The only reason we've gotten this far is because he's *let* us. Galbatorix *wants* us to go to Urû'baen. He *wants* us to bring you to him. If he cared about stopping us, he would have flown out to meet us at the Burning Plains and crushed us then and there. And once he has you in his reach, he'll do just that: crush us."

The air in the tent seemed to grow taut between them.

Careful, said Saphira to Eragon. *He'll leave the pack if you can't convince him otherwise.*

Arya appeared similarly worried.

Eragon spread his hands flat on the table and took a moment to gather his thoughts. He did not want to lie, but at the same time he had to find a way to inspire hope in Orrin, which was difficult when Eragon felt little himself. *Is this what it was like for Nasuada all those times she rallied us to the cause, convinced us to keep going even when we couldn't see a way clear?*

"Our position isn't quite as . . . precarious as you make it out to be," said Eragon.

Orrin snorted and drank from his goblet.

"The Dauthdaert *is* a threat to Galbatorix," continued Eragon, "and that's to our advantage. He'll be wary of it. Because of that, we can force him to do what we want, perhaps just a bit. Even if we can't use it to kill him, we might be able to kill Shruikan. Theirs isn't a true pairing of dragon and Rider, but Shruikan's death would still wound him to the core."

"It'll never happen," said Orrin. "He knows that we have the Dauthdaert now, and he'll take the appropriate precautions."

"Maybe not. I doubt Murtagh and Thorn recognized it."

"No, but Galbatorix will when he examines their memories."

And he'll also know of Glaedr's existence, if they haven't told him already, Saphira said to Eragon.

Eragon's spirits sank further. He had not thought of that, but she was right. *So much for any hope of surprising him. We have no more secrets.*

Life is full of secrets. Galbatorix cannot predict exactly how we will choose to fight him. In that, at least, we can confound him.

"Which of the death spears have you found, O Shadeslayer?" asked Grimrr in a seemingly bored tone.

"Du Niernen—the Orchid."

The werecat blinked, and Eragon had the impression that he was surprised, although Grimrr's expression remained blank as ever. "The Orchid. Is that so? How very strange to find such a weapon in this age, especially that . . . particular weapon."

"Why so?" asked Jörmundur.

Grimrr's small pink tongue passed over his fangs. "Niernen is *notoriousss.*" He drew out the end of the word into a short hiss.

Before Eragon could press the werecat for more information, Garzhvog spoke, his voice grinding like boulders: "What is this death spear you speak of, Firesword? Is it the lance that wounded Saphira in Belatona? We heard tales of it, but they were odd indeed."

Eragon belatedly remembered that Nasuada had told neither the Urgals nor the werecats what Niernen truly was. *Oh well,* he thought. *It can't be helped.*

He explained to Garzhvog about the Dauthdaert, then insisted everyone in the pavilion swear an oath in the ancient language that they would not discuss the spear with anyone else without permission. There was some grumbling, but in the end they all complied, even the werecat. Trying to hide the spear from Galbatorix might have been pointless, but Eragon could see no good in allowing the Dauthdaert to become general knowledge.

When the last of them had finished their oaths, Eragon resumed speaking, "So. First, we have the Dauthdaert, and that's more than we had before. Second, I don't plan on facing Murtagh and Galbatorix together; I've never planned to. When we arrive at Urû'baen, we'll lure Murtagh out of the city, and then we'll surround him, with the whole army if necessary—the elves included—and we'll kill or capture him once and for all." He looked round at the gathered faces, trying to impress them with the force of his conviction. "Third—and this is what you have to believe deep in your hearts—Galbatorix isn't invulnerable, however powerful he is. He might have cast thousands upon thousands of wards to protect himself, but in spite of all his knowledge and cunning, there are still spells that can kill him, if only we are clever enough to think of them. Now, maybe I'll be the one to find the spell that is his undoing, but it might just as well be an elf or a member of Du Vrangr Gata. Galbatorix seems untouchable, I know, but there's always a weakness—there's always a crevice you can slip a blade through and thus stab your foe."

"If the Riders of old couldn't find his weakness, what is the likelihood we can?" demanded King Orrin.

Eragon spread his hands, palms upward. "Maybe we can't. Nothing is certain in life, much less in war. However, if the combined spellcasters of our five races can't kill him, then we might as well accept that Galbatorix is going to rule as long as he pleases, and nothing we can do is going to change that."

Silence pervaded the tent, short and profound.

Then Roran stepped forward. "I would speak," he said.

Eragon saw the others around the table exchange glances.

"Say what you will, Stronghammer," said Orik, to King Orrin's evident annoyance.

"It is this: too much blood and too many tears have been shed for us to turn back now. It would be disrespectful, both to the dead and to those who remember the dead. This may be a battle between gods"—he appeared perfectly serious to Eragon as he said this—"but I for one will keep fighting until the gods strike me down, or until I strike them down. A dragon might kill ten thousand wolves one at a time, but ten thousand wolves together can kill a dragon."

Not likely, Saphira snorted in the privacy of her and Eragon's shared mind space.

Roran smiled without humor. "And we have a dragon of our own. Decide as you wish. But I, for one, am going to Urû'baen, and I'll face Galbatorix, even if I have to do it by myself."

"Not by yourself," said Arya. "I know I speak for Queen Islanzadí when I say that our people will stand with you."

"As will ours," rumbled Garzhvog.

"And ours," affirmed Orik.

"And ours," Eragon said in a tone that he hoped would discourage dissent.

When, after a pause, the four of them turned toward Grimrr, the werecat sniffed and said, "Well, I suppose we'll be there too." He inspected his sharp nails. "Someone has to sneak past enemy lines, and it certainly won't be the dwarves bumbling around in their iron boots."

Orik's eyebrows rose, but if he was offended, he hid it well.

Two more drinks Orrin quaffed; then he wiped his mouth with the back of his hand and said, "Very well, as you wish; we'll continue on to Urû'baen." His cup empty, he reached for the bottle in front of him.

A MAZE WITHOUT END

Eragon and the others spent the rest of the conclave discussing practicalities: lines of communication—who was supposed to answer to whom; assignments of duty; rearrangements of the camp wards and sentinels to prevent Thorn or Shruikan from sneaking up on them again; and how to secure new equipment for the men whose belongings had been burned or squashed during the attack. By consensus they decided to hold off announcing what had happened to Nasuada until the following day; it was more important for the warriors to get what sleep they could before dawn brightened the horizon.

And yet, the one thing they never discussed was whether they should try to rescue Nasuada. It was obvious that the only way to free her would be to seize Urû'baen, and by then she would probably be dead, injured, or bound to Galbatorix in the ancient language. So they avoided the subject entirely, as if to mention it was forbidden.

Nevertheless, she was a constant presence in Eragon's thoughts. Every time he closed his eyes, he saw Murtagh striking her, then the scaly fingers of Thorn's paw closing round her, and then the red dragon flying off into the night. The memories only made Eragon more miserable, but he could not stop himself from reliving them.

As the conclave dispersed, Eragon motioned to Roran, Jörmundur, and Arya. They followed him without question back to his tent, where Eragon spent some time asking their advice and planning for the day to come.

"The Council of Elders will give you some trouble, I'm sure,"

Jörmundur said. "They don't consider you as skilled at politics as Nasuada, and they'll try to take advantage of that." The long-haired warrior had appeared preternaturally calm since the attack, so much so that Eragon suspected he was on the verge of either tears or rage, or perhaps a combination of both.

"I'm not," Eragon said.

Jörmundur inclined his head. "Nevertheless, you must hold strong. I can help you some, but much will depend on how you comport yourself. If you allow them to unduly influence your decisions, they'll think *they* have inherited the leadership of the Varden, not you."

Eragon glanced at Arya and Saphira, concerned.

Never fear, said Saphira to them all. *No one shall get the better of him while I stand watch.*

When their smaller, secondary meeting came to an end, Eragon waited until Arya and Jörmundur had filed out of the tent; then he caught Roran by the shoulder. "Did you mean what you said about this being a battle of the gods?"

Roran stared at him. "I did. . . . You and Murtagh and Galbatorix—you're too powerful for any normal person to defeat. It's not right. It's not fair. But so it is. The rest of us are like ants under your boots. Have you any idea how many men you've killed single-handedly?"

"Too many."

"Exactly. I'm glad you're here to fight for us, and I'm glad to count you as my brother in all but name, but I wish we didn't have to rely on a Rider or an elf or any sort of magician to win this war for us. No one should be at the mercy of another person. Not like this. It unbalances the world."

Then Roran strode out of the tent.

Eragon sank onto his cot, feeling as if he had been struck in the chest. He sat there for a while, sweating and thinking, until the strain of his overactive thoughts caused him to spring upright and hurry outside.

As he exited the tent, the six Nighthawks jumped to their feet, readying their weapons to accompany him wherever he might be going.

Eragon motioned for them to stay put. He had protested, but Jörmundur insisted upon assigning Nasuada's guards, in addition to Blödhgarm and the other elves, to protect him. "We can't be too careful," he had said. Eragon disliked having even more people follow him around, but he had been forced to agree.

Walking past the guards, Eragon hurried over to where Saphira lay curled on the ground.

She opened one eye as he neared and then lifted her wing so he could crawl under it and nestle against her warm belly. *Little one,* she said, and began to hum softly.

Eragon sat against her, listening to her humming and to the soft rustle of air flowing in and out of her mighty lungs. Behind him, her belly rose and fell with a gentle, soothing cadence.

At any other time, her presence would have been enough to calm him, but not now. His mind refused to slow, his pulse continued to hammer, and his hands and feet were uncomfortably hot.

He kept his feelings to himself, to avoid disturbing Saphira. She was tired after her two fights with Thorn, and she soon fell into a deep slumber, her humming fading into the ever-present sound of her breathing.

And still Eragon's thoughts would not give him rest. Over and over, he returned to the same impossible, incontrovertible fact: *he* was the leader of the Varden. He, who had been nothing more than the youngest member of a poor farming family, was now the leader of the second-largest army in Alagaësia. That it had happened at all seemed outrageous, as if fate was toying with him, baiting him into a trap that would destroy him. He had never wanted it, never sought it, and yet events had thrust it upon him.

What was Nasuada thinking when she chose me as her successor? he wondered. He remembered the reasons she had given him, but they did nothing to alleviate his doubts. *Did she really believe I could take*

*her place? Why not Jörmundur? He's been with the Varden for decades,
and he knows so much more about command and strategy.*

Eragon thought of when Nasuada had decided to accept the
Urgals' offer of an alliance in spite of all the hate and grief that existed between their two races, and even though it had been Urgals
who had killed her father. *Could I have done that?* He imagined
not—not then, at least. *Can I make those sorts of decisions now, if
they're what's required to defeat Galbatorix?*

He was not sure.

He made an effort to still his mind. Closing his eyes, he concentrated on counting his breaths in batches of ten. It was difficult to
keep his attention focused on the task; every few seconds, another
thought or sensation would threaten to distract him, and he often
forgot the count.

In time, however, his body began to relax, and almost without his
realizing it, the shifting, rainbow visions of his waking dreams crept
over him.

Many things he saw, some grim and unsettling, as his dreams reflected the events of the past day. Others were bittersweet: memories of what had been or what he wished could have been.

Then, like a sudden change of wind, his dreams rippled and became harder and more substantial, as if they were tangible realities
that he could reach out and touch. Everything around him faded
away, and he beheld another time and place—one that seemed
both strange and familiar, as if he had seen it once long before, and
then it had passed from recollection.

Eragon opened his eyes, but the images stayed with him, obscuring his surroundings, and he knew that he was experiencing no normal dream:

*A dark and lonely plain lay before him, cut by a single strip of water
that flowed slow-moving into the east: a ribbon of beaten silver bright
beneath the glare of a full moon. . . . Floating on the nameless river, a
ship, tall and proud, with pure white sails raised and ready. . . . Ranks
of warriors holding lances, and two hooded figures walking among them,*

as if in a stately procession. The smell of willows and cottonwoods, and a sense of passing sorrow. . . . Then a man's anguished cry, and a flash of scales, and a muddle of motion that concealed more than it revealed.

And then nothing but silence and blackness.

Eragon's sight cleared, and he again found himself looking at the underside of Saphira's wing. He released his pent-up breath—which he had not realized he was holding—and with a shaky hand wiped the tears from his eyes. He could not understand why the vision had affected him so strongly.

Was that a premonition? he wondered. *Or something actually happening at this very moment? And why is it of any importance to me?*

Thereafter, he was unable to continue resting. His worries returned in force and assailed him without reprieve, gnawing at his mind like a host of rats, each bite of which seemed to infect him with a creeping poison.

At last he crawled out from under Saphira's wing—taking care not to wake her—and wandered back to his tent.

As before, the Nighthawks rose when they saw him. Their commander, a thickset man with a crooked nose, came forward to meet Eragon. "Is there anything you need, Shadeslayer?" he asked.

Eragon dimly remembered that the man's name was Garven and something Nasuada had told him about the man losing his senses after examining the minds of the elves. The man appeared well enough now, although his gaze had a certain dreamy quality. Still, Eragon assumed Garven was capable of carrying out his duties; otherwise, Jörmundur would never have allowed him to return to his post.

"Not at the moment, Captain," Eragon said, keeping his voice low. He took another step forward, then paused. "How many of the Nighthawks were killed tonight?"

"Six, sir. An entire watch. We'll be shorthanded for a few days until we can find suitable replacements. And we'll need more recruits in addition to that. We want to double the force around you."

A look of anguish perturbed Garven's otherwise distant gaze. "We failed her, Shadeslayer. If there had been more of us there, maybe—"

"We all failed her," said Eragon. "And if there had been more of you there, more of you would have died."

The man hesitated, then nodded, his expression miserable.

I failed her, thought Eragon as he ducked into his tent. Nasuada was his liegelord; it was his duty to protect her even more than it was that of the Nighthawks. And yet the one time she had needed his help, he had been unable to save her.

He cursed once, viciously, to himself.

As her vassal, he ought to be searching for a way to rescue her, to the exclusion of all else. But he also knew that she would not want him to abandon the Varden just for her sake. She would rather suffer and die than allow her absence to harm the cause to which she had devoted her life.

Eragon cursed again and began to pace back and forth within the confines of the tent.

I'm the leader of the Varden.

Only now that she was gone did Eragon realize that Nasuada had become more than just his liegelord and commander; she had become his friend, and he felt the same urge to protect her that he often felt with Arya. If he tried, however, he could end up costing the Varden the war.

I'm the leader of the Varden.

He thought of all the people who were now his responsibility: Roran and Katrina and the rest of the villagers from Carvahall; the hundreds of warriors whom he had fought alongside, and many more as well; the dwarves; the werecats; and even the Urgals. All now under his command and dependent on him to make the right decisions in order to defeat Galbatorix and the Empire.

Eragon's pulse surged, causing his vision to flicker. He stopped pacing and clutched at the pole in the center of the tent, then dabbed the sweat from his brow and upper lip.

He wished he had someone to talk to. He considered waking

Saphira but discounted the idea. Her rest was more important than listening to him complain. Nor did he want to burden Arya or Glaedr with problems they could do nothing to solve. In any event, he doubted he would find a sympathetic listener in Glaedr when their last exchange had been so barbed.

Eragon resumed his monotonous circuit: three steps forward, turn, three steps back, turn, and repeat.

He had lost the belt of Beloth the Wise. He had allowed Murtagh and Thorn to capture Nasuada. And now he was in charge of the Varden.

Again and again, the same few thoughts kept running through his mind, and with each repetition, his sense of anxiety increased. He felt as if he were caught in a maze without end, and round every unseen corner lurked monsters waiting to pounce. Despite what he had said during the meeting with Orik, Orrin, and the others, he could not see how he, the Varden, or their allies could defeat Galbatorix.

I wouldn't even be able to rescue Nasuada, assuming I had the freedom to chase after her and try. Bitterness welled up inside him. The task before them seemed hopeless. *Why did this have to fall to us?* He swore and bit the inside of his mouth until he could not bear the pain.

He stopped pacing and crumpled to the ground, wrapping his hands around the back of his neck. "It can't be done. It can't be done," he whispered, rocking from side to side upon his knees. "It can't."

In his despair, Eragon thought of praying to the dwarf god Gûntera for help, even as he had done before. To lay his troubles at the feet of one greater than himself and to trust his fate to that power would be a relief. Doing so would allow him to accept his fate—as well as the fates of those he loved—with greater equanimity, for he would no longer be directly responsible for whatever happened.

But Eragon could not bring himself to utter the prayer. He *was* responsible for their fates, whether he liked it or not, and he felt it would be wrong to pass off his responsibility to anyone else, even a god—or the idea of a god.

The problem was, he did not think he could do what needed to be done. He could command the Varden; of that, he was reasonably sure. But as for how he might go about capturing Urû'baen and killing Galbatorix, there he was at a loss. He did not have the strength to go up against Murtagh, much less the king, and it seemed unlikely in the extreme that he could think of a way around either of their wards. Capturing their minds, or at least Galbatorix's, seemed equally improbable.

Eragon dug his fingers into the nape of his neck, stretching and scratching his skin as he frantically considered every possibility, no matter how unlikely.

Then he thought of the advice Solembum had given him in Teirm, so long ago. The werecat had said, *Listen closely and I will tell you two things. When the times comes and you need a weapon, look under the roots of the Menoa tree. Then, when all seems lost and your power is insufficient, go to the Rock of Kuthian and speak your name to open the Vault of Souls.*

His words concerning the Menoa tree had proven true; under it Eragon had found the brightsteel he needed for the blade of his sword. Now a desperate hope flared inside Eragon as he pondered the second of the werecat's pronouncements.

If ever my power was insufficient, and if ever all seemed lost, it is now, thought Eragon. However, he still had no idea where or what the Rock of Kuthian or the Vault of Souls were. He had asked both Oromis and Arya at different times, but they had never returned an answer.

Eragon reached out with his mind then, and searched through the camp until he found the distinctive feel of the werecat's mind. *Solembum,* he said, *I need your help! Please come to my tent.*

After a moment, he felt a grudging acknowledgment from the werecat, and he severed the contact.

Then Eragon sat alone in the dark . . . and waited.

FRAGMENTS,
HALF-SEEN AND INDISTINCT

Over a quarter of an hour passed before the flap to Eragon's tent stirred and Solembum pushed his way inside, his padded feet nearly silent upon the ground.

The tawny werecat walked past Eragon without looking at him, jumped onto his cot, and settled among his blankets, whereupon he began to lick the webbing between the claws of his right paw. Still not looking at Eragon, he said, *I am not a dog to come and go at your summons, Eragon.*

"I never thought you were," Eragon replied. "But I have need of you, and it is urgent."

Mmh. The rasping of Solembum's tongue grew louder as he concentrated on the leathery palm of his foot. *Speak then, Shadeslayer. What do you want?*

"One moment." Eragon stood and went over to the pole where his lantern hung. "I'm going to light this," he warned Solembum. Then Eragon spoke a word in the ancient language, and a flame sprang to life atop the wick of the lantern, filling the tent with a warm, flickering illumination.

Both Eragon and Solembum squinted while they waited for their eyes to adjust to the increase in brightness. When the light no longer felt quite so uncomfortable, Eragon seated himself on his stool, not far from the cot.

The werecat, he was puzzled to see, was watching him with ice-blue eyes.

"Weren't your eyes a different color?" he asked.

Solembum blinked once, and his eyes changed from blue to gold. Then he resumed cleaning his paw. *What do you want, Shadeslayer?*

The night is for the doing of things, not sitting and talking. The tip of his tasseled tail lashed from side to side.

Eragon wet his lips, his hope making him nervous. "Solembum, you told me that when all seemed lost and my power was insufficient, I should go to the Rock of Kuthian and open the Vault of Souls."

The werecat paused in his licking. *Ah, that.*

"Yes, that. And I need to know what you meant by it. If there's anything that can help us against Galbatorix, I need to know about it now—not later, not once I manage to solve one riddle or another, but *now*. So, where can I find the Rock of Kuthian, how do I open the Vault of Souls, and what will I find inside it?"

Solembum's black-tipped ears angled backward slightly, and the claws on the paw he was cleaning extended halfway from their sheaths. *I don't know.*

"You don't know?!" exclaimed Eragon in disbelief.

Must you repeat everything I say?

"How can you not know?"

I don't know.

Leaning forward, Eragon grabbed Solembum's large, heavy paw. The werecat's ears flattened, and he hissed and curled his paw inward, digging his claws into Eragon's hand. Eragon smiled tightly and ignored the pain. The werecat was stronger than he had expected, almost strong enough to pull him off the stool.

"No more riddles," Eragon said. "I need the truth, Solembum. Where did you get this information and what does it mean?"

The fur along Solembum's spine bristled. *Sometimes riddles are the truth, you thick-headed human. Now let me go, or I'll tear your face off and feed your guts to the crows.*

Eragon maintained his grip for a moment longer, then he released Solembum's paw and leaned back. He clenched his hand to help dull the pain and stop the bleeding.

Solembum glared at him with slitted eyes, all pretense of detachment gone. *I said I don't know because, despite what you might think,*

I do not know. I have no knowledge of where the Rock of Kuthian might lie, nor how you might open the Vault of Souls, nor what the vault might contain.

"Say that in the ancient language."

Solembum's eyes narrowed even farther, but he repeated himself in the tongue of the elves, and then Eragon knew he was speaking the truth.

So many questions occurred to Eragon, he hardly knew which to ask first. "How did you learn of the Rock of Kuthian, then?"

Again Solembum's tail lashed from side to side, flattening wrinkles in the blanket. *For the last time, I do not know. Nor do any of my kind.*

"Then how . . . ?" Eragon trailed off, overcome by confusion.

Soon after the fall of the Riders, a certain conviction came upon the members of our race that, should we encounter a new Rider, one who was not beholden to Galbatorix, we should tell him or her what I told you: of the Menoa tree and of the Rock of Kuthian.

"But . . . where did the information come from?"

Solembum's muzzle wrinkled as he bared his teeth in an unpleasant smile. *That we cannot say, only that whoever or whatever was responsible for it meant well.*

"How can you know that?" exclaimed Eragon. "What if it was Galbatorix? He could be trying to trick you. He could be trying to trick Saphira and me, so as to capture us."

No, said Solembum, and his claws sank into the blanket under him. *Werecats are not so easily fooled as others. Galbatorix is not the one behind this. Of that, I am sure. Whoever wanted you to have this information is the same person or creature who arranged for you to find the brightsteel for your sword. Would Galbatorix have done that?*

Eragon frowned. "Haven't you tried to find out who is behind this?"

We have.

"And?"

We failed. The werecat ruffled his fur. *There are two possibilities.*

One, that our memories were altered against our will and we are the pawns of some nefarious entity. Or two, that we agreed to the alteration, for whatever reason. Perhaps we even excised the memories ourselves. I find it difficult and distasteful to believe that anyone could have succeeded in meddling with our minds. A few of us, I could understand. But our entire race? No. It cannot be.

Why would you, the werecats, have been entrusted with this information?

Because, I would guess, we have always been friends of the Riders and friends of the dragons. . . . We are the watchers. The listeners. The wanderers. We walk alone in the dark places of the world, and we remember what is and what has been.

Solembum's gaze shifted away. Understand this, Eragon. None of us have been happy with the situation. We long debated whether it would cause more harm than good to pass on this information should the moment arise. In the end, the decision was mine, and I decided to tell you, for it seemed you needed all the help you could get. Make of it what you will.

"But what am I supposed to do?" said Eragon. "How am I supposed to find the Rock of Kuthian?"

That I cannot say.

"Then what use is the information? I might as well have never heard it."

Solembum blinked, once. There is one other thing I can tell you. It may mean nothing, but perhaps it can show you the way.

"What? What is it?"

If you but wait, I will tell you. When I first met you in Teirm, I had a strange feeling that you ought to have the book Domia abr Wyrda. It took me time to arrange it, but it was I who was responsible for Jeod giving the book to you. Then the werecat lifted his other paw and, after a cursory examination, began to lick it.

"Have you gotten any other strange feelings in the past few months?" asked Eragon.

Only the urge to eat a small red mushroom, but it passed quickly enough.

Eragon grunted and bent down to retrieve the book from under his cot, where he kept it with the rest of his writing supplies. He stared at the large, leather-bound volume before opening it to a random page. As usual, the thicket of runes within made little sense to him at first glance. It was only with a concerted effort that he was able to decipher even a few of them:

> . . . which, if *Taladorous is to be believed, would mean that the mountains themselves were the result of a spell. That, of course, is absurd, for* . . .

Eragon growled with frustration and closed the book. "I don't have time for this. It's too big, and I'm too slow of a reader. I've already gone through a fair number of chapters, and I've seen nothing having to do with the Rock of Kuthian or the Vault of Souls."

Solembum eyed him for a moment. *You could ask someone else to read it for you, but if there is a secret hidden in* Domia abr Wyrda, *you may be the only one who can see it.*

Eragon resisted the desire to curse. Springing up from the stool, he began to pace again. "Why didn't you tell me about all this sooner?"

It didn't seem important. Either my advice concerning the vault and the rock would be of help or it wouldn't, and knowing the origins of that information—or lack thereof—would . . . have . . . changed . . . nothing!

"But if I had known it had something to do with the Vault of Souls, I would have spent more time reading it."

But we don't know that it does, said Solembum. His tongue slipped out of his mouth and passed over the whiskers on each side of his face, smoothing them. *The book may have nothing to do with the Rock of Kuthian or the Vault of Souls. Who can say? Besides, you were already reading it. Would you really have spent more time with it if I had said that I had a feeling—and mind you, nothing more—that the book was of some significance to you? Hmm?*

"Maybe not . . . but you still should have told me."

The werecat tucked his front paws under his breast and did not answer.

Eragon scowled, gripping the book and feeling as if he wanted to tear it apart. "This can't be everything. There has to be some other piece of information that you've forgotten."

Many, but none, I think, related to this.

"In all your travels around Alagaësia, with Angela and without, you've never found anything that might explain this mystery? Or even just something that might be of use against Galbatorix."

I found you, didn't I?

"That's not funny," growled Eragon. "Blast it, you have to know something more."

I do not.

"Think, then! If I can't find some sort of help against Galbatorix, we'll lose, Solembum. We'll lose, and most of the Varden, including the werecats, will die."

Solembum hissed again. *What do you expect of me, Eragon? I cannot invent help where none exists. Read the book.*

"We'll be at Urû'baen before I can finish it. The book might as well not exist."

Solembum's ears flattened again. *That is not my fault.*

"I don't care if it is. I just want a way to keep us from ending up dead or enslaved. Think! You have to know something else!"

Solembum uttered a low, warbling growl. *I do not. And—*

"You have to, or we're doomed!"

Even as Eragon uttered the words, he saw a change come over the werecat. Solembum's ears swiveled until they were upright, his whiskers relaxed, and his gaze softened, losing its hard-edged brilliance. At the same time, the werecat's mind grew unusually empty, as if his consciousness had been stilled or removed.

Eragon froze, uncertain.

Then he felt Solembum say, with thoughts that were as flat and colorless as a pool of water beneath a wintry, cloud-ridden sky: *Chapter forty-seven. Page three. Start with the second passage thereon.*

Solembum's gaze sharpened, and his ears returned to their previous position. *What?* he said with obvious irritation. *Why are you gaping at me like that?*

"What did you just say?"

I said that I do not know anything else. And that—

"No, no, the other thing, about the chapter and page."

Do not toy with me. I said no such thing.

"You did."

Solembum studied him for several seconds. Then, with thoughts that were overly calm, he said, *Tell me exactly what you heard, Dragon Rider.*

So, Eragon repeated the words as closely as he could. When he finished, the werecat was silent for a while. *I have no memory of that,* he said.

"What do you think it means?"

It means that we should look and see what's on page three of chapter forty-seven.

Eragon hesitated, then nodded and began to flip through the pages. As he did, he remembered the chapter in question; it was the one devoted to the aftermath of the Riders' secession from the elves, following the elves' brief war with the humans. Eragon had read the beginning of the section, but it had seemed to be nothing more than a dry discussion of treaties and negotiations, so he had left it for another time.

Soon enough, he arrived at the proper page. Tracing the lines of runes with the tip of his finger, Eragon slowly read out loud:

> . . . *The island is remarkably temperate compared with areas of the mainland at the same latitude. Summers are often cool and rainy, but then the winters are mild and tend not to assume the brutal cold of the northern reaches of the Spine, which means that crops could be grown for a goodly portion of the year. By all*

accounts, the soil is rich and fertile—the one benefit of the fire
mountains that are known to erupt from time to time and cover
the island with a thick layer of ash—and the forests were full
of large game such as the dragons preferred to hunt, including
many species not found elsewhere in Alagaësia.

Eragon paused. "None of this seems relevant."

Keep reading.

Frowning, Eragon continued on to the next paragraph:

It was there, in the great cauldron at the center of Vroengard,
that the Riders built their far-famed city, Doru Araeba.

Doru Araeba! The only city in history designed to house
dragons as well as elves and humans. Doru Araeba! A place of
magic and learning and ancient mysteries. Doru Araeba! The
very name seems to hum with excitement. Never was there a
city like it before, and never shall there be again, for now it is
lost, destroyed—ground to dust by the usurper Galbatorix.

The buildings were constructed in the elvish style—with
some influence from human Riders in later years—but out of
stone, not wood; wooden buildings, as must be obvious to the
reader, fare poorly around creatures with razor-sharp claws
and the ability to breathe fire. The most notable feature of
Doru Araeba, however, was its enormous scale. Every street
was wide enough for at least two dragons to walk abreast, and
with few exceptions, rooms and doorways were large enough to
accommodate dragons of most any size.

As a result, Doru Araeba was a vast, sprawling affair, dotted
with buildings of such immense proportions, even a dwarf would
have been impressed. Gardens and fountains were common
throughout the city, on account of the elves' irrepressible love of
nature, and there were many soaring towers among the Riders'
halls and holds.

Upon the peaks surrounding the city, the Riders placed

watchtowers and eyries—to guard against attack—and more
than one dragon and Rider had a well-appointed cave high in
the mountains, where they lived apart from the rest of their
order. The older, larger dragons were especially partial to this
arrangement, as they often preferred solitude, and living above
the floor of the cauldron made it easier for them to take flight.

Frustrated, Eragon broke off. The description of Doru Araeba was
interesting enough, but he had read other, more detailed accounts
of the Riders' city during his time in Ellesméra. Nor did he enjoy
having to decipher the cramped runes, a painstaking process even
at the best of times.

"This is pointless," he said, lowering the book.

Solembum looked as annoyed as Eragon felt. *Don't give up yet.
Read another two pages. If there's nothing by then, then you can stop.*

Eragon took a breath and agreed. He ran his finger down the page
until he found his place, whereupon he began to again pick out the
sounds of the words:

> The city contained many marvels, from the Singing Fountain of
> Eldimírim to the crystal fortress of Svellhjall to the rookeries of
> the dragons themselves, but for all their splendor, I believe that
> Doru Araeba's greatest treasure was its library. Not, as one
> might assume, because of its imposing structure—although it
> was indeed imposing—but because over the centuries the Riders
> collected one of the most comprehensive stores of knowledge
> in the whole of the land. By the time of the Riders' fall, there
> were only three libraries that rivaled it—that of Ilirea, that of
> Ellesméra, and that of Tronjheim—and none of those three
> contained as much information about the workings of magic as
> did the one in Doru Araeba.
>
> The library was located on the northwestern edge of the city,
> near the gardens that surrounded Moraeta's Spire, also known
> as the Rock of Kuthian . . .

Eragon's voice died in his throat as he stared at the name. After a moment, he began again, even slower:

> . . . also known as the Rock of Kuthian (see chapter twelve), and not far from the high seat, where the leaders of the Riders held court when various kings and queens came to petition them.

A sense of awe and fear came over Eragon. Some person or some thing had arranged for him to learn this particular piece of information, the same person or thing that had made it possible for him to find the brightsteel for his sword. The thought was intimidating, and now that Eragon knew where to go, he was no longer quite so sure that he wanted to.

What, he wondered, lay waiting for them on Vroengard? He was afraid to speculate, lest he raise hopes that were impossible to fulfill.

QUESTIONS UNANSWERED

E ragon searched through *Domia abr Wyrda* until he found the reference to Kuthian in the twelfth chapter. To his disappointment, all it said was that Kuthian had been one of the first Riders to explore Vroengard Island.

Afterward, he closed the book and sat staring at it, thumbing a ridge embossed across the spine. On the cot, Solembum was silent as well.

"Do you think that the Vault of Souls contains spirits?" asked Eragon.

Spirits are not the souls of the dead.

"No, but what else could they be?"

Solembum rose from where he had been sitting and stretched, a wave of motion moving through his body from his head to his tail. *If you find out, I would be interested to hear what you discover.*

"Do you think Saphira and I should go, then?"

I cannot tell you what you should do. If this is a trap, then most of my race has been broken and enslaved without them realizing it, and the Varden might as well surrender now, because they will never outwit Galbatorix. If not, then this may be an opportunity to find assistance where we thought none was to be had. I cannot say. You have to decide on your own whether it is a chance worth taking. As for me, I have had enough of this mystery.

He jumped down from the cot and walked over to the opening of the tent, where he paused and glanced back at Eragon. *There are many strange forces at work in Alagaësia, Shadeslayer. I have seen things that defy belief: whirlwinds of light spinning in caverns deep below*

*the ground, men who age backward, stones that speak, and shadows
that creep. Rooms that are bigger on the inside than the outside. . . .
Galbatorix is not the only power in the world to be reckoned with, and he
may not even be the strongest. Choose carefully, Shadeslayer, and if you
choose to go, walk softly.*

And then the werecat slipped out of the tent and vanished into
the darkness.

Eragon released his breath and leaned back. He knew what he had
to do; he had to go to Vroengard. But he could not make that decision without consulting Saphira.

With a gentle nudge of his mind, he woke her, and once he had
assured her that nothing was amiss, he shared his memories of
Solembum's visit. Her astonishment was as great as his.

When he finished, she said, *I do not like the thought of playing the
puppet to whoever has enchanted the werecats.*

*Neither do I, but what other choice do we have? If Galbatorix is behind
this, then we'll be placing ourselves in his hands. But if we stay, then we'll
be doing exactly the same, only when we arrive at Urû'baen.*

The difference is, we would have the Varden and the elves with us.

That's true.

Silence fell between them for a time. Then Saphira said, *I agree.
I agree; we should go. We need longer claws and sharper teeth if we
are to best Galbatorix and Shruikan in addition to Murtagh and Thorn.
Besides, Galbatorix expects us to rush straight to Urû'baen in hope of
rescuing Nasuada. And if there is one thing that makes my scales itch, it
is doing what our enemies expect.*

Eragon nodded. *And if this is a trap?*

A soft growl sounded outside the tent. *Then we will teach whoever
set it to fear our names, even if it is Galbatorix.*

He smiled. For the first time since Nasuada's abduction, he felt
a sense of purposeful direction. Here was something they could
do—a means by which they could influence the unfolding of events,

389

instead of just sitting by as passive observers. "Right, then," he muttered.

Arya arrived at his tent mere seconds after he contacted her. Her speed puzzled him until she explained that she had been keeping watch with Blödhgarm and the other elves, lest Murtagh and Thorn return.

With her there, Eragon reached out with his mind to Glaedr and coaxed him into joining their conversation, though the surly dragon was in no mood to talk.

Once the four of them, including Saphira, were all joined by their thoughts, Eragon finally burst out, *I know where the Rock of Kuthian is!*

What rock is this? Glaedr rumbled, his tone sour.

The name seems familiar, said Arya, *but I cannot place it.*

Eragon frowned slightly. Both of them had heard him speak of Solembum's advice before. It was not like either of them to forget.

Nevertheless, Eragon repeated the story of his encounter with Solembum in Teirm, and then he told them about the werecat's most recent revelations and read them the pertinent section from the book *Domia abr Wyrda*.

Arya tucked a strand of hair behind one of her pointed ears. Speaking both with her mind and her voice, she said, "And what is the name of this place again?"

". . . Moraeta's Spire, or the Rock of Kuthian," replied Eragon in the same manner. He hesitated for a half second, briefly thrown by her question. "It's a long flight, but—"

—if Eragon and I leave forthwith— said Saphira.

"—we can travel there and back—"

—before the Varden arrive at Urû'baen. This—

"—is our only chance to go."

We'll not have the time—

"—to make the trip later on."

Where would you be flying to, though? asked Glaedr.

"What . . . what do you mean?"

Exactly what I said, the dragon growled, the field of his mind darkening. *For all your yammering, you've yet to tell us where this mysterious . . . thing is located.*

"I have, though!" said Eragon, bewildered. "It's on Vroengard Island!"

At last, a straightforward answer . . .

A frown creased Arya's brow. "But what would you *do* on Vroengard?"

"I don't know!" said Eragon, his temper rising. He debated whether it was worth confronting Glaedr about his remarks; the dragon seemed to be needling Eragon on purpose. "It depends on what we find. Once we're there, we'll try to open the Rock of Kuthian and discover whatever secrets it contains. If it's a trap . . ." He shrugged. "Then we'll fight."

Arya's expression grew increasingly troubled. "The Rock of Kuthian . . . The name seems weighted with significance, but I cannot say why; it echoes in my mind, like a song I once knew but have since forgotten." She shook her head and put her hands to her temples. "Ah, now it is gone. . . ." She looked up. "Forgive me, what were we speaking of?"

"Going to Vroengard," Eragon said slowly.

"Ah, yes . . . but for what purpose? You're needed here, Eragon. In any case, nothing of value remains on Vroengard."

Aye, said Glaedr. *It is a dead and abandoned place. After the destruction of Doru Araeba, the few of us who had escaped returned to search for anything that might be of use, but the Forsworn had already picked the ruins clean.*

Arya nodded. "Whatever put this idea in your head in the first place? I don't understand how you could believe deserting the Varden now, when they're at their most vulnerable, could possibly be wise. And for what? To fly to the far ends of Alagaësia without cause or reason? I had thought better of you. . . . You cannot leave just because you are uncomfortable with your new station, Eragon."

Eragon decoupled his mind from Arya and Glaedr, and signaled to Saphira to do the same. *They don't remember!* . . . *They can't remember!*

It is magic. Deep magic, like the spell that hides the names of the dragons who betrayed the Riders.

But you haven't forgotten about the Rock of Kuthian, have you?

Of course not, she said, her mind flashing green with pique. *How could I when we are so closely joined?*

A sense of vertigo gripped Eragon as he considered the implications. *In order to be effective, the spell would have to erase the memories of everyone who knew about the rock in the first place and also the memories of anyone who heard or read about it thereafter. Which means . . . the whole of Alagaësia is in the thrall of this enchantment. No one can escape its reach.*

Except for us.

Except for us, he agreed. *And the werecats.*

And, perhaps, Galbatorix.

Eragon shivered; it felt as if spiders made of ice crystals were crawling up and down his spine. The size of the deception astounded him and left him feeling small, vulnerable. To cloud the minds of elves, dwarves, humans, and dragons alike, and without arousing the slightest hint of suspicion, was a feat so difficult, he doubted it could have been accomplished by a deliberate application of craft; rather, he believed it could only have been done by instinct, for such a spell would be far too complicated to put into words.

He *had* to know who was responsible for manipulating the minds of everyone in Alagaësia, and why. If it was Galbatorix, then Eragon feared that Solembum was right and the Varden's defeat was inevitable.

Do you think this was the work of dragons, as was the Banishing of the Names? he asked.

Saphira was slow to answer. *Perhaps. But then, as Solembum said to you, there are many powers in Alagaësia. Until we go to Vroengard, we won't know for certain one way or another.*

If ever we do.

Aye.

Eragon ran his fingers through his hair. He suddenly felt exceptionally tired. *Why does everything have to be so hard?* he wondered.

Because, said Saphira, *everyone wants to eat, but no one wants to be eaten.*

He snorted, grimly amused.

Despite the speed with which he and Saphira could exchange thoughts, their conversation had lasted long enough for Arya and Glaedr to notice.

"Why have you closed your minds to us?" asked Arya. Her gaze flicked toward one wall of the tent—the wall nearest to where Saphira lay curled in the darkness beyond. "Is something wrong?"

You seem perturbed, Glaedr added.

Eragon stifled a humorless chuckle. "Perhaps because I am." Arya watched with concern as he went over to the cot and sat on the edge. He let his arms hang limp and heavy between his legs. He was silent for a moment as he made the shift from the language of his birth to that of the elves and magic, whereupon he said, "Do you trust Saphira and me?"

The resulting pause was gratifyingly brief.

"I do," replied Arya, also in the ancient language.

As do I, Glaedr likewise said.

Shall I, or shall you? Eragon quickly asked Saphira.

You want to tell them, so tell them.

Eragon looked up at Arya. Then, still in the ancient language, he said to both her and Glaedr, "Solembum has told me the name of a place, a place on Vroengard, where Saphira and I may find someone or something to help us defeat Galbatorix. However, the name is enchanted. Every time I say the name, you soon forget it." A faint expression of shock appeared on Arya's face. "Do you believe me?"

"I believe you," Arya slowly said.

I believe that you believe what you are saying, Glaedr growled. *But that does not necessarily make it so.*

"How else can I prove it? You won't remember if I tell you the name or share my memories with you. You could question Solembum, but again, what good would it do?"

What good? For one, we can prove that you haven't been tricked or deceived by something that only appeared to be Solembum. And as for the spell, there may be a way to demonstrate its existence. Summon the werecat, and then we shall see what can be done.

Will you? Eragon asked Saphira. He thought that the werecat would be more likely to come if Saphira asked him.

A moment later, he felt her searching with her mind through the camp, and then he sensed the touch of Solembum's consciousness against Saphira's. After she and the werecat exchanged a brief, wordless communication, Saphira announced, *He is on his way.*

They waited in silence, Eragon staring down at his hands as he compiled a list of supplies he would need for the trip to Vroengard.

When Solembum pushed aside the flaps to the tent and entered, Eragon was surprised to see that he was now in his human form: that of a young boy, dark-eyed and insolent. In his left hand, the werecat held a leg of roast goose, on which he was gnawing. A ring of grease coated his lips and chin, and drops of melted fat had splattered his bare chest.

As he chewed on a strip of flesh, Solembum motioned with his sharp, pointed chin toward the patch of dirt where Glaedr's heart of hearts lay buried. *What is it you want, firebreather?* he asked.

To know if you are who you seem to be! said Glaedr, and the dragon's consciousness seemed to surround Solembum's, pressing inward like piles of black clouds around a brightly burning but wind-battered flame. The dragon's strength was immense, and from personal experience, Eragon knew that few could hope to withstand him.

With a gargled yowl, Solembum spat out his mouthful of meat and sprang backward, as if he had stepped on a viper. He stood where he was, then, trembling with effort, his sharp teeth bared, and a look of such fury in his tawny eyes, Eragon placed his hand on the hilt of Brisingr as a precaution. The flame dimmed but held: a white-hot point of light amid a sea of churning thunderheads.

After a minute, the storm diminished and the clouds withdrew, although they did not disappear entirely.

My apologies, werecat, said Glaedr, *but I had to know for certain.*

Solembum hissed, and the hair on his head fluffed and spiked so that it resembled the blossom of a thistle. *If you still had your body, old one, I would cut off your tail for that.*

You, little cat? You could not have done more than scratch me.

Again Solembum hissed, and then he turned on his heel and stalked toward the entrance, his shoulders hunched close to his ears.

Wait, said Glaedr. *Did you tell Eragon about this place on Vroengard, this place of secrets that none can remember?*

The werecat paused, and without turning around, he growled and brandished the goose leg over his head in an impatient, dismissive gesture. *I did.*

And did you tell him the page in Domia abr Wyrda *wherein he found the location of this place?*

So it seems, but I have no memory of it, and I hope that whatever is on Vroengard singes your whiskers and burns your paws.

The entrance to the tent made a loud flapping sound as Solembum swatted it aside; then his small form melted into the shadows, as if he had never existed.

Eragon stood and, with the toe of his boot, pushed the scrap of half-eaten meat out of the tent.

"You should not have been so rough with him," said Arya.

I had no other choice, said Glaedr.

"Didn't you? You could have asked his permission first."

And given him the opportunity to prepare? No. It is done; let it be, Arya.

"I cannot. His pride is wounded. You should attempt to placate him. It would be dangerous to have a werecat as your enemy."

It is even more dangerous to have a dragon as your enemy. Let it be, elfling.

Troubled, Eragon exchanged looks with Arya. Glaedr's tone bothered him—and her as well, he could see—but Eragon could not decide what to do about it.

Now, Eragon, the golden dragon said, *will you allow me to examine the memories of your conversation with Solembum?*

"If you want, but . . . why? You'll only end up forgetting."

Perhaps. And then again, perhaps not. We shall see. Addressing Arya, Glaedr said, *Separate your mind from ours, and do not allow Eragon's memories to taint your consciousness.*

"As you wish, Glaedr-elda." As Arya spoke, the music of her thoughts grew ever more distant. A moment later, the eerie singing faded to silence.

Then Glaedr returned his attention to Eragon. *Show me,* he commanded.

Ignoring his trepidation, Eragon cast his mind back to when Solembum had first arrived at the tent, and he carefully recalled everything that had transpired between the two of them thereafter. Glaedr's consciousness melded with Eragon's so that the dragon could relive the experiences along with him. It was an unsettling sensation; it felt as if he and the dragon were two images stamped onto the same side of a coin.

When he finished, Glaedr withdrew somewhat from Eragon's mind and then, to Arya, said, *When I have forgotten, if I do, repeat to me the words "Andumë and Fíronmas at the hill of sorrows, and their flesh like glass." This place on Vroengard . . . I know of it. Or I once did. It was something of importance, something . . .* The dragon's thoughts grayed for a second, as if a layer of mist had been blown over the hills and valleys of his being, obscuring them. *Well?* he demanded, regaining his former brusque attitude. *Why do we tarry? Eragon, show me your memories.*

"I already have."

Even as Glaedr's mood turned to disbelief, Arya said, "Glaedr, remember: 'Andumë and Fíronmas at the hill of sorrows, and their flesh like glass.'"

How— Glaedr started, and then he growled with such force, Eragon almost expected to hear the sound out loud. *Argh. I hate spells that interfere with one's memory. They're the worst form of magic, always leading to chaos and confusion. Half the time they seem to end with family members killing one another without realizing it.*

What does the phrase you used mean? Saphira asked.

Nothing, except to me and Oromis. But that was the point; no one would know of it unless I told them.

Arya sighed. "So the spell is real. I suppose you have to go to Vroengard, then. To ignore something of this importance would be folly. If nothing else, we need to know who the spider is at the center of this web."

I shall go as well, said Glaedr. *If someone means to harm you, they may not expect to fight two dragons instead of one. In any event, you will need a guide. Vroengard has become a dangerous place since the destruction of the Riders, and I would not have you fall prey to some forgotten evil.*

397

Eragon hesitated as he noticed a strange yearning in Arya's gaze, and he realized that she wanted to accompany them as well. "Saphira will fly faster if she only has to carry one person," he said in a quiet voice.

"I know. . . . Only, I always wanted to visit the home of the Riders."

"I'm sure you will. Someday."

She nodded. "Someday."

Eragon took a moment to marshal his energy and reflect on everything that needed to be done before he, Saphira, and Glaedr could leave. Then he drew a deep breath and rose from the cot.

"Captain Garven!" he called. "Will you please join us?"

DEPARTURE

First, Eragon had Garven, with all secrecy, send one of the Nighthawks to collect provisions for the trip to Vroengard. Saphira had eaten after the capture of Dras-Leona, but she had not gorged herself, else she would have been too slow and too heavy to fight if the need arose, as indeed it had. She was well enough fed, then, to fly to Vroengard without stopping, but once there, Eragon knew she would have to find food on or around the island, which worried him.

I can always fly back on an empty stomach, she assured him, but he was not so certain.

Next Eragon sent a runner to bring Jörmundur and Blödhgarm to his tent. Once they arrived, it took Eragon, Arya, and Saphira another hour to explain the situation to them and—harder still—to convince them that the trip was necessary. Blödhgarm was the easiest to win over to their point of view, whereas Jörmundur objected vociferously. Not because he doubted the veracity of the information from Solembum, nor even because he doubted its importance—on both those points he accepted Eragon's word without question—but, as he argued with increasing vehemence, because it would destroy the Varden if they woke to find not only that Nasuada had been kidnapped but that Eragon and Saphira had vanished to parts unknown.

"Furthermore, we don't dare let Galbatorix think that you've left us," Jörmundur said. "Not when we're so close to Urû'baen. He might send Murtagh and Thorn to intercept you. Or he might take the opportunity to crush the Varden once and for all. We can't risk it."

His concerns, Eragon was forced to acknowledge, were valid.

After much discussion, they finally arrived at a solution: Blödhgarm and the other elves would create apparitions of both Eragon and Saphira, even as they had created one of Eragon when he had gone to the Beor Mountains to participate in the election and coronation of Hrothgar's successor.

The images would apear to be perfect living, breathing, thinking replicas of Eragon and Saphira, but their minds would be empty, and if anyone peered into them, the ruse would be discovered. As a result, the image of Saphira would be unable to speak, and although the elves could feign speech on the part of Eragon, that too would be better to avoid, lest some oddity of diction alert those listening that all was not as it seemed. The limitations of the illusions meant that they would work best at a distance and that the people who had reason to interact with Eragon and Saphira on a more personal basis—such as the kings Orrin and Orik—would soon realize that something was amiss.

So Eragon ordered Garven to wake all the Nighthawks and bring them to him as discreetly as possible. When the whole company was gathered before his tent, Eragon explained to the motley group of men, dwarves, and Urgals why he and Saphira were leaving, although he was purposefully vague about the details and he kept their destination a secret. Then he explained how the elves were going to conceal their absence, and he had the men swear oaths of secrecy in the ancient language. He trusted them, but one could never be too careful where Galbatorix and his spies were concerned.

Afterward, Eragon and Arya visited Orrin, Orik, Roran, and the sorceress Trianna. As with the Nighthawks, they explained the situation and from each of them extracted oaths of secrecy.

King Orrin, as Eragon expected, proved to be the most intransigent. He expressed outrage at the prospect of either Eragon or Saphira traveling to Vroengard and railed at length against the idea. He questioned Eragon's bravery, questioned the value of Solembum's information, and threatened to withdraw his forces from the Varden if Eragon continued to pursue such a foolish, misguided course. It took over an hour of threats, flattery, and coaxing to bring him around, and even then, Eragon feared Orrin might go back on his word.

The visits to Orik, Roran, and Trianna went faster, but Eragon and Arya still had to spend what seemed to Eragon an unreasonable amount of time talking with them. Impatience made him curt and restless; he wanted to be off, and every minute that passed only increased his sense of urgency.

As he and Arya went from person to person, Eragon was also aware, through his link with Saphira, of the elves' faint, lilting chanting, which underlay everything he heard, like a strip of cunningly woven fabric hidden beneath the surface of the world.

Saphira had remained at his tent, and the elves were ringed about her, their arms outstretched and the tips of their fingers touching while they sang. The purpose of their long, complicated spell was to collect the visual information they would need in order to create an accurate representation of Saphira. It was difficult enough to imitate the shape of an elf or a human; a dragon was harder still, especially given the refractive nature of her scales. Even so, the most complicated part of the illusion, as Blödhgarm had told Eragon, would be reproducing the effects of Saphira's weight on her surroundings every time her apparition took off or landed.

When at last Eragon and Arya had finished making their rounds, night had already given way to day, and the morning sun hung a handsbreadth above the horizon. By its light, the damage wrought upon the camp during the attack seemed even greater.

Eragon would have been happy to depart with Saphira and Glaedr then, but Jörmundur insisted that he address the Varden at least once, properly, as their new leader.

Therefore, soon afterward, once the army was assembled, Eragon found himself standing in the back of an empty wagon, looking out over a field of upturned faces—some human and some not—and wishing he were anywhere but there.

Eragon had asked Roran for advice beforehand, and Roran had told him, "Remember, they're not your enemies. You have nothing to fear from them. They *want* to like you. Speak clearly, speak honestly, and whatever you do, keep your doubts to yourself. That's the way to win them over. They're going to be frightened and dismayed once you tell them about Nasuada. Give them the reassurance they need, and they'll follow you through the very gates of Urû'baen."

Despite Roran's encouragement, Eragon still felt apprehensive before his speech. He had rarely spoken to large groups before, and never for more than a few lines. As he gazed at the sun-darkened, battle-worn warriors before him, he decided that he would rather fight a hundred enemies by himself than have to stand up in public and risk the disapproval of others.

Until the moment he opened his mouth, Eragon was not sure what he was going to say. Once he started, the words seemed to pour out of their own accord, but he was so tense, he could not remember much of what he said. The speech passed in a blur; his main impressions were of heat and sweat, the groans of the warriors when they learned of Nasuada's fate, the ragged cheers when he exhorted them to victory, and the general roar from the crowd when he finished. With relief, he jumped down from the back of the wagon to where Arya and Orik were waiting next to Saphira.

As he did, his guards formed a circle around the four of them, shielding them from the crowd and holding back those who wished to speak with him.

"Well done, Eragon!" said Orik, clapping him on the arm.

"Was it?" Eragon asked, feeling dazed.

"You were most eloquent," said Arya.

Eragon shrugged, embarrassed. It intimidated him to remember that Arya had known most of the leaders of the Varden, and he could not help but think that Ajihad or his predecessor, Deynor, would have done a better job with the speech.

Orik pulled on his sleeve. Eragon bent toward the dwarf. In a voice barely loud enough to be heard over the crowd, Orik said, "I hope that whatever you find is worth the trip, my friend. Take care you don't get yourselves killed, eh?"

"I'll try not to."

To Eragon's surprise, Orik grabbed him by the forearm and pulled him into a rough embrace. "May Gûntera watch over you." As they separated, Orik reached over and slapped the palm of his hand against Saphira's side. "And you as well, Saphira. Safe journeys to the both of you."

Saphira responded with a low hum.

Eragon looked over at Arya. He suddenly felt awkward, unable to think of anything but the most obvious things to say. The beauty of her eyes still captivated him; the effect she had on him never seemed to lessen.

Then she took his head in her hands, and she kissed him once, formally, on the brow.

Eragon stared at her, dumbstruck.

"Guliä waíse medh ono, Argetlam." Luck be with you, Silverhand.

As she released him, he caught her hands in his own. "Nothing bad is going to happen to us. I won't let it. Not even if Galbatorix is waiting for us. If I have to, I'll tear apart mountains with my bare hands, but I promise, we're going to make it back safely."

Before she could respond, he let go of her hands and climbed onto Saphira's back. The crowd began to cheer again as they saw him settle into the saddle. He waved to them, and they redoubled their efforts, stamping their feet and pounding their shields with the pommels of their swords.

Eragon saw Blödhgarm and the other elves gathered in a close-knit group, half hidden behind a nearby pavilion. He nodded to them, and they nodded in return. The plan was simple: He and Saphira would set off as if they intended to patrol the skies and scout the land ahead—as they normally did when the army was on the march—but after circling the camp a few times, Saphira would fly into a cloud, and Eragon would cast a spell that would render her invisible to those watching from below. Then the elves would create the hollow wraiths that would take Eragon and Saphira's place while they continued on with their journey, and it would be the wraiths that onlookers would see emerge from the cloud. Hopefully, none would notice the difference.

With practiced ease, Eragon tightened the straps around his legs and checked that the saddlebags behind him were properly secured. He took special care with the one on his left, for packed within it—well swaddled with clothes and blankets—was the velvet-lined chest that contained Glaedr's precious heart of hearts, his Eldunarí.

Let us be off, the old dragon said.

To Vroengard! Saphira exclaimed, and the world pitched and plunged around Eragon as she leaped off the ground, and a rush of air buffeted him as she flapped her massive, batlike wings, driving them higher and higher into the sky.

Eragon tightened his grip on the neck spike in front of him, lowered his head against the speed-induced wind, and stared at the polished leather of his saddle. He took a deep breath and tried to stop worrying about what lay behind them and what lay before them. There was nothing he could do now but wait—wait and hope that Saphira could fly to Vroengard and back before the Empire attacked the Varden again; hope that Roran and Arya would be safe; hope that he might somehow still be able to rescue Nasuada; and hope that going to Vroengard was the right decision, for the time was fast approaching when he would finally have to face Galbatorix.

✦ ✦ ✦

THE TORMENT OF UNCERTAINTY

Nasuada opened her eyes.

Tiles covered the dark, vaulted ceiling, and upon the tiles were painted angular patterns of red, blue, and gold: a complex matrix of lines that trapped her gaze for a mindless while.

At last she mustered the will to look away.

A steady orange glow emanated from a source somewhere behind her. The glow was just strong enough to reveal the shape of the octagonal room, but not so bold as to dispel the shadows that clung like gauze to the corners above and below.

She swallowed and found her throat was dry.

The surface she lay on was cold, smooth, and uncomfortably hard; it felt like stone against her heels and the pads of her fingers. A chill had crept into her bones, and it was that which caused her to realize the only thing she wore was the thin white shift she slept in.

Where am I?

The memories returned all at once, without sense or order: an unwelcome cavalcade that thundered into her mind with a force almost physical in its intensity.

She gasped and tried to sit upright—to bolt, to flee, to fight if she had to—but found she was unable to move more than a fraction of an inch in any direction. There were padded manacles around her wrists and ankles, and a thick leather belt held her head firmly against the slab, preventing her from lifting or turning it.

She strained against her bonds, but they were too strong for her to break.

Letting out her breath, she went limp and stared at the ceiling again. Her pulse hammered in her ears, like a maddened drumbeat.

Heat suffused her body; her cheeks burned, and her hands and feet felt as if they were filled with molten tallow.

So this is how I die.

For a moment, despair and self-pity bedeviled her. She had barely begun her life, yet now it was about to end, and in the vilest, most miserable manner possible. What was worse, she had accomplished none of the things she had hoped to. Not war, not love, not birth, not life. Her only offspring were battles and corpses and trundling supply trains; stratagems too numerous to remember; oaths of friendship and fealty now worth less than a mummer's promise; and a halting, fractious, all-too-vulnerable army led by a Rider younger than she was herself. It seemed a poor legacy for the memory of her name. And a memory would be all that remained. She was the last of her line. When she died, there would be no one left to continue her family.

The thought pained her, and she berated herself for not having borne children when she could.

"I'm sorry," she whispered, seeing the face of her father before her.

Then she disciplined herself and put aside her despair. The only control she had over the situation was self-control, and she was not about to relinquish it for the dubious pleasure of indulging her doubts, fears, and regrets. As long as she was the master of her thoughts and feelings, she was not entirely helpless. It was the smallest of freedoms—that of one's own mind—but she was grateful for it, and knowing that it might soon be torn away made her all the more determined to exercise it.

In any event, she still had one final duty to perform: to resist her interrogation. To that end, she would need to be in full command of herself. Otherwise, she would break quickly.

She slowed her breathing and concentrated on the regular flow of air through her throat and nostrils, letting that sensation crowd out all others. When she felt appropriately calm, she set about deciding what was safe to think about. So many subjects were dangerous—dangerous to her, dangerous to the Varden, dangerous to their allies, or dangerous to Eragon and Saphira. She did not review the things she ought to avoid, which might have given her jailers the information they wanted then and there. Instead, she picked a handful of thoughts and memories that seemed benign and strove to ignore the rest—strove to convince herself that everything she was, and had ever been, consisted of only those few elements.

In essence, she attempted to create a new and simpler identity for herself so that, when asked questions about this or that, she could, with complete honesty, plead ignorance. It was a dangerous technique; for it to work, she had to believe her own deception, and if she was ever freed, it might be difficult to reclaim her true personality.

But then, she had no hope of rescue or release. All she dared hope for was to frustrate the designs of her captors.

Gokukara, give me the strength to endure the trials before me. Watch over your little owlet, and should I die, carry me safely from this place . . . carry me safely to the fields of my father.

Her gaze wandered about the tile-covered room as she studied it in greater detail. She guessed she was in Urû'baen. It was only logical that Murtagh and Thorn would have taken her there, and it would explain the elvish look of the room; the elves had built much of Urû'baen, the city they called Ilirea, either before their war with the dragons—long, long ago—or after the city had become the capital of the Broddring Kingdom and the Riders had established a formal presence therein.

Or so her father had told her. She remembered nothing of the city herself.

Still, she might be somewhere else entirely: one of Galbatorix's private estates, perhaps. And the room might not even exist as she perceived it. A skilled magician could manipulate everything she saw, felt, heard, and smelled, could distort the world around her in ways she would never notice.

Whatever happened to her—whatever *seemed* to happen to

her—she would not allow herself to be tricked. Even if Eragon broke down the door and cut her loose, she would still believe that it was a ruse of her captors. She dared not trust the evidence of her senses.

The moment Murtagh had taken her from the camp, the world had become a lie, and there was no telling when the lie would end, if ever it did. The only thing she could be certain of was that she existed. All else was suspect, even her own thoughts.

After her initial shock subsided, the tedium of waiting began to wear on her. She had no way to tell time other than her hunger and thirst, and her hunger waxed and waned at seemingly irregular intervals. She tried marking off the hours by counting numbers, but the practice bored her, and she always seemed to forget her place once she reached the tens of thousands.

Despite the horrors she was sure awaited her, she wished her captors would hurry up and show themselves. She shouted for minutes on end, but heard only plaintive echoes in response.

The dull light behind her never wavered, never dimmed; she assumed it was a flameless lantern similar to those the dwarves made. The glow made it hard to sleep, but eventually exhaustion overcame her and she dozed off.

The prospect of dreaming terrified her. She was most vulnerable when asleep, and she feared that her unconscious mind would conjure up the very information she was trying to keep hidden. She had little choice in the matter, however. Sooner or later, she had to sleep, and forcing herself to stay awake would only end up making her feel worse.

So she slept. But her rest was fitful and unsatisfying, and she still felt tired when she woke.

A boom startled her.

Somewhere above and behind her, she heard a latch being lifted, and then the creak of a door swinging open.

Her pulse quickened. As best she could tell, over a day had passed since she had first regained consciousness. She was painfully thirsty, her tongue felt swollen and sticky, and her entire body ached from being confined in one position for so long.

Footsteps descending stairs. Soft-soled boots shuffling against stone. . . . A pause. Metal clinked. Keys? Knives? Something worse? . . . Then the footsteps resumed. Now they were approaching her. Drawing closer . . . closer . . .

A portly man dressed in a gray woolen tunic entered her field of vision, carrying a silver platter with an assortment of food: cheese, bread, meat, wine, and water. He stooped and placed the platter by the base of the wall, then turned and walked over to her, his stride short, quick, and precise. Dainty, almost.

Wheezing slightly, he leaned against the edge of the slab and stared down at her. His head was like a gourd: bulbous at the top, bulbous at the bottom, and narrow in the middle. He was clean-shaven and mostly bald, except for a fringe of dark, close-cropped hair that ran about his skull. The upper part of his forehead was shiny, his fleshy cheeks were ruddy, and his lips were as gray as his tunic. His eyes were unremarkable: brown and close-set.

He smacked his tongue, and she saw that his teeth met on end, like the jaws of a clamp, and that they protruded farther than normal from the rest of his face, giving him a slight but noticeable muzzle.

On his warm, moist breath hung the smell of liver and onions. In her famished condition, she found the odor nauseating.

She was acutely aware of her state of undress as the man's gaze roamed over her body. It made her feel vulnerable, as if she were a toy or a pet laid out for his enjoyment. Anger and humiliation brought a hot flush to her cheeks.

Determined not to wait for him to make his intentions known, she tried to speak, to ask him for water, but her throat was too parched; all she could do was croak.

The gray-suited man tutted and, to her astonishment, began to undo her restraints.

The moment she was free, she sat up on the slab, formed a blade with her right hand, and swung it toward the side of the man's neck.

He caught her wrist in midair, seemingly without effort. She growled and jabbed at his eyes with the fingers of her other hand.

Again he caught her wrist. She wrenched back and forth, but his grip was too strong to break; her wrists might as well have been encased in stone.

Frustrated, she lunged forward and sank her teeth into the man's right forearm. Hot blood gushed into her mouth, salty and coppery. She choked but kept biting down even as blood leaked out from under her lips. Between her teeth and against her tongue, she could feel the muscles of the man's forearm flexing like so many trapped snakes trying to escape.

Other than that, he failed to react.

At last she released his arm, drew back her head, and spat his blood onto his face.

Even then the man continued to regard her with the same flat expression, neither blinking nor showing any sign of pain or anger.

She wrenched at his hands once more, then swung her hips and legs around on the slab to kick him in the stomach.

Before she could land the blow, he let go of her left wrist and slapped her across the face, hard.

A white light flashed behind her eyes, and a soundless explosion seemed to erupt around her. Her head snapped to one side, her teeth clacked together, and pain lanced down her spine from the base of her skull.

When her sight cleared, she sat glaring at the man, but she made no move to attack him again. She understood she was at his mercy. . . . She understood she needed to find something to cut his throat or stab him through the eye if she was going to overpower him.

He let go of her other wrist and reached into his tunic to retrieve a dull white kerchief. He dabbed at his face, wiping off every drop of blood and spittle. Then he tied the kerchief around his injured forearm, using his clamplike teeth to hold one end of the cloth.

She flinched as he reached out and grasped her by the upper arm, his large, thick fingers encircling her limb. He pulled her off the ash-colored slab, and her legs gave way as she struck the floor. She hung like a doll from the man's grip, her arm twisted at an awkward angle above her head.

He hoisted her onto her feet. This time her legs held. Half supporting her, he guided her around to a small side door she had been unable to see from where she lay on her back. Next to it was a short flight of stairs that led to a second, larger door—the same door through which her jailer had entered. It was closed, but there was a small metal grate in the middle, and through it she glimpsed a well-lit tapestry hanging against a smooth stone wall.

The man pushed open the side door and escorted her into a narrow privy chamber. To her relief, he left her there alone. She searched the bare room for anything she could use as a weapon or a means to escape but, to her disappointment, found only dust, wood shavings, and, more ominously, dried bloodstains.

So she did what she was expected to do, and when she emerged from the privy chamber, the sweating, gray-suited man took her arm again and walked her back to the slab.

As they neared it, she began to kick and struggle; she would rather be hit than allow him to restrain her as before. For all her efforts, however, she could not stop or slow the man. His limbs were like iron beneath her blows, and even his seemingly soft paunch gave but little when she struck it.

Handling her as easily as if she were a small child, he lifted her onto the slab, pressed her shoulders flat against the stone, and then locked the manacles around her wrists and ankles. Lastly, he pulled the leather belt over her forehead and cinched it down, hard enough to hold her head in place but not so hard as to cause her pain.

She expected him to go and eat his lunch—or supper, or whatever meal it was—but instead he picked up the platter, carried it over to her, and offered her a drink of watered wine.

It was difficult to swallow while lying on her back, so she had to quickly sip the liquid from the silver chalice he pressed to her mouth. The feeling of the diluted wine coursing down her dry throat was one of cool, soothing relief.

When the chalice was empty, the man put it aside, cut slices of bread and cheese, and held them out toward her.

"What . . . ," she said, her voice finally responding to her commands. "What is your name?"

The man gazed at her without emotion. His bulbous forehead gleamed like polished ivory in the light of the flameless lantern.

He pushed the bread and cheese toward her.

"Who are you? . . . Is this Urû'baen? Are you a prisoner like me? We could help each other, you and I. Galbatorix isn't all-knowing. Together we could find a way to escape. It may seem impossible, but it isn't, I promise." She continued to speak in a low, calm voice, hoping to say something that would either gain the man's sympathy or appeal to his self-interest.

411

She knew she could be persuasive—long hours of negotiating on the Varden's behalf had proven that to her satisfaction—but her words seemed to have no effect on the man. Save for his breathing, he might as well have been dead as he stood there, bread and cheese extended. That he was deaf occurred to her, but he had noticed when she tried to ask for water, so she dismissed the possibility.

She talked until she exhausted every argument and appeal she could think of, and when she stopped—pausing to find a different approach—the man placed the cheese and bread against her lips and held it there. Furious, she willed him to take it away, but his hand never budged, and he continued to stare at her with the same blank, disinterested look.

The nape of her neck prickled as she realized his manner was not an affectation; she really did mean nothing to him. She would have understood if he hated her, or if he had taken a perverse pleasure in tormenting her, or if he had been a slave reluctantly carrying out Galbatorix's orders, but none of those things seemed true. Rather, he was indifferent, devoid of even the slightest shred of empathy. He would, she had no doubt, kill her just as readily as he would tend to her, and with no more concern than one might have for crushing an ant.

Silently cursing the necessity of it, she opened her mouth and allowed him to place the pieces of bread and cheese on her tongue, despite the urge she felt to bite his fingers.

He fed her. Like a child. By hand, putting each morsel of food into her mouth as carefully as if it were a hollow orb of glass that might shatter at any sudden movement.

A deep sense of loathing gathered within her. To go from being the leader of the greatest alliance in the history of Alagaësia to— No, no, none of that existed. She was her father's daughter. She had lived in Surda in the dust and the heat, among the echoing calls of the merchants in the bustling marketplace streets. That was all. She had no reason to be haughty, no reason to resent her fall.

Nevertheless, she hated the man looming over her. She hated that he insisted on feeding her when she could have done so herself. She hated that Galbatorix, or whoever was overseeing her captivity, was trying to strip her of her pride and dignity. And she hated that, to a degree, they were succeeding.

She was, she decided, going to kill the man. If she could accomplish only one more thing in her life, she wanted it to be the death of her jailer. Short of escape, nothing else would give her as much satisfaction. *Whatever it takes, I'll find a way.*

The idea pleased her, and she ate the rest of the meal with relish, all the while plotting how she might arrange the man's demise.

When she was finished, the man took the tray and left.

She listened to his footsteps recede, to the door opening and closing behind her, to the *snick* of the latch snapping shut, and then to the heavy, doom-laden sound of a beam falling into place across the outside of the door.

Then once again she was alone, with nothing to do but wait and dwell upon the ways of murder.

For a while, she amused herself by tracing one of the lines painted on the ceiling and attempting to determine whether it had a beginning or an end. The line she chose was blue; the color appealed to her because of its associations with the one person whom, above all else, she dared not think of.

In time, she grew bored with the lines and with her fantasies of revenge, and she closed her eyes and slipped into an uneasy half sleep, where the hours seemed, with the paradoxical logic of nightmares, to pass both faster and slower than normal.

When the man in the gray tunic returned, she was almost glad to see him, a reaction for which she despised herself, considering it a weakness.

She was not sure how long she had been waiting—could not be sure unless someone told her—but she knew it had been a shorter period than before. Still, the wait had felt interminable, and she had feared that she was to be left strapped down and isolated—though not ignored, surely not that—for the same drawn-out stretch. To her disgust, she found herself grateful that the man was going to visit her more often than she had originally thought. Lying motionless on a flat piece of stone for so many hours was painful enough, but to be denied contact with any other living creature—even one as lumpish and abhorrent as her jailer—was a torture in and of itself and was by far the harder trial to bear.

As the man unlocked her from her restraints, she noted that the wound on his forearm had been healed; the skin was as smooth and pink as a suckling pig's.

She refrained from fighting, but on the way to the privy room, she pretended to stumble and fall, hoping to get near enough to the platter that she might steal the small paring knife the man used to cut the food. However, the platter proved too far away, and the man was too heavy for her to drag toward it without alerting him to her intentions. Her ploy having failed, she forced herself to submit calmly to the rest of the man's ministrations; she needed to convince him that she had given up so he would grow complacent and, if she was lucky, careless.

While he fed her, she studied his fingernails. Previously, she had been too angry to pay them heed, but now that she was calmer, the oddity of them fascinated her.

His nails were thick and highly arched. They were set deep within the flesh, and the white moons by the cuticles were large and broad. In all, no different from the nails of many of the men and dwarves she had dealt with.

When had she dealt with them? . . . She did not remember.

What set his nails apart was the care with which they had been cultivated. And *cultivated* seemed the right description to her, as if the nails were rare flowers a gardener had devoted long hours to tending. The cuticles were neat and trim, with no sign of tears, while the nails themselves had been cut straight across—not too long, not too short—and the edges smoothly beveled. The tops of the nails had been polished until they shone like glazed pottery, and the skin surrounding them looked as if oil or butter had been rubbed into it.

Except for elves, she had never seen a man with such perfect nails.

Elves? She shook off the thought, irritated with herself. She knew no elves.

The nails were an enigma; a strangeness in an otherwise understandable setting; a mystery that she wanted to solve, even though it was probably futile to try.

She wondered who was responsible for the nails' exemplary condition. Was it the man himself? He seemed overly fastidious, and she could not imagine he had a wife or daughter or servant or anyone else close to him who would lavish so much attention on the caps of his fingers. Of course, she realized she might be mistaken. Many a battle-scarred veteran—grim, close-mouthed men whose only loves seemed to be wine, women, and war—had surprised her with some facet of their character that was at odds with their outward guise: a knack for wood carving, a tendency to memorize romantic poems, a fondness for hounds, or a fierce devotion to a family that they kept hidden from the rest of the world. It had been years before she had learned that Jör—

She cut off the thought before it went any further.

In any event, the question she kept turning over in her mind was a simple one: why? Motivation was telling, even when such small things as fingernails were concerned.

If the nails were the work of someone else, then they were a labor of either great love or great fear. But she doubted that was the case; somehow it felt wrong.

If, instead, they were the work of the man himself, then any number of explanations were possible. Perhaps his nails were a way for him to exert a modicum of control over a life that was no longer his own. Or perhaps he felt they were the only part of himself that was or could be attractive. Or perhaps caring for them was merely a nervous tic, a habit that served no other purpose except to while away the hours.

Whatever the truth might be, the fact remained that *someone* had cleaned and trimmed and buffed and oiled his fingernails, and it had not been a casual or inattentive effort.

She continued to ponder the matter while she ate, barely tasting her food. Occasionally, she glanced up to search the man's heavy face for one clue or another, but always without success.

Upon feeding her the last piece of bread, the man pushed himself off the edge of the slab, picked up the platter, and turned away.

She chewed and swallowed the bread as fast as she could without choking; then, her voice hoarse and creaky from disuse, she said, "You have nice fingernails. They're very . . . shiny."

The man paused in midstep, and his large, ponderous head

swiveled toward her. For a moment, she thought he might strike her again, but then his gray lips slowly split and he smiled at her, showing both his upper and lower rows of teeth.

She suppressed a shudder; he looked as if he were about to bite the head off a chicken.

Still with the same unsettling expression, the man continued out of her range of sight, and a few seconds later, she heard the door to her cell open and close.

Her own smile crept across her lips. Pride and vanity were weaknesses that she could exploit. If there was one thing she was skilled at, it was the ability to bend others to her will. The man had given her the tiniest of handholds—no more than a fingerhold, really, or rather a finger*nail*-hold, as it were—but it was all she needed. Now she could begin to climb.

THE HALL OF THE SOOTHSAYER

The third time the man visited her, Nasuada was sleeping. The sound of the door banging open caused her to jolt awake, heart pounding.

It took her a few seconds to remember where she was. When she did, she frowned and blinked, trying to clear her eyes. She wished she could rub them.

Her frown deepened as she looked down her body and saw that there was still a small damp spot on her shift where a drop of watered wine had fallen during her meal.

Why has he returned so soon?

Her heart sank as the man walked past her carrying a large copper brazier full of charcoal, which he set upon its legs a few feet away from the slab. Resting in the charcoal were three long irons.

The time she had dreaded had finally arrived.

She tried to catch his eye, but the man refused to look at her as he took flint and steel from a pouch on his belt and lit a nest of shredded tinder in the center of the brazier. As sparks smoldered and spread, the tinder glowed like a ball of red-hot wires. The man bent, puckered his lips, and blew on the incipient fire, gentle as a mother kissing her child, and the sparks sprang into lambent flames.

For several minutes, he tended the fire, building a bed of coals several inches thick, the smoke rising to a grate far above. She watched with morbid fascination, unable to tear her gaze away, despite what she knew awaited her. Neither he nor she spoke; it was as if they were both too ashamed of what was about to take place for either to acknowledge it.

He blew on the coals again, then turned as if to approach her.

Don't give in, she told herself, stiffening.

She clenched her fists and held her breath as the man walked toward her . . . closer . . . closer . . .

A feather-like touch of wind brushed her face as he strode past her, and she listened to his footsteps dwindle into silence as he climbed the stairs and left the room.

A faint gasp escaped her as she relaxed slightly. Like lodestones, the bright coals drew her gaze back toward them. A dull, rust-colored glow was creeping up the iron rods that stuck out of the brazier.

She wet her mouth and thought how nice a drink of water would be.

One of the coals jumped and split in two, but otherwise the chamber was quiet.

As she lay there, unable to fight or escape, she strove not to think. Thinking would only weaken her resolve. Whatever was going to happen was going to happen, and no amount of fear or anxiety could change that.

New footsteps sounded in the hallway outside the chamber: a group of them this time, some marching in rhythm, some not. Together they created a host of raucous echoes that made it impossible to determine the number of people approaching. The procession stopped by the doorway, and she heard voices murmuring, and then two sets of clacking footsteps—the product of hard-soled riding boots, she guessed—entered the room.

The door closed with a hollow thud.

Down the stairs the footsteps came, steady and deliberate. She saw someone's arm place a carved wooden chair at the very edge of her vision.

A man sat in it.

He was large: not fat, but broad-shouldered. A long black cape hung draped around him. It looked heavy, as if backed with mail. Light from the coals and from the flameless lantern gilded the edges of his form, but his features remained too dark to make out. Still, the shadows did nothing to hide the outline of the sharp, pointed crown that rested upon his brow.

Her heart skipped a beat. With a struggle, it resumed its previous rapid tempo.

A second man, this one dressed in a maroon jerkin and leggings—both trimmed with gold thread—walked over to the brazier and stood with his back to her while he stirred the coals with one of the iron rods.

One by one, the man in the chair tugged on the fingers of his gauntlets. Then he pulled off the gloves. Underneath, his hands were the color of tarnished bronze.

When he spoke, his voice was low, rich, and commanding. Any bard who possessed such a mellifluous instrument would have his name praised throughout the land as a master of masters. The sound of it caused her skin to prickle; his words seemed to wash over her like warm waves of water, caressing her, beguiling her, binding her. Listening to him, she realized, was as perilous as listening to Elva.

"Welcome to Urû'baen, Nasuada, daughter of Ajihad," said the man in the chair. "Welcome to this, my home, 'neath these ancient, piled rocks. Long has it been since a guest as distinguished as yourself has graced us with their presence. My energies have been occupied elsewhere, but I assure you, from now on, I shall not neglect my duties as host." At the last, a note of menace crept into his voice, like a claw emerging from its sheath.

She had never seen Galbatorix in person, only heard descriptions and studied drawings, but the effect the man's speech had on her was so visceral, so powerful, she had no doubt that he indeed was the king.

In both his accent as well as his diction, there was something of the *other,* as if the language he spoke was not the language he had been raised with. It was a subtle difference, but impossible to ignore once she noticed. Perhaps, she decided, it was because the language

419

had changed in the years since he had been born. That seemed the most reasonable explanation, as his way of speaking reminded her—No, no, it reminded her of nothing.

He leaned forward, and she could feel his gaze boring into her.

"You are younger than I expected. I knew you had but recently come of age, but still, you are no more than a child. Most seem as children to me these days: prancing, preening, foolhardy children who know not what is best for them—children who need the guidance of those who are older and wiser."

"Such as yourself?" she said in a scornful tone.

She heard him chuckle. "Would you rather the elves ruled over us? I am the only one of our race who can hold them at bay. By their reckoning, even our oldest graybeards would be considered untested youths, unfit for the responsibilities of adulthood."

"By their reckoning, so would you." She did not know where her courage came from, but she felt strong and defiant. Whether or not the king would punish her for it, she was determined to speak her mind.

"Ah, but I contain more than my share of years. The memories of hundreds are mine. Life piled upon life: loves, hates, battles, victories, defeats, lessons learned, mistakes made—all lie within my mind, whispering their wisdom into my ears. I remember *eons*. In the whole of recorded history, there has never been one such as I, not even among the elves."

"How is that possible?" she whispered.

He shifted in the chair. "Do not think to pretend with me, Nasuada. I know that Glaedr gave his heart of hearts to Eragon and Saphira, and that he is there, with the Varden, even now. You understand whereof I speak."

She suppressed a thrill of fear. The fact that Galbatorix was willing to discuss such things with her—that he was willing to refer, even obliquely, to the source of his power—eliminated what little hope she still had that he ever intended to release her.

Then he gestured at the room with his gauntlets. "Before we

proceed, you should know something of the history of this place. When the elves first ventured to this part of the world, they discovered a crevice buried deep within the escarpment that looms over the plains hereabout. The escarpment they prized as defense against the attacks of dragons, but the crevice they prized for an entirely different reason. By happenstance, they discovered that the vapors rising out of the crack in the stone increased the chances that those who slept near it might catch a glimpse, if however confused, of future events. So, over two and a half thousand years ago, the elves built this room atop the fissure, and an oracle came to live here for many hundreds of years, even after the elves abandoned the rest of Ilirea. She sat where you now lie, and she whiled away the centuries dreaming of all that had been and all that might be.

"In time, the air lost its potency and the oracle and her attendants departed. Who she was and where she went, none can say for sure. She had no name other than the title Soothsayer, and certain stories lead me to believe she was neither elf nor dwarf but something else entirely. Be that as it may, during her residency, this chamber came to be called, as you might expect, the Hall of the Soothsayer, and so it still is today—only now *you* are the soothsayer, Nasuada, daughter of Ajihad."

Galbatorix spread his arms. "This is a place for truths to be told . . . and heard. I will tolerate no lies within these walls, not even the simplest of falsehoods. Whosoever rests upon that hard block of stone becomes the latest soothsayer, and though many have found that role difficult to accept, in the end, none have refused. You will be no different."

The legs of the chair scraped over the floor, and then she felt Galbatorix's breath warm against her ear. "I know this will be painful for you, Nasuada, painful beyond belief. You will have to unmake yourself before your pride will allow you to submit. In all the world, nothing is harder than changing one's own self. I understand this, for I have reshaped myself on more than one occasion. However, I will be here to hold your hand and help you through this transition.

You need not take the journey alone. And you may console yourself with the knowledge that I will never lie to you. None of us shall. Not within this room. Doubt me if you wish, but in time you will come to believe me. I consider this a hallowed place, and I would no more desecrate the idea it represents than cut off my own hand. You may ask whatever you want, and I promise you, Nasuada, daughter of Ajihad, that we shall answer truthfully. As king of these lands, I give you my sworn word."

She worked her jaw back and forth, trying to decide how to answer. Then, from between clenched teeth, she said, "I'll never tell you what you want to know!"

A slow, deep chuckle filled the room. "You misunderstand; I didn't have you brought here because I seek information. There's nothing you could say that I don't already know. The number and disposition of your troops; the state of your provisions; the locations of your supply trains; the manner in which you plan to lay siege to this citadel; Eragon and Saphira's duties, habits, and abilities; the Dauthdaert you acquired in Belatona; even the powers of the witch-child, Elva, whom you have kept by your side until but recently—all this I know, and more. Shall I quote the figures to you? . . . No? Well then. My spies are more numerous and more highly placed than you imagine, and I have other means of gathering intelligence withal. You have no secrets from me, Nasuada, none whatsoever; therefore, it is pointless to insist upon holding your tongue."

His words struck her like hammerblows, but she strove not to let them dishearten her. "Why, then?"

"Why did I have you brought here? Because, my dear, you have the gift of command, and that is far deadlier than any spell. Eragon is no threat to me, nor are the elves, but you . . . you are dangerous in a way they are not. Without you, the Varden will be like a blinded bull; they will snort and rage, and they will charge straight ahead, heedless of what lies in their way. Then I will catch them and, with their folly, destroy them.

"But the destruction of the Varden is not the reason I had you abducted. No, you are here because you have proven yourself worthy of my attention. You are fierce, tenacious, ambitious, and intelligent—the very qualities I prize most in my servants. I wish to have you by my side, Nasuada, as my foremost adviser and as the general of my army as I move to implement the final stages of the great plan I have been laboring upon for nigh on a century. A new order is about to descend upon Alagaësia, and I would have you be a part of it. Ever since the last of the Thirteen died, I have searched for those who were fit to take their place. Until recently, my efforts have been in vain. Durza was a useful tool, but being a Shade, he had certain limitations: a lack of concern for his own preservation to name but one. Of all the candidates I have examined, Murtagh was the first I considered eligible and the first to survive the tests I set before him. You shall be the next, I am sure. And Eragon, the third."

Horror crept through her as she listened to him. What he was proposing was far worse than she had envisioned.

The maroon-clad man at the brazier startled her by shoving one of the iron rods into the coals with such force, the tip banged against the copper bowl underneath.

Galbatorix continued speaking: "Should you live, you shall have a chance to accomplish more than you ever could with the Varden. Think of it! In my service, you could help bring peace to the whole of Alagaësia, and you would be my chief architect for accomplishing these changes."

"I would rather let a thousand vipers bite me before I would agree to serve you." And she spat into the air.

His chuckle echoed throughout the room once more: the sound of a man who feared nothing, not even death. "We shall see."

She flinched as she felt a finger touch the inside of her elbow. It slowly traced a circle, then slid down to the first of her scars on her forearm and paused atop the ridge of flesh, warm against her skin. The finger tapped three times before proceeding to the next few scars, then back again, running over them like a washboard.

"You have defeated an opponent in the Trial of the Long Knives," said Galbatorix, "and with more cuts than any have endured in recent memory. That means both that you are exceptionally strong-willed and that you are able to suspend the functioning of your imagination—for it is an overactive imagination that turns men into cowards, not a surfeit of fear, as most believe. However, neither of these traits will be of help to you now. On the contrary, they are a hindrance. Everyone has a limit, whether physical or mental. The only question is how long it takes to reach that point. And you will reach it, I promise you. Your strength may delay the moment, but it cannot avert it. Nor will your wards avail you while you are within my power. Why, then, should you suffer needlessly? No one questions your courage; you have already demonstrated it to all the world. Give in now. There is no shame in accepting the inevitable. To continue would be to subject yourself to an array of torments for no other reason but to appease your sense of duty. Let your duty be appeased now, and give me your oath of fealty in the ancient language, and ere the hour is out, you will have a dozen servants to command, robes of silk and damask to wear, a set of chambers to live in, and a place at my table when we dine."

He paused then, waiting for her answer, but she stared at the lines painted on the ceiling and refused to speak.

On her arm, the finger continued its exploration, moving from her scars to the hollow of her wrist, where it rested heavily upon a vein.

"Very well. As you wish." The pressure on her wrist vanished. "Murtagh, come, show yourself. You're being impolite to our guest."

Ah, not him too, she thought, suddenly feeling a great sadness.

At the brazier, the man in red slowly turned, and though he wore a silver mask over the upper half of his face, she saw it was indeed Murtagh. His eyes were nearly lost in shadows, and his mouth and jaw were fixed in a grim expression.

"Murtagh was somewhat reluctant when he first entered my service, but he has since proven to be a most apt student. He has his father's talents. Isn't that so?"

"Yes, sir," said Murtagh, his voice rough.

"He surprised me when he killed old King Hrothgar on the Burning Plains. I didn't expect him to turn on his former friends with such eagerness, but then, our Murtagh is full of rage and bloodlust, he is. He would tear out the throat of a Kull with his bare hands if I gave him the chance, and I have. Nothing pleases you so much as killing, now does it?"

The muscles in Murtagh's neck tensed. "No, sir."

Galbatorix laughed softly. "Murtagh Kingkiller . . . 'Tis a fine name, a name fit for a legend, but not one you should seek to earn again, except at my direction." Then to her: "Until now I have neglected his instruction in the subtle arts of persuasion, which is why I brought him here with me today. He has some experience as the object of such arts, but never as the practitioner, and it is high time he learns to master them. And what better way to learn than here, with you? It was Murtagh, after all, who convinced me that you were worthy of joining my newest generation of disciples."

A strange sense of betrayal crept over her. Despite what had transpired, she had thought better of Murtagh. She searched his face for an explanation, but he stood stiff as a guard on watch and kept his gaze averted; she could glean nothing from his expression.

Then the king motioned toward the brazier and, in a conversational tone of voice, said, "Take up an iron."

Murtagh's hands curled into fists. Other than that, he did not move.

A word rang in Nasuada's ears, like the clap of a great bell. The very warp and weft of the world seemed to vibrate at the sound, as if a giant had plucked the threads of reality and set them a-quivering. For a moment, she felt as if she were falling, and the air before her shimmered like water. Despite its power, she could not remember the letters that made up the word nor even what language it belonged to, for the word passed clean through her mind, leaving behind only the memory of its effects.

Murtagh shuddered; then he twisted, grasped one of the iron

rods, and pulled it from the brazier with a halting motion. Sparks sprayed into the air as the iron came free of the coals, and several glittering embers fell spiraling toward the floor like pine seeds from their cones.

The end of the rod glowed a bright, pale yellow that, even as she watched, darkened to a ruddy orange. The light from the hot metal reflected off Murtagh's polished half mask, giving him a grotesque, inhuman appearance. She saw herself reflected in the mask as well, her form distorted into a crabbed torso with spindly legs that dwindled away into thin black lines along the curve of Murtagh's cheek.

Futile as it was, she could not help but pull against her restraints as he advanced toward her.

"I don't understand," she said to Galbatorix with feigned calm. "Aren't you going to use your mind against me?" Not that she wanted him to, but she would rather defend herself from an attack on her consciousness than withstand the pain of the iron.

"There will be time for that later, if need be," said Galbatorix. "For now, I am curious to discover how brave you really are, Nasuada, daughter of Ajihad. Besides, I would prefer not to seize control of your mind and force you to swear fealty to me. Instead, I want you to make this decision of your own free will and while still in possession of your faculties."

"Why?" she croaked.

"Because it pleases me. Now, for the last time, will you submit?"

"Never."

"So be it. Murtagh?"

The rod descended toward her, the tip like a giant, sparkling ruby.

They had given her nothing to bite on, so she had no choice but to scream, and the eight-sided chamber reverberated with the sounds of her agony until her voice gave out and an all-consuming darkness enveloped her in its folds.

✦　✦　✦

ON THE WINGS OF A DRAGON

Eragon lifted his head, took a deep breath, and felt a portion of his worries recede.

Riding a dragon was far from restful, but being so close to Saphira was calming for both him and her. The simple pleasure of physical contact comforted them in a way few things did. Also, the constant sound and motion of her flight helped distract him from the black thoughts that had been dogging him.

Despite the urgency of their trip and the precarious nature of their circumstances in general, Eragon was glad to be away from the Varden. The recent bloodshed had left him feeling as if he was no longer quite himself.

Ever since he had rejoined the Varden at Feinster, he had spent the bulk of his time fighting or waiting to fight, and the strain was beginning to wear on him, especially after the violence and horror of Dras-Leona. On the Varden's behalf, he had killed hundreds of soldiers—few of whom had stood even the slightest chance of harming him—and though his actions had been justified, the memories troubled him. He did not want every fight to be desperate and every opponent to be his equal or his better—far from it—but at the same time, the easy slaughter of so many made him feel more like a butcher than a warrior. Death, he had come to believe, was a corrosive thing, and the more he was around it, the more it gnawed away at who he was.

However, being alone with Saphira—and Glaedr, although the golden dragon had kept to himself since their departure—helped Eragon regain a sense of normalcy. He felt most comfortable alone or in small groups, and he preferred not to spend time in a town or a city or even a camp like the Varden's. Unlike the majority of people, he did not hate or fear the wilderness; as harsh as the empty lands were, they possessed a grace and a beauty that no artifice could compete with and that he found restorative.

So he let Saphira's flying distract him, and for the better part of the day, he did nothing more important than watch the landscape slide past.

From the Varden's camp by the banks of Leona Lake, Saphira set out across the broad expanse of water, angling northwest and climbing so high that Eragon had to use a spell to shield himself from the cold.

The lake appeared patchy: shining and sparkling in areas where the angle of the waves reflected the sunlight toward Saphira, dull and gray where it did not. Eragon never tired of staring at the constantly changing patterns of light; nothing else in the world was quite like it.

Fisher hawks, cranes, geese, ducks, starlings, and other birds often flew by underneath them. Most ignored Saphira, but a few of the hawks spiraled upward and accompanied her for a short while, seeming more curious than frightened. Two were even so bold as to swerve in front of her, mere feet from her long, sharp teeth.

In many ways, the fierce, hook-clawed, yellow-beaked raptors reminded Eragon of Saphira herself, an observation that pleased her, for she admired the hawks as well, though not so much for their appearance as for their hunting prowess.

The shore behind them gradually faded to a hazy purple line, then vanished altogether. For over half an hour, they saw only birds and clouds in the sky and the vast sheet of wind-hammered water that covered the surface of the earth.

Then, ahead and to their left, the jagged gray outline of the Spine began to appear along the horizon, a welcome sight to Eragon. Although these were not the mountains of his childhood, they still belonged to the same range, and seeing them, he felt not quite so far from his old home.

The mountains grew in size until the stony, snowcapped peaks loomed before them like the broken battlements of a castle wall. Down their dark, green-covered flanks, dozens of white streams tumbled, wending their way through the creases in the land until they joined with the great lake that lay pressed against their foothills. A half-dozen villages sat upon the shore or close thereby, but on account of Eragon's magic, the people below remained oblivious to Saphira's presence as she sailed overhead.

As he looked at the villages, it struck Eragon just how small and isolated they were and, in hindsight, how small and isolated Carvahall had been as well. Compared to the great cities he had visited, the villages were little more than clusters of hovels, barely fit for even the meanest of paupers. Many of the men and women within them, he knew, had never traveled more than a few miles from their birthplace and would live their whole lives in a world bound by the limits of their sight.

What a blinkered existence, he thought.

And yet, he wondered if it was perhaps better to remain in one place and learn all you could about it rather than to constantly roam across the land. Was a broad but shallow education superior to one that was narrow but deep?

He was not sure. He remembered Oromis once telling him that the whole of the world could be deduced from the smallest grain of sand, if one studied it closely enough.

The Spine was only a fraction of the height of the Beor Mountains, yet the slab-sided peaks still towered a thousand feet or more above Saphira as she threaded her way between them, following the shadow-filled gorges and valleys that split the range. Now and then, she had to soar upward to clear a bare, snowy pass, and when she did and Eragon's range of view widened, he thought the mountains looked like so many molars erupting from the brown gums of the earth.

As Saphira glided over a particularly deep valley, he saw at the bottom a glade with a ribbony stream wandering across the field of grass. And along the edges of the glade, he glimpsed what he thought might have been houses—or perhaps tents; it was hard to tell—hidden under the eaves of the heavy-boughed spruce trees that populated the flanks of the neighboring mountains. A single spot of firelight shone through a gap in the branches, like a tiny chip of gold embedded within the layers of black needles, and he thought he spied a lone figure lumbering away from the stream. The figure appeared strangely bulky, and its head seemed too large for its body.

I think that was an Urgal.

Where? Saphira asked, and he sensed her curiosity.

In the clearing behind us. He shared the memory with her. *I wish we had the time to go back and find out. I'd like to see how they live.*

She snorted. Hot smoke streamed out of her nostrils, then rolled down her neck and over him. *They might not take kindly to a dragon and Rider landing among them without warning.*

He coughed and blinked as his eyes watered. *Do you mind?*

She did not answer, but the line of smoke trailing from her nostrils ceased, and the air around him soon cleared.

Not long afterward, the shape of the mountains began to look familiar to Eragon, and then a large rift opened up before Saphira and he realized they were flying across the pass that led to Teirm—the same pass he and Brom had twice ridden through on horseback. It was much as he remembered it: the western branch of the Toark River still flowed fast and strong toward the distant sea, the surface of the water streaked with white mare's tails where boulders interrupted its course. The crude road he and Brom had followed by the side of the river was still a pale, dusty line barely wider than a deer trail. He even thought he recognized a clump of trees where they had stopped to eat.

Saphira turned westward and proceeded down the river until the mountains dropped away to lush, rain-soaked fields, whereupon she adjusted her course to a more northerly direction. Eragon did not question her decision; she never seemed to lose her bearing, not even on a starless night or when deep underground in Farthen Dûr.

The sun was close to the horizon when they flew out of the Spine. As dusk settled over the land, Eragon occupied himself by trying to devise ways to trap, kill, or fool Galbatorix. After a time, Glaedr emerged from his self-imposed isolation and joined him in his efforts. They spent an hour or so discussing various strategies, and then they practiced attacking and defending each other with their minds. Saphira participated in the exercise as well, but with limited success, as flying made it difficult for her to concentrate on anything else.

Later, Eragon stared at the cold white stars for a while. Then he asked Glaedr, *Could the Vault of Souls contain Eldunarí that the Riders hid from Galbatorix?*

No, said Glaedr without hesitation. *It's impossible. Oromis and I would have known if Vrael had sanctioned such a plan. And if any Eldunarí had been left on Vroengard, we would have found them when we returned to search the island. It's not so easy to hide a living creature as you seem to think.*

Why not?

If a hedgehog rolls into a ball, that doesn't mean that he becomes invisible, now does it? Minds are no different. You can shield your thoughts from others, but your existence is still apparent to anyone who searches the area.

Surely with a spell you could—

If a spell had tampered with our senses, we would have known, for we had wards to prevent that from happening.

So, no Eldunarí, Eragon concluded glumly.

Unfortunately not.

They flew on in silence as the waxing three-quarter moon rose above the jagged peaks of the Spine. By its light, the land looked as if it were made out of pewter, and Eragon amused himself by imagining that it was an immense sculpture the dwarves had carved and stored within a cave as large as Alagaësia itself.

Eragon could feel the pleasure Glaedr took in their flight. Like Eragon and Saphira, the old dragon seemed to welcome the opportunity to leave behind their concerns on the ground, if even only for a short while, and to soar freely through the sky.

It was Saphira who spoke next. Between the slow, heavy flaps of her wings, she said to Glaedr, *Tell us a story, Ebrithil.*

What manner of story would you hear?

The tale of how you and Oromis were captured by the Forsworn, and how you then escaped.

At this, Eragon's interest increased. He had always been curious about the matter himself, but he had never worked up the courage to ask Oromis.

Glaedr was quiet for a span, then said, *When Galbatorix and Morzan returned from the wilds and began their campaign against our order, we did not at first realize the severity of the threat. We were concerned, of course, but no more than if we had discovered that a Shade was stalking the land. Galbatorix was not the first Rider to go mad, although he was the first to have acquired a disciple such as Morzan. That alone should have warned us of the danger we faced, but the truth was only apparent in hindsight.*

At the time, we failed to consider that Galbatorix might have gathered other followers or that he would even attempt such a thing. It seemed absurd that any of our brethren could prove susceptible to Galbatorix's poisonous whisperings. Morzan was still a novice; his weakness was understandable. But those who were already Riders in full? We never questioned their loyalties. For only when they were tempted did they reveal the extent to which their spite and weaknesses had corrupted them. Some wanted revenge for old hurts; others believed that, by virtue of our power, dragons and Riders deserved to rule over the whole of Alagaësia; and others, I am afraid to say, simply enjoyed the chance to tear down what was and indulge themselves however they wanted.

The old dragon paused, and Eragon sensed ancient hates and sorrows shading his mind. Then Glaedr continued: *Events at that point were . . . confusing. Little was known, and what reports we received were so larded with rumors and speculation as to be useless. Oromis and I began to suspect that something far worse was afoot than most realized. We tried to convince several of the older dragons and Riders, but they disagreed and dismissed our concerns. Fools they were not, but centuries of peace had clouded their vision, and they were unable to see that the world was shifting around us.*

Frustrated with the lack of information, Oromis and I left Ilirea to discover what we could for ourselves. We brought two younger Riders with us, both elves and accomplished warriors, who had recently returned from scouting the northern reaches of the Spine. It was partly at their urging that we ventured forth on our expedition. Their names you might recognize, for they were Kialandí and Formora.

"Ah," said Eragon, suddenly understanding.

Yes. After a day and a half of traveling, we stopped at Edur Naroch, a watchtower built of old to stand guard over Silverwood Forest. Unbeknownst to us, Kialandí and Formora had visited the tower beforehand and slain the three elven rangers stationed there. Then they had placed a trap upon the stones that ringed the tower, a trap that caught us the moment my claws touched the grass upon the knoll. It was a clever spell; Galbatorix had taught it to them himself. We had no defense against it, for it caused us no harm, only held us and slowed us, like honey poured over our bodies and minds. While we were thus snared, minutes passed as seconds. Kialandí, Formora, and their dragons flitted around us faster than hummingbirds; they appeared as no more than dark blurs at the edges of our vision.

When they were ready, they released us. They had cast dozens of spells—spells to bind us in place, spells to blind us, and spells to prevent Oromis from speaking, so as to make it more difficult for him to cast spells. Again, their magic did not hurt us, and thus we had no defense against it. . . . The moment we could, we attacked Kialandí, Formora, and their dragons with our minds, and they us, and for hours thereafter, we strove against them. The experience was . . . not pleasant. They were weaker and less skilled than Oromis and I, but there were two of them for each of us, and they had with them the heart of hearts of a dragon named Agaravel—whose Rider they had slain—and her strength added to their own. As a result, we were hard-pressed to defend ourselves. Their intent, we discovered, was to force us to help Galbatorix and the Forsworn enter Ilirea unnoticed, so that they might catch the Riders by surprise and capture the Eldunarí who were then living in the city.

"How did you escape?" asked Eragon.

In time, it became clear that we would not be able to defeat them. So, Oromis decided to risk using magic in an attempt to free us, even though he knew it would provoke Kialandí and Formora into attacking us with magic in return. It was a desperate ploy, but it was the only choice we had.

At a certain point, without knowing of Oromis's plans, I struck back at our attackers, seeking to hurt them. Oromis had been waiting for just such a moment. He had long known the Rider who had instructed Kialandí and Formora in the ways of magic, and he was well familiar with Galbatorix's twisted reasoning. From that knowledge, he was able to guess at how Kialandí and Formora had worded their spells, and where the flaws in their enchantments were likely to lie.

Oromis had only seconds to act; the moment he began to use magic, Kialandí and Formora realized what he was about, panicked, and began to cast their own spells. It took Oromis three tries to break our bonds. How exactly he did it, I cannot say. I doubt whether he really understood it himself. Most simply, he shifted us a finger's-breadth away from where we had been standing.

Like how Arya sent my egg from Du Weldenvarden to the Spine? asked Saphira.

Yes, and no, Glaedr replied. Yes, he transported us from one place to another without moving us through the intervening space. But he did not just shift our position, he also shifted the very substance of our flesh, rearranged it so that we were no longer what we once were. Many of the smallest parts of our bodies can be exchanged for one another without ill effect, and so he did with every muscle, bone, and organ.

Eragon frowned. Such a spell was a feat of the highest order, a wonder of magical dexterity that few in history could have hoped to carry out. Still, as impressed as Eragon was, he could not help but ask, "How could that have worked, though? You would still be the same person as before."

You would, and yet you would not. The difference between who we had been and who we then were was slight, but it was enough to render useless the enchantments Kialandí and Formora had woven about us.

What of the spells they cast once they noticed what Oromis was doing? asked Saphira.

An image came to Eragon of Glaedr ruffling his wings, as if he were tired of sitting in one position for so long. *The first spell, Formora's, was meant to kill us, but our wards stopped it. The second, which was from Kialandí . . . that was a different matter. It was a spell Kialandí had learned from Galbatorix, and he from the spirits who possessed Durza. This I know, for I was in contact with Kialandí's mind even when he wrought his enchantment. It was a clever, fiendish spell, the purpose of which was to prevent Oromis from touching and manipulating the flow of energy around him, and thereby to prevent him from using magic.*

"Did Kialandí do the same to you?"

He would have, but he feared it would either kill me or sever my connection with my heart of hearts and thus create two independent versions of me that they would then have to subdue. Even more than elves, dragons depend on magic for our existence; without it, we would soon die.

Eragon could sense Saphira's curiosity was aroused. *Has that ever happened? Has the connection between a dragon and the dragon's Eldunarí ever been severed while the dragon's body was still alive?*

It has, but that is a tale for another time.

Saphira subsided, but Eragon could tell that she intended to raise the question again at the soonest opportunity.

"But Kialandí's spell didn't stop Oromis from being able to use magic, did it?"

Not entirely. It was supposed to, but Kialandí cast the spell even as Oromis shifted us from place to place, and so its effect was somewhat lessened. Still, it kept him from working all but the smallest of magics, and as you know, the spell remained with him for the rest of his life, despite the efforts of our wisest healers.

"Why didn't his wards protect him?"

Glaedr seemed to sigh. *That is a mystery. No one had done such a thing before, Eragon, and of those still living, only Galbatorix now knows the secret of it. The spell was bound to Oromis's mind, but it may not have affected him directly. Instead, it may have worked upon the energy around him or upon his link to the same. The elves have long studied magic, but even they do not fully understand how the material and immaterial worlds interact. It is a riddle that will likely never be solved. However, it seems reasonable to assume that the spirits know more than we about both the material and the immaterial, considering that they are the embodiment of the second and that they occupy the first when in the form of a Shade.*

Whatever the truth may be, the outcome was this: Oromis cast his spell, and he freed us, but the effort was too much for him, and a fit came over him, the first of many. Never again was he able to cast such a powerful spell, and ever after, he suffered a weakness of the flesh that would have killed him if not for his skill with magic. The weakness was already in him when Kialandí and Formora captured us, but when he shifted us and reshuffled the parts of our bodies, he brought it to the fore. Otherwise, the malady might have lain dormant for many more years.

Oromis fell to the ground, as helpless as a hatchling, even as Formora and her dragon, an ugly brown thing, ran at us, the others close behind. I leaped over Oromis, and I attacked. If they had realized he was crippled, they would have taken advantage of his condition to slip into his mind and make it their own. I had to distract them until Oromis recovered. . . . I have never fought harder than I did that day. There were four of them arrayed against me, five if you include Agaravel in the tally. Both of my kin, the brown and Kialandí's purple, were smaller than me, but their teeth were sharp and their claws were fast. Still, my rage gave me a strength greater than normal, and I dealt grave wounds to them both. Kialandí was foolish enough to come within my reach, and I grasped him with my talons and threw him at his own dragon. Glaedr made a sound of amusement. His magic did not protect him against that. One of the spikes on the purple's back impaled him, and I might have killed him then and there had not the brown forced me to retreat.

We must have fought for almost five minutes before I heard Oromis shout that we must flee. I kicked up dirt in the faces of my enemies, then returned to Oromis and grasped him in my right forepaw and took flight from Edur Naroch. Kialandí and his dragon could not follow, but Formora and the brown could and did.

They caught us less than a mile from the watchtower. We closed several times, and then the brown flew underneath me, and I saw Formora about to strike at my right leg with her sword. She was trying to force me to drop Oromis, I think, or perhaps she wanted to kill him. I twisted to evade the blow, and instead of my right leg, her sword struck my left, cutting it off.

The memory that passed through Glaedr's mind was that of a hard, cold, pinching sensation, as if Formora's blade had been forged of ice, not steel. The feeling made Eragon queasy. He swallowed and tightened his grip on the front of the saddle, grateful that Saphira was safe.

It hurt less than you might imagine, but I knew that I could not continue to fight, so I turned and raced toward Ilirea as fast as my wings could carry me. In a way, Formora's victory worked against her, for without the burden of my leg, I was able to outdistance the brown and thus escape.

Oromis was able to stop the bleeding, but no more, and he was too weak to contact Vrael or the other elder Riders and warn them of Galbatorix's plans. Once Kialandí and Formora reported to him, we knew that Galbatorix would attack Ilirea soon thereafter. If he waited, it would only give us time to fortify, and strong as he was, surprise was still Galbatorix's greatest weapon in those days.

When we arrived at Ilirea, we were dismayed to find that few of our order were still there; in our absence, more had left to search for Galbatorix or to consult with Vrael in person on Vroengard. We convinced those who remained of the danger, and we had them warn Vrael and the other elder dragons and Riders. They were loath to believe that Galbatorix had the forces needed to attack Ilirea—or that he would dare do such a thing—but in the end, we were able to make them see the truth of the matter. As a result, they decided that all of the Eldunarí in Alagaësia should be taken to Vroengard for safekeeping.

It seemed a prudent measure, but we should have sent them to Ellesméra instead. If nothing else, we should have left the Eldunarí that were already in Du Weldenvarden where they were. At least then some of them would have remained free of Galbatorix. Alas, none of us thought that they would be safer among the elves than on Vroengard, at the very center of our order.

Vrael ordered every dragon and Rider who was within a few days journey of Ilirea to hurry to the aid of the city, but Oromis and I feared they would be too late. Nor were we in any state to help defend Ilirea. So we gathered what supplies we needed, and with our two remaining students—Brom and the dragon who is your namesake, Saphira—we left the city that very night. You have seen, I think, the fairth Oromis made as we departed.

Eragon nodded absently as he remembered the image of the beautiful, tower-filled city clustered about the base of an escarpment and lit by a rising harvest moon.

And that is how it came to be that we were not in Ilirea when Galbatorix and the Forsworn attacked a few hours later. And it is also why we were not at Vroengard when the oath-breakers defeated the combined might of all our forces and sacked Doru Araeba. From Ilirea, we went to Du Weldenvarden in the hope that the elven healers might be able to cure Oromis's ailment and restore his ability to use magic. When they could

not, we decided to remain where we were, for it seemed safer than flying
all the way to Vroengard when both of us were hampered by our injuries
and we might be ambushed at any point along the journey.

Brom and Saphira did not stay with us, though. Despite our advice
to the contrary, they went to join the fight, and it was in that fighting
that your namesake died, Saphira. . . . And now you know how the
Forsworn captured us and how we escaped.

After a moment, Saphira said, *Thank you for the story, Ebrithil.*

You are welcome, Bjartskular, but never ask it of me again.

When the moon was nearing its zenith, Eragon saw a nest of dim
orange lights floating in the darkness. It took him a moment to realize they were the torches and lanterns of Teirm, many miles away.
And, high above the other lights, a bright yellow spot appeared for
a second, like a great eye glaring at him; then it vanished and reappeared, flashing on and off in a never-changing cycle, as if the eye
were blinking.

The lighthouse at Teirm is lit, he said to both Saphira and Glaedr.

Then a storm is brewing, said Glaedr.

Saphira's flapping ceased, and Eragon felt her tip forward and begin a long, slow glide toward the ground.

A half hour elapsed before she landed. By then, Teirm was a faint
glow to the south, and the beam from the lighthouse was no brighter
than a star.

Saphira alit on an empty beach strewn with twisted driftwood.
By the light of the moon, the hard, flat strand appeared almost
white, while the waves that crashed into it were gray and black and
seemed angry, as if the ocean were trying to devour the land with
each breaker it sent forth.

Eragon unbuckled the straps around his legs, then slid off Saphira,
grateful for the opportunity to stretch his muscles. He noted the
smell of brine as he sprinted down the strand toward a large chunk
of driftwood, his cloak flapping behind him. At the piece of wood,
he spun around and sprinted back to Saphira.

She sat where he had left her, staring out to sea. He paused, wondering if she was going to speak—for he could feel a great strain within her—but when she remained silent, he turned on his heel and again sprinted to the driftwood. She would talk when she was ready.

Back and forth Eragon ran, until he was warm all over and his legs felt wobbly.

And yet the whole time Saphira kept her gaze fixed on some point in the distance.

As Eragon threw himself down on a patch of sedge next to her, Glaedr said, *It would be foolish to try.*

Eragon cocked his head, unsure to whom the dragon was speaking. *I know I can do it*, said Saphira.

You have never before been to Vroengard, said Glaedr. *And if there is a storm, it might drive you far out to sea, or worse. More than one dragon has perished because of overweening confidence. The wind is not your friend, Saphira. It can help you, but it can also destroy you.*

I am not a hatchling to be instructed about the wind!

No, but you are still young, and I do not think you are ready for this.

The other way would take too long!

Perhaps, but better to get there safely than not at all.

"What are you talking about?" Eragon asked.

The sand under Saphira's front feet made a gritty, rustling sound as she flexed her claws, sinking them deep into the earth.

We have a choice to make, said Glaedr. *From here, Saphira can either fly straight to Vroengard or follow the coastline north until she reaches the point on the mainland closest to the island and then—only then—turn west and cross the sea.*

Which path would be faster? Eragon asked, although he had already guessed the answer.

Flying straight there, said Saphira.

But if she does, then she would be over the water the whole time.

Saphira bristled. *It's no farther than it was from the Varden to here. Or am I wrong?*

You're more tired now, and if there is a storm—

Then I'll fly around it! she said, and huffed, releasing a spike of blue and yellow flame from her nostrils.

The flame branded itself into Eragon's vision, leaving behind a flashing afterimage. "Ah! Now I can't see." He rubbed his eyes as he tried to help the afterimage fade away. *Would flying straight there really be all that dangerous?*

It could be, rumbled Glaedr.

How much longer would it take to go along the coastline?

Half a day, maybe a bit more.

Eragon scratched the stubble on his chin as he stared at the forbidding mass of water. Then he looked up at Saphira and, in a low voice, said, "Are you sure you can do this?"

She twisted her neck and returned his gaze with one huge eye. Her pupil had expanded until it was nearly circular; it was so large and black, Eragon felt as if he could crawl into it and disappear altogether.

As sure as I can be, she said.

He nodded and ran his hands through his hair as he accustomed himself to the idea. *Then we have to chance it. . . . Glaedr, if need be, you can guide her? You can help her?*

The old dragon was quiet for a while; then he surprised Eragon by humming in his mind, even as Saphira hummed when she was pleased or amused. *Very well. If we are to tempt fate, then let us not be cowards about it. Across the sea it is.*

The matter settled, Eragon climbed back onto Saphira, and with a single bound, she left behind the safety of solid land and took flight over the trackless waves.

◆ ◆ ◆

THE SOUND OF HIS VOICE, THE TOUCH OF HIS HAND

"**A**ggghhh!"

. . .

"Will you swear your fealty to me in the ancient language?"

"Never!"

His question and her answer had become a ritual between them, a call-and-response such as children might use in a game, except that in this game she lost even when she won.

Rituals were all that allowed Nasuada to maintain her sanity. By them, she ordered her world—by them, she was able to endure from one moment to the next, for they gave her something to hold on to when all else had been stripped from her. Rituals of thought, rituals of action, rituals of pain and relief: these had become the framework upon which her life depended. Without them, she would have been lost, a sheep without a shepherd, a devotee bereft of faith . . . a Rider separated from her dragon.

Unfortunately, this particular ritual always ended in the same way: with another touch of the iron.

She screamed and bit her tongue, and blood filled her mouth. She coughed, trying to clear her throat, but there was too much blood and she began to choke. Her lungs burned from a lack of air, and the lines on the ceiling wavered and grew dim, and then her memory ceased and there was nothing, not even darkness.

Afterward, Galbatorix spoke to her while the irons heated.

This too had become one of their rituals.

442

He had healed her tongue—at least, she thought it had been him and not Murtagh—for as he said, "It wouldn't do if you were unable to speak, now would it? How else will I know when you are ready to serve me?"

As before, the king sat to her right, at the very edge of her vision, where all she could see of him was a gold-edged shadow, his form partially hidden beneath the long, heavy cape he wore.

"I met your father, you know, when he was steward of Enduriel's chief estate," said Galbatorix. "Did he tell you of that?"

She shuddered and closed her eyes and felt tears seep from the corners. She hated listening to him. His voice was too powerful, too seductive; it left her wanting to do whatever he desired just so she could hear him utter a tiny morsel of praise.

"Yes," she murmured.

"I took little notice of him at the time. Why would I? He was a servant, no one of significance. Enduriel allowed him a fair bit of freedom, the better to manage the affairs of the estate—too much freedom, as it turned out." The king made a dismissive gesture, and the light caught his lean, clawlike hand. "Enduriel always was overly permissive. It was his dragon who was the cunning one; Enduriel merely did as he was told. . . . What a strange, amusing series of events fate has arranged. To think, the man who saw to it that my boots were brightly polished went on to become my foremost enemy after Brom, and now here you are, his daughter, returned to Urû'baen and about to enter my service, even as did your father. How very ironic, would you not agree?"

"My father escaped, and he nearly killed Durza when he did," she said. "All your spells and oaths could not hold him any more than you'll be able to hold me."

She thought Galbatorix might have frowned. "Yes, that was unfortunate. Durza was quite put out about it at the time. Families seem to make it easier for people to change who they are and thus their true names, which is why I now choose my household servants only from those who are barren and unwed. However, you are sorely mistaken if you think to slip your bonds. The only ways to leave the Hall of the Soothsayer are by swearing loyalty to me or by dying."

"Then I will die."

"How very shortsighted." The gilded shadow of the king leaned toward her. "Have you never entertained the thought, Nasuada, that the world would have been worse off had I not overthrown the Riders?"

"The Riders kept the peace," she said. "They protected the whole of Alagaësia from war, from plague . . . from the threat of Shades. In times of famine, they brought food to the starving. How is this land a better place without them?"

"Because there was a price attached to their service. You of all people should know that everything in this world must be paid for, whether in gold, time, or blood. Nothing is without its price, not even the Riders. *Especially* not the Riders.

"Aye, they kept the peace, but they also stifled the races of this land, the elves and dwarves just as much as us humans. What is always said in praise of the Riders when the bards bemoan their passing? That their reign extended for thousands of years, and that during this much-vaunted 'golden age,' little changed besides the names of the kings and queens who sat smug and secure upon their thrones. Oh, there were little alarms: a Shade here, an incursion by Urgals there, a skirmish between two dwarf clans over a mine no one but they cared about. But on the whole, the order of things remained exactly the same as it had been when the Riders first rose to prominence."

She heard the *clink* of metal against metal as Murtagh stirred the coals in the brazier. She wished she could see his face so that she could gauge his reaction to Galbatorix's words, but as was his habit, he stood with his back to her, staring down at the coals. The only time he looked at her was when he had to apply the white-hot metal to her flesh. That was his particular ritual, and she suspected he needed it as much as she needed hers.

And still Galbatorix kept talking: "Does that not seem the most evil thing to you, Nasuada? Life is change, and yet the Riders suppressed it so that the land lay in an uneasy slumber, unable to shake off the chains that bound it, unable to advance or retreat as nature intended . . . unable to become something new. I saw with my own eyes scrolls in the vaults at Vroengard and here, in the vaults of Ilirea, that detailed discoveries—magical, mechanical, and from every sphere of natural philosophy—discoveries that the Riders kept hidden because they feared what might happen if those things became generally known. The Riders were cowards wedded to an old way of life and an old way of thinking, determined to defend it unto their dying breath. Theirs was a gentle tyranny, but a tyranny nevertheless."

"Were murder and betrayal really the solution, though?" she asked, not caring if he punished her for it.

He laughed, seeming genuinely amused. "Such hypocrisy! You condemn me for the very thing you seek to do. If you could, you would kill me where I sit, and with no more hesitation than were I a rabid dog."

"You're a traitor; I'm not."

"I am the victor. In the end, nothing else matters. We are not so different as you think, Nasuada. You wish to kill me because you believe my death would be an improvement for Alagaësia, and because you—who are still almost a child—believe you can do a better job of ruling the Empire than I. Your arrogance would cause others to despise you. But not me, for I understand. I took up arms against the Riders for those very same reasons, and I was right to do so."

"Did vengeance have nothing to do with it?"

She thought he smiled. "It might have provided the initial inspiration, but neither hate nor revenge was my guiding motive. I was concerned by what the Riders had become and convinced, as I still am, that only when they were gone could we flourish as a race."

For a moment, the pain from her wounds made it impossible for her to talk. Then she managed to whisper: "If what you say is true—and I have no cause to believe you, but if it is—then you are no better than the Riders. You pillaged their libraries and gathered up their stores of knowledge, and as of yet, you have shared none of that lore with anyone else."

He moved nearer to her, and she felt his breath upon her ear. "That is because, scattered throughout their hoard of secrets, I found hints of a greater truth, a truth that could provide an answer to one of the most perplexing questions in history."

A shiver ran down her spine. "What . . . question?"

He leaned back in his chair and tugged at the edge of his cape. "The question of how a king or a queen can enforce the laws they enact when there are those among their subjects who can use magic. When I realized what the hints alluded to, I put aside all else and committed myself to hunting down this truth, this answer, for I knew it was of paramount importance. That is why I have kept the Riders' secrets to myself; I have been busy with my search. The answer to this problem must be set into place before I make known any of those other discoveries. The world is already a troubled place, and it is better to soothe the waters before disturbing them once more. . . . It took me nearly a hundred years to find the information I needed, and now that I have, I shall use it to reshape the whole of Alagaësia.

"Magic is the great injustice in the world. It would not be so unfair if the ability only occurred among those who were weak—for then it would be a compensation for what chance or circumstance had robbed them of—but it doesn't. The strong are just as likely to be able to use magic, and they gain more from it besides. One need only look to the elves to see this is true. The problem is not confined to individuals; it also plagues the relationships between the races. The elves find it easier than us to maintain order within their society, for most every elf can use magic, and, therefore, few of them are ever at the mercy of another. In this regard, they are fortunate, but it is not so fortunate for us, for the dwarves, or even for the accursed Urgals. We have only been able to live here in Alagaësia because the elves permitted it. If they wanted, they could have swept us from the face of the earth as easily as a flood might sweep away an anthill. But no more, not while I am here to oppose their might."

"The Riders would never have let them kill us or drive us away."

"No, but while the Riders existed, we were dependent upon their goodwill, and it is not right that we should have to rely on others for our safekeeping. The Riders began as a means to keep the peace between elves and dragons, but in the end, their main purpose became upholding the rule of law throughout the land. They were, however, insufficient to the task, as are my own spellcasters, the Black Hand. The problem is too far-reaching for any one group to combat. My own life is proof enough of that. Even if there were a trustworthy band of spellcasters adept enough to watch over all the other magicians in Alagaësia—ready to intervene at the slightest hint of malfeasance—we would still be reliant upon the very ones whose powers we sought to restrain. Ultimately, the land would be no safer than it is now. No, in order to solve this problem, it must be addressed on a deeper, more fundamental level. The ancients knew how that might be done, and now so do I."

Galbatorix shifted in the chair, and she caught a sharp gleam from his eye, as from a lantern set deep within a cave. "I shall make it so that no magician will be able to harm another person, whether human, dwarf, or elf. None shall be able to cast a spell unless they have permission, and only magics that are benign and beneficial shall be allowed. Even the elves will be bound by this precept, and they shall learn to measure their words carefully or speak not at all."

"And who will grant permission?" she asked. "Who will decide what is allowed and what is not? You?"

"Someone must. It was I who recognized what was needed, I who discovered the means, and I who shall implement them. You sneer at the thought? Well then, ask yourself this, Nasuada: have I been a bad king? Be honest now. By the standards of my forebears, I have not been excessive."

"You have been cruel."

"That is not the same thing. . . . You have led the Varden; you understand the burdens of command. Surely you have realized the threat that magic poses to the stability of any kingdom? To give but one example, I have spent more time laboring over the enchantments that protect the coin of the realm from being forged than I have upon most any other aspect of my duties. And yet, no doubt, there is a clever-minded conjurer somewhere who has found a way to circumvent my wards and who is busy making bags of lead coins with which he can fool nobles and commoners alike. Why else do you think I have been so careful to restrict the use of magic throughout the Empire?"

"Because it is a threat to you."

"No! There you are exactly wrong. It is no threat to me. No one and nothing is. However, spellcasters *are* a threat to the proper functioning of this realm, and that I shall not tolerate. Once I have bound every magician in the world to the laws of the land, imagine the peace and prosperity that shall reign. No more shall men or dwarves have to fear elves. No more shall Riders be able to impose their will on others. No more shall those who cannot use magic be prey for those who can. . . . Alagaësia will be transformed, and with our newfound safety, we will build a more wondrous tomorrow, one you could be a part of.

"Enter into my service, Nasuada, and you will have the opportunity to oversee the creation of a world such as has never existed before—a world where a man will stand or fall based upon the strength of his limbs and the keenness of his mind, and not whether chance has granted him skill with magic. Man may build up his limbs and man may improve his mind, but never can he learn to use magic if he was born lacking the ability. As I said, magic is the great injustice, and for the good of all, I will impose limits upon every magician there is."

She stared at the lines on the ceiling and tried to ignore him. So much of what he said *was* similar to what she had thought herself. He was right: magic was the most destructive force in the world, and if it could be regulated, Alagaësia would be a better place for it. She hated that there had been nothing to stop Eragon from—

Blue. Red. Patterns of interwoven color. The throbbing of her burns. She strove desperately to concentrate upon anything other than . . . than nothing. Whatever she had been about to think of was nothing, did not exist.

"You call me evil. You curse my name and seek to overthrow me. But remember this, Nasuada: it was not I who started this war, and I am not responsible for those who have lost their lives as a result. I did not seek this out. You did. I would have been content to devote myself to my studies, but the Varden insisted upon stealing Saphira's egg from my treasure house, and you and your kind are responsible for all of the blood and sorrow that have followed. You are the ones, after all, who have been rampaging across the countryside, burning and pillaging as you please, not I. And yet you have the audacity to claim that I am in the wrong! Were you to go into the homes of the peasants, they would tell you that it is the Varden they fear most. They would talk about how they look to my soldiers for protection and how they hope the Empire will defeat the Varden and all shall be as it was."

Nasuada wet her lips. Even though she knew her boldness might cost her, she said, "It seems to me you protest too much. . . . If the welfare of your subjects were your main concern, you would have flown out to confront the Varden weeks ago, instead of letting an army roam loose within your borders. That is, unless you are not so sure of your might as you pretend. Or is it you fear the elves will take Urû'baen while you are gone?" As had become her habit, she spoke of the Varden as if she knew no more about them than any random person in the Empire.

Galbatorix shifted, and she could tell he was about to respond, but she was not yet finished.

"And what of the Urgals? You cannot convince me your cause is just when you would exterminate an entire race in order to ease your pain at the death of your first dragon. Have you no answer for that, Oath-breaker? . . . Speak to me of the dragons, then. Explain why you slew so many that you doomed their kind to a slow and inevitable extinction. And finally, explain your mistreatment of the Eldunarí you captured." In her anger, she allowed herself that one slip. "You have bent and broken them and chained them to your will. There is no rightness in what you do, only selfishness and a never-ending hunger for power."

Galbatorix regarded her in silence for a long, uncomfortable while. Then she saw his outline move as he crossed his arms. "I think the irons ought to be sufficiently hot by now. Murtagh, if you would . . ."

She clenched her fists, digging her nails into her skin, and her muscles began to tremble, despite her best efforts to hold them still. One of the iron rods scraped against the lip of the brazier as Murtagh pulled it free. He turned to face her, and she could not help but stare at the tip of the glowing metal. Then she looked into Murtagh's eyes, and she saw the guilt and self-loathing they contained, and a sense of profound sorrow overcame her.

What fools we are, she thought. *What sorry, miserable fools.*

After that, she had no more energy for thinking, and so she fell back to her well-worn rituals, clinging to them for survival even as a drowning man might cling to a piece of wood.

When Murtagh and Galbatorix departed, she was in too much pain to do more than gaze mindlessly at the patterns on the ceiling while she struggled not to cry. She was sweating and shivering at the same time, as if she had a fever, and she found it impossible to concentrate upon any one thing for more than a few seconds. The pain from her burns did not subside as it would have if she had been cut or bruised; indeed, the throbbing from her wounds seemed to grow worse with time.

She closed her eyes and concentrated upon slowing her breathing as she tried to calm her body.

The first time Galbatorix and Murtagh had visited her, she had been far more courageous. She had cursed and taunted them and done all she could to hurt them with her words. However, through Murtagh, Galbatorix had made her suffer for her insolence, and she had soon lost her taste for open rebellion. The iron made her timid; even the memory of it made her want to curl into a tight little ball. During their second, most recent visit, she had said as little as possible until her final, imprudent outburst.

She had tried to test Galbatorix's claim that neither he nor Murtagh would lie to her. She did this by asking them questions about the Empire's inner workings, facts that her spies had informed her of but that Galbatorix had no reason to believe she knew. So far as she could determine, Galbatorix and Murtagh had told her the truth, but she was not about to trust anything the king said when there was no way to verify his claims.

As for Murtagh, she was not quite so sure. When he was with the king, she gave no credence to his words, but when he was by himself . . .

Several hours after her first, agonizing audience with King Galbatorix—when she had at long last fallen into a shallow, troubled sleep—Murtagh had come alone to the Hall of the Soothsayer, bleary-eyed and smelling of drink. He had stood by the monolith upon which she lay, and he had stared at her with such a strange, tormented expression, she had not been sure what he was going to do.

At last he had turned away, walked to the nearest wall, and slid down it to the floor. There he sat, with his knees pulled up against his chest, his long, shaggy hair obscuring most of his face, and blood oozing from the torn skin on the knuckles of his right hand. After what felt like minutes, he had reached into his maroon jerkin—for he was wearing the same clothes as earlier, although without the mask—and drawn forth a small stone bottle. He drank several times and then began to talk.

He talked, and she listened. She had no choice, but she did not allow herself to believe what he said. Not at first. For all she knew, everything he said or did was a sham designed to win her confidence.

Murtagh had started by telling her a rather garbled story about a man named Tornac, which involved a riding mishap and some sort of advice Tornac had given him regarding how an honorable man ought to live. She had been unable to make out whether Tornac was a friend, a servant, a distant relative, or some combination thereof, but whatever he was, it was obvious that he had meant a great deal to Murtagh.

When he concluded his story, Murtagh had said, "Galbatorix was going to have you killed. . . . He knew Elva wasn't guarding you as she used to, so he decided it was the perfect time to have you assassinated. I only found out about his plan by chance; I happened to be with him when he gave the orders to the Black Hand." Murtagh shook his head. "It's my fault. I convinced him to have you brought here instead. He liked that; he knew you would lure Eragon here that much faster. . . . It was the only way I could keep him from killing you. . . . I'm sorry. . . . I'm sorry." And he buried his head in his arms.

"I would rather have died."

"I know," he said in a hoarse voice. "Will you forgive me?"

That she had not answered. His revelation only made her more uneasy. Why should he care to save her life, and what did he expect in return?

Murtagh had said nothing more for a while. Then, sometimes weeping and sometimes raging, he told her of his upbringing in Galbatorix's court, of the distrust and jealousy he had faced as the son of Morzan, of the nobles who had sought to use him to win favor with the king, and of his longing for the mother he barely remembered. Twice he mentioned Eragon and cursed him for a fool favored by fortune. "He would not have done so well if our places had been reversed. But our mother chose to take *him* to Carvahall, not me." He spat on the floor.

She found the whole episode maudlin and self-pitying, and his weakness did nothing but inspire contempt in her until he recounted how the Twins had abducted him from Farthen Dûr, how they had mistreated him on the way to Urû'baen, and how Galbatorix had broken him once they arrived. Some of the tortures he described were worse than her own and, if true, gave her a slight measure of sympathy for his own plight.

"Thorn was my undoing," Murtagh finally confessed. "When he hatched for me and we bonded . . ." He shook his head. "I love him. How could I not? I love him even as Eragon loves Saphira. The moment I touched him, I was lost. Galbatorix used him against me. Thorn was stronger than me. He never gave up. But I could not bear to see him suffer, so I swore my loyalty to the king, and after that . . ." Murtagh's lips curled with revulsion. "After that, Galbatorix went into my mind. He learned everything about me, and then he taught me my true name. And now I am his. . . . His forever."

Then he leaned his head against the wall and closed his eyes, and she watched the tears roll down his cheeks.

453

Eventually, he stood, and as he walked toward the door, he paused next to her and touched her on the shoulder. His nails, she noted, were clean and trimmed, but nowhere near as well cared for as her jailer's. He murmured a few words in the ancient language, and a moment later, her pain melted away, although her wounds looked the same as ever.

As he took his hand away, she said, "I cannot forgive . . . but I understand."

Whereupon he nodded and stumbled away, leaving her to wonder if she had found a new ally.

SMALL REBELLIONS

As Nasuada lay on the slab, sweating and shivering, every part of her body aching with pain, she found herself wishing that Murtagh would return, if only so he could again free her from her agony.

When at last the door to the eight-sided chamber swung open, she was unable to suppress her relief, but her relief turned to bitter disappointment when she heard the shuffling footsteps of her jailer descending the stairs that led into the room.

As he had once before, the stocky, narrow-shouldered man bathed her wounds with a wet cloth, then bound them with strips of linen. When he released her from the restraints so that she could visit the privy room, she found she was too weak to make any attempt to grab the knife on the tray of food. Instead, she contented herself with thanking the man for his help and, for the second time, complimenting him on his nails, which were even shinier than before and which he quite obviously wanted her to see, for he kept holding his hands where she could not help but look at them.

After he fed her and departed, she tried to sleep, but the constant pain of her wounds made it impossible for her to do more than doze.

Her eyes snapped open as she heard the bar to the door of the chamber being thrown open.

Not again! she thought, panic welling up inside her. *Not so soon! I can't bear it. . . . I'm not strong enough.* Then she reined in her fear and told herself, *Don't. Don't say such things or else you'll start to believe them.* Still, although she was able to master her conscious reactions, she could not stop her heart from pounding at twice its normal speed.

A single pair of footsteps echoed in the room, and then Murtagh appeared at the corner of her vision. He wore no mask, and his expression was somber.

This time he healed her first, without waiting. The relief she felt as her pain abated was so intense, it bordered on ecstasy. In all her life, she had never experienced a sensation quite so pleasurable as the draining away of the agony.

She gasped slightly at the feeling. "Thank you."

Murtagh nodded; then he went over to the wall and sat in the same spot as before.

She studied him for a minute. The skin on his knuckles was smooth and whole again, and he appeared sober, if grim and close-mouthed. His clothes had once been fine, but they were now torn, frayed, and patched, and she spotted what looked like several cuts in the undersides of his sleeves. She wondered if he had been fighting.

"Does Galbatorix know where you are?" she finally asked.

"He might, but I doubt it. He's busy playing with his favorite concubines. That, or he's asleep. It's the middle of the night right now. Besides, I cast a spell to keep anyone from listening to us. He could break it if he wants, but I would know."

"What if he finds out?"

Murtagh shrugged.

"He will find out, you know, if he wears down my defenses."

"Then don't let him. You're stronger than me; you have no one he can threaten. You can resist him, unlike me. . . . The Varden are fast approaching, as are the elves from the north. If you can hold out for another few days, there's a chance . . . there's a chance maybe they can free you."

"You don't believe they can, do you?"

He shrugged again.

". . . Then help me escape."

A bark of hard laughter erupted from his throat. "How? I can't do much more than put on my boots without Galbatorix's permission."

"You could loosen my cuffs, and when you leave, perhaps you could forget to secure the door."

His upper lip curled in a sneer. "There are two men stationed outside, there are wards set upon this room to warn Galbatorix if a prisoner steps outside it, and there are hundreds of guards between here and the nearest gate. You'd be lucky to make it to the end of the hallway, if that."

"Perhaps, but I'd like to try."

"You'd only get yourself killed."

"Then help me. If you wanted, you could find a way to fool his wards."

"I can't. My oaths won't let me use magic against him."

"What of the guards, though? If you held them off long enough for me to reach the gate, I could hide myself in the city, and it wouldn't matter if Galbatorix knew—"

"The city is his. Besides, wherever you went, he could find you with a spell. The only way you would be safe from him would be to get far away from here before the alarm roused him, and that you could not do even on dragonback."

"There must be a way!"

"If there were . . ." He smiled sourly and looked down. "It's pointless to consider."

Frustrated, she shifted her gaze to the ceiling for a few moments. Then, "At least let me out of these cuffs."

He released his breath in a sound of exasperation.

"Just so I can stand up," she said. "I hate lying on this stone, and it's making my eyes ache having to look at you down there."

He hesitated, and then he rose to his feet in a single graceful movement, came over to the slab, and began to unfasten the padded restraints around her wrists and ankles. "Don't think you can kill me," he said in a low voice. "You can't."

As soon as she was free, he retreated to his former position and again lowered himself onto the floor, where he sat staring into the distance. It was, she thought, his attempt to give her some privacy as she sat up and swung her legs over the edge of the slab. Her shift was in tatters—burned through in dozens of locations—and it did a poor job of concealing her form, not that it had covered much to begin with.

The marble floor was cool against the soles of her feet as she made her way over to Murtagh and sat next to him. She wrapped her arms around herself in an attempt to preserve her modesty.

"Was Tornac really your only friend growing up?" she asked.

Murtagh still did not look at her. "No, but he was as close to a father as I've ever had. He taught me, comforted me . . . berated me when I was too arrogant, and saved me from making a fool of myself more times than I can remember. If he were still alive, he would have beaten me silly for getting as drunk as I did the other day."

"You said he died during your escape from Urû'baen?"

He snorted. "I thought I was being clever. I bribed one of the watchmen to leave a side gate open for us. We were going to slip out of the city under the cover of darkness, and Galbatorix was only supposed to find out what had happened once it was too late to catch us. He knew from the very start, though. How, I'm not sure, but I guess he was scrying me the whole while. When Tornac and I went through the gate, we found soldiers waiting for us on the other side. . . . Their orders were to bring us back unharmed, but we fought, and one of them killed Tornac. The finest swordsman in all the Empire brought down by a knife in the back."

"But Galbatorix let you escape."

"I don't think he expected us to fight. Besides, his attention was directed elsewhere that night."

She frowned as she saw the oddest half smile appear on Murtagh's face.

"I counted the days," he said. "That was when the Ra'zac were in

Palancar Valley, searching for Saphira's egg. So you see, Eragon lost his foster father almost at the same time I lost mine. Fate has a cruel sense of humor, don't you think?"

"Yes, it does. . . . But if Galbatorix could scry you, why didn't he track you down and bring you back to Urû'baen later on?"

"He was playing with me, I think. I went to stay at the estate of a man I believed I could trust. As usual, I was mistaken, though I only found that out later, once the Twins brought me back here. Galbatorix knew where I was, and he knew I was still angry over Tornac's death, so he was content to leave me at the estate while he hunted for Eragon and Brom. . . . I surprised him, though; I left, and by the time he learned of my disappearance, I was already on my way to Dras-Leona. That's why Galbatorix went to Dras-Leona, you know. It wasn't to chastise Lord Tábor over his behavior—although he certainly did—it was to find me. But he was too late. By the time he arrived at the city, I had already met up with Eragon and Saphira, and we had set off for Gil'ead."

"Why did you leave?" she asked.

"Didn't Eragon tell you? Because—"

"No, not Dras-Leona. Why did you leave the estate? You were safe there, or so you thought. So why did you leave?"

Murtagh was quiet for a while. "I wanted to strike back at Galbatorix, and I wanted to make a name for myself apart from my father's. My whole life, people have looked at me differently because I am the son of Morzan. I wanted them to respect me for my deeds, not his." He finally looked at her, a quick glance out of the corner of one eye. "I suppose I got what I wanted, but again, fate has a cruel sense of humor."

She wondered if there had been anyone else in Galbatorix's court whom he had cared for, but she decided it would be a dangerous topic to broach. So, instead, she asked, "How much does Galbatorix really know about the Varden?"

"Everything, so far as I can tell. He has more spies than you think."

She pressed her arms against her belly as her gut twisted. "Do you know of any way to kill him?"

"A knife. A sword. An arrow. Poison. Magic. The usual ways. The problem is, he has too many spells wound about himself for anyone or anything to have a chance of harming him. Eragon is luckier than most; Galbatorix doesn't want to kill him, so he may get to attack the king more than once. But even if Eragon could attack him a hundred times, he wouldn't find a way past Galbatorix's wards."

"Every puzzle has a solution, and every man has a weakness," Nasuada insisted. "Does he love any of his concubines?"

The look on Murtagh's face answered her well enough. Then he said, "Would it be so bad if Galbatorix remains king? The world he envisions is a good world. If he defeats the Varden, the whole of Alagaësia will finally be at peace. He'll put an end to the misuse of magic; elves, dwarves, and humans will no longer have cause to hate each other. What's more, if the Varden lose, Eragon and I can be together as brothers ought to be. But if they win, it'll mean the death of Thorn and me. It'll have to."

"Oh? And what of me?" she asked. "If Galbatorix wins, shall I become his slave, to order about as he wills?" Murtagh refused to answer, but she saw the tendons on the back of his hands tighten. "You can't give up, Murtagh."

"What other choice do I have!" he shouted, filling the room with echoes.

She stood and stared down at him. "You can fight! Look at me. . . . Look at me!"

He reluctantly lifted his gaze.

"You can find ways to work against him. That's what you can do! Even if your oaths will allow only the smallest of rebellions, the smallest of rebellions might still prove to be his undoing." She restated his question for effect. "What other choice do you have? You can go around feeling helpless and miserable for the rest of your life.

You can let Galbatorix turn you into a monster. Or you can fight!" She spread her arms so that he could see all of the burn marks on her. "Do you enjoy hurting me?"

"No!" he exclaimed.

"Then fight, blast you! You have to fight or you *will* lose everything you are. As will Thorn."

She held her ground as he sprang to his feet, lithe as a cat, and moved toward her until he was only a few inches away. The muscles in his jaw bunched and knotted while he glowered at her, breathing heavily through his nostrils. She recognized his expression, for it was one she had seen many times before. His was the look of a man whose pride had been offended and who wanted to lash out at the person who had insulted him. It was dangerous to keep pushing him, but she knew she had to, for she might never get the chance again.

"If I can keep fighting," she said, "then so can you."

"Back to the stone," he said in a harsh voice.

"I know you're not a coward, Murtagh. Better to die than to live as a slave to one such as Galbatorix. At least then you might accomplish some good, and your name might be remembered with a measure of kindness after you're gone."

"Back to the stone," he growled, grabbing her by the arm and dragging her over to the slab.

She allowed him to push her onto the ash-colored block, fasten the restraints around her wrists and ankles, and then tighten the strap around her head. When he finished, he stood looking at her, his eyes dark and wild, the lines of his body like cords stretched taut.

"You have to decide whether you are willing to risk your life in order to save yourself," she said. "You and Thorn both. And you have to decide now, while there is still time. Ask yourself: what would Tornac have wanted you to do?"

Without answering, Murtagh extended his right arm and placed his hand upon the upper part of her chest, his palm hot against her skin. Her breath hitched at the shock of the contact.

Then, hardly louder than a whisper, he began to speak in the ancient language. As the strange words tumbled from his lips, her fear grew ever stronger.

He spoke for what seemed like minutes. She felt no different when he stopped, but that was neither a favorable nor an unfavorable sign where magic was concerned.

Cool air washed over the patch on her chest, chilling it as Murtagh lifted his hand away. He stepped back then and started to walk past her, toward the entrance of the chamber. She was about to call out to him—to ask what he had done to her—when he paused and said, "That should shield you from the pain of most any wound, but you'll have to pretend otherwise, or Galbatorix will discover what I've done."

And then he left.

"Thank you," she whispered to the empty room.

She spent a long time pondering their conversation. It seemed unlikely that Galbatorix had sent Murtagh to talk with her, but unlikely or not, it remained a possibility. Also, she found herself torn as to whether Murtagh was, at heart, a good person or a bad one. She thought back to King Hrothgar—who had been like an uncle to her when she was growing up—and how Murtagh had killed him on the Burning Plains. Then she thought of Murtagh's childhood and the many hardships he had faced, and how he had allowed Eragon and Saphira to go free when he could have just as easily brought them to Urû'baen.

Yet even if Murtagh had once been honorable and trustworthy, she knew that his enforced servitude might have corrupted him.

In the end, she decided she would ignore Murtagh's past and judge him on his actions in the present and those alone. Good, bad, or some combination thereof, he was a potential ally, and she needed his help if she could get it. If he proved false, then she would be no worse off than she already was. But if he proved true, then she might be able to escape from Urû'baen, and that was well worth the risk.

In the absence of pain, she slept long and deep for the first time since her arrival at the capital. She awoke feeling more hopeful than before, and again fell to tracing the lines painted on the ceiling. The thin blue line she was following led her to notice a small white shape on the corner of a tile that she had previously overlooked. It took her a moment to realize that the discoloration was where a chip had fallen free.

The sight amused her, for she found it humorous—and somewhat comforting—to know that Galbatorix's perfect chamber was not quite so perfect after all, and that, despite his pretensions otherwise, he was not omniscient or infallible.

When the door to the chamber next opened, it was her jailer, bringing what she guessed was a midday meal. She asked him if she could eat first, before he let her up, for she said she was more hungry than anything else, which was not entirely untrue.

To her satisfaction, he agreed, though he uttered not a word, only smiled his hideous, clamplike smile and seated himself on the edge of the slab. As he spooned warm gruel into her mouth, her mind raced as she tried to plan for every contingency, for she knew she would have only one chance at success.

Anticipation made it difficult for her to stomach the bland food. Nevertheless, she managed, and when the bowl was empty and she had drunk her fill, she readied herself.

The man had, as always, placed the food tray by the base of the far wall, close to where Murtagh had been sitting and perhaps ten feet from the door to the privy room.

Once she was free of her manacles, she slid off the block of stone. The gourd-headed man reached over to take hold of her left arm, but she raised a hand and, in her sweetest voice, said, "I can stand by myself now, thank you."

Her jailer hesitated, then he smiled again and clacked his teeth together twice, as if to say, "Well then, I'm happy for you!"

They started toward the privy room, she in the front and he

slightly to the rear. As she took her third step, she deliberately twisted her right ankle and stumbled diagonally across the room. The man shouted and tried to catch her—she felt his thick fingers close on the air above her neck—but he was too slow, and she eluded his grasp.

She fell lengthwise onto the tray, breaking the pitcher—which still held a fair amount of watered wine—and sending the wooden bowl clattering across the floor. By design, she landed with her right hand underneath her, and as soon as she felt the tray, she began to search with her fingers for the metal spoon.

"Ah!" she exclaimed, as if hurt, then turned to look up at the man, doing her best to appear chagrined. "Maybe I wasn't ready after all," she said, and gave him an apologetic smile. Her thumb touched the handle of the spoon, and she grabbed hold of it even as the man pulled her upright by her other arm.

He looked her over and wrinkled his nose, appearing disgusted by her wine-soaked shift. While he did, she reached behind herself and slid the handle of the spoon through a hole near the hem of her garment. Then she held up her hand, as if to show that she had taken nothing.

The man grunted, grabbed her other arm, and marched her to the privy room. As she entered, he shuffled back toward the tray, muttering under his breath.

The moment she had closed the door, she pulled the spoon out of her shift and placed it between her lips, holding it there as she plucked several strands of hair from the back of her head, where they were longest. Moving as fast as she could, she pinched one end of the gathered hairs between the fingers of her left hand and then rolled the loose strands down her thighs with the palm of her right, twisting them together into a single cord. Her skin grew cold as she realized the cord was too short. Fumbling in her urgency, she tied off the ends, then placed the cord on the ground.

She plucked another group of hairs and rolled them into a second cord, which she tied off like the first.

Knowing that she had only seconds remaining, she dropped to one knee and knotted the two strands together. Then she took the spoon from her mouth and, with the slim length of thread, she bound the spoon to the outside of her left leg, where the edge of her shift would cover it.

It had to go on her left leg because Galbatorix always sat to her right.

She stood and checked that the spoon remained hidden, and then she took a few steps to make sure it would not fall.

It did not.

Relieved, she allowed herself to exhale. Now her challenge was to return to the slab without letting her jailer notice what she had done.

The man was waiting for her when she opened the door to the privy room. He scowled at her, and his sparse eyebrows met, forming a single straight line.

"Spoon," he said, mashing the word with his tongue as if it were a piece of overcooked parsnip.

She lifted her chin and pointed toward the rear of the privy room.

His scowl deepened. He went into the room and carefully examined the walls, floors, ceiling, and all else before stomping back out. He clacked his teeth together again and scratched his bulbous head, appearing unhappy and, she thought, a little hurt that she would bother to throw away the spoon. She had been kind to him, and she knew an act of such petty defiance would puzzle him and make him angry.

She resisted the urge to pull away when he stepped forward, put his weighty hands on her head, and combed through her hair with his fingers. When he did not find the spoon, his face drooped. He grabbed her arm then and walked her over to the slab and again placed her in the manacles.

Then, his expression sullen, he picked up the tray and shuffled out of the room.

She waited until she was absolutely sure he was gone before she reached out with the fingers of her left hand and, inch by inch, pulled up the edge of her shift.

A broad smile passed across her face as she felt the bowl of the spoon with the tip of her index finger.

Now she had a weapon.

◆　◆　◆

A CROWN OF ICE AND SNOW

When the first pale rays of light streaked across the surface of the dimpled sea, illuminating the crests of the translucent waves—which glittered as if carved from crystal—then Eragon roused himself from his waking dreams and looked to the northwest, curious to see what the light revealed of the clouds building in the distance.

What he beheld was disconcerting: the clouds encompassed nearly half the horizon, and the largest of the dense white plumes looked as tall as the peaks of the Beor Mountains, too tall for Saphira to climb over. The only open sky lay behind her, and even that would be lost to them as the arms of the storm closed in.

We shall have to fly through it, Glaedr said, and Eragon felt Saphira's trepidation.

Why not try to go around? she asked.

Through Saphira, Eragon was aware of Glaedr examining the structure of the clouds. At last the golden dragon said, *I do not want you flying too far off course. We still have many leagues to cover, and if your strength fails you—*

Then you can lend me yours to keep us aloft.

Hmph. Even so, it is best to be cautious in our recklessness. I have seen the likes of this storm before. It is larger than you think. To skirt it, you would have to fly so far to the west that you would end up beyond Vroengard, and it would probably take another day to reach land.

The distance to Vroengard isn't that great, she said.

No, but the wind will slow us. Besides, my instincts tell me that the storm extends all the way to the island. One way or another, we shall have to fly through it. However, there's no need to go through its very heart. Do you see the notch between those two small pillars off to the west?

Yes.

Go there, and perhaps we can then find a safe path through the clouds.

Eragon grasped the front of the saddle as Saphira dropped her left shoulder and turned westward, aiming herself toward the notch Glaedr had indicated. He yawned and rubbed his eyes as she leveled out; then he twisted round and dug out an apple and a few strips of dried beef from the bags strapped behind him. It was a meager breakfast, but his hunger was slight, and eating a large meal while riding Saphira often made him queasy.

While he ate, he alternated between watching the clouds and gazing at the sparkling sea. He found it unsettling that there was nothing but water beneath them and that the nearest solid ground—the mainland—was, by his estimate, over fifty miles away. He shivered as he imagined sinking down and down into the cold, clutching depths of the sea. He wondered what lay at the bottom, and it occurred to him that with his magic, he could likely travel there and find out, but the thought held no appeal. The watery abyss was too dark and too dangerous for his liking. It was not, he felt, a place where his sort of life ought to venture. Better, instead, to leave it to whatever strange creatures already lived there.

As the morning wore on, it became apparent that the clouds were farther away than they had first seemed and that, as Glaedr had said, the storm was larger than either Eragon or Saphira had originally imagined.

A light headwind sprang up, and Saphira's flight became somewhat more labored, but she continued to make good progress.

When they were still some leagues from the leading edge of the storm, Saphira surprised Eragon and Glaedr by slipping into a shallow dive and flying down close to the surface of the water.

As she descended, Glaedr said, *Saphira, what are you about?*

I'm curious, she replied. *And I would like to rest my wings before entering the clouds.*

She skimmed over the waves, her reflection below and her shadow in front mirroring her every move like two ghostly companions, one dark and one light. Then she swiveled her wings on edge and, with three quick flaps, slowed herself and landed upon the water. A fan of spray shot up on either side of her neck as her chest plowed into the waves, sprinkling Eragon with hundreds of droplets.

The water was cold, but after so long aloft, the air felt pleasantly warm—so warm, in fact, that Eragon unwrapped his cloak and pulled off his gloves.

Saphira folded her wings and floated along peacefully, bobbing up and down with the motion of the waves. Eragon spotted several clumps of brown seaweed off to the right. The plants were branched like scrub brush and had berry-sized bladders at joints along the stems.

Far overhead, near the height Saphira had been, Eragon spotted a pair of albatrosses with black-tipped wings flying away from the massive wall of clouds. The sight only deepened his unease; the seabirds reminded him of the time he had seen a pack of wolves running alongside a herd of deer as the animals fled a forest fire in the Spine.

If we had any sense, he said to Saphira, *we would turn around.*

If we had any sense, we would leave Alagaësia and never return, she rejoined.

Arching her neck, she dipped her muzzle into the seawater, then shook her head and ran her crimson tongue in and out of her mouth several times, as if she had tasted something unpleasant.

Then Eragon felt a sense of panic from Glaedr, and the old dragon roared in his mind: *Take off! Now, now, now! Take off!*

Saphira wasted no time on questions. With a sound like thunder, she opened her wings and began to beat them as she reared out of the water.

Leaning forward, Eragon grabbed the edge of the saddle to keep from being thrown backward. The flapping of Saphira's wings threw up a screen of mist that half blinded him, so he used his mind to search for whatever had alarmed Glaedr.

From deep below, rising toward Saphira's underside faster than Eragon would have believed possible, he felt something that was cold and huge . . . and filled with a ravenous, insatiable hunger. He tried to frighten it, tried to turn it away, but the creature was alien and implacable and seemed not to notice his efforts. In the strange, lightless caverns of its consciousness, he glimpsed memories of uncounted years spent lurking alone in the icy sea, hunting and being hunted.

His own panic mounting, Eragon groped for the hilt of Brisingr even as Saphira wrenched herself free from the grasp of the water and began to climb into the air. *Saphira! Hurry!* he silently shouted.

She slowly gained speed and altitude, and then a fountain of white water erupted behind her, and Eragon saw a pair of shiny gray jaws emerge from within the plume. The jaws were large enough for a horse and rider to pass through unscathed and were filled with hundreds of glinting white teeth.

Saphira was aware of what he saw, and she twisted violently to the side in an attempt to escape the gaping maw, clipping the water with the tip of her wing. An instant later, Eragon heard and felt the creature's jaws snap shut.

The needle-like teeth missed Saphira's tail by inches.

As the monster fell back into the water, more of its body became visible: The head was long and angular. A bony crest jutted out over the eyes, and from the outer part of each crest grew a ropy tendril that Eragon guessed to be over six feet in length. The neck of the creature reminded him of a giant, rippling snake. What was visible of the creature's torso was smooth and powerfully built and looked incredibly dense. A pair of oar-shaped flippers extended from the sides of its chest, flailing helplessly in the air.

The creature landed upon its side, and a second, even larger burst of spray flew toward the sky.

Just before the waves closed over the monster's shape, Eragon looked into its one upward-facing eye, which was as black as a drop of tar. The malevolence contained therein—the sheer hate and fury and *frustration* that he perceived in the creature's unblinking gaze—was enough to make Eragon shiver and wish he were in the center of the Hadarac Desert. For only there, he felt, would he be safe from the creature's ancient hunger.

Heart pounding, he relaxed his grip on Brisingr and slumped over the front of the saddle. "What was that?"

A Nïdhwal, said Glaedr.

Eragon frowned. He did not remember reading about any such thing in Ellesméra. *And what is a Nïdhwal?!*

They are rare and not often spoken about. They are to the sea what the Fanghur are to the air. Both are cousins to the dragons. Though the differences in our appearance are greater, the Nïdhwal are closer to us than are the screeching Fanghur. They are intelligent, and they even have a structure similar to the Eldunarí within their chest, which we believe enables them to remain submerged for extended periods of time at great depth.

Can they breathe fire?

No, but like the Fanghur, they often use the power of their minds to incapacitate their prey, which more than one dragon has discovered to their dismay.

They would eat their own kind! Saphira said.

To them, we are nothing alike, Glaedr replied. *But they do eat their own, which is one reason there are so few Nïdhwalar. They have no interest in happenings outside their own realm, and every attempt to reason with them has met with failure. It is odd to encounter one so close to shore. There was a time when they were only found several days' flight from land, where the sea is the deepest. It seems they have grown either bold or desperate since the fall of the Riders.*

Eragon shivered again as he remembered the feel of the Nïdhwal's mind. *Why did neither you nor Oromis ever teach us of them?*

There is much we did not teach you, Eragon. We had only so much time, and it was best spent trying to arm you against Galbatorix, not every dark creature that haunts the unexplored regions of Alagaësia.

Then there are other things like the Nïdhwal that we don't know about?

A few.

Will you tell us of them, Ebrithil? Saphira asked.

I will make a pact with you, Saphira, and with you, Eragon. Let us wait a week, and if we are still alive and still possessed of our freedom, I will happily spend the next ten years teaching you about every single race I know of, including every variety of beetle, of which there are multitudes. But until then, let us concentrate upon the task before us. Are we agreed?

Eragon and Saphira reluctantly agreed, and they spoke of it no more.

The headwind strengthened into a blustery gale as they neared the front of the storm, slowing Saphira until she was flying at half her normal speed. Now and then, powerful gusts rocked her and sometimes stopped her dead in her course for a few moments. They always knew when the gusts were about to strike, for they could see a silvery, scalelike pattern rushing toward them across the surface of the water.

Since dawn, the clouds had only increased in size, and up close, they were even more intimidating. Near the bottom, they were dark and purplish, with curtains of driving rain connecting the storm with the sea like a gauzy umbilical cord. Higher up, the clouds were the color of tarnished silver, while the very tops were a pure, blinding white and appeared as solid as the flanks of Tronjheim. To the north, over the center of the storm, the clouds had formed a gigantic flat-topped anvil that loomed over all else, as if the gods themselves intended to forge some strange and terrible instrument.

As Saphira soared between two bulging white columns—beside which she was no more than a speck—and the sea vanished beneath a field of pillow-like clouds, the headwind abated and the air grew rough and choppy, swirling about them without an identifiable direction. Eragon clenched his teeth to keep them from clacking, and his stomach lurched as Saphira dropped a half-dozen feet and then, just as quickly, rose more than twenty feet straight up.

Glaedr said, *Have you any experience storm-flying other than the time you were caught in a thunderstorm between Palancar Valley and Yazuac?*

No, said Saphira, short and grim.

Glaedr seemed to have expected her answer, for without hesitation he began to instruct her about the intricacies of navigating the fantastic cloudscape. *Look for patterns of movement and take note of the formations around you,* he said. *By them, you may guess where the wind is strongest and the direction it is blowing.*

Much of what he said Saphira already knew, but as Glaedr kept talking, the old dragon's calm demeanor steadied both her and Eragon. Had they felt alarm or fear in the old dragon's mind, it would have caused them to doubt themselves, and perhaps Glaedr was aware of that.

A stray, wind-torn scrap of cloud lay across Saphira's path. Instead of flying around it, she went straight through, piercing the cloud like a glittering blue spear. As the gray mist enveloped them, the sound of the wind grew muted, and Eragon squinted and held a hand before his face to keep his eyes clear.

When they shot out of the cloud, millions of tiny droplets clung to Saphira's body, and she sparkled as if diamonds had been affixed to her already dazzling scales.

Her flight continued to be unsettled; one moment she would be level, but the next the unruly air might shove her sideways, or an unexpected updraft might lift one wing and send her slewing off in the opposite direction. Just sitting on her back as she fought against the turbulence was tiring, while for Saphira herself, it was a miserable, frustrating struggle made all the more difficult by knowing that it was far from over and that she had no choice but to continue on.

After an hour or two they still had not sighted the far side of the tempest. Glaedr said, *We have to turn. You've gone as far west as is prudent, and if we're to dare the full wrath of the storm, we had best do it now, before you are any more exhausted.*

Without a word, Saphira wheeled north toward the vast, towering cliff of sunlit clouds that occupied the heart of the giant storm. As they neared the ridged face of the cliff—which was the largest single thing Eragon had ever seen, larger even than Farthen Dûr—blue flashes illuminated the folds within as lightning crawled upward, toward the top of the anvil head.

A moment later, a clap of thunder shook the sky, and Eragon covered his ears with his hands. He knew that his wards would protect them from the lightning, but he still felt apprehensive about venturing near the crackling bolts of energy.

If Saphira was frightened, he did not sense it. All he could feel was her determination. She quickened the beat of her wings, and a few minutes later they arrived at the face of the cliff and then plunged through it and into the center of the storm.

Twilight surrounded them, gray and featureless.

It was as if the rest of the world had ceased to exist. The clouds made it impossible for Eragon to judge any distance past the tips of Saphira's nose, tail, and wings. They were effectively blind, and only the constant pull of their weight let them differentiate up from down.

Eragon opened his mind and allowed his consciousness to expand as far as he could, but he felt no other living thing besides Saphira and Glaedr, not even a single stray bird. Fortunately, Saphira retained her sense of direction; they would not get lost. And by continuing to search with his mind for other beings, whether plant or animal, Eragon could ensure that they would not fly straight into the side of a mountain.

He also cast a spell that Oromis had taught him, a spell that informed him and Saphira exactly how close they were to the water—or the ground—at any given moment.

From the moment they entered the cloud, the ever-present moisture began to accumulate on Eragon's skin and soak into his woolen clothes, weighing them down. It was an annoyance he could have ignored had not the combination of water and wind been so

473

chilling, it would have soon drained the heat from his limbs and killed him. Therefore, he cast another spell, which filtered the air around him of any visible droplets, as well as—at her request—the air around Saphira's eyes, for the moisture kept collecting on their surface, forcing her to blink all too frequently.

The wind inside the anvil head was surprisingly gentle. Eragon made a comment to that effect to Glaedr, but the old dragon stayed as grim as ever. *We have yet to encounter the worst of it.*

The truth of his words soon became evident when a ferocious updraft slammed into Saphira's underside and carried her thousands of feet higher, where the air was too thin for Eragon to breathe properly and the mist froze into countless tiny crystals that stung his nose and cheeks and the webbing of Saphira's wings like so many razor-sharp knives.

Pinning her wings against her sides, Saphira dove forward, trying to escape the updraft. After a few seconds, the pressure underneath her vanished, only to be replaced by an equally powerful downdraft, which shoved her toward the waves at a frightful speed.

As they fell, the ice crystals melted, forming large, globular raindrops that seemed to float weightlessly alongside Saphira. Lightning flared nearby—an eerie blue glow through the veil of clouds—and Eragon shouted with pain as the thunder boomed around them. His ears still ringing, he ripped two small pieces off the edge of his cloak, then rolled up the scraps of cloth and screwed them into his ears, forcing them in as far as he could.

Only near the bottom of the clouds did Saphira manage to break free of the fast-flowing stream of air. As soon as she did, a second updraft seized hold of her and, like a giant hand, pushed her skyward.

Then and for a long while after, Eragon lost all track of time. The raging wind was too strong for Saphira to resist, and she continued to rise and fall in the cycling air, like a piece of flotsam caught in a whirlpool. She made some headway—a few scant miles, dearly won and with great effort retained—but every time she extricated herself from one of the looping currents, she found herself trapped in another.

It was humbling for Eragon to realize that he, Saphira, and Glaedr were helpless before the storm and that, for all their might, they could not hope to match the power of the elements.

Twice, the wind nearly drove Saphira into the crashing waves. On both occasions, the downdrafts cast her out of the underbelly of the storm into the squalls of rain that pummeled the sea below. The second time it happened, Eragon looked over Saphira's shoulder and, for an instant, he thought he saw the long, dark shape of the Nïdhwal resting upon the heaving water. However, when the next burst of lightning came, the shape was gone, and he wondered whether the shadows had played a trick upon him.

As Saphira's strength waned, she fought the wind less and less and, instead, allowed it to take her where it would. She only made an effort to defy the storm when she got too close to the water. Otherwise, she stilled her wings and exerted herself as little as possible. Eragon felt when Glaedr began to feed her a thread of energy to help sustain her, but even that was not enough to allow her to do more than hold her place.

Eventually, what light there was began to fade, and despair settled upon Eragon. They had spent the better part of the day being tossed about by the storm, and still it showed no sign of subsiding, nor did it seem as if Saphira was anywhere close to its perimeter.

Once the sun had set, Eragon could not even see the tip of his nose, and there was no difference between when his eyes were open and when they were closed. It was as if a huge pile of black wool had been packed around him and Saphira, and indeed, the darkness seemed to have a weight to it, as if it were a palpable substance pressing against them from all sides.

Every few seconds, another flash of lightning split the gloom, sometimes hidden within the clouds, sometimes streaking across their field of vision, glaring with the brightness of a dozen suns and leaving the air tasting like iron. After the searing brightness of the closer discharges, the night seemed twice as dark, and Eragon and Saphira alternated between being blinded by the light and being blinded by the utter black that followed. As close as the bolts came, they never struck Saphira, but the constant roll of thunder left Eragon and Saphira feeling sick from the noise.

How long they continued like that, Eragon could not tell.

Then, at some point in the night, Saphira entered a torrent of rising air that was far larger and far stronger than any they had previously encountered. As soon as it struck them, Saphira began to struggle against it in an attempt to escape, but the force of the wind was so great, she could barely hold her wings level.

At last, frustrated, she roared and loosed a jet of flame from her maw, illuminating a small area of the surrounding ice crystals, which glittered like gems.

Help me, she said to Eragon and Glaedr. *I can't do this by myself.*

So the two of them melded their minds and, with Glaedr supplying the needed energy, Eragon shouted, "Gánga fram!"

The spell propelled Saphira forward, but ever so slowly, for moving at right angles to the wind was like swimming across the Anora River during the height of the spring snowmelt. Even as Saphira advanced horizontally, the current continued to sweep her upward at a dizzying rate. Soon Eragon began to notice that he was growing short of breath, and yet they remained caught within the torrent of air.

This is taking too long and it's costing us too much energy, said Glaedr. *End the spell.*

But—

End the spell. We can't win free before the two of you faint. We'll have to ride the wind until it weakens enough for Saphira to escape.

How? she asked while Eragon did as Glaedr instructed. The exhaustion and sense of defeat that muddied her thoughts made Eragon feel a pang of concern for her.

Eragon, you must amend the spell you are using to warm yourself to include Saphira and me. It is going to grow cold, colder than even the bitterest winter in the Spine, and without magic, we shall freeze to death.

Even you?

I will crack like a piece of hot glass dropped in snow. Next you must cast a spell to gather the air around you and Saphira and to hold it there, so you may still breathe. But it must also allow the stale air to escape, or else you will suffocate. The wording of the spell is complicated, and you must not make any mistakes, so listen carefully. It goes as such—

Once Glaedr had recited the necessary phrases in the ancient language, Eragon repeated them back to him, and when the dragon was satisfied with his pronunciation, Eragon cast the spell. Then he amended his other piece of magic as Glaedr had instructed, so the three of them were shielded from the cold.

They waited, then, while the wind lifted them higher and higher. Minutes passed, and Eragon began to wonder if they would ever stop, or if they would keep hurtling upward until they were level with the moon and the stars.

It occurred to him that perhaps this was how shooting stars were made: a bird or a dragon or some other earthly creature snatched upward by the inexorable wind and thrown skyward with such speed, they flamed like siege arrows. If so, then he guessed he, Saphira, and Glaedr would make the brightest, most spectacular shooting star in living memory, if anyone was close enough to see their demise so far out to sea.

The howling of the wind gradually grew softer. Even the bone-jarring claps of thunder seemed muted, and when Eragon dug the scraps of cloth out of his ears, he was astonished by the hushed silence that surrounded them. He still heard a faint susurration in the background, like the sound of a small forest brook, but other than that, it was quiet, blessedly quiet.

As the clamor of the angry storm faded, he also noticed that the strain imposed by his spells was increasing—not so much from the enchantment that prevented their bodily heat from dissipating too quickly, but from the enchantment that collected and compressed the atmosphere in front of him and Saphira so that they could fill their lungs as they normally did. For whatever reason, the energy required to maintain the second spell multiplied out of all proportion to the first, and he soon felt the symptoms that indicated the magic was upon the verge of stealing away what little remained of his life force: a coldness of his hands, an uncertainty in the beating of his heart, and an overwhelming sense of lethargy, which was perhaps the most worrying sign of all.

Then Glaedr began to assist him. With relief, Eragon felt his burden decrease as the dragon's strength flowed into him, a flush of fever-like heat that washed away his lethargy and restored the vigor of his limbs.

And so they continued.

At long last, Saphira detected a slackening of the wind—slight but noticeable—and she began to prepare to fly out of the stream of air.

Before she could, the clouds above them thinned, and Eragon glimpsed a few glittering specks: stars, white and silvery and brighter than any he had seen before.

Look, he said. Then the clouds opened up around them, and Saphira rose out of the storm and hung above it, balancing precariously atop the column of rushing wind.

Laid out below them, Eragon saw the whole of the storm, extending for what must have been a hundred miles in every direction. The center appeared as an arching, mushroom-like dome, smoothed off by the vicious crosswinds that swept west to east and threatened to topple Saphira from her uncertain perch. The clouds both near and far were milky and seemed almost luminous, as if lit from within. They looked beautiful and benign—placid, unchanging formations that betrayed nothing of the violence inside.

Then Eragon noticed the sky, and he gasped, for it contained more stars than he had thought existed. Red, blue, white, gold, they lay strewn upon the firmament like handfuls of sparkling dust. The constellations he was familiar with were still present but now set among thousands of fainter stars, which he beheld for the very first time. And not only did the stars appear brighter, the void between them appeared darker. It was as if, whenever he had looked at the sky before, there had been a haze over his eyes that had kept him from seeing the true glory of the stars.

He stared at the spectacular display for several moments, awe-struck by the glorious, random, unknowable nature of the twinkling lights. Only when he finally lowered his gaze did it occur to him that there was something unusual about the purple-hued horizon. Instead of the sky and the sea meeting in a straight line—as they ought to and always had before—the juncture between them curved, like the edge of an unimaginably big circle.

It was such a strange sight, it took Eragon a half-dozen seconds to understand what he was seeing, and when he did, his scalp tingled and he felt as if the breath had been knocked out of him.

"The world is round," he whispered. "The sky is hollow and the world is round."

So it would appear, Glaedr said, but he seemed equally impressed. *I heard tell of this from a wild dragon, but I never thought to see it myself.*

To the east, a faint yellow glow tinted a section of the horizon, presaging the return of the sun. Eragon guessed that if Saphira held her position for another four or five minutes, they would see it rise, even though it would still be hours before the warm, life-giving rays reached the water below.

Saphira balanced there for a moment more, the three of them suspended between the stars and the earth, floating in the silent twilight like dispossessed spirits. They were in a nowhere place, neither part of the heavens nor part of the world below—a mote passing through the margin separating two immensities.

Then Saphira tipped forward and half flew, half fell northward, for the air was so sparse that her wings could not fully support her weight once she left the stream of rising wind.

As she hurtled downward, Eragon said, *If we had enough jewels, and if we stored enough energy in them, do you think we could fly all the way to the moon?*

Who knows what is possible? said Glaedr.

When Eragon was a child, Carvahall and Palancar Valley had been all he had known. He had heard of the Empire, of course, but it had never seemed quite real until he began to travel within it. Later still, his mental picture of the world had expanded to include the rest of Alagaësia and, vaguely, the other lands he had read of. And now he realized that what he had thought of as so large was actually but a small part of a much greater whole. It was as if his point of view had, within a few seconds, gone from that of an ant to that of an eagle.

For the sky was hollow, and the world was round.

It made him reevaluate and recategorize . . . everything. The war between the Varden and the Empire seemed inconsequential when compared with the true size of the world, and he thought how petty were most of the hurts and concerns that bedeviled people, when looked at from on high.

To Saphira, he said, *If only everyone could see what we have seen, perhaps there would be less fighting in the world.*

You cannot expect wolves to become sheep.

No, but neither do the wolves have to be cruel to the sheep.

Saphira soon dropped back into the darkness of the clouds, but she managed to avoid getting caught in another cycle of rising and falling air. Instead, she glided for many miles, skipping off the tops of the other, lower updrafts packed within the storm, using them to help conserve her strength.

An hour or two later, the fog parted, and they flew out of the huge mass of clouds that formed the center of the storm. They descended to skim over the insubstantial foothills piled about its base, which gradually flattened into a quilted blanket that covered everything in sight, with the sole exception of the anvil head itself.

By the time the sun finally appeared above the horizon, neither Eragon nor Saphira had the energy to pay much attention to their surroundings. Nor was there anything in the sameness below to attract their attention.

It was Glaedr, then, who said, *Saphira, there, to your right. Do you see it?*

Eragon lifted his head off his folded arms and squinted as his eyes adjusted to the brightness.

Some miles to the north, a ring of mountains rose out of the clouds. The peaks were clad in snow and ice, and together they looked like an ancient, jagged crown resting atop the layers of mist. The eastward-facing scarps shone brilliantly in the light of the morning sun, while long blue shadows cloaked the western sides and stretched dwindling into the distance, tenebrous daggers upon the billowy, snow-white plain.

Eragon straightened in his seat, hardly daring to believe that their journey might be at an end.

Behold, said Glaedr, *Aras Thelduin, the fire mountains that guard the heart of Vroengard. Fly quickly, Saphira, for we have but a little farther to go.*

✦ ✦ ✦

BURROW GRUBS

They caught her at the intersection of two identical corridors, both lined with pillars and torches and scarlet pennants bearing the twisting gold flame that was Galbatorix's insignia.

Nasuada had not expected to escape, not really, but she could not help but feel disappointed at her failure. If nothing else, she had hoped to cover more distance before they recaptured her.

She fought the whole way as the soldiers dragged her back to the chamber that had been her prison. The men wore chest plates and vambraces, but she still managed to scratch their faces and bite their hands, wounding a pair of the men rather severely.

The soldiers uttered exclamations of dismay when they entered the Hall of the Soothsayer and saw what she had done to her jailer. Careful not to step in the pooling blood, they carried her to the slab of stone, strapped her down, then hurried away, leaving her alone with the corpse.

She shouted at the ceiling and yanked at her restraints, angry with herself for not having done better. Still simmering, she glanced at the body on the floor, then quickly looked away. In death, the man's expression seemed accusatory, and she could not bear to gaze upon it.

After she stole the spoon, she had spent hours grinding the end of the handle against the stone slab. The spoon had been made of soft iron, so it was easy to shape.

She had thought that Galbatorix and Murtagh would visit her next, but instead it was her jailer, bringing her what might have been a late dinner. He had started to undo her manacles in preparation for escorting her to the privy room. The moment he freed her left hand, she stabbed him underneath the chin with the sharpened handle of the spoon, burying the utensil in the folds of his wattle. The man squealed, a horrible, high-pitched sound that reminded her of a pig at slaughter, and spun thrice around, flailing his arms, then fell to the floor, where he lay thrashing and frothing and drumming his heels for what seemed an unreasonably long time.

Killing him had troubled her. She did not think the man had been evil—she was not sure what he had been—but there had been a simpleness to him that made her feel as if she had taken advantage of him. Still, she had done what was necessary, and though she now found it unpleasant to consider, she remained convinced that her actions had been justified.

As the man lay convulsing in his death throes, she had unfastened the rest of the restraints and jumped off the slab. Then, steeling her nerve, she pulled the spoon out of the man's neck, which— like a stopper removed from the bung of a barrel—released a spray of blood that splattered her legs and caused her to jump backward while stifling a curse.

The two guards outside the Hall of the Soothsayer had been easy enough to deal with. She had caught them by surprise and killed the right-hand guard in much the same way she had killed her jailer. Then she had drawn the dagger from the guard's belt and attacked the other man even as he struggled to bring his pike to bear upon her. Up close, a pike was no match for a dagger, and she had unseamed him before he had a chance to escape or raise the alarm.

She had not gotten very far after that. Whether because of Galbatorix's spells or just plain bad luck, she ran headlong into a group of five soldiers, and they had quickly, if not easily, subdued her.

It could not have been more than half an hour later when she heard a large group of men in iron-shod boots march up to the door of the chamber, and then Galbatorix stormed in, followed by several guards.

As always, he stopped at the edge of her line of sight, and there he stood, a tall, dark figure with an angular face, only the outlines of which were visible. She saw his head turn as he took in the scene; then, in a cold voice, he said, "How did this happen?"

A soldier with a plume on his helm scurried in front of Galbatorix, knelt, and held out her sharpened spoon. "Sire, we found this in one of the men outside."

The king took the spoon and turned it over in his hands. "I see." His head swiveled toward her. He gripped the ends of the spoon and, without discernible effort, bent it until it snapped in two. "You knew you could not escape, and yet you insisted upon trying. I'll not have you killing my men merely to spite me. You have not the right to take their lives. You have not the right to do *anything* unless I allow it." He flung the pieces of metal upon the floor. Then he turned and stalked out of the Hall of the Soothsayer, his heavy cape flapping behind him.

Two of the soldiers removed her jailer's body, then scoured the chamber of his blood, cursing her as they scrubbed.

Once they had left and she was again alone, she allowed herself a sigh, and some of the tension in her limbs vanished.

She wished she had had a chance to eat, for now that the excitement was over, she found she was hungry. Worse, she suspected she would have to wait hours before she could hope to have her next meal, assuming that Galbatorix did not decide to punish her by withholding food.

Her musings about bread and roasts and tall glasses of wine were short-lived, as she again heard the sound of many boots in the passageway outside her cell. Startled, she tried to mentally prepare herself for whatever unpleasantness was about to come, for it *would* be unpleasant, she was sure.

The door to the chamber crashed open, and two sets of footsteps echoed in the octagonal room as Murtagh and Galbatorix walked over to her. Murtagh positioned himself where he usually did, but without the brazier to occupy himself, he crossed his arms, leaned against the wall, and glared at the floor. What she could see of his expression beneath his silver half mask did not comfort her; the lines of his face seemed even harder than normal, and there was something about the cast of his mouth that sent a chill of fear into her bones.

Instead of sitting, as was his wont, Galbatorix stood behind and somewhat to the side of her head, where she could feel his presence more than she could see it.

He extended his long, clawlike hands over her. In them, he held a small box decorated with lines of carved horn that might have formed glyphs from the ancient language. Most disconcerting of all, a faint *skree-skree* sound came from within the container, soft as the scratching of a mouse, but no less distinct.

With the pad of his thumb, Galbatorix pushed open the box's sliding lid. Then he reached inside and pulled out what appeared to be a large, ivory-colored maggot. The creature was almost three inches long, and it had a tiny mouth at one end, with which it uttered the *skree-skree* she had heard before, announcing its displeasure to the world. It was plump and pleated, like a caterpillar, but if it had any legs, they were so small as to be invisible.

As the creature wiggled in a vain attempt to free itself from between Galbatorix's fingers, the king said, "This is a burrow grub. It is not what it appears to be. Few things are, but in the case of burrow grubs, that is all the more true. They are found in only one place in Alagaësia and are far more difficult to capture than you might suppose. Take it, then, as a sign of my regard for you, Nasuada, daughter of Ajihad, that I deign to use one on you." His voice dropped in tone, becoming even more intimate. "I would not, however, wish to exchange places with you."

The *skree-skree* of the burrow grub increased in volume as Galbatorix dropped it onto the bare skin of her right arm, just below the elbow. She flinched as the disgusting creature landed on her; it was heavier than it looked, and its underside gripped her with what felt like hundreds of little hooks.

The burrow grub squalled for a moment more; then it gathered up its body in a tight bundle and *hopped* several inches up her arm.

She wrenched at her bonds, hoping to dislodge the grub, but it continued to cling to her.

Again it hopped.

And again, and now it was on her shoulder, the hooks pinching and digging into her skin like a strip of minute cockleburs. Out of the corner of her eye, she saw the burrow grub lift up its eyeless head and point it toward her face, as if testing the air. Its tiny mouth opened, and she saw that it had sharp cutting mandibles behind its upper and lower lips.

Skree-skree? said the burrow grub. *Skree-skra?*

"Not there," Galbatorix said, and he spoke a word in the ancient language.

On hearing it, the burrow grub swung away from her head, for which she felt a measure of relief. Then it began to worm its way back down her arm.

Few things frightened her. The touch of the hot iron frightened her. The thought that Galbatorix might reign forevermore in Urû'baen frightened her. Death, of course, frightened her, although not so much because she feared the end of her existence as because she feared leaving undone all the things she still hoped to accomplish.

But, for whatever reason, the sight and feel of the burrow grub unnerved her in a way that, until that very moment, nothing else had. Every muscle in her body seemed to burn and tingle, and she felt an overwhelming urge to run, to flee, to put as much distance between herself and the creature as she could, for there seemed to be something profoundly *wrong* about the burrow grub. It did not move as it should, and its obscene little mouth reminded her of a child's, and the sound it made, the horrible, horrible sound, elicited a primal loathing within her.

The burrow grub paused by her elbow.

Skree-skree!

Then its fat, limbless body contracted, and it hopped four, five inches straight up into the air and then dove headfirst toward the inner part of her elbow.

As it landed, the burrow grub divided into a dozen small, bright green centipedes, which swarmed over her arm before each chose a spot to sink its mandibles into her flesh and bore its way through her skin.

The pain was too great for her to bear; she struggled against her restraints and screamed at the ceiling, but she could not escape her torment, not then and not for a seemingly endless span of time thereafter. The iron had hurt more, but she would have preferred its touch, for the hot metal was impersonal, inanimate, and predictable, all things the burrow grub was not. There was a special horror in knowing that the cause of her pain was a creature *chewing* on her, and worse, that it was inside her.

At the last, she lost her pride and self-control and cried out to the goddess Gokukara for mercy, and then she began to babble as a child might, unable to stop the flow of random words coming from her mouth.

And behind her, she heard Galbatorix laughing, and his enjoyment of her suffering made her hate him all the more.

She blinked, slowly coming back to herself.

After several moments, she realized that Murtagh and Galbatorix were gone. She had no recollection of their departure; she must have lost consciousness.

The pain was less than before, but she still hurt terribly. She glanced down her body, then averted her eyes, feeling her pulse quicken. Where the centipedes had been—she was not sure whether individually they were still considered burrow grubs—her flesh was swollen and lines of purple blood filled the tracks they had left underneath the surface of her skin, and every track burned. It felt as if she had been lashed across the front of her body with a metal whip.

She wondered if perhaps the burrow grubs were still inside of her, lying dormant while they digested their meal. Or perhaps they were metamorphosing, like maggots into flies, and they would turn into something even worse. Or, and this seemed the most terrible possibility, perhaps they were laying eggs within her, and *more* of them would soon hatch and begin to feast on her.

She shuddered and cried out with fear and frustration.

The wounds made it difficult for her to remain coherent. Her vision faded in and out, and she found herself weeping, which disgusted her, but she could not stop, no matter how hard she tried. As a distraction, she fell to talking to herself—nonsense mostly— anything to bolster her resolve or focus her mind on other subjects. It helped, if only a little.

She knew that Galbatorix did not want to kill her, but she feared that in his anger he had gone further than he intended. She was shaking, and her entire body felt inflamed, as if she had been stung by hundreds of bees. Willpower could sustain her for only so long; no matter how determined she was, there was a limit to what her frame could withstand, and she felt that she was well past that point. Something deep inside her seemed to have broken, and she was no longer confident that she could recover from her injuries.

The door to the chamber scraped open.

She forced her eyes to focus as she strained to see who was approaching.

It was Murtagh.

He looked down at her, his lips pinched, his nostrils flared, and a furrow between his brows. At first she thought he was angry, but then she realized he was actually worried and afraid, deathly so. The strength of his concern surprised her; she knew he regarded her with a certain liking—why else would he have convinced Galbatorix to keep her alive?—but she had not suspected that he cared for her quite so much.

She tried to reassure him with a smile. It must not have come out right, for as she did, Murtagh clenched his jaw, as if he was struggling to contain himself.

"Try not to move," he said, and lifted his hands over her and began to murmur in the ancient language.

As if I could, she thought.

His magic soon took effect, and wound by wound, her pain abated, but it did not disappear entirely.

She frowned at him, puzzled, and he said, "I'm sorry. I can do no more. Galbatorix would know how, but it's beyond me."

"What . . . what about your Eldunarí?" she asked. "Surely they can help."

He shook his head. "Young dragons all, or they were when their bodies died. They knew little of magic then, and Galbatorix has taught them almost nothing since. . . . I'm sorry."

"Are those *things* still in me?"

"No! No, they're not. Galbatorix removed them once you passed out."

489

Her relief was profound. "Your spell didn't stop the pain." She tried not to sound accusatory, but she could not prevent a note of anger from creeping into her voice.

He grimaced. "I'm not sure why. It ought to have. Whatever that creature is, it doesn't fit into the normal pattern of the world."

"Do you know where it's from?"

"No. I only learned of it today, when Galbatorix fetched it from his inner chambers."

She closed her eyes for a moment.

"Let me up."

"Are you s—"

"Let me up."

Without a word, he undid her restraints. Then she got to her feet and stood swaying next to the slab while she waited for an attack of light-headedness to recede.

"Here," said Murtagh, handing her his cape. She wrapped it

around her body, covering herself for both modesty and warmth, and also so that she did not have to look at the burns, scabs, blisters, and blood-filled lines that disfigured her.

Limping—for, among other places, the burrow grub had visited the soles of her feet—she walked to the edge of the chamber. She leaned against the wall and slowly lowered herself to the floor.

Murtagh joined her, and the two of them sat staring at the opposite wall.

Despite herself, she began to cry.

After a while, she felt him touch her shoulder, and she jerked away. She could not help it. He had hurt her more in the past few days than anyone else ever had, and though she knew he had not wanted to do it, she could not forget that it was he who had wielded the hot iron.

Even so, when she saw how her reaction stung him, she relented and reached out and took his hand. He gave her fingers a gentle squeeze, then put his arm around her shoulders and drew her close. She resisted for a moment, then relaxed into his embrace and laid her head on his chest as she continued to cry, her quiet sobs echoing in the bare stone room.

Some minutes later, she felt him move beneath her as he said, "I'll find a way to free you, I swear. It's too late for Thorn and me. But not for you. As long as you don't pledge fealty to Galbatorix, there's still a chance I can spirit you out of Urû'baen."

She looked up at him and decided he meant what he said. "How?" she whispered.

"I haven't the slightest idea," he admitted with a roguish smile. "But I will. Whatever it takes. You have to promise me, though, that you won't give up—not until I've tried. Agreed?"

"I don't think I can endure that . . . *thing* again. If he puts it on me again, I'll give him whatever he wants."

"You won't have to; he doesn't intend to use the burrow grubs again."

". . . What does he intend?"

Murtagh was silent for a minute more. "He's decided to start manipulating what you see, hear, feel, and taste. If that doesn't work, then he'll attack your mind directly. You won't be able to resist him if he does. No one ever has. Before it comes to that, though, I'm sure I'll be able to rescue you. All you have to do is keep fighting for another few days. That's it—just another few days."

"How can I if I can't trust my senses?"

"There is one sense he cannot feign." Murtagh twisted to look at her more directly. "Will you let me touch your mind? I won't try to read your thoughts. I only want you to know what my mind feels like, so you can recognize it—so you can recognize *me*—in the future."

She hesitated. She knew that this was a turning point. Either she would agree to trust him, or she would refuse and perhaps lose her only chance to avoid becoming Galbatorix's slave. Still, she remained wary of granting anyone access to her mind. Murtagh could be trying to lull her into lowering her defenses so that he could more easily install himself in her consciousness. Or it might be that he hoped to glean some piece of information by eavesdropping on her thoughts.

Then she thought: *Why should Galbatorix resort to such tricks? He could do either of those things himself. Murtagh is right; I wouldn't be able to resist him. . . . If I accept Murtagh's offer, it may mean my doom, but if I refuse, my doom is inevitable. One way or another, Galbatorix will break me. It's only a matter of time.*

"Do as you will," she said.

Murtagh nodded and half closed his eyes.

In the silence of her mind, she began to recite the scrap of verse she used whenever she wanted to hide her thoughts or defend her consciousness from an intruder. She concentrated on it with all her might, determined to repel Murtagh if need be and also determined not to think about any of the secrets it was her duty to keep hidden.

In El-harím, there lived a man, a man with yellow eyes.
To me, he said, "Beware the whispers, for they whisper lies.

> Do not wrestle with the demons of the dark,
> Else upon your mind they'll place a mark;
> Do not listen to the shadows of the deep,
> Else they haunt you even when you sleep."

When Murtagh's consciousness pressed against hers, she stiffened and began to recite the lines of the verse even faster. To her surprise, his mind felt familiar. The similarities between his consciousness and— No, she could not say whose, but the similarities were striking, as were the equally prominent differences. Foremost among the differences was his anger, which lay at the center of his being like a cold black heart, clenched and unmoving, with veins of hatred snaking out to entangle the rest of his mind. But his concern for her outshone his anger. Seeing it convinced her that his solicitude was genuine, for to dissemble with one's inner self was incredibly difficult, and she did not believe that Murtagh could have deceived her so convincingly.

True to his word, he made no attempt to force himself deeper into her mind, and after a few seconds, he withdrew and she again found herself alone with her thoughts.

Murtagh's eyes opened fully, and he said, "There now. Will you be able to recognize me if I reach out to you again?"

She nodded.

"Good. Galbatorix can do many things, but even he cannot imitate the feeling of another person's mind. I'll try to warn you before he starts to alter your senses, and I'll contact you when he stops. That way, he won't be able to confuse you as to what is real and what is not."

"Thank you," she said, unable to express the full extent of her gratitude in so short a phrase.

"Fortunately, we have some time. The Varden are only three days hence, and the elves are fast approaching from the north. Galbatorix has gone to oversee the final placement of Urû'baen's defenses and to discuss strategy with Lord Barst, who has command of the army now that it's garrisoned here in the city."

She frowned. That boded ill. She had heard of Lord Barst; he had a fearsome reputation among the nobles of Galbatorix's court. He was said to be both keen-minded and bloody-handed, and those who were foolish enough to oppose him, he crushed without mercy.

"Not you?" she asked.

"Galbatorix has other plans for me, although he's yet to share them."

"How long will he be busy with his preparations?"

"The rest of today and all of tomorrow."

"Do you think you can free me before he returns?"

"I don't know. Probably not." A pause fell between them. Then he said, "Now I have a question for you: why did you kill those men? You knew you wouldn't make it out of the citadel. Was it just to spite Galbatorix, as he said?"

She sighed and pushed herself off Murtagh's chest so she was sitting upright. With some reluctance, he released his hold around her shoulders. She sniffed, then looked him square in the eyes. "I couldn't just lie there and let him do whatever he wanted to me. I had to fight back; I had to show him that he hadn't broken me, and I wanted to hurt him however I could."

"So it *was* spite!"

"In part. What of it?" She expected him to express disgust or condemnation at her actions, but instead he gave her an appraising look and his lips curved in a small, knowing smile.

"Then I say well done," he replied.

After a moment, she returned his smile.

"Besides," she said, "there was always a chance I *might* escape."

He snorted. "And dragons might start eating grass."

"Even so, I had to try."

"I understand. If I could have, I would have done the same when the Twins first brought me here."

493

"And now?"

"I still can't, and even if I could, what purpose would it serve?"

To that, she had no answer. Silence followed, and then she said, "Murtagh, if it's not possible to free me from here, then I want your promise that you'll help me escape by . . . other means. I wouldn't ask . . . I wouldn't place this burden upon you, but your assistance would make the task easier, and I may not have the opportunity to do it myself." His lips grew thin and hard as she spoke, but he did not interrupt. "Whatever happens, I won't allow myself to become a plaything for Galbatorix to order about as he will. I'll do anything, anything at all to avoid that fate. Can you understand that?"

His chin dipped in a short nod.

"Then do I have your word?"

He looked down and clenched his fists, his breathing ragged. "You do."

494   Murtagh was taciturn, but eventually she succeeded in drawing him out again, and they passed the time talking about matters of little import. Murtagh told her of the alterations he had made to the saddle Galbatorix had given him for Thorn—changes that Murtagh was justifiably proud of, as they allowed him to mount and dismount faster, as well as to draw his sword with less inconvenience. She told him about the market streets in Aberon, the capital of Surda, and how, as a child, she had often run away from her nurse to explore them. Her favorite of the merchants had been a man of the wandering tribes. His name was Hadamanara-no Dachu Taganna, but he had insisted that she call him by his familiar name, which was Taganna. He sold knives and daggers, and he always seemed to delight in showing her his wares, even though she never bought any.

As she and Murtagh continued to talk, their conversation grew easier and more relaxed. Despite their unpleasant circumstances, she found that she enjoyed speaking with him. He was smart and well educated, and he had a mordant wit that she appreciated, especially given her current predicament.

Murtagh seemed to enjoy their conversation as much as she did. Still, the time came when they both recognized that it would be foolish to keep talking, for fear of being caught. So she returned to the slab, where she lay down and allowed him to strap her to the unforgiving block of stone once again.

As he was about to leave, she said, "Murtagh."

He paused and turned to regard her.

She hesitated for a moment, then mustered her courage and said, "Why?" She thought he understood her meaning: Why her? Why save her, and now why try to rescue her? She had guessed at the answer, but she wanted to hear him say it.

He stared at her for the longest while, and then, in a low, hard voice, he said, "You know why."

✦   ✦   ✦

AMID THE RUINS

The thick gray clouds parted, and from his place on Saphira's back, Eragon beheld the interior of Vroengard Island.

Before them was a huge bowl-shaped valley, encircled by the steep mountains they had seen poking through the tops of the clouds. A dense forest of spruce, pine, and fir trees blanketed the sides of the mountains as well as the foothills below, like an army of prickly soldiers marching down from the peaks. The trees were tall and mournful, and even from a distance Eragon could see the beards of moss and lichen that hung from their heavy branches. Scraps of white mist clung to the sides of the mountains, and in several places throughout the valley, diffuse curtains of rain drifted from the ceiling of clouds.

High above the valley floor, Eragon could see a number of stone structures among the trees: tumbled, overgrown entrances to caves; the husks of burnt-out towers; grand halls with collapsed roofs; and a few smaller buildings that looked as if they might still be habitable.

A dozen or more rivers flowed out of the mountains and wandered across the verdant ground until they poured into a large, still lake near the center of the valley. Around the lake lay the remnants of the Riders' city, Doru Araeba. The buildings were immense—great empty halls of such enormous proportions that many could have encompassed the whole of Carvahall. Every door was like the mouth to a vast, unexplored cavern. Every window was as tall and wide as a castle gate, and every wall was a sheer cliff.

Thick mats of ivy strangled the blocks of stone, and where there was no ivy there was moss, which meant that the buildings blended into the landscape and looked as if they had grown out of the earth itself. What little of the stone was bare tended to be a pale ocher, although patches of red, brown, and dusky blue were also visible.

As with all elf-made structures, the buildings were graceful and flowing and more attenuated than those of dwarves or humans. But they also possessed a solidity and authority that the treehouses of Ellesméra lacked; in some of them, Eragon descried similarities to houses in Palancar Valley, and he remembered that the earliest human Riders had come from that very part of Alagaësia. The result was a unique style of architecture, neither entirely elvish nor entirely human.

Almost all the buildings were damaged, some more severely than others. The damage seemed to radiate outward from a single point near the southern edge of the city, where a wide crater sank more than thirty feet into the ground. A copse of birch trees had taken root in the depression, and their silvery leaves shook in the gusts of the directionless breeze.

The open areas within the city were overgrown with weeds and brush, while a fringe of grass surrounded each of the flagstones that formed the streets. Where the buildings had sheltered the Riders' gardens from the blast that had ravaged the city, dull-colored flowers still grew in artful designs, their shapes no doubt governed by the dictates of some long-forgotten spell.

Altogether, the circular valley presented a dismal picture.

Behold the ruins of our pride and glory, said Glaedr. Then: *Eragon, you must cast another spell. The wording of it goes thus—* And he uttered several lines in the ancient language. It was an odd spell; the phrasing was obscure and convoluted, and Eragon was unable to determine what it was supposed to accomplish.

When he asked Glaedr, the old dragon said, *There is an invisible poison here, in the air you breathe, in the ground you walk upon, and in the food you may eat and the water you may drink. The spell will protect us against it.*

What . . . poison? asked Saphira, her thoughts as slow as the beats of her wings.

Eragon saw from Glaedr an image of the crater by the city, and the dragon said, *During the battle with the Forsworn, one of our own, an elf by the name of Thuviel, killed himself with magic. Whether by design or by accident has never been clear, but the result is what you see and what you cannot see, for the resulting explosion rendered the area unfit to live in. Those who remained here soon developed lesions upon their skin and lost their hair, and many died thereafter.*

Concerned, Eragon cast the spell—which required little energy—before he said, *How could any one person, elf or not, cause so much damage? Even if Thuviel's dragon helped him, I can't think how it would be possible, not unless his dragon was the size of a mountain.*

His dragon did not help him, said Glaedr. *His dragon was dead. No, Thuviel wrought this destruction by himself.*

But how?

The only way he could have: he converted his flesh into energy.

He made himself into a spirit?

No. The energy was without thought or structure, and once unbound, it raced outward until it dispersed.

I had not realized that a single body contained so much force.

It is not well known, but even the smallest speck of matter is equal to a great amount of energy. Matter, it seems, is merely frozen energy. Melt it, and you release a flood few can withstand. . . . It was said that the explosion here was heard as far away as Teirm and that the cloud of smoke that followed rose as high as the Beor Mountains.

Was it the blast that killed Glaerun? Eragon asked, referring to the one member of the Forsworn who he knew had died on Vroengard.

It was. Galbatorix and the rest of the Forsworn had a moment of warning, and so were able to shield themselves, but many of our own were not as fortunate and thus perished.

As Saphira glided downward from the underside of the low-slung clouds, Glaedr instructed her where to fly, so she altered her course, turning toward the northwestern part of the valley. Glaedr named each of the mountains that she flew past: Ilthiaros, Fellsverd, and

Nammenmast, along with Huildrim and Tírnadrim. He also named many of the holds and fallen towers below, and he gave something of their history to Eragon and Saphira, although only Eragon paid heed to the old dragon's narration.

Within Glaedr's consciousness, Eragon felt an ancient sorrow re-awaken. The sorrow was not so much for the destruction of Doru Araeba as for the deaths of the Riders, the near extinction of the dragons, and the loss of thousands of years of knowledge and wisdom. The memory of what had been—of the companionship he had once shared with the other members of his order—exacerbated Glaedr's loneliness. That, along with his sorrow, created a mood of such desolation, Eragon began to feel saddened as well.

He withdrew slightly from Glaedr, but still the valley seemed gloomy and melancholy, as if the land itself were mourning the fall of the Riders.

The lower Saphira flew, the larger the buildings appeared. As their true size became evident, Eragon realized that what he had read in *Domia abr Wyrda* was no exaggeration: the grandest of them were so enormous, Saphira would be able to fly within them.

Near the edge of the abandoned city, he began to notice piles of giant white bones upon the ground: the skeletons of dragons. The sight filled him with revulsion, and yet he could not bring himself to look elsewhere. What struck him most was their size. A few of the dragons had been smaller than Saphira, but most had been far larger. The biggest he saw was a skeleton with ribs that he guessed were at least eighty feet long and perhaps fifteen wide at their thickest. The skull alone—a huge, fierce thing covered with blotches of lichen, like a rough crag of stone—was longer and taller than the main part of Saphira's body. Even Glaedr, when he was still clothed in flesh, would have appeared diminutive next to the slain dragon.

There lies Belgabad, greatest of us all, said Glaedr as he noticed the object of Eragon's attention.

Eragon vaguely remembered the name from one of the histories he had read in Ellesméra; the author had written only that Belgabad had been present at the battle and that he perished in the fighting, as so many had.

Who was his Rider? he asked.

He had no Rider. He was a wild dragon. For centuries, he lived alone in the icy reaches of the north, but when Galbatorix and the Forsworn began to slaughter our kind, he flew to our aid.

Was he the largest dragon ever?

Ever? No. But at the time, yes.

How did he find enough to eat?

At that age and at that size, dragons spend most of their time in a sleep-like trance, dreaming of whatever happens to capture their fancy, be it the turning of the stars, or the rise and fall of the mountains over the eons, or even something as small as the motion of a butterfly's wings. Already I feel the lure of such repose, but awake I am needed and awake I shall stay.

Did . . . you . . . know . . . Belgabad? asked Saphira, forcing the words through her fatigue.

I met him, but I did not know him. Wild dragons did not, as a rule, consort with those of us who were bonded with Riders. They looked down on us for being too tame and too compliant, while we looked down on them for being too driven by their instincts, although sometimes we admired them for the same. Also, you must remember, they had no language of their own, and that created a greater difference between us than you might think. Language alters your mind in ways that are hard to explain. Wild dragons could communicate as effectively as any dwarf or elf, of course, but they did so by sharing memories, images, and sensations, not words. Only the more cunning of them chose to learn this or any other tongue.

Glaedr paused, and then he added, *If I recall correctly, Belgabad was a distant ancestor of Raugmar the Black, and Raugmar, as I'm sure you remember, Saphira, was the great-great-great-grandsire of your mother, Vervada.*

In her exhaustion, Saphira was slow to react, but at last she twisted her neck to again look at the vast skeleton. *He must have been a good hunter to grow so big.*

He was the very best, said Glaedr.

Then . . . I am glad to be of his blood.

The number of bones scattered across the ground staggered Eragon. Until then, he had fully comprehended neither the extent of the battle nor how many dragons there had once been. The sight renewed his hate for Galbatorix, and once again Eragon swore that he would see the king dead.

Saphira sank through a band of mist, the white haze rolling off the tips of her wings like tiny whirlpools set within the sky. Then a field of tangled grass rushed up at her and she landed with a heavy jolt. Her right foreleg gave way beneath her, and she lurched to the side and fell onto her chest and shoulder, plowing into the ground with such force that Eragon would have impaled himself on the neck spike in front of him, had it not been for his wards.

Once her forward slide ceased, Saphira lay motionless, stunned by the impact. Then she slowly rolled onto her feet, folded her wings, and settled into a low crouch. The straps on the saddle creaked as she moved, the sound unnaturally loud in the hushed atmosphere that pervaded the interior of the island.

Eragon pulled loose the bands around his legs, then jumped all the way to the ground. It was wet and soft, and he dropped to one knee as his boots sank into the damp earth.

"We made it," he said, amazed. He walked forward to Saphira's head, and when she lowered her neck so that she could look him in the eye, he placed his hands on either side of her long head and pressed his forehead against her snout.

Thank you, he said.

He heard the *snick* as her eyelids closed, and then her head began to vibrate as she hummed deep in her chest.

After a moment, Eragon released her and turned to look at their surroundings. The field Saphira had landed in was on the northern outskirts of the city. Pieces of cracked masonry—some as large as Saphira herself—lay scattered throughout the grass; Eragon was relieved she had avoided striking any.

The field sloped upward, away from the city, to the base of the nearest foothill, which was covered with forest. Where field and hill met, a large paved square had been cut flat into the ground, and at the far side of the square sat a massive pile of dressed stone that stretched to the north for over half a mile. Intact, the building would have been one of the largest on the island, and certainly one of the most ornate, for among the square blocks of stone that had formed the walls, Eragon spotted dozens of fluted pillars, as well as carved panels depicting vines and flowers, and a whole host of statues, most of which were missing some combination of body parts, as if they too had participated in the battle.

There lies the Great Library, said Glaedr. *Or what remains after Galbatorix plundered it.*

Eragon slowly turned as he inspected the surrounding area. To the south of the library, he saw the faint lines of abandoned footpaths underneath the shaggy pelt of grass. The paths led away from the library to a grove of apple trees that hid the ground from view, but rising behind the trees was a jagged spar of stone well over two hundred feet tall, upon which grew several gnarled junipers.

A spark of excitement formed within Eragon's chest. He was sure, but still he asked, *Is that it? Is that the Rock of Kuthian?*

He could feel Glaedr using his eyes to look at the formation, and then the dragon said, *It seems oddly familiar, but I cannot remember when I might have seen it before. . . .*

Eragon needed no other confirmation. "Come on!" he said. He waded through the waist-high grass toward the nearest path.

There the grass was not quite so thick, and he could feel hard cobblestones under his feet instead of rain-soaked earth. With Saphira close behind, he hurried down the path, and together they walked through the shadowed grove of apple trees. Both of them stepped with care, for the trees seemed alert and watchful, and something about the shape of their branches was ominous, as if the trees were waiting to ensnare them with splintered claws.

Without meaning to, Eragon breathed a sigh of relief when they emerged from the grove.

The Rock of Kuthian stood upon the edge of a large clearing wherein grew a tangled pool of roses, thistles, raspberries, and water hemlock. Behind the stone prominence stood row upon row of drooping fir trees, which extended all the way back to the mountain that loomed high above. The angry chatter of squirrels echoed among the boles of the forest, but of the animals themselves, not so much as a whisker was to be seen.

Three stone benches—their shapes half hidden beneath layers of roots, vines, and creepers—were situated at equal distances around the clearing. Off to the side was a willow tree, whose latticework trunk had once served as a bower where the Riders might sit and enjoy the view; but in the past hundred years, the trunk had grown too thick for any man, elf, or dwarf to slip into the space within.

Eragon stopped at the edge of the clearing and stared at the Rock of Kuthian. Beside him, Saphira whuffed and dropped onto her belly, shaking the ground and causing him to bend his knees to keep his balance. He rubbed her on the shoulder, then turned his gaze back to the tower of rock. A sense of nervous anticipation welled up inside him.

Opening his mind, Eragon searched the clearing and the trees beyond for anyone who might be waiting to ambush them. The only living things he sensed were plants, insects, and the moles, mice, and garter snakes that lived among the brush in the clearing.

Then he started to compose the spells that he hoped would allow him to detect any magical traps in the area. Before he had put more than a few words together, Glaedr said, *Stop. You and Saphira are too tired for this now. Rest first; tomorrow we can return and see what we may discover.*

But—

The two of you are in no condition to defend yourselves if we must fight. Whatever we are supposed to find will still be here in the morn.

Eragon hesitated, then reluctantly abandoned the spell. He knew Glaedr was right, but he hated to wait any longer when the completion of their quest was so close at hand.

Very well, he said, and climbed back onto Saphira.

With a weary *huff*, she rose to her feet, then slowly turned around and trudged once more through the grove of apple trees. The heavy impact of her steps shook loose withered leaves from the canopy, one of which landed in Eragon's lap. He picked it up and was about to throw it away when he noticed that the leaf was shaped differently than it ought to be: the teeth along the edge were longer and wider than those of any apple leaf he had seen before, and the veins formed seemingly random patterns, instead of the regular network of lines he would have expected.

He picked another leaf, this one still green. Like its desiccated cousin, the fresh leaf had larger serrations and a confused map of veins.

Ever since the battle, things here have not been as they once were, said Glaedr.

Eragon frowned and tossed away the leaves. Again he heard the chatter of the squirrels, and again he failed to see any among the trees, nor was he able to feel them with his mind, which concerned him.

If I had scales, this place would make them itch, he said to Saphira.

A small puff of smoke rose from her nostrils as she snorted with amusement.

From the grove, she walked south until she came to one of the many streams that flowed out of the mountains: a thin white brook that burbled softly as it tumbled over its bed of rocks. There Saphira turned and followed the water upstream to a sheltered meadow near the forefront of the evergreen forest.

Here, said Saphira, and she sank to the ground.

SNALGLÍ FOR TWO

It was late afternoon when Eragon opened his eyes. The blanket of clouds had broken in several places, and beams of golden light planked the valley floor, illuminating the tops of the ruined buildings. Though the valley still looked cold and wet and unwelcoming, the light gave it a newfound majesty. For the first time, Eragon understood why the Riders had chosen to settle on the island.

He yawned, then glanced over at Saphira and lightly touched her mind. She was still asleep, lost in a dreamless slumber. Her consciousness was like a flame that had dimmed until it was little more than a smoldering coal, a coal that might just as easily go out as flare up again.

The feeling unsettled him—it reminded him too much of death—so he returned to his own mind and restricted their contact to a narrow thread of thought: just enough so that he could be sure of her safety.

In the forest behind him, a pair of squirrels began to swear at each other with a series of high-pitched shrieks. He frowned as he listened; their voices sounded a bit too sharp, a bit too fast, a bit too warbly. It was as if some other creature was imitating the cries of the squirrels.

The thought made his scalp prickle.

He lay where he was for over an hour, listening to the shrieks and chattering that emanated from the woods and watching the patterns of light as they played across the hills, fields, and mountains of the bowl-shaped valley. Then the gaps in the clouds closed, the sky darkened, and snow began to fall on the upper flanks of the mountains, painting them white.

It looked a good place to make camp, and Saphira
condition to keep searching, so Eragon agreed and dismou
paused for a moment to appreciate the view over the vall
he removed the saddle and the saddlebags from Saphira, whe
she shook her head, rolled her shoulders, and then twisted her
to nibble at a spot on the side of her chest where the straps had l
chafing.

Without further ado, she curled up in the grass, tucked her hea
under her wing, and wrapped her tail around herself. *Do not wake
me unless something is trying to eat us*, she said.

Eragon smiled and patted her on the tail, then turned to look
at the valley again. He stood there for a long while, barely thinking, content to observe and exist without making any effort to coax
meaning from the world around him.

At last he fetched his bedroll, which he laid out beside Saphira.
Will you keep watch for us? he asked Glaedr.

I shall keep watch. Rest, and do not worry.

Eragon nodded, even though Glaedr could not see him, and then
he lowered himself onto the blankets and allowed himself to drift
off into the embrace of his waking dreams.

Eragon rose and said to Glaedr, *I'm going to gather some firewood. I'll be back in a few minutes.*

The dragon acknowledged him, and Eragon carefully made his way across the meadow to the forest, doing his best to be quiet so as not to disturb Saphira. Once he was at the trees, he quickened his pace. Although there were plenty of dead branches along the verge of the forest, he wanted to stretch his legs and, if he could, find the source of the chattering.

Shadows lay heavy under the trees. The air was cool and still, like that of a cave deep underground, and it smelled of fungus, rotting wood, and oozing sap. The moss and lichen that trailed from the branches were like lengths of tattered lace, stained and sodden but still possessed of a certain delicate beauty. They partitioned the interior of the woods into cells of varying size, which made it difficult to see more than fifty feet in any direction.

Eragon used the burbling of the brook to determine his bearings as he worked his way deeper into the forest. Now that he was close to them, he saw that the evergreens were unlike those from the Spine or even from Du Weldenvarden; they had clusters of seven needles instead of three, and though it might have been a trick of the fading light, it seemed to him as if darkness clung to the trees, like a cloak wrapped around their trunks and branches. Also, everything about the trees, from the cracks in the bark to their protruding roots to their scaled cones—everything about them had a peculiar angularity and a fierceness of line that made them appear as if they were about to pull themselves free of the earth and stride down to the city below.

Eragon shivered and loosened Brisingr in its scabbard. He had never before been in a forest that felt so menacing. It was as if the trees were *angry* and—as with the apple grove earlier—as if they wanted to reach out and rend his flesh from his bones.

With the back of his hand, he brushed aside a swath of yellow lichen as he cautiously made his way forward.

So far he had seen no sign of game, nor had he found any evidence of wolves or bears, which puzzled him. That close to the stream, there should have been trails leading to the water.

Maybe the animals avoid this part of the woods, he thought. *But why?*

A fallen log lay across his path. He stepped over it, and his boot sank ankle-deep into a carpet of moss. An instant later, the gedwëy ignasia on his palm began to itch, and he heard a tiny chorus of *skree-skree!* and *skree-skra!* as a half-dozen white, wormlike grubs—each the size of one of his thumbs—burst out of the moss and began to hop away from him.

Old instincts took hold, and he stopped as he would if he had chanced upon a snake. He did not blink. He did not even breathe as he watched the fat, obscene-looking grubs flee. At the same time, he racked his memory for any mention of them during his training in Ellesméra, but he could recall no such thing.

Glaedr! What are these? And he showed the dragon the grubs. *What is their name in the ancient language?*

To Eragon's dismay, Glaedr said, *They are unknown to me. I have not seen their like before, nor have I ever heard tell of them. They are new to Vroengard, and new to Alagaësia. Do not let them touch you; they may be more dangerous than they appear.*

Once they had put several feet between them and Eragon, the nameless grubs hopped higher than usual and with a *skree-skro!* dove back into the moss. As they landed, they split, dividing into a swarm of green centipedes, which quickly disappeared within the tangled strands of moss.

Only then did Eragon allow himself to breathe.

They should not be, said Glaedr. He sounded troubled.

Eragon slowly lifted his boot off the moss and retreated behind the log. Examining the moss with greater care, he saw that what he had originally taken as the tips of old branches poking out of the blanket of vegetation were actually pieces of broken ribs and antlers—the remains, he thought, of one or more deer.

After a moment's consideration, Eragon turned around and began to retrace his steps, this time making sure to avoid every scrap of moss along the way, which was no easy task.

Whatever had been chattering in the forest was not worth risking his life to find—especially since he suspected that there was worse than the grubs lurking among the trees. His palm kept itching, and from experience, he knew that meant there was still *something* dangerous close by.

When he could see the meadow and the blue of Saphira's scales between the trunks of the evergreens, he turned aside and walked to the brook. Moss covered the bank of the stream, so he stepped from log to stone until he was standing on a flat-topped rock in the midst of the water.

There he squatted, removed his gloves, and washed his hands, face, and neck. The touch of the icy water was bracing, and within moments his ears flushed and his whole body began to feel warm.

A loud chattering rang forth over the stream as he wiped the last few droplets from his neck.

Moving as little as possible, he looked toward the top of the trees on the opposite bank.

Thirty feet up, four shadows sat on a branch. The shadows had large barbed plumes that extended in every direction from the black ovals of their heads. A pair of white eyes, slanted and slit-like, glowed within the middle of each oval, and the blankness of their gaze made it impossible to determine where they were looking. Most disconcerting yet, the shadows, like all shadows, had no depth. When they turned to the side, they disappeared.

Without taking his eyes off them, Eragon reached across his body and grasped Brisingr's hilt.

The leftmost shadow ruffled its plumes and then uttered the same shrieking chatter he had mistaken for a squirrel. Two more of the wraiths did likewise, and the forest echoed with the strident clamor of their cries.

Eragon considered trying to touch their minds, but remembering the Fanghur on his way to Ellesméra, he discarded the idea as fool-hardy.

In a low voice, he said, "Eka aí fricai un Shur'tugal." I am a Rider and a friend.

The shadows seemed to fix their glowing eyes upon him, and for a moment, all was silent, save the gentle murmuring of the brook. Then they began to chatter again, and their eyes increased in brightness until they were like pieces of white-hot iron.

When, after several minutes, the shadows had made no move to attack him and, moreover, showed no indication of departing, Eragon rose to his feet and carefully reached out with one foot toward the stone behind him.

The motion seemed to alarm the wraiths; they shrieked in unison. Then they shrugged and shook themselves, and in their place appeared four large owls, with the same barbed plumes surrounding their mottled faces. They opened their yellow beaks and chattered at him, scolding him even as squirrels might; then they took wing and flew silently off into the trees and soon vanished behind a screen of heavy boughs.

"Barzûl," said Eragon. He jumped back the way he had come and hurried to the meadow, stopping only to pick up an armful of fallen branches.

As soon as he reached Saphira, he placed the wood on the ground, knelt, and began to cast wards, as many as he could think of. Glaedr recommended a spell that he had overlooked, then said, *None of these creatures were here when Oromis and I returned after the battle. They are not as they should be. The magic that was cast here has twisted the land and those who live on it. This is an evil place now.*

What creatures? asked Saphira. She opened her eyes and yawned, an intimidating sight. Eragon shared his memories with her, and she said, *You should have brought me with you. I could have eaten the grubs and the shadow birds, and then you would have had nothing to fear from them.*

Saphira!

She rolled an eye at him. *I'm hungry. Magic or not, is there any reason I should not eat these strange things?*

Because they might eat you instead, Saphira Bjartskular, said Glaedr. *You know the first law of hunting as well as I: do not stalk your prey until you are sure that it is prey. Otherwise, you might well end up as a meal for something else.*

"I wouldn't bother looking for deer either," said Eragon. "I doubt there are many left. Besides, it's almost dark, and even if it weren't, I'm not sure hunting here would be safe."

She growled softly. *Very well. Then I shall keep sleeping. But in the morning, I shall hunt, no matter the danger. My belly is empty, and I must eat before crossing the sea again.*

True to her word, Saphira closed her eyes and promptly returned to sleep.

Eragon built a small fire, then ate a meager supper and watched the valley grow black. He and Glaedr talked about their plans for the following day, and Glaedr told him more about the history of the island, going back to the time before the elves had arrived in Alagaësia, when Vroengard had been the province of the dragons alone.

Before the last of the light had faded from the sky, the old dragon said, *Would you like to see Vroengard as it was during the age of the Riders?*

I would, said Eragon.

Then look, said Glaedr, and Eragon felt the dragon take hold of his mind and into it pour a stream of images and sensations. Eragon's vision shifted, and atop the landscape, he beheld a ghostly twin of the valley. The memory was of the valley in twilight, even as it was at the present, but the sky was free of clouds, and a multitude of stars shone twinkling and gleaming over the great ring of fire mountains, Aras Thelduin. The trees of long ago appeared taller, straighter, and less foreboding, and throughout the valley, the Riders' buildings stood intact, glowing like pale beacons in the dusk with the soft light from the elves' flameless lanterns. Less ivy and moss covered the ocher stone then, and the halls and towers seemed noble in a way that the ruins did not. And along the cobblestone pathways and high overhead, Eragon discerned the glittering shapes of numerous dragons: graceful giants with the treasure of a thousand kings upon their hides.

The apparition lasted for a moment longer; then Glaedr released Eragon's mind, and the valley once more appeared as it was.

It was beautiful, said Eragon.

That it was, but no more.

Eragon continued to study the valley, comparing it to what Glaedr had shown him, and he frowned when he saw a line of bobbing lights—lanterns, he thought—within the abandoned city. He whispered a spell to sharpen his sight and was able to make out a line of hooded figures in dark robes walking slowly through the ruins. They seemed solemn and unearthly, and there was a ritualistic quality to the measured beats of their strides and to the patterned sway of their lanterns.

Who are they? he asked Glaedr. He felt as if he was witnessing something not meant for others to see.

I do not know. Perhaps they are the descendants of those who hid during the battle. Perhaps they are men of your race who thought to settle here after the fall of the Riders. Or perhaps they are those who worship dragons and Riders as gods.

Are there really such?

There were. We discouraged the practice, but even so, it was common in many of the more isolated parts of Alagaësia. . . . It is good, I think, that you placed the wards you did.

Eragon watched as the hooded figures wound their way across the city, which took almost an hour. Once they arrived at the far side, the lanterns winked out one by one, and where the lantern holders had gone, Eragon could not see, even with the assistance of magic.

Then Eragon banked the fire with handfuls of dirt and crawled under his blankets to rest.

* * *

Eragon! Saphira! Rouse yourselves!

Eragon's eyes snapped open. He sat upright and grabbed Brisingr.

All was dark, save for the dull red glow of the bed of coals to his right and a ragged patch of starry sky off to the east. Though the light was faint, Eragon was able to make out the general shape of the forest and the meadow . . . and the monstrously large snail that was sliding across the grass toward him.

Eragon yelped and scrambled backward. The snail—whose shell was over five and a half feet tall—hesitated, then slimed toward him as fast as a man could run. A snakelike hiss came from the black slit of its mouth, and its waving eyeballs were each the size of his fist.

Eragon realized that he would not have time to get to his feet, and on his back he did not have the space he needed to draw Brisingr. He prepared to cast a spell, but before he could, Saphira's head arrowed past him and she caught the snail about the middle with her jaws. The snail's shell cracked between her fangs with a sound like breaking slate, and the creature uttered a faint, quavering shriek.

513

With a twist of her neck, Saphira tossed the snail into the air, opened her mouth as wide as it would go, and swallowed the creature whole, bobbing her head twice as she did, like a robin eating an earthworm.

Lowering his gaze, Eragon saw four more giant snails farther down upon the rise. One of the creatures had retreated within its shell; the others were hurrying away upon their undulating, skirtlike bellies.

"Over there!" shouted Eragon.

Saphira leaped forward. Her entire body left the ground for a moment, and then she landed upon all fours and snapped up first one, then two, then three of the snails. She did not eat the last snail, the one hiding in its shell, but drew back her head and bathed it in a stream of blue and yellow flame that lit up the land for hundreds of feet in every direction.

She maintained the flame for no more than a second or two;

then she picked up the smoking, steaming snail between her jaws—as gently as a mother cat picking up a kitten—carried it over to Eragon, and dropped it at his feet. He eyed it with distrust, but it appeared well and truly dead.

Now you can have a proper breakfast, said Saphira.

He stared at her, then began to laugh—and he kept laughing until he was doubled over, resting his hands on his knees and heaving for breath.

What is so amusing? she asked, and sniffed the soot-blackened shell.

Yes, why do you laugh, Eragon? asked Glaedr.

He shook his head and continued to wheeze. At last he was able to say, "Because—" And then he shifted to speaking with his mind so that Glaedr would hear as well. *Because . . . snail and eggs!* And he began to giggle again, feeling very silly. *Because, snail steaks! . . . Hungry? Have a stalk! Feeling tired? Eat an eyeball! Who needs mead when you have slime?! I could put the stalks in a cup, like a bunch of flowers, and they would . . .* He was laughing so hard, he found it impossible to continue, and he dropped to one knee while he gasped for air, tears of mirth streaming from his eyes.

Saphira parted her jaws in a toothy approximation of a smile, and she made a soft choking sound in her throat. *You are very odd sometimes, Eragon.* He could feel his merriment infecting her. She sniffed the shell again. *Some mead would be nice.*

"At least you ate," he said, both with his mind and his tongue.

Not enough, but enough to return to the Varden.

As his laughter subsided, Eragon poked at the snail with the tip of his boot. *It's been so long since there were dragons on Vroengard, it must not have realized what you were and thought to make an easy meal of me. . . . That would have been a sorry death indeed, to end up as dinner for a snail.*

But memorable, said Saphira.

But memorable, he agreed, feeling his mirth return.

And what did I say is the first law of hunting, younglings? asked Glaedr.

Together Eragon and Saphira replied, *Do not stalk your prey until you are sure that it is prey.*

Very good, said Glaedr.

Then Eragon said, *Hopping grubs, shadow birds, and now giant snails . . . How could the spells cast within the battle have created them?*

The Riders, the dragons, and the Forsworn loosed an enormous amount of energy during the conflict. Much of it was bound in spells, but much of it was not. Those who lived to tell of it said that, for a time, the world went mad and nothing they saw or heard could be trusted. Some of that energy must have settled on the ancestors of the grubs and the birds you saw today and altered them. However, you are mistaken to include the snails among their ranks. The snalglí, as they are known, have always lived here on Vroengard. They were a favorite food of ours, of the dragons, for reasons I'm sure, Saphira, you understand.

She hummed and licked her chops.

515

And not only is their flesh soft and tasty, but the shells are good for the digestion.

If they're just ordinary animals, then why didn't my wards stop them? asked Eragon. *At the very least, I should have been warned of approaching danger.*

That, replied Glaedr, *may be a result of the battle. Magic did not create the snalglí, but that does not mean they have remained unaffected by the forces that have wracked this place. We should not linger here any longer than necessary. Better we leave before whatever else is lurking on the island decides to test our mettle.*

With Saphira's help, Eragon cracked open the shell of the burnt snail and, by the glow of a red werelight, cleaned the spineless carcass within, which was a messy, slimy exercise that left him covered in gore up to his elbows. Then Eragon had Saphira bury the meat close to the bed of coals.

Afterward, Saphira returned to the spot in the grass where she had been lying, curled up once again, and went to sleep. This time Eragon joined her. Carrying his blankets and the saddlebags, one of which contained Glaedr's heart of hearts, he crawled under her wing and settled in the warm, dark nook between her neck and her body. And there he spent the rest of the night, thinking and dreaming.

The following day was as gray and gloomy as the previous one. A light dusting of snow covered the sides of the mountains and the tops of the foothills, and the air had a chill that led Eragon to believe it would snow again later that day.

Tired as she was, Saphira did not stir until the sun was already a handsbreadth above the mountains. Eragon was impatient, but he let her sleep. It was more important for her to recover from the flight to Vroengard than for them to get an early start.

Once she was awake, Saphira dug up the snail carcass for him, and he cooked a large breakfast of snail . . . he was not sure what to call it: snail bacon? Whatever the name for it, the strips of meat were delicious, and he ate more than he usually would. Saphira devoured what was left, and then they waited an hour, for it would not be wise to enter a fight with food in their stomachs.

Finally, Eragon rolled up his blankets and strapped the saddle back onto Saphira, and together with Glaedr they set off for the Rock of Kuthian.

THE ROCK OF KUTHIAN

The walk to the apple grove seemed shorter than it had the previous day. The gnarled trees were as ominous as ever, and Eragon kept his hand on Brisingr the whole time they were in the thicket.

As before, he and Saphira stopped at the edge of the tangled clearing that fronted the Rock of Kuthian. A flock of crows was perched upon the rough crag of stone, and at the sight of Saphira, they rose cawing into the air—as ill an omen as Eragon could imagine.

For half an hour, Eragon stood fixed in place as he cast spell after spell, searching for any magic that could cause him, Saphira, or Glaedr harm. Woven throughout the clearing, the Rock of Kuthian, and—so far as he could tell—the rest of the island, he found a daunting array of enchantments. Some of the spells embedded in the depths of the earth had such power that it felt as if a great river of energy was flowing beneath his feet. Others were small and seemingly innocuous, sometimes affecting only a single flower or a single branch of a tree. More than half of the enchantments were dormant—because they lacked energy, no longer had an object upon which to act, or were waiting for a certain set of circumstances that had yet to arrive—and a number of the spells seemed to conflict, as if the Riders, or whoever had cast them, had sought to modify or negate earlier pieces of magic.

Eragon was unable to determine the purpose of most of the spells. No record remained of the words used to cast them, only the structures of energy that the long-dead magicians had so carefully created, and those structures were difficult, if not impossible, to interpret. Glaedr was of some help, as he was familiar with many of the older, larger pieces of magic that had been placed on Vroengard, but otherwise Eragon was forced to guess. Fortunately, even though he could not always figure out what a spell was supposed to do, he was often able to establish whether it would affect him, Saphira, or Glaedr. It was a complicated process that required complicated incantations, though, and it took him another hour to examine all the spells.

What most worried him—and Glaedr as well—were the spells that they might not have been able to detect. Ferreting out other magicians' enchantments grew vastly more difficult if they had tried to hide their work.

At last, when Eragon was as confident as he could be that there were no traps on or around the Rock of Kuthian, he and Saphira walked across the clearing to the base of the jagged, lichen-covered spire.

Eragon tilted his head back and looked toward the top of the formation. It seemed incredibly far away. He saw nothing unusual about the stone, nor did Saphira.

Let us say our names and be done with it, she said.

Eragon sent a questioning thought to Glaedr, and the dragon responded: *She is right. There is no reason to delay. Speak your name, and Saphira and I shall do likewise.*

Feeling nervous, Eragon clenched his hands twice, then unslung his shield from his back, drew Brisingr, and dropped into a crouch.

"My name," he said in a loud, clear voice, "is Eragon Shadeslayer, son of Brom."

My name is Saphira Bjartskular, daughter of Vervada.

And mine Glaedr Eldunarí, son of Nithring, she of the long tail.

They waited.

Off in the distance, the crows cawed, as if mocking them. Unease stirred within Eragon, but he ignored it. He had not really expected opening the vault to be quite so simple.

Try again, but this time say your piece in the ancient language, advised Glaedr.

So Eragon said, "Nam iet er Eragon Sundavar-Vergandí, sönr abr Brom."

And then Saphira repeated her name and lineage in the ancient language, as did Glaedr.

Again nothing happened.

Eragon's unease deepened. If their trip had been in vain . . . No, it did not bear thinking about. Not yet. *Maybe all of our names have to be uttered out loud,* he said.

How? asked Saphira. *Am I supposed to roar at the stone? And what of Glaedr?*

I can say your names for you, said Eragon.

It seems unlikely that is what is required, but we may as well attempt it, said Glaedr.

In this or the ancient language?

The ancient language, I would think, but try both to be certain.

Two times then Eragon recited their names, yet the stone remained as stolid and unchanging as ever. Finally, frustrated, he said, *Maybe we're in the wrong place; maybe the entrance to the Vault of Souls is on the other side of the stone. Or maybe it's on the very top.*

519

If that were the case, wouldn't the directions contained within Domia abr Wyrda *have mentioned it?* asked Glaedr.

Eragon lowered his shield. *When are riddles ever easy to understand?*

What if only you are supposed to give your name? Saphira said to Eragon. *Did not Solembum say, ". . . when all seems lost and your power is insufficient, go to the Rock of Kuthian and speak your name to open the Vault of Souls." Your name, Eragon, not mine or Glaedr's.*

Eragon frowned. *It's possible, I suppose. But if only my name is needed, then perhaps I have to be by myself when I say it.*

With a growl, Saphira leaped into the air, ruffling Eragon's hair and battering the plants in the clearing with the wind from her wings. *Then try, and be quick about it!* she said as she flew east, away from the rock.

When she was a quarter mile away, Eragon looked back at the uneven surface of the rock, once more raised his shield, and once more pronounced his name, first in his own tongue and then in that of the elves.

No door or passageway revealed itself. No cracks or fissures appeared within the stone. No symbols traced themselves upon its surface. In every respect, the towering spire seemed to be nothing more than a solid piece of granite, devoid of any secrets.

Saphira! Eragon shouted with his mind. Then he swore and stalked back and forth within the clearing, kicking at loose stones and branches.

He returned to the base of the rock as Saphira swooped down to the clearing. The talons on her hind legs cut deep gouges in the soft earth as she landed, back-flapping to slow herself to a halt. Leaves and blades of grass swirled about her, as if caught in a whirlwind.

Once she had dropped to all fours and folded her wings, Glaedr said, *I take it you did not meet with success?*

No, snapped Eragon, and he glared at the spire.

The old dragon seemed to sigh. *I was afraid this would be the case. There is only one explanation—*

That Solembum lied to us? That he sent us off on a wild chase so that Galbatorix could destroy the Varden while we're gone?

No. That in order to open this . . . this . . .

Vault of Souls, said Saphira.

Yes, this vault he told you about—that in order to open it, we must speak our true names.

The words fell between them like weighty stones. For a time, none of them spoke. The thought intimidated Eragon, and he was reluctant to address it, as if doing so would somehow make the situation worse.

But if it's a trap— said Saphira.

Then it is a most devilish trap, said Glaedr. *The question you must decide is this: do you trust Solembum? For to proceed is to risk more than our lives; it is to risk our freedom. If you do trust him, can you be honest enough with yourselves to discover your true names, and quickly too? And are you willing to live with that knowledge, however unpleasant*

*it might be? Because if not, then we should leave this very moment. I
have changed since Oromis's death, but I know who I am. But do you,
Saphira? Do you, Eragon? Can you really tell me what it is that makes
you the dragon and Rider you are?*

Dismay crept through Eragon as he gazed up at the Rock of
Kuthian.

Who am *I?* he wondered.

✦ ✦ ✦

AND ALL THE WORLD A DREAM

Nasuada laughed as the starry sky spun around her and she fell tumbling toward a crevice of brilliant white light miles below.

Wind tore at her hair, and her shift flapped wildly, the ragged ends of the sleeves snapping like whips. Great big bats, black and dripping, flocked about her, nipping at her wounds with teeth that cut and stabbed and burned like ice.

And still she laughed.

The crevice widened and the light engulfed her, blinding her for a minute. When her eyes cleared, she found herself standing in the Hall of the Soothsayer, looking at herself lying strapped to the ash-colored slab. Next to her limp body stood Galbatorix: tall, broad-shouldered, with a shadow where his face ought to be and a crown of crimson fire upon his head.

He turned toward where she was standing and extended a gloved hand. "Come, Nasuada, daughter of Ajihad. Unbend your pride and pledge your fealty to me, and I shall give you everything you have ever wanted."

She uttered a derisive noise and lunged toward him with her hands outstretched. Before she could tear out his throat, the king vanished in a cloud of black mist.

"What I want is to kill you!" she shouted toward the ceiling.

The chamber rang with Galbatorix's voice as it emanated from every direction at once: "Then here you shall stay until you realize the error of your ways."

* * *

Nasuada opened her eyes. She was still on the slab, her wrists and ankles chained down and the wounds from the burrow grub throbbing as if they had never stopped.

She frowned. Had she been unconscious, or had she just been talking with the king? It was so difficult to tell when—

In one corner of the chamber, she saw the tip of a thick green vine force its way between the painted tiles, cracking them. More vines appeared next to the first; they poked through the wall from the outside and spread across the floor, covering it in a sea of writhing, snakelike appendages.

Watching them crawl toward her, Nasuada began to chuckle. *Is this all he can think of? I have stranger dreams nearly every night.*

As if in response to her scorn, the slab beneath her melted into the floor and the thrashing tendrils closed over her, wrapping around her limbs and holding them more securely than any chains. Her sight grew dark as the vines atop her multiplied, and the only thing she could hear was the sound of them sliding against one another: a dry, shifting sound, like that of falling sand.

The air around her grew thick and hot, and she felt as if she was having trouble breathing. Had she not known that the vines were only an illusion, she might have panicked then. Instead, she spat into the darkness and cursed Galbatorix's name. Not for the first time. Nor for the last, she was sure. But she refused to allow him the pleasure of knowing he had unbalanced her.

Light . . . Golden sunbeams streaming across a series of rolling hills patched with fields and vineyards. She was standing by the edge of a small courtyard, underneath a trellis laden with blooming morning glories, the vines of which seemed uncomfortably familiar. She was wearing a beautiful yellow dress. There was a crystal goblet of wine in her right hand and the musky, cherry taste of wine upon her tongue. A slight breeze was blowing from the west. The air smelled of warmth and comfort and freshly tilled land.

"Ah, there you are," said a voice behind her, and she turned to see Murtagh striding toward her from a grand estate. Like her, he held a goblet of wine. He was dressed in black hose and a doublet of maroon satin trimmed with gold piping. A gem-encrusted dagger hung from his studded belt. His hair was longer than she remembered, and he appeared relaxed and confident in a way she had not seen before. That, and the light upon his face, made him appear strikingly handsome—noble, even.

He joined her under the trellis and placed a hand on her bare arm. The gesture seemed casual and intimate. "You minx, abandoning me to Lord Ferros and his interminable stories. It took me half an hour to escape." Then he paused and looked at her closer, and his expression became one of concern. "Are you feeling ill? Your cheeks look gray."

She opened her mouth, but no words came to her. She could not think how to react.

Murtagh's brow furrowed. "You had another one of your attacks, didn't you?"

"I—I don't know. . . . I can't remember how I got here, or . . ." She trailed off as she saw the pain that appeared in Murtagh's eyes, and which he quickly hid.

He slid his hand down to the small of her back as he moved around her to stare out at the hilly landscape. With a swift motion, he drained his goblet. Then, in a low voice, he said, "I know how confusing this is for you. . . . It isn't the first time this has happened, but—" He took a deep breath and shook his head slightly. "What is the last thing you remember? Teirm? Aberon? The siege of Cithrí? . . . The gift I gave you that night in Eoam?"

A terrible sense of uncertainty overcame her. "Urû'baen," she whispered. "The Hall of the Soothsayer. That is my last memory."

For an instant, she felt his hand tremble against her back, but his face betrayed no reaction.

"Urû'baen," he repeated hoarsely. He looked at her. "Nasuada . . . it's been eight years since Urû'baen."

No, she thought. *It can't be.* And yet everything she saw and felt seemed so real. The motion of Murtagh's hair as the wind tousled it, the scent of the fields, the touch of her dress against her skin—it all seemed exactly as it should. But if she was actually there, then why hadn't Murtagh reassured her of it by reaching out to her mind, as he had done before? Had he forgotten? If eight years had elapsed, he might not remember the promise he made to her so long ago in the Hall of the Soothsayer.

"I—" she started to say, and then she heard a woman call out: "My Lady!"

She looked over her shoulder and saw a portly maid hurrying down from the estate, the front of her white apron flapping. "My Lady," said the maid, and curtsied. "I'm sorry to disturb you, but the children hoped that you would watch them put on their play for the guests."

"Children," she whispered. She looked back at Murtagh to see his eyes shining with tears.

"Aye," he said. "Children. Four of them, all strong and healthy and full of high spirits."

She shuddered, overcome with emotion. She could not help it. Then she lifted her chin. "Show me what I have forgotten. Show me *why* I have forgotten."

Murtagh smiled at her with what seemed like pride. "It would be my pleasure," he said, and kissed her on the forehead. He took her goblet and gave both glasses to the maid. Then he grasped her hands in his, closed his eyes, and bowed his head.

An instant later, she felt a *presence* pressing against her mind, and then she knew: it was not him. It could never have been him.

Angered by the deception and by the loss of what could never be, she pulled her right hand free of Murtagh's, grabbed his dagger, and shoved the blade into his side. And she shouted:

> *In El-harím, there lived a man, a man with yellow eyes!*
> *To me, he said, "Beware the whispers, for they whisper lies!"*

Murtagh regarded her with a curiously blank expression, and then he faded away before her. Everything around her—the trellis, the courtyard, the estate, the hills with the vineyards—vanished, and she found herself floating in a void without light or sound. She tried to continue her litany, but no sound came from her throat. She could not even hear the pounding of her pulse in her veins.

Then she felt the darkness *twist*, and—

She stumbled and fell onto her hands and knees. Sharp rocks scraped her palms. Blinking as her eyes adjusted to the light, she rose to her feet and looked around.

Haze. Ribbons of smoke drifting across a barren field similar to the Burning Plains.

She was once more clothed in her tattered shift, and her feet were bare.

Something roared behind her, and she spun around to see a twelve-foot-tall Kull charging toward her, swinging an ironbound club as large as she was. Another roar came from her left, and she saw a second Kull, as well as four smaller Urgals. Then a pair of cloaked, hunchbacked figures scurried out of the whitish haze and darted in her direction, chittering and waving their leaf-bladed swords. Although she had never seen them before, she knew they were the Ra'zac.

She laughed again. Now Galbatorix was just trying to punish her.

Ignoring the oncoming enemies—whom she knew she would never be able to kill or escape—she sat cross-legged on the ground and began to hum an old dwarvish tune.

Galbatorix's initial attempts to deceive her had been subtle affairs that might very well have succeeded in leading her astray had Murtagh not warned her beforehand. To keep Murtagh's help a secret, she had pretended to be ignorant of the fact that Galbatorix was manipulating her perception of reality, but regardless of what she saw or felt, she refused to allow the king to trick her into thinking of the things she should not or, far worse, giving him her loyalty.

Defying him had not always been easy, but she held to her rituals of thought and speech and, with them, she had been able to thwart the king.

The first illusion had been of another woman, Rialla, who joined her in the Hall of the Soothsayer as a fellow prisoner. The woman claimed she was secretly wedded to one of the Varden's spies in Urû'baen, and that she had been captured while carrying a message for him. Over what seemed like the course of a week, Rialla tried to ingratiate herself with Nasuada and, in a sideways manner, convince her that the Varden's campaign was doomed, that their reasons for fighting were flawed, and that it was only right and proper to submit to Galbatorix's authority.

In the beginning, Nasuada had not realized that Rialla herself was an illusion. She assumed that Galbatorix was distorting the woman's words or appearance, or perhaps that he was tampering with her own emotions to make her more susceptible to Rialla's arguments.

As the days had dragged on, and Murtagh neither visited nor contacted her, she had grown to fear that he had abandoned her to Galbatorix's clutches. The thought caused her more anguish than she would have liked to admit, and she found herself worrying about it at nearly every turn.

Then she had begun to wonder why Galbatorix had not come to torture her during the week, and it occurred to her that if a week *had* elapsed, then the Varden and the elves would have attacked Urû'baen. And if *that* had happened, Galbatorix surely would have mentioned it, if only to gloat. Moreover, Rialla's somewhat odd behavior, combined with a number of inexplicable gaps in her memory, Galbatorix's forbearance, and Murtagh's continued silence—for she could not bring herself to believe that he would break his word to her—convinced her, as outlandish as it seemed, that Rialla was an apparition and that time was no longer what it seemed.

It had shaken her to realize that Galbatorix could alter the number of days she thought had passed. She loathed the idea. Her sense of time had grown vague during her imprisonment, but she had retained a general awareness of its passage. To lose that, to become unmoored in time, meant she was even more at Galbatorix's mercy, for he could prolong or contract her experiences as he saw fit.

Still, she remained determined to resist Galbatorix's attempts at coercion, no matter how much time seemed to go by. If she had to endure a hundred years in her cell, then a hundred years she would endure.

When she had proven immune to Rialla's insidious whisperings—and indeed finally denounced the woman for being a coward and a traitor—the figment was taken from her chamber, and Galbatorix moved on to another ploy.

Thereafter, his deceptions had grown increasingly elaborate and improbable, but none broke the laws of reason and none conflicted with what he had already shown her, for the king was still trying to keep her ignorant of his meddling.

His efforts culminated when he seemed to take her from the chamber to a dungeon cell elsewhere in the citadel, where she saw what appeared to be Eragon and Saphira bound in chains. Galbatorix had threatened to kill Eragon unless she swore fealty to him, the king. When she refused, much to Galbatorix's displeasure—and, she thought, his surprise—Eragon shouted a spell that somehow freed the three of them. After a brief duel, Galbatorix fled—which she doubted he ever would do in reality—and then she, Eragon, and Saphira started to fight their way out of the citadel.

It had been rather dashing and exciting, and she had been tempted to find out how the sequence of events would resolve itself, but by then she felt she had played along with Galbatorix's false show for long enough. So she seized upon the first discrepancy she noticed—the shape of the scales around Saphira's eyes—and used it as an excuse to feign a realization that the world around her was only a pretense.

"You promised you would not lie to me while I was in the Hall of the Soothsayer!" she had shouted into the air. "What is this but a lie, Oath-breaker?"

Galbatorix's wrath at her discovery had been prodigious; she had heard a growl like that of a mountain-sized dragon, and then he abandoned all subtlety, and for the rest of the session he subjected her to a series of fantastical torments.

At last the apparitions had ceased, and Murtagh had contacted her to let her know she could once again trust her senses. She had never been so happy to feel the touch of his mind.

That night, he had come to her, and they spent hours sitting together and talking. He told her of the Varden's progress—they were nearly upon the capital—and of the Empire's preparations, and he explained that he believed he had discovered a means of freeing her. When she pressed him for details, he refused to elaborate, saying, "I need another day or two to see if it will work. But there *is* a way, Nasuada. Take heart in that."

She had taken heart in his earnestness and his concern for her. Even if she never escaped, she was glad to know that she was not alone in her captivity.

529

After she recounted some of the things Galbatorix had done to her and the means by which she had foiled him, Murtagh chuckled. "You've proven more of a challenge than he anticipated. It's been a long time since anyone has given him this much of a fight. I certainly didn't. . . . I understand little about it, but I know it's incredibly difficult to create believable illusions. Any competent magician can make it seem as if you're floating in the sky or that you're cold or hot or that there's a flower growing in front of you. Small complicated things or large simple things are the most any one person can hope to create, and it requires a great deal of concentration to maintain the illusion. If your attention wavers, all of a sudden the flower has four petals instead of ten. Or it might vanish altogether. Details are the hardest thing to replicate. Nature is filled with infinite details, but our minds can only hold so much. If you're ever in doubt as to whether what you're seeing is real, look at the details. Look for the seams in the world, where the spellcaster either does not know or has forgotten what should be there, or has taken a shortcut to conserve energy."

"If it's so difficult, then how does Galbatorix manage it?"

"He's using the Eldunarí."

"All of them?"

Murtagh nodded. "They provide the energy and the details needed, and he directs them as he wants."

"So then, the things I see are built on the memories of dragons?" she asked, feeling slightly awed.

He nodded again. "That and the memories of their Riders, for those who had Riders."

The following morning, Murtagh had woken her with a swift bolt of thought to tell her that Galbatorix was about to start again. Thereafter, phantoms and illusions of every sort had beset her, but as the day wore on, she noticed that the visions—with a few notable exceptions, such as that of her and Murtagh at the estate—had grown increasingly fuzzy and simple, as if either Galbatorix or the Eldunarí were growing tired.

And now she sat upon the barren plain, humming a dwarven tune as Kull, Urgals, and Ra'zac bore down on her. They caught her, and it felt as if they beat and cut her, and at times she screamed and wished her pain would end, but not once did she consider giving in to Galbatorix's desires.

Then the plain vanished, as did most of her suffering, and she reminded herself: *It is only in my mind. I shall not give in. I am not an animal; I am stronger than the weakness of my flesh.*

A dark cave lit by glowing green mushrooms appeared around her. For several minutes, she heard a large creature snuffling and padding about in the shadows between the stalagmites, and then she felt the creature's warm breath against the back of her neck, and she smelled the odor of carrion.

530

She started to laugh again, and she continued to laugh even as Galbatorix forced her to confront horror after horror in an attempt to find the particular combination of pain and fear that would break her. She laughed because she knew her will was stronger than his imagination, and she laughed because she knew she could count on Murtagh's help, and with him as her ally, she did not fear the spectral nightmares Galbatorix inflicted upon her, no matter how terrible they seemed at the time.

✦　✦　✦

A QUESTION OF CHARACTER

Eragon's foot slipped out from under him as he stepped on a patch of slick mud, and he fell onto his side in the wet grass with brutal suddenness. He uttered a grunt and winced as his hip began to throb. The impact was sure to leave a bruise.

"Barzûl," he said as he rolled to his feet and carefully stood. *At least I didn't land on Brisingr*, he thought as he pried scales of cold mud from his leggings.

Feeling glum, he resumed trudging toward the ruined building where they had decided to camp, in the belief it would be safer than by the forest.

As he strode through the grass, he startled a number of bullfrogs, who sprang out of hiding and fled hopping to either side. The bull-frogs were the only other strange creature they had encountered on the island; each had a hornlike projection above its reddish eyes, and from the center of its forehead sprouted a curving stalk—much like a fisherman's rod—upon the end of which hung a small, fleshy organ that at night glowed either white or yellow. The light allowed the bullfrogs to lure hundreds of flying insects within the reach of their tongues, and as a result of their easy access to food, the frogs grew enormously large. He had seen some the size of a bear's head, great fleshy lumps with staring eyes and mouths as wide as both his outstretched hands put together.

The frogs reminded him of Angela the herbalist, and he suddenly wished that she were there on Vroengard Island with them. *If anyone could tell us our true names, I bet she could.* For some reason, he always felt as if the herbalist could see right through him, as if she understood everything about him. It was a disconcerting sensation, but at the moment, he would have welcomed it.

He and Saphira had decided to trust Solembum and stay on Vroengard for another three days at most while they tried to discover their true names. Glaedr had left the decision up to them; he said, *You know Solembum better than I do. Stay or do not. Either way, the risk is great. There are no more safe paths.*

It was Saphira who ultimately made the choice. *The werecats would never serve Galbatorix,* she said. *They prize their freedom too highly. I would trust their word before that of any other creature, even an elf.*

So they had stayed.

They spent the rest of that day, and now most of the next, sitting, thinking, talking, sharing memories, examining each other's minds, and trying various combinations of words in the ancient language, all in the hope that they would be able to either consciously work out their true names or—if they were lucky—strike upon them by accident.

Glaedr had offered his help when asked, but for the most part he kept to himself and gave Eragon and Saphira privacy for their conversations, many of which Eragon would have been embarrassed for anyone else to hear. *The finding of one's true name ought to be something one does by oneself,* said Glaedr. *If I think of either of yours, I will tell you—for we have no time to waste—but it would be better if you discover them on your own.*

As of yet, neither of them had succeeded.

Ever since Brom had explained to him about true names, Eragon had wanted to learn his own. Knowledge, particularly self-knowledge, was ever a useful thing, and he hoped his true name would allow him to better master his thoughts and feelings. Still, he could not help but feel a certain amount of trepidation about what he might discover.

Assuming that he *could* discover his name in the next few days, of which he was not entirely sure. He hoped he could, both for the success of their mission and because he did not want Glaedr or Saphira to figure it out for him. If he was to hear his whole being described in a word or phrase, then he wanted to arrive at that knowledge on his own, instead of having it thrust upon him.

Eragon sighed as he climbed the five broken steps that led up to the building. The structure had been a nesting house, or so Glaedr had said, and by the standards of Vroengard, it was so small as to be entirely unnoteworthy. Still, the walls were over three stories high, and the interior was large enough for Saphira to move about with ease. The southeastern corner had collapsed inward, taking part of the ceiling with it, but otherwise the building was sound.

Eragon's steps echoed as he walked through the vaulted entryway and made his way across the glassy floor of the main chamber. Embedded within the transparent material were swirling blades of color that formed an abstract design of dizzying complexity. Every time he looked at it, he felt as if the lines were about to resolve into a recognizable shape, but they never did.

The surface of the floor was covered with a fine web of cracks that radiated outward from the rubble beneath the gaping hole where the walls had given way. Long tendrils of ivy hung from the edges of the broken ceiling like lengths of knotted rope. Water dripped from the ends of the vines to fall into shallow, misshapen puddles, and the sound of the droplets striking echoed throughout the building, a constant, irregular beat that Eragon thought would drive him mad if he had to listen to it for more than a few days.

Against the north-facing wall was a half circle of stones Saphira had dragged and pushed into place to protect their camp. When he reached the barrier, Eragon jumped onto the nearest block, which stood over six feet tall. Then he dropped down to the other side, landing heavily.

Saphira paused in the midst of licking her forefoot, and he felt a questioning thought from her. He shook his head, and she returned to her grooming.

Undoing his cloak, Eragon walked over to the fire he had built close to the wall. He spread the sodden garment on the floor, then removed his mud-caked boots and set them out to dry as well.

Does it look as if it will start raining again? Saphira asked.

Probably.

He squatted by the fire for a bit, and then sat on his bedroll and leaned against the wall. He watched Saphira as she worked her crimson tongue around the flexible cuticle at the base of each of her talons. An idea occurred to him, and he murmured a phrase in the ancient language, but to his disappointment, he felt no charge of energy in the words, nor did Saphira react to their utterance, as had Sloan when Eragon had spoken his true name.

Eragon closed his eyes and tipped his head back.

It frustrated him that he was unable to puzzle out Saphira's true name. He could accept that he did not fully understand himself, but he had known Saphira since the moment she had hatched, and he had shared nearly all of her memories. How could there be parts of her that were still a mystery to him? How could he have been better able to understand a murderer like Sloan than his own spell-bonded partner? Was it because she was a dragon and he was a human? Was it because Sloan's identity had been simpler than Saphira's?

Eragon did not know.

One of the exercises he and Saphira had done—on Glaedr's recommendation—was to tell each other all of the flaws they had noticed: he in her and she in him. It had been a humbling exercise. Glaedr had also shared his observations, and though the dragon had been kind, Eragon could not help but feel a sense of wounded pride upon hearing Glaedr list his various failings. And that too Eragon knew he needed to take into account when trying to discover his true name.

For Saphira, the hardest thing to come to terms with had been her vanity, which she had refused to acknowledge as such for the longest time. For Eragon, it had been the arrogance Glaedr claimed he sometimes displayed, his feelings concerning the men he had killed, and all the petulance, selfishness, anger, and other short-comings to which he, like so many others, was prey.

And yet, though they had examined themselves as honestly as they could, their introspection had yielded no results.

Today and tomorrow, that's all we have. The thought of returning to the Varden empty-handed depressed him. *How are we supposed to best Galbatorix?* he wondered, as he had so many times before. *Another few days and our lives may no longer be our own. We'll be slaves, like Murtagh and Thorn.*

He swore under his breath and surreptitiously punched a fist against the floor.

Be calm, Eragon, said Glaedr, and Eragon noticed the dragon was shielding his thoughts so that Saphira did not hear.

How can I? he growled.

It is easy to be calm when there is nothing to worry about, Eragon. The true test of your self-control, however, is whether you can remain calm in a trying situation. You cannot allow anger or frustration to cloud your thoughts, not at the moment. Right now, you need your mind to be clear.

Have you always been able to remain calm at times like this?

The old dragon seemed to chuckle. *No. I used to growl and bite and knock down trees and tear up the ground. Once, I broke the top off of a mountain in the Spine; the other dragons were rather upset with me for that. But I have had many years to learn that losing my temper rarely helps. You have not, I know, but allow my experience to guide you in this. Let go of your worries and focus only on the task at hand. The future will be what it will, and fretting about it will only make your fears more likely to come true.*

I know, Eragon sighed, *but it's not easy.*

Of course not. Few things of worth are. Then Glaedr withdrew and left him to the silence of his own mind.

Eragon fetched his bowl from the saddlebags, hopped over the half circle of stones, and walked barefoot to one of the puddles underneath the opening in the ceiling. A light drizzle had begun to fall, coating that part of the floor with a slippery layer of water. He squatted by the edge of the puddle and began to scoop water into the bowl with his bare hands.

Once the bowl was full, Eragon retreated a few feet and set it on a piece of stone that was the height of a table. Then he fixed an image of Roran in his mind and murmured, "Draumr kópa."

The water in the bowl shimmered, and an image of Roran appeared against a pure white background. He was walking next to Horst and Albriech, leading his horse, Snowfire. The three men looked tired and footsore, but they still carried weapons, so Eragon knew the Empire had not captured them.

He next scryed Jörmundur, then Solembum—who was tearing at a freshly killed robin—and then Arya, but Arya's wards hid her from his sight, and all he saw was blackness.

At last Eragon released the spell and tossed the water back into the puddle. As he climbed over the barrier surrounding their camp, Saphira stretched and yawned, arching her back like a cat, and said, *How are they?*

"Safe, as far as I can tell."

He dropped the bowl on the saddlebags, then lay on his bedroll, closed his eyes, and returned to scouring his mind for ideas as to what his true name might be. Every few minutes, he thought of a different possibility, but none touched a chord within him, so he discarded them and began anew. All of the names contained a few constants: the fact that he was a Rider; his affection for Saphira and Arya; his desire to vanquish Galbatorix; his relationships with Roran, Garrow, and Brom; and the blood he shared with Murtagh. But no matter in what combination he placed those elements, the name did not speak to him. It was obvious that he was missing some crucial aspect of himself, so he kept making the names longer and longer in the hope that he might stumble across whatever it was he was overlooking.

When the names began to take him more than a minute to say, he realized he was wasting his time. He needed to reexamine his basic assumptions once again. He was convinced that his mistake lay in failing to notice some fault, or in not giving enough consideration to a fault he was already aware of. People, he had observed, were rarely willing to acknowledge their own imperfections, and he knew the same was true of himself. Somehow he had to cure himself of that blindness while he yet had time. It was a blindness born of pride and self-preservation, as it allowed him to believe the best of himself as he went about his life. However, he could no longer afford to indulge in such self-deception.

Thus he thought and continued to think as the day wore on, but his efforts met only with failure.

The rain grew heavier. Eragon disliked the sound of it drumming against the puddles, for the featureless noise made it difficult to hear if anyone was trying to sneak up on them. Since their first night on Vroengard, he had seen no sign of the strange, hooded figures whom he had watched wending their way through the city, nor had he felt any hint of their minds. Nevertheless, Eragon remained conscious of their presence, and he could not help feeling that he and Saphira were about to be attacked at any moment.

The gray light of day slowly faded to dusk, and a deep, starless night settled across the valley. Eragon heaped more wood onto the fire; it was the only illumination within the nesting house, and the cluster of yellow flames was like a tiny candle within the huge, echoing space. Close to the fire, the glassy floor reflected the glow of the burning branches. It gleamed like a sheet of polished ice, and the blades of color within often distracted Eragon from his brooding.

Eragon ate no dinner. He was hungry, but he was too tense for food to sit well in his stomach, and in any case, he felt that a meal would slow his thinking. Never was his mind so keen as when his belly was empty.

He would not, he decided, eat again until he knew his true name, or until they had to leave the island, whichever came first.

Several hours passed. They spoke little amongst themselves, although Eragon remained conscious of the general drift of Saphira's moods and thoughts, even as she remained conscious of his.

Then, as Eragon was about to enter into his waking dreams—both to rest and out of hope that the dreams might provide some insight—Saphira uttered a *yowl*, reached forward with her right paw, and slapped it upon the floor. Several branches within the fire crumbled and fell apart, sending a burst of sparks toward the black ceiling.

Alarmed, Eragon sprang to his feet and drew Brisingr while he searched the darkness beyond the half circle of stones for enemies. An instant later, he realized that Saphira's mood was not one of concern or anger but of triumph.

I have done it! exclaimed Saphira. She arched her neck and loosed a jet of blue and yellow flame into the upper reaches of the building. *I know my true name!* She spoke a single line in the ancient language, and the inside of Eragon's mind seemed to ring with a sound like a bell, and for a moment, the tips of Saphira's scales gleamed with an inner light, and she looked as if she were made of stars.

The name was grand and majestic, but also tinged with sadness, for it named her as the last female of her kind. In the words, Eragon could hear the love and devotion she felt for him, as well as all the other traits that made up her personality. Most he recognized; a few he did not. Her flaws were as prominent as her virtues, but overall, the impression was one of fire and beauty and grandeur.

Saphira shivered from the tip of her nose to the tip of her tail, and she shuffled her wings.

I know who I am, she said.

Well done, Bjartskular, said Glaedr, and Eragon could sense how impressed he was. *You have a name to be proud of. I would not say it again, however, not even to yourself, until we are at the . . . at the spire we have come to see. You must take great care to keep your name hidden now that you know it.*

Saphira blinked and shuffled her wings again. *Yes, Master.* The excitement running through her was palpable.

Eragon sheathed Brisingr and walked over to her. She lowered her head until it was at his level. He stroked the line of her jaw, and then pressed his forehead against her hard snout and held her as tightly as he could, her scales sharp against his fingers. Hot tears began to slide down his cheeks.

Why do you cry? she asked.

Because . . . I'm lucky enough to be bonded with you.

Little one.

They talked for a while longer, as Saphira was eager to discuss what she had learned about herself. Eragon was happy to listen, but he could not help feeling a little bitter that he still had not been able to divine his own true name.

Then Saphira curled up on her side of the half circle and went to sleep, leaving Eragon to ruminate by the light of the dying campfire. Glaedr remained awake and aware, and sometimes Eragon consulted with him, but for the most part, he kept to himself.

The hours crawled past, and Eragon grew increasingly frustrated. His time was running out—ideally he and Saphira should have left for the Varden the previous day—and yet no matter what he tried, he seemed unable to describe himself as he was.

It was nearly midnight, by his reckoning, when the rain ceased.

Eragon fidgeted, trying to make up his mind; then he bounded to his feet, too wound up to bear sitting any longer. *I'm going for a walk,* he said to Glaedr.

He expected the dragon to object, but instead Glaedr said, *Leave your weapons and armor here.*

Why?

Whatever you find, you need to face it by yourself. You cannot learn what you are made of if you rely on anyone or anything else to help you.

Glaedr's words made sense to Eragon, but still he hesitated before he unbuckled his sword and dagger and pulled off his mail hauberk. He donned his boots and his damp cloak, and then he dragged the saddlebags that contained Glaedr's heart of hearts closer to Saphira.

As Eragon started to leave the half circle of stones, Glaedr said, *Do what you must, but be careful.*

* * *

Outside the nesting house, Eragon was pleased to see patches of stars and enough moonlight shining through the gaps in the clouds for him to make out his surroundings.

He bounced on the balls of his feet a few times, wondering where to go, and then he set off at a brisk trot toward the heart of the ruined city. After a few seconds, his frustration got the better of him and he increased his pace to an all-out run.

As he listened to the sound of his breathing and of his footsteps pounding against the paving stones, he asked himself, *Who am I?* But no answer came to him.

He ran until his lungs began to fail, and then he ran some more, and when neither his lungs nor his legs would sustain him any longer, he stopped by a weed-filled fountain and leaned on his arms against it while he recovered his breath.

Around him loomed the shapes of several enormous buildings: shadowy hulks that looked like a range of ancient, crumbling mountains. The fountain stood in the center of a vast square courtyard, much of which was littered with pieces of broken stone.

He pushed himself off the fountain and slowly turned in a circle. In the distance, he could hear the deep, resonant croaking of the bullfrogs, an odd booming sound that grew especially loud whenever one of the larger frogs participated.

A cracked slab of stone several yards away caught his eye. He walked over, grasped it by the edges, and, with a heave, picked it off the ground. The muscles in his arms burning, he staggered to the edge of the courtyard and threw the slab onto the grass beyond.

It landed with a soft but satisfying *thump*.

He strode back to the fountain, unclasped his cloak, and draped it over the edge of the sculpture. Then he strode to the next piece of rubble—a jagged wedge that had cleaved off a larger block—and he fit his fingers underneath it and lifted it onto his shoulder.

For over an hour, he labored to clear the courtyard. Some of the fallen masonry was so big, he had to use magic to move it, but for the most part he was able to use his hands. He was methodical about it; he worked back and forth across the courtyard, and every piece of rubble he encountered, no matter how large or small, he stopped to remove.

The effort soon left him drenched in sweat. He would have removed his tunic, but the edges of the stone were often sharp and would have cut him. As it was, he accumulated a host of bruises across his chest and shoulders, and he scraped his hands in numerous places.

The exertion helped calm his mind and, since it required little thought, left him free to mull over all that he was and all that he might be.

In the midst of his self-appointed task, as he was resting after having shifted a particularly heavy length of cornice, he heard a threatening *hiss,* and he looked up to see a snalglí—this one with a shell at least six feet tall—gliding out of the darkness with startling speed. The creature's boneless neck was fully extended, its lipless mouth was like a slash of darkness splitting its soft flesh, and its bulbous eyes were pointed directly at him. By the light of the moon, the snalglí's exposed flesh gleamed like silver, as did the track of slime it left behind.

"Letta," said Eragon, and he straightened upright and shook drops of blood from his torn hands. "Ono ach *néiat* threyja eom verrunsmal edtha, O snalglí."

As he spoke his warning, the snail slowed and retracted its eyes several inches. It paused when it was a few yards away, hissed again, and began to circle around to his left.

"Oh no you don't," he muttered, turning with it. He glanced over his shoulders to make sure no other snalglí were approaching from behind.

The giant snail seemed to realize that it could not catch him by surprise, for it stopped and sat hissing and waving its eyeballs at him.

"You sound like a teapot left to boil," he said to it.

The snalglí's eyeballs waved even faster, and then it charged at him, the edges of its flat belly undulating.

Eragon waited until the last moment, then jumped to the side and let the snalglí slide past. He laughed and slapped the back of its shell. "Not too bright, are you?" Dancing away from it, he began to taunt the creature in the ancient language, calling it all sorts of insulting but perfectly accurate names.

The snail seemed to puff up with rage—its neck thickened and bulged, and it opened its mouth even farther and began to sputter as well as hiss.

Again and again, it charged at Eragon, and every time he jumped out of the way. At last the snalglí grew tired of the game. It withdrew a half-dozen yards and sat staring at him with its fist-sized eyeballs.

"How do you ever catch anything when you're so slow?" Eragon asked in a mocking tone, and he stuck his tongue out at the snail.

The snalglí hissed once more, and then it turned around and slid off into the darkness.

Eragon waited several minutes to be sure it was gone before he returned to clearing the rubble. "Maybe I should just call myself Snail Vanquisher," he muttered as he rolled a section of a pillar across the courtyard. "Eragon Shadeslayer, Vanquisher of Snails. . . . I would strike fear into the hearts of men wherever I went."

It was the deepest part of the night when he finally dropped the last piece of stone onto the border of grass that edged the courtyard. There he stood, panting. He was cold and hungry and tired, and the scrapes on his hands and wrists smarted.

He had ended by the northeastern corner of the courtyard. To the north was an immense hall that had been mostly destroyed during the battle; all that remained standing was a portion of the back walls and a single, ivy-covered pillar where the entryway had been.

He stared at the pillar for the longest time. Above it, a cluster of stars—red, blue, and white—shone through an opening in the clouds, gleaming like cut diamonds. He felt a strange attraction to them, as if their appearance signified something that he ought to be aware of.

Without bothering to consider his action, he walked to the base of the pillar—scrambling over piles of rubble—then reached as high as he could and grasped the thickest part of the ivy: a stem as big around as his forearm and covered with thousands of tiny hairs.

He tugged on the vine. It held, so he jumped off the ground and began to climb. Hand over hand, he scaled the pillar, which must have been three hundred feet tall, but which felt taller the farther he got from the ground.

He knew he was being reckless, but then, he felt reckless.

Halfway up, the smaller tendrils of vine began to peel off the stone when he put his full weight on them. After that, he was careful to only grab hold of the main stem and some of the thicker side branches.

His grip had almost given out by the time he arrived at the top. The crown of the pillar was still intact; it formed a square, flat surface large enough to sit on, with over a foot to spare on each side.

Feeling somewhat shaky from the exertion, Eragon crossed his legs and rested his hands palm upward on his knees, allowing the air to soothe his torn skin.

Below him lay the ruined city: a maze of shattered husks that often echoed with strange, forlorn cries. In a few places where there were ponds, he could see the faint, glowing lights of the bullfrogs' lures, like lanterns viewed from a great distance.

Angler frogs, he thought suddenly in the ancient language. *That's what their name is: angler frogs*. And he knew he was right, for the words seemed to fit like a key in a lock.

Then he shifted his gaze to the cluster of stars that had inspired his climb. He slowed his breathing and concentrated on maintaining a steady, never-ending flow of air in and out of his lungs. The cold, his hunger, and his trembling exhaustion gave him a peculiar sense of clarity; he seemed to float apart from his body, as if the bond between his consciousness and his flesh had grown attenuated, and there came upon him a heightened awareness of the city and the island around him. He was acutely sensitive to every motion of the wind and to every sound and smell that wafted past the top of the pillar.

As he sat there, he thought of more names, and though none fully described him, his failures did not upset him, for the clarity he felt was too deep-seated for any setback to perturb his equanimity.

How can I include everything I am in just a few words? he wondered, and he continued to ponder the question as the stars turned.

Three warped shadows flew across the city—like small, moving rifts in reality—and landed upon the roof of the building to his left. Then the dark, owl-shaped silhouettes spread their barbed plumes and stared at him with luminous, evil-looking eyes. The shadows chattered softly to one another, and two of them scratched their empty wings with claws that had no depth. The third held the remains of a bullfrog between its ebony talons.

He watched the menacing birds for several minutes, and they watched him in return, and then they took flight and ghosted away to the west, making no more noise than a falling feather.

Near dawn, when Eragon could see the morning star between two peaks to the east, he asked himself, "What do I want?"

Until then, he had not bothered to consider the question. He wanted to overthrow Galbatorix: that, of course. But should they succeed, what, then? Ever since he had left Palancar Valley, he had thought that he and Saphira would one day return, to live near the mountains he so loved. However, as he pondered the prospect, he slowly realized that it no longer appealed to him.

He had grown up in Palancar Valley, and he would always consider it home. But what was left there for him or Saphira? Carvahall was destroyed, and even if the villagers rebuilt it someday, the town would never be the same. Besides, most of the friends he and Saphira had made lived elsewhere, and the two of them had obligations to the various races of Alagaësia—obligations that they could not ignore. And after all the things they had done and seen, he could not imagine that either of them would be content to live in such an ordinary, isolated place.

For the sky is hollow and the world is round. . . .

Even if they did return, what would they do? Raise cows and farm wheat? He had no desire to eke out a living from the land as his family had during his childhood. He and Saphira were a Rider and dragon; their doom and their destiny was to fly at the forefront of history, not to sit before a fire and grow fat and lazy.

And then there was Arya. If he and Saphira lived in Palancar Valley, he would see her rarely, if at all.

"No," said Eragon, and the word was like a hammerblow in the silence. "I don't want to go back."

A cold tingle crawled down his spine. He had known he had changed since he, Brom, and Saphira had set out to track down the Ra'zac, but he had clung to the belief that, at his core, he was still the same person. Now he understood that this was no longer true. The boy he had been when he first set foot outside of Palancar Valley had ceased to exist; Eragon did not look like him, he did not act like him, and he no longer wanted the same things from life.

He took a deep breath and then released it in a long, shuddering sigh as the truth sank into him.

"I am not who I was." Saying it aloud seemed to give the thought weight.

Then, as the first rays of dawn brightened the eastern sky over the ancient island of Vroengard, where the Riders and dragons had once lived, he thought of a name—a name such as he had not thought of before—and as he did, a sense of certainty came over him.

He said the name, whispered it to himself in the deepest recesses of his mind, and all his body seemed to vibrate at once, as if Saphira had struck the pillar beneath him.

And then he gasped, and he found himself both laughing and crying—laughing that he had succeeded and for the sheer joy of comprehension; crying because all his failings, all the mistakes he had made, were now obvious to him, and he no longer had any delusions to comfort himself with.

"I am not who I was," he whispered, gripping the edges of the column, "but I know who I am."

The name, his true name, was weaker and more flawed than he would have liked, and he hated himself for that, but there was also much to admire within it, and the more he thought about it, the more he was able to accept the true nature of his self. He was not the best person in the world, but neither was he the worst.

"And I *won't* give up," he growled.

He took solace in the fact that his identity was not immutable; he could improve himself if he wished. And right then, he swore to himself that he would do better in the future, be it ever so hard.

Still laughing, still crying, he turned his face toward the sky and spread his arms out to either side. In time, the tears and the laughter stopped, and in their place he felt a sense of deep calm overlaid with a tinge of happiness and resignation. Despite Glaedr's admonition, he again whispered his true name, and once more his entire being shook from the force of the words.

Keeping his arms outstretched, he stood atop the pillar, and then he tipped forward and fell headfirst toward the ground. Just before he struck, he said, "Vëoht," and he slowed, rotated, and alit upon the cracked stone as gently as if he were stepping out of a carriage.

He returned to the fountain in the center of the courtyard and retrieved his cloak. Then, as light spread through the ruined city, he hurried back toward the nesting house, eager to wake Saphira and tell her and Glaedr of his discovery.

THE VAULT OF SOULS

Eragon lifted his sword and shield, eager to proceed, but also somewhat afraid.

As before, he and Saphira stood at the base of the Rock of Kuthian while Glaedr's heart of hearts sat in the small chest hidden within the saddlebags upon Saphira's back.

It was still early morning, and the sun shone brightly through large tears in the canopy of clouds. Eragon and Saphira had wanted to go directly to the Rock of Kuthian once Eragon had returned to the nesting house, but Glaedr had insisted that Eragon eat first, and that they then wait for the food to settle in his stomach.

But now they were finally at the jagged spire of stone, and Eragon was tired of waiting, as was Saphira.

Ever since they had shared their true names, the bond between them seemed to have grown stronger, perhaps because they had both heard how much they cared for each other. It was something they had always known, but nevertheless, to have it stated in such irrefutable terms had increased the sense of closeness they shared.

Somewhere to the north, a raven called.

I'll go first, said Glaedr. *If it's a trap, I might be able to spring it before it catches either of you.*

Eragon started to pull his mind away from Glaedr, as did Saphira, to allow the dragon to utter his true name without being overheard. But Glaedr said, *No, you have told me your names. It is only right you should know mine.*

Eragon looked at Saphira, and then they both said, *Thank you, Ebrithil.*

Then Glaedr spoke his name, and it boomed forth in Eragon's

mind like a fanfare of trumpets, regal and yet discordant, colored throughout by Glaedr's grief and anger at Oromis's death. His name was longer than either Eragon's or Saphira's; it went on for several sentences—a record of a life that had stretched over centuries and which had contained joys and sorrows and accomplishments too numerous to count. His wisdom was evident in his name, but also contradictions: complexities that made it difficult to fully grasp his identity.

Saphira felt the same sense of awe upon hearing Glaedr's name as did Eragon; the sound of it made them both realize how young they still were and how far they had to go before they could hope to match Glaedr's knowledge and experience.

I wonder what Arya's true name is. Eragon thought to himself.

They watched the Rock of Kuthian intently, but saw no change.

Saphira went next. Arching her neck and pawing at the ground like a high-spirited charger, she proudly stated her true name. Even in the daylight, her scales again shimmered and sparkled at the proclamation.

Hearing her and Glaedr say their true names made Eragon less self-conscious about his own. None of them were perfect, and yet they did not condemn each other for their shortcomings, but rather acknowledged and forgave them.

Again, nothing happened after Saphira uttered her name.

Lastly, Eragon stepped forward. A cold sweat coated his brow. Knowing that it might be his final act as a free man, he spoke his name with his mind, as had Glaedr and Saphira. They had agreed beforehand that it would be safer for him to avoid saying his name out loud, so as to reduce the chance that anyone might overhear it.

As Eragon formed the last word with his thoughts, a thin, dark line appeared at the base of the spire.

It ran upward fifty feet and then split in two and arched down to either side, tracing the outline of two broad doors. Upon the doors appeared row after row of glyphs limned in gold: wards against both physical and magical detection.

Once the outline was complete, the doors swung outward upon hidden hinges, scraping aside the dirt and plants that had accumulated before the spire since the doors had last opened, whenever that had been. Through the doorway was a huge vaulted tunnel that descended at a steep angle into the bowels of the earth.

The doors ground to a halt, and the clearing fell silent again.

Eragon stared at the dark tunnel, feeling a sense of increasing apprehension. They had found what they were looking for, but he still was not sure if it was a trap or not.

Solembum did not lie, said Saphira. Her tongue darted out as she tasted the air.

Yes, but what's waiting for us inside? asked Eragon.

This place should not exist, said Glaedr. *We and the Riders hid many secrets on Vroengard, but the island is too small for a tunnel as large as this to have been built without others knowing. And yet I have never heard of it before.*

Eragon frowned and glanced about. They were still alone; no one was trying to sneak up on them. *Could it have been built before the Riders made Vroengard their home?*

Glaedr thought for a moment. *I do not know. . . . Perhaps. It is the only explanation that makes sense, but if so, then it is ancient indeed.*

The three of them searched the passageway with their minds, but they felt no living thing within it.

Right then, said Eragon. The sour taste of dread filled his mouth, and his palms were slick within his gloves. Whatever they were about to find at the other end of the tunnel, he wanted to know once and for all. Saphira was also nervous, but less than he.

Let us dig out the rat hiding in this nest, she said.

Together then, they walked through the doorway and into the tunnel.

As the last inch of Saphira's tail slid over the threshold, the doors swung shut behind them and closed with a loud crack of stone meeting stone, plunging them into darkness.

"Ah, no, no, no!" growled Eragon, rushing back to the doors. "Naina hvitr," he said, and a directionless white light illuminated the entrance to the tunnel.

The inner surfaces of the doors were perfectly smooth, and no matter how he pushed and pounded on them, they refused to budge. "Blast it. We should have used a log or a boulder to wedge them open," he lamented, berating himself for not thinking of it beforehand.

If we have to, we can always break them down, said Saphira.

That I very much doubt, said Glaedr.

Eragon regripped Brisingr. *Then I guess we have no choice but to go forward.*

When have we ever had any choice but to go forward? asked Saphira.

Eragon altered his spell so that the werelight emanated from a single point near the ceiling—otherwise the lack of shadows made it difficult for him and Saphira to judge depth—and then, together, they started down the slanting tunnel.

The floor of the passageway was somewhat knobbly, which made it easy for them to maintain their footing in the absence of steps. Where the floor and the walls met, they flowed together as if the stone had been melted, which told Eragon that it was most likely elves who had excavated the tunnel.

Down they went, deeper and deeper into the earth, until Eragon guessed they had passed under the foothills behind the Rock of Kuthian and burrowed into the roots of the mountain beyond. The tunnel neither turned nor branched, and the walls remained utterly bare.

At last Eragon felt a hint of warm air rising toward them from farther down the tunnel, and he noticed a faint orange glow in the distance. "Letta," he murmured, and extinguished the werelight.

The air continued to warm as they descended, and the glow before them waxed in brightness. Soon they were able to see an end to the tunnel: a huge black arch that was covered entirely with sculpted glyphs, which made the arch look as if it were wrapped in thorns. The smell of brimstone tainted the air, and Eragon felt his eyes begin to water.

They stopped before the archway; through it, all they could see was a flat gray floor.

Eragon glanced back the way they had come, then returned his gaze to the arch. The jagged structure made him nervous, and Saphira as well. He tried to read the glyphs, but they were too jumbled and too densely packed to make sense of, nor could he detect any energy stored within the black structure. Yet he had difficulty believing that it was not enchanted. Whoever built the tunnel had succeeded in hiding the latch spell for the doors to the outside, which meant they could have done the same with any spells they had placed upon the arch.

He exchanged a quick look with Saphira, and he wet his lips as he remembered what Glaedr had said: *There are no more safe paths*.

Saphira snorted, releasing a small jet of flame from the pit of each nostril, and then, as one, she and Eragon walked through the archway.

LACUNA, PART THE FIRST

Eragon noticed several things at once.

First, that they were standing at one side of a circular chamber over two hundred feet across with a large pit in the center, from which radiated a dull orange glow. Second, that the air was stiflingly hot. Third, that around the outer part of the room were two concentric rings of benchlike tiers—the back one higher than the front—upon which rested numerous dark objects. Fourth, that the wall behind this tier sparkled in numerous places, as if decorated with colored crystal. But he had no opportunity to examine either the wall or the dark objects, for in the open area next to the glowing pit there stood a man with the head of a dragon.

The man was made of metal, and he gleamed like polished steel. He wore no clothes other than a segmented loincloth fashioned out of the same lustrous material as his body, and his chest and limbs rippled with muscles like those of a Kull. In his left hand, he held a metal shield, and in his right, an iridescent sword that Eragon recognized as the blade of a Rider.

Behind the man, set within the far side of the room, Eragon vaguely saw a throne with the outline of the creature's body worn into its back and seat.

The dragon-headed man strode forward. His skin and joints moved as smoothly as flesh, but every step sounded as if a great weight was being dropped onto the floor. He stopped thirty feet from Eragon and Saphira and stared at them with eyes that flickered like a pair of crimson flames. Then, lifting his scaled head, he uttered a peculiar metallic roar that echoed until it seemed as if a dozen creatures were bellowing at them.

Even as Eragon was wondering whether they were supposed to fight the creature, he felt a strange, vast mind touch his. The consciousness was unlike any he had encountered before, and it seemed to contain a host of shouting voices, a great, disjointed chorus that reminded him of the wind inside a storm.

Before he could react, the mind stabbed through his defenses and seized control of his thoughts. For all the time he had spent practicing with Glaedr, Arya, and Saphira, he could not stop the attack; he could not even slow it. He might as well have tried to hold back the tide with his bare hands.

A blur of light and a roar of incoherent noise surrounded him as the yammering chorus forced itself into every nook and cranny of his being. Then it felt as if the invader tore his mind into a half-dozen pieces—each of which remained aware of the others, but none of which was free to do as it wished—and his vision fragmented, as if he were seeing the chamber through the facets of a jewel.

Six different memories began to race through his fractured consciousness. He had not chosen to recall them; they simply appeared, and they flew past faster than he could follow. At the same time, his body bent and flexed in various poses, and then his arm lifted Brisingr to where his eyes could see, and he beheld six identical versions of the sword. The invader even had him cast a spell, the purpose of which he did not and could not understand, for the only thoughts he had were those the other allowed. Nor did he feel any emotion but that of fading alarm.

For what seemed like hours, the alien mind examined every one of his memories, from the moment he had set out from his family's farm to hunt deer in the Spine—three days before he had found Saphira's egg—up until the present. In the back of his mind, Eragon could sense the same thing happening to Saphira, but the knowledge meant nothing to him.

At last, long after he would have given up hope of release if he still had command of his thoughts, the whirling chorus carefully rejoined the pieces of his mind and then withdrew.

Eragon staggered forward and dropped to one knee before he was able to regain his balance. Beside him, Saphira lurched and snapped at the air.

How? he thought. *Who?* To capture both of them at once, and Glaedr as well, he assumed, was something he did not believe even Galbatorix was capable of.

Again the consciousness pressed against Eragon's mind, but this time it did not attack. This time it said, *Our apologies, Saphira. Our apologies, Eragon, but we had to be certain of your intentions. Welcome to the Vault of Souls. Long have we waited for you. And welcome to you as well, cousin. We are glad that you are still alive. Take now your memories, and know that your task is at long last complete!*

A bolt of energy flashed between Glaedr and the consciousness. An instant later, Glaedr uttered a mental bellow that made Eragon's temples throb with pain. A surge of jumbled emotions rushed forth from the golden dragon: sorrow, triumph, disbelief, regret, and, overriding them all, a sense of joyous relief so intense, Eragon found himself smiling without knowing why. And brushing against Glaedr's mind, he felt not just one strange mind but a multitude, all whispering and murmuring.

"Who?" whispered Eragon. Before them, the man with the head of a dragon had not shifted so much as an inch.

Eragon, said Saphira. *Look at the wall. Look . . .*

He looked. And he saw that the circular wall was not decorated with crystal, as he had first taken it to be. Rather, dozens upon dozens of alcoves dotted the wall, and within each alcove rested a glittering orb. Some were large, some were small, but they all pulsed with a soft inner glow, like coals smoldering in a dying campfire.

Eragon's heart skipped a beat as comprehension dawned upon him.

He lowered his gaze to the dark objects on the tiers below; they were smooth and ovoid and appeared to have been sculpted from stone of differing colors. As with the orbs, some were large and some were small, but regardless of their size, their shape was one he would have recognized anywhere.

A hot flush crept over him, and his knees grew weak. *It cannot be.* He wanted to believe what he saw, but he feared that it might be an illusion created to prey on his hopes. And yet the possibility that what he beheld was actually there took his breath away and left him staggered and overwhelmed to such a degree that he knew not what to do or say. Saphira's reaction was much the same, if not stronger.

Then the mind spoke again: *You are not mistaken, hatchlings, nor do your eyes deceive you. We are the secret hope of our race. Here lie our hearts of hearts—the last free Eldunarí in the land—and here lie the eggs that we have guarded for over a century.*

LACUNA, PART THE SECOND

or a moment, Eragon was unable to move or breathe.

Then he whispered, "Eggs, Saphira. . . . Eggs."

She shivered, as if with cold, and the scales along her spine prickled and lifted their tips slightly from her hide.

Who are you? he asked the mind. *How do we know if we can trust you?*

They speak the truth, Eragon, said Glaedr in the ancient language. *I know, for Oromis was among those who devised the plan for this place.*

Oromis . . . ?

Before Glaedr could elaborate, the other mind said, *My name is Umaroth. My Rider was the elf Vrael, leader of our order before our doom came upon us. I speak for the others but I do not command them, for while many of us were bonded with Riders, more were not, and our wild brethren acknowledge no authority but their own.* This he said with a hint of exasperation. *It would be too confusing for all of us to speak at once, so my voice will stand for the rest.*

Are you . . . ? And Eragon indicated the silvery, dragon-headed man in front of him and Saphira.

Nay, replied Umaroth. *He is Cuaroc, Hunter of the Nïdhwal and Bane of the Urgals. Silvarí the Enchantress fashioned for him the body he now wears, so that we would have a champion to defend us should Galbatorix or any foes force their way into the Vault of Souls.*

As Umaroth spoke, the dragon-headed man reached across his torso with his right hand, undid a hidden latch, and pulled open the front of his chest, as if he were pulling open the door to a cupboard. Within Cuaroc's chest nestled a purple heart of hearts, which was surrounded by thousands of silver wires, each no thicker than a hair.

Then Cuaroc swung shut his breastplate, and Umaroth said, *No, I am over here*, and he directed Eragon's vision toward an alcove that contained a large white Eldunarí.

Eragon slowly sheathed Brisingr.

Eggs and Eldunarí. Eragon could not seem to grasp the enormity of the revelation all at once. His thoughts felt slow and sluggish, as if he had taken a blow to the head—which, in a way, he supposed he had.

He started toward the tiers to the right of the black, glyph-covered arch, then paused before Cuaroc and said, both out loud and with his mind, "May I?"

The dragon-headed man clacked his teeth together and retreated with crashing steps to stand by the glowing pit in the center of the room. He kept his sword out, however, something of which Eragon remained constantly aware.

A sense of wonder and reverence gripped Eragon as he approached the eggs. He leaned against the lower tier and released a shuddering breath while he stared at a gold and red egg that was almost five feet tall. Struck by a sudden urge, he peeled off a glove and placed the palm of his bare hand against the egg. It was warm to the touch, and when he extended his mind along with his hand, he could feel the slumbering consciousness of the unhatched dragon within.

Saphira's hot breath passed across his neck as she joined him.

Your egg was smaller than this, he said.

That is because my mother was not so old and not so large as the dragon who laid this one.

Ahh. I hadn't thought of that.

He looked out over the rest of the eggs and felt his throat tighten. "There are so many," he whispered. He pressed his shoulder against Saphira's massive jaw and felt the quivers coursing through her. She wanted, he could tell, nothing more than to rejoice and embrace the minds of her kin, but like him, she could hardly bring herself to believe that what she beheld was real.

She snorted and swung her head around until she was looking

at the rest of the room, and then she uttered a roar that shook dust from the ceiling. *How?!* she growled with her mind. *How could you have escaped Galbatorix? We dragons do not hide when we fight. We are not cowards to run from danger. Explain yourselves!*

Not so loudly, Bjartskular, or you will upset the younglings in their eggs, chided Umaroth.

Saphira's muzzle creased as she snarled. *Then speak, old one, and tell us how this can be.*

For a moment, Umaroth seemed amused, but when the dragon answered her, his words were somber. *You are correct: we are not cowards, and we do not hide when we fight, but even dragons may lie in wait so as to catch their prey by surprise. Would you not agree, Saphira?*

She snorted again and lashed her tail from side to side.

And we are not like the Fanghur or the lesser vipers who abandon their young to live or die according to the whims of fate. Had we joined the battle for Doru Araeba, we would only have been destroyed. Galbatorix's victory would have been absolute—as indeed he believes it was—and our kind would have passed forever from the face of the earth.

Once the true extent of Galbatorix's power and ambition became evident, said Glaedr, *and once we realized that he and the traitors with him intended to attack Vroengard, then Vrael, Umaroth, Oromis, and I, and a few others, decided that it would be best to hide the eggs of our race, as well as a number of the Eldunarí. It was easy to convince the wild dragons; Galbatorix had been hunting them, and they had no defense against his magic. They came here, and they gave charge of their unhatched offspring to Vrael, and those who could laid eggs when otherwise they would have waited, for we knew that the survival of our race was threatened. Our precautions, it seems, were well thought of.*

Eragon rubbed his temples. "Why didn't you know of this before? Why didn't Oromis? And how is it possible to hide their minds? You told me it couldn't be done."

It can't, replied Glaedr, *or at least not with magic alone. In this instance, however, where magic fails, distance may yet succeed. That is why we are far underground, a mile below Mount Erolas. Even if*

559

Galbatorix or the Forsworn had thought to search with their minds in such an unlikely location, the intervening rock would have made it difficult for them to feel much more than a confused flux of energy, which they would have attributed to eddies within the blood of the earth, which lies close beneath us. Moreover, before the Battle of Doru Araeba, more than a hundred years ago, all of the Eldunarí were placed in a trance so deep as to be akin to death, which made them that much more difficult to find. Our plan was to rouse them after the fighting was over, but those who built this place also cast a spell that would wake them from their trance once several moons had passed.

As it did, said Umaroth. The Vault of Souls was placed here for another reason as well. The pit you see before you opens onto a lake of molten stone that has lain beneath these mountains since the world was born. It provides the warmth needed to keep the eggs comfortable, and it also provides the light needed for us Eldunarí to maintain our strength.

Addressing Glaedr, Eragon said, You still haven't answered my question: why didn't you or Oromis remember this place?

Umaroth was the one who answered: Because all who knew of the Vault of Souls agreed to have the knowledge removed from their minds and replaced with a false memory, including Glaedr. It was not an easy decision, especially for the mothers of the eggs, but we could not allow anyone outside this room to remain in possession of the truth, lest Galbatorix should learn of us from them. So we said farewell to our friends and comrades, knowing full well that we might never see them again and that, if the worst came to pass, they would die believing we had entered into the void. . . . As I said, it was not an easy decision. We also erased from all memory the names of the rock that marks the entrance to this sanctuary, even as we had earlier erased the names of the thirteen dragons who chose to betray us.

I've spent the last hundred years believing that our kind was doomed to oblivion, said Glaedr. Now, to know that all my anguish was for naught . . . I am glad, though, that I was able to help safeguard our race through my ignorance.

Then Saphira said to Umaroth, *Why didn't Galbatorix notice that you and the eggs were missing?*

He thought we were killed in the battle. We were but a small portion of the Eldunarí on Vroengard, not enough for him to become suspicious of our absence. As for the eggs, no doubt he was enraged by their loss, but he would have had no reason to believe trickery was involved.

Ah yes, said Glaedr sadly. *That was why Thuviel agreed to sacrifice himself: to conceal our deception from Galbatorix.*

"But didn't Thuviel kill many of his own?" said Eragon.

He did, and it was a great tragedy, said Umaroth. *However, we had agreed that he was not to act unless it was obvious that defeat was unavoidable. By immolating himself, he destroyed the buildings where we normally kept the eggs, and he also rendered the island poisonous to ensure that Galbatorix would not choose to settle here.*

"Did he know why he was killing himself?"

At the time, no, only that it was necessary. One of the Forsworn had slain Thuviel's dragon a month before. Though he had refrained from passing into the void, as we needed every warrior we had to fight Galbatorix, Thuviel no longer wished to continue living. He was glad for the task then; it granted him the release he yearned for while also allowing him to serve our cause. By the gift of his life, he secured a future for both our race and the Riders. He was a great and courageous hero, and his name shall someday be sung in every corner of Alagaësia.

And after the battle, you waited, said Saphira.

And then we waited, Umaroth agreed. The thought of spending over a hundred years within a single room buried deep underground made Eragon quail. *But we have not been idle. When we woke from our trance, we began to cast our minds out, slowly at first, and then with ever-greater confidence once we realized Galbatorix and the Forsworn had left the island. Together our strength is great, and we have been able to observe much of what has transpired throughout the land in the years since. We cannot scry, not normally, but we can see the skeins of tangled energy strewn across Alagaësia, and we can often listen to the thoughts*

561

of those who make no effort to defend their minds. In that way, we have gathered our information.

As the decades crawled past, we began to despair that anyone would be able to kill Galbatorix. We were prepared to wait for centuries if needed, but we could sense the Egg-breaker's power growing, and we feared that our wait might be one of thousands of years instead of hundreds. That, we agreed, would be unacceptable, both for the sake of our sanity and for the sake of the younglings in the eggs. They are bound with magic that slows their bodies, and they can remain as they are for years more, but it is not good for them to stay within their shells for too long. If they do, their minds can grow twisted and strange.

Thus spurred by our concern, we began to intervene in the events we saw. At first only in small ways: a nudge here, a whispered suggestion there, a sense of alarm to one about to be ambushed. We did not always succeed, but we were able to help those who still fought Galbatorix, and as time progressed, we grew more adept and more confident with our tampering. On a few rare occasions, our presence was noticed, but no one was ever able to determine who or what we were. Thrice we were able to arrange the death of one of the Forsworn; when not ruled by his passions, Brom was a useful weapon for us.

"You helped Brom!" Eragon exclaimed.

We did, and many others as well. When the human known as Hefring stole Saphira's egg from Galbatorix's treasure room—nigh on twenty years ago—we aided his escape, but we went too far, for he noticed us and became frightened. He fled and did not meet with the Varden as he was supposed to. Later, after Brom had rescued your egg, and the Varden and the elves started to bring younglings before it in an attempt to find the one for whom you would hatch, we decided that we should make certain preparations for that eventuality. So we reached out to the werecats, who have long been friends of the dragons, and we spoke with them. They agreed to help us, and to them we gave the knowledge of the Rock of Kuthian and the brightsteel beneath the roots of the Menoa tree, and then we removed all memory of our conversation from their minds.

"You did all that, from here?" said Eragon, wondering.

And more. Have you never wondered why Saphira's egg happened to appear in front of you while you were in the midst of the Spine?

That was your doing? said Saphira, her shock as strong as Eragon's.

"I thought it was because Brom is my father, and Arya mistook me for him."

Nay, said Umaroth. *The spells of elves do not so easily go astray. We altered the flow of magic so that you and Saphira would meet. We thought there was a chance—a small one, but a chance nevertheless—that you might prove a fit match for her. We were right.*

"Why didn't you bring us here sooner, though?" asked Eragon.

Because you needed time for your training, and otherwise we risked alerting Galbatorix to our presence before you or the Varden were ready to confront him. If we had contacted you after the Battle of the Burning Plains, for example, what good would it have done, with the Varden still so far from Urû'baen?

There was silence for a minute.

Eragon slowly said, "What else have you done for us?"

A few nudges, warnings mostly. Visions of Arya in Gil'ead, when she needed your aid. The healing of your back during the Agaetí Blödhren.

A feeling of disapproval emanated from Glaedr. *You sent them to Gil'ead, untrained and without wards, knowing that they would have to face a Shade?*

We thought Brom would be with them, but even once he died, we could not stop them, for they still had to go to Gil'ead to find the Varden.

"Wait," said Eragon. "You were responsible for my . . . transformation?"

In part. We touched the reflection of our race that the elves summon during the celebration. We provided the inspiration, and she-he-it provided the strength for the spell.

Eragon looked down and clenched his hand for a moment, not angry, but so filled with other emotions that he could not remain still. Saphira, Arya, his sword, the very shape of his body—he owed them all to the dragons within the room. "Elrun ono," he said. Thank you.

You are most welcome, Shadeslayer.

"Have you helped Roran as well?"

Your cousin has required no assistance from us. Umaroth paused. *We have watched both of you, Eragon and Saphira, for many years now. We have watched you grow from hatchlings to mighty warriors, and we are proud of all you have accomplished. You, Eragon, have been all we hoped for in a new Rider. And you, Saphira, have proven yourself worthy of being counted among the greatest members of our race.*

Saphira's joy and pride mingled with Eragon's. He sank to one knee, even as she pawed at the floor and dipped her head. Eragon felt like jumping and shouting and otherwise celebrating, but he did none of those things. Instead, he said, "My sword is yours—"

—*And my teeth and claws,* said Saphira.

"To the end of our days," they concluded in unison. "What would you have of us, Ebrithilar?"

Satisfaction came from Umaroth, and he replied, *Now that you have found us, our days of hiding are over; we would go with you to Urû'baen and fight alongside you to kill Galbatorix. The time has come for us to leave our den and once and for all confront that traitorous eggbreaker. Without us, he would be able to pry open your minds as easily as did we, for he has many Eldunarí at his command.*

I cannot carry all of you, said Saphira.

You shall not have to, said Umaroth. *Five of us will stay to watch over the eggs, along with Cuaroc. In the event we should fail to defeat Galbatorix, they will tamper no more with the skeins of energy, but will content themselves with waiting until it is again safe for dragons to venture forth in Alagaësia. But you need not worry; we shall not be a burden to you, for we will provide the strength to move our weight.*

"How many of you are there?" asked Eragon, gazing around the room.

One hundred and thirty-six. But do not think we will be able to best the Eldunarí Galbatorix has enslaved. We are too few, and those who were chosen to be placed within this vault were either too old and too valuable to risk in the fighting or too young and too inexperienced to participate in the battle. That is why I elected to join them; I provide a bridge between the groups, a point of common understanding that otherwise would be lacking. Those who are older are wise and powerful indeed, but their minds wander down strange paths, and it is often hard to convince them to concentrate upon anything outside of their dreams. Those who are younger are more unfortunate: they parted from their bodies before they should have; thus their minds remain limited by the size of their Eldunarí, which can never grow or expand once it leaves the flesh. Let that be a lesson to you, Saphira, not to disgorge your Eldunarí unless you have reached a respectable size or face the direst of emergencies.

"So we are still outmatched," said Eragon grimly.

Yes, Shadeslayer. But now Galbatorix cannot force you to your knees the moment he sees you. We may not be able to best them, but we will be able to hold off his Eldunarí long enough for you and Saphira to do what you must. And have hope; we know many things, many secrets, about war and magic and the workings of the world. We will teach you what we can, and it may be that some piece of our knowledge will allow you to slay the king.

Thereafter, Saphira inquired of the eggs and learned that two hundred and forty-three had been saved. Twenty-six were set to be joined with Riders; the rest were unbonded. Then they fell to discussing the flight to Urû'baen. While Umaroth and Glaedr advised Saphira as to the quickest way to reach the city, the dragon-headed man sheathed his sword, laid down his shield, and, one by one, began to remove the Eldunarí from their alcoves in the wall. He placed each of the gemlike orbs in the silk purse upon which it had been resting, then piled them gently on the floor next to the glowing pit. The girth of the largest Eldunarí was so immense, the metal-bodied dragon was unable to wrap his arms all the way around it.

As Cuaroc worked, and as they talked, Eragon continued to feel a sense of dazed incredulousness. He had hardly dared to dream that there were any other dragons hiding in Alagaësia. Yet here they were, the remnants of a lost age. It was as if the stories of old had come to life, and he and Saphira were caught in the midst of them.

Saphira's emotions were more complicated. Knowing that her race was no longer doomed to extinction had lifted a shadow from her mind—a shadow that had lain there for as long as Eragon could remember—and her thoughts soared with a joy so profound, it seemed to make her eyes and scales sparkle brighter than normal. Still, a curious defensiveness tempered her elation, as though she was self-conscious before the Eldunarí.

Even through his daze, Eragon was aware of Glaedr's change of mood; he did not seem to have entirely forgotten his sorrow, but he was the happiest Eragon had felt him since Oromis had died. And while Glaedr was not deferential to Umaroth, he treated the other dragon with a level of respect that Eragon had not witnessed from him before, not even when Glaedr had spoken with Queen Islanzadí.

When Cuaroc was nearly done with his task, Eragon walked to the edge of the pit and peered into it. He saw a circular shaft that sank through the stone for over a hundred feet, then opened onto a cave half filled with a sea of glowing stone. The thick yellow liquid bubbled and splattered like a pot of boiling glue, and tails of swirling fumes rose from its heaving surface. He thought he saw a light, like that of a spirit, flit across the face of the burning sea, but it vanished so quickly, he could not be sure.

Come, Eragon, said Umaroth as the dragon-headed man set the last of the Eldunarí who were to travel with them upon the pile. *You must cast a spell now. The words are as follows—*

Eragon frowned as he listened. "What is the . . . *twist* in the second line? What am I supposed to twist, the air?"

Umaroth's explanation left Eragon even more confused. Umaroth attempted again, but Eragon still could not understand the concept. Other, older Eldunarí joined in the conversation, but their explanations made even less sense, for they came mainly as a torrent of overlapping images, sensations, and strange, esoteric comparisons that left Eragon hopelessly bewildered.

Somewhat to his relief, Saphira and Glaedr seemed similarly

puzzled, although Glaedr said, *I think I understand, but it is like trying to catch hold of a frightened fish; whenever I think I have it, it slips out between my teeth.*

At last Umaroth said, *This is a lesson for another time. You know what the spell is supposed to do, if not how. That will have to suffice. Take from us the strength needed and cast it, and then let us be off.*

Nervous, Eragon fixed the words of the spell in his mind to avoid making mistakes, and then he began to speak. As he uttered the lines, he drew upon the reserves of the Eldunarí, and his skin tingled as an enormous rush of energy poured through him, like a river of water both hot and cold.

The air around the uneven pile of Eldunarí rippled and shimmered; then the pile seemed to fold in on itself and it winked out of sight. A gust of wind tousled Eragon's hair, and a soft, dull *thud* echoed throughout the chamber.

Astonished, Eragon watched as Saphira pushed her head forward and swung it through the spot where the Eldunarí had just been. They had disappeared, completely and utterly, as if they had never existed, and yet he and she could still feel the dragons' minds close at hand.

Once you leave the vault, said Umaroth, *the entrance to this pocket of space will remain at a fixed distance above and behind you at all times, save when you are in a confined area or when a person's body should happen to pass through that space. The entrance is no larger than a pinprick, but it is more deadly than any sword; it would cut right through your flesh were you to touch it.*

Saphira sniffed. *Even your scent has gone.*

"Who discovered how to do this?" Eragon asked, amazed.

A hermit who lived on the northern coast of Alagaësia twelve hundred years ago, Umaroth replied. *It is a valuable trick if you want to hide something in plain sight, but dangerous and difficult to do correctly.* The dragon was silent for a moment thereafter, and Eragon could feel him gathering his thoughts. Then Umaroth said, *There is one more thing you and Saphira need to know. The moment you pass through the great arch behind you—the Gate of Vergathos—you will begin to forget about Cuaroc and the eggs hidden here, and by the time you reach the stone doors at the end of the tunnel, all memory of them will have vanished from your minds. Even we Eldunarí will forget about the eggs. If we succeed in killing Galbatorix, the gate will restore our memories, but until then, we must remain ignorant of them.* Umaroth seemed to rumble. *It is . . . unpleasant, I know, but we cannot allow Galbatorix to learn of the eggs.*

Eragon disliked the idea, but he could not think of a reasonable alternative.

Thank you for telling us, said Saphira, and Eragon added his thanks to hers.

Then the great metal warrior, Cuaroc, picked up his shield from the floor, drew his sword, and walked over to his ancient throne and sat thereon. After laying his naked blade across his knees and leaning his shield against the side of the throne, he placed his hands flat upon his thighs and grew as still as a statue, save for the dancing sprites of his crimson eyes, which gazed out over the eggs.

Eragon shivered as he turned his back on the throne. There was something haunting about the sight of the lone figure at the far side of the chamber. Knowing that Cuaroc and the other Eldunarí who were staying behind might have to remain there by themselves for another hundred years—or longer—made it difficult for Eragon to leave.

Farewell, he said with his mind.

Farewell, Shadeslayer, five whispers answered. *Farewell, Brightscales. Luck be with you.*

Then Eragon squared his shoulders, and together he and Saphira strode through the Gate of Vergathos and thus departed the Vault of Souls.

RETURN

Eragon frowned as he stepped out of the tunnel into the early-afternoon sunlight that bathed the clearing before the Rock of Kuthian.

He felt as if he had forgotten something important. He tried to remember what, but nothing came to mind, only a sense of emptiness that unsettled him. Had it to do with . . . no, he could not recall. *Saphira, did you . . .* he started to say, then trailed off.

What?

Nothing. I just thought . . . Never mind; it doesn't matter.

Behind them, the doors to the tunnel swung shut with a hollow boom, and the lines of glyphs upon them faded away, and the rough, mossy spire once again appeared to be a solid piece of stone.

Come, said Umaroth, *let us be away. The day grows long, and many leagues lie between here and Urû'baen.*

Eragon glanced around the clearing, still feeling as if he was missing something; then he nodded and climbed into Saphira's saddle.

As he tightened the straps around his legs, the eerie chatter of a shadow bird sounded among the heavy-boughed fir trees to the right. He looked, but the creature was nowhere to be seen. He made a face. He was glad to have visited Vroengard, but he was equally glad to be leaving. The island was an unfriendly place.

Shall we? asked Saphira.

Let's, he said with a sense of relief.

With a sweep of her wings, Saphira jumped into the air and took flight over the grove of apple trees at the other side of the clearing. She rose quickly above the floor of the bowl-shaped valley, circling the ruins of Doru Araeba as she climbed. Once she was high enough to soar over the mountains, she turned east and set off for the mainland and Urû'baen, leaving behind the remains of the Riders' once-glorious stronghold.

THE CITY OF SORROWS

The sun was still near its zenith when the Varden arrived at Urû'baen.

Roran heard the cries from the men at the head of his column as they crested a ridge. Curious, he looked up from the heels of the dwarf in front of him, and when he arrived at the top of the ridge, he paused to take in the view, as had each of the warriors before him.

The land sloped gently downward for several miles, flattening out into a broad plain dotted with farms, mills, and grand stone estates that reminded him of the ones near Aroughs. Some five miles away, the plain arrived at the outer walls of Urû'baen.

Unlike those of Dras-Leona, the walls of the capital were long enough to encompass the whole of the city. They were taller, too; even from a distance, Roran could see that they dwarfed those of both Dras-Leona and Aroughs. He guessed that they stood at least three hundred feet tall. Upon the wide battlements, he spotted ballistae and catapults mounted at regular intervals.

The sight worried him. The machines would be difficult to take down—no doubt they were protected from magical attacks—and he knew from experience just how deadly such weapons could be.

Behind the walls was an odd mixture of human-built structures and those he guessed the elves had made. The most prominent of the elven buildings were six tall, graceful towers—made of a malachite-green stone—which were scattered in an arc throughout what he assumed was the oldest part of the city. Two of the towers were missing their roofs, and he thought he saw the stumps of two more partially buried among the jumble of houses below.

What interested him most, however, was not the wall or the buildings, but the fact that much of the city lay shadowed underneath a huge stone shelf, which must have been over half a mile wide and five hundred feet thick at its narrowest. The overhang formed one end of a massive, sloping hill that stretched off to the northeast for several miles. Atop the craggy lip of the shelf stood another wall, like that which surrounded the city, and several thick watchtowers.

At the back of the cavelike recess underneath the shelf was an enormous citadel adorned with a profusion of towers and parapets. The citadel rose high above the rest of the city, high enough that it almost scraped the underside of the shelf. Most intimidating of all was the gate set within the front of the fortress: a great, gaping cavern that looked large enough for Saphira and Thorn to walk through side by side.

Roran's gut tightened. If the gate was any indication, Shruikan was big enough to wipe out their whole army by himself. *Eragon and Saphira had better hurry up*, he thought. *And the elves too.* From what he had seen, the elves might be able to hold their own against the king's black dragon, but even they would be hard-pressed to kill him.

All that and more Roran took in as he paused on the ridge. Then he tugged on Snowfire's reins. Behind him, the white stallion snorted and followed as Roran resumed his weary march, following the winding road as it descended to the lowlands.

He could have ridden—was supposed to ride, actually, as captain of his battalion—but after his trip to Aroughs and back, he had come to loathe sitting in a saddle.

As he walked, he tried to figure out how best to attack the city. The pocket of stone Urû'baen sat nestled within would prevent assaults from the sides and the rear and would interfere with attacks from above, which was surely why the elves had chosen to settle in that location to begin with.

If we could somehow break off the overhang, we could crush the citadel and most of the city, he thought, but he deemed that unlikely, as the stone was too thick. *Still, we might be able to take the wall at the top of the hill. Then we could drop stones and pour boiling oil onto those below. It wouldn't be easy, though. Uphill fighting, and those walls . . . Maybe the elves could manage it. Or the Kull. They might enjoy it.*

The Ramr River was several miles north of Urû'baen, too far to be of any help. Saphira could dig a ditch large enough to divert it, but even she would need weeks to complete such a project, and the Varden did not have weeks' worth of food. They had only a few days left. After that, they would have to starve or disband.

Their only option was to attack before the Empire did. Not that Roran believed Galbatorix *would* attack. So far the king had seemed content to allow the Varden to come to him. *Why should he risk his neck? The longer he waits, the weaker we grow.*

Which meant a frontal assault—a brazen fool's charge over open ground toward walls too thick to breach and too tall to climb while archers and war machines shot at them the whole time. Just imagining it made a sweat break out on his brow. They would die in droves. He cursed. *We'll dash ourselves to pieces, and all the while Galbatorix will sit laughing in his throne room. . . . If we can get close to the walls, the soldiers won't be able to hit us with their foul contraptions, but then we'll be vulnerable to pitch and oil and rocks being dropped on our heads.*

Even if they managed to breach the walls, they would still have the whole of Galbatorix's army to overcome. More important than the defenses of the city, then, would be the character and quality of the men the Varden would face. Would they fight to their last breath? Could they be frightened? Would they break and flee if pushed hard enough? What manner of oaths and spells bound them?

The Varden's spies had reported that Galbatorix had placed an earl by the name of Lord Barst in command of the troops within Urû'baen. Roran had never heard of Barst before, but the information seemed to dismay Jörmundur, and the men in Roran's battalion had shared enough stories to persuade him of Barst's villainy. Supposedly, Barst had been lord of a rather large estate near Gil'ead, which the invasion of the elves had forced him to abandon. His vassals had lived in mortal fear of him, for Barst had a tendency to resolve disputes and punish criminals in the harshest manner possible, often choosing to simply execute those he believed were in the wrong. Of itself, that was hardly notable; many a lord throughout the Empire had a reputation for brutality. Barst, however, was not only ruthless but strong—impressively strong—and cunning to boot. In everything Roran had heard about Barst, the man's intelligence had been clear. Barst might be a bastard, but he was a smart bastard, and Roran knew it would be a mistake to underestimate him. Galbatorix would not have chosen a weakling or a dullard to command his men.

And then there were Thorn and Murtagh. Galbatorix might not stir from his stronghold, but the red dragon and his Rider were sure to defend the city. *Eragon and Saphira will have to lure them away. Otherwise, we'll never make it over the walls.* Roran frowned. That would be a problem. Murtagh was stronger than Eragon now. Eragon would need the help of the elves to kill him.

Once again, Roran felt bitter anger and resentment welling up inside him. He hated that he was at the mercy of those who could use magic. At least when it came to strength and cunning, a man might make up for a lack of one with a surfeit of the other. But there was no making up for the absence of magic.

Frustrated, he scooped up a pebble from the ground and, as Eragon had taught him, said, "Stenr rïsa." The pebble remained motionless.

The pebble *always* remained motionless.

He snorted and tossed it by the side of the road.

His wife and unborn child were with the Varden, and yet there was nothing he could do to kill either Murtagh or Galbatorix. He clenched his fists and imagined breaking things. Bones, mostly.

Maybe we should flee. It was the first time the thought had occurred to him. He knew there were lands to the east beyond Galbatorix's reach—fertile plains where none but nomads lived. If the other villagers came with him and Katrina, they could start anew, free of the Empire and Galbatorix. The idea made him sick to consider, however. He would be abandoning Eragon, his men, and the land that he called home. *No. I won't allow our child to be born into a world where Galbatorix still holds sway. Better to die than to live in fear.*

Of course, that still did not solve the problem of how to capture Urû'baen. Always before, there had been a weakness he could exploit. In Carvahall, it had been the Ra'zac's failure to understand that the villagers would fight. When he wrestled the Urgal Yarbog, it had been the creature's horns. In Aroughs, it had been the canals. But here at Urû'baen, he saw no weaknesses, no place where he could turn his opponents' strength against them.

If we had the supplies, I would wait and starve them out. That would be the best way. Anything else is madness. But as he knew, war was a catalog of madness.

Magic is the only way, he finally concluded. *Magic and Saphira. If we can kill Murtagh, then either she or the elves will have to help us past the walls.*

He scowled, a sour taste in his mouth, and quickened his stride. The faster they made camp, the better. His feet were sore from walking, and if he was going to die in a senseless charge, then at least he wanted a hot meal and a good night's sleep beforehand.

The Varden set up their tents a mile from Urû'baen, by a small stream that fed the Ramr River. Then the men, dwarves, and Urgals began constructing defenses, a process that would continue until night and then resume in the morning. In fact, as long as they stayed in one location, they would continue to work on reinforcing their perimeter. The warriors detested the labor, but it kept them busy and, moreover, it might save their lives.

Everyone thought the orders came from the shadow-Eragon. Roran knew they actually came from Jörmundur. He had come to respect the older warrior since Nasuada's abduction and Eragon's departure. Jörmundur had been fighting the Empire nearly his whole life, and he had a deep understanding of tactics and logistics. He and Roran got along well; they were both men of steel, not magic.

And then there was King Orrin, with whom—after the initial defenses had been established—Roran found himself arguing. Orrin never failed to irritate him; if anyone was going to get them killed, it was him. Roran knew that offending a king was not the healthiest thing to do, but the fool wanted to send a messenger to the front gates of Urû'baen and issue a formal challenge, the way they had at Dras-Leona and Belatona.

"Do you *want* to provoke Galbatorix?" Roran growled. "If we do that, he might respond!"

"Well, of course," said King Orrin, drawing himself upright. "It's only proper that we announce our intentions and provide him with the opportunity to parley for peace."

Roran stared; then he turned away in disgust and said to Jörmundur, "Can't you make him see reason?"

The three of them were gathered in Orrin's pavilion, where the king had summoned them.

"Your Majesty," said Jörmundur, "Roran is right. It would be best to wait to contact the Empire."

"But they can see us," protested Orrin. "We're camped right outside their walls. It would be . . . *rude* not to send an envoy to state our position. You are both commoners; I would not expect you to understand. Royalty demands certain courtesies, even if we are at war."

An urge to strike the king swept through Roran. "Are you so puffed up as to believe Galbatorix considers you an equal? Bah! We're insects to him. He cares nothing for your courtesy. You forget, Galbatorix was a commoner like us before he overthrew the Riders. His ways are not your ways. There is no one like him in the world, and you think to predict him? You think to placate him? Bah!"

Orrin's face colored, and he threw aside his goblet of wine, dashing it against the rug upon the ground. "You go too far, Stronghammer. No man has the right to insult me like that."

"I have the right to do whatever I want," growled Roran. "I'm not one of your subjects. I don't answer to you. I'm a free man, and

I'll insult anyone I choose, whenever I choose, however I choose—even you. It would be a mistake to send that messenger, and I—"

There was a screech of sliding steel as King Orrin tore his sword from its scabbard. He did not catch Roran entirely unawares; Roran already had his hand on his hammer, and as he heard the sound, he yanked the weapon from his belt.

The king's blade was a silver blur in the dim light of the tent. Roran saw where Orrin was going to strike and stepped out of the way. Then he rapped the flat of the king's sword, causing it to flex and ring and leap out of Orrin's hand.

The jeweled weapon fell onto the rug, the blade quivering.

"Sire," cried one of the guards outside. "Are you all right?"

"I just dropped my shield," replied Jörmundur. "There's no need for concern."

"Sir, yes sir."

Roran stared at the king; there was a wild, hunted look on Orrin's face. Without taking his eyes off him, Roran returned his hammer to his belt. "Contacting Galbatorix is stupid and dangerous. If you try, I'll kill whomever you send before he reaches the city."

"You wouldn't dare!" said Orrin.

"I would, and I will. I won't let you endanger the rest of us just to satisfy your royal . . . *pride*. If Galbatorix wants to talk, then he knows where to find us. Otherwise, *let him be*."

Roran stormed out of the pavilion. Outside, he stood with his hands on his hips and gazed at the puffy clouds while he waited for his pulse to subside. Orrin was like a yearling mule: stubborn, over-confident, and all too willing to kick you in the gut if you gave him the opportunity.

And he drinks too much, thought Roran.

He paced in front of the pavilion until Jörmundur emerged. Before the other man could speak, Roran said, "I'm sorry."

"As well you should be." Jörmundur drew a hand over his face, then removed a clay pipe from the purse on his belt and began to fill it with cardus weed, which he tamped down with the ball of his thumb. "It took me this whole time to convince him not to send an envoy just to spite you." He paused for a moment. "Would you really kill one of Orrin's men?"

"I don't make idle threats," said Roran.

"No, I didn't think so. . . . Well, let's hope it doesn't come to that." Jörmundur started down the path between the tents, and Roran followed. As they walked, men moved out of their way and respectfully dipped their heads. Gesturing with his unlit pipe, Jörmundur said, "I admit, I've wanted to give Orrin a good tongue-lashing on more than one occasion." His lips stretched in a thin smile. "Unfortunately, discretion has always gotten the better of me."

"Has he always been so . . . intractable?"

"Hmm? No, no. In Surda, he was far more reasonable."

"What happened, then?"

"Fear, I think. It does strange things to men."

"Aye."

"It may offend you to hear this, but you acted rather stupidly yourself."

"I know. My temper got the better of me."

"And you've earned yourself a king as a foe."

"You mean *another* king."

Jörmundur uttered a low laugh. "Yes, well, I suppose when you have Galbatorix as a personal enemy, all others seem rather harmless. Nevertheless . . ." He stopped by a campfire and pulled a thin burning branch from the midst of the flames. Tipping the end of the branch into the bowl of his pipe, he puffed several times, setting the flame, then threw the branch back into the fire. "Nevertheless, I wouldn't ignore Orrin's anger. He was willing to kill you back there. If he holds a grudge, and I think he will, he may seek his revenge. I'll post a guard by your tent for the next few days. After that, though . . ." Jörmundur shrugged.

"After that, we may all be dead or enslaved."

They walked in silence for a few more minutes, Jörmundur puffing on his pipe the whole while. As they were about to part, Roran said, "When you see Orrin next . . ."

"Yes?"

"Perhaps you can let him know that if he or his men hurt Katrina, I'll rip out his guts in front of the whole camp."

Jörmundur tucked his chin against his breast and stood thinking for a moment, then he looked up and nodded. "I think I might find a way to do that, Stronghammer."

"My thanks."

"You're most welcome. As always, this was a unique pleasure."

"Sir."

Roran sought out Katrina and convinced her to bring their dinner to the northern embankment, where he kept vigil for any messengers Orrin might send. They ate on a cloth that Katrina spread over the freshly turned soil, then sat together as the shadows grew long and the stars began to appear in the purple sky above the overhang.

"I'm glad to be here," she said, leaning her head against his shoulder.

"Are you? Really?"

"It's beautiful, and I have you all to myself." She squeezed his arm.

He drew her closer, but the shadow in his heart remained. He could not forget the danger that threatened her and their child. The knowledge that their greatest foe was but a few miles distant burned within him; he wanted nothing more than to leap up, run to Urû'baen, and kill Galbatorix.

But that was impossible, so he smiled and laughed and hid his fear, even as he knew she hid hers.

Blast it, Eragon, he thought, *you'd better hurry, or I swear I'll haunt you from the grave.*

◆ ◆ ◆

WAR COUNCIL

On the flight from Vroengard to Urû'baen, Saphira did not have to battle her way through a storm and was fortunate enough to have a tailwind to speed her progress, for the Eldunarí told her where to find the fast-moving stream of air, which they said blew nearly every day of the year. Also, the Eldunarí fed her a constant supply of energy, so she never flagged or grew tired.

As a result, the city first came into sight on the horizon a mere two days after they departed the island.

Twice during the trip, when the sun was at its brightest, Eragon thought he glimpsed the entrance to the pocket of space where the Eldunarí floated hidden behind Saphira. It appeared as a single dark point, so small that he could not keep his eyes fixed upon it for more than a second. At first he assumed it was a mote of dust, but then he noticed that the point never varied in its distance from Saphira, and when he saw it, it was always in the same place.

As they flew, the dragons had, through Umaroth, poured memory after memory into Eragon and Saphira: a cascade of experiences—battles won and battles lost, loves, hates, spells, events witnessed throughout the land, regrets, realizations, and ponderings concerning the workings of the world. The dragons possessed thousands of years of knowledge, and they seemed driven to share every last bit.

It's too much! Eragon had protested. *We can't remember it all, much less understand it.*

No, said Umaroth. *But you can remember some, and it may be that some will be what you need to defeat Galbatorix. Now, let us continue.*

The torrent of information was overwhelming; at times Eragon felt as if he was forgetting who he was, for the dragons' memories far outnumbered his own. When that happened, he would separate his mind from theirs and repeat his true name to himself until he again felt secure in his identity.

The things he and Saphira learned amazed and troubled him and oftentimes caused him to question his own beliefs. But he never had time to dwell on such thoughts, for there was always another memory to take their place. It would, he knew, take him years to begin to make sense of what the dragons were showing them.

The more he learned about the dragons, the more he regarded them with awe. Those who had lived for hundreds of years were strange in their ways of thinking, and the oldest were as different from Glaedr and Saphira as Glaedr and Saphira were from the Fanghur in the Beor Mountains. Interacting with these elders was confusing and unsettling; they made jumps, associations, and comparisons that seemed meaningless but that Eragon knew made sense at some deep level. He was rarely able to figure out what they were trying to say, and the ancient dragons did not deign to explain themselves in terms that he could understand.

After a while, he realized that they *couldn't* express themselves in any other way. Over the centuries, their minds had changed; what was simple and straightforward for him often seemed complicated for them, and the same was true in reverse. Listening to their thoughts, he felt, must be like listening to the thoughts of a god.

When he made that particular observation, Saphira snorted and said to him, *There is a difference.*

What?

Unlike gods, we take part in the events of the world.

Perhaps the gods choose to act without being seen.

Then what good are they?

You believe that dragons are better than gods? he asked, amused.

When we are fully grown, yes. What creature is greater than us? Even Galbatorix depends upon us for his strength.

What of the Nïdhwal?

She sniffed. *We can swim, but they cannot fly.*

The very oldest of the Eldunarí, a dragon by the name of Valdr—which meant "ruler" in the ancient language—spoke to them directly only once. From him, they received a vision of beams of light turning into waves of sand, as well as a disconcerting sense that everything that seemed solid was mostly empty space. Then Valdr showed them a nest of sleeping starlings, and Eragon could feel their dreams flickering in their minds, fast as the blink of an eye. At first Valdr's emotion was one of contempt—the starlings' dreams seemed tiny, petty, and inconsequential—but then his mood changed and became warm and sympathetic, and even the smallest of the starlings' concerns grew in importance until it seemed equal to the worries of kings.

Valdr lingered over the vision, as if to make sure that Eragon and Saphira would remember it amid all the other memories. Yet neither of them was certain what the dragon was trying to say, and Valdr refused to explain himself further.

When at last Urû'baen came into view, the Eldunarí ceased sharing their memories with Eragon and Saphira, and Umaroth said, *Now you would be best served by studying the lair of our foe.*

This they did as Saphira descended toward the ground over the course of many leagues. What they saw did not encourage either of them, nor did their moods improve when Glaedr said, *Galbatorix has built much since he drove us from this place. The walls were not so thick nor so tall in our day.*

To which Umaroth added: *Nor was Ilirea this heavily fortified during the war between our kind and the elves. The traitor has burrowed deep and piled a mountain of stone about his hole. He will not come out of his own accord, I think. He is like a badger who has retreated into his den and who will bloody the nose of anyone who tries to dig him out.*

A mile southwest from the walled shelf and the city beneath lay the Varden's camp. It was significantly larger than Eragon remembered, which puzzled him until he realized that Queen Islanzadí and her army must have finally joined forces with the Varden. He gave a small sigh of relief. Even Galbatorix was wary of the might of the elves.

When he and Saphira were a league or so from the tents, the Eldunarí helped Eragon extend the range of his thoughts until he was able to feel the minds of the men, dwarves, elves, and Urgals gathered within the camp. His touch was too light for anyone to notice unless they were deliberately watching for it, and the moment he located the distinctive strain of wild music that marked Blödhgarm's thoughts, he narrowed his focus to the elf alone.

Blödhgarm, he said. *It is I, Eragon.* The more formal phrasing seemed natural to him after so long spent reliving experiences from ages past.

Shadeslayer! Are you safe? Your mind feels most strange. Is Saphira with you? Is she hurt? Has something happened to Glaedr?

They are both well, as am I.

Then— Blödhgarm's confusion was evident.

Cutting him off, Eragon said, *We're not far, but I've hidden us from sight for the time being. Is the illusion of Saphira and me still visible to those below?*

Yes, Shadeslayer. We have Saphira circling the tents a mile above. Sometimes we hide her in a bank of clouds, or we make it seem as if you and she have gone off on patrol, but we dare not let Galbatorix think you've left for long. We will make your images fly away now, so that you may rejoin us without arousing suspicion.

No. Rather, wait and maintain your spells for a while longer.

Shadeslayer?

We are not returning directly to the camp. Eragon glanced at the ground. *There is a small hill perhaps two miles to the southeast. Do you know it?*

Yes, I can see it.

Saphira will land behind it. Have Arya, Orik, Jörmundur, Roran, Queen Islanzadí, and King Orrin join us there, but make sure they do not leave the camp all at once. If you could help hide them, that would be best. You should come as well.

As you wish. . . . Shadeslayer, what did you find on—

No! Do not ask me. It would be dangerous to think of it here. Come and I will tell you, but I do not want to blare the answer where others might be listening.

I understand. We will meet with you as quickly as we can, but it may take some time to stagger our departures correctly.

Of course. I trust you'll do what's best.

Eragon severed their connection and leaned back in the saddle. He smiled slightly as he imagined Blödhgarm's expression when he learned of the Eldunarí.

With a whirl of wind, Saphira landed in the hollow by the base of the hill, startling a flock of nearby sheep, who scurried away while uttering plaintive bleats.

As she folded her wings, Saphira looked after the sheep and said, *It would be easy to catch them, since they cannot see me.* She licked her chops.

"Yes, but where would the sport be in that?" Eragon asked, loosening the straps around his legs.

Sport does not fill your belly.

"No, but then you aren't hungry, are you?" The energy from the Eldunarí, though insubstantial, had suppressed her desire to eat.

She released a great amount of air in what seemed to be a sigh. *No, not really. . . .*

While they waited, Eragon stretched his sore limbs, then ate a light lunch from what remained of his provisions. He knew that Saphira was sprawled her full, sinuous length on the ground next to him, though he could not see her. Her presence was betrayed only by the shadowed impression her body left upon the flattened stalks of grass, like a strangely shaped hollow. He was not sure why, but the sight amused him.

As he ate, he gazed out at the pleasant fields around the hill, watching the stir of air in the stalks of wheat and barley. Long, low walls of piled stone separated the fields; it must have taken the local farmers hundreds of years to dig so many stones out of the ground.

At least that wasn't a problem we had in Palancar Valley, he thought.

A moment later, one of the dragons' memories returned to him, and he knew exactly how old the stone walls were; they dated to the time when humans had come to live in the ruins of Ilirea, after the elves had defeated King Palancar's warriors. He could see, as if he had been there, lines of men, women, and children combing over freshly tilled fields and carrying the rocks they found over to where the walls would be.

After a time, Eragon allowed the memory to fade away, and then he opened his mind to the ebb and flow of energy around them. He listened to the thoughts of the mice in the grass and the worms in the earth and the birds that fluttered past overhead. It was a slightly risky thing to do, for he could end up alerting any nearby enemy spellcasters to their presence, but he preferred to know who and what was close, so that no one could attack them by surprise.

Thus he sensed the approach of Arya, Blödhgarm, and Queen Islanzadí, and he was not alarmed when the shadows of their footsteps moved toward him from around the western side of the hill.

The air rippled like water, and then the three elves appeared before him. Queen Islanzadí stood in the lead, as regal as ever. She was garbed in a golden corselet of scale armor, with a jeweled helm upon her head and her red, white-trimmed cape clasped about her shoulders. A long, slim sword hung from her narrow waist. She carried a tall, white-bladed spear in one hand and a shield shaped like a birch leaf—its edges were even serrated like a leaf—in the other.

Arya, too, was clad in fine armor. She had exchanged her usual dark clothes for a corselet like her mother's—although Arya's was the gray of bare steel, not gold—and she wore a helm decorated with embossed knotwork upon the brow and nosepiece and a pair of stylized eagle wings that swept back from her temples. Compared with the splendor of Islanzadí's raiment, Arya's was somber, but all the more deadly because of it. Together, mother and daughter were like a pair of matched blades, where one was adorned for display and one fitted for combat.

Like the two women, Blödhgarm wore a shirt of scale armor, but his head was bare, and he carried no weapon besides a small knife on his belt.

"Show yourself, Eragon Shadeslayer," said Islanzadí, looking toward the spot where he stood.

Eragon released the spell that concealed him and Saphira, then bowed to the elf queen.

She ran her dark eyes over him, studying him as if he were a prize draft horse. Unlike before, he had no difficulty holding her gaze. After a few seconds, the queen said, "You have improved, Shadeslayer."

He gave a second, shorter bow. "Thank you, Your Majesty." As always, the sound of her voice sent a thrill through him. It seemed to hum with magic and music, as if every word were part of an epic poem. "Such a compliment means much from one so wise and fair as you."

Islanzadí laughed, showing her long teeth, and the hill and the fields rang with her mirth. "And you have grown eloquent as well! You did not tell me he had become so well spoken, Arya!"

A faint smile touched Arya's face. "He is still learning." Then to Eragon, she said, "It is good to see you safely returned."

The elves plied him, Saphira, and Glaedr with numerous questions, but the three of them refused to provide answers until the others had arrived. Still, Eragon thought that the elves sensed something of the Eldunarí, for he noticed that they sometimes glanced in the direction of the hearts of hearts, although they seemed not to realize it.

Orik was the next to join them. He rode from the south on a shaggy pony that was lathered and panting. "Ho, Eragon! Ho, Saphira!" the dwarf king cried, raising a fist. He slid down from his exhausted mount, stomped over, and pulled Eragon into a rough embrace, pounding him on the back.

When they had finished greeting each other—and Orik had

given Saphira a rub on her nose, which made her hum—Eragon asked, "Where are your guards?"

Orik gestured over his shoulder. "Braiding their beards by a farmhouse a mile west of here, and none too happy about it, I dare say. I'd trust every last one of them—they're clanmates of mine—but Blödhgarm said I should best come alone, so alone I've come. Now tell me, why this secrecy? What did you discover on Vroengard?"

"You'll have to wait for the rest of our council to find out," said Eragon. "But I am glad to see you again." And he clapped Orik on the shoulder.

Roran arrived on foot soon afterward, looking grim and dusty. He gripped Eragon's arm and welcomed him, then pulled him aside and said, "Can you stop them from hearing us?" He motioned with his chin toward Orik and the elves.

It took Eragon only a few seconds to cast a spell that shielded them from listeners. "Done." At the same time, he separated his mind from Glaedr and the other Eldunarí, although not from Saphira.

Roran nodded and looked off over the fields. "I had some words with King Orrin while you were gone."

"Words? How so?"

"He was being a fool, and I told him so."

"I take it he didn't react very kindly."

"You could say that. He tried to stab me."

"He *what?*!"

"I managed to knock his sword out of his hand before he could land a blow, but if he had had his way, he would have killed me."

"Orrin?" Eragon had trouble imagining the king doing any such thing. "Did you hurt him badly?"

For the first time, Roran smiled: a brief expression that quickly vanished under his beard. "I scared him, which might be worse."

Eragon grunted and clenched the pommel of Brisingr. He realized that he and Roran were mirroring each other's posture; they both had their hands on their weapons, and they both stood with their weight on the opposite leg. "Who else knows of this?"

"Jörmundur—he was there—and whomever Orrin has told."

Frowning, Eragon began to pace back and forth as he tried to decide what to do. "The timing of this couldn't be worse."

"I know. I wouldn't have been so blunt with Orrin, but he was about to send 'royal greetings' to Galbatorix and other such nonsense. He would have put us all in danger. I couldn't allow that to happen. You would have done the same."

"Maybe so, but this just makes things all the more difficult. I'm the leader of the Varden now. An attack on you or any of the other warriors under my command is the same as an attack on me. Orrin knows that, and he knows we're of the same blood. He might as well have thrown a gauntlet in my face."

"He was drunk," said Roran. "I'm not sure he was thinking of that when he drew his sword."

Eragon saw Arya and Blödhgarm giving him curious glances. He stopped pacing and turned his back to them.

"I'm worried about Katrina," Roran added. "If Orrin is angry enough, he might send his men after me or her. Either way, she could get hurt. Jörmundur already posted a guard at our tent, but that's not enough protection."

Eragon shook his head. "Orrin wouldn't dare hurt her."

"No? He can't harm you, and he doesn't have the stomach to confront me directly, so what does that leave? An ambush. Knives in the dark. Killing Katrina would be an easy way for Orrin to have his revenge."

"I doubt that Orrin would resort to knives in the dark—or harming Katrina."

"You can't say for sure, though."

Eragon thought for a moment. "I'll place some spells on Katrina to keep her safe, and I'll let Orrin know that I've placed them. That should put a stop to any plans he might have."

The tension in Roran seemed to drain away. "I'd appreciate that."

"I'll give you some new wards as well."

"No, save your strength. I can take care of myself."

Eragon insisted, but Roran kept refusing. Finally, Eragon said, "Blast it! Listen to me. We're about to go into battle against Galbatorix's men. You have to have *some* protection, if only against magic. I'm going to give you wards whether you like it or not, so you might as well smile and thank me for them!"

Roran glowered at him, then he grunted and raised his hands. "Fine, as you wish. You never did know when it was sensible to give up."

"Oh, and you do?"

A chuckle came from within the depths of Roran's beard. "I suppose not. I guess it runs in the family."

"Mmh. Between Brom and Garrow, I don't know who was the more stubborn."

"Father was," said Roran.

"Eh . . . Brom was as— No, you're right. It was Garrow."

They exchanged grins, remembering their life on the farm. Then Roran shifted his stance and gave Eragon an odd, sideways look. "You seem different than before."

"Do I?"

"Yes, you do. You seem more sure of yourself."

"Perhaps it's because I understand myself better than I once did."

To that, Roran had no answer.

Half an hour later, Jörmundur and King Orrin rode up together. Eragon greeted Orrin as politely as ever, but Orrin responded with a curt reply and avoided his gaze. Even from a distance of several feet, Eragon could smell wine on his breath.

Once they were all assembled before Saphira, Eragon began. First, he had everyone swear oaths of secrecy in the ancient language. Then he explained the concept of an Eldunarí to Orik, Roran, Jörmundur, and Orrin, and he recounted a brief history of the dragons' gemlike hearts with the Riders and Galbatorix.

The elves appeared uneasy with Eragon's willingness to discuss the Eldunarí before the others, but none protested, which pleased him. He had earned that much trust, at least. Orik, Roran, and Jörmundur reacted with surprise, disbelief, and dozens of questions. Roran in particular acquired a sharp gleam in his eye, as if the information had given him a host of new ideas on how to kill Galbatorix.

Throughout, Orrin was surly and remained stridently unconvinced of the existence of the Eldunarí. In the end, the only thing that quelled his doubts was when Eragon removed Glaedr's heart of hearts from the saddlebags and introduced the dragon to the four of them.

The awe they displayed at meeting Glaedr gratified Eragon. Even Orrin seemed impressed, although after exchanging a few words with Glaedr, he turned on Eragon and said, "Did Nasuada know of this?"

"Yes. I told her at Feinster."

As Eragon expected, the admission displeased Orrin. "So once again the two of you chose to ignore me. Without the support of my men and the food of my nation, the Varden would have had no hope of confronting the Empire. I'm the sovereign ruler of one of only four countries in Alagaësia, my army makes up a goodly portion of our forces, and yet neither of you deemed it appropriate to inform me of this!"

Before Eragon could respond, Orik stepped forward. "They did not tell me about it either, Orrin," the dwarf king rumbled. "And mine people have helped the Varden for longer than yours. You should not take offense. Eragon and Nasuada did what they thought was best for our cause; they meant no disrespect."

Orrin scowled and looked as if he was going to continue arguing, but Glaedr preempted him by saying, *They did as I asked, King of the Surdans. The Eldunarí are the greatest secret of our race, and we do not share it lightly with others, even kings.*

"Then why have you chosen to do so now?" demanded Orrin. "You could have gone into battle without ever revealing yourself."

In answer, Eragon recounted the story of their trip to Vroengard, including their encounter with the storm at sea and the sight they had witnessed at the very top of the clouds. Arya and Blödhgarm seemed the most interested in that part of his story, whereas Orik was the most uncomfortable.

"Barzûl, but that sounds a nasty experience," he said. "It makes me shiver just to think of it. The ground is the proper place for a dwarf, not the sky."

I agree, said Saphira, which caused Orik to scowl suspiciously and twist the braided ends of his beard.

Resuming his tale, Eragon told of how he, Saphira, and Glaedr had entered the Vault of Souls, though he refrained from divulging that this had required their true names. And when he at last revealed what the vault had contained, there was a moment of shocked silence.

Then Eragon said, "Open your minds."

A moment later, the sound of whispering voices seemed to fill the air, and Eragon felt the presence of Umaroth and the other hidden dragons surround them.

The elves staggered, and Arya dropped to one knee, pressing a hand to the side of her head as if she had been struck. Orik uttered a cry and looked about, wild-eyed, while Roran, Jörmundur, and Orrin stood dumbfounded.

Queen Islanzadí knelt, adopting a pose much like her daughter's. In his mind, Eragon heard her speaking to the dragons, greeting many by name and welcoming them as old friends. Blödhgarm did likewise, and for several minutes a flurry of thoughts passed between the dragons and those gathered at the base of the hill.

The mental cacophony was so great, Eragon shielded himself from it and retreated to sit on one of Saphira's forelegs while he waited for the noise to subside. The elves seemed most affected by the revelation: Blödhgarm stared into the air with an expression of joy and wonder, while Arya continued to kneel. Eragon thought he saw a line of tears on each of her cheeks. Islanzadí beamed with a triumphant radiance, and for the first time since he had met her, Eragon thought she seemed truly happy.

Orik shook himself then and broke from his reverie. Looking over at Eragon, he said, "By Morgothal's hammer, this puts a new twist on things! With their help, we might actually be able to kill Galbatorix!"

"You didn't think we could before?" Eragon asked mildly.

"Of course I did. Only not so much as I do now."

Roran shook himself, as if waking from a dream. "I didn't. . . . I knew that you and the elves would fight as hard as you could, but I didn't believe you could win." He met Eragon's gaze. "Galbatorix has defeated so many Riders, and you're but one, and not that old. It didn't seem possible."

"I know."

"Now, though . . ." A wolfish look came into Roran's eyes. "Now we have a chance."

"Aye," said Jörmundur. "And just think: we no longer have to worry so much about Murtagh. He's no match for you and the dragons combined."

Eragon drummed his heels against Saphira's leg and did not answer. He had other ideas on that front. Besides, he did not like to consider having to kill Murtagh.

Then Orrin spoke up. "Umaroth says that you have devised a battle plan. Do you intend to share it with us, *Shadeslayer*?"

"I would like to hear it as well," said Islanzadí in a kinder tone.

"And I," said Orik.

Eragon stared at them for a moment, then nodded. To Islanzadí, he said, "Is your army ready to fight?"

"It is. Long we have waited for our vengeance; we need wait no longer."

"And ours?" Eragon asked, directing his words toward Orrin, Jörmundur, and Orik.

"Mine knurlan are eager for battle," proclaimed Orik.

Jörmundur glanced at King Orrin. "Our men are tired and hungry, but their will is unbroken."

"The Urgals too?"

"Them too."

"Then we attack."

"When?" demanded Orrin.

"At first light."

For a moment, no one spoke.

Roran broke the silence. "Easy to say, hard to do. How?"

Eragon explained.

When he finished, there was another silence.

Roran squatted and began to draw in the dirt with the tip of a finger. "It's risky."

"But bold," said Orik. "Very bold."

"There are no safe paths anymore," said Eragon. "If we can catch Galbatorix unprepared, even a bit, it might be enough to tip the scales."

Jörmundur rubbed his chin. "Why not kill Murtagh first? That's the part I don't understand. Why not finish him and Thorn while we have the chance?"

"Because," Eragon replied, "then Galbatorix would know of *them*." And he motioned toward where the hidden Eldunarí floated. "We would lose the advantage of surprise."

"What of the child?" Orrin asked harshly. "What makes you think that she will accommodate you? She hasn't before."

"This time she will," Eragon promised, more confidently than he felt.

The king grunted, unconvinced.

Then Islanzadí said, "Eragon, it is a great and terrible thing you propose. Are you willing to do this? I ask not because I doubt your dedication or your bravery, but because this is something to be undertaken only after much consideration. So I ask you: are you willing to do this, even knowing what the cost may be?"

Eragon did not rise, but he allowed a bit of steel to enter his voice. "I am. It must be done, and we are the ones to whom the task has fallen. Whatever the cost, we cannot turn away now."

As a sign of her agreement, Saphira opened her jaws a few inches and then snapped them shut, punctuating the end of his sentence.

Islanzadí turned her face toward the sky. "And do you and those you speak for approve of this, Umaroth-elda?"

We do, replied the white dragon.

"Then here we go," Roran murmured.

A MATTER OF DUTY

The ten of them—including Umaroth—continued to talk for another hour. Orrin required more convincing, and there were numerous details to decide: questions of timing and placement and signaling.

Eragon was relieved when Arya said, "Unless either you or Saphira object, I will accompany you tomorrow."

"We would be glad to have you," he said.

Islanzadí stiffened. "What good would that accomplish? Your talents are needed elsewhere, Arya. Blödhgarm and the other spellcasters I assigned to Saphira and Eragon are more skilled at magic than you and more experienced in battle as well. Remember, they fought against the Forsworn, and unlike many, they lived to tell of it. Many of the elder members of our race would volunteer to take your place. It would be selfish to insist upon going when there are others better suited for the task who are willing and close at hand."

"I think no one is as suited for the task as Arya," Eragon said in a calm voice. "And there is no one, other than Saphira, I would rather have by my side."

Islanzadí kept her gaze upon Arya and to Eragon said, "You are still young, Shadeslayer, and you are allowing your emotions to cloud your judgment."

"No, Mother," said Arya. "It is you who are allowing your emotions to cloud your judgment." She moved toward Islanzadí with long, graceful steps. "You are right, there are others who are stronger, wiser, and more experienced than I. But it was I who ferried Saphira's egg about Alagaësia. I who helped save Eragon from the Shade Durza. And I who, with Eragon's help, killed the Shade

Varaug in Feinster. Like Eragon, I am now a Shadeslayer, and you well know that I swore myself in service to our people long ago. Who else among our kind can claim as much? Even if I wanted to, I would not turn away from this. I would sooner die. I am as prepared for this challenge as any of our elders, for it is to this I have devoted the whole of my life, as has Eragon."

"And the whole of your life has been so short," said Islanzadí. She put a hand up to Arya's face. "You have devoted yourself to fighting Galbatorix all these years since your father's death, but you know little of the joys life can provide. And in those years, we have spent such a small amount of time together: a handful of days scattered throughout a century. It is only since you brought Saphira and Eragon to Ellesméra that we have begun to speak once more, as a mother and daughter ought. I would not lose you again so soon, Arya."

"It was not I who chose to remain apart," said Arya.

"No," said Islanzadí, and she took her hand away. "But it was you who chose to leave Du Weldenvarden." Her expression softened. "I do not wish to argue, Arya. I understand that you see this as your duty, but please, for my sake, will you not allow another to take your place?"

Arya lowered her gaze and was silent for a time. Then she said, "I cannot allow Eragon and Saphira to go without me any more than you can allow your army to march into battle without you at its head. I cannot. . . . Would you have it said of me that I am a coward? Those of our family do not turn away from what must be done; do not ask me to shame myself."

The shine in Islanzadí's eyes looked suspiciously like tears to Eragon. "Yes," said the queen, "but to fight Galbatorix . . ."

"If you are so afraid," said Arya, but not unkindly, "then come with me."

"I cannot. I must stay to command my troops."

"And I must go with Eragon and Saphira. But I promise you, I shall not die." Arya placed her hand on Islanzadí's face even as her mother had done to her. *"I shall not die."* Once more Arya repeated the phrase, but this time in the ancient language.

Arya's determination impressed Eragon; to say what she had in the ancient language meant that she believed it without qualification. Islanzadí also appeared impressed, and proud too. She smiled and kissed Arya once on each cheek. "Then go, and go with my blessings. And take no more risks than you must."

"Nor you." And the two of them embraced.

As they separated, Islanzadí looked at Eragon and Saphira and said, "Watch over her, I implore you, for she has not a dragon or the Eldunarí to protect her."

We will, both Eragon and Saphira replied, in the ancient language.

Once they had settled what needed to be settled, the war council broke and its various members began to disperse. From where he sat by Saphira, Eragon watched the others mill about. Neither he nor she made an effort to move. Saphira was going to remain hidden behind the hill until the attack, while he intended to wait for dark before he ventured into the camp.

Orik was the second to depart, after Roran. Before he did, the dwarf king came over to Eragon and gave him a rough hug. "Ah, I wish I were going with the two of you," he said, his eyes solemn above his beard.

"And I wish you were coming," said Eragon.

"Well, we'll see each other afterward and toast our victory with barrels of mead, eh?"

"I look forward to it."

As do I, said Saphira.

"Good," said Orik, and he nodded firmly. "That's settled, then. You'd better not let Galbatorix get the better of you, or I'll be honor-bound to march in after you."

"We'll be careful," Eragon said with a smile.

"I should hope so, because I doubt I could do much more than tweak Galbatorix on the nose."

That I would like to see, said Saphira.

Orik grunted. "May the gods watch over you, Eragon, and you as well, Saphira."

"And you, Orik, Thrifk's son." Then Orik slapped Eragon on the shoulder and stomped off to where he had tied his pony to a bush.

When Islanzadí and Blödhgarm left, Arya stayed. She was deep in conversation with Jörmundur, and so Eragon thought little of it. When Jörmundur rode off, however, and Arya still lingered nearby, he realized that she wanted to talk to them alone.

Sure enough, once everyone else had gone, she looked at him and Saphira and said, "Did something else happen to you while you were gone, something that you didn't want to speak of in front of Orrin or Jörmundur . . . or my mother?"

"Why do you ask?"

She hesitated. "Because . . . you both seem to have changed. Is it the Eldunarí, or does it have to do with your experience in the storm?"

Eragon smiled at her perception. He consulted with Saphira, and when she approved, he said, "We learned our true names."

Arya's eyes widened. "You did? And . . . were you pleased with them?"

In part, said Saphira.

"We learned our true names," Eragon repeated. "We saw that the earth is round. And during the flight here, Umaroth and the other Eldunarí shared many of their memories with us." He allowed himself a wry smile. "I can't say we understand all of them, but they make things seem . . . different."

"I see," murmured Arya. "Do you think the change is for the better?"

"I do. Change itself is neither good nor bad, but knowledge is always useful."

"Was it difficult to find your true names?"

So he told her how they had accomplished it, and he also told her about the strange creatures they had encountered on Vroengard Island, which interested her greatly.

As Eragon spoke, an idea occurred to him, one that resonated within him too strongly to ignore. He explained it to Saphira, and once again she granted him her permission, although somewhat more reluctantly than before.

Must you? she asked.

Yes.

Then do as you will, but only if she agrees.

When they finished speaking of Vroengard, he looked Arya in the eyes and said, "Would you like to hear my true name? I would like to share it with you."

The offer seemed to shock her. "No! You shouldn't tell it to me or anyone else. Especially not when we're so close to Galbatorix. He might steal it from my mind. Besides, you should only give your true name to . . . to one whom you trust above all others."

"I trust you."

"Eragon, even when we elves exchange our true names, we do not do so until we have known each other for many, many years. The knowledge they provide is too personal, too intimate, to bandy about, and there is no greater risk than sharing it. When you teach someone your true name, you place everything you are in their hands."

"I know, but I may never have the chance again. This is the only thing I have to give, and I would give it to you."

"Eragon, what you are proposing . . . It is the most precious thing one person can give another."

"I know."

A shiver ran through Arya, and then she seemed to withdraw within herself. After a time, she said, "No one has ever offered me such a gift before. . . . I'm honored by your trust, Eragon, and I understand how much this means to you, but no, I must decline. It would be wrong for you to do this and wrong for me to accept just because tomorrow we may be killed or enslaved. Danger is no reason to act foolishly, no matter how great our peril."

Eragon inclined his head. Her reasons were good reasons, and he would respect her choice. "Very well, as you wish," he said.

599

"Thank you, Eragon."

A moment passed. Then he said, "Have you ever told anyone your true name?"

"No."

"Not even your mother?"

Her mouth twisted. "No."

"Do you know what it is?"

"Of course. Why would you think otherwise?"

He half shrugged. "I didn't. I just wasn't sure." Silence came between them. Then, "When . . . how did you learn your true name?"

Arya was quiet for so long, he began to think that she would refuse to answer. Then she took a breath and said, "It was a number of years after I left Du Weldenvarden, when I finally had become accustomed to my role among the Varden and the dwarves. Faolin and my other companions were away, and I had a great deal of time to myself. I spent most of it exploring Tronjheim, wandering in the empty reaches of the city-mountain, where others rarely tread. Tronjheim is bigger than most realize, and there are many strange things within it: rooms, people, creatures, forgotten artifacts. . . . As I wandered, I thought, and I came to know myself better than ever I had before. One day I discovered a room somewhere high in Tronjheim—I doubt I could locate it again, even if I tried. A beam of sunlight seemed to pour into the room, though the ceiling was solid, and in the center of the room was a pedestal, and upon the pedestal was growing a single flower. I do not know what kind of flower it was; I have never seen its like before or since. The petals were purple, but the center of the blossom was like a drop of blood. There were thorns upon the stem, and the flower exuded the most wonderful scent and seemed to hum with a music all its own. It was such an amazing and unlikely thing to find, I stayed in the room, staring at the flower for longer than I can remember, and it was then and there that I was finally able to put words to who I was and who I am."

"I would like to see that flower someday."

"Perhaps you will." Arya glanced toward the Varden's camp. "I should go. There is much yet to be done."

He nodded. "We'll see you tomorrow, then."

"Tomorrow." Arya began to walk away. After a few steps, she paused and looked back. "I'm glad that Saphira chose you as her Rider, Eragon. And I'm proud to have fought alongside you. You have become more than any of us dared hope. Whatever happens tomorrow, know that."

Then she resumed her stride, and soon she disappeared around the curve of the hill, leaving him alone with Saphira and the Eldunarí.

FIRE IN THE NIGHT

hen darkness fell, Eragon cast a spell to hide himself. Then he patted Saphira on the nose and set out on foot for the Varden's camp.

Be careful, she said.

Invisible as he was, it was easy to slip past the warriors who kept watch around the periphery of the camp. As long as he was quiet, and as long as the men did not catch sight of his footprints or shadows, he could move about freely.

He wound his way between the woolen tents until he found Roran and Katrina's. He rapped his knuckles against the central pole, and Roran popped his head out.

"Where are you?" whispered Roran. "Hurry in!"

Releasing the flow of magic, Eragon revealed himself. Roran flinched, then grabbed him by the arm and pulled him into the dark interior of the tent.

"Welcome, Eragon," said Katrina, rising from where she sat on their tiny cot.

"Katrina."

"It's good to see you again." She gave him a quick embrace.

"Will this take long?" Roran asked.

Eragon shook his head. "It shouldn't." Squatting on his heels, he thought for a moment, then began to chant softly in the ancient language. First, he placed spells around Katrina, to protect her against any who might harm her. He made the spells more extensive than he had originally planned, in an attempt to ensure that she and her unborn child would be able to escape Galbatorix's forces should something happen to both him and Roran. "These wards will shield you from a certain number of attacks," he told her. "I can't tell you how many exactly, because it depends on the strength of the blows or spells. I've given you another defense as well. If you're in danger, say the word *frethya* two times and you'll vanish from sight."

"Frethya," she murmured.

"Exactly. It won't hide you completely, however. The sounds you make can still be heard, and your footprints will still be visible. No matter what happens, don't go into water or your position will be obvious at once. The spell will draw its energy from you, which means that you'll tire faster than usual, and I wouldn't recommend sleeping while it's active. You might not wake up again. To end the spell, simply say *frethya letta*."

"Frethya letta."

"Good."

Then Eragon turned his attention to Roran. He spent longer placing the wards around his cousin—for it was likely Roran would confront a greater number of threats—and he endowed the spells with more energy than he thought Roran would have approved of, but Eragon did not care. He could not bear the thought of defeating Galbatorix only to find that Roran had died during the battle.

Afterward, he said, "I did something different this time, something I should have thought of long ago. In addition to the usual wards, I gave you a few that will feed directly off your own strength. As long as you're alive, they'll shield you from danger. But"—he lifted a finger—"they'll only activate once the other wards are exhausted, and if the demands placed upon them are too great, you'll fall unconscious and then you'll die."

"So in trying to save me, they may kill me?" Roran asked.

Eragon nodded. "Don't let anyone drop another wall on you, and you'll be fine. It's a risk, but worth it, I think, if it keeps a horse from trampling you or a javelin from going through you. Also, I gave you the same spell as Katrina. All you have to do is say *frethya* twice and *frethya letta* to turn yourself invisible and visible at will." He shrugged. "You might find that useful during the battle."

Roran gave an evil chuckle. "That I will."

"Just make sure the elves don't mistake you for one of Galbatorix's spellcasters."

As Eragon rose to his feet, Katrina stood as well. She surprised him by grasping one of his hands and pressing it against her chest. "Thank you, Eragon," she said softly. "You're a good man."

He flushed, embarrassed. "It's nothing."

"Guard yourself well tomorrow. You mean a great deal to both of us, and I expect you to be around to act the doting uncle for our child. I'll be most put out if you get yourself killed."

He laughed. "Don't worry. Saphira won't let me do anything foolish."

"Good." She kissed him on both cheeks, then released him. "Farewell, Eragon."

"Farewell, Katrina."

Roran accompanied him outside. Motioning toward the tent, Roran said, "Thank you."

"I'm glad I could help."

They gripped each other by the forearms and hugged; then Roran said, "Luck be with you."

Eragon took a long, unsteady breath. "Luck be with you." He tightened his grip on Roran's forearm, reluctant to let go, for he knew that they might never meet again. "If Saphira and I don't come back," he said, "will you see to it that we're buried at home? I wouldn't want our bones to lie here."

Roran raised his brows. "Saphira would be difficult to lug all the way back."

"The elves would help, I'm sure."

"Then yes, I promise. Is there anywhere in particular you would like?"

"The top of the bald hill," said Eragon, referring to a foothill near their farm. The bare-topped hill had always seemed like an excellent location for a castle, something they had discussed at great length when younger.

Roran nodded. "And if I don't come back—"

"We'll do the same for you."

"That's not what I was going to ask. If I don't . . . you'll see to Katrina?"

"Of course. You know that."

"Aye, but I had to be sure." They gazed at each other for another minute. Finally, Roran said, "We'll be expecting you for dinner tomorrow."

"I'll be there."

Then Roran slipped back into the tent, leaving Eragon standing alone in the night.

He looked up at the stars and felt a touch of grief, as if he had already lost someone close to him.

After a few moments, he padded away into the shadows, relying upon the darkness to conceal him.

He searched through the camp until he found the tent Horst and Elain shared with their baby girl, Hope. The three of them were still awake, as the infant was crying.

"Eragon!" Horst exclaimed softly when Eragon made his presence known. "Come in! Come in! We haven't seen much of you since Dras-Leona! How are you?"

Eragon spent the better part of an hour talking with them—he did not tell them of the Eldunarí, but he did tell them of his trip to Vroengard—and when Hope finally fell asleep, he bade them farewell and returned to the night.

He next sought out Jeod, whom he found reading scrolls by candlelight while his wife, Helen, slept. When Eragon knocked and stuck his face into the tent, the scarred, thin-faced man put aside his scrolls and left the tent to join Eragon.

Jeod had many questions, and while Eragon did not answer them all, he answered enough that he thought Jeod would be able to guess much of what was about to happen.

Afterward, Jeod laid a hand on Eragon's shoulder. "I don't envy you the task that lies ahead. Brom would be proud of your courage."

"I hope so."

"I'm sure of it. . . . If I don't see you again, you should know: I've written a small account of your experiences and of the events that led to them—mainly my adventures with Brom in recovering Saphira's egg." Eragon gave him a look of surprise. "I may not get the opportunity to finish it, but I thought it would make a useful addition to Heslant's work in *Domia abr Wyrda*."

Eragon laughed. "I think that would be most fitting. However, if you and I are both alive and free after tomorrow, there are some things I should tell you which will make your account that much more complete and that much more interesting."

"I'll hold you to it."

Eragon wandered through the camp for another hour or so, pausing by the fires where men, dwarves, and Urgals still sat awake. He spoke briefly with each of the warriors he met, inquired whether they were being fairly treated, commiserated about their sore feet and short rations, and sometimes exchanged a quip or two. He hoped that by showing himself among them, he could lift the warriors' spirits and strengthen their resolve, and thus spread a sense of optimism throughout the army. The Urgals, he found, were in the best mood; they seemed delighted about the upcoming battle and the opportunities for glory that it would provide.

He had another purpose as well: to spread false information. Whenever someone asked him about attacking Urû'baen, he hinted that he and Saphira would be among the battalion to besiege the northwestern section of the city wall. He hoped that Galbatorix's spies would repeat the lie to the king as soon as the alarms woke Galbatorix the following morn.

As he looked into the faces of those listening to him, Eragon could not help but wonder which, if any, were Galbatorix's servants. The thought made him uncomfortable, and he found himself listening for footsteps behind him when he moved from one fire to the next.

At last, when he was satisfied that he had spoken to enough

warriors to ensure that the information would reach Galbatorix, he left the fires behind and made his way to a tent that was set slightly away from the others by the southern edge of the camp.

He knocked on the center pole: once, twice, three times. There was no response, so he knocked again, this time louder and longer.

A moment later, he heard a sleepy groan and the rustle of shifting blankets. He waited patiently until a small hand pulled aside the entrance flap and the witch-child, Elva, emerged. She wore a dark robe much too large for her, and by the faint light of a torch some yards away, he could see a frown upon her sharp little face.

"What do you want, Eragon?" she demanded.

"Can't you tell?"

Her frown deepened. "No, I can't, only that you want something badly enough to wake me in the middle of the night, which even an idiot could see. What is it? I get little enough rest as is, so this had best be important."

"It is."

He spoke without interruption for several minutes, describing his plan, then said, "Without you, it won't work. You're the point upon which it all turns."

She gave an ugly laugh. "Such irony, the mighty warrior relying upon a child to kill the one he cannot."

"Will you help?"

The girl looked down and scuffed her bare foot against the ground.

"If you do, all this" —he motioned toward the camp and the city beyond—"may end far sooner, and then you will not have to endure quite so much—"

"I'll help." She stamped her foot and glared at him. "You don't have to bribe me. I was going to help anyway. I'm not about to let Galbatorix destroy the Varden just because I don't like you. You're not *that* important, Eragon. Besides, I made a promise to Nasuada, and I intend to keep it." She cocked her head. "There's something you're not telling me. Something you're afraid Galbatorix will find out before we attack. Something about—"

The sound of clanking chains interrupted her.

For a moment, Eragon was confused. Then he realized the sound was coming from the city.

He put his hand on his sword. "Ready yourself," he said to Elva. "We may have to leave at once."

Without argument, the girl turned around and disappeared inside the tent.

Reaching out with his mind, Eragon contacted Saphira. *Do you hear it?*

Yes.

If we have to, we'll meet you by the road.

The clanking continued for a short while, then there was a hollow boom, followed by silence.

Eragon listened as intently as he could but heard nothing more. He was just about to cast a spell to increase the sensitivity of his ears when there was a dull *thud*, accompanied by a series of sharp clacks.

Then another . . .

And another . . .

A shiver of horror ran down Eragon's spine. The sound was unmistakably that of a dragon walking on stone. But what a dragon, to hear its steps from over a mile away!

Shruikan, he thought, and his gut clenched with dread.

Throughout the camp, alarm horns blared, and men, dwarves, and Urgals lit torches as the army scrambled to wakefulness.

Eragon spared Elva a sideways glance as she hurried out of the tent, followed by Greta, the old woman who was her caretaker. The girl had donned a short red tunic, over which she wore a mail hauberk just her size.

The footsteps in Urû'baen ceased. The dragon's shadowy bulk blotted out most of the lanterns and watchlights in the city. *How big is he?* Eragon wondered, dismayed. Bigger than Glaedr, that was certain. As big as Belgabad? Eragon could not tell. Not yet.

Then the dragon leaped up and out from the city, and he unfurled his massive wings, and their opening was like a hundred black sails filling with wind. When he flapped, the air shook as if from a clap of thunder, and throughout the countryside, dogs bayed and roosters crowed.

Without thinking, Eragon crouched, feeling like a mouse hiding from an eagle.

Elva tugged on the hem of his tunic. "We should go," she insisted.

"Wait," he whispered. "Not yet."

Great swaths of stars vanished as Shruikan wheeled across the sky, climbing higher and higher. Eragon tried to guess the dragon's size from the outline of his shape, but the night was too dark and the distance too hard to determine. Whatever Shruikan's exact proportions, he was frighteningly large. At only a century of age, he ought to have been smaller than he was, but Galbatorix seemed to have accelerated his growth, even as he had Thorn's.

As he watched the shadow drifting above, Eragon hoped with all his might that Galbatorix was not with the dragon, or if he was, that he would not bother to examine the minds of those below. If he did, he would discover—

"Eldunarí," gasped Elva. "That's what you're hiding!" Behind her, the girl's caretaker frowned with puzzlement and started to ask a question.

"Quiet!" growled Eragon. Elva opened her mouth, and he clamped his hand over it, silencing her. "Not here, not now," he warned. She nodded, and he removed his hand.

At that very moment, a bar of fire as wide as the Anora River arced across the sky. Shruikan whipped his head back and forth, spraying the torrent of blinding flames above the camp and the surrounding fields, and the night filled with a sound like a crashing waterfall. Heat stung Eragon's upturned face. Then the flames evaporated, like mist in the sun, leaving behind a throbbing afterimage and a smoky, sulfurous smell.

The huge dragon turned and flapped once more—shaking the air—before his formless black shape glided back down toward the city and settled among the buildings. Footsteps followed, then the clanking of the chains, and finally the echoing crack of a gate slamming shut.

Eragon released the breath he had been holding and swallowed, though his throat was dry. His heart was pounding so hard, it was painful. *We have to fight . . . that?* he thought, all his old fears rushing back.

"Why didn't he attack?" asked Elva in a small, fearful voice.

"He wanted to frighten us." Eragon frowned. "Or distract us." He searched through the minds of the Varden until he found Jörmundur, then gave the warrior instructions to check that all the sentries were still at their posts and to redouble the watch for the remainder of the night. To Elva, he said, "Were you able to feel anything from Shruikan?"

The girl shuddered. "Pain. Great pain. And anger too. If he could, he would kill every creature he met and burn every plant, until there were none left. He's utterly mad."

"Is there no way to reach him?"

"None. The kindest thing to do would be to release him from his misery."

The knowledge made Eragon sad. He had always hoped that they might be able to save Shruikan from Galbatorix. Subdued, he said, "We had best be off. Are you ready?"

Elva explained to her caretaker that she was leaving, which displeased the old woman, but Elva soothed her worries with a few quick words. The girl's power to see into others' hearts never ceased to amaze Eragon, and trouble him as well.

Once Greta had granted her consent, Eragon hid both Elva and himself with magic, and then they set off together toward the hill where Saphira was waiting.

OVER THE WALL AND
INTO THE MAW

"Must you do that?" asked Elva.

Eragon paused in the midst of checking the leg straps on Saphira's saddle and looked over to where the girl sat cross-legged on the grass, toying with the links of her mail shirt.

"What?" he asked.

She tapped her lip with a small, pointed fingernail. "You keep chewing on the inside of your mouth. It's distracting." After a moment's consideration, she said, "And disgusting."

With some surprise, he realized that he had bitten the inner surface of his right cheek until it was covered with several bloody sores. "Sorry," he said, and healed himself with a quick spell.

He had spent the deepest part of the night meditating—thinking not of what was to come nor of what had been, but only of what was: the touch of the cool air against his skin, the feel of the ground beneath him, the steady flow of his breath, and the slow beat of his heart as it marked off the remaining moments of his life.

Now, however, the morning star, Aiedail, had risen in the east—heralding the arrival of dawn's first light—and the time had come to ready themselves for battle. He had inspected every inch of his equipment, adjusted the harness of the saddle until it was perfectly comfortable for Saphira, emptied the saddlebags of everything but the chest that contained Glaedr's Eldunarí and a blanket for padding, and buckled and rebuckled his sword belt at least five times.

He finished examining the straps on the saddle, then jumped off Saphira. "Stand up," he said. Elva gave him a look of annoyance but did as he asked, brushing grass from the side of her tunic. Moving quickly, he ran his hands over her thin shoulders and tugged on the edge of her mail hauberk to ensure that it was sitting properly. "Who made this for you?"

"A pair of charming dwarf brothers called Ûmar and Ulmar." Her cheeks dimpled as she smiled at him. "They didn't think I needed it, but I was *very* persuasive."

I'm sure she was, Saphira said to Eragon. He suppressed a smile. The girl had spent a goodly portion of the night talking with the dragons, beguiling them as only she could. However, Eragon could tell that they also feared her—even the older ones, such as Valdr— for they had no defense against Elva's power. No one did.

"And did Ûmar and Ulmar give you a blade to fight with?" he asked.

Elva frowned. "Why would I want that?"

He stared at her for a moment, then he fetched his old hunting knife, which he used when eating, and had her tie it around her waist with a leather thong. "Just in case," he said when she protested. "Now, up you go."

She obediently climbed onto his back and locked her arms around his neck. He had carried her to the hill in that manner, which had been uncomfortable for them both, but she could not keep pace with him on foot.

He carefully climbed up Saphira's side to the peak of her shoulders. As he clung to one of the spikes that protruded from her neck, he twisted his body so that Elva was able to pull herself into the saddle.

Once he felt the girl's weight leave him, Eragon dropped back to the ground. He tossed his shield up to her, then lunged forward, arms outstretched, when it nearly pulled her off Saphira.

"Have you got it?" he asked.

"Yes," she said, tugging the shield onto her lap. She made a shooing motion with one hand. "Go, go."

Holding Brisingr's pommel to keep the sword from tangling

between his legs, Eragon ran to the top of the hill and knelt on one knee, staying as low as he could. Behind him, Saphira crawled partway up the rise, then pressed herself flat against the ground and snaked her head through the grass until it was next to him and she could see what he saw.

A thick column of humans, dwarves, elves, Urgals, and werecats streamed out of the Varden's camp. In the flat gray light of early dawn, the figures were difficult to make out, especially because they carried no lights. The column marched across the sloping fields toward Urû'baen, and when the warriors were about half a mile from the city, they divided into three lines. One positioned itself before the front gate, one turned toward the southeastern part of the curtain wall, and one went toward the northwestern part.

It was the last group that Eragon had hinted he and Saphira were going to accompany.

The warriors had wrapped rags around their feet and weapons, and they kept their voices to a whisper. Still, Eragon could hear the occasional bray of a donkey or the whinny of a horse, and a number of dogs were barking at the procession. The soldiers on the walls would soon notice the activity—most likely when the warriors began to move the catapults, ballistae, and siege towers that the Varden had already assembled and placed in the fields before the city.

Eragon was impressed that the men, dwarves, and Urgals were still willing to go into battle after seeing Shruikan. *They must have a great deal of faith in us,* he said to Saphira. The responsibility weighed heavily upon him, and he was keenly aware that if he and those with him failed, few of the warriors would survive.

Yes, but if Shruikan flies out again, they will scatter like so many frightened mice.

Then we'd best not let that happen.

A horn sounded in Urû'baen, and then another and another, and lights began to appear throughout the city as lanterns were unshuttered and torches lit.

"Here we go," Eragon murmured, his pulse quickening.

Now that the alarm had been raised, the Varden abandoned all attempts at secrecy. To the east, a group of elves on horseback set off at a gallop toward the hill that backed the city, planning to ride up the side of it and attack the wall along the top of the immense shelf that hung over Urû'baen.

In the center of the Varden's mostly empty camp, Eragon saw what appeared to be Saphira's glittering shape. On the illusion sat a lone figure—which he knew bore a perfect copy of his own features—holding a sword and shield.

The duplicate of Saphira raised her head and spread her wings; then she took flight and loosed a stirring roar.

They do a good job of it, don't they? he said to Saphira.

Elves understand how a dragon is supposed to look and behave . . . unlike some humans.

The shadow-Saphira landed next to the northernmost group of warriors, although Eragon noticed the elves were careful to keep her some distance from the men and dwarves, so that they would not brush up against her and discover that she was as insubstantial as a rainbow.

The sky lightened as the Varden and their allies gathered in orderly formations at each of the three locations outside the walls. Inside the city, Galbatorix's soldiers continued to prepare for the assault, but it was obvious as they ran about the battlements that they were panicked and disorganized. However, Eragon knew their confusion would not last long.

Now, he thought. *Now! Don't wait any longer.* He swept his gaze over the buildings, searching for the slightest scrap of red, but none met his eye. *Where are you, blast it?! Show yourself!*

Three more horns sounded, this time the Varden's. A great chorus of shouts and cries rose from the army, and then the Varden's war machines launched their projectiles at the city, archers loosed their arrows, and the ranks of warriors broke and charged toward the seemingly impenetrable curtain wall.

The stones, javelins, and arrows appeared to move slowly as they arced across the ground that separated the army from the city. None of the missiles hit the outer wall; it would be pointless to try to batter it down, so the engineers aimed above and beyond. Some of the stones shattered as they struck within Urû'baen, sending dagger-like shards in every direction, while others punched through buildings and bounced up the streets like giant marbles.

Eragon thought how horrible it would be to wake amid such confusion, with large chunks of stone raining down. Then activity elsewhere caught his attention as the shadow-Saphira took flight over the running warriors. With three flaps of her wings, she climbed above the wall and bathed the battlements with a tongue of flame that, to Eragon's eye, appeared somewhat brighter than normal. The fire, he knew, was real enough, conjured into being by the elves close to the northern part of the wall, who had created and were sustaining the illusion.

The apparition of Saphira swooped back and forth over the same stretch of wall, clearing it of soldiers. Once she had, a band of twenty-some elves flew from the ground outside the city up to the top of one of the wall towers, so they could continue to keep watch on the apparition as it ranged deeper into Urû'baen.

If Murtagh and Thorn don't show themselves soon, they're going to start wondering why we're not attacking the other parts of the wall, he said to Saphira.

They will think we're defending the warriors trying to breach this section, she replied. *Give it time.*

Elsewhere along the wall, soldiers fired arrows and javelins at the army below, felling dozens of the Varden. The deaths were unavoidable, but Eragon regretted them all the same, for the warriors' attacks were merely a distraction; they had little chance of actually surmounting the city's defenses. Meanwhile, the siege towers trundled closer, and flights of arrows leaped between their upper levels and the men on the battlements.

From above, a ribbon of burning pitch fell across the edge of the overhang and disappeared among the buildings below. Eragon looked up and saw flashes of light atop the wall that guarded the lip of the precipice. Even as he watched, he saw four bodies tumble over the side; they looked like understuffed dolls as they plummeted toward the ground. The sight pleased Eragon, for it meant the elves had taken the upper wall.

The shadow-Saphira looped over the city, lighting several buildings on fire. As she did, a flock of arrows shot up from archers stationed on a nearby rooftop. The apparition swerved to avoid the darts and, seemingly by accident, crashed into one of the six green elf towers scattered throughout Urû'baen.

The collision looked perfectly real. Eragon winced with sympathy as he saw the dragon's left wing break against the tower, the bones snapping like stalks of dry grass. The imitation Saphira roared and thrashed as she spiraled down to the streets. The buildings hid her after that, but her roars were audible for miles around, and the flame she seemed to breathe painted the sides of the houses and lit the underside of the stone shelf that hung over the city.

I would never have been so clumsy, sniffed Saphira.

I know.

A minute passed. The tension within Eragon increased to a nearly unbearable level. "Where are they?" he growled, clenching his fist. With every passing second, it became increasingly likely the soldiers would discover that the dragon they thought they had forced down did not actually exist.

Saphira saw them first. *There,* she said, showing him with her mind.

Like a ruby blade dropped from above, Thorn plunged out of an opening hidden within the overhang. He fell straight down for several hundred feet, then unfolded his wings just enough to slow himself to a safe speed before landing in a square close to where the shadow-Saphira and the shadow-Eragon had fallen.

Eragon thought he spotted Murtagh on the red dragon, but the distance was too great to be sure. They would have to hope it was

Murtagh, because if it was Galbatorix, their plan was almost certainly doomed to failure.

There must be tunnels in the stone, he said to Saphira.

More dragon fire erupted from between the buildings; then the apparition of Saphira hopped above the rooftops and, like a bird with an injured wing, fluttered a short distance before sinking to the ground again. Thorn followed.

Eragon did not wait to see more.

He spun around, ran back along Saphira's neck, and threw himself into the saddle behind Elva. It took just a few seconds to slip his legs into the straps and tighten two on each side. He left the rest loose; they would only slow him later. The uppermost strap held Elva's legs also.

Swiftly chanting the words, he cast a spell to hide the three of them. When the magic took effect, he experienced the usual sense of disorientation as his body vanished. It looked to him as if he were hanging a number of feet above a dark, dragon-shaped pattern pressed into the plants of the hill.

The moment he finished the spell, Saphira surged forward. She jumped off the crest of the hill and flapped hard, struggling to gain height.

"It's not very comfortable, is it?" said Elva as Eragon took his shield from her.

"No, not always!" he replied, raising his voice to be heard over the wind.

In the back of his mind, he could feel Glaedr and Umaroth and the other Eldunarí watching as Saphira angled downward and dove toward the Varden's camp.

Now we will have our revenge, said Glaedr.

Eragon hunched low over Elva as Saphira gained speed. Gathered in the center of the camp, he saw Blödhgarm and his ten elven spellcasters, as well as Arya—who carried the Dauthdaert. They each had a thirty-foot-long piece of rope tied around their chests, under their arms. At the other end, all the ropes were bound to a log as thick as Eragon's thigh and equal in length to a fully grown Urgal.

When Saphira swooped toward the camp, Eragon signaled them with his mind and two of the elves threw the log into the air. Saphira caught it with her talons, the elves jumped, and a moment later, Eragon felt a jolt and Saphira dipped as she took up their weight.

Through her body, Eragon saw the elves, the ropes, and the log wink out of sight as the elves cast a spell of invisibility, the same as he had.

Flapping mightily, Saphira climbed a thousand feet above the ground, high enough that she and the elves below could easily clear the walls and buildings of the city.

To their left, Eragon glimpsed first Thorn and then the shadow-Saphira as they chased each other on foot through the northern part of the city. The elves controlling the apparition were trying to keep Thorn and Murtagh so busy physically that neither of them would have the opportunity to attack with their minds. If they did, or if they caught the apparition, they would quickly realize they had been fooled.

Just a few more minutes, Eragon thought.

Over the fields flew Saphira. Over the catapults with their devoted attendants. Over banks of archers with their arrows stuck in the ground in front of them, like tufts of white-topped reeds. Over a siege tower, and over the warriors on foot: men, dwarves, and Urgals hiding beneath their shields as they rushed ladders toward the curtain wall, and among them elves: tall and slender, with their bright helms and their long-bladed spears and narrow-bladed swords.

Then Saphira soared past the wall itself. Eragon felt a strange twinge as Saphira reappeared beneath him, and he found himself looking at the back of Elva's head. He assumed that Arya and the other elves hanging below them had become visible as well. Eragon bit off a curse and ended the spell that had concealed them. Galbatorix's wards, it seemed, would not allow them to enter the city unseen.

Saphira hastened her flight toward the citadel's massive gate.

Below them, Eragon heard shouts of fear and astonishment, but he paid them no heed. Murtagh and Thorn were the ones he was worried about, not the soldiers.

Bringing in her wings, Saphira dove toward the gate. Just when it looked as if she was going to slam into it, she turned and reared upright while back-flapping to slow herself. When she had reached a near stop, she allowed herself to drift downward until the elves were safely on the ground.

Once they had cut themselves free of the ropes and moved out of the way, Saphira landed in the courtyard before the gate, jarring both Eragon and Elva with the force of the impact.

Eragon yanked on the buckles of the straps that held him and Elva in the saddle. Then he helped the girl down from Saphira's back and they hurried after the elves toward the gate.

The entrance to the citadel took the form of two giant black doors, which met in a point high above. They looked to be made of solid iron and were studded with hundreds, if not thousands, of spiked rivets, each the size of Eragon's head. The sight was daunting; Eragon could not imagine a less inviting entrance.

Spear in hand, Arya ran to the sally port set within the left-hand door. The port was visible only as a thin, dark seam that outlined a rectangle barely wide enough for a single man to pass through. Within the rectangle was a horizontal strip of metal, perhaps three fingers wide and thrice as long, that was slightly lighter than its surroundings.

As Arya neared the door, the strip sank inward a half inch, then slid to the side with a rusty scrape. A pair of owlish eyes peered out of the dark interior.

"Who are you, then?" demanded a haughty voice. "State your business or be gone!"

Without hesitation, Arya jabbed the Dauthdaert through the open slot. A gurgle emanated from within; then Eragon heard the sound of a body falling to the floor.

Arya pulled the lance back and shook the blood and scraps

of flesh from the barbed blade. Then she grasped the haft of the weapon with both hands, placed the tip of it along the right seam of the sally port, and said, "Verma!"

Eragon squinted and turned aside as a fierce blue flame appeared between the lance and the gate. Even from several feet away, he could feel the heat.

Her face contorted with strain, Arya pressed the blade of the spear into the gate, slowly cutting through the iron. Sparks and drops of molten metal poured out from underneath the blade and skittered across the paved ground like grease on a hot pan, causing Eragon and the others to step back.

As she worked, Eragon glanced in the direction of Thorn and the shadow-Saphira. He could not see them, but he could still hear roars and the crash of breaking masonry.

Elva sagged against him, and he looked down to see that she was shaking and sweating, as if she had a fever. He knelt next to her. "Do you want me to carry you?"

She shook her head. "I'll be better once we're inside and away from . . . that." She motioned in the direction of the battle.

At the edges of the courtyard, Eragon saw a number of people—they did not look like soldiers—standing in the spaces between the grand houses, watching what they were doing. *Scare them off, would you?* he asked Saphira. She swung her head around and gave a low growl, and the onlookers scurried away.

When the fountain of sparks and white-hot metal ceased, Arya kicked at the sally port until—on the third kick—the door fell inward and landed on the body of the gatekeeper. A second later, the smell of burning wool and skin wafted out.

Still holding the Dauthdaert, Arya stepped through the dark portal. Eragon held his breath. Whatever wards Galbatorix had placed on the citadel, the Dauthdaert ought to allow her to pass through them without harm, even as it had allowed her to cut open the sally port. But there was always a chance that the king had cast a spell the Dauthdaert would be unable to counter.

To his relief, nothing happened as Arya entered the citadel.

Then a group of twenty soldiers rushed toward her, pikes out-stretched. Eragon drew Brisingr and ran to the sally port, but he dared not cross the threshold of the citadel to join her, not yet.

Wielding the spear with the same proficiency as her sword, Arya fought her way through the men, dispatching them with impressive speed.

"Why didn't you warn her?" exclaimed Eragon, never taking his eyes off the fight.

Elva joined him by the hole in the gate. "Because they won't hurt her."

Her words proved prophetic; none of the soldiers managed to land a blow. The last two men tried to flee, but Arya bounded after them and slew them before they had gone more than a dozen yards down the immense hallway, which was even larger than the four main corridors of Tronjheim.

When all of the soldiers were dead, Arya pulled the bodies aside so that there was a clear path to the sally port. Then she walked down the hallway a good forty feet, placed the Dauthdaert on the floor, and slid it back out to Eragon.

As her hand left the spear, she tensed as if in preparation for a blow, but she seemed to remain unaffected by whatever magics were in the area.

"Do you feel anything?" Eragon called. His voice echoed in the interior of the hall.

She shook her head. "As long as we stay clear of the gate, we should be fine."

Eragon handed the spear to Blödhgarm, who took it and entered through the sally port. Together Arya and the fur-covered elf went into the rooms on either side of the gate and worked the hidden mechanisms to open it, a task that would have been beyond the same number of humans.

The clanking of chains filled the air as the giant iron doors slowly swung outward.

Once the gap was wide enough for Saphira, Eragon shouted, "Stop!" and the doors ground to a halt.

Blödhgarm emerged from the room to the right and—keeping a safe distance from the threshold—slid the Dauthdaert to another of the elves.

In that fashion, they entered the citadel one by one.

When only Eragon, Elva, and Saphira remained outside, a terrible roar sounded in the northern part of the city, and for a moment, the whole of Urû'baen fell silent.

"They have discovered our deception," cried the elf Uthinarë. He tossed the spear to Eragon. "Hurry, Argetlam!"

"You next," said Eragon, handing the Dauthdaert to Elva.

Cradling it in the crooks of her arms, she scurried over to join the elves, then pushed the spear back to Eragon, who grabbed it and ran across the threshold. Turning, he was alarmed to see Thorn rise above the buildings by the far edge of the city. Eragon dropped to one knee, placed the Dauthdaert on the floor, and rolled it to Saphira. "Quickly!" he shouted.

A number of seconds were lost as Saphira fumbled with the lance, struggling to pick it up between the tips of her jaws. At last she got it between her teeth, and she leaped into the gigantic corridor, scattering the bodies of the soldiers.

In the distance, Thorn bellowed and flapped furiously, racing toward the citadel.

Speaking in unison, Arya and Blödhgarm cast a spell. A deafening clatter sounded within the stone walls, and the iron doors swung shut many times faster than they had opened. They closed with a *boom* that Eragon felt through his feet, and then a metal bar—three feet thick and six feet wide—slid out of each wall and through brackets bolted to the inside of the doors, securing them in place.

"That should hold them for a while," said Arya.

"Not for that long," said Eragon, looking at the open sally port.

Then they turned to see what lay before them.

The hallway ran for what Eragon guessed was close to a quarter mile, which would take them deep inside the hill behind Urû'baen. At the far end was another set of doors, just as large as the first but covered in patterned gold that glowed beautifully in the light of the flameless lanterns mounted at regular intervals along the walls. Dozens of smaller passageways branched off to either side, but none were large enough for Shruikan, although Saphira could have fit in many of them. Red banners embroidered with the outline of the twisting flame that Galbatorix used as his sigil hung along the walls every hundred feet. Otherwise, the hall was bare.

The sheer size of the passageway was intimidating, and its emptiness made Eragon that much more nervous. He assumed the throne room was on the other side of the golden doors, but he did not think it would be as easy to reach as it appeared. If Galbatorix was even half as cunning as his reputation implied, he would have littered the corridor with dozens, if not hundreds, of traps.

Eragon found it puzzling that the king had not already attacked them. He did not feel the touch of any mind save those of Saphira and his companions, but he remained acutely aware of how close they were to the king. The entire citadel seemed to be watching them.

"He must know we're here," he said. "*All* of us."

"Then we had best make haste," said Arya. She took the Dauthdaert from Saphira's mouth. The weapon was covered in saliva. "Thurra," said Arya, and the slime fell to the floor.

Behind them, outside the iron gate, there was a loud crash as Thorn landed in the courtyard. He uttered a roar of frustration, then something heavy struck the gate, and the walls rang with the noise.

Arya trotted to the front of their group, and Elva joined her. The dark-haired girl placed a hand on the shaft of the spear—so that she too shared its protective powers—and the two of them started forward, leading the way down the long hall as they hurried ever deeper into Galbatorix's lair.

◆　◆　◆

THE STORM BREAKS

"Sir, it's time."

Roran opened his eyes and nodded at the boy with a lantern who had stuck his head into the tent. The boy hurried off, and Roran leaned over and kissed Katrina on the cheek; she kissed him back. Neither of them had slept.

Together they rose and dressed. She finished first, for it took him longer to don his armor and weapons.

As he pulled on his gloves, she handed him a slice of bread, a wedge of cheese, and a cup of lukewarm tea. He ignored the bread, took a single bite of cheese, and downed the whole cup of tea at once.

They held each other for a moment, and he said, "If it's a girl, name her something fierce."

"And if it's a boy?"

"The same. Boy or girl, you have to be strong in order to survive in this world."

"I'll do it. I promise." They released each other, and she looked him in the eye. "Fight well, my husband."

He nodded, then turned and left before he lost his composure.

The men under his command were assembling by the northern entrance to the camp when he joined them. The only light they had was from the faint glow above and the torches planted along the outer breastwork. In the dim, flickering illumination, the warriors' figures seemed like a pack of shuffling beasts, threatening and alien.

Among their ranks were a large number of Urgals, including some Kull. His battalion contained a greater share of the creatures than most, as Nasuada had deemed them more likely to follow orders from him than from anyone else. The Urgals carried the long and heavy siege ladders that would be used to climb over the city walls.

Also among the men were a score of elves. Most of their kind would be fighting on their own, but Queen Islanzadí had granted permission for some to serve in the Varden's army as protection against attack by Galbatorix's spellcasters.

Roran welcomed the elves and took the time to ask each their name. They answered politely enough, but he had a feeling they did not think very highly of him. That was all right. He did not care for them either. There was something about them he did not trust; they were too aloof, too well practiced, and above all, too *different*. The dwarves and Urgals, at least, he understood. But not the elves. He could not tell what they were thinking, and that bothered him.

"Greetings, Stronghammer!" said Nar Garzhvog in a whisper that could be heard at thirty paces. "Today we shall win much glory for our tribes!"

"Yes, today we will win much glory for our tribes," Roran agreed, moving on. The men were nervous; some of the younger ones looked as if they might be sick—and some were, which was only to be expected—but even the older men seemed tense, short-tempered, and either overly talkative or overly withdrawn. The cause was obvious enough: Shruikan. There was little Roran could do to help them other than to hide his own fears and hope that the men did not lose courage entirely.

The sense of anticipation that clung to everyone there, himself included, was dreadful. They had sacrificed much in order to reach this point, and it was not just their lives that were at risk in the battle to come. It was the safety and well-being of their families and descendants, as well as the future of the land itself. All of their prior battles had been similarly fraught, but this was the final one. This was the end. One way or another, there would be no more battles with the Empire after this day.

The thought hardly felt real. Never again would they have the chance to kill Galbatorix. And while confronting Galbatorix had seemed fine enough in conversations late at night, now that the moment was almost upon them, the prospect was terrifying.

Roran sought out Horst and the other villagers from Carvahall, and the lot of them formed a knot within the battalion. Birgit was among the men, clutching an ax that looked freshly sharpened. He acknowledged her by lifting his shield, as he might a mug of ale. She returned the gesture, and he allowed himself a grim smile.

The warriors muffled their boots and feet with rags, then stood waiting for the order to depart.

It soon arrived, and they marched out of the camp, doing their best to keep their arms and armor from making noise. Roran led his warriors across the fields to their place before the front gate of Urû'baen, where they joined two other battalions, one led by his old commander Martland Redbeard and one led by Jörmundur.

The alarm went up in Urû'baen soon afterward, so they pulled the rags off their weapons and feet and prepared to attack. A few minutes later, the Varden's horns sounded the advance and they set off at a run across the dark ground toward the immensity of the city wall.

Roran took a place at the forefront of the charge. It was the fastest way to get himself killed, but the men needed to see him braving the same dangers they faced. It would, he hoped, stiffen their spines and keep them from breaking rank at the first sign of serious opposition. For whatever happened, Urû'baen would *not* be easy to take. Of that, he was sure.

They ran past one of the siege towers, the wheels of which were over twenty feet high and creaked like a set of rusty hinges, and then they were on open ground. Arrows and javelins rained upon them from the soldiers atop the battlements.

The elves shouted in their strange tongue, and by the faint light of dawn, Roran saw many of the arrows and spears turn and bury themselves harmlessly in the dirt. But not all. A man behind him uttered a desperate cry, and Roran heard a clatter of armor as men and Urgals leaped aside to avoid stepping on the fallen warrior.

Roran did not look back, nor did he or those with him slow their headlong dash toward the wall.

An arrow struck the shield he held over his head. He barely felt the impact.

When they arrived at the wall, he moved to the side, shouting, "Ladders! Make way for the ladders!"

The men parted to allow the Urgals carrying the ladders to move forward. The ladders' great length meant that the Kull had to use poles made of trees lashed together to push them upright. Once the ladders touched the wall, they sagged inward under their own weight, so that the upper two-thirds lay flat against the dressed stone and slid from side to side, threatening to fall.

Roran elbowed his way back through the men and grabbed one of the elves, Othíara, by the arm. She gave him a look of anger, which he ignored. "Keep the ladders in place!" he shouted. "Don't let the soldiers push them away!"

She nodded and began to chant in the ancient language, as did the other elves.

Turning, Roran hurried back to the wall. One of the men was already starting to climb the nearest ladder. Roran grabbed him by the belt and pulled him off. "I'll go first," he said.

"Stronghammer!"

Roran slung his shield over his back, then began to climb, hammer in hand. He had never been fond of heights, and as the men and Urgals grew smaller below him, he felt increasingly uneasy. The feeling just grew worse when he reached the section of the ladder that lay flat against the wall, for he could no longer wrap his hands all the way around the rungs, nor could he get a good foothold— only the first few inches of his boots would fit on the bark-covered branches, and he had to move carefully to ensure that they did not slip off.

A spear flew past him, close enough that he felt the wind on his cheek.

He swore and kept climbing.

He was less than a yard from the battlements when a soldier with blue eyes leaned over the edge and looked straight at him.

"Bah!" Roran shouted, and the soldier flinched and stepped back. Before the man had time to recover, Roran scrambled up the remaining rungs and hopped over the battlements to land on the walkway along the top of the wall.

The soldier he had scared stood several feet in front of him, holding a short archer's sword. The man's head was turned to the side as he shouted at a group of soldiers farther down the wall.

Roran's shield was still on his back so he swung his hammer at the man's wrist. Without the shield, Roran knew he would have difficulty fending off a trained swordsman; his safest course was to disarm his opponent as quickly as possible.

The soldier saw what he intended and parried the blow. Then he stabbed Roran in the belly.

Or rather, he tried to. Eragon's spells stopped the tip of the blade a quarter inch from Roran's gut. Roran grunted, surprised, then knocked aside the blade and brained the man with three rapid strikes.

He swore again. It was a bad beginning.

Up and down the wall, more of the Varden tried to climb over the battlements. Few made it. Clumps of soldiers waited at the top of most every ladder, and reinforcements were streaming onto the walkway from the stairs to the city.

Baldor joined him—he had used the same ladder as Roran—and together they ran toward a ballista manned by eight soldiers. The ballista was mounted near the base of one of the many towers that rose out of the wall, each of which stood about two hundred feet apart. Behind the soldiers and the tower, Roran saw the illusion of Saphira that the elves had created, flying over and around the wall, breathing fire on it.

The soldiers were smart; they grabbed their spears and poked at him and Baldor, keeping them at a distance. Roran tried to catch one of the spears, but the man wielding it was too fast, and Roran nearly got stabbed again. A moment more and he knew the soldiers would overwhelm him and Baldor.

Before that could happen, an Urgal pulled himself over the edge of the wall behind the soldiers, then lowered his head and charged, bellowing and swinging the ironbound club he carried.

The Urgal struck one man in the chest, breaking his ribs, and another on the hip, breaking his pelvis. Either injury ought to have incapacitated the soldiers, but as the Urgal bulled past them, the two men picked themselves off the stone as if nothing had happened and proceeded to stab the Urgal in the back.

A sense of doom settled upon Roran. "We'll have to bash in their skulls or take off their heads if we're going to stop them," he growled to Baldor. Keeping his eyes on the soldiers, he shouted to the Varden behind them, "They can't feel pain!"

Out over the city, the illusionary Saphira crashed into a tower. Everyone but Roran paused to look; he knew what the elves were doing.

Jumping forward, he slew one of the soldiers with a blow to the temple. He used his shield to shove the next soldier aside; then he was too close for their spears to be of any use, and he was able to make short work of them with his hammer.

Once he and Baldor had killed the rest of the soldiers around the ballista, Baldor looked at him with an expression of despair. "Did you see? Saphira—"

"She's fine."

"But—"

"Don't worry about it. She's fine."

Baldor hesitated, then accepted Roran's word, and they rushed at the next clump of soldiers.

Soon afterward, Saphira—the *real* Saphira—appeared over the southern part of the wall as she flew toward the citadel, prompting cheers of relief from the Varden.

Roran frowned. She was supposed to remain hidden for the whole of her flight. "Frethya. Frethya," he said quickly under his breath. He remained visible. *Blast it*, he thought.

Turning, he said, "Back to the ladders!"

"Why?" demanded Baldor as he grappled with another soldier. Uttering a ferocious shout, he pushed the man off the wall, into the city.

"Stop asking questions! Move!"

Side by side, they fought their way through the line of soldiers that separated them from the ladders. It was bloody and difficult, and Baldor received a cut on his left calf, behind his greave, and a severe bruise on one of his shoulders, where a spear nearly pierced his mail shirt.

The soldiers' immunity to pain meant that killing them was the only sure way to stop them, and killing them was no easy task. Also, it meant that Roran dared not show mercy. More than once, he thought he had killed a soldier, only to have the wounded man rear up and strike at him while he was engaged with another opponent. And there were so many soldiers on the walkway, he began to fear that he and Baldor would never make it off.

When they reached the nearest ladder, he said, "Here! Stay here."

If Baldor was puzzled, he did not show it. They held off the soldiers by themselves until another two men climbed up the ladder and joined them, then a third, and at last Roran began to feel as if they had a good chance of pushing back the soldiers and capturing that segment of the wall.

Even though the attack had been devised as only a distraction, Roran saw no reason to treat it as such. If they were going to risk their lives, they might as well get something out of it. They needed to clear the walls anyway.

Then they heard Thorn roar with rage, and the red dragon appeared above the tops of the buildings, winging his way toward the citadel. Roran saw a figure he thought was Murtagh on his back, crimson sword in hand.

"What does it mean?" shouted Baldor between sword strokes.

"It means the game is up!" Roran replied. "Brace yourself; these bastards are in for a surprise!"

He had barely finished speaking when the voices of the elves sounded above the noise of the battle, eerie and beautiful as they sang in the ancient language.

Roran ducked under a spear and poked the end of his hammer into a soldier's belly, knocking the wind from the man's lungs. The soldiers might not be able to feel pain, but they still had to breathe. As the soldier struggled to recover, Roran slipped past his guard and crushed his throat with the rim of his shield.

He was about to attack the next man when he felt the stone tremble beneath his feet. He retreated until his back was pressed against the battlements, then widened his stance for balance.

One of the soldiers was foolish enough to rush him at that very moment. As the man ran toward him, the trembling grew stronger, then the top of the wall rippled, like a blanket being tossed, and the onrushing soldier, as well as most of his companions, fell and remained prone, helpless to rise as the earth continued to shake.

631

From the other side of the wall tower that separated them from Urû'baen's main gate came a sound like a mountain breaking. Fan-shaped jets of water sprayed into the air, and then with a great noise, the wall over the gate shuddered and began to crumble inward.

And still the elves sang.

As the motion beneath his feet subsided, Roran sprang forward and killed three of the soldiers before they were able to stand. The rest turned and fled back down the stairs that led into the city.

Roran helped Baldor to his feet, then shouted, "After them!" He grinned, tasting blood. Maybe it wasn't such a bad start after all.

THAT WHICH DOES NOT KILL...

"Stop," said Elva.

Eragon froze with his foot in the air. The girl waved him back, and he retreated.

"Jump to there," said Elva. She pointed at a spot a yard in front of him. "By the scrollwork."

He crouched, then hesitated as he waited for her to tell him whether it was safe.

She stamped her foot and made a sound of exasperation. "It won't work if you don't mean it. I can't tell if something is going to hurt you unless you actually intend to put yourself in danger." She gave him a smile that he found less than reassuring. "Don't worry; I won't let anything happen to you."

Still doubtful, he flexed his legs again and was just about to spring forward when—

"Stop!"

He cursed and waved his arms as he tried to keep from falling onto the section of floor that would trigger the spikes hidden both above and below.

The spikes were the third trap Eragon and his companions had encountered in the long hallway leading to the golden doors. The first had been a set of hidden pits. The second had been blocks of stone in the ceiling that would have squished them flat. And now the spikes, much like those that had killed Wyrden in the tunnels beneath Dras-Leona.

They had seen Murtagh enter the hallway through the open sally port, but he had made no effort to pursue them without Thorn. After watching for a few seconds, he had disappeared into one of the side rooms where Arya and Blödhgarm had broken the gears and wheels used to open and close the stronghold's main gate.

It might take Murtagh an hour to fix the mechanisms, or it might take him minutes. Either way, they dared not dawdle.

"Try a little bit farther out," said Elva.

Eragon grimaced, but did as she suggested.

"Stop!"

This time he would have fallen had Elva not grabbed the back of his tunic.

"Even farther," she said. Then, "Stop! Farther."

"I can't," he growled, his frustration increasing. "Not without a running start." But with a running start, it would be impossible to stop himself in time, should Elva determine that the jump was dangerous. "What now? If the spikes go all the way to the doors, we'll never reach them." They had already thought of using magic to float over the trap, but even the smallest spell would set it off, or so Elva claimed, and they had no choice but to trust her.

"Maybe the trap is meant for a walking dragon," said Arya. "If it's only a yard or two long, Saphira or Thorn could step right over without ever realizing it was there. But if it's a hundred feet long, it would be sure to catch them."

Not if I jump, said Saphira. *A hundred feet is an easy distance.*

Eragon exchanged concerned glances with Arya and Elva. "Just make sure you don't let your tail touch the floor," he said. "And don't go too far, or you might run into another trap."

Yes, little one.

Saphira crouched and gathered herself in, lowering her head until it was only a foot or so above the stone. Then she dug her claws into the floor and leaped down the hallway, opening her wings just enough to give herself a bit of lift.

To Eragon's relief, Elva remained silent.

When Saphira had gone two full lengths of her body, she folded her wings and dropped to the floor with a resounding clatter.

Safe, she said. Her scales scraped on the floor as she turned around. She jumped back, and Eragon and the others moved out of the way to give her room to land on her return. *Well?* she said. *Who's first?*

It took her four trips to ferry them all across the bed of spikes. Then they continued forward at a swift trot, Arya and Elva again in the lead. They encountered no more traps until they were three-quarters of the way to the gleaming doors, at which point Elva shuddered and raised her small hand. They immediately stopped.

"Something will cut us in two if we continue," she said. "I'm not sure where it will come from . . . the walls, I think."

Eragon frowned. That meant that whatever would cut them had enough weight or strength behind it to overcome their wards—hardly an encouraging prospect.

"What if we—" he started to say, then stopped as twenty black-robed humans, men and women alike, filed out of a side passageway and formed a line in front of them, blocking the way.

Eragon felt a blade of thought stab into his mind as the enemy magicians began to chant in the ancient language. Opening her jaws, Saphira raked the spellcasters with a torrent of crackling flame, but it passed harmlessly around them. One of the banners along the wall caught fire, and scraps of smoldering fabric fell to the floor.

Eragon defended himself, but he did not attack in turn; it would take too long to subdue the magicians one by one. Moreover, their chanting concerned him: if they were willing to cast spells before they had seized control of his mind—as well as those of his companions—then they no longer cared if they lived or died, only that they stopped the intruders.

He dropped to one knee next to Elva. She was speaking to one of the spellcasters, saying something about the man's daughter.

"Are they standing over the trap?" he asked, keeping his voice low.

She nodded, never pausing in her speech.

Reaching out, he slapped the palm of his hand against the floor. He had expected something to happen, but still he recoiled when a horizontal sheet of metal—thirty feet long and four inches thick—shot out of each wall with a terrible *screech*. The plates of metal caught the magicians between them and cut them in two, like a pair of giant tin snips, then just as quickly retreated back into their hidden slots.

The suddenness of it shocked Eragon. He averted his eyes from the shambles before them. *What a horrible way to die.*

Next to him, Elva gurgled, then slumped forward in a faint. Arya caught her before her head hit the floor. Cradling her with one arm, Arya began to murmur to her in the ancient language.

Eragon consulted with the other elves about how best to bypass the trap. They decided that the safest way would be to jump over it, as they had with the bed of spikes.

Four of them climbed onto Saphira, and she was just about to spring forward when Elva cried out in a weak voice: "Stop! Don't!"

Saphira flicked her tail but remained where she was.

Elva slid out of Arya's grasp, staggered a few feet away, leaned over, and was sick. She wiped her mouth on the back of her hand, then stared at the mangled bodies that lay before them, as if fixing them in her memory.

Still staring at them, she said, "There is another trigger, halfway across, in the air. If you jump"—she clapped her hands together, a loud, sharp sound, and made an ugly face—"blades come out from high on the walls, as well as lower."

A thought began to bother Eragon. "Why would Galbatorix try to kill us? . . . If you weren't here," he said, looking at Elva, "Saphira might be dead right now. Galbatorix wants her alive, so why this?" He gestured at the bloody floor. "Why the spikes and the blocks of stone?"

"Perhaps," said the elf woman Invidia, "he expected the pits to capture us before we reached the rest of the traps."

"Or perhaps," said Blödhgarm in a grim voice, "he knows that Elva is with us and what she is capable of."

The girl shrugged. "What of it? He can't stop me."

635

A chill crept through Eragon. "No, but if he knows of you, then he might be scared, and if he's scared—"

Then he might really be trying to kill us, Saphira finished.

Arya shook her head. "It doesn't matter. We still have to find him."

They spent a minute discussing how to get past the blades, whereupon Eragon said, "What if I used magic to transport us over there, the way Arya sent Saphira's egg to the Spine?" He gestured toward the area past the bodies.

It would require too much energy, said Glaedr.

Better to conserve our strength for when we face Galbatorix, Umaroth added.

Eragon gnawed on his lip. He looked back over his shoulder and was alarmed to see, far behind them, Murtagh running from one side of the hallway to the other. *We don't have long.*

"Maybe we could put something into the walls, to keep the blades from coming out."

"The blades are sure to be protected from magic," Arya pointed out. "Besides, we don't have anything with us that could hold them back. A knife? A piece of armor? The plates of metal are too big and heavy. They would tear past whatever was in front of them as if it were not there."

Silence fell upon them.

Then Blödhgarm licked his fangs and said, "Not necessarily." He turned and placed his sword on the floor in front of Eragon, then motioned for the elves under his command to do the same.

Eleven blades in total they laid before Eragon. "I can't ask you to do this," he said. "Your swords—"

Blödhgarm interrupted with a raised hand, his fur glossy in the soft light of the lanterns. "We fight with our minds, Shadeslayer, not our bodies. If we encounter soldiers, we can take what weapons we need from them. If our swords are of more use here and now, then we would be foolish to retain them merely for reasons of sentiment."

Eragon inclined his head. "As you wish."

To Arya, Blödhgarm said, "It should be an even number, if we are to have the best chance of success."

She hesitated, then drew her own thin-bladed sword and placed it among the others. "Consider carefully what you are about to do, Eragon," she said. "These are storied weapons all. It would be a shame to destroy them and gain nothing by it."

He nodded, then frowned, concentrating as he recalled his lessons with Oromis. *Umaroth*, he said, *I'll need your strength*.

What is ours is yours, the dragon replied.

The illusion that hid the slots from which the sheets of metal slid out was too well constructed for Eragon to pierce. This was as he expected—Galbatorix was not one to overlook such a detail. On the other hand, the enchantments responsible for the illusion were easy enough to detect, and by them he was able to determine the exact placement and dimensions of the openings.

He could not tell exactly how far back the sheets of metal lay within the slots. He hoped it was at least an inch or two from the outer surface of the wall. If they were closer, his idea would fail, for the king was sure to have protected the metal against outside tampering.

Summoning the words he needed, Eragon cast the first of the twelve spells he intended to use. One of the elves' swords—Laufin's, he thought—disappeared with a faint breath of wind, like a tunic being swung through the air. A half second later, a solid *thud* emanated from the wall to their left.

Eragon smiled. It had worked. If he had tried to send the sword through the sheet of metal, the reaction would have been substantially more dramatic.

Speaking faster than before, he cast the rest of the spells, embedding six swords within each wall, each sword five feet from the next. The elves watched him intently as he spoke; if the loss of their weapons upset them, they did not show it.

When he had finished, Eragon knelt by Arya and Elva—who

were both once more holding the Dauthdaert—and said, "Get ready to run."

Saphira and the elves tensed. Arya had Elva climb onto her back while still maintaining her hold on the green lance; then Arya said, "Ready."

Reaching forward, Eragon again slapped the floor.

A jarring crash sounded from each wall, and threads of dust fell from the ceiling, blossoming into hazy plumes.

The moment he saw that the swords had held, Eragon dashed forward. He had barely taken two steps when Elva screamed, "Faster!"

Roaring with the effort, he forced his feet to strike the ground even harder. To his right, Saphira ran past, head and tail low, a dark shadow at the edge of his vision.

Just as he reached the far side of the trap, he heard the *snap* of breaking steel and then the cringe-inducing shriek of metal scraping against metal.

Behind him, someone shouted.

He twisted as he flung himself away from the noise, and he saw that everyone had crossed the space in time, save the silver-haired elf woman Yaela, who had been caught between the last six inches of the two pieces of metal. The space around her flared blue and yellow, as if the air itself was burning, and her face contorted with pain.

"Flauga!" shouted Blödhgarm, and Yaela flew out from between the sheets of metal, which snapped together with a ringing clang. Then they retreated into the walls with the same terrible shrieking that had accompanied their appearance.

Yaela had landed on her hands and knees close to Eragon. He helped her to her feet; to his surprise, she seemed unharmed. "Are you hurt?" he asked.

She shook her head. "No, but . . . my wards are gone." She lifted her hands and stared at them with an expression close to wonder. "I've not been without wards since . . . since I was younger than you are now. Somehow the blades stripped them from me."

"You're lucky to be alive," said Eragon. He frowned.

Elva shrugged. "We would have all died, except for *him*"—she pointed at Blödhgarm—"if I hadn't told you to move faster."

Eragon grunted.

They continued on their way, expecting with every step to find another trap. But the rest of the hallway proved to be free of obstacles, and they reached the doors at the end without further incident.

Eragon looked up at the shining expanse of gold. Embossed across the doors was a life-sized oak tree, the leaves of which formed an arching canopy that joined with the roots below to inscribe a great circle about the trunk. Sprouting from either side of the trunk's midsection were two thick bundles of branches, which divided the space within the circle into quarters. In the top-left quarter was a carving of an army of spear-bearing elves marching through a thick forest. In the top-right quarter were humans building castles and forging swords. In the bottom left, Urgals—Kull, mostly—burning down a village and killing the inhabitants. In the bottom right, dwarves mining caves filled with gems and veins of ore. Amid the roots and branches of the oak, Eragon spotted werecats and the Ra'zac, as well as a few small strange-looking creatures that he failed to recognize. And coiled in the very center of the bole of the tree was a dragon that held the end of its tail in its mouth, as if biting itself. The doors were beautifully crafted. Under different circumstances, Eragon would have been content to sit and study them for most of a day.

As it was, the sight of the shining doors filled him with dread as he contemplated what might lie on the other side. If it was Galbatorix, then their lives were about to change forever and nothing would ever be the same—not for them, and not for the rest of Alagaësia.

I'm not ready, Eragon said to Saphira.

When will we ever be ready? she replied. She flicked out her tongue, tasting the air. He could feel her nervous anticipation. *Galbatorix and Shruikan must be killed, and we are the only ones who might be able to do it.*

What if we can't?

Then we can't, and what will be will be.

He nodded and took a long breath. *I love you, Saphira.*

I love you too, little one.

Eragon stepped forward. "Now what?" he asked, trying to hide his uneasiness. "Should we knock?"

"First, let's see if it's open," said Arya.

They arranged themselves in a formation suitable for battle. Then Arya, with Elva next to her, grasped a handle set within the left-hand door and prepared to pull.

As she did, a column of shimmering air appeared around Blödhgarm and each of his ten spellcasters. Eragon shouted with alarm, and Saphira released a short hiss, as if she had stepped upon something sharp. The elves seemed unable to move within the columns: even their eyes remained motionless, fixed upon whatever they had been looking at when the spell took effect.

With a heavy clank, a door in the wall to the left slid open, and the elves began to move toward it, like a procession of statues gliding across ice.

Arya lunged toward them, barbed spear extended before her, in an attempt to cut through the enchantments binding the elves, but she was too slow, and she could not catch them.

"Letta!" shouted Eragon. Stop! The simplest spell he could think of that might help. However, the magic that imprisoned the elves proved too strong for him to break, and they disappeared within the dark opening, the door slamming shut behind them.

Dismay swept through Eragon. Without the elves . . .

Arya pounded on the door with the butt of the Dauthdaert, and she even tried to find the seam between the door and the wall with the tip of the blade—as she had with the sally port—but the wall seemed solid, immovable.

When she turned around, her expression was one of cold fury. *Umaroth*, she said. *I need your help to open this wall.*

No, said the white dragon. *Galbatorix is sure to have hidden your* companions well. *Trying to find them will only waste energy and place us in even greater danger.*

Arya's slanting eyebrows drew closer as she scowled. *Then we play into his hand, Umaroth-elda. He wants to divide us and make us weaker. If we continue without them, it will be that much easier for Galbatorix to defeat us.*

Yes, little one. But think you not also that the Egg-breaker might want us to pursue them? He might want us to forget him in our anger and concern, and thus to rush blindly into another of his traps.

Why would he go to so much trouble? He could have captured Eragon, Saphira, you, and the rest of the Eldunarí, even as he captured Blödhgarm and the others, but he didn't.

Perhaps because he wants us to exhaust ourselves before we confront him or before he attempts to break us.

Arya lowered her head for a moment, and when she looked up, her fury had vanished—at least on the surface—replaced by her usual controlled watchfulness. *What, then, should we do, Ebrithil?*

We hope that Galbatorix will not kill Blödhgarm or the others—not immediately, at least—and we continue on until we find the king.

Arya acquiesced, but Eragon could tell that she found it distasteful. He could not blame her; he felt the same.

"Why didn't you sense the trap?" he asked Elva in an undertone. He thought he understood, but he wanted to hear it from her.

"Because it didn't hurt them," she said.

He nodded.

Arya strode back to the golden doors and again grasped the handle on the left. Joining her, Elva wrapped her small hand around the shaft of the Dauthdaert.

Leaning away from the door, Arya pulled and pulled, and the massive structure slowly began to swing outward. No one human, Eragon was sure, could have opened it, and even Arya's strength was barely sufficient.

When the door reached the wall, Arya released it, and then she and Elva joined Eragon in front of Saphira.

On the other side of the cavernous archway was a huge, dark chamber. Eragon was unsure of its size, for the walls lay hidden in velvet shadows. A line of flameless lanterns mounted on iron poles ran straight out from either side of the entranceway, illuminating the patterned floor and little else, while a faint glow came from above through crystals set within the distant ceiling. The two rows of lanterns ended over five hundred feet away, near the base of a broad dais, upon which rested a throne. On the throne sat a single black figure, the only figure in the whole room, and on his lap lay a bare sword, a long white splinter that seemed to emit a faint glow.

Eragon swallowed and tightened his grip on Brisingr. He gave Saphira's jaw a quick rub with the edge of his shield, and she flicked out her tongue in response. Then, by unspoken consent, the four of them started forward.

The moment they were all in the throne room, the golden door swung shut behind them. Eragon had expected as much, but still, the noise of it closing made him start. As the echoes faded to dusky silence within the high presence chamber, the figure upon the throne stirred, as if waking from sleep, and then a voice—a voice such as Eragon had never heard before: deep and rich and imbued with authority greater than that of Ajihad or Oromis or Hrothgar, a voice that made even the elves' seem harsh and discordant—rang forth from the far side of the throne room.

And it said, "Ah, I have been expecting you. Welcome to my abode. And welcome to you in particular, Eragon Shadeslayer, and to you, Saphira Brightscales. I have much desired to meet with you. But I am also glad to see you, Arya—daughter of Islanzadí, and Shadeslayer in your own right—and you as well, Elva, she of the Shining Brow. And of course, Glaedr, Umaroth, Valdr, and those others who travel with you unseen. I had long believed them to be dead, and I am most glad to learn otherwise. Welcome, all! We have much to talk about."

✦ ✦ ✦

THE HEART OF THE FRAY

Along with the warriors of his battalion, Roran fought his way down off Urû'baen's outer wall to the streets below. There they paused to regroup; then he shouted, "To the gate!" and pointed with his hammer.

He and several men from Carvahall, including Horst and Delwin, took the lead as they trotted along the inside of the wall toward the breach the elves had created with their magic. Arrows flitted over their heads as they ran, but none were aimed at them specifically, and he did not hear any of their group take a wound.

They encountered dozens of soldiers in the narrow space between the wall and the stone houses. A few paused to fight, but the rest ran, and even those who fought soon retreated down the adjoining alleyways.

At first the savage intensity of slaughter and victory blinded Roran to all else. But when the soldiers they met continued to flee, a sense of unease began to gnaw at his stomach, and he began to look around with greater alertness, searching for anything that seemed different from what it ought to be.

Something was wrong. He was sure of it.

"Galbatorix wouldn't let them give up this easily," he muttered to himself.

"What?" asked Albriech, who was next to him.

"I said, Galbatorix wouldn't let them give up this easily." Twisting his head around, Roran shouted to the rest of the battalion, "Pin back your ears and look sharp! Galbatorix has a surprise or two in store for us, I wager. We won't let ourselves get caught unawares, though, now will we?"

"Stronghammer!" they shouted in return, and pounded their weapons against their shields. All but the elves, that was. Satisfied, he quickened the pace even as he continued to scan the rooftops.

They soon broke out into the rubble-strewn street that led to what had once been the main gate of the city. Now all that was left was a gaping hole several hundred feet wide at the top, with a pile of broken stones at the bottom. Through the gap streamed the Varden and their allies: men, dwarves, Urgals, elves, and werecats, fighting alongside one another for the first time in history.

Arrows rained down on the army as it poured into the city, but the elves' magic stopped the deadly darts before they could cause harm. The same did not hold true for Galbatorix's soldiers; Roran saw a number of them fall to the Varden's archers, although some appeared to have wards that protected them from the arrows. Galbatorix's favorites, he assumed.

As his battalion joined the rest of the army, Roran spotted Jörmundur riding in the press of warriors. Roran called out greetings, and Jörmundur replied in kind and shouted, "Once we reach that fountain"—he pointed with his sword toward a large, ornate edifice that stood in a courtyard several hundred yards in front of them—"take your men and head off to the right. Clear the southern part of the city, then meet back up with us at the citadel."

Roran nodded, exaggerating the movement so Jörmundur could see. "Sir!"

He felt safer now that they had the company of other warriors, but still his sense of unease continued. *Where are they?* he wondered, looking at the mouths of the empty streets. Galbatorix had supposedly gathered the whole of his army in Urû'baen, but Roran had yet to see evidence of a large force of men. There had been surprisingly few soldiers on the walls, and those who were present had fled far sooner than they should have.

He's luring us in, Roran realized with sudden certainty. *It's all a play designed to trick us.* Catching Jörmundur's attention again, he shouted, "Something's wrong! Where are the soldiers?"

Jörmundur frowned and turned to speak with King Orrin and Queen Islanzadí, who had ridden up to him. Oddly enough, a white raven sat on Islanzadí's left shoulder, his claws hooked into her corselet of golden armor.

And still the Varden continued to march deeper and deeper into Urû'baen.

"What is the matter, Stronghammer?" growled Nar Garzhvog as he pushed his way over to Roran.

Roran glanced up at the heavy-headed Kull. "I'm not sure. Galbatorix—"

He forgot whatever else he was going to say when a horn sounded among the buildings ahead of them. It blared for the better part of a minute, a low, ominous tone that caused the Varden to pause and look around with concern.

Roran's heart sank. "This is it," he said to Albriech. Turning, he waved his hammer, motioning toward the side of the street. "Move over!" he bellowed. "Get between the buildings and take cover!"

It took his battalion longer to extricate itself from the column of warriors than it had to join it. Frustrated, Roran continued shouting, trying to get them to move faster. "Quickly, you sorry dogs! Quickly!"

The horn sounded again, and Jörmundur finally called a halt to the army.

By then, Roran's warriors were safely wedged into three streets, where they stood clustered behind buildings, waiting for his orders. He stood by the side of a house, along with Garzhvog and Horst, peering around the corner as he tried to see what was happening.

Once more the horn sounded, and then the tramp of many feet echoed through Urû'baen.

Dread crawled through Roran as he saw rank after rank of soldiers march into the streets leading from the citadel, the rows of men brisk and orderly, their faces devoid of even the slightest hint of fear. At their head rode a squat, broad-shouldered man upon a gray charger. He wore a gleaming breastplate that bulged over a foot outward, as if to accommodate a large belly. In his left hand, he carried a shield painted with the device of a crumbling tower upon a bare stone peak. In his right hand, he carried a spiked mace that most men would have found difficult to lift but that he swung back and forth with ease.

Roran wet his lips. He guessed that the man was none other than Lord Barst, and if even half the things he had heard about the man were true, then Barst would never ride straight at an opposing force unless he was utterly certain of destroying it.

Roran had seen enough. Pushing himself off the corner of the building, he said, "We're not going to wait. Tell the others to follow us."

"You mean to run away, Stronghammer?" rumbled Nar Garzhvog.

"No," said Roran. "I mean to attack from the side. Only a fool would attack an army like that head-on. Now go!" He gave the Urgal a shove, then hurried down the cross street to take his position at the front of his warriors. *And only a fool would go head to head with the man Galbatorix has chosen to lead his forces.*

As they made their way between the densely packed buildings, Roran heard the soldiers start to chant, "Lord Barst! Lord Barst! Lord Barst!" And they stamped the ground with their hobnail boots and banged their swords against their shields.

Better and better, Roran thought, wishing he were anywhere but there.

Then the Varden shouted in return, the air filled with cries of "Eragon!" and "The Riders!" and the city rang with the sounds of clashing metal and the screams of wounded men.

When his battalion was level with what Roran guessed was the midpoint of the Empire's army, he had them turn and start in the direction of their enemies. "Stay together," he ordered. "Form a wall with your shields, and whatever you do, make sure you protect the spellcasters."

They soon spotted the soldiers in the street—spearmen, mostly—

pressed close against one another as they shuffled toward the front of the battle.

Nar Garzhvog let out a ferocious bellow, as did Roran and the other warriors in the battalion, and they charged toward the ranks of men. The soldiers shouted with alarm, and panic spread among them as they scrambled backward, trampling their own kind as they tried to find room to fight.

Howling, Roran fell upon the first row of men. Blood sprayed around him as he swung his hammer and felt metal and bone give way. The soldiers were so tightly packed that they were nearly help-less. He killed four of them before even one managed to swing a sword at him, which he blocked with his shield.

By the edge of the street, Nar Garzhvog knocked down six men with a single blow of his club. The soldiers started to climb back to their feet, ignoring injuries that would have crippled them had they been able to feel pain, and Garzhvog struck again, pounding them to a pulp.

Roran was aware of nothing but the men in front of him, the weight of his hammer in his hand, and the slipperiness of the blood-coated cobblestones under his feet. He broke and he battered; he ducked and he shoved; he growled and he shouted and he killed and he killed and he killed—until, to his surprise, he swung his hammer and found nothing but empty air before him. His weapon bounced against the ground, striking sparks from the cobblestones, and a painful jolt ran up his arm.

Roran shook his head, his battle rage clearing; he had fought his way completely through the mass of soldiers.

Spinning around, he saw that most of his warriors were still en-gaged with soldiers to his right and left. Loosing another howl, he dove back into the fray.

Three soldiers closed in on him: two with spears, one with a sword. Roran lunged at the man with the sword, but his foot slipped beneath him as he stepped on something soft and wet. Even as he fell, he swung his hammer at the ankles of the nearest man. The soldier danced back and was about to bring his sword down on Roran when an elf leaped forward and, with two quick strokes, beheaded all three soldiers.

It was the same elf woman he had spoken to outside the city walls, only now splattered with stripes of gore. Before he could thank her, she darted past, her sword a blur as she cut down more of the soldiers.

After watching them in action, Roran decided that each elf was worth at least five men, not even counting their ability to cast spells. As for the Urgals, he just did his best to stay out of their way, especially the Kull. They seemed to make little distinction between friend and foe once roused, and the Kull were so big, it was easy for them to kill someone without meaning to. He saw one of them crush a soldier between his leg and the side of a building and not even notice. Another time, he saw a Kull behead a soldier with an inadvertent swipe of a shield while turning about.

The fighting continued for another few minutes, whereupon the only soldiers remaining in the area were dead soldiers.

Wiping the sweat from his brow, Roran glanced up and down the street. Farther into the city, he saw remnants of the force they had destroyed disappearing between the houses as the men ran to join another part of Galbatorix's army. He considered pursuing them, but the main battle lay closer to the edge of the city, and he wanted to fall upon the rear of the attacking soldiers and disrupt their lines.

"This way!" he shouted, raising his hammer and starting down the street.

An arrow buried itself in the edge of his shield, and he looked up to see the silhouette of a man sliding below the peak of a nearby roof.

When Roran emerged from between the close-set buildings into the open area before the remnants of Urû'baen's front gate, he found a scene of such confusion that he hesitated, unsure of what to do.

The two armies had mingled together until it was impossible to determine lines or ranks or even where the front of the battle was. The crimson tunics of the soldiers were scattered throughout the square, sometimes singly, sometimes in large clusters, and the fighting had spilled into all of the nearby streets, the armies spreading outward like a stain. Among the combatants Roran expected to see, he also spotted scores of cats—ordinary cats, not werecats—attacking the soldiers, as savage and frightening a sight as he had ever beheld. The cats, he knew, followed the direction of the werecats.

And in the center of the square, sitting upon his gray charger, was Lord Barst, his large round breastplate gleaming with the light of the fires burning in nearby houses. He swung his mace again and again, faster than any human ought to have been able to, and with every blow he slew at least one of the Varden. Arrows fired at him vanished in puffs of sickly orange flame, swords and spears bounced off him as if he were made of stone, and even the strength of a charging Kull was not enough to knock him off his steed. Roran watched with astonishment as, with a casual swipe of his mace, the armor-clad man brained an attacking Kull, breaking his horns and skull as easily as an eggshell.

Roran frowned. *How can he be so strong and fast?* Magic was the obvious answer, but that magic had to have a source. There were no gems upon Barst's mace or armor, nor could Roran believe that Galbatorix would be feeding energy to Barst from a distance. Roran remembered his conversation with Eragon the night before they rescued Katrina from Helgrind. Eragon had told him that it was basically impossible to alter a human's body to have the speed and strength of an elf, even if the human was a Rider—which made what the dragons had done to Eragon during the Blood-oath Celebration all the more amazing. It seemed unlikely that Galbatorix could have managed a similar transformation with Barst, which again made Roran wonder, where was the source of Barst's unnatural might?

Barst pulled on the reins of his steed, turning the horse around. The light moving across the surface of his swollen breastplate caught Roran's attention.

Roran's mouth went dry, and he felt a sense of despair. From what he knew, Barst was not the sort of man to have a belly. He would not let himself go soft, nor would Galbatorix have chosen such a man to defend Urû'baen. The only explanation that made sense, then, was that Barst had an Eldunarí strapped to his body underneath his oddly shaped breastplate.

Then the street shook and split, and a dark crevice appeared beneath Barst and his charger. The hole would have swallowed them both, with room to spare, but the horse remained standing upon thin air, as if its hooves were still planted firmly upon the ground. A wreath of different colors flickered around Barst, like a nimbus of tattered rainbows. Alternating waves of heat and cold emanated from his location, and Roran saw tendrils of ice crawling up from the ground, seeking to wrap themselves around the horse's legs and hold them in place. But the ice could not grip the horse, nor did any of the magic seem to have an effect on either the man or the animal.

Barst pulled on the reins again, then spurred his horse toward a group of elves who stood beside a nearby house, chanting in the ancient language. It was they, Roran assumed, who had been casting the spells against Barst.

Lifting his mace above his head, Barst charged into the midst of the elves. They scattered, seeking to defend themselves, but to no avail, for Barst split their shields and broke their swords, and when he struck, the mace crushed the elves as if their bones were as thin and hollow as those of birds.

Why didn't their wards protect them? Roran wondered. *Why can't they stop him with their minds? He's only one man, and there's only one Eldunarí with him.*

A few yards away, a large round stone crashed into the sea of struggling bodies, leaving behind a bright red smear, and bounced into the front of a building, where it shattered the statues above the doorframe.

Roran ducked and cursed as he looked for where the stone had come from. Halfway across the city, he saw that Galbatorix's soldiers had retaken the catapults and other war machines mounted on the curtain wall. *They're firing into their own city,* he thought. *They're firing at their own men!*

With a growl of disgust, he turned away from the square, so that he was facing the interior of the city. "We can't help here!" he shouted to the battalion. "Leave Barst to the others. Take the street over there!" He pointed to his left. "We'll fight our way to the wall and make our stand there!"

If the warriors responded, he did not hear, for he was already moving. Behind him, another stone crashed into the fighting armies, causing even more screams of pain.

The street Roran had chosen was full of soldiers, as well as a few elves and werecats, who were clumped together by the front door of a hatter's shop, hard-pressed to fend off the large number of enemies around them. The elves shouted something, and a dozen soldiers fell to the ground, but the rest remained standing.

Diving into the midst of the soldiers, Roran again lost himself in the red-tinged haze of battle. He leaped over one of the fallen soldiers and brought his hammer down on the helm of a man with his back turned. Confident that the man was dead, Roran used his shield to shove the next soldier back and then jabbed with the end of his hammer at the man's throat, crushing it.

Next to him, Delwin caught a spear in his shoulder and went down on one knee with a cry of pain. Swinging his hammer even faster than normal, Roran drove back the spearman while Delwin pulled the weapon out and got back to his feet.

"Fall back," Roran told him.

Delwin shook his head, teeth bared. "No!"

"Fall back, blast you! That's an order."

Delwin cursed, but he obeyed, and Horst took his place. The

smith, Roran noticed, was bleeding from cuts on his arms and legs, but they did not seem to interfere with his ability to move.

Evading a sword thrust, Roran took a step forward. He seemed to hear a faint rushing sound behind him, and then a thunderclap went off in his ears, and the earth spun around him and everything went black.

He woke with a throbbing head. Above, he saw the sky—bright now with light from the rising sun—and the dark underside of the crevice-lined overhang.

Groaning with pain, he pushed himself upright. He was lying at the base of the city's outer wall, next to the bloody fragments of a stone from a catapult. His shield was missing, as was his hammer, which concerned him in a befuddled sort of way.

Even as he tried to regain his bearings, a group of five soldiers rushed at him, and one of the men stabbed him in the chest with a spear. The point of the weapon drove him back against the wall, but it did not pierce his skin.

"Grab him!" shouted the soldiers, and Roran felt hands take hold of his arms and legs. He thrashed, trying to wrench free, but he was still weak and disoriented, and there were too many soldiers for him to overpower.

The soldiers struck at him again and again, and he felt his strength fading as his wards shielded him from the blows. The world grew gray, and he was about to lose consciousness again when the blade of a sword sprouted from the mouth of one of the soldiers.

The soldiers dropped him, and Roran saw a dark-haired woman whirling among them, swinging her sword with the practiced ease of a seasoned warrior. Within seconds, she killed the five men, although one of them managed to give her a shallow cut along her left thigh.

Afterward, she offered him her hand and said, "Stronghammer."

As he grasped her forearm, he saw that her wrist—where her worn bracer did not cover it—was layered with scars, as if she had been burned or whipped nearly to the bone. Behind the woman stood a pale-faced teenage girl clad in a piecemeal collection of armor, and also a boy who looked a year or two younger than the girl.

"Who are you?" he asked, standing. The woman's face was striking: broad and strong-boned, with the bronzed, weather-beaten look of one who had spent most of her life outdoors.

"A passing stranger," she said. Bending at the knees, she picked up one of the soldiers' spears and handed it to him.

"My thanks."

She nodded, and then she and her young companions trotted off among the buildings, heading farther into the city.

Roran stared after them for a half second, wondering, then shook himself and hurried back along the street to rejoin his battalion.

The warriors greeted him with shouts of astonishment and, heartened, attacked the soldiers with renewed vigor. However, as Roran took his place along with the other men from Carvahall, he discovered that the stone that had struck him had also killed Delwin. His sorrow quickly turned to rage, and he fought with even greater ferocity than before, determined to help end the battle as soon as possible.

✦   ✦   ✦

THE NAME OF ALL NAMES

Afraid but determined, Eragon strode forward with Arya, Elva, and Saphira toward the dais where Galbatorix sat relaxed upon his throne.

It was a long walk, long enough that Eragon had time to consider a number of strategies, most of which he discarded as impractical. He knew that strength alone would not be enough to defeat the king; it would require cunning as well, and that was the one thing he felt he most lacked. Still, they had no choice now but to confront Galbatorix.

The two rows of lanterns that led to the dais were wide enough apart that the four of them were able to walk side by side. For that Eragon was glad, as it meant Saphira would be able to fight next to them if need be.

As they approached the throne, Eragon continued to study the chamber around them. It was, he thought, a strange room for a king to receive guests in. Aside from the bright path that lay before them, most of the space was hidden within impenetrable gloom—even more so than the halls of the dwarves beneath Tronjheim and Farthen Dûr—and the air contained a dry, musky scent that seemed familiar, even though he could not place it.

"Where is Shruikan?" he said in an undertone.

Saphira sniffed. *I can smell him, but I don't hear him.*

Elva frowned. "Nor can I feel him."

When they were perhaps thirty feet from the dais, they halted. Behind the throne hung thick black curtains made of velvety material, which stretched up toward the ceiling.

A shadow lay over Galbatorix, concealing his features. Then he leaned forward, into the light, and Eragon saw his face. It was long and lean, with a deep brow and a bladelike nose. His eyes were hard as stones, and they showed little white around the irises. His mouth was thin and wide with a slight downturn at the corners, and he had a close-cropped beard and mustache, which, like his clothes, were black as pitch. In age, he appeared to be in his fourth decade: still at the height of his strength, yet near the beginning of his decline. There were lines on his brow and on either side of his nose, and his tanned skin had a thin look to it, as if he had eaten nothing but rabbit meat and turnips through the winter. His shoulders were broad and well built, and his waist trim.

Upon his head was a crown of reddish gold set with all manner of jewels. The crown appeared old—older even than the hall, and Eragon wondered if perhaps it had once belonged to King Palancar, many hundreds of years ago.

On Galbatorix's lap rested his sword. It was a Rider's sword, that much was obvious, but Eragon had never seen its like before. The blade, hilt, and crossguard were stark white, while the gem within the pommel was as clear as a mountain spring. Altogether, there was something about the weapon that Eragon found unsettling. Its color—or rather its *lack* of color—reminded him of a sun-bleached bone. It was the color of death, not life, and it seemed far more dangerous than any shade of black, be it ever so dark.

Galbatorix examined them each in turn with his sharp, unblinking gaze. "So, you have come to kill me," he said. "Well then, shall we begin?" He lifted his sword and spread his arms to either side in a welcoming gesture.

Eragon widened his stance and raised his sword and shield. The king's invitation unsettled him. *He's playing with us.*

Still keeping hold of the Dauthdaert, Elva stepped forward and began to speak. However, no sound came from her mouth, and she looked at Eragon with an expression of alarm.

Eragon tried to touch her mind with his own, but he could feel nothing of her thoughts; it was as if she were no longer in the room with them.

Galbatorix laughed, then returned his sword to his lap and leaned back in his throne. "Did you truly believe that I was ignorant of your ability, child? Did you really think you could render me helpless with such a petty, transparent trick? Oh, I have no doubt your words could harm me, but only if I can hear them." His bloodless lips curved in a cruel, humorless smile. "Such folly. *This* is the extent of your plan? A girl who cannot speak unless I grant her leave, a spear more suited for hanging on a wall than carrying into battle, and a collection of Eldunarí half out of their minds with age? Tut-tut. I had thought better of you, Arya. And you, Glaedr, but then I suppose your emotions have clouded your reason since I used Murtagh to slay Oromis."

To Eragon, Saphira, and Arya, Glaedr said, *Kill him.* The golden dragon felt perfectly calm, but his very serenity betrayed an anger that surpassed all other emotions.

Eragon exchanged a quick glance with Arya and Saphira, and then the three of them started toward the dais, even as Glaedr, Umaroth, and the other Eldunarí attacked Galbatorix's mind.

Before Eragon managed to take more than a few steps, the king rose up from his velvet seat and shouted a Word. The Word reverberated within Eragon's mind, and every part of his being seemed to thrum in response, as if he were an instrument upon which a bard had struck a chord. Despite the intensity of his response, Eragon was unable to remember the Word; it faded from his mind, leaving behind only the knowledge of its existence and how it had affected him.

Galbatorix uttered other words after the first, but none seemed to have the same power, and Eragon was too dazed to comprehend their meaning. As the last phrase left the king's lips, a force gripped Eragon, stopping him in mid-stride. The jolt shook a yelp of surprise from him. He tried to move, but his body might as well have been encased in stone. All he could do was breathe, look, and as he had already discovered, speak.

He did not understand; his wards should have protected him from the king's magic. That they did not left him feeling as if he were teetering on the edge of a vast abyss.

Next to him, Saphira, Arya, and Elva appeared likewise immobilized.

Enraged by how easily the king had caught them, Eragon joined his mind with the Eldunarí as they battered at Galbatorix's consciousness. He felt a vast number of minds opposing them—dragons all, who crooned and babbled and shrieked in a mad, disjointed chorus that contained such pain and sorrow, Eragon wanted to pull himself away lest they drag him down into their insanity. They were strong too, as if most of them had been Glaedr's size or larger.

The opposing dragons made it impossible to attack Galbatorix directly. Every time Eragon thought he felt the touch of the king's thoughts, one of the enslaved dragons would throw itself at Eragon's mind and—gibbering all the while—force him to retreat. Fighting the dragons was difficult on account of their wild and incoherent thoughts; subduing any one of them was like trying to hold down a rabid wolf. And there were so many of them, far more than the Riders had hidden in the Vault of Souls.

Before either side could gain the advantage, Galbatorix, who seemed entirely unaffected by the invisible struggle, said, "Come out, my dears, and meet our guests."

A boy and a girl emerged from behind the throne and came to stand by the king's right hand. The girl looked about six, the boy perhaps eight or nine. They shared a close resemblance, and Eragon guessed they were brother and sister. Both were dressed in their night garments. The girl clung to the boy's arm and half hid behind him, while the boy appeared frightened but determined. Even as he struggled against Galbatorix's Eldunarí, Eragon could feel the minds of the children—could feel their terror and confusion—and he knew they were real.

657

"Isn't she charming?" asked Galbatorix, lifting the girl's chin with one long finger. "Such large eyes and such pretty hair. And isn't he a handsome young lad?" He put his hand on the boy's shoulder. "Children, it is said, are a blessing to us all. I do not happen to share that belief. It has been my experience that children are every bit as cruel and vindictive as adults. They only lack the strength to subjugate others to their will.

"Perhaps you agree with me, perhaps you don't. Regardless, I know that you of the Varden pride yourselves on your virtue. You see yourselves as upholders of justice, defenders of the innocent—as if any are truly innocent—and as noble warriors fighting to right an ancient wrong. Very well, then; let us test your convictions and see if you are what you claim to be. Unless you stop your attack, I shall kill these two"—he shook the boy's shoulder—"and I shall kill them if you dare attack me again. . . . In fact, if you displease me excessively, I shall kill them anyway, so I advise you to be courteous." The boy and the girl appeared sick at his words, but they made no attempt to flee.

Eragon looked over at Arya, and he saw his despair mirrored in her eyes.

Umaroth! they cried out.

No, growled the white dragon, even as he wrestled with the mind of another Eldunarí.

You have to stop, said Arya.

No!

He'll kill them, said Eragon.

No! We will not give up. Not now!

Enough! roared Glaedr. *There are hatchlings in danger!*

And more hatchlings will be in danger if we do not kill the Egg-breaker.

Yes, but now is the wrong time to try, said Arya. *Wait a little while, and perhaps we can find a way to attack him without risking the lives of the children.*

And if not? asked Umaroth.

Neither Eragon nor Arya could bring themselves to answer.

Then we will do what we must, said Saphira. Eragon hated it, but he knew she was right. They could not place the two children before the whole of Alagaësia. If possible, they would save the boy and the girl, but if not, then they would still attack. They had no other choice.

As Umaroth and the Eldunarí he spoke for grudgingly subsided, Galbatorix smiled. "There, that's better. Now we may speak as civilized beings, without worrying about who is trying to kill whom." He patted the boy on the head and then pointed toward the steps of the dais. "Sit." Without arguing, the two children settled on the lowest step, as far from the king as they could get. Then Galbatorix motioned and said, "Kausta," and Eragon slid forward until he was standing at the base of the dais, as did Arya, Elva, and Saphira.

Eragon continued to be bewildered that their wards were not protecting them. He thought of the Word—whatever it might have been—and a horrible suspicion began to take root within him. Hopelessness quickly followed. For all their plans, for all their talking and worrying and suffering, for all their sacrifices, Galbatorix had captured them as easily as he might a litter of newborn kittens. And if Eragon's suspicion was true, the king was even more formidable than they had suspected.

Still, they were not entirely helpless. Their minds were, for the moment, their own. And so far as he could tell, they could still use magic . . . one way or another.

Galbatorix's gaze settled upon Eragon. "So you are the one who has given me so much trouble, Eragon, son of Morzan. . . . You and I should have met long ago. Had your mother not been so foolish as to hide you in Carvahall, you would have grown up here, in Urû'baen, as a child of the nobility, with all the riches and responsibilities that entails, instead of whiling away your days grubbing in the dirt.

"Be that as it may, you are here now, and those things shall at last be yours. They are your birthright, your inheritance, and I shall see to it that you receive them." He seemed to study Eragon with greater intensity, and then he said, "You look more like your mother than your father. With Murtagh, the opposite holds true. Still, it matters little. Whichever one you resemble most, it is only right that you and your brother should serve me, even as did your parents."

"Never," said Eragon with a clenched jaw.

A thin smile appeared on the king's face. "Never? We shall see." His gaze shifted. "And you, Saphira. Of all my guests today, I am gladdest to see you. You have grown to a fine adulthood. Do you remember this place? Do you remember the sound of my voice? I spent many a night talking to you and the other eggs in my charge during the years when I was securing my rule over the Empire."

I . . . I remember a little, said Saphira, and Eragon relayed her words to the king. She did not want to communicate directly with the king, nor would the king have allowed it. Keeping their minds separate was the best way to protect themselves when not in open conflict.

Galbatorix nodded. "And I am sure you will remember more the longer you stay within these walls. You may not have been fully aware of it at the time, but you spent most of your life in a room not far from here. This is your home, Saphira. It is where you belong. And it is where you will build your nest and lay your eggs."

Saphira's eyes narrowed, and Eragon felt a strange yearning from her, mixed with a burning hatred.

The king moved on. "Arya Dröttningu. Fate, it seems, has a sense of humor, for here you are, even as I ordered you to be brought so long ago. Your path was a roundabout one, but still you have come, and of your own accord. I find that rather amusing. Don't you?"

Arya pressed her lips together and refused to answer.

Galbatorix chuckled. "I admit you have been a thorn in my side for quite some time now. You've not caused as much mischief as that bumbling meddler Brom, but neither have you been idle. One might even say that this whole situation is your fault, as it was you who sent Saphira's egg to Eragon. However, I hold no enmity toward you. If not for you, Saphira might not have hatched and I might never have been able to flush the last of my enemies from hiding. For that, I thank you.

"And then there is you, Elva. The girl with the sigil of a Rider upon her brow. Dragon-marked and blessed with the wherewithal to perceive all that pains a person and all that *will* pain them. How you must have suffered these past months. How you must despise those around you for their weaknesses, even as you are forced to share in their misery. The Varden have used you poorly. Today I shall end the battles that have so tormented you, and you shall no longer have to endure the mistakes and misfortunes of others. That I promise. On occasion, I may have need of your skill, but in the main, you may live as you please, and peace shall be yours."

Elva frowned, but it was obvious that the king's offer tempted her. Listening to Galbatorix, Eragon realized, could be as dangerous as listening to Elva herself.

Galbatorix paused and fingered the wire-wrapped hilt of his sword while he regarded them with a hooded gaze. Then he looked past them toward the point in the air where the Eldunarí floated hidden from sight, and his mood seemed to darken. "Convey my words to Umaroth as I speak them," he said. "Umaroth! We are ill met once again. I thought I killed you on Vroengard."

Umaroth responded, and Eragon began to relay his words: "He says—"

"—that you killed only his body," Arya finished.

"That much is obvious," said Galbatorix. "Where did the Riders hide you and those with you? On Vroengard? Or was it elsewhere? My servants and I searched the ruins of Doru Araeba most closely."

Eragon hesitated to deliver the dragon's answer, as it was sure to displease the king, but he could think of no other option. "He says . . . that he will never share that information with you of his own free will."

Galbatorix's eyebrows met above his nose. "Does he now? Well, he'll tell me soon enough, whether he wishes to or not." The king tapped the pommel of his glaringly white sword. "I took this blade from his Rider, you know, when I killed him—when I killed Vrael—in the watchtower that overlooks Palancar Valley. Vrael had his own name for this sword. He called it Islingr, 'Light-bringer.' I thought Vrangr was more . . . appropriate."

Vrangr meant "awry," and Eragon agreed that it fitted the sword better.

A dull boom sounded behind them, and Galbatorix smiled again. "Ah, good. Murtagh and Thorn shall be joining us shortly, and then we can begin properly." Another sound filled the chamber, then a great gusting noise that seemed to come from several directions at once. Galbatorix glanced over his shoulder and said, "It was inconsiderate of you to attack so early in the morning. I was already awake—I rise well before dawn—but you woke Shruikan. He gets rather irritated when he's tired, and when he's irritated, he tends to eat people. My guards learned long ago not to disturb him when he's resting. You would have done well to follow their example."

As Galbatorix spoke, the curtains behind his throne shifted and rose toward the ceiling.

With a sense of shock, Eragon realized that they were actually Shruikan's wings.

The black dragon lay curled on the floor with his head close to the throne, the bulk of his massive body forming a wall too steep and too high for any to climb without magic. His scales had not the radiance of Saphira's or Thorn's but rather sparkled with a dark, liquid brilliance. Their inky color made them almost opaque, which gave them an appearance of strength and solidity that Eragon had not seen in a dragon's scales before; it was as if Shruikan were plated with stone or metal, not gems.

The dragon was enormous. Eragon at first had difficulty comprehending that the entire shape before them was a single living creature. He saw part of Shruikan's corded neck and thought he was seeing the main part of the dragon's body; he saw the side of one of Shruikan's hind feet and mistook it for a shin. A fold of a wing was an entire wing in his mind. Only when he looked up and found the spikes atop the dragon's spine did Eragon grasp the full extent of Shruikan's size. Each spike was as wide as the trunk of an ancient oak tree; the scales surrounding them were a foot thick, if not more.

Then Shruikan opened an eye and looked down at them. His iris was a pale blue white, the color of a high mountain glacier, and it appeared startlingly bright amid the black of his scales.

The dragon's huge slitted orb darted back and forth as he studied their faces. His gaze seemed to contain nothing but fury and madness, and Eragon felt certain that Shruikan would kill them in an instant if Galbatorix allowed it.

The stare of the enormous eye—especially when it held such evident malice—made Eragon want to run and hide in a burrow deep, deep underground. It was, he imagined, very much how a rabbit must feel when confronted by a large, toothy creature.

Beside him, Saphira growled, and the scales along her back rippled and lifted like hackles.

In response, jets of fire appeared in the yawning pits of Shruikan's nostrils, and then he growled as well, drowning out Saphira and filling the chamber with a rumble like that of a rockslide.

On the dais, the two children squeaked and curled into balls, tucking their heads between their knees.

"Peace, Shruikan," said Galbatorix, and the black dragon grew silent again. His eyelid descended, but it did not close completely; the dragon continued to watch them through a gap a few inches wide, as if waiting for the right moment to pounce.

"He does not like you," said Galbatorix. "But then, he does not like anyone . . . do you now, Shruikan?" The dragon snorted, and the smell of smoke tinged the air.

Hopelessness again overwhelmed Eragon. Shruikan could kill Saphira with a bat of his paw. And as large as the chamber was, it was still too small for Saphira to evade the great black dragon for long.

His hopelessness turned to frustrated rage, and he wrenched at his invisible bonds. "How is it you can do this?" he shouted, straining every muscle in his body.

"I would like to know that as well," said Arya.

Galbatorix's eyes seemed to gleam beneath the dark eaves of his brow. "Can you not guess, elfling?"

"I would prefer an answer to a guess," she replied.

"Very well. But first you must do something so that you may know that what I say is indeed the truth. You must try to cast a spell, both of you, and then I shall tell you." When neither Eragon nor Arya made to speak, the king gestured with his hand. "Go on; I promise that I will not punish you for it. Now try. . . . I insist."

Arya went first. "Thrautha," she said, her voice hard and low. She was, Eragon guessed, trying to send the Dauthdaert flying toward Galbatorix. The weapon, however, remained fixed to her hand.

Then Eragon spoke: "Brisingr!" He thought that perhaps his bond with his sword would allow him to use magic where Arya could not, but to his disappointment, the blade remained as it was, glittering dimly in the dull light of the lanterns.

Galbatorix's gaze grew more intense. "The answer must be obvious to you now, elfling. It has taken me most of the past century, but at long last I have found what I was searching for: a means of governing the spellcasters of Alagaësia. The search was not easy; most men would have given up in frustration or, if they had the required patience, fear. But not I. I persisted. And through my study, I discovered what I had for so long desired: a tablet written in another land and another age, by hands that were neither elf nor dwarf nor human nor Urgal. And upon that tablet, there was scribed a certain Word—a name that magicians throughout the ages have hunted for with nothing but bitter disappointment as their reward." Galbatorix lifted a finger. "The name of all names. The name of the ancient language."

Eragon bit back a curse. He had been right. *That's what the Ra'zac was trying to tell me,* he thought, remembering what one of the insect-like monsters had said to him in Helgrind: "He has almossst found the *name*. . . . The true *name!*"

As disheartening as Galbatorix's revelation was, Eragon clung to the knowledge that the name could not stop him or Arya—or Saphira for that matter—from using magic *without* the ancient language. Not that it would do much good. The king's wards were sure to protect him and Shruikan from any spells they might cast. Still, if the king did not know that it was possible to use magic without the ancient language, or even if he did but he believed that *they* did not, then they might be able to surprise him and maybe distract him for a moment, although Eragon was not sure how that might help.

Galbatorix continued: "With this Word, I can reshape spells as easily as another magician might command the elements. All spells shall be subject to me, but I am subject to none, except for those of my choosing."

Perhaps he doesn't *know*, Eragon thought, a spark of determination kindling in his heart.

"I shall use the name of names to bring every magician in Alagaësia to heel, and no one shall cast a spell but with my blessing, not even the elves. At this very moment, the magicians of your army are discovering the truth of this. Once they venture a certain distance into Urû'baen, past the front gate, their spells cease to work as they should. Some of their enchantments fail outright, while others twist and end up affecting your troops instead of mine." Galbatorix tilted his head and his gaze grew distant, as if he were listening to someone whispering in his ear. "It has caused much confusion among their ranks."

Eragon fought the urge to spit at the king. "It doesn't matter," he growled. "We'll still find a way to stop you."

Galbatorix seemed grimly amused. "Is that so. How? And why? Think what you are saying. You would stop the first opportunity that Alagaësia has had for true peace in order to sate your over-developed sense of vengeance? You would allow magicians everywhere to continue to have their way, regardless of the harm they cause others? That seems far worse than anything I have done. But this is idle speculation. The finest warriors of the Riders could not defeat me, and you are far from their equal. You never had any hope of overthrowing me. None of you did."

"I killed Durza, and I killed the Ra'zac," said Eragon. "Why not you?"

"I am not as weak as those who serve me. You could not even trounce Murtagh, and he is but a shadow of a shadow. Your father, Morzan, was far more powerful than either of you, and even he could not withstand my might. Besides," said Galbatorix as a cruel expression settled on his face, "you are mistaken if you think you destroyed the Ra'zac. The eggs in Dras-Leona weren't the only ones I took from the Lethrblaka. I have others, hidden elsewhere. Soon they shall hatch, and soon the Ra'zac shall once more roam the earth to do my bidding. As for Durza, Shades are easy to make, and they are often more trouble than they are worth. So you see, you have won *nothing*, boy—nothing but false victories."

Above all, Eragon hated Galbatorix's smugness and his air of overwhelming superiority. He wanted to rage at the king and curse him with every oath he knew, but for the sake of the children's safety, he held his tongue.

Do you have any ideas? he asked Saphira, Arya, and Glaedr.

No, said Saphira. The others remained silent.

Umaroth?

Only that we should attack while we still can.

A minute passed wherein no one spoke. Galbatorix leaned on one elbow and rested his chin on his fist while he continued to watch them. By his feet, the boy and the girl cried softly. Above, Shruikan's eye remained fixed on Eragon and those with him, like a great ice-blue lantern.

Then they heard the doors to the chamber open and close, and the sound of approaching footsteps—the footsteps of both a man and a dragon.

Murtagh and Thorn soon appeared in their field of vision. They stopped next to Saphira, and Murtagh bowed. "Sir."

The king motioned, and Murtagh and Thorn walked over to the right of the throne.

As Murtagh took up his position, he gave Eragon a look of disgust; then he clasped his hands behind his back and stared toward the far end of the chamber, ignoring him.

"You took longer than I expected," said Galbatorix in a deceptively mild voice.

Without looking, Murtagh said, "The gate was more damaged than I originally thought, sir, and the spells you placed on it made it difficult to repair."

"Do you mean that it's my fault you are tardy?"

Murtagh's jaw tightened. "No, sir. I only mean to explain. Also, part of the hallway was rather . . . messy, and that slowed us."

"I see. We shall speak of this later, but for now, there are other matters we must attend to. For one, it is time our guests meet the final member of our party. Moreover, it is high time we had some proper light in here."

And Galbatorix struck the flat of his blade against one arm of his throne, and in a deep voice, he cried, "Naina!"

At his command, hundreds of lanterns sprang to life along the walls of the chamber, bathing it with warm, candle-like illumination. The room was still dim about the corners, but for the first time Eragon could make out the details of their surroundings. Scores of pillars and doorways lined the walls, and all about were sculptures and paintings and gilt scrollwork. Gold and silver had been used with abundance, and Eragon glimpsed the sparkle of many jewels. It was a staggering display of wealth, even when compared with the riches of Tronjheim or Ellesméra.

After a moment, he noticed something else: a block of gray stone—granite perhaps—eight feet tall, which stood off to their right, beyond where the light had previously reached. And chained standing to the block was Nasuada, wearing a simple white tunic.

She was watching them with wide-open eyes, though she could not speak, for a knotted cloth was tied over her mouth. She looked worn and tired but otherwise healthy.

Relief shot through Eragon. He had not dared hope to find her alive. "Nasuada!" he shouted. "Are you all right?"

She nodded.

"Has he forced you to swear fealty to him?"

She shook her head.

"Do you think I would let her tell you if I had?" asked Galbatorix. As Eragon looked back at the king, he saw Murtagh cast a quick, concerned glance toward Nasuada, and he wondered at its significance.

"Well, have you?" Eragon asked in a challenging tone.

"As it so happens, no. I decided to wait until I had gathered all of you together. Now that I have, none shall leave until you have pledged yourself in service to me, nor shall you leave until I have learned the true name of each and every one of you. *That* is why you are here. Not to kill me, but to bow down before me and to finally put an end to this noisome rebellion."

Saphira growled again, and Eragon said, "We won't give in." Even to his own ears, his words seemed weak and toothless.

"Then they will die," Galbatorix replied, pointing at the two children. "And in the end, your defiance will change nothing. You do not seem to understand; you have already lost. Outside, the battle fares badly for your friends. Soon my men will force them to surrender, and this war will arrive at its destined conclusion. Fight if you wish. Deny what is before you if it comforts you. But nothing you do can change your fate, or that of Alagaësia."

Eragon refused to believe that he and Saphira would have to spend the rest of their lives answering to Galbatorix. Saphira felt the same, and her anger joined with his, burning away every last bit of his fear and caution, and he said, "Vae weohnata ono vergarí, eka thäet otherúm." We will kill you, I swear it.

For a moment, Galbatorix appeared aggravated; then he spoke

the Word again—as well as other words in the ancient language besides—and the vow Eragon had uttered seemed to lose all meaning; the words lay in his mind like a handful of dead leaves, devoid of any power to impel or inspire.

The king's upper lip curved in a sneer. "Swear all the oaths you want. They shall not bind you, not unless I allow them to."

"I'll still kill you," Eragon muttered. He understood that if he continued to resist, it might mean the lives of the two children, but Galbatorix *had* to be killed, and if the price of his death was the deaths of the boy and the girl, then that was a cost Eragon was willing to accept. He knew he would hate himself for it. He knew that he would see the faces of the children in his dreams for the rest of his life. But if he did not challenge Galbatorix, then all would be lost.

Do not hesitate, said Umaroth. *Now is the time to strike.*

Eragon raised his voice. "Why won't you fight me? Are you a coward? Or are you too weak to match yourself against me? Is that why you hide behind these children like a frightened old woman?"

Eragon . . . , said Arya in a warning tone.

"I am not the only one who brought a child here today," replied the king, the lines on his face deepening.

"There is a difference: Elva agreed to come. But you didn't answer the question. Why won't you fight? Is it that you've spent so long sitting on your throne and eating sweets that you've forgotten how to swing a sword?"

"You would not want to fight me, youngling," growled the king.

"Prove it, then. Release me and meet me in honest battle. Show that you are still a warrior to be reckoned with. Or live with the knowledge that you are a sniveling coward who dares not face even a single opponent without the help of your Eldunarí. You killed Vrael himself! Why should you fear me? Why should—"

"Enough!" said Galbatorix. A flush had crept onto his hollow cheeks. Then, like quicksilver, his mood changed, and he bared his teeth in a fearsome approximation of a smile. He rapped the arm of his seat with his knuckles. "I did not gain this throne by accepting every challenge put to me. Nor have I held it by meeting my foes in 'honest battle.' What you have yet to learn, youngling, is that it does not matter how you achieve victory, only that you achieve it."

"You're wrong. It does matter," said Eragon.

"I will remind you of that when you are sworn to me. However . . ." Galbatorix tapped the pommel of his sword. "Since you wish so badly to fight, I will grant your request." The flare of hope that Eragon felt vanished when Galbatorix added, "But not with me. With Murtagh."

At those words, Murtagh flashed an angry look at Eragon.

The king stroked the fringe of his beard. "I would like to know, once and for all, which of you is the better warrior. You will fight as you are, without magic or Eldunarí, until one of you is unable to continue. You may not kill each other—that I forbid—but short of death, I will allow most anything. It will be rather entertaining, I think, to watch brother fight brother."

"No," said Eragon. "Not brothers. Half brothers. Brom was my father, not Morzan."

For the first time, Galbatorix appeared surprised. Then one corner of his mouth twisted upward. "Of course. I should have seen it; the truth is in your face for any who know what to look for. This duel will be all the more fitting, then. The son of Brom pitted against the son of Morzan. Fate indeed has a sense of humor."

Murtagh also reacted with surprise. He controlled his face too well for Eragon to determine whether the information pleased or upset him, but Eragon knew that it had thrown him off balance. That had been his plan. If Murtagh was distracted, it would be that much easier for Eragon to defeat him. And he did intend to defeat him, regardless of the blood they shared.

"Letta," said Galbatorix with a slight motion of his hand.

Eragon staggered as the spell holding him vanished.

Then the king said, "Gánga aptr," and Arya, Elva, and Saphira slid backward, leaving a wide space between them and the dais. The king muttered a few other words, and most of the lanterns in the chamber dimmed so that the area in front of the throne was the brightest spot in the room.

"Come now," said Galbatorix to Murtagh. "Join Eragon, and let us see which of you is the more skilled."

Scowling, Murtagh walked to a spot several yards from where Eragon stood. He drew Zar'roc—the blade of the crimson sword looked as if it were already coated in blood—then lifted his shield and settled into a crouch.

After glancing at Saphira and Arya, Eragon did the same.

"Now fight!" cried Galbatorix, and clapped his hands.

Sweating, Eragon began to move toward Murtagh, even as Murtagh moved toward him.

MUSCLE AGAINST METAL

Roran yelped and jumped aside as a brick chimney smashed to the ground in front of him, followed by the body of one of the Empire's archers.

He shook the sweat from his eyes, then moved around the body and the pile of scattered bricks, hopping from one patch of open ground to the next, much as he used to hop along the stones by the Anora River.

The battle was going badly. That much was obvious. He and his warriors had remained close to the outer wall for at least a quarter of an hour, fighting off the advancing waves of soldiers, but then they had allowed the soldiers to lure them back among the buildings. In retrospect, that had been a mistake. Fighting in the streets was desperate and bloody and confusing. His battalion had become spread out, and only a small number of his warriors remained close by—men from Carvahall, mostly, along with four elves and several Urgals. The rest were scattered among the nearby streets, fighting on their own, without direction.

Worse, for some reason that the elves and other spellcasters could not explain, magic no longer seemed to be working as it should. They had discovered this when one of the elves had tried to kill a soldier with a spell, only to have a Varden warrior fall down dead instead, consumed by the swarm of beetles the elf had summoned forth. His death had sickened Roran; it was a horrible, senseless way to die, and it might have happened to any of them.

Off to their right, closer to the main gate, Lord Barst was still rampaging through the main body of the Varden's army. Roran had caught sight of him several times: on foot now, striding among the humans, elves, and dwarves and dashing them aside like so many ninepins with his huge black mace. No one had been able to stop the hulking man, much less wound him, and those around him scrambled to stay out of reach of his fearsome weapon.

Roran had also seen King Orik and a group of dwarves hewing their way through a group of soldiers. Orik's jeweled helm flashed in the light as he swung his mighty war hammer, Volund. Behind him, his warriors shouted, "Vor Orikz korda!"

Fifty feet past Orik, Roran had glimpsed Queen Islanzadí whirling through the battle, her red cape flying and her shining armor as bright as a star amid the dark mass of bodies. About her head had flitted the white raven that was her companion. What little Roran saw of Islanzadí impressed him with her skill, ferocity, and bravery. She reminded him of Arya, but he thought that the queen might be the greater warrior.

A cluster of five soldiers charged around the corner of a house and nearly ran into Roran. Shouting, they leveled their spears and did their best to skewer him like a roast chicken. He ducked and dodged and, with his own spear, caught one of the men in the throat. The soldier remained on his feet for a minute more, but he could not breathe properly and soon he fell to the ground, tangling the legs of his companions.

Roran seized the opportunity, stabbing and cutting with abandon. One of the soldiers managed to land a blow on Roran's right shoulder, and Roran felt the familiar decrease in his strength as his wards deflected the blade.

He was surprised that the wards protected him. Only a few moments before, they had failed to stop the rim of a shield from tearing open the skin on his left cheek. He wished that whatever was happening with the magic would resolve itself one way or another. As it was, he dared not risk leaving himself open for even the slightest blow.

Roran advanced toward the last two soldiers, but before he reached them, there was a blur of steel, and then their heads dropped to the cobblestones, surprised expressions on their faces. The bodies collapsed, and behind them Roran saw the herbalist Angela, garbed in her green and black armor and carrying her sword-staff. Close by her side were a pair of werecats, one in the shape of a brindle-haired girl with sharp, bloodstained teeth and a long dagger, the other in the shape of an animal. He thought it might have been Solembum, but he was not sure.

"Roran! How nice to see you," said the herbalist with a smile that seemed altogether too cheery considering the circumstances. "Imagine meeting here!"

"Better here than in the grave!" he shouted, picking up an extra spear and heaving it at a man farther down the street.

"Well said!"

"I thought you went with Eragon?"

She shook her head. "He didn't ask me, and I wouldn't have gone if he had. I'm no match for Galbatorix. Besides, Eragon has the Eldunarí to help him."

"You know?" he asked, shocked.

She winked at him from under the lip of her helm. "I know lots of things."

He grunted and tucked his shoulder behind his shield as he rammed into another group of soldiers. The herbalist and the werecats joined him, as did Horst, Mandel, and several others.

"Where's your hammer?" shouted Angela as she spun her bladed staff, blocking and cutting at the same time.

"Lost! I dropped it."

Someone howled with pain behind him. As soon as he dared, Roran looked back and saw Baldor clutching the stump of his right arm. On the ground, his hand lay twitching.

Roran ran back to him, leaping over several corpses along the way. Horst was already by his son's side, fending off the soldier who had severed Baldor's hand.

Drawing his dagger, Roran cut a strip of cloth from the tunic of a fallen soldier, then said, "Here!" and tied it around the stump of Baldor's arm, stanching the bleeding.

The herbalist knelt next to them, and Roran said, "Can you help him?"

She shook her head. "Not here. If I use magic, it might end up killing him. If you can get him out of the city, though, the elves can probably save his hand."

Roran hesitated. He was not sure he dared spare anyone to escort Baldor safely out of Urû'baen. However, without a hand, Baldor would face a hard life, and Roran had no desire to condemn him to that.

"If you won't take him, I will," bellowed Horst.

Roran ducked as a stone the size of a hog flew past overhead and glanced off the front of a house, scattering pieces of masonry through the air. Inside the building, someone screamed.

"No. We need you." Turning, Roran whistled and picked two warriors: the old cobbler Loring and an Urgal. "Get him to the elves' healers as fast as you can," he said, pushing Baldor toward them. As he went, Baldor picked up his hand and tucked it under his hauberk.

The Urgal snarled and said in a thick accent that Roran barely understood, "No! I stay. I fight!" He struck his sword against his shield.

Roran stepped over, grabbed one of the creature's horns, and pulled on it until he had twisted the Urgal's head halfway around. "You'll do as I say," Roran growled. "Besides, it's not an easy task. Protect him and you'll win much glory for you and your tribe."

The Urgal's eyes seemed to brighten. "Much glory?" he said, mashing the words between his heavy teeth.

"Much glory!" Roran confirmed.

"I do it, Stronghammer!"

With a sense of relief, Roran watched the three of them depart, heading toward the outer wall, so that they might skirt most of the fighting. He was also pleased to see the human-shaped werecat follow after them, the feral, brindle-haired girl swinging her head from side to side as she scented the air.

Then another group of soldiers attacked, and all thoughts of Baldor left Roran's mind. He hated fighting with a spear instead of a hammer, but he made do, and after a time, the street again grew calm. He knew the respite would be short.

He took the opportunity to sit on the front doorstep of a house and try to regain his breath. The soldiers seemed as fresh as ever, but he could feel exhaustion dragging on his limbs. He doubted he could keep going for much longer without making a fatal mistake.

As he sat panting, he listened to the shouts and screams coming from the direction of Urû'baen's ruined front gate. It was difficult to tell what was happening from the general clamor, but he suspected the Varden were getting pushed back, for the noise seemed to be receding slightly. Amid the commotion, he could hear the regular *crack* of Lord Barst's mace striking warrior after warrior, and then the increase in cries that invariably followed.

Roran made himself stand. If he sat for much longer, his muscles would start to stiffen. A moment after he moved away from the doorstep, the contents of a chamber pot splashed across the spot where he had just been.

"Murderers!" shouted a woman above him, and then a pair of shutters banged shut.

Roran snorted and picked his way around bodies as he led his remaining warriors over to the nearest cross street.

They paused, wary, when a soldier raced past, panic upon his face. Close behind, a pack of yowling housecats chased after him, blood dripping from the fur around their mouths.

Roran smiled and started forward again.

He stopped a second later when a group of dwarves with red beards ran toward them from deeper within the city. "Ready yourself!" one shouted. "We have a whole pack of soldiers nipping at our heels, a few hundred of them, at least."

Roran looked back up the empty cross street. "Perhaps you lost—" he began to say, and then stopped when a line of crimson tunics appeared around the corner of a building a few hundred feet away. More and more soldiers followed, pouring into the street like a swarm of red ants.

"Back!" Roran shouted. "Back!" *We have to find somewhere defensible.* The outer wall was too far away, and none of the houses were large enough to have enclosed courtyards.

As Roran ran down the street with his warriors, a dozen or so arrows landed around them.

Roran stumbled and fell, writhing, as a bolt of pain shot up his spine from the small of his back. It felt as if someone had jabbed him with a large iron bar.

A second later, the herbalist was by his side. She tugged at something behind him, and Roran screamed. Then the pain decreased, and he found himself able to see clearly again.

The herbalist showed him an arrow with a bloody tip before throwing it away. "Your mail stopped most of it," she said as she helped him to his feet.

Gritting his teeth, Roran ran with her to rejoin their group. Every step pained him now, and if he bent at the waist too far, his back spasmed and he found it almost impossible to move.

He saw no good places to make a stand, and the soldiers were getting closer, so at last he shouted, "Stop! Form up! Elves to the sides! Urgals front and center!"

Roran took his place near the front, along with Darmmen, Albriech, the Urgals, and one of the red-bearded dwarves.

"So you are the one they call Stronghammer," said the dwarf as they watched the advance of the soldiers. "I fought alongside your hearth-brother in Farthen Dûr. It is mine honor to fight with you as well."

Roran grunted. He just hoped he could stay on his feet.

Then the soldiers crashed into them, shoving them back through sheer weight. Roran set his shoulder against his shield and pushed with all his might. Swords and spears stuck through the gaps in the wall of overlapping shields; he felt one scrape against his side, but his hauberk protected him.

The elves and the Urgals proved invaluable. They broke the soldiers' lines and earned Roran and the other warriors room to swing their weapons. At the edge of his vision, Roran saw the dwarf stabbing the soldiers in the legs, feet, and groin, causing many to fall.

The supply of soldiers seemed endless, however, and Roran found himself forced backward step by step. Not even the elves could stem the tide of men, try though they might. Othíara, the elf woman Roran had spoken to outside the city wall, died from an arrow in the neck, and the remaining elves received many wounds.

Roran was injured several more times himself: a cut on the upper part of his right calf, which would have hamstrung him if it had been a little bit higher; another cut on the thigh of the same leg, where a sword had slipped under the edge of his hauberk; a nasty scrape on his neck, where he hit himself with his own shield; a stab wound on the inner part of his right leg that fortunately missed the major arteries; and more bruises than he could count. He felt as if every part of himself had been beaten soundly with a wooden mallet and then a pair of clumsy men had used him as a target for knife throwing.

He dropped back from the front line a few times to rest his arms and catch his breath, but he always rejoined the fight soon afterward.

Then the buildings opened up around them, and Roran realized that the soldiers had succeeded in driving them into the square before Urû'baen's broken gate, and that there were now enemies behind them as well as before them.

He chanced a look over his shoulder and saw the elves and the Varden retreating before Barst and his soldiers.

"Right!" shouted Roran. "Right! Up against the buildings!" He pointed with his bloody spear.

With some difficulty, the warriors packed behind him edged to the side and onto the steps of a huge stone building fronted with a double row of pillars as tall as any of the trees in the Spine. Between the pillars, Roran glimpsed the dark, yawning shape of an open archway big enough to accommodate Saphira, if not Shruikan.

"Up! Up!" Roran shouted, and the men, dwarves, elves, and Urgals ran with him to the top of the stairs. There they set themselves among the pillars and repelled the wave of soldiers that charged after them. From their vantage point, which was perhaps twenty feet above the level of the streets, Roran saw that the Empire had nearly forced the Varden and the elves back out the gaping hole in the outer wall.

We're going to lose, he thought with sudden desperation.

The soldiers charged up the steps once again. Roran dodged a spear and kicked its owner in the belly, knocking the soldier and two other men down the stairs.

From one of the ballistae on a nearby wall tower, a javelin streaked down toward Lord Barst. When it was still a few yards from him, the javelin burst into flames, then crumbled into dust, as did every arrow shot at the armored man.

We have to kill him, thought Roran. If Barst fell, then the soldiers would likely break and lose confidence. But given that both the elves and the Kull had failed to stop him, it seemed doubtful that anyone other than Eragon could.

Even as he continued to fight, Roran kept glancing at the large, armored figure, hoping to see something that might provide a way to defeat him. He noticed that Barst walked with a slight hitch in his stride, as if he had once injured his left knee or hip. And the man seemed a hair slower than before.

So he does have his limits, thought Roran. *Or rather, the Eldunarí does.*

With a shout, he parried the sword of the soldier who had been pressing him. Jerking his shield up, he caught the soldier underneath the jaw, killing the man instantly.

Roran was out of breath and faint from his wounds, so he withdrew behind one of the pillars and leaned against it. He coughed and spat; his spittle contained blood, but he thought that was just from where he had bitten the inside of his mouth and not from a punctured lung. At least he hoped so. His ribs felt sore enough that one of them might be broken.

A great shout rose from the Varden, and Roran looked around the pillar to see Queen Islanzadí and eleven other elves riding through the battle toward Lord Barst. Again upon Islanzadí's left shoulder sat the white raven, and he cawed and lifted his wings, the better to balance upon his moving perch. In her hand, Islanzadí carried her sword, while the rest of the elves carried spears with banners attached close to their leaf-shaped blades.

Roran leaned against the pillar, hope rising within him. "Kill him," he growled.

Barst made no move to avoid the elves but stood waiting for them with his feet spread wide and his mace and shield by his sides, as if he had no need to defend himself.

Throughout the streets, the fighting slowed to a standstill as everyone turned to watch what was about to happen.

The two elves in the lead lowered their spears, and their horses sprang forward into a gallop, the muscles beneath their glossy hides flexing and relaxing as they raced across the short distance that separated them from Barst. For a moment, it looked as if Barst would surely fall; it seemed impossible that anyone on foot could withstand such a charge.

The spears never touched Barst. His wards stopped them an arm's length from his body, and the hafts shattered in the elves' hands, leaving them holding useless shards of wood. Then Barst lifted his mace and his shield, and with them he struck the horses on the sides of their heads, breaking their necks and killing them.

The horses fell, and the elves upon them jumped free, twisting in the air as they did.

The next two elves did not have time to change course before they reached Barst. Like their predecessors, they split their spears on his wards, and then they too jumped free of their horses as Barst struck the animals down.

By then, the eight other elves, including Islanzadí, had managed to turn and rein in their steeds. They trotted in a circle around Barst, keeping their weapons pointed at him, while the four elves on the ground drew their swords and cautiously advanced toward Barst.

The man laughed and hefted his shield as he prepared for their attack. The light caught his face under his helm, and even from a distance Roran could see that it was broad and heavy-browed, with prominent cheekbones. In some ways, it reminded him of the face of an Urgal.

The four elves ran at Barst, each from a different direction, and they cut and stabbed at him in unison. Barst caught one of the swords on his shield, deflected another with his mace, and let his wards stop the blades of the two elves behind him. He laughed again and swung his weapon.

A silver-haired elf threw himself to the side, and the mace flew past harmlessly.

Twice more Barst swung, and twice more the elves evaded him. Barst showed no signs of frustration, but hunched behind his shield and bided his time, like a cave bear waiting for whosoever might be foolish enough to venture into his lair.

Outside the ring of elves, a block of halberd-wielding soldiers took it upon themselves to run screaming toward Queen Islanzadí and her companions. Without pause, the queen lifted her sword over her head, and at her signal, a swarm of buzzing arrows shot out from the ranks of the Varden and felled the soldiers.

Roran shouted with excitement, along with many of the Varden.

Barst had been edging ever closer to the bodies of the four horses he had slain, and now he stepped into their midst so that the bodies formed a low, tumbled wall on either side of him. The elves to his left and his right would have no choice but to leap over the horses if they wished to attack him.

Clever, Roran thought, frowning.

The elf in front of Barst darted forward, shouting something in the ancient language. Barst seemed to hesitate, and his hesitation encouraged the elf to come closer. Then Barst lunged forward, his mace came crashing down, and the elf crumpled to the ground, broken.

A groan went up from the elves.

The three remaining elves on foot were more cautious thereafter. They continued to circle Barst, running in to attack him on occasion, but mostly keeping their distance.

"Surrender!" exclaimed Islanzadí, and her voice could be heard throughout the streets. "There are more of us than you. No matter how strong you are, in time you will tire and your wards will fail. You cannot win, human."

"No?" said Barst. He straightened and dropped his shield with a loud clatter.

Sudden dread filled Roran. *Run*, he thought. "Run!" he shouted a half second later.

He was too late.

Bending at the knees, Barst grabbed the neck of one of the horses and, with his left arm alone, threw the horse at Queen Islanzadí.

If she spoke in the ancient language, Roran did not hear it, but she lifted her hand—and the body of the horse stopped in midair, then dropped to the cobblestones, where it landed with an unpleasant sound. On her shoulder, the raven screeched.

Barst was not looking, however. As soon as the carcass left his hand, he scooped up his shield and sprinted toward the nearest of the mounted elven riders. One of the three remaining elves on foot—a woman with a red sash tied around her upper arm—ran toward him and slashed at his back. Barst ignored her.

Over a flat stretch of land, the elves' horses might have been able to outdistance Barst, but in the limited space between the buildings and the closely packed warriors, Barst was both faster and more nimble. He rammed his shoulder into the ribs of one of the horses, toppling it over, and then swung his mace at an elf upon another horse, knocking the elf from his seat. A horse screamed.

The circle of elven riders disintegrated, each turning in a different direction as they tried to calm their mounts and address the threat before them.

A half-dozen elves ran out from the nearby press of warriors and surrounded Barst, all hacking at him with frenzied speed. Barst disappeared behind them for a moment; then his mace rose up, and three of the elves flew tumbling away. Then another two, and Barst strode forward, blood and gore clinging to the flanges of his black weapon.

"Now!" roared Barst, and throughout the square, hundreds of soldiers ran forward and assailed the elves, forcing them to defend themselves.

"No," Roran growled, agonized. He would have gone with his warriors to help, but too many bodies—both living and dead—separated them from Barst and the elves. He glanced over at the herbalist, who looked as worried as he felt, and said, "Can't you do something?"

"I could, but it would mean my life and that of everyone here."

"Galbatorix as well?"

"He's too well shielded, but our army would be destroyed along with most everyone in Urû'baen, and even those at our camp might die. Is that what you want?"

Roran shook his head.

"I thought not."

Moving with uncanny speed, Barst struck elf after elf, felling them with ease. With one of his swings, he caught the shoulder of the elf woman with the red sash and knocked her sprawling onto her back. She pointed at Barst and screamed in the ancient language, but the spell went awry, for another elf slumped forward and toppled out of his saddle, the front of his body split from head to seam.

Barst slew the elf woman with a jab of his mace and then continued to run from horse to horse until he reached Islanzadí on her white mare.

The elf queen did not wait for Barst to kill her steed. She leaped out of her saddle, her red cape billowing, and her companion, the white raven, beat his wings as he took flight from her shoulder.

Before she alit, Islanzadí lashed out at Barst, her sword a streak of shining steel. Her blade rang as it collided with his wards.

Barst retaliated with a counterstroke, which Islanzadí parried with a deft turn of her wrist, sending the spiked ball of his mace crashing into the cobblestones. Around them, a space formed as friend and foe alike paused to watch them duel. Overhead, the raven circled, shrieking and cursing in the harsh manner of his kind.

Never had Roran seen such a fight. The blows from both Islanzadí and Barst were too fast to follow—only a blur was visible when they struck—and the sound of their weapons clashing was louder than all of the other noises in the city.

Again and again, Barst tried to crush Islanzadí with his mace, even as he had crushed the other elves. But she was too fast for him to catch, and she seemed, if not his equal in strength, at least strong enough to knock aside his blows without difficulty. The other elves, Roran thought, must be aiding her, for she appeared not to tire, despite her exertions.

A Kull and two elves joined Islanzadí. Barst paid them no mind, other than to kill them, one by one, when they made the mistake of venturing within his reach.

Roran found himself gripping the pillar so hard, his hands began to cramp.

Minutes passed as Islanzadí and Barst fought back and forth across the street. In motion, the elf queen was glorious: swift, lithe, and powerful. Unlike Barst, she could not afford to make a single mistake—nor did she—for her wards would not protect her. With every moment, Roran's admiration for Islanzadí increased, and he felt he was witnessing a battle that would be sung about for centuries to come.

The raven often dove at Barst, seeking to distract him from Islanzadí. After the raven's first few attempts, Barst ignored the bird, for the maddened creature could not touch him, and it took pains to keep away from his mace.

The raven seemed to grow frustrated; it shrieked louder and more frequently, and was bolder with its attacks, and with each sally, it edged ever closer to Barst's head and neck.

Finally, as the bird again swooped toward Barst, the man twisted his mace upward, changing its path in midair, and clipped the raven on its right wing. The bird cried out in pain and dropped a foot toward the ground before struggling to climb back into the sky.

Barst swung at the raven again, but Islanzadí stopped his mace with her sword, and they stood facing each other with their weapons locked together at the top, the blade of her sword wedged between the flanges of his mace.

Elf and human swayed as they pushed against one another. Neither was able to gain the advantage. Then Queen Islanzadí shouted a word in the ancient language, and where their weapons met, a harsh, brilliant light shone forth.

Squinting, Roran shaded his eyes with his hand and averted his gaze.

For a minute, the only sounds were the cries of the wounded and a ringing, bell-like tone that grew louder and louder until it was nearly unbearable. To the side, Roran saw the werecat with Angela cringing and covering its tasseled ears with its paws.

When the sound was at the very height of its intensity, the blade of Islanzadí's sword cracked, and the light and the bell-like tone vanished.

Then the elf queen smote at Barst's face with the broken end of her sword, and she said, "Thus I curse you, Barst, son of Berengar!"

Barst allowed her sword to fall upon his wards. Then he swung his mace once more and caught Queen Islanzadí between her neck and her shoulder, and she collapsed to the ground, blood staining her corselet of golden scale armor.

And all was still.

The white raven circled once over Islanzadí's body and uttered a doleful cry, then flew slowly toward the breach in the outer wall, the feathers of its wounded wing red and crumpled.

A great wail went up from the Varden. Throughout the streets, men cast down their weapons and fled. The elves shouted with rage and grief—a most terrible sound—and every elf with a bow began to fire arrows toward Barst. The arrows burst into flame before they touched him. A dozen elves charged him, but he swatted them aside as if they weighed no more than children. In that moment, another five elves darted in, lifted up Islanzadí's body, and bore her away upon their leaf-shaped shields.

A sense of disbelief gripped Roran. Of them all, Islanzadí was the one he had least expected to die. He glared at the men who were fleeing and silently cursed them for traitors and cowards; then he returned his gaze to Barst, who was rallying his troops in preparation for driving the Varden and their allies back out of Urû'baen.

The pit in Roran's stomach grew larger. The elves might continue to fight, but the men, dwarves, and Urgals no longer had a taste for battle. He could see it in their faces. They would break and retreat, and Barst would slaughter them by the hundreds from behind. Nor, Roran was sure, would Barst halt at the city walls. No, he would continue on to the fields beyond and chase the Varden back to their camp, scattering and killing as many as he could.

It was what Roran would do.

Worse, if Barst reached the camp, Katrina would be in danger, and Roran had no illusions as to what would happen if the soldiers caught her.

Roran stared down at his bloody hands. Barst had to be stopped. But how? Roran thought and he thought, running through everything he knew about magic until, at last, he remembered how it had felt when the soldiers were holding him and striking him.

Roran took a deep, shuddering breath.

There was a way, but it was dangerous, incredibly dangerous. If he did what he was contemplating, he knew that he would probably never see Katrina again, much less their unborn child. Yet the knowledge brought him a certain peace. His life for theirs was a fair trade, and if he could help save the Varden at the same time, then he would be happy to give it.

Katrina . . .

The decision was an easy one.

Raising his head, he strode over to the herbalist. She looked as shocked and grief-ridden as any of the elves. He touched her on the shoulder with the edge of his shield and said, "I need your help."

She gazed at him with red-rimmed eyes. "What do you intend to do?"

"Kill Barst." His words captivated all of the warriors nearby.

"Roran, no!" exclaimed Horst.

The herbalist nodded. "I'll help however I can."

"Good. I want you to fetch Jörmundur, Garzhvog, Orik, Grimrr, and one of the elves who still has some authority."

The curly-haired woman sniffed and wiped her eyes. "Where do you want them to meet you?"

"Right here. And hurry, before any more men flee!"

Angela nodded, then she and the werecat trotted away, sticking close to the sides of the buildings for protection.

"Roran," said Horst, clutching his arm, "what do you have in mind?"

"I'm not going to go up against him by myself, if that's what you're thinking," said Roran, nodding toward Barst.

Horst appeared somewhat relieved. "Then what are you going to do?"

"You'll see."

Several soldiers carrying pikes ran up the steps of the building, but the red-haired dwarves who had joined Roran's force held them off with ease, the steps for once giving them the advantage of height over their opponents.

While the dwarves fenced with the soldiers, Roran went to a

nearby elf who—with a snarl fixed on his face—was emptying his quiver at a prodigious speed, sending each of his arrows arcing toward Barst. None of them, of course, found their mark.

"Enough," said Roran. When the dark-haired elf ignored him, Roran grabbed the elf's right hand, his bow hand, and pulled it to the side. "That's enough, I said. Save your arrows."

A growl sounded, and then Roran felt a hand around his throat. "Do not touch me, human."

"Listen to me! I can help you kill Barst. Just . . . let me go."

After a second or two, the fingers gripping Roran's neck relaxed. "How, Stronghammer?" The bloodthirstiness of the elf's voice contrasted with the tears on his cheeks.

"You'll find out in a minute. But I have a question for you first. Why can't you kill Barst with your minds? He's only one man, and there are so many of you."

An anguished expression crossed the elf's face. "Because his mind is hidden from us!"

"How?"

"I do not know. We can feel nothing of his thoughts. It is as if there is a sphere around his mind. We can see nothing within the sphere, nor can we pierce it."

Roran had expected something like that. "Thank you," he said, and the elf made a slight motion of his head in acknowledgment.

Garzhvog was the first to reach the building; he emerged from a nearby street and ran up the steps with two huge strides, then turned and roared at the thirty soldiers following him. Seeing the Kull safe among friends, the soldiers wisely dropped back.

"Stronghammer!" exclaimed Garzhvog. "You asked, and I have come."

After a few more minutes, the others Roran had sent the herbalist to fetch arrived at the great stone building. The silver-haired elf who presented himself was one Roran had seen with Islanzadí on several occasions. Lord Däthedr was his name. The six of them, all bloody and weary, stood in a clump among the fluted pillars.

"I have a plan to kill Barst," Roran said, "but I need your help, and we have little time. Can I count on you?"

"That depends on your plan," said Orik. "Tell it to us first."

So Roran explained it as quickly as he could. When he finished, he asked Orik, "Can your engineers aim the catapults and ballistae as accurately as needed?"

The dwarf made a noise in his throat. "Not with how humans build their war machines. We can put a stone within twenty feet of the target, but any closer than that is up to luck."

Roran looked at the elf lord Däthedr. "Will the others of your kind follow you?"

"They will obey my orders, Stronghammer. Do not doubt it."

"Then will you send some of your magicians to accompany the dwarves and help guide the stones?"

"There would be no guarantee of success. The spells might easily fail or go astray."

"We'll have to risk it." Roran swept his gaze over the group. "So, I ask again: can I count on you?"

Out by the city wall, a chorus of fresh screams erupted as Barst smashed his way through a bank of men.

Garzhvog surprised Roran by being the first to answer. "You are battle-mad, Stronghammer, but I will follow you," he said. He made a *ruk-ruk* sound that Roran thought might be laughter. "There will be much glory in killing Barst."

Then Jörmundur said, "Aye, I'll follow you as well, Roran. We have no other choice, I think."

"Agreed," said Orik.

"Agrrreed," said Grimrr, king of the werecats, drawing the word out into a throaty growl.

"Agreed," said Lord Däthedr.

"Then go!" said Roran. "You know what you need to do! Go!"

As the others departed, Roran called his warriors together and told them his plan. Then they hunkered between the pillars and waited.

It took three or four minutes—precious time in which Barst and his soldiers pushed the Varden ever closer to the breach in the outer wall—but then Roran saw groups of dwarves and elves run up to twelve of the nearest ballistae and catapults on the walls and free them from the soldiers.

Several more tense minutes passed. Then Orik hurried up the steps to the building, along with thirty of his dwarves, and said to Roran, "They're ready."

Roran nodded. To everyone with him, he said, "Take your places!"

The remnants of Roran's battalion formed a dense wedge, with him at the tip and the elves and Urgals directly behind him. Orik and his dwarves took up the rear.

Once all of the warriors were in place, Roran shouted, "Forward!" and trotted down the steps into the midst of the enemy soldiers, knowing that the rest of the group was close behind him.

The soldiers had not been expecting the charge; they parted before Roran like water before the prow of a ship.

One man tried to bar Roran's way, and Roran stabbed him through the eye without breaking stride.

When they were about fifty feet from Barst, who had his back turned, Roran stopped, as did the warriors behind him. To one of the elves, he said, "Make it so everyone in the square can hear me."

The elf muttered in the ancient language, then said, "It is done."

"Barst!" shouted Roran, and was relieved to hear his voice echo over the whole of the battle. The fighting throughout the streets came to a halt, save for a few individual skirmishes here and there.

Sweat dripped down Roran's brow and his heart was pounding, but he refused to feel afraid. "Barst!" he shouted again, and slapped the front of his shield with his spear. "Turn and fight me, you maggot-ridden cur!"

A soldier ran at him. Roran blocked his sword and, in one easy motion, swept the man off his feet and dispatched him with two quick jabs. Pulling his spear free, Roran repeated his call: "Barst!"

The broad, heavy figure slowly turned to face him. Now that he was closer, Roran could see the sly intelligence that lay in Barst's eyes and the small, mocking smile that lifted the corners of his childlike mouth. His neck was as thick as Roran's thigh, and beneath his mail hauberk, his arms were knotted with muscles. The reflections from his protruding breastplate kept snaring Roran's gaze, despite his efforts to ignore them.

"Barst! My name is Roran Stronghammer, cousin to Eragon Shadeslayer! Fight me if you dare, or be branded a coward before all here today."

"No man scares me, Stronghammer. Or should I say Lackhammer, for I see no hammer upon you."

Roran drew himself up. "I need no hammer to kill you, you beardless bootlicker."

"Is that so?" Barst's tiny smile grew wider. "Give us room!" he shouted, and waved his mace at the soldiers and Varden alike.

With the soft thunder of thousands of feet treading backward, the armies withdrew, and a wide, circular area formed around Barst. He pointed his mace at Roran. "Galbatorix told me of you, Lackhammer. He said that I was to break every bone in your body before I killed you."

"What if we break *your* bones instead?" said Roran. *Now!* he thought as hard as he could, trying to shout his thoughts into the darkness that surrounded his mind. He hoped the elves and the other spellcasters were listening as promised.

Barst frowned and opened his mouth. Before he could speak, a low, whistling noise sounded over the city, and six stone projectiles—each the size of a barrel—hurtled over the tops of the houses from the catapults on the walls. A half-dozen javelins accompanied the stones.

Five of the stones landed directly on Barst. The sixth missed and went bouncing across the square like a rock across water, bowling over men and dwarves alike.

The stones cracked and exploded as they struck Barst's wards, sending fragments flying in every direction. Roran ducked behind his shield and nearly fell as a fist-sized chunk of stone slammed into it, bruising his arm. The javelins vanished in a flare of yellow fire, which gave a ghoulish light to the clouds of dust that floated upward from Barst's location.

When he was sure it was safe, Roran looked over his shield.

Barst was lying on his back amid the rubble, his mace on the ground next to him.

"Get him!" Roran bellowed, and ran forward.

Many of the gathered Varden started toward Barst, but the soldiers they had been fighting shouted and attacked, stopping them from covering more than a few steps. With a roar, the two armies turned on each other once again, both factions inflamed with a desperate anger.

As they did, Jörmundur emerged from a side street, leading a hundred men whom he had collected from the edges of the battle. He and those with him would help hold back the scrum of combatants while Roran and the others dealt with Barst.

From the opposite side of the square, Garzhvog and six other Kull charged out from behind the houses they had been using for cover. Their pounding footsteps shook the ground, and men of both the Empire and the Varden scrambled to move out of their way.

Then hundreds of werecats, most in their animal forms, slipped out from the main body of the intermingled armies and streamed across the cobblestones, teeth bared, toward where Barst lay.

Barst had just begun to stir when Roran reached him. Grabbing his spear with both hands, Roran brought it down on Barst's neck.

The blade of the weapon stopped a foot away, and the tip bent and snapped as if it had struck a block of granite.

Roran cursed and continued to stab as quickly as he could, trying to keep the Eldunarí within Barst's breastplate from recovering its strength.

Barst groaned.

"Hurry!" Roran bellowed at the Urgals.

Once they were close enough, Roran sprang aside so that the Kull would have the room they needed. Taking turns, each of the massive Urgals struck at Barst with their weapons. His wards blocked them, but the Kull continued to hammer away. The sound was deafening.

Werecats and elves gathered around Roran. Behind them, he was half-aware of the warriors he had brought with him holding off the soldiers, along with Jörmundur's men.

Just when Roran was beginning to think that Barst's wards would never give way, one of the Kull uttered a triumphant shout, and Roran saw the creature's ax glance off the front of Barst's armor, denting it.

"Again!" shouted Roran. "Now! Kill him!"

The Kull lifted his ax out of the way, and Garzhvog swung his ironbound club toward Barst's head.

Roran saw a flurry of motion, and then there was a loud *thud* as the club struck Barst's shield, which the man had pulled over himself.

Blast it!

Before the Urgals could attack again, Barst rolled up against the legs of one of the Kull, and his hand latched on to the back of the Kull's right knee. The Kull bellowed with pain and hopped backward, pulling Barst out of the knot of Kull.

The Urgals and two elves closed in around Barst once more, and for a number of heartbeats, it seemed as if they might subdue him.

Then one of the elves went flying, her neck crooked at an odd angle. A Kull fell onto his side, shouting in his native language. Bone protruded from his left forearm. Garzhvog snarled and jumped back, blood streaming from a fist-sized hole in his side.

No! thought Roran, going cold. *It can't end like this. I won't let it!*

Shouting, he ran forward and slipped between two of the giant Urgals. He barely had time to see Barst—bloody and enraged, with his shield in one hand and a sword in the other—before Barst swung his shield and struck Roran on the left side of his body.

The air rushed out of Roran's lungs, and the sky and the ground spun around him, and he felt his helmet-covered head bouncing against the cobblestones.

The world seemed to keep moving beneath him even when he rolled to a stop.

He lay where he was for a time, struggling to breathe. At last he was able to fill his lungs with air, and he thought he had never been so grateful for anything as he was for that breath. He gasped. Then he howled as his body filled with pain. His left arm felt numb, but every other muscle and sinew burned with agony.

He tried to push himself upright and fell back onto his stomach, too dizzy and hurt to stand. Before him was a fragment of yellowish stone, veined with coiled branches of red agate. He stared at it for a while, panting, and the whole time, the only thought running through his mind was: *Have to get up. Have to get up. Have to get up. . . .*

When he felt ready, he tried again. His left arm refused to work, so he was forced to rely on his right alone. Hard as it was, he got his legs underneath him, and then he slowly rose to his feet, shaking and unable to take more than shallow breaths.

As he straightened, something pulled in his left shoulder, and he uttered a silent scream. It felt as if a red-hot knife were buried in the joint. Looking down, he saw that his arm was dislocated. Of his shield, nothing remained but a splintered board still attached to the strap around his forearm.

Roran turned, searching for Barst, and saw the man thirty yards away, covered in clawing werecats.

Satisfied that Barst would be occupied for at least a few more seconds, Roran returned his gaze to his dislocated arm. At first he could not remember what his mother had taught him, but then her words returned to him, faint and blurred by the passage of time. He pulled off the remnants of his shield.

"Make a fist," mumbled Roran, and he did so with his left hand.

"Bend your arm so your fist points forward." That he did, though it worsened his pain. "Then turn your arm outward, away from your . . ." He screamed a curse as his shoulder grated, the muscles and tendons pulling in ways they were not supposed to stretch. He kept turning his arm and he kept clenching his fist, and after a few seconds, the bone popped back into the socket.

His relief was immediate. He still hurt elsewhere—especially his lower back and ribs—but at least he could use his arm again, and the pain was not so excruciating.

Then Roran looked toward Barst again.

What he saw sickened him.

Barst was standing in a circle of dead werecats. Blood streaked his dented breastplate, and clumps of fur clung to his mace, which he had retrieved. His cheeks were scratched deeply, and the right sleeve of his mail hauberk was torn, but otherwise he appeared unharmed. The few werecats who still faced him were careful to keep their distance, and it looked to Roran as if they were about to turn tail and run. Behind Barst lay the bodies of the Kull and the elves he had been fighting. All of Roran's warriors seemed to have disappeared, for none but soldiers surrounded Roran, Barst, and the werecats: a seething mass of crimson tunics, the men pushing and shoving as they struggled against the eddies of the battle.

"Shoot him!" Roran shouted, but no one seemed to hear.

Barst noticed, however, and he began to lumber toward Roran. "Lackhammer!" he roared. "I'll have your head for this!"

Roran saw a spear on the ground. He knelt and picked it up. The motion made him light-headed. "Let's see you try!" he replied. But the words sounded hollow, and his mind filled with thoughts of Katrina and their child who was yet to be.

Then one of the werecats—who was in the form of a white-haired woman no taller than Roran's elbow—ran forward and cut Barst along the side of his left thigh.

Barst snarled and twisted, but the werecat was already retreating, hissing at him while she did. A moment more Barst waited, to ensure that she would not trouble him again, and then he continued walking toward Roran, limping now as his new wound exacerbated the hitch in his stride. Blood sheeted down his leg.

Roran wet his lips, unable to look away from his approaching foe. He had only the spear. He had no shield. He could not outrun Barst, and he could not hope to match Barst's unnatural strength or speed. Nor was there anyone nearby to help him.

It was an impossible situation, but Roran refused to admit defeat. He had given up once before, and he would never do so again, even though reason told him that he was about to die.

Then Barst was upon him, and Roran stabbed at his right knee, in the desperate hope that he might by some chance cripple him. Barst deflected the spear with his mace, then swung at Roran.

Roran had anticipated the counterattack and was already stumbling backward as fast as his legs would allow. A gust of wind touched his face as the head of the mace swept past, inches from his skin.

Barst showed his teeth in a grim smile, and he was about to strike again when a shadow fell on him from above, and he looked up.

Islanzadí's white raven dropped out of the sky and landed on Barst's face. The raven screeched with fury as it pecked and clawed at Barst, and Roran was astonished to hear the raven say, "Die! Die! Die!"

Barst swore and dropped his shield. With his free hand, he batted the raven away, breaking its already-injured wing. Ribbons of flesh hung loose from his brow, and blood painted his cheeks and chin crimson.

Roran lunged forward and stabbed Barst's other hand with his spear, causing Barst to drop his mace as well.

Then Roran seized his chance and stabbed at Barst's exposed throat. However, Barst caught the spear with one hand, tore it from Roran's grip, and broke it between his fingers as easily as Roran might break a dry twig.

"Now you die," said Barst, spitting blood. His lips were torn and his right eye was ruined, but he could still see out of his remaining orb.

The man reached for Roran, seeking to envelop him in a deadly embrace. Roran could not have escaped even if he had wanted to, but as Barst's arms closed about him, Roran grasped Barst's waist and twisted with all his might, putting as much weight and pressure as he could on Barst's wounded leg, the leg with the hitch.

Barst held for a moment; then his knee buckled, and with a cry of pain, he fell forward onto one leg and caught himself with his left hand. Squirming around, Roran slipped out from under Barst's right arm. The blood on Barst's breastplate made it that much easier to work free, despite the man's immense strength.

Roran tried to grab Barst's throat from behind, but Barst tucked his chin, preventing Roran from getting a grip. So, instead, Roran wrapped his arms around Barst's chest, hoping to restrain him until someone else could help kill him.

Barst growled and threw himself onto his side, jarring Roran's injured shoulder and causing him to grunt with pain. The cobblestones dug into Roran's arms and back as Barst rolled three times. When the bulk of the man was atop him, Roran had trouble breathing. Yet still Roran maintained his grip. One of Barst's elbows slammed into his side, and Roran felt several of his ribs break.

Roran clenched his teeth and tightened his arms, squeezing as hard as he could.

Katrina, he thought.

Again Barst's elbow slammed into him.

Roran howled, and flashing lights appeared before his eyes. He squeezed even harder.

Again the elbow, like an anvil pounding into his side.

"You . . . shall . . . not . . . win, . . . Lackhammer," grunted Barst. He staggered to his feet, dragging Roran with him.

Though he thought he might tear the muscles from his bones, Roran tightened his embrace even further. He screamed, but he could not hear his voice, and he felt veins pop and tendons snap.

And then Barst's breastplate caved in, giving way where the Kull had dented it, and there was the sound of crystal breaking.

"No!" shouted Barst even as a pure white light erupted from the edges of his armor. He went rigid, as if chains had pulled every limb to its farthest reach, and he began to shake uncontrollably.

The light blinded Roran and burned his arms and face. He released Barst and fell to the ground, where he covered his eyes with his forearm.

The light continued to pour out from under Barst's breastplate until the edges of the metal began to glow. Then the blaze ceased, leaving the world darker than before, and what little remained of Lord Barst tumbled backward and lay smoking on the cobblestones.

Roran blinked as he stared at the featureless sky. He knew he should rise, for there were soldiers nearby, but the cobblestones seemed soft beneath him, and all he really wanted to do was to close his eyes and rest. . . .

When he next opened his eyes, he saw Orik and Horst and a number of elves gathered around him.

"Roran, can you hear me?" said Horst, peering at him with concern.

Roran tried to speak, but he could not form the words.

"Can you hear me? Listen to me. You have to stay awake. Roran! Roran!"

Again Roran felt himself sinking into blackness. It was a comforting sensation, like wrapping himself in a soft woolen blanket. Warmth spread through him, and the last thing he remembered was Orik bending over him and saying something in Dwarvish that sounded like a prayer.

✦ ✦ ✦

THE GIFT OF KNOWLEDGE

Eyes locked, Eragon and Murtagh slowly circled each other, trying to anticipate where and how the other would move. Murtagh appeared fit as ever, but there were dark circles under his eyes and his face was haggard; Eragon suspected that he had been under a great strain. He wore the same pieces of armor as did Eragon: mail hauberk, gauntlets, bracers, and greaves, but his shield was longer and thinner than Eragon's. As for their swords, Brisingr, with its hand-and-a-half hilt, had the advantage of length, while Zar'roc, with its wider blade, had the advantage of weight.

They began to edge closer, and when they were about ten feet apart, Murtagh, who had his back to Galbatorix, said in a low, anger-filled voice, "What are you doing?"

"Buying time," Eragon muttered, keeping his lips as still as possible.

Murtagh scowled. "You're a fool. He'll watch us cut each other to shreds, and what will it change? *Nothing*."

Instead of answering, Eragon shifted his weight forward and twitched his sword arm, causing Murtagh to flinch in response.

"Blast you," growled Murtagh. "If you had waited just one more day, I could have freed Nasuada."

That surprised Eragon. "Why should I believe you?"

The question angered Murtagh further, for his lip curled and he quickened his step, causing Eragon to increase his pace as well. Then, in a louder tone, Murtagh said, "So, you finally found a proper sword for yourself. The elves made it for you, didn't they?"

"You know they d—"

Murtagh lunged toward him, swinging Zar'roc at his gut, and Eragon skipped backward, barely parrying the red sword.

Eragon replied with a looping, overhead blow—he allowed his hand to slide down to Brisingr's pommel to give himself more reach—and Murtagh danced out of the way.

They both paused to see if the other would attack again. When neither did, they resumed circling, Eragon more wary than before.

From their exchange, it was obvious that Murtagh was still as fast and as strong as Eragon—or an elf. Galbatorix's prohibition on the use of magic apparently did not extend to the spells that fortified Murtagh's limbs. For selfish reasons, Eragon disliked the king's edict, but he could understand the rationale behind it; the fight would hardly have been fair otherwise.

But Eragon did not want a fair fight. He wanted to control the course of the duel so that he could decide when it should end, and how. Unfortunately, Eragon doubted that he would have the opportunity, given Murtagh's skill with a blade, and even if he did, he was not sure how he could use the fight to strike against Galbatorix. Nor did he have time to think about it, though he trusted that Saphira, Arya, and the dragons would try to devise a solution for him.

Murtagh feinted with his left shoulder, and Eragon ducked behind his shield. An instant later, he realized that it had been a ruse and that Murtagh was moving around toward his right in an attempt to get past his guard.

Eragon twisted and saw Zar'roc arcing toward his neck, the edge a glittering, wire-thin line. He knocked it aside with a clumsy push of Brisingr's crossguard. Then he retaliated with a quick slash at Murtagh's lower arm. To his grim delight, he struck Murtagh on the side of his wrist. Brisingr failed to cut through Murtagh's gauntlet and the sleeve of the tunic beneath, but the impact still hurt Murtagh and pushed his arm away from his body, leaving his chest exposed.

Eragon stabbed, and Murtagh used his shield to deflect the attack.

Three more times Eragon stabbed, but Murtagh stopped each blow, and when Eragon drew back his arm to strike again, Murtagh countered with a backhanded cut at his knee, which would have crippled him had it landed.

Seeing what Murtagh intended, Eragon altered his swing and stopped Zar'roc an inch from his leg. Then he countered with a cut of his own.

For several minutes, they exchanged blows, trying to disrupt each other's rhythms, but to no avail. They knew each other too well. Whatever Eragon attempted, Murtagh was able to thwart, and the same was true in reverse. It was like a game where they both had to think many moves in advance, which fostered a certain sense of intimacy as Eragon focused on divining the inner workings of Murtagh's mind and, from them, predicting, what Murtagh would do next.

Right from the beginning, Eragon noticed that Murtagh was playing the game differently than the previous times they'd fought. He attacked with a ruthlessness that heretofore had been lacking, as if, for the first time, he wanted to defeat Eragon, and quickly too. Moreover, after his initial outburst, his anger seemed to vanish, and he displayed only a cool, implacable determination.

Eragon found himself fighting to the limit of his abilities, and though he was able to hold Murtagh off, he ended up on the defensive more than he would have liked.

After a while, Murtagh lowered his sword and turned toward the throne and Galbatorix.

Eragon kept his guard up, but he hesitated, unsure whether it was appropriate to attack.

In that moment of hesitation, Murtagh leaped toward him. Eragon stood his ground and swung. Murtagh caught the blow on his shield, and then, instead of following up with a strike of his own as Eragon expected, he slammed his shield against Eragon's and pushed.

Eragon growled and pushed back. He would have reached around his shield to slash at Murtagh's back or legs, but Murtagh was shoving too hard for Eragon to risk it. Murtagh was an inch or two taller, and the extra height allowed him to bear down on Eragon's shield in a way that made it difficult for Eragon to keep from sliding back across the polished stone floor.

At last, with a roar and a mighty heave, Murtagh sent Eragon stumbling away. As Eragon flailed and struggled to regain his balance, Murtagh stabbed at his neck.

"Letta!" said Galbatorix.

The tip of Zar'roc stopped less than a finger's-breadth from Eragon's skin. He froze, panting, not sure what had just happened.

"Restrain yourself, Murtagh, or I shall do it for you," said Galbatorix from where he sat watching. "I dislike having to repeat myself. You are not to kill Eragon, nor is he to kill you. . . . Now, continue."

The realization that Murtagh had just tried to kill him—and that he would have succeeded if not for Galbatorix's intervention—shocked Eragon. He searched Murtagh's face for an explanation, but Murtagh remained stubbornly expressionless, as if Eragon meant little or nothing to him.

Eragon could not understand. Murtagh was definitely playing the game differently than he ought to be. Something had changed in him, but what it was, Eragon could not tell.

In addition, the knowledge that he had lost—and that, by all rights, he should be dead—undermined Eragon's confidence. He had confronted death many times before, but never in such a stark and uncompromising manner. There was no question of it; Murtagh had bested him, and only Galbatorix's mercy—such as it was—had saved him.

Eragon, do not dwell on it, said Arya. *You had no reason to suspect he would try to kill you. Nor were you trying to kill him. If you had, the fight would have gone differently, and Murtagh would never have had the chance to attack you as he did.*

Doubtful, Eragon glanced over to where she stood by the edge of the pool of light, along with Elva and Saphira. Then Saphira said,

If he wishes to rip out your throat, then cut his hamstrings and make sure that he cannot do it again.

Eragon nodded, acknowledging what they had said.

He and Murtagh separated and again took up their positions opposite each other while Galbatorix looked on approvingly.

This time Eragon was the first to attack.

They fought for what felt like hours. Murtagh did not attempt any more killing blows, whereas Eragon—to his satisfaction—succeeded in touching Murtagh on the collarbone, although he stopped the blow before Galbatorix saw fit to do so himself. Murtagh looked unsettled by the touch, and Eragon allowed himself a brief smile at Murtagh's reaction.

There were other blows that they failed to block as well. For all their speed and skill, neither he nor Murtagh was infallible, and without an easy means to end the fight, it was inevitable that they would make mistakes and that those mistakes would result in injuries.

The first wound was a cut Murtagh gave Eragon on his right thigh, in the gap between the edge of his hauberk and the upper part of his greave. It was a shallow cut, but exceedingly painful, and every time Eragon put his weight on the leg, blood surged from the wound.

The second wound was also Eragon's: a gash above one eyebrow after Murtagh landed a blow upon his helm and the edge of it drove into his flesh. Of the two wounds, Eragon found the second by far the most aggravating, because blood kept dripping into his eye, obscuring his vision.

Then Eragon caught Murtagh on the wrist again and, this time, sliced all the way through the cuff of his gauntlet, the sleeve of his tunic, and a thin layer of skin to the bone beneath. He failed to sever any muscles, but the wound seemed to pain Murtagh a great deal, and the blood that seeped into his gauntlet caused him to lose his grip at least twice.

Eragon took a nick to his right calf, and then—when Murtagh

was still recovering from a failed attack—he moved around to Murtagh's shield side and brought down Brisingr as hard as he could upon the middle of Murtagh's left greave, denting the steel.

Murtagh howled and jumped back on one leg. Eragon followed, swinging Brisingr in an attempt to batter him to the floor. Despite his injury, Murtagh was able to defend himself, and a few seconds later, Eragon was the one who was hard-pressed to remain on his feet.

For a time, their shields resisted the relentless pounding— Galbatorix, Eragon was pleased to realize, had left intact the enchantments upon their swords and armor—but then the spells on Eragon's shield gave way, as did those on Murtagh's, which was apparent from the chips and splinters that flew every time their swords landed. Soon afterward, Eragon cracked Murtagh's shield with a particularly heavy blow. His victory was short-lived, for Murtagh grasped Zar'roc with both hands and struck at Eragon's own shield twice in quick succession, and it split as well, leaving them equally matched once again.

As they fought, the stone beneath them grew slippery with smears and splashes of blood, and it became increasingly difficult to keep their footing. The massive presence chamber returned distant echoes of their clashing weapons—like the sounds of a long-forgotten battle—and it felt as if they were the center of all that existed, for theirs was the only light, and the two of them were alone within its compass.

And all the while, Galbatorix and Shruikan continued to watch from within the bordering shadows.

Without their shields, Eragon found it easier to land blows upon Murtagh—mainly upon his arms and legs—even as it was easier for Murtagh to do the same to him. For the most part, their armor protected them from cuts, but it did not protect them from lumps and bruises, of which they accrued many.

In spite of the wounds he gave Murtagh, Eragon began to suspect that, of the two of them, Murtagh was the better swordsman. Not by much, but enough that Eragon was never really able to gain the upper hand. If the course of their duel continued, Murtagh would end up wearing him down until he was too hurt or too tired to go on, an outcome that seemed to be fast approaching. With every step, Eragon could feel the blood gushing over his knee from the cut on his thigh, and with every moment that passed, it became harder to defend himself.

He had to end the duel now or else he would be unable to take on Galbatorix afterward. As it was, he doubted he would pose much of a challenge to the king, but he had to try. If nothing else, he had to try.

The heart of the problem, he realized, was that Murtagh's reasons for fighting were a mystery to him, and unless he could figure them out, Murtagh would continue to catch him by surprise.

Eragon thought back to what Glaedr had told him outside Dras-Leona: *You must learn to see what you are looking at.* And also: *The way of the warrior is the way of knowing.*

So he looked at Murtagh. He looked at him with the same intensity with which he had gazed upon Arya during their sparring sessions, the same intensity with which he had studied himself during his long night of introspection on Vroengard. By it, he sought to decipher the hidden language of Murtagh's body.

He met with some success; it was clear that Murtagh was drawn and hard-worn, and his shoulders were hunched in a way that spoke of deep-rooted anger, or perhaps it was fear. And then there was his ruthlessness, hardly a new characteristic, but newly applied to Eragon. Those things Eragon discerned, along with other, subtler details, and then he strove to reconcile them with what he knew of Murtagh from days past, with his friendship and his loyalty and his resentment of Galbatorix's control.

It took a few seconds—seconds filled with strained breathing and a pair of awkward blows that gained him another bruise on his elbow—until the truth came to Eragon. It seemed so obvious when it did. There had to be something in Murtagh's life, something their duel would affect, that was so important to Murtagh, he felt compelled to win by any means necessary, even if that meant killing his own half brother. Whatever that something was—and Eragon had his suspicions, some more disturbing than others—it meant that Murtagh would never give up. It meant Murtagh would fight like a cornered animal until his very last breath, and it meant Eragon would never be able to defeat him through conventional measures, for the duel did not mean as much to him as it did to Murtagh. For Eragon, the duel was a convenient distraction, and he cared little who won or lost as long as he was still able to face Galbatorix afterward. But for Murtagh, the duel was of far more significance, and from experience, Eragon knew that determination such as his was costly, if not impossible, to overcome by force alone.

The question, then, was how to stop a man who was resolved to persist and prevail in spite of whatever obstacles barred his way.

It was an unsolvable conundrum until, at last, Eragon realized that the only way to best Murtagh was to give him what he wanted. In order to achieve his own desire, Eragon would have to accept defeat.

But not entirely. He could not leave Murtagh free to carry out Galbatorix's bidding. Eragon would grant Murtagh his victory, and then he would take his own.

As she listened to his thoughts, Saphira's anguish and concern grew more pronounced, and she said, *No, Eragon. There must be another way.*

Then tell me what it is, he said, *for I cannot see it.*

She snarled, and Thorn growled back at her from across the pool of light.

Choose wisely, said Arya, and Eragon understood her meaning.

Murtagh rushed at him, and their blades met with a clamorous ring, and then they disengaged and paused a moment to gather their strength. As they started toward each other once again, Eragon sidled to Murtagh's right, while at the same time allowing his sword arm to drift away from the side of his body, as if through exhaustion or carelessness. It was a slight motion, but he knew that Murtagh would notice and that he would attempt to exploit the opening he had provided.

At that moment, Eragon felt nothing. He still registered the pain from his wounds, but at a remove, as if the sensations were not his own. His mind was like a pool of deep water on a breathless day, flat and motionless, and yet filled with the reflection of those things around it. What he saw, he registered without conscious thought. The need for that had passed. He understood all that was before him, and further contemplation would only hamper him.

As Eragon expected, Murtagh lunged toward him, stabbing at the middle of his belly.

When the time was ripe, Eragon turned. He moved neither fast nor slow but at just the right speed the situation required. The motion felt preordained, as if it were the only action he could have taken.

Instead of striking him in the gut, as Murtagh had intended, Zar'roc struck Eragon in the muscles along his right side, directly below his ribcage. The impact felt like a hammerblow, and there was a steely slither as Zar'roc slid past the broken links of his mail and into his flesh. The coldness of the metal made Eragon gasp more than the pain itself.

Behind him, the tip of the blade tugged at his hauberk as it emerged from his body.

Murtagh stared, seemingly taken aback.

Before Murtagh could recover, Eragon drew back his arm and thrust Brisingr into Murtagh's abdomen, close to his navel: a far worse wound than the one Eragon had just received.

Murtagh's face went slack. His mouth opened as if he were going to speak, and he fell to his knees, still clutching Zar'roc.

Off to the side, Thorn roared.

Eragon pulled Brisingr free, then stepped back and grimaced in a soundless howl as Zar'roc slid out of his body.

There was a clatter as Murtagh released Zar'roc and it dropped to the floor. Then he wrapped his arms around his waist, doubled over, and pressed his head against the polished stone.

Now Eragon was the one to stare, hot blood dripping into one eye.

From on his throne, Galbatorix said, "Naina," and dozens of lanterns throughout the chamber sprang to life, once again revealing the pillars and carvings along the walls and the block of stone where Nasuada stood chained.

Eragon staggered over to Murtagh and knelt next to him.

"And to Eragon goes the victory," said the king, his sonorous voice filling the great hall.

Murtagh looked up at Eragon, his sweat-beaded face contorted with pain. "You couldn't just let me win, could you?" he growled in an undertone. "You can't beat Galbatorix, but you still had to prove that you are better than me. . . . Ah!" He shuddered and began to rock back and forth upon his shins.

Eragon put a hand on his shoulder. "Why?" he asked, knowing that Murtagh would understand the question.

The answer came as a barely audible whisper: "Because I hoped to gain his favor so that I could save *her*." Tears blurred Murtagh's eyes, and he looked away.

At that, Eragon realized that Murtagh had been telling the truth earlier, and he felt a sense of dismay.

Another moment passed, and Eragon was aware of Galbatorix watching them with keen interest.

Then Murtagh said, "You tricked me."

"It was the only way."

Murtagh grunted. "That was always the difference between you and me." He eyed Eragon. "You were willing to sacrifice yourself. I wasn't. . . . Not then."

"But now you are."

"I'm not the person I once was. I have Thorn now, and . . ." Murtagh hesitated; then his shoulders rose and fell in a tiny shrug. "I'm not fighting for myself anymore. . . . It makes a difference." He took a shallow breath and winced. "I used to think you were a fool to keep risking your life as you have. . . . I know better now. I understand . . . why. I understand. . . ." His eyes widened and his grimace relaxed, as if his pain was forgotten, and an inner light seemed to illuminate his features. "I understand—*we* understand," he whispered, and Thorn uttered a strange sound that was half whimper and half growl.

Galbatorix stirred on his throne, as if uneasy, and in a harsh voice, he said, "Enough of this talk. Your duel is over, and Eragon has won. Now the time has arrived for our guests to bend their knees and give to me their oaths of fealty. . . . Come closer, the both of you, and I shall heal your wounds, and then we shall proceed."

Eragon started to stand, but Murtagh grabbed his forearm, stopping him.

"Now!" said Galbatorix, his heavy brows drawing together. "Or I will leave you to suffer from your wounds until we have finished."

Ready yourself, Murtagh mouthed to Eragon.

Eragon hesitated, not sure what to expect; then he nodded and warned Arya, Saphira, Glaedr, and the other Eldunarí

Then Murtagh pushed Eragon aside, and he rose up on his knees, still clutching his belly. He looked at Galbatorix. And he shouted the Word.

Galbatorix recoiled and lifted a hand, as if to shield himself.

Still shouting, Murtagh voiced other words in the ancient language, speaking too quickly for Eragon to understand the purpose of the spell.

The air around Galbatorix flashed red and black, and for an instant, his body appeared to be wreathed in flames. There was a sound like that of a high summer wind stirring the branches of an evergreen forest. Then Eragon heard a series of thin shrieks as twelve orbs of light appeared around Galbatorix's head and fled outward from him and passed through the walls of the chamber and thus vanished. They looked like spirits, but Eragon saw them for such a brief span, he could not be certain.

Thorn spun around—as fast as a cat whose tail has been stepped

709

on—and he pounced on Shruikan's immense neck. The black dragon bellowed and scrambled backward, shaking his head in an attempt to throw Thorn off. The noise of his growls was painfully loud, and the floor shook from the weight of the two dragons.

On the steps of the dais, the two children screamed and covered their ears with their hands.

Eragon saw Arya, Elva, and Saphira lurch forward, no longer bound by Galbatorix's magic. Dauthdaert in hand, Arya started toward the throne, while Saphira loped toward where Thorn clung to Shruikan. Meanwhile, Elva put her hand to her mouth and seemed to say something to herself, but what it was Eragon could not hear over the sound of the dragons.

Fist-sized drops of blood rained down around them and lay smoking on the stone.

Eragon rose from where Murtagh had pushed him, and he followed Arya toward the throne.

Then Galbatorix spoke the name of the ancient language, along with the word *letta.* Invisible bonds seized hold of Eragon's limbs, and throughout the chamber, silence fell as the king's magic restrained everyone, even Shruikan.

Rage and frustration boiled within Eragon. They had been so close to striking at the king, and still they were helpless before his spells. "*Get him!*" he shouted, both with his mind and his tongue. They had already tried to attack Galbatorix and Shruikan; the king would kill the two children whether or not they continued. The only path left to Eragon and those with him—the only hope of victory that yet remained—was to break past Galbatorix's mental barriers and seize control of his thoughts.

Along with Saphira and Arya and the Eldunarí they had brought with them, Eragon stabbed outward with his consciousness toward the king, pouring all his hate, anger, and pain into the single, burning ray that he drove into the center of Galbatorix's being.

For an instant, Eragon felt the king's mind: a terrible, shadow-ridden vista swept with bitter cold and searing heat—ruled by bars of iron, hard and unyielding, which portioned off areas of his consciousness.

Then the dragons under Galbatorix's command, the mad, howling, grief-stricken dragons, attacked Eragon's mind and forced him to withdraw within himself to avoid being torn to pieces.

Behind him, Eragon heard Elva start to say something, but she had barely uttered a sound when Galbatorix said, "Theyna!" and she stopped with a choked gurgle.

"I stripped him of his wards!" shouted Murtagh. "He's—"

Whatever Galbatorix said, it was too fast and too low for Eragon to catch, but Murtagh ceased speaking, and a moment later, Eragon heard him fall to the floor with a tinkle of mail and the sharp clink of his helm striking stone.

"I have plenty of wards," said Galbatorix, his hawklike face dark with fury. "You cannot harm me." He rose from his seat and strode down the steps of the dais toward Eragon, his cape billowing around him and his sword, Vrangr, white and deathly in his hand.

In the brief time he had, Eragon tried to capture the mind of at least one of the dragons battering at his consciousness, but there were too many, and his attempt left him scrambling to repel the horde of Eldunarí before they completely subjugated his thoughts.

Galbatorix stopped a foot in front of him and glared at him, a thick, forked vein prominent on his brow, the muscles of his heavy jaw knotting. "Think you to challenge me, *boy?*" he growled, fairly spitting with rage. "Think you to be my equal? That you could lay me low and steal my throne?" The cords in Galbatorix's neck stood out like a skein of twisted rope. He plucked at the edge of his cape. "I cut this mantle from the wings of Belgabad himself, and my gloves too." He lifted Vrangr and held its bleak blade before Eragon's eyes. "I took this sword from Vrael's hand, and I took this crown from the head of the mewling wretch who wore it before me. And yet you think to outwit me? *Me?* You come to my castle, and you kill my men, and you act as if you are *better* than I. As if you are more *noble* or *virtuous.*"

Eragon's head rang, and a constellation of throbbing, swirling crimson motes appeared before his eyes as Galbatorix struck him on the cheek with Vrangr's pommel, tearing his skin.

"You need to be taught a lesson in humility, boy," said Galbatorix, moving closer, until his gleaming eyes were mere inches from Eragon's.

He struck Eragon on the other cheek, and for a second, all Eragon could see was a black immensity littered with flashing lights.

"I shall *enjoy* having you in my service," said Galbatorix. In a lower voice, he said, "Gánga," and the pressure from the Eldunarí assailing Eragon's mind vanished, leaving him free to think as he would. But not so the others, as he could see from the strain on their faces.

Then a blade of thought, honed to an infinitesimal point, pierced Eragon's consciousness and sheathed itself in the marrow of his being. The blade twisted and, like a cocklebur lodged within a batt of felt, it tore at the fabric of his mind, seeking to destroy his will, his identity, his very awareness.

It was an attack unlike any Eragon had experienced. He shrank from it and concentrated upon a single thought—revenge—as he struggled to protect himself. Through their contact, he could feel Galbatorix's emotions: anger, mainly, but also a savage joy at being able to hurt Eragon and watch him writhe in discomfort.

The reason, Eragon realized, that Galbatorix was so good at breaking the minds of his enemies was because it gave him a perverse pleasure.

The blade dug deeper into Eragon's being and he howled, unable to help himself.

Galbatorix smiled, the edges of his teeth translucent, like fired clay.

Defense alone was no way to win a fight, and so, despite the searing pain, Eragon forced himself to attack Galbatorix in return. He dove into the king's consciousness and grasped at his razor-sharp thoughts, trying to pin them in place and prevent the king from moving or thinking without his approval.

Galbatorix made no attempt to guard himself, however. His cruel smile widened, and he twisted the blade in Eragon's mind even further.

It felt to Eragon as if a nest of briars were ripping him apart from the inside. A scream racked his throat, and he went limp in the grip of Galbatorix's spell.

"Submit," said the king. He grabbed Eragon's chin with fingers of steel. "Submit." The blade twisted yet again, and Eragon screamed until his voice gave out.

The king's probing thoughts closed in around Eragon's consciousness, restricting him to an ever-smaller part of his mind, until all that was left to him was a small, bright nub overshadowed by the looming weight of Galbatorix's presence.

"Submit," the king whispered, almost lovingly. "You have nowhere to go, nowhere to hide. . . . This life is at an end for you, Eragon Shadeslayer, but a new one awaits. Submit, and all shall be forgiven."

Tears distorted Eragon's vision as he stared into the featureless abyss of Galbatorix's pupils.

They had lost. . . . *He* had lost.

The knowledge was more painful than any of the wounds he had received. A hundred years' worth of striving—all for naught. Saphira, Elva, Arya, the Eldunarí: none of them could overcome Galbatorix. He was too strong, too knowledgeable. Garrow and Brom and Oromis had all died in vain, as had the many warriors of different races who had laid down their lives in the course of fighting the Empire.

The tears spilled from Eragon's eyes.

"Submit," whispered the king, and his grip tightened.

More than anything, it was the injustice of the situation that Eragon hated. It seemed *wrong* on a fundamental level that so many had suffered and died in pursuit of a hopeless goal. It seemed *wrong* that Galbatorix alone should be the cause of so much misery. And it seemed *wrong* that he should escape punishment for his misdeeds.

Why? Eragon asked himself.

He remembered, then, the vision the oldest of the Eldunarí, Valdr, had shown him and Saphira, where the dreams of starlings were equal to the concerns of kings.

"Submit!" shouted Galbatorix, and his mind bore down on Eragon with even greater force as splinters of ice and fire lanced through him from every direction.

Eragon cried out, and in his desperation he reached for Saphira and the Eldunarí—their minds besieged by the crazed dragons of Galbatorix's command—and without intending to, he drew from their stores of energy.

And with that energy, he cast a spell.

It was a spell without words, for Galbatorix's magic would not allow otherwise, and no words could have described what Eragon wanted, nor what he felt. A library of books would have been insufficient to the task. His was a spell of instinct and emotion; language could not contain it.

What he wanted was both simple and complex: he wanted Galbatorix to *understand* . . . to understand the wrongness of his actions. The spell was not an attack; it was an attempt to communicate. If Eragon was going to spend the rest of his life as a slave to the king, then he wanted Galbatorix to comprehend what he had done, fully and completely.

As the magic took effect, Eragon felt Umaroth and the Eldunarí turn their attention to his spell, fighting to ignore Galbatorix's dragons. A hundred years of inconsolable grief and anger welled up within the Eldunarí, like a roaring wave, and the dragons melded their minds with Eragon's and began to alter the spell, deepening it, widening it, and building upon it until it encompassed far more than he originally intended.

Not only would the spell show Galbatorix the wrongness of his actions; now it would also compel him to experience all the feelings, both good and bad, that he had aroused in others since the day he had been born. The spell was beyond any Eragon could have invented on his own, for it contained more than a single person, or a single dragon, could conceive of. Each Eldunarí contributed to the enchantment, and the sum of their contributions was a spell that extended not only across the whole of Alagaësia but also back through every moment in time between then and Galbatorix's birth.

It was, Eragon thought, the greatest piece of magic the dragons had ever wrought, and he was their instrument; he was their weapon.

The power of the Eldunarí rushed through him, like a river as wide as an ocean, and he felt a hollow and fragile vessel, as if his skin might tear with the force of the torrent he channeled. If not for Saphira and the other dragons, he would have died in an instant, drained of all strength by the voracious demands of the magic.

Around them, the light of the lanterns dimmed, and in his mind, Eragon seemed to hear the echo of thousands of voices: an unbearable cacophony of pains and joys innumerable, echoing forth from both the present and the past.

The lines upon Galbatorix's face deepened, and his eyes began to bulge from their sockets. "What have you done?" he said, his voice hollow and strained. He stepped back and put his fists to his temples. *"What have you done!"*

With an effort, Eragon said, "Made you understand."

The king stared at him with an expression of horror. The muscles of his face jumped and twitched, and his whole body began to shake with tremors. Baring his teeth, he growled, "You will not get the better of me, boy. You . . . will . . . not. . . ." He groaned and staggered, and all at once the spell holding Eragon vanished and he fell to the floor, even as Elva, Arya, Saphira, Thorn, Shruikan, and the two children began to move again as well.

A deafening roar from Shruikan filled the chamber, and the huge black dragon shook Thorn off his neck, sending the red dragon flying halfway across the room. Thorn landed on his left side, and the bones in his wing broke with a loud *snap*.

"I . . . shall . . . not . . . give . . . in," said Galbatorix. Behind the king, Eragon saw Arya—who was closer to the throne than Eragon—hesitate and look back at them. Then she sprinted past the dais and ran with Saphira toward Shruikan.

Thorn struggled to his feet and followed.

His face contorted like a madman's, Galbatorix strode toward Eragon and swung Vrangr at him.

Eragon rolled to the side and heard the sword strike the stone by his head. He kept rolling for another few feet, then pushed himself into a standing position. Only the energy from the Eldunarí allowed him to remain upright.

Shouting, Galbatorix charged at him, and Eragon deflected the king's clumsy blow. Their swords rang like bells, sharp and clear amid the roars of dragons and the whispers of the dead.

Saphira leaped high into the air and batted at Shruikan's enormous snout, bloodying it, then dropped back to the floor. He swung a paw at her, talons extended, and she hopped backward, half spreading her wings.

Eragon ducked a savage crosscut and stabbed at Galbatorix's left armpit. To his astonishment, he scored a hit, wetting the tip of Brisingr with the king's blood.

A spasm in Galbatorix's arm threw off his next strike, and they ended up with their swords locked at the hilt, both striving to push each other off balance. The king's face was twisted almost beyond recognition, and there were tears on his cheeks.

A sheet of flame erupted over their heads, and the air grew hot around them.

Somewhere the children were screaming.

Eragon's wounded leg gave way, and he fell back onto his hands and feet, bruising the fingers with which he held Brisingr.

He expected the king to be upon him within a second, but instead Galbatorix remained where he was, swaying from side to side.

"No!" cried the king. "I didn't. . . ." He looked at Eragon and shouted, "Make it stop!"

Eragon shook his head even while he scrambled back onto his feet.

Pain shot through his left arm, and he looked over to see Saphira with a bloody gash on her corresponding foreleg. On the other side of the room, Thorn sank his teeth into Shruikan's tail, causing the black dragon to snarl and turn on him. While Shruikan's attention was directed elsewhere, Saphira sprang upward and landed atop his neck, close to the base of his bony skull. She hooked her claws under his scales and then bit down on his neck between two of the spikes that ran along his spine.

Shruikan let out a rumbling, savage yowl and began to thrash about even more.

Once again Galbatorix ran at Eragon, slashing at him as he did. Eragon blocked one blow, then another, and then took a hit on his ribs, which nearly caused him to black out.

"Make it stop," said Galbatorix, his tone more pleading than threatening. "The pain . . ."

Another yowl, this one more frantic than the last, came from Shruikan. Behind the king, Eragon saw Thorn clinging to Shruikan's neck, opposite Saphira. The combined weight of the two dragons pulled down Shruikan's head until it was close to the floor. However, the black dragon was still too large and strong for them to subdue. Moreover, his neck was so thick, Eragon did not think either Saphira or Thorn would be able to hurt him much with their teeth.

Then, like a shadow flitting through a forest, Eragon saw Arya dart out from behind a pillar and run toward the dragons. In her left hand, the green Dauthdaert glowed with its usual starry nimbus.

Shruikan saw her coming and jerked his body, trying to dislodge Saphira and Thorn. When they remained affixed, he snarled and opened his jaws and painted the area in front of him with a torrent of fire.

Arya dove forward, and for a moment, Eragon lost sight of her behind the wall of flames. Then she came into view again, not far from where Shruikan's head hung above the floor. The ends of her hair were on fire, but she seemed not to notice.

With three bounding steps, she leaped onto Shruikan's left fore-foot, and from there flung herself toward the side of his head, trailing fire like a comet. Uttering a shout that could be heard throughout the throne room, Arya threw the Dauthdaert into the center of Shruikan's great, gleaming ice-blue eye and buried the full length of the spear within his skull.

Shruikan bellowed and twitched, and then he slowly fell side-ways, liquid fire pouring from his mouth.

Saphira and Thorn jumped clear a moment before the gigantic black dragon struck the floor.

Pillars cracked; chunks of stone fell from the ceiling and shat-tered. A number of lanterns broke, and gouts of some molten sub-stance dribbled out of them.

Eragon nearly fell as the room shuddered. He had not been able to see what had happened to Arya, but he feared that Shruikan's bulk might have crushed her.

"Eragon!" shouted Elva. "Duck!"

He ducked, and he heard a whistle of wind as Galbatorix's white blade swung over his lowered back.

Rising, Eragon lunged forward . . .

. . . and stabbed Galbatorix in the center of his stomach, even as he had stabbed Murtagh.

The king grunted, and then he stepped back, pulling himself off Eragon's blade. He touched the wound with his free hand and stared at the blood on the tips of his fingers. Then he looked back at Eragon and said, "The voices . . . the voices are terrible. I can't bear it. . . ." He closed his eyes, and fresh tears streamed down his cheeks. "Pain . . . so much pain. So much grief. . . . Make it stop! *Make it stop!*"

"No," said Eragon. Elva joined him, as did Saphira and Thorn from the other end of the room. With them, Eragon was relieved to see, was Arya, burned and bloodied, but otherwise unhurt.

Galbatorix's eyes snapped open—round and rimmed with an unnatural amount of white—and he stared into the distance, as if Eragon and those before him no longer existed. He shook and trembled and his jaw worked, but no sound came from his throat.

Two things happened at once, then. Elva let out a shriek and fainted, and Galbatorix shouted, "Waíse néiat!"

Be not.

Eragon had no time for words. Again drawing upon the Eldunarí, he cast a spell to drag himself, Saphira, Arya, Elva, Thorn, Murtagh, and the two children on the dais over to the block of stone where Nasuada was chained. And he also cast a spell to stop or deflect whatever might harm them.

They were only halfway to the block when Galbatorix vanished in a flash of light brighter than the sun. Then all went black and silent as Eragon's protective spell took effect.

✦　✦　✦

DEATH THROES

Roran sat on a litter that the elves had placed upon one of the many blocks of stone just inside the ruined gate of Urû'baen, giving orders to the warriors in front of him.

Four of the elves had carried him out of the city, where they could use magic without fear of Galbatorix's enchantments distorting their spells. They had healed his dislocated arm and broken ribs, as well as the other wounds Barst had inflicted, although they warned him that it would be weeks before his bones were as strong as before, and they insisted that he remain off his feet for the rest of the day.

Likewise, he had insisted upon rejoining the battle. The elves argued with him, but he told them, "Either you take me back or I'll walk there myself." Their displeasure had been obvious, but at last they agreed and carried him to where he now sat looking over the square.

As Roran expected, the soldiers had lost their will to fight with the death of their commander, and the Varden were able to push them back up the narrow streets. By the time Roran returned, the Varden had already cleared a third or more of the city and were fast approaching the citadel.

They had lost many—the dead and dying littered the street, and the gutters ran red with blood—but with their recent advances, a renewed sense of victory gripped the army; Roran could see it in the faces of the men and dwarves and Urgals, though not the elves, who maintained a cold fury at the death of their queen.

The elves worried Roran; he had seen them kill soldiers who were trying to surrender, cutting them down without the slightest compunction. Once loosed, their bloodlust seemed to have few bounds.

Soon after Barst fell, King Orrin had taken a bolt to the chest while storming a guardhouse deeper within the city. It was a serious wound, one that even the elves, apparently, were unsure they could heal. The king's soldiers had taken Orrin back to the camp, and so far, Roran had heard no word of his fate.

Although he could not fight, Roran could still give orders. Of his own accord, he had started to organize the army from the rear, gathering up stray warriors and sending them on missions throughout Urû'baen—the first being to capture the rest of the catapults along the walls. When he received a piece of information that he thought Jörmundur or Orik or Martland Redbeard or any of the other captains within the army ought to know, now he had runners seek them out among the buildings and convey the news.

"—and if you see any soldiers near the big domed building by the market, be sure to tell Jörmundur that as well," he said to the thin, high-shouldered swordsman who stood in front of him.

"Yes, sir," said the man, and the knob in his neck bobbed as he swallowed.

Roran stared for a moment, fascinated by the movement, then he waved and said, "Go."

As the man trotted away, Roran frowned and looked over the peaked roofs of the houses toward the citadel at the base of the overhanging shelf.

Where are you? he wondered. Nothing had been seen of Eragon or those with him since they entered the stronghold, and the length of their absence worried Roran. He could think of numerous explanations for the delay, but none boded well. The most benign was that Galbatorix was simply hiding, and that Eragon and his companions were having to search for the king. But after seeing the might of Shruikan during the previous night, Roran could not imagine that Galbatorix would flee from his enemies.

If his worst fears had come to pass, then the Varden's victories would be short-lived, and Roran knew it was unlikely that he or any of the other warriors within their army would live through the day.

One of the men he had sent off earlier—a bare-headed, sandy-haired archer with a ruddy spot in the center of each cheek—ran out of a street to Roran's right. The archer stopped in front of the block of stone and ducked his head while he panted for breath.

"You found Martland?" Roran asked.

The archer nodded again, his hair flopping over his glistening forehead.

"And you gave him my message?"

"Sir, yes sir. Martland told me to tell you that"—he paused for breath—"the soldiers have retreated from the baths, but now they've barricaded themselves in a hall close to the southern wall."

Roran shifted on the litter and a pang ran through his newly healed arm. "What of the wall towers between the baths and the granaries? Have they been secured yet?"

"Two of them; we're still fighting for the rest. Martland convinced a few elves to go and help, though. He also—"

A muffled roar from within the stone hill interrupted the man.

The archer blanched, save for the spots of color on his cheeks, which appeared even brighter and redder than before, like daubs of paint on the skin of a corpse. "Sir, is that—"

"Shh!" Roran cocked his head, listening. Only Shruikan could have roared that loud.

For a few moments, they heard nothing else of note. Then another roar sounded from inside the citadel, and Roran thought he could make out other, fainter noises, although he was not sure what they were.

Throughout the area in front of the ruined gate, men, elves, dwarves, and Urgals paused and looked toward the citadel.

Another roar, even louder than the last, rang forth.

Roran clutched the edge of the litter, his body rigid. "Kill him," he muttered. "Kill the bastard."

A vibration, subtle but noticeable, passed through the city, as if a great weight had struck the ground. With it, Roran heard what he thought was something breaking.

Then silence settled over the city, and every second that passed felt longer than the last.

". . . Do you think he needs our help?" the archer asked in a soft voice.

"There's nothing we can do for them," said Roran, keeping his eyes fixed on the citadel.

"Couldn't the elves—"

The ground rumbled and shook; then the front of the citadel exploded outward in a wall of white and yellow flame so bright, Roran saw the bones within the archer's neck and head, his flesh like a red gooseberry held before a candle.

Roran grabbed the archer and rolled off the edge of the stone block, pulling the other man with him.

A blast of sound struck them as they fell. It felt as if spikes were being driven into Roran's ears. He screamed, but he could not hear himself—nor, after the initial clap of thunder, could he hear anything else. The cobblestones bucked underneath them, a cloud of dust and debris hurtled over them, blotting out the sun, and a massive wind tore at Roran's clothes.

The dust forced Roran to squeeze his eyes shut. All he could do was cling to the archer and wait for the upheaval to subside. He tried to take a breath, but the heated wind snatched the air from his lips and nose before he could fill his lungs. Something struck his head, and he felt his helmet fly off.

The shaking went on and on, but at last the ground grew still again, and Roran opened his eyes, afraid of what he would see.

The air was gray and dim; objects past a few hundred feet were lost in the haze. Small chunks of wood and stone rained from the sky, along with flakes of ash. A piece of timber that lay across the street from him—part of a flight of stairs the elves had broken when they destroyed the gate—was burning. The heat of the explosion had already charred the beam along its full length. The warriors who had been standing in the open now lay flat on the ground, some still moving, others clearly dead.

Roran glanced at the archer. The man had bitten through his bottom lip; blood coated his chin.

They helped each other off the ground, and Roran looked toward where the citadel had been. He could see nothing but gray darkness. *Eragon!* Could he and Saphira have survived the explosion? Could anyone who had been close to the heart of such an inferno?

Roran opened his mouth several times, trying to clear his ears—which rang and hurt badly—but to no avail. When he touched his right ear, his fingers came away bloody.

"Can you hear me?" he shouted at the archer, the words nothing but a vibration in his mouth and throat.

The archer frowned and shook his head.

A spate of dizziness caused Roran to lean over and prop himself against the block of stone. As he waited for his balance to return, he thought of the shelf hanging over them, and it suddenly occurred to him that the whole city might be in danger.

We have to leave before it falls, he thought. He spat blood and dirt onto the cobblestones. Then he looked in the direction of the citadel again. The dust still hid it. And grief clutched at his heart.

Eragon!

✦ ✦ ✦

A SEA OF NETTLES

Darkness, and in that darkness, silence.

Eragon felt himself slide to a stop, then . . . nothing. He could breathe, but the air was stale and lifeless, and when he tried to move, the strain upon his spell increased.

He touched the minds of everyone around him, checking that he had managed to save them all. Elva was unconscious, and Murtagh nearly so, but they were alive, as were the rest.

It was the first time Eragon had come into contact with Thorn's mind. As he did, the red dragon seemed to recoil. His thoughts felt darker, more contorted than Saphira's, but there was a strength and nobility to him that impressed Eragon.

We cannot maintain this spell for much longer, said Umaroth, his voice tense.

You have to, said Eragon. *If you don't, we'll die.*

Seconds more passed.

Without warning, light flooded Eragon's eyes, and an onslaught of noise assailed his ears.

He winced and blinked while his eyes adjusted.

Through the smoke-filled air, he saw a huge glowing crater where Galbatorix had been standing. The incandescent stone pulsed like living flesh as breaths of air wafted over its surface. The ceiling glowed as well, and the sight unnerved Eragon; it was as if they were standing inside a giant crucible.

The air smelled like the taste of iron.

The walls of the room were cracked, and the pillars, carvings, and lanterns had been pulverized. At the back of the chamber lay Shruikan's corpse, much of the flesh stripped from his soot-blackened bones. At the front, the explosion had shattered the stone walls, as well as the walls beyond for hundreds of feet, exposing a veritable warren of tunnels and rooms. The beautiful golden doors that had guarded the entrance to the chamber had been blown off their hinges, and Eragon thought he glimpsed daylight at the far end of the quarter-mile-long hallway that led to the outside.

As he got to his feet, he noticed that his ward was still drawing strength from the dragons, but not so quickly as before.

A piece of stone the size of a house fell from the ceiling and landed next to Shruikan's skull, where it split into a dozen pieces. Around them, more cracks spread through the walls, ominous shrieks and groans sounding from every side.

Arya went to the two children, grabbed the boy around his waist, and climbed with him up onto Saphira's back. Once there, she pointed at the girl and said to Eragon, "Throw her to me!"

Eragon lost a second as he struggled to sheathe Brisingr. Then he grabbed the girl and tossed her to Arya, who caught her in outstretched arms.

Eragon turned and sidestepped Elva as he hurried over to Nasuada. "Jierda!" he said, placing a hand on the manacles that held her to the block of gray stone. The spell had no apparent effect, so he ended it quickly before it consumed too much energy.

Nasuada made an urgent sound, and he pulled the knotted cloth out of her mouth. "You have to find the key!" she said. "Galbatorix's jailer has it on him."

"We'll never find him in time!" Eragon drew Brisingr again and swung at the chain connected to the manacle around her left hand. The sword bounced off the links with a harsh reverberation, leaving not so much as a scratch on the dull metal. He swung a second time, but the chain was impervious to his blade.

Another piece of rock fell from the ceiling and struck the floor with a loud *crack*.

A hand gripped his arm, and he turned to see Murtagh standing behind him, one arm pressed against the wound in his stomach. "Move aside," he growled. Eragon did, and Murtagh spoke the name of all names, as he had before, as well as *jierda,* and the iron cuffs opened and fell from Nasuada's limbs.

Murtagh took her by the wrist, and he began to lead her toward Thorn. After his first step, she slipped under his arm and allowed him to lean his weight on her shoulders.

Eragon opened his mouth, then closed it. He would ask his questions later.

"Wait!" cried Arya, and she leaped down from Saphira and ran over to Murtagh. "Where is the egg? And the Eldunarí? We can't leave them!"

Murtagh frowned, and Eragon felt the information pass between him and Arya.

Arya spun around, her burnt hair flying, and sprinted toward a doorway on the opposite side of the room.

"It's too dangerous!" Eragon shouted after her. "This place is fall- ing apart! Arya!"

Go, she said. *Get the children to safety. Go! You haven't much time!*

Eragon cursed. At the very least, he wished she had taken Glaedr with her. He slid Brisingr back into its scabbard, then bent and picked up Elva, who was just beginning to stir.

"What's happening?" she asked as Eragon carried her up onto Saphira's back behind the two other children.

"We're leaving," he said. "Hold on."

Saphira had already started moving. Limping because of her wounded foreleg, she trotted around the crater. Thorn followed close behind her, Murtagh and Nasuada upon his back.

"Look out!" shouted Eragon as he saw a chunk of the glowing ceiling break loose directly overhead.

Saphira shied to her left, and the jagged piece of stone landed next to her and sent a burst of straw-yellow shards in every direc- tion. One of them struck Eragon in the side and lodged in his mail.

He plucked it out and threw it away. Smoke trailed from the fingers of his gloves, and he smelled burnt leather. More pieces of stone fell elsewhere in the chamber.

When Saphira arrived at the mouth of the hallway, Eragon twisted and looked back at Murtagh. "What of the traps?" he shouted.

Murtagh shook his head and waved for them to continue.

Piles of broken stone covered the floor along much of the hall-way, which slowed the dragons. To either side, Eragon could see into the rubble-filled rooms and tunnels that the explosion had torn open. Within them, tables, chairs, and other pieces of furniture burned. The limbs of the dead and dying stuck out at odd angles from beneath the tumbled stones, occasionally a grimy face or the back of a head.

He looked for Blödhgarm and his spellcasters but saw no sign of them, either dead or alive.

Farther down the hallway, hundreds of people—soldiers and ser-vants alike—poured out of the adjoining doorways and ran toward the now-gaping entrance. Broken limbs were common among them, as were burns, scrapes, and other wounds. The survivors moved aside for Saphira and Thorn, but otherwise ignored the dragons.

Saphira was nearly at the end of the hall when a thunderous crash sounded behind them, and Eragon looked back to see that the throne room had caved in on itself, burying the chamber floor under a pile of stone fifty feet thick.

Arya! thought Eragon. He tried to find her with his mind, but without success. Either too much material separated them, or one of the spells woven throughout the mined-out crag blocked his mental probe, or—the one alternative he hated to consider—she was dead. She had not been in the room when it collapsed; that much he knew, but he wondered if she would be able to find her way back out again, now that the throne room was blocked.

As they emerged from the citadel, the air cleared and Eragon was able to see the destruction that the blast had wreaked on Urû'baen. It had ripped off the slate roofs of many nearby buildings and set fire to the beams underneath. Scores of fires dotted the rest of the city. The threads and plumes of smoke drifted upward until they collided with the underside of the shelf above. There they pooled and flowed along the angled surface of the stone, like water over a streambed. By the southeastern edge of the city, the smoke caught the light of the morning sun as it seeped around the side of the overhang, and there the smoke glowed with the reddish-orange color of a fire opal.

The people of Urû'baen were fleeing their houses, streaming through the streets toward the hole in the outer wall. The soldiers and servants from the citadel hurried to join them, giving Saphira and Thorn a wide berth as they ran across the courtyard in front of the fortress. Eragon paid them little attention; as long as they remained peaceful, he did not care what they did.

Saphira stopped in the middle of the quadrangle, and Eragon lowered Elva and the two nameless children to the ground. "Do you know where your parents are?" he asked, kneeling by the siblings.

They nodded, and the boy pointed toward a large house on the left side of the courtyard.

"Is that where you live?"

The boy nodded again.

"Go on, then," said Eragon, and gave them a gentle push on the back. Without further prompting, the brother and sister ran across the courtyard to the building. The door to the house flew open, and a balding man with a sword at his belt stepped out and wrapped the two of them in his arms. He gave Eragon a glance, then hurried the children inside.

That was easy, Eragon said to Saphira.

Galbatorix must have had his men find the nearest hatchlings, she replied. *We didn't give him time to do much else.*

I suppose.

Thorn sat a number of yards away from Saphira, and Nasuada helped Murtagh down from his back. Then Murtagh slumped against Thorn's belly. Eragon heard him begin to recite spells of healing.

Eragon likewise attended to Saphira's wounds, ignoring his own, for hers were more serious. The gash on her left foreleg was as wide as both his hands put together, and a pool of blood was forming about her foot.

Tooth or claw? he asked as he examined the wound.

Claw, she said.

He used her strength, as well as Glaedr's, to mend the gash. When he finished, he turned his attention to his own wounds, starting with the burning line of pain in his side, where Murtagh had stabbed him.

As he worked, he kept an eye on Murtagh—watched as Murtagh healed his gut wound, Thorn's broken wing, and the dragon's other injuries. Nasuada stayed by him the whole while, her hand on his shoulder. He had, Eragon saw, somehow reacquired Zar'roc on the way out of the throne room.

Eragon then turned to Elva, who was standing nearby. She appeared pained, but he saw no blood upon her. "Are you hurt?" he asked.

Her brow furrowed, and she shook her head. "No, but many of them are." And she pointed at the people fleeing the citadel.

"Mmh." Eragon glanced over at Murtagh again. He and Nasuada were standing now, talking to each other.

Nasuada frowned.

Then Murtagh reached out, grasped the neck of her tunic, and pulled it to the side, tearing the fabric.

Eragon had drawn Brisingr halfway out of its sheath before he saw the map of angry-looking welts below Nasuada's collarbone. The sight struck him like a blow; it reminded him of the wounds on Arya's back after he and Murtagh had rescued her from Gil'ead.

Nasuada nodded and bowed her head.

Again Murtagh began to speak, this time, Eragon was sure, in the ancient language. He placed his hands upon various parts of Nasuada's body, his touch gentle—even hesitant—and her expression of relief was all the evidence Eragon needed to understand how much pain she had been suffering.

Eragon watched for a minute longer, then a sudden rush of emotion swept through him. His knees grew weak, and he sat on Saphira's right paw. She lowered her head and nuzzled his shoulder, and he leaned his head against her.

We did it, she said in a quiet tone.

We did it, he said, hardly able to believe the words.

He could feel Saphira thinking about Shruikan's death; as dangerous as Shruikan had been, she still mourned the passing of one of the last remaining members of her race.

Eragon gripped her scales. He felt light, almost dizzy, as if he might float away from the surface of the earth. *What now . . . ?*

Now we will rebuild, said Glaedr. His own emotions were a curious mixture of satisfaction, grief, and weariness. *You acquitted yourself well, Eragon. No one else would have thought to attack Galbatorix as you did.*

"I just wanted him to understand," he murmured wearily. But if Glaedr heard, he chose not to respond.

At last, the Oath-breaker is dead, crowed Umaroth.

It seemed impossible that Galbatorix was no more. As Eragon contemplated the fact, something within his mind seemed to release, and he remembered—as if he had never forgotten—everything that had transpired during their time in the Vault of Souls.

A tingle passed through him. *Saphira—*

I know, she said, her excitement rising. *The eggs!*

Eragon smiled. Eggs! Dragon eggs! As a race, they would not pass into the void. They would survive, and flourish, and return to their former glory, as they had been before the fall of the Riders.

Then a horrible suspicion occurred to him. *Did you make us forget anything else?* he asked Umaroth.

If we did, how would we know? replied the white dragon.

"Look!" cried Elva, pointing.

Eragon turned and saw Arya walking out of the dark maw of the citadel. With her were Blödhgarm and his spellcasters, bruised and scraped, but alive. In her arms, Arya carried a wooden chest fitted with gold hasps. A long line of metal boxes—each the size of the back of a wagon—floated along behind the elves, a few inches above the floor.

Elated, Eragon sprang up and ran over to meet them. "You're alive!" He surprised Blödhgarm by grabbing the fur-covered elf and embracing him.

Blödhgarm regarded him for a moment with his yellow eyes, and then he smiled, showing his fangs.

"We are alive, Shadeslayer."

"Are those the . . . Eldunarí?" Eragon asked, speaking the word softly.

Arya nodded. "They were in Galbatorix's treasure room. We will have to go back at some point; there are many wonders hidden therein."

"How are they? The Eldunarí, I mean."

"Confused. It will take them years to recover, if ever they do."

"And is that . . . ?" Eragon motioned toward the chest she carried.

Arya glanced around to make sure no one was close enough to see; then she lifted the lid the width of a finger. Inside, nestled in velvet, Eragon saw a beautiful green dragon egg, webbed with veins of white.

The joy in Arya's face lifted Eragon's heart. He grinned and beckoned to the other elves. When they had gathered close to him, he whispered in the ancient language and told them of the eggs on Vroengard.

They did not shout or laugh, but their eyes gleamed, and as a group, they seemed to vibrate with excitement. Still grinning, Eragon bounced on his heels, delighted by their reaction.

Then Saphira said, *Eragon!*

At the same time, Arya frowned and said, "Where are Thorn and Murtagh?"

Eragon shifted his gaze and saw Nasuada standing alone in the courtyard. Next to her was a pair of saddlebags that Eragon did not remember seeing on Thorn. Wind swept over the courtyard and he heard the sound of wings flapping, but of Murtagh and Thorn, nothing was visible.

Eragon cast his thoughts out toward where he thought they were. He felt them at once, for their minds were not hidden, but they refused to speak or listen to him.

"Blast it," muttered Eragon as he ran over to Nasuada. There were tears on her cheeks, and she seemed on the verge of losing her composure.

"Where are they going?!"

"Away." Her chin trembled. Then she took a breath, released it, and stood taller than before.

Cursing again, Eragon bent and pulled open the saddlebags. Within, he found a number of smallish Eldunarí enclosed in padded cases. "Arya! Blödhgarm!" he shouted, pointing at the saddlebags. The two elves nodded.

Eragon ran over to Saphira. He did not have to explain himself; she understood. She spread her wings as he climbed onto her back, and the moment he was settled in the saddle, she took flight from the courtyard.

Cheers rose from the city as the Varden caught sight of her.

Saphira flapped quickly, following Thorn's musky scent trail through the air. It led her south, out from under the shadow of the overhang, and then it turned and curved up and around the great stone outcrop, heading north, toward the Ramr River.

For several miles, the trail ran straight and level. When the broad, tree-lined river was almost underneath them, the scent began to angle downward.

Eragon studied the ground ahead and saw a flash of red by the foot of a small hill on the other side of the river. *Over there*, he said to Saphira, but she had already spotted Thorn.

She spiraled down and landed softly atop the hill, where she had the advantage of height. The air off the water was cool and moist, carrying with it the scent of moss, mud, and sap. Between the hill and the river lay a sea of nettles. The plants grew in such thick profusion, the only way to pass through them would have been to cut a path. Their dark, sawtooth leaves rubbed against each other with a gentle susurration that blended with the sound of the rushing river.

By the edge of the nettles sat Thorn. Murtagh stood next to him, adjusting the girth on his saddle.

Eragon loosened Brisingr in its sheath, then cautiously approached.

Without turning around, Murtagh said, "Have you come to stop us?"

"That depends. Where are you going?"

"I don't know. North, maybe . . . somewhere away from other people."

"You could stay."

Murtagh uttered a bark of mirthless laughter. "You know better than that. It would only cause Nasuada problems. Besides, the dwarves would never stand for it. Not after I killed Hrothgar." He glanced over his shoulder at Eragon. "Galbatorix used to call me Kingkiller. You're Kingkiller as well now."

"It seems to run in the family."

"You'd better keep an eye on Roran, then. . . . And Arya is a dragonkiller. That can't be easy for her—an elf killing a dragon. You should talk to her and make sure she's all right."

Murtagh's insight surprised Eragon. "I will."

"There," said Murtagh, giving the strap a final tug. Then he turned to face Eragon, and Eragon saw that he had been holding Zar'roc close against his body, drawn and ready to use. "So, again: have you come to stop us?"

"No."

Murtagh gave a thin smile and sheathed Zar'roc. "Good. I would hate to have to fight you again."

"How were you able to break free of Galbatorix? It was your true name, wasn't it?"

Murtagh nodded. "As I said, I'm not . . . *we're* not"—he touched Thorn's side—"what we once were. It just took a while to realize it."

"And Nasuada."

Murtagh frowned. Then he turned away and stared out over the sea of nettles. As Eragon joined him, Murtagh said in a low voice, "Do you remember the last time we were at this river?"

"It would be hard to forget. I can still hear the screams of the horses."

"You, Saphira, Arya, and me, all together and sure that nothing could stop us. . . ."

In the back of his mind, Eragon could feel Saphira and Thorn talking to each other. Saphira, he knew, would tell him later what had passed between them.

"What will you do?" he asked Murtagh.

"Sit and think. Maybe I'll build a castle. I have the time."

"You don't have to leave. I know it would be . . . difficult, but you have family here: me and also Roran. He's your cousin as well as mine, and you've never even met him. . . . You belong as much to Carvahall and Palancar Valley as you do to Urû'baen, maybe more."

Murtagh shook his head and continued to stare over the nettles. "It wouldn't work. Thorn and I need time alone; we need time to heal. If we stay, we'd be too busy to figure things out for ourselves."

"Good company and staying busy are often the best cure for a sickness of the soul."

"Not for what Galbatorix did to us. . . . Besides, it would be painful to be around Nasuada right now, for both her and me. No, we have to leave."

"How long do you think you'll be gone?"

"Until the world no longer seems quite so hateful and we no longer feel like tearing down mountains and filling the sea with blood."

To that, Eragon had no response. They stood looking at the river, where it lay behind a line of low willow trees. The rustling of the nettles grew louder, stirred by the westward wind.

Then Eragon said, "When you no longer wish to be alone, come find us. You'll always be welcome at our hearth, wherever that may be."

"We will. I promise." To Eragon's surprise, he saw a gleam appear in Murtagh's eyes. It vanished a second later. "You know," Murtagh said, "I never thought you could do it . . . but I'm glad you did."

"I was lucky. And it wouldn't have been possible without your help."

"Even so. . . . You found the Eldunarí in the saddlebags?"

Eragon nodded.

"Good."

Should we tell them? Eragon asked Saphira, hoping that she would agree.

She thought for a moment. *Yes, but do not say where. You tell him, and I will tell Thorn.*

As you wish. To Murtagh, Eragon said, "There's something you should know."

Murtagh gave him a sideways glance.

"The egg that Galbatorix had—it isn't the only one in Alagaësia. There are more, hidden in the same place where we found the Eldunarí we brought with us."

Murtagh turned toward him, disbelief evident on his face. At the same time, Thorn arched his neck and uttered a joyful trumpet that scared a flight of swallows from the branches of a nearby tree.

"How many more?"

"Hundreds."

For a moment, Murtagh seemed unable to speak. Then: "What will you do with them?"

"Me? I think Saphira and the Eldunarí will have some say in the matter, but probably find somewhere safe for the eggs to hatch, and start to rebuild the Riders."

"Will you and Saphira train them?"

Eragon shrugged. "I'm sure the elves will help. You could as well, if you join us."

Murtagh tilted his head back and released a long breath. "The dragons are going to return, and the Riders as well." He laughed softly. "The world is about to change."

"It has already changed."

"Aye. So you and Saphira will become the new leaders of the Riders, while Thorn and I will live in the wilderness." Eragon tried to say something, to comfort him, but Murtagh stopped him with a look. "No, it is as it should be. You and Saphira will make better teachers than we would."

"I'm not so sure of that."

"Mmh . . . Promise me one thing, though."

"What?"

"When you teach them—teach them not to fear. Fear is good in small amounts, but when it is a constant, pounding companion, it cuts away at who you are and makes it hard to do what you know is right."

"I'll try."

Then Eragon noticed that Saphira and Thorn were no longer speaking. The red dragon shifted and moved around her until he was able to peer down at Eragon. With a mental voice that was surprisingly musical, Thorn said, *Thank you for not killing my Rider, Eragon-Murtagh's-brother.*

737

"Yes, thank you," Murtagh said dryly.

"I'm glad I didn't have to," Eragon said, looking Thorn in one glittering, blood-red eye.

The dragon snorted, then bent and touched Eragon on the top of his head, tapping his scales against Eragon's helm. *May the wind and the sun always be at your back.*

"And at yours."

A sense of great anger, grief, and ambivalence pressed heavily against Eragon as Glaedr's consciousness enveloped his mind and, it seemed, those of Murtagh and Thorn, for they tensed, as if in anticipation of battle. Eragon had forgotten that Glaedr, along with the other Eldunarí—hidden within their invisible pocket of space— were present and listening.

Would that I could thank you for the same, said Glaedr, his words as bitter as an oak gall. *You killed my body and you killed my Rider*. The statement was flat and simple and all the more terrible because of it.

Murtagh said something with his thoughts, but Eragon did not know what it was, for it was directed to Glaedr alone, and Eragon was privy only to Glaedr's reaction.

No, I cannot, said the gold dragon. *However, I understand that it was Galbatorix who drove you to it and that it was he who swung your arm, Murtagh. . . . I cannot forgive, but Galbatorix is dead and with him my desire for vengeance. Yours has always been a hard path, since each of you hatched. But today you showed that your misfortunes have not broken you. You turned against Galbatorix when it might have gained you only pain, and by it you allowed Eragon to kill him. Today you and Thorn proved yourselves worthy of being considered Shur'tugal in full, though you never had the proper instruction or guidance. That is . . . admirable.*

Murtagh bowed his head slightly, and Thorn said, *Thank you, Ebrithil*, which Eragon heard. Thorn's use of the honorific *ebrithil* seemed to startle Murtagh, for Murtagh looked back at the dragon and opened his mouth as if he was going to say something.

Then Umaroth spoke. *We know much of the difficulties you have faced, Thorn and Murtagh, for we have watched you from afar, even as we have watched Eragon and Saphira. There are many things we would teach you once you are ready, but until then, we will tell you this: in your wanderings, avoid the barrows of Anghelm, where the one and only Urgal king, Kulkarvek, lies in state. Avoid too the ruins of Vroengard and of El-harím. Beware the deeps, and tread not where the ground grows black and brittle and the air smells of brimstone, for in those places evil lurks. Do this and, unless you are greatly unfortunate, you shall not encounter danger beyond your ability to master.*

Murtagh and Thorn thanked Umaroth, and then Murtagh cast a glance in the direction of Urû'baen and said, "We should be off." He looked at Eragon again. "Can you remember the name of the ancient language now, or is Galbatorix's magic still clouding your mind?"

"I can *almost* remember it, but . . ." Eragon shook his head with frustration.

Then Murtagh spoke the name of names twice: first to remove the spell of forgetfulness Galbatorix had placed on Eragon, and then again so that Eragon and Saphira might learn the name for themselves. "I wouldn't share it with anyone else," he said. "If every magician knew the name of the ancient language, the language would be worse than useless."

Eragon nodded, agreeing.

Then Murtagh held out his hand and Eragon grasped him by the forearm. They stood like that for a moment, gazing at each other.

"Be careful," Eragon said.

"You too . . . Brother."

Eragon hesitated, then nodded again. "Brother."

Murtagh checked the straps on Thorn's harness once more before he climbed up into the saddle. As Thorn spread his wings and started to move away, Murtagh called out, "See to it that Nasuada is well protected. Galbatorix had many servants, more than he ever told me about, and not all of them were bound to him by magic alone. They will seek revenge for the death of their master. Be on your guard at all times. There are those among them who are even more dangerous than the Ra'zac!"

Then Murtagh raised a hand in farewell. Eragon did likewise, and Thorn took three loping steps away from the sea of nettles and leaped into the sky, leaving tracklike gouges in the soft earth below.

The sparkling red dragon circled over them once, twice, three times and then he turned and set off to the north, flapping with a slow, steady beat.

Eragon joined Saphira on the crest of the low hill, and together they watched as Thorn and Murtagh dwindled to a single starlike speck close to the horizon.

With a sense of sadness upon them both, Eragon took his place on Saphira's back, and they departed from the knoll and returned thence to Urû'baen.

HEIR TO THE EMPIRE

Eragon slowly climbed the worn steps of the green tower. It was close to sunset, and through the windows that pierced the curving wall to his right, he could see the shadow-streaked buildings of Urû'baen, as well as the hazy fields outside the city and, as he spiraled around, the dark mass of the stone hill that rose up behind it.

The tower was tall, and Eragon was tired. He wished he could have flown with Saphira to the top. It had been a long day, and right then, he wanted nothing more than to sit with Saphira and drink a cup of hot tea while watching the light fade from the sky. But, as always, there was still work to be done.

He had seen Saphira only twice since they landed back at the citadel after parting with Murtagh and Thorn. She had spent most of the afternoon helping the Varden kill or capture the remainder of the soldiers and, later, gather into camps the families who had fled their homes and scattered across the countryside while they waited to see if the overhang would break and fall.

That it had not, the elves told Eragon, was because of spells they had embedded within the stone in ages past—when Urû'baen was yet known as Ilirea—and also because of the overhang's sheer size, which had allowed it to weather the force of the blast without significant damage.

The hill itself had helped contain the harmful residue from the explosion, although a large amount had still escaped through the entrance to the citadel, and most everyone who had been in or around Urû'baen needed healing with magic, else they would soon sicken and die. Already many had fallen ill. Along with the elves, Eragon had worked to save as many as possible; the strength of the Eldunarí had allowed him to cure a large portion of the Varden, as well as many inhabitants of the city.

At that very moment, the elves and the dwarves were walling up the front of the citadel to prevent any further contamination from seeping out. This after having searched the building for survivors, of whom there had been many: soldiers, servants, and hundreds of prisoners from the dungeons below. The great store of treasures that lay within the citadel, including the contents of Galbatorix's vast library, would have to be retrieved at a later date. It would be no easy task. The walls of many rooms had collapsed; countless others, though still standing, were so damaged that they posed a danger to any who ventured near. Moreover, magic would be required to fend off the poison that had permeated the air, the stone, and all of the objects within the sprawling warren of the fortress. And more magic would be required to cleanse whatever items they chose to bring out.

Once the citadel was closed off, the elves would purge the city and the land thereabouts of the harmful residue that had settled upon it so that the area would again be safe to live in. Eragon knew that he would have to help with that too.

Before he had joined in the effort to heal and place wards of protection around everyone in and around Urû'baen, he had spent over an hour using the name of the ancient language to find and dismantle the many spells Galbatorix had bound to the buildings and the people of the city. Some of the enchantments seemed benign, even helpful—such as one spell whose only apparent purpose was to keep the hinges of a door from creaking, and which drew its power from an egg-sized piece of crystal set within the face of the door—but Eragon dared not leave any of the king's spells intact, no matter how harmless they appeared. Especially not those that lay upon the men and women of Galbatorix's command. Among them, oaths of fealty were the most common, but there were also wards, enchantments to grant skills beyond the ordinary, and other, more mysterious spells.

As Eragon had released nobles and commoners alike from their bondage, he occasionally felt a cry of anguish, as if he had taken something precious from them.

There had been a moment of crisis when he stripped Galbatorix's strictures from the Eldunarí the king had enslaved. The dragons immediately began to lash out and assail the minds of the people within the city, attacking without regard for who was friend or who was foe. In those moments, a great pall of dread spread over Urû'baen, causing everyone, even the elves, to crouch and turn white with fear.

Then Blödhgarm and his ten remaining spellcasters had tied the convoy of metal boxes that contained the Eldunarí to a pair of horses and ridden out of Urû'baen, where the dragons' thoughts no longer had such a strong effect. Glaedr insisted upon accompanying the maddened dragons, as did several of the Eldunarí from Vroengard. That had been the second time Eragon had seen Saphira since their return, when he amended the spell that hid Umaroth and those with him so that five of the Eldunarí could be portioned out and given over to Blödhgarm's safekeeping. Glaedr and the five were of the opinion that they could calm and communicate with the dragons that Galbatorix had for so long tormented. Eragon was less sure, but he hoped they were right.

As the elves and Eldunarí were on their way out of the city, Arya had contacted him, casting a questioning thought from outside the ruined gate, where she was in conference with the captains of her mother's army. In that brief time when their minds touched, he felt her desolation at Islanzadí's death, as well as the regret and anger that eddied beneath her grief, and he saw how her emotions threatened to overwhelm her reason and how she struggled to restrain them. He sent her what comfort he could, but it seemed paltry when compared to her loss.

Then and now, and ever since Murtagh's departure, a sense of emptiness had gripped Eragon. He had expected to feel jubilant if they killed Galbatorix, and though he was glad—and he *was* glad—with the king gone, he no longer knew what he was supposed to do. He had reached his goal. He had climbed the unclimbable mountain. And now, without that purpose to guide him, to drive him, he was at a loss. What were he and Saphira to make of their lives now? What would give them meaning? He knew that, in time, he and Saphira were to raise the next generation of dragons and Riders, but the prospect seemed too distant to be real.

Pondering those questions made him feel queasy and overwhelmed. He turned his thoughts elsewhere, but the questions continued to nibble at the edges of his mind, and his sense of emptiness persisted.

Maybe Murtagh and Thorn had the right idea.

It seemed as if the stairs of the green tower would never end. He trudged upward, round and round, until the people in the streets appeared as small as ants and his calves and the backs of his ankles burned from the repetitive motion. He saw the nests of swallows built within the narrow windows, and beneath one window, he found a pile of small skeletons: the leavings of a hawk or an eagle.

When at last the top of the winding staircase appeared—a large lancet door, black with age—he paused to gather his thoughts and allow his breathing to slow. Then he climbed the last few feet, lifted the latch, and pushed forward into the large round chamber atop the elven watchtower.

Waiting for him were six people, along with Saphira: Arya and the silver-haired elf lord Däthedr, King Orrin, Nasuada, King Orik, and the king of the werecats, Grimrr Halfpaw. They stood—or in the case of King Orrin, sat—in a widely spaced circle, with Saphira directly opposite the stairs, before the southern-facing window that had allowed her to land within the tower. The light from the dying sun streamed sideways through the chamber, illuminating the elven carvings upon the walls and the intricate pattern of colored stone set within the chipped floor.

Except for Saphira and Grimrr, everyone appeared tense and uncomfortable. In the tightness of the skin around Arya's eyes and the hard line of her tawny throat, Eragon saw evidence of her grief and upset. He wished he could do something to ease her pain. Orrin sat in a deep-seated chair, holding his bandaged chest with his left hand and a cup of wine with his right. He moved with exaggerated care, as if afraid of hurting himself, but his eyes were bright and clear, so Eragon guessed it was his wound, and not the drink, that made him cautious. Däthedr was tapping the pommel of his sword with one finger while Orik stood with his hands folded atop the butt of Volund's haft—the hammer rested upright on the floor before him—staring into his beard. Nasuada had her arms crossed, as if she was cold. To the right, Grimrr Halfpaw stared out a window, seemingly oblivious to the others.

As Eragon opened the door, they all looked at him, and a smile broke across Orik's face. "Eragon!" he exclaimed. He hefted Volund onto his shoulder, trundled over to Eragon, and grasped him by a forearm. "I knew you could kill him! Well done! Tonight we celebrate, eh! Let the fires burn bright, and let our voices ring forth until the heavens themselves echo with the sound of our feasting."

Eragon smiled and nodded, and Orik clapped him on the arm once more, then returned to his place as Eragon crossed the room to stand by Saphira.

Little one, she said, brushing his shoulder with her snout.

He reached up and touched her hard, scaled cheek, taking comfort from her closeness. Then he extended a tendril of thought toward the Eldunarí she still had with her. Like him, they were weary from the day's events, and he could tell they preferred to watch and listen rather than to actively participate in the discussion that was about to take place.

The Eldunarí acknowledged his presence, and Umaroth said, *Eragon*, but thereafter he was silent.

No one in the room seemed willing to speak first. From the city below, Eragon heard a horse whinny. Off by the citadel came the rapping of picks and chisels. King Orrin shifted uncomfortably in his chair and sipped his wine. Grimrr scratched one pointed ear, then sniffed, as if testing the air.

Finally, Däthedr broke the silence. "We have a decision to make," he said.

"That we know, elf," rumbled Orik.

"Let him speak," said Orrin, and gestured with his jeweled goblet. "I would hear his thoughts on how he thinks we should proceed." A bitter, somewhat mocking smile appeared on his face. He tilted his head toward Däthedr, as if to grant him permission to speak.

Däthedr inclined his head in return. If the elf took offense at the king's tone, it did not show. "There is no hiding that Galbatorix is dead. Even now, word of our victory wings its way across the land. By the end of the week, Galbatorix's demise shall be known throughout the greater part of Alagaësia."

"As it should be," said Nasuada. She had changed out of the tunic her jailers had given her and into a dark red dress, which made the weight she had lost during her captivity all the more apparent, for the dress hung loosely off her shoulders and her waist was painfully small. But though she appeared frail, she seemed to have regained some of her strength. When Eragon and Saphira had returned to the citadel, Nasuada had been on the verge of collapse, from both mental and physical exhaustion. The moment Jörmundur had seen her, he bundled her off to their camp, and she spent the rest of the day in seclusion. Eragon had been unable to consult with her before the meeting, so he was not sure of her opinion on the subject they had assembled to discuss. If he had to, he would contact her directly with his thoughts, but he hoped to avoid that, for he did not want to intrude on her privacy. Not then. Not after what she had endured.

"As it should be," said Däthedr, his voice strong and clear beneath the vaulted ceiling of that high, round chamber. "However, as people learn that Galbatorix has fallen, the first question they shall ask is who has taken his place." Däthedr looked around at their faces. "We must provide them with an answer now before unrest begins to spread. Our queen is dead. King Orrin, you are wounded. Rumors aplenty are afoot, I am sure. It is important that we quell them before they cause harm. To delay would be disastrous. We cannot allow every lord with a measure of troops to believe that he can set himself up as ruler of his own petty monarchy. Should that happen, the Empire will disintegrate into a hundred different kingdoms. None of us want that. A successor must be chosen—chosen and named, however difficult that may be."

Without turning around, Grimrr said, "You cannot lead a pack if you are weak."

King Orrin smiled again, but the smile did not touch his eyes. "And what part do you seek to play in this, Arya, Lord Däthedr? Or you, King Orik? Or you, King Halfpaw? We are grateful for your friendship and your help, but this is a matter for humans to decide, not you. We rule ourselves, and we do not let others choose our kings."

Nasuada rubbed her crossed arms and, to Eragon's surprise, said, "I agree. This is something we must settle on our own." She looked across the room at Arya and Däthedr. "Surely you can understand. You would not allow us to tell you whom you ought to appoint as your new king or queen." She looked at Orik. "Nor would the clans have allowed us to select you as Hrothgar's successor."

"No," said Orik. "That they wouldn't have."

"The decision is, of course, yours to make," said Däthedr. "We would not presume to dictate what you should or should not do. However, as your friends and allies, have we not earned the right to offer our advice upon such a weighty matter, especially when it shall affect us all? Whatever you decide will have far-reaching implications, and you would do well to understand those implications ere you make your choice."

Eragon understood well enough. It was a threat. Däthedr was saying that if they made a decision the elves disapproved of, there would be unpleasant consequences. Eragon resisted the urge to scowl. The elves' stance was only to be expected. The stakes were high, and a mistake now could end up causing problems for decades more.

"That . . . seems reasonable," said Nasuada. She glanced over at King Orrin.

Orrin stared into his goblet as he tilted it around, swirling the liquid within. "And just *how* would you advise us to choose, Lord Däthedr? Do tell; I am most curious."

The elf paused. In the low, warm light from the setting sun, his silver hair glowed in a diffuse halo around his head. "Whoever is to wear the crown must have the skill and experience needed to rule effectively from the start. There is no time to instruct someone in the ways of command, nor can we afford the mistakes of a novice. In addition, this person must be morally fit to assume such a high office; he or she must be an acceptable choice to the warriors of the Varden and, to a lesser extent, the people of the Empire; and if at all possible, this person should also be one whom we and your other allies will find agreeable."

"You limit our choices a great deal with your requirements," said King Orrin.

"They merely make for good statesmanship. Or do you see it differently?"

"I see several options you have overlooked or disregarded, perhaps because you consider them distasteful. But no matter. Continue."

Däthedr's eyes narrowed, but his voice remained as smooth as ever. "The most obvious choice—and the one the people of the Empire will likely expect—is the person who actually killed Galbatorix. That is, Eragon."

The air in the chamber grew brittle, as if it were made of glass.

Everyone looked at Eragon, even Saphira and the werecat, and he could feel Umaroth and the other Eldunarí observing him closely too. He stared back at the people around him, neither frightened nor angered by their scrutiny. He searched Nasuada's face for a hint as to her reaction, but other than the seriousness of her expression, he could discern nothing of what she thought or felt.

It unsettled him to realize that Däthedr was correct: he could become king.

For a moment, Eragon allowed himself to entertain the possibility. There was no one who could stop him from taking the throne, no one except Elva and perhaps Murtagh—but he now knew how to counter Elva's ability, and Murtagh was no longer there to challenge him. Saphira, he could sense from her mind, would not oppose him, whatever he chose. And though he could not read Nasuada's expression, he had a strange feeling that, for the first time, she would be willing to step aside and allow him to take command.

What do you want? asked Saphira.

Eragon thought about it. *I want . . . to be of use. But power and dominion over others—those things that Galbatorix sought—they hold little appeal for me. In any case, we have other responsibilities.*

Shifting his attention back to those watching, he said, "No. It would not be right."

King Orrin grunted and took another swig of his wine, while Arya, Däthedr, and Nasuada seemed to relax, if however slightly. Like them, the Eldunarí seemed pleased with his decision, although they did not comment upon it with words.

"I am glad to hear you say it," said Däthedr. "No doubt you would make a fine ruler, but I do not think it would be good for your kind, nor for the other races of Alagaësia, were another Dragon Rider to assume the crown."

Then Arya motioned to Däthedr. The silver-haired elf stepped back slightly, and Arya said, "Roran would be another obvious choice."

"Roran!" said Eragon, incredulous.

Arya gazed at him, her eyes solemn and—in the sideways light—bright and fierce, like emeralds cut in a rayed pattern. "It was by his actions that the Varden captured Urû'baen. He is the hero of Aroughs and of many other battles besides. The Varden and the rest of the Empire would follow him without hesitation."

"He's rude and overconfident, and he hasn't the experience needed," said Orrin. Then he glanced over at Eragon with a slightly guilty expression. "He is a good warrior, though."

Arya blinked, once, like an owl. "I believe you would find that his rudeness depends upon those he is dealing with . . . Your Majesty. However, you are correct; Roran lacks the experience needed. That leaves but two choices, then: you, Nasuada; and you, King Orrin."

King Orrin shifted again in his deep-seated chair, and his brow furrowed more severely than before, while Nasuada's expression remained unchanged.

"I assume," said Orrin to Nasuada, "that you wish to assert your claim."

She lifted her chin. "I do." Her voice was as calm as smooth water.

"Then we are at an impasse, for so do I. And I will not relent." Orrin rolled the stem of his goblet between his fingers. "The only way I can see to resolve the matter without bloodshed is for you to renounce your claim. If you insist upon pursuing it, you will end up destroying everything we have won today, and you will have none to blame but yourself for the havoc that will follow."

"You would turn upon your own allies for no other reason than to deny Nasuada the throne?" asked Arya. King Orrin might not have recognized it, but Eragon saw her cold, hard demeanor for what it was: a readiness to strike and kill at a moment's notice.

"No," Orrin replied. "I would turn upon the Varden in order to *win* the throne. There is a difference."

"Why?" asked Nasuada.

"Why?" The question seemed to outrage Orrin. "My people have housed, fed, and equipped the Varden. They have fought and died alongside your warriors and, as a country, we have risked far more than the Varden. The Varden have no home; if Galbatorix had defeated Eragon and the dragons, you could have fled and hid. But we had nowhere to go other than Surda. Galbatorix would have fallen

749

upon us like a bolt from on high, and he would have laid waste to the entire region. We wagered *everything*—our families, our homes, our wealth, and our freedom—and after all that, after all our sacrifices, do you truly believe we will be satisfied to return to our fields with no other rewards than a pat on the head and your royal thanks? Bah! I'd sooner crawl. We've watered the ground between here and the Burning Plains with our blood, and now we'll have our recompense." He clenched his fist. "Now we'll have the just spoils of war."

Orrin's words did not seem to upset Nasuada; indeed, she looked thoughtful, almost sympathetic.

Surely she won't give this snarling cur what he wants, said Saphira.

Wait and see, said Eragon. *She's yet to lead us astray.*

Arya said, "I would hope that the two of you could come to an amicable agreement, and—"

"Of course," said King Orrin. "I hope for that as well." His gaze flicked toward Nasuada. "But I fear that Nasuada's single-minded determination will not allow her to realize that, in this, she must finally submit."

Arya continued: "—and as Däthedr said, we would not think of interfering with your race as you choose your next ruler."

"I remember," said Orrin with a hint of a smug smile.

"However," said Arya, "as sworn allies of the Varden, I must tell you that we regard any attack on them as an attack on ourselves, and we will respond in kind."

Orrin's face drew inward, as if he had bitten into something sour.

"The same holds true for us the dwarves," said Orik. The sound of his voice was like stones grinding against one another deep underground.

Grimrr Halfpaw lifted his mangled hand before his face and inspected the clawlike nails on his three remaining fingers. "We do not care who becomes king or queen as long as we are given the seat next to the throne that was promised to us. Still, it was with Nasuada that we made our bargain, and it is Nasuada we shall continue to support until such time as she is no longer pack leader of the Varden."

"Ah-ha!" exclaimed King Orrin, and he leaned forward with his hand on one knee. "But she isn't the leader of the Varden. Not anymore. Eragon is!"

Again all eyes turned to Eragon. He grimaced slightly and said, "I thought it was understood that I gave my authority back to Nasuada the moment she was free. If not, then let there be no mistake: Nasuada is the leader of the Varden, not me. And I believe that she ought to be the one to inherit the throne."

"You *would* say that," said King Orrin, sneering. "You've sworn fealty to her. Of course you believe she should inherit the throne. You're nothing more than a loyal servant standing up for his master, and your opinions carry no more weight than the opinions of my own servants."

"No!" said Eragon. "There you're wrong. If I thought that you or anyone else would make a better ruler, then I would say so! Yes, I gave my oath to Nasuada, but that doesn't stop me from speaking the truth as I see it."

"Maybe not, but your loyalty to her still clouds your judgment."

"Even as your loyalty to Surda clouds yours," said Orik.

King Orrin scowled. "Why is it that you always turn against me?" he demanded, looking from Eragon to Arya to Orik. "Why is it that, in every dispute, you side with her?" Wine sloshed over the rim of his goblet as he gestured toward Nasuada. "Why is it that *she* commands your respect, and not I or the people of Surda? Always it is Nasuada and the Varden you favor, and before her, it was Ajihad. Were my father still alive—"

"Were your father, King Larkin, still alive," said Arya, "he would not be sitting there bemoaning how others see him; he would be doing something about it."

"Peace," said Nasuada before Orrin could utter a retort. "There is no need for insults here. . . . Orrin, your concerns are reasonable.

You are right; the Surdans have contributed much to our cause. I freely admit that without your help, we never would have been able to attack the Empire as we did, and you deserve recompense for what you have risked, spent, and lost over the course of this war."

King Orrin nodded, appearing satisfied. "You will yield, then?"

"No," said Nasuada, calm as ever. "That, I will not. But I have a counterproposal, one that perhaps will satisfy all our interests." Orrin made a noise of dissatisfaction, but he did not interrupt further. "My proposal is this: much of the land we have captured shall become part of Surda. Aroughs, Feinster, and Melian will all be yours, as well as the isles to the south, once they are under our governance. By this acquisition, Surda will nearly double in size."

"And in return?" asked King Orrin, lifting an eyebrow.

"In return, you will swear allegiance to the throne here in Urû'baen and whoever sits upon it."

Orrin's mouth twisted. "You would set yourself up as High Queen over the land."

"These two realms—the Empire and Surda—must be reunited if we are to avoid future hostilities. Surda would remain yours to command as you see fit, save for one exception: the magicians of both our countries would be subject to certain restrictions, the exact nature of which we would decide upon at a later date. Along with those laws, Surda would of necessity have to contribute to the defense of our combined territories. Should either of us be attacked, the other would be required to provide aid in the form of men and materiel."

King Orrin placed his goblet upright in his lap and stared down at it. "Again I ask: why should *you* be the one to take the throne instead of me? My family has ruled Surda since Lady Marelda won the Battle of Cithrí and thereby established both Surda and the House of Langfeld, and we can trace our ancestry all the way back to Thanebrand the Ring Giver himself. We faced and fought the Empire for an entire century. Our gold and our weapons and our armor allowed the Varden to exist in the first place and have sustained you through the years. Without us, it would have been impossible for you to resist Galbatorix. The dwarves could not have provided everything you needed, nor the elves, as far away as they were. So again I ask, why should this prize fall to you, Nasuada, and not me?"

"Because," said Nasuada, "I believe I can make a good queen. And because—as with everything I have done while leading the Varden—I believe it is what is best for our people and for the whole of Alagaësia."

"You have a very high opinion of yourself."

"False modesty is never admirable, and least of all among those who command others. Have I not amply demonstrated my ability to lead? If not for me, the Varden would still be cowering inside Farthen Dûr, waiting for a sign from above that it was the right time to advance on Galbatorix. I shepherded the Varden from Farthen Dûr to Surda, and I built them into a mighty army. With your help, yes, but I am the one who led them, and it was I who secured the help of the dwarves, the elves, and the Urgals. Could you have done as much? Whosoever rules in Urû'baen will have to treat with every race in the land, not just our own. Again, this I have done and this I can do." Then Nasuada's voice softened, although her expression remained as strong as ever. "Orrin, why do you want this? Would it make you any happier?"

"It isn't a question of happiness," he growled.

"But it is, in part. Do you really want to govern the whole of the Empire in addition to Surda? Whoever takes the throne will have a huge task ahead. There is a country to rebuild: treaties to negotiate, cities still to capture, nobles and magicians to subdue. It will take a lifetime to even begin to undo the damage Galbatorix has wrought. Is that something you are really willing to undertake? It seems to me that you would prefer your life as it once was." Her gaze shifted to the goblet in his lap and then back to his face. "If you accept my offer, you can return to Aberon and your experiments in natural philosophy. Wouldn't you like that? Surda will be larger and richer, and you will have the freedom to pursue your interests."

"We don't always get to do what we like. Sometimes we have to do what is right, not what we want," said King Orrin.

"True, but—"

"Besides, if I were king in Urû'baen, I would be able to pursue my interests here just as easily as I could in Aberon." Nasuada frowned, but before she could speak, Orrin overrode her: "You don't understand. . . ." He scowled and took another sip of wine.

Then explain it to us, said Saphira, her impatience conspicuous in the color of her thoughts.

Orrin snorted, drained his goblet, and then threw it against the door to the staircase, denting the gold of the cup and knocking several of the jewels from their settings so that they spun jittering across the floor. "I can't," he growled, "and I don't care to try." He glared around the room. "None of you would understand. You are too bound up in your own importance to see. How could you, when you've never experienced what I have?" He sank back into his chair, his eyes like dark coals beneath the eaves of his brow. To Nasuada, he said, "You are determined? You will not withdraw your claim?"

She shook her head.

"And if I choose to pursue my own claim?"

"Then we will be in conflict."

"And the three of you will side with her?" asked Orrin, looking in turn at Arya, Orik, and Grimrr.

"If the Varden are attacked, we will fight alongside them," said Orik.

"As will we," said Arya.

King Orrin smiled a smile that was more a baring of his teeth than anything. "But you would not think to tell us who we ought to choose as our ruler, now would you?"

"Of course not," said Orik, and his own teeth flashed white and dangerous within his beard.

"Of course not." Then Orrin returned his attention to Nasuada. "I want Belatona, along with the other cities you mentioned."

Nasuada thought for a moment. "You're already gaining two

port cities with Feinster and Aroughs, three if you count Eoam on Beirland Isle. I'll give you Furnost instead, and then you'll have the whole of Lake Tüdosten, even as I will have the whole of Leona Lake."

"Leona is more valuable than Tüdosten, as it grants access to the mountains and the northern coast," Orrin pointed out.

"Aye. But you already have access to Leona Lake from Dauth and the Jiet River."

King Orrin stared at the floor in the center of the room and was silent. Outside, the top of the sun slipped below the edge of the horizon, leaving a few attenuated clouds illuminated by its light. The sky began to darken, and the first few stars appeared in the gloaming: faint pinpricks of light in the purple vastness. A slight breeze started, and in the sound of it brushing against the sides of the tower, Eragon heard the rustling of the sawtooth nettles.

The longer they waited, the more likely it seemed to Eragon that Orrin would reject Nasuada's offer, or that he would remain sitting there, silent, for the entire night.

Then the king shifted his weight and looked up. "Very well," he said in a low voice. "As long as you honor the terms of our agreement, I shall not challenge you for Galbatorix's throne . . . Your Majesty."

A shiver passed through Eragon as he heard Orrin utter those words.

Her expression somber, Nasuada walked forward until she stood in the center of the open room. Then Orik struck the butt of Volund's haft against the floor and proclaimed, "The king is dead, long live the queen!"

"The king is dead, long live the queen!" cried Eragon, Arya, Däthedr, and Grimrr. The werecat's lips stretched, baring his sharp fangs, and Saphira uttered a loud, triumphant bugle, which echoed off the angled ceiling and out over the dusk-ridden city below. A sense of approval emanated from the Eldunarí.

Nasuada stood tall and proud, her eyes gleaming with tears in the graying light. "Thank you," she said, and looked at each of them, holding their gaze. Still, her thoughts seemed to be directed elsewhere, and about her was an air of sadness that Eragon doubted the others noticed.

And all across the land, darkness sank, leaving the top of their tower a lone beacon of light high above the city.

A Fitting Epitaph

After their victory at Urû'baen, the months passed both quickly and slowly for Eragon. Quickly because there was much for him and Saphira to do, and rare was the day that they were not exhausted by sundown. Slowly because he continued to feel a lack of purpose—despite the many tasks Queen Nasuada gave them—and it seemed to him as if they were idling in a patch of becalmed water, waiting for something, anything, to push them back into the main current.

He and Saphira stayed in Urû'baen for another four days after Nasuada was chosen queen, helping establish the Varden's presence there and throughout the surrounding area. Much of that time they spent dealing with the inhabitants of the city—usually placating crowds who were furious with some action of the Varden's—and hunting groups of soldiers who had fled Urû'baen and were preying upon travelers, peasants, and nearby estates to support themselves. He and Saphira also participated in the effort to rebuild the city's massive front gate, and at Nasuada's behest, he cast several spells designed to prevent those still loyal to Galbatorix from working against her. The spells applied only to the people within the city and the adjacent lands, but having them in place made everyone in the Varden feel safer.

Eragon noticed that the Varden, the dwarves, and even the elves treated him and Saphira differently than they had before Galbatorix's death. They were more respectful and deferential, especially the humans, and they regarded him and Saphira with what he slowly came to understand was a sense of awe. He enjoyed it at first—Saphira did not seem to care one way or another—but it began to bother him when he realized that many of the dwarves and humans were so eager to please him, they would tell him whatever they thought he wanted to hear and not the actual truth. The discovery unsettled him; he felt unable to trust anyone other than Roran, Arya, Nasuada, Orik, Horst, and of course, Saphira.

He saw little of Arya during those days. The few times they met, she seemed withdrawn, which he recognized was her way of dealing with her grief. They never had a chance to talk in private, and the only condolences he was able to offer were brief and awkward. He thought she appreciated them, but it was hard to tell.

As for Nasuada, she seemed to regain much of her former drive, spirit, and energy after a single night's sleep, which amazed Eragon. His opinion of her increased tremendously upon hearing her account of her ordeal in the Hall of the Soothsayer, as did his regard for Murtagh, of whom Nasuada spoke not a word thereafter. She complimented Eragon on his leadership of the Varden in her absence—although he protested that he had been gone most of that time—and thanked him for rescuing her as quickly as he had, for as she admitted late in their conversation, Galbatorix had nearly succeeded in breaking her.

Upon the third day, Nasuada was coronated in a great square near the center of the city, in full view of a vast crowd of humans, dwarves, elves, werecats, and Urgals. The explosion that had ended Galbatorix's life had destroyed the ancient crown of the Broddrings, so the dwarves had forged a new crown from gold found in the city and from jewels the elves had taken from their helms or from the pommels of their swords.

The ceremony was simple, but all the more effective for it. Nasuada approached on foot from the direction of the ruined citadel. She wore a dress of royal purple—cut short at the elbows so that all might see the scars that lined her forearms—with a train fringed with mink, which Elva carried, for Eragon had heeded Murtagh's warning and insisted that the girl stay as close to Nasuada as possible.

A slow drumbeat sounded as Nasuada walked up to the dais that had been erected in the center of the square. At the top of the dais, next to the carved chair that would serve as her throne, stood Eragon, with Saphira close behind. In front of the raised platform were the kings Orrin, Orik, and Grimrr, along with Arya, Däthedr, and Nar Garzhvog.

Nasuada ascended the dais, then knelt before Eragon and Saphira. A dwarf of Orik's clan presented Eragon with the newly made crown, which he placed upon Nasuada's head. Then Saphira arched her neck and, with her snout, touched Nasuada upon the brow, and both she and Eragon said:

"Rise now as queen, Nasuada, daughter of Ajihad and Nadara."

A fanfare of trumpets rang forth, and the gathered crowd—which had been deathly silent—began to cheer. It was a strange cacophony, what with the bellows of Urgals intermingled with the melodious voices of the elves.

Then Nasuada sat upon the throne. King Orrin came before her and swore his allegiance, followed by Arya, King Orik, Grimrr Halfpaw, and Nar Garzhvog, who each pledged the friendship of their respective races.

The event affected Eragon strongly. He found himself holding back tears as he gazed at Nasuada sitting regnant on her throne. Only with her coronation did it feel as if the specter of Galbatorix's oppression had begun to recede.

Afterward, they feasted, and the Varden and their allies celebrated throughout the night and into the next day. Eragon remembered little of the festivities, save the dancing of the elves, the pounding of the dwarves' drums, and the four Kull who climbed a tower along the city wall and there stood blowing horns made from the skulls of their fathers. The people of the city joined in the celebrations as well, and among them, Eragon saw relief and jubilation that Galbatorix was no longer king. And underlying their emotions, and those of everyone present, was an awareness of the importance of the moment, for they knew they were witnessing the end of one age and the beginning of another.

Upon the fifth day, when the gate was nearly rebuilt and the city seemed reasonably secure, Nasuada ordered Eragon and Saphira to fly to Dras-Leona, and thence to Belatona, Feinster, and Aroughs, and in each place to use the name of the ancient language to release from their oaths everyone who had sworn fealty to Galbatorix. She also asked Eragon to bind the soldiers and nobles with spells—even as he had bound the people of Urû'baen—to keep them from trying to undermine the newly established peace. That, Eragon had refused, for he felt it was too similar to how Galbatorix had controlled those who served him. In Urû'baen, the risk of hidden killers or other loyalists was great enough that Eragon had been willing to do as she wished. But not elsewhere. To his relief, Nasuada agreed with him after some consideration.

He and Saphira took with them over half the Eldunarí from Vroengard; the rest remained behind with the hearts of hearts that had been rescued from Galbatorix's treasure room. Blödhgarm and his spellcasters—who were no longer bound to defend Eragon and Saphira—moved those Eldunarí to a castle several miles northeast of Urû'baen, where it would be easy to protect the hearts against any who might seek to steal them, and where the thoughts of the mad dragons would not affect the minds of any but their caretakers.

Only once Eragon and Saphira were satisfied that the Eldunarí were safe did they depart.

When they arrived at Dras-Leona, Eragon was astounded by the number of spells he found woven throughout the city, as well as in the dark tower of stone, Helgrind. Many of them, he guessed, were hundreds of years old, if not older: forgotten enchantments from ages past. He left those that seemed harmless and removed those that did not, but ofttimes it was difficult to tell, and he was reluctant to tamper with spells whose purpose he did not understand. Here the Eldunarí proved helpful; in several cases, they remembered who had cast a spell and why, or else they were able to divine its purpose from information that meant nothing to him.

When it came to Helgrind and the various holdings of the priests—who had gone into hiding as soon as news of Galbatorix's demise had reached them—Eragon did not bother trying to determine which spells were dangerous and which were not; he removed them all. He also used the name of names to search for the belt of Beloth the Wise in the ruins of the great cathedral, but without success.

They stayed in Dras-Leona for three days, then they proceeded to Belatona. There too Eragon removed Galbatorix's enchantments, as well as at Feinster and Aroughs. In Feinster, someone tried to kill him with a poisoned drink. His wards protected him, but the incident angered Saphira.

If I ever corner the rat-coward who did this, I'll eat him alive from the toes up, she growled.

On the return trip to Urû'baen, Eragon suggested a slight change of direction. Saphira agreed and altered her course, tilting so the horizon stood on end and the world was divided equally between the dark blue sky and the green and brown earth.

It took a half day of searching, but at last Saphira found the cluster of sandstone hills and, among them, one hill in particular: a tall, sloping mound of reddish stone with a cave halfway up its side. And upon its crest, a glittering tomb of diamond.

The hill looked exactly as Eragon remembered. When he gazed upon it, he felt his chest grow tight.

Saphira landed next to the tomb. Her claws scraped against the pitted stone, chipping off flakes.

With slow fingers, Eragon unbuckled his legs. Then he slid to the ground. A wave of dizziness passed through him at the smell of the warm stone, and for a moment, he felt as if he were in the past.

Then he shook himself, and his mind cleared. He walked to the tomb and looked into its crystal depths, and there he saw Brom.

There he saw his father.

Brom's appearance had not changed. The diamond that encased his body protected him from the ravages of time, and his flesh showed no hint of decay. The skin of his lined face was firm, and it had a rosy tint, as if hot blood still coursed beneath the surface. At any moment, it seemed as if Brom might open his eyes and rise to his feet, ready to continue on their unfinished journey. In a way, he had become deathless, for he no longer aged as others did, but would remain forever the same, caught in a dreamless sleep.

Brom's sword lay atop his chest and the long white pennant of his beard, with his hands folded over the hilt, just as Eragon had placed them. By his side was his gnarled staff, carved, Eragon now realized, with dozens of glyphs from the ancient language.

Tears welled in Eragon's eyes. He fell to his knees and wept quietly for a timeless while. He heard Saphira join him, felt her with his mind, and he knew that she too mourned Brom's passing.

762

At last Eragon got to his feet and leaned against the edge of the tomb as he studied the shape of Brom's face. Now that he knew what to look for, he could see the similarities between their features, blurred and obscured by age and by Brom's beard, but still unmistakable. The angle of Brom's cheekbones, the crease between his eyebrows, the way his upper lip curved; all those Eragon recognized. He had not inherited Brom's hooked nose, however. His nose he had gotten from his mother.

Eragon looked down, breathing heavily as his eyes again grew blurry. "It's done," he said in an undertone. "I did it. . . . *We* did it. Galbatorix is dead, Nasuada is on the throne, and both Saphira and I are unharmed. That would please you, wouldn't it, you old fox?" He laughed shortly and wiped his eyes with the back of his wrist. "What's more, there are dragon eggs in Vroengard. Eggs! The dragons aren't going to die out. And Saphira and I will be the ones to raise them. You never foresaw *that*, now did you?" He laughed again, feeling silly and grief-stricken at the same time. "What would you think of this all, I wonder? You're the same as ever, but we're not. Would you even recognize us?"

Of course he would, said Saphira. *You are his son.* She touched him with her snout. *Besides, your face isn't so different that he would mistake you for someone else, even if your scent has changed.*

"It has?"

You smell more like an elf now. . . . . Anyway, he would hardly think I was Shruikan or Glaedr, now would he?

"No."

Eragon sniffed and pushed himself off the tomb. Brom looked so lifelike within the diamond, the sight of him inspired an idea: a wild, improbable idea that he almost dismissed but that his emotions would not let him ignore. He thought of Umaroth and the Eldunarí—of all their collected knowledge and of what they had accomplished with his spell in Urû'baen—and a spark of desperate hope kindled within his heart.

Speaking both to Saphira and Umaroth, he said, *Brom had only just died when we buried him. Saphira didn't turn the stone to diamond until the following day, but he was still encased in stone, away from the air, through the night. Umaroth, with your strength and your knowledge, maybe . . . maybe we could still heal him.* Eragon shivered as if he were in the grip of a fever. *I didn't know how to mend his wound before, but now—now I think I could.*

It would be more difficult than you imagine, said Umaroth.

Yes, but you could do it! said Eragon. *I've seen you and Saphira accomplish amazing things with magic. Surely this isn't beyond you!*

You know that we cannot use magic on command, said Saphira.

And even if we succeeded, said Umaroth, *there is every chance that we would be unable to restore Brom's mind to what it was. Minds are complicated things, and he might easily end up with his wits muddled or his personality altered. And then what? Would you want him to live like that? Would he? No, it is best to let him be, Eragon, and to honor him with your thoughts and actions, as you have. You wish it were otherwise. So do all who have lost one they care about. However, it is the way of things. Brom lives on in your memories, and if he was the man you showed us, he would be content with that. Let you be content with that as well.*

But—

It was not Umaroth who interrupted, but the oldest of the Eldunarí, Valdr. He surprised Eragon by speaking not in images or feelings, but in words of the ancient language, strained and labored, as if each was foreign to him. And he said, *Leave the dead to the earth. They are not for us.* Then he spoke no more, but Eragon felt from him a great sadness and sympathy.

Eragon let out a long sigh and closed his eyes for a moment. Then, in his heart, he allowed himself to release his misguided hope and again accept the fact that Brom was gone.

"Ah," he said to Saphira. "I didn't think this would be so difficult."

It would be strange if it were not. He felt her warm breath ruffle the hair on the top of his head as she touched his back with the side of her muzzle.

He smiled weakly and gathered up his courage to look at Brom again.

"Father," he said. The word tasted strange in his mouth; he had never had cause to say it to anyone before. Then Eragon shifted his gaze to the runes he had set into the spire at the head of the tomb, which read:

HERE LIES BROM
Who was a Dragon Rider
And like a father
To me.
May his name live on in glory.

He smiled painfully at how close he had come to the truth. Then he spoke in the ancient language, and he watched the diamond shimmer and flow as a new pattern of runes formed upon its surface. When he finished, the inscription had changed to:

HERE LIES BROM
Who was
A Rider bonded to the dragon Saphira
Son of Holcomb and Nelda
Beloved of Selena
Father of Eragon Shadeslayer
Founder of the Varden
And Bane of the Forsworn.
May his name live on in glory.
Stydja unin mor'ranr.

It was a less personal epitaph, but it seemed more fitting to Eragon. Then he cast several spells to protect the diamond from thieves and vandals.

He continued to stand next to the tomb, reluctant to turn away and feeling as if there ought to be something *more*—some event or emotion or realization that would make it easier for him to say farewell to his father and thus to leave.

At last he put his hand atop the cool diamond, wishing that he could reach through it to touch Brom one final time. And he said, "Thank you for everything you taught me."

Saphira snorted and bowed her head until her snout tapped against the hard jewel.

Then Eragon turned and, with a sense of finality, he slowly climbed onto Saphira's back.

He was somber for a time as Saphira took off and flew northeast, toward Urû'baen. When the patch of sandstone hills was no more than a smudge on the horizon, he let out a long breath and looked up into the azure sky.

A smile split his face.

What is so amusing? asked Saphira, and she swung her tail back and forth.

The scale on your snout is regrowing.

Her delight was evident. Then she sniffed and said, *I always knew it would. Why would it not?* However, he could feel her sides vibrating against his heels as she hummed with satisfaction, and he patted her and laid his chest against her neck, feeling the warmth from her body seeping into his.

PIECES ON A BOARD

When he and Saphira arrived at Urû'baen, Eragon was surprised to discover that Nasuada had restored its name to Ilirea, out of respect for its history and heritage.

Also, he was dismayed to learn that Arya had departed for Ellesméra, along with Däthedr and many of the other high elf lords, and that she had taken with her the green dragon egg they had found in the citadel.

She had left a letter for him with Nasuada. In it, Arya explained that she needed to accompany her mother's body back to Du Weldenvarden for a proper burial. As for the dragon egg, she wrote:

> . . . and because Saphira chose you, a human, to be her Rider,
> it is only right that an elf should be the next Rider, if the dragon
> within this egg agrees. I wish to give it that chance without delay.
> Already, it has spent far too long within its shell. Since there are
> many more eggs elsewhere—I shall not name the place—I hope
> you do not believe that I have acted presumptuously or that I
> have been overly prejudiced in favor of my own race. I consulted
> with the Eldunarí upon this matter, and they agreed with my
> decision.
>
> In any event, with both Galbatorix and my mother having
> passed into the void, I no longer wish to continue as ambassador
> to the Varden. Rather, I wish to resume my task of ferrying
> a dragon egg throughout the land, as I did with Saphira's.
> Of course, an ambassador between our races is still needed.
> Therefore, Däthedr and I have appointed as my replacement
> a young elf named Vanir, whom you met during your time in

Ellesméra. He has expressed a desire to learn more about the people of your race, and that seems to me as good a reason as any for him to have the post—so long as he does not prove completely incompetent, that is.

The letter continued for several more lines, but Arya gave no indication of when, if ever, she might return to the western half of Alagaësia. Eragon was pleased that she had thought enough of him to write, but he wished that she could have waited until their return before she had departed. With her gone, there was a hole in his world, and though he spent a fair amount of time with Roran and Katrina, as well as Nasuada, the aching emptiness within him refused to subside. That, along with his continued sense that he and Saphira were merely biding their time, left him with a feeling of detachment. It often seemed as if he were watching himself from outside his body, as might a stranger. He understood the cause of his feelings, but he could think of no cure other than time.

During their recent trip, it had occurred to him that—with the command of the ancient language bestowed by the name of names—he could remove from Elva the last vestiges of his blessing that had proved a curse. So he went to the girl, where she was living in Nasuada's grand hall, and he told her his idea, then asked her what she wanted.

She did not react with the delight he expected, but sat staring at the floor, a frown upon her pale face. She remained silent for the better part of an hour—he sitting across from her, waiting without complaint.

Then she looked at him and said, "No. I would rather stay as I am. . . . I am grateful that you thought to ask, but this is too large a part of me, and I cannot give it up. Without my ability to sense others' pain, I would be only an oddity—a misbegotten aberration, good for nothing but satisfying the low-minded curiosity of those who consented to have me around, of those who *tolerated* me. With it, I am still an oddity, but I can be useful as well, and I have a power that others fear and a control over my own destiny, which many of my sex do not." She gestured at the ornate room where she was staying. "Here I can live in comfort—I can live in peace—and yet I can continue to do some good by helping Nasuada. If you take away my ability, then what would I have? What would I do? What would I be? To remove your spell would be no blessing, Eragon. No, I will stay as I am, and I will bear the trials of my gift of my own free will. But I do thank you."

Two days after he and Saphira alit in what was now Ilirea, Nasuada sent them out once more, first to Gil'ead and then to Ceunon—the two cities that the elves had captured—so that Eragon could again use the name of names to clear away Galbatorix's spells.

Both Eragon and Saphira found Gil'ead unpleasant to visit. It reminded them of when the Urgals had captured Eragon at Durza's orders, and also of Oromis's death.

Eragon and Saphira slept in Ceunon for three nights. It was unlike any other city they had seen before. The buildings were mainly wood, with steep, shingled roofs that, in the case of the larger houses, had several layers. The peaks of the roofs were often decorated with a stylized carving of a dragon head, while the doors were carved or painted with elaborate, knotlike patterns.

When they departed, Saphira was the one who suggested a change of path. She did not have to try very hard to convince Eragon; he was happy to agree once she explained that the side trip would not take too long.

From Ceunon, Saphira flew westward, across the Bay of Fundor: a broad, white-capped expanse of water. The gray and black humps of great sea-fish often breached the waves, like small, leathery islands. Then they would spray water from their blowholes and lift their flukes high into the air before slipping back into the silent depths.

Across the Bay of Fundor, through winds cold and blustery, and then across the mountains of the Spine, each of which Eragon knew by name. And thus to Palancar Valley for the first time since they had set off in pursuit of the Ra'zac, along with Brom, what seemed like a lifetime ago.

The valley smelled like home to Eragon; the scent of the pines and the willows and the birches reminded him of his childhood, and the bitter bite of the air told him that winter was near.

They landed in the charred ruins of Carvahall, and Eragon wandered along streets fringed with encroaching grass and weeds.

A pack of wild dogs trotted out of a nearby stand of birch. They stopped when they saw Saphira, then snarled, yelped, and ran for cover. Saphira growled and loosed a puff of smoke but made no move to chase them.

A piece of burnt wood cracked under Eragon's foot as he dragged his boot through a pile of ashes. The destruction of the town left him saddened. But most of the villagers who had escaped were still alive. If they returned, Eragon knew that they would rebuild Carvahall and make it better than it had been. The buildings he had grown up with, though, were gone forever. Their absence exacerbated his feeling that he no longer belonged in Palancar Valley, and the empty spaces where they ought to have been left him with a sense of wrongness, as if he were in a dream where everything was off-kilter.

"The world is out of joint," he murmured.

Eragon built a small campfire next to what had been Morn's tavern, and he cooked a large pot of stew. While he ate, Saphira prowled the surrounding landscape, sniffing at whatever she found interesting.

When the stew was gone, Eragon carried his pot, bowl, and spoon to the Anora River and washed them in the icy water. He sat squatting on the rocky shore and stared at the drifting white plume at the head of the valley: the Igualda Falls, which stretched upward for a half mile before disappearing over a shoulder of stone high on Narnmor Mountain. Seeing it brought back the evening he had returned from the Spine with Saphira's egg in his pack, knowing nothing of what lay before the two of them, or even that there would *be* two of them.

"Let's go," he said to Saphira, rejoining her by the caved-in well in the center of the town.

Do you want to visit your farm? she asked as he took his place on her back.

He shook his head. "No. I would rather think of it as it was, not as it is."

She agreed. However, by unspoken consent she flew south following the same path as when they had left Palancar Valley. Along the way, Eragon glimpsed the clearing where his home had been, but it was distant and obscure enough that he was able to pretend that perhaps the house and barn were still intact.

At the southern end of the valley, Saphira rode a pillar of rising air up to the top of the huge, bare mountain, Utgard, where stood the crumbling turret the Riders had built to keep watch over mad King Palancar. The turret had once been known as Edoc'sil, but now bore the name Ristvak'baen, or the "Place of Sorrow," as it was there that Galbatorix had slain Vrael.

In the ruins of the turret, Eragon, Saphira, and the Eldunarí with them paid their respects to the memory of Vrael. Umaroth in particular was somber, but he said, *Thank you for bringing me here, Saphira. I never thought to see the place where my Rider fell.*

Then Saphira spread her wings and leaped out of the turret and soared away from the valley and over the grassy plains beyond.

Halfway to Ilirea, Nasuada contacted them through one of the Varden's magicians and ordered them to join a large group of warriors she had sent to march from the capital to Teirm.

Eragon was pleased to learn that Roran commanded the warriors and that among their ranks were Jeod, Baldor—who had regained full use of his hand after the elves reattached it—and several more of the villagers.

Somewhat to Eragon's surprise, the people of Teirm refused

to surrender, even after he released them from their oaths to Galbatorix, and even though it was obvious that the Varden, with Saphira and Eragon to help, could easily capture the city if they wished. Instead, the governor of Teirm, Lord Risthart, demanded that they be allowed to become an independent city-state with the freedom to choose its own rulers and set its own laws.

In the end, after several days of negotiations, Nasuada agreed to his terms, provided that Lord Risthart swore allegiance to her as high queen, even as King Orrin had, and consented to abide by her laws concerning magicians.

From Teirm, Eragon and Saphira accompanied the warriors south, along the narrow coast, until they arrived at the city of Kuasta. They repeated the process from Teirm, but unlike Teirm, the governor of Kuasta yielded and agreed to join Nasuada's new kingdom.

Then Eragon and Saphira flew alone to Narda, far to the north, and extracted the same promise from them before finally return-ing to Ilirea, where they stayed for some weeks in a hall next to Nasuada's.

When time allowed, he and Saphira left the city and went to the castle, where Blödhgarm and the other spellcasters guarded the Eldunarí rescued from Galbatorix. There Eragon and Saphira aided in the effort to heal the minds of the dragons. They made prog-ress, but it was slow, and some of the Eldunarí responded faster than others. Many of them, Eragon worried, simply did not care about life anymore, or were so lost within the labyrinths of their minds that it was almost impossible to communicate with them in a mean-ingful manner, even for the elder dragons such as Valdr. To prevent the hundreds of maddened dragons from overwhelming those who were trying to help them, the elves kept most of the Eldunarí in a trancelike state, choosing to interact with only a few at a time.

Eragon also labored alongside the magicians of Du Vrangr Gata to empty the citadel of its treasures. Much of the work fell to him, as none of the other spellcasters had the knowledge or experience needed to deal with many of the enchanted artifacts Galbatorix had left behind. But Eragon did not mind; he enjoyed exploring the damaged fortress and discovering the secrets that lay hidden therein. Galbatorix had collected a host of wonders over the past century, some more dangerous than others, but all of them interesting. Eragon's favorite was an astrolabe that, when put to his eye, allowed him to see the stars, even in daylight.

He kept the existence of the most perilous artifacts a secret between him, Saphira, and Nasuada, deeming it too risky to allow knowledge of them to spread.

Nasuada put the trove of riches they recovered from the citadel to immediate use feeding and clothing her warriors, as well as rebuilding the defenses of the cities they had captured during their invasion of the Empire. In addition, she gave a gift of five gold crowns to every one of her subjects: a trifling amount to the nobles, but a veritable fortune to the poorer farmers. The gesture, Eragon knew, earned her their respect and allegiance in a way Galbatorix would never have understood.

They also recovered several hundred Riders' swords: swords of every color and shape, made for both humans and elves. It was a breathtaking find. Eragon and Saphira personally carried the weapons to the castle where the Eldunarí were, in anticipation of the day when they would again be needed by Riders.

Rhunön, Eragon thought, would be pleased to know that so much of her handiwork had survived.

And there were the thousands of scrolls and books that Galbatorix had collected, which the elves and Jeod helped to catalog, setting aside those that contained secrets about the Riders or the inner workings of magic.

As they sorted through Galbatorix's great hoard of knowledge, Eragon kept hoping that they would find some mention of where the king had hidden the rest of the Lethrblaka's eggs. However, the only mentions of the Lethrblaka or the Ra'zac he saw were in works by the elves and the Riders from ages past, where they discussed the dark menace of the night and wondered what was to be done about a foe that could not be detected with magic of any sort.

Now that Eragon could speak openly with him, he found himself talking with Jeod on a regular basis, confiding in him all that had happened with the Eldunarí and the eggs, and even going so far as to tell him about the process of finding his true name on Vroengard. Talking with Jeod was a comfort, especially as he was one of the few people who had known Brom well enough to call him a friend.

Eragon found it interesting, in a rather abstract way, to watch what went into ruling and rebuilding the kingdom Nasuada had formed from the remnants of the Empire. The amount of effort required to manage such an enormous and diverse country was tremendous, and the task never seemed finished; there was always more that needed doing. Eragon knew that he would have hated the demands of the position, but Nasuada appeared to thrive upon them. Her energy never flagged, and she always seemed to know how to solve the problems that came before her. Day by day, he saw her stature grow among the emissaries, functionaries, nobles, and commoners with whom she dealt. She seemed perfectly suited for her new role, although he was not sure how happy she really was, and he worried about her because of it.

He watched how she rendered judgment upon the nobles who had worked with Galbatorix—willingly or not—and he approved of the fairness and mercy she displayed, as well as the punishments she meted out when necessary. Most she stripped of their lands, titles, and the better portion of their ill-gotten wealth, but she did not have them executed, for which Eragon was glad.

He stood by her side when she granted Nar Garzhvog and his people vast swaths of land along the northern coast of the Spine, as well as along the fertile plains between the lake Fläm and the Toark River, where few if any people now lived. And that too Eragon approved of.

Like King Orrin and Lord Risthart, Nar Garzhvog had sworn fealty to Nasuada as his high queen. However, the huge Kull said, "My people agree with this, Lady Nightstalker, but they have thick blood and short memories, and words will not bind them forever."

In a cold voice, Nasuada replied, "Do you mean to say your people will break the peace? Am I to understand our races will once again be enemies?"

"No," said Garzhvog, and shook his massive head. "We do not want to fight you. We know that Firesword would kill us. But . . . when our young ones have grown, they will want battles in which to prove themselves. If there are no battles, then they will start them. I am sorry, Nightstalker, but we cannot change what we are."

The exchange troubled Eragon—and Nasuada as well—and he spent several nights thinking about the Urgals, trying to solve the problem they presented.

As the weeks rolled by, Nasuada continued to send him and Saphira to various locations within Surda and her kingdom, often using them as her personal representatives to King Orrin, Lord Risthart, and the other nobles and groups of soldiers throughout the land.

Wherever they went, they searched for a place that could serve as a home for the Eldunarí in the centuries to come and as nesting and proving grounds for the dragons hidden on Vroengard. There were areas of the Spine that showed promise, but most were too close to humans or Urgals, or else were so far north, Eragon thought it would be miserable to live there year-round. Besides, Murtagh and Thorn had gone north, and Eragon and Saphira did not want to cause them additional difficulty.

The Beor Mountains would have been perfect, but it seemed doubtful that the dwarves would welcome hundreds of ravenous dragons hatching within the bounds of their realm. No matter where they went in the Beors, they would still be a short flight from at least one dwarven city, and it would not do if a young dragon were to start raiding the dwarves' flocks of Feldûnost—which, knowing Saphira, Eragon deemed more than likely.

The elves would, he thought, have no objection to the dragons living on or around one of the mountains in Du Weldenvarden, but Eragon still worried about their nearness to the elven cities. Also, he disliked the idea of placing the dragons and the Eldunarí within the territory of any one race. Doing so would give the appearance that they were lending support to that race in particular. The Riders of the past had never done that, nor—Eragon believed—should the Riders of the future.

The only location that was far enough away from every town and city and that no race had yet claimed was the ancestral home of the dragons: the heart of the Hadarac Desert, where stood Du Fells Nángoröth, the Blasted Mountains. It would, Eragon was sure, be a fine place to raise hatchlings. However, it had three drawbacks. First, they would not be able to find enough food in the desert to feed the young dragons. Saphira would have to spend most of her time carrying deer and other wild animals to the mountains. And of course, once the hatchlings grew larger, they would have to start flying out on their own, which would take them close to the lands of either the humans, the elves, or the dwarves. Second, everyone who had traveled widely—and many who had not—knew where the mountains were. And third, it was not unduly difficult to reach the mountains, especially in the winter. The last two points concerned Eragon the most and made him wonder how well they would be able to protect the eggs, the hatchlings, and the Eldunarí.

It would be better if we were high up on one of the peaks in the Beors, where only a dragon could fly, he said to Saphira. *Then no one would be able to sneak up on us, no one except for Thorn, Murtagh, or some other magician.*

Some other magician, like every elf in the land? Besides, it would be cold all the time!

I thought you didn't mind the cold.

I don't. But I don't want to live in the snow year-round either. Sand is better for your scales; Glaedr told me. It helps polish them and keep them clean.

Mmh.

Day by day, the weather grew colder. Trees shed their leaves, flocks of birds flew south for the year, and winter thus came upon the land. It was a cruel, harsh winter, and for a long while it felt as if the whole of Alagaësia was locked in slumber. At the first fall of snow, Orik and his army returned to the Beor Mountains. All of the elves who were still in Ilirea—save Vanir and Blödhgarm and his ten spellcasters—likewise left for Du Weldenvarden. The Urgals had departed weeks earlier. Last to go were the werecats. They seemed to simply disappear; no one saw them leave, and yet one day they were all gone, except for a large, fat werecat by the name of Yelloweyes, who sat on the padded cushion next to Nasuada, purring, napping, and listening to everything that went on in the throne room.

Without the elves and the dwarves, the city felt depressingly empty to Eragon as he walked along the streets, ragged flakes of snow drifting sideways underneath the shelf of creviced stone overhead.

And still Nasuada continued to dispatch him and Saphira upon missions. But never did she send them to Du Weldenvarden, the one place Eragon wanted to go. They had had no word from the elves as to who had been chosen as Islanzadí's successor, and when asked, Vanir would only say, "We are not a hasty people, and for us, appointing a new monarch is a difficult, complicated process. As soon as I learn what our councils have decided, I will tell you."

It had been so long since Eragon had seen or heard from Arya, he considered using the name of the ancient language to bypass the wards around Du Weldenvarden so that he could communicate with, or at least scry, her. However, he knew the elves would not look kindly on the intrusion, and he feared Arya would not appreciate him contacting her in that way without a pressing need.

Therefore, he instead wrote her a short letter, asking after her and telling her some of what he and Saphira had been doing. He gave the letter to Vanir, and Vanir promised that he would have it sent to Arya at once. Eragon was sure that Vanir kept his word—for they had been speaking in the ancient language—but he received no response from Arya, and as the moons waxed and waned, he began to think that, for some unknown reason, she had decided to end their friendship. The thought hurt him terribly, and it caused him to concentrate on the work Nasuada gave him with even greater intensity, hoping to forget his misery.

In the deepest part of winter, when swordlike icicles hung from the shelf above Ilirea and deep drifts of snow lay upon the surrounding landscape, when the roads were nearly impassable and the fare at their tables had grown lean, three attempts were made on Nasuada's life, as Murtagh had warned might happen.

The attempts were clever and well thought out, and the third one—which involved a net full of stones falling on Nasuada—nearly succeeded. But with Eragon's wards and Elva to protect her, Nasuada survived, although the last attack cost her several broken bones.

During the third attempt, Eragon and the Nighthawks managed to kill two of Nasuada's attackers—the exact number of which remained a mystery—but the rest escaped.

Eragon and Jörmundur went to extraordinary lengths to ensure Nasuada's safety after that. They increased the number of her guards once again, and wherever she went, at least three spellcasters accompanied her. Nasuada herself grew ever more wary, and Eragon saw in her a certain hardness that had not been apparent before.

There were no more attacks upon Nasuada's person, but a month after winter broke and the roads were again clear, a displaced earl by the name of Hamlin, who had gathered up several hundred of the Empire's former soldiers, started launching raids against Gil'ead and attacking the travelers on the roads thereabouts.

At the same time, another, slightly larger rebellion began to brew in the south, led by Tharos the Quick of Aroughs.

The uprisings were more of a nuisance than anything, but they still took several months to quell, and they resulted in a number of unexpectedly savage fights, although Eragon and Saphira attempted to settle matters peacefully whenever they could. After the battles they had already participated in, neither of them was thirsty for more blood.

Soon after the end of the uprisings, Katrina gave birth to a large, healthy girl with a lock of red hair atop her head, the same as her mother. The girl bawled louder than any infant Eragon had ever heard, and she had a grip like iron. Roran and Katrina named her Ismira, after Katrina's mother, and whenever they looked at her, the joy in their faces made Eragon grin as well.

The day after Ismira's birth, Nasuada summoned Roran to her throne room and surprised him by granting him the title of earl, along with the whole of Palancar Valley as his domain.

"As long as you and your descendants remain fit to rule, the valley shall be yours," she said.

Roran bowed and said, "Thank you, Your Majesty." The gift, Eragon could see, meant almost as much to Roran as had the birth of his daughter, for after his family, the thing Roran prized most was his home.

Nasuada also tried to give Eragon various titles and lands, but he refused them, saying, "It is enough to be a Rider; I need nothing more."

A few days later, Eragon was standing with Nasuada in her study, examining a map of Alagaësia and discussing matters of concern throughout the land, when she said, "Now that things are somewhat more settled, I think it's time to address the role of magicians within Surda, Teirm, and my own kingdom."

"Oh?"

"Yes. I've spent a great deal of time thinking about it and have reached a decision. I have decided to form a group, much like the Riders, but for magicians alone."

"And what will this group do?"

Nasuada picked up a quill from her desk and rolled it between her fingers. "Again, much the same as the Riders: travel through the land, keep the peace, resolve disputes of law, and most important, watch over their fellow spellcasters, so as to ensure they do not use their ability for ill."

Eragon frowned slightly. "Why not just leave that to the Riders?"

"Because it will be years before we have more of them, and even then there won't be enough to mind every petty conjurer and hedge witch. . . . You still haven't found a place to raise the dragons, have you?"

Eragon shook his head. Both he and Saphira had been feeling increasingly impatient, but as of yet, they and the Eldunarí had been unable to agree upon a location. It was becoming a sore point between them, for the infant dragons needed to hatch as soon as possible.

"I thought not. We have to do this, Eragon, and we cannot afford to wait. Look at the havoc Galbatorix wrought. Magicians are the most dangerous creatures in this world, even more dangerous than dragons, and they have to be held accountable. If not, we'll always be at their mercy."

"Do you really believe you will be able to recruit enough magicians to watch over all of the other spellcasters here and in Surda?"

"I think so, if you ask them to join. Which is one of the reasons I want you to lead this group."

"Me?"

She nodded. "Who else? Trianna? I don't fully trust her, nor does she have the strength needed. An elf? No, it has to be one of our own. You know the name of the ancient language, you're a Rider, and you have the wisdom and authority of the dragons behind you.

I cannot think of a better person to lead the spellcasters. I've spoken to Orrin about this, and he agrees."

"I can't imagine the idea pleases him."

"No, but he understands that it is necessary."

"Is it?" Eragon picked at the edge of her desk, troubled. "How do you intend to keep watch over the magicians who don't belong to this group?"

"I hoped you might have some suggestions. I thought perhaps with spells and scrying mirrors, so that we could track their where-abouts and supervise their use of magic, lest they use it to better themselves at the expense of others."

"And if they do?"

"Then we see to it that they make amends for their crime, and we have them swear in the ancient language to give up the use of magic."

"Oaths in the ancient language won't necessarily stop anyone from using magic."

"I know, but it's the best we can do."

He nodded. "And what if a spellcaster refuses to be watched? What, then? I can't imagine very many would agree to be spied upon."

A sigh escaped Nasuada, and she put down her quill. "There's the difficult part. What would you do, Eragon, if you were in my place?"

None of the solutions he thought of were very palatable. "I don't know. . . ."

Her expression grew sad. "Nor do I. This is a difficult, painful, messy problem, and no matter what I choose, someone will end up hurt. If I do nothing, the magicians will remain free to manipulate others with their spells. If I force them to submit to oversight, many will hate me for it. However, I think you will agree with me that its better to protect the majority of my subjects at the expense of a few."

"I don't like it," he murmured.

"I don't like it either."

"You're talking about binding every human spellcaster to your will, regardless of who they are."

She did not blink. "For the good of the many."

"What about people who can only hear thoughts, and nothing more? That's a form of magic as well."

"Them too. The potential for them to abuse their power is still too great." Nasuada sighed then. "I know this isn't easy, Eragon, but easy or not, it's something we have to address. Galbatorix was mad and evil, but he was right about one thing: the magicians need to be reined in. But not as Galbatorix intended. Something needs to be done, though, and I think my plan is the best solution possible. If you can think of another, better way to enforce the rule of law among spellcasters, I would be delighted. Otherwise, this is the only path available to us, and I need your help to do it. . . . So, will you accept charge of this group, for the good of the country, and the good of our race as a whole?"

Eragon was slow to answer. At last he said, "If you don't mind, I'd like to think about it for a while. And I need to consult with Saphira."

"Of course. But don't think for too long, Eragon. Preparations are already under way, and you will soon be needed."

Afterward, Eragon did not return directly to Saphira but wandered through the streets of Ilirea, ignoring the bows and the greetings from the people he passed. He felt . . . uneasy, both with Nasuada's proposal and with life in general. He and Saphira had been idling for too long. The time had come for a change, and circumstances would no longer allow them to wait. They had to decide what they were going to do, and whatever they chose, it would affect the rest of their lives.

He spent several hours walking and thinking, mainly about his ties and obligations. In late afternoon, he made his way back to Saphira and, without speaking, climbed onto her back.

She leaped out of the courtyard of the hall and flew high above

Ilirea, high enough that they could see for hundreds of miles in every direction. There she stayed, circling.

They spoke without words, exchanging their mind-states. Saphira shared many of his concerns, but she was not as worried as he about their bonds with others. Nothing was as important to her as protecting the eggs and the Eldunarí, and doing what was right for him and her. Yet Eragon knew that they could not just ignore the effects their choices would have, both political and personal.

Finally, he said, *What should we do?*

Saphira dipped as the wind underneath her wings slowed. *What we need to do, as has always been the case.* She said nothing more, but turned then and began to descend toward the city.

Eragon appreciated her silence. The decision would be harder for him to make than for her, and he needed to think about it on his own.

When they landed in the courtyard, Saphira nudged him with her snout and said, *If you need to talk, I'll be here.*

He smiled and rubbed the side of her neck, and then slowly walked to his rooms, while staring at the floor.

That night, when the waxing moon had just appeared beneath the edge of the cliff over Ilirea and Eragon was sitting against the end of his bed, reading a book about the saddle-making techniques of the early Riders, a flicker by the edge of his sight—like the flapping of a drape—caught his attention.

He sprang to his feet, drawing Brisingr from its sheath.

Then, in his open window, he saw a small three-masted ship, woven from stalks of grass. He smiled and sheathed his sword. He held out his hand, and the ship sailed across the room and landed upon his palm, where it listed to one side.

The ship was different from the one Arya had made during their travels together in the Empire, after he and Roran rescued Katrina from Helgrind. It had more masts, and it also had sails fashioned from the blades of grass. Though the grass was limp and browning, it had not dried out entirely, which led him to think that it had been picked only a day or two earlier.

Tied to the middle of the deck was a square of folded paper. Eragon carefully removed it, his heart pounding, then unfolded the paper on the floor. It read, in glyphs of the ancient language:

> Eragon,
>
> We have finally decided upon a leader, and I am on my way to Ilirea to arrange an introduction with Nasuada. I would like to talk with you and Saphira first. This message should reach you four days before the half moon. If you would, meet me the day after you receive it, at the easternmost point of the Ramr River. Come alone, and do not tell anyone else where you are going.
>
> Arya

Eragon smiled without meaning to. Her timing had been perfect; the ship had arrived exactly when she intended. Then his smile faded, and he reread the letter several more times. She was hiding something; that much was obvious. But what? Why meet in secret?

Maybe Arya doesn't approve of the elves' next ruler, he thought. *Or maybe there's some other problem.* And though Eragon was eager to see her again, he could not forget how she had ignored him and Saphira. He supposed that, from Arya's point of view, the intervening months were a trifling amount of time, but he could not help feeling hurt.

He waited until the first hint of sunlight appeared in the sky, then hurried down to wake Saphira and tell her the news. She was as curious as he, if not quite as excited.

He saddled her, and then they left the city and set off to the northeast, having told no one of their plans, not even Glaedr or the other Eldunarí.

FÍRNEN

It was early in the afternoon when they arrived at the location Arya had designated: a gentle curve in the Ramr River that marked its farthest excursion eastward.

Eragon strained to look over Saphira's neck as he searched for a glimpse of anyone below. The land appeared empty, save for a herd of wild oxen. When the animals caught sight of Saphira, they fled, lowing and kicking up plumes of dust. They and a few other, smaller animals scattered about the countryside were the only living creatures Eragon could sense. Disappointed, he shifted his gaze to the horizon but saw no sign of Arya.

Saphira landed on a slight rise fifty yards from the banks of the river. She sat, and Eragon sat with her, resting his back against her side.

On the top of the rise was an outcropping of soft, slatelike rock. While they waited, Eragon amused himself by grinding a thumb-sized flake into the shape of an arrowhead. The stone was too soft for the arrowhead to be anything other than decorative, but he enjoyed the challenge. When he was satisfied with the simple, triangular point, he set it aside and began to grind a larger piece into a leaf-bladed dagger, similar to those the elves carried.

They did not have to wait as long as he first thought.

An hour after their arrival, Saphira lifted her head from the ground and peered across the plains in the direction of the not-so-distant Hadarac Desert.

Her body stiffened against his, and he felt a strange emotion within her: a sense of impending momentousness.

Look, she said.

Keeping hold of his half-finished dagger, he clambered to his feet and peered eastward.

He saw nothing but grass, dirt, and a few lone, windswept trees between them and the horizon. He broadened his area of scrutiny but still saw nothing of interest.

What— he started to ask, then cut himself off as he looked up.

High in the eastern sky, he saw a wink of green fire, like an emerald glimmering in the sun. The point of light arced through the blue mantle of the heavens, approaching at a rapid pace, bright as a star at night.

Eragon dropped the stone dagger and, without taking his eyes off the glittering spark, climbed onto Saphira's back and strapped his legs into her saddle. He wanted to ask her what she thought the point of light was—to force her to put into words what he suspected—but he could not bring himself to speak any more than she could.

Saphira held her position, although she unfolded her wings and, keeping them bent nearly in half, lifted them in preparation to take off.

As it grew larger, the spark proliferated, dividing into a cluster of dozens, then hundreds, then thousands of tiny points of light. After a few minutes, the true shape of it became visible, and they saw that it was a dragon.

Saphira could wait no longer. She uttered a resonant trumpet, leaped off the rise, and flapped downward.

Eragon clutched the neck spike in front of him as she ascended at a nearly vertical angle, desperate to intercept the other dragon as quickly as possible. Both he and she alternated between elation and a wariness born of too many battles. In their caution, it pleased them that they had the sun to their backs.

Saphira continued to climb until she was slightly above the green dragon, whereupon she leveled off and concentrated upon speed.

Closer, Eragon saw that the dragon, while well built, still had some of the gangly look of youth—his limbs had yet to acquire the stocky weight of Glaedr's or Thorn's—and he was smaller than Saphira.

The scales upon his sides and back were a dark forest green, while those upon his belly and the pads of his feet were lighter, with the smallest ones verging upon white. When against his body, his wings were the color of holly leaves, but when the light shone through them, they were the color of oak leaves in the spring.

At the juncture between the dragon's neck and back was a saddle much like Saphira's, and on the saddle sat a figure that looked to be Arya, her dark hair streaming from her head. The sight filled Eragon's heart with joy, and the emptiness he had labored under for so long vanished like the darkness of night before the rising sun.

As the dragons swooped past each other, Saphira roared, and the other dragon roared in response. They turned and began to circle— as if chasing each other's tails—Saphira still slightly above the green dragon, who made no attempt to climb above her. If he had, Eragon would have feared he was attempting to gain the advantage before attacking.

He grinned and shouted into the wind. Arya shouted back and raised an arm. Then Eragon touched her mind, just to be sure, and he *knew* in an instant that it really was Arya, and that she and the dragon meant them no harm. He withdrew a moment later, for it would have been rude to prolong the mental contact without her consent; she would answer his questions when they spoke on the ground.

Saphira and the green dragon roared again, and the green dragon lashed his whiplike tail; then they chased each other through the air until they reached the Ramr River. There Saphira took the lead and spiraled down until she landed upon the same rise where she and Eragon had been waiting.

The green dragon landed a hundred feet away, settling into a low crouch while Arya freed herself from her saddle.

Eragon tore the straps off his legs and jumped to the ground, banging the sheath of Brisingr against his leg. He ran over to Arya, and she to him, and they met in the middle between the two dragons, who followed at a more sedate pace, their steps weighing heavily on the ground.

As he drew near, Eragon saw that, in place of the leather strip that Arya usually wore to keep her hair back, a circlet of gold rested upon her brow. In the center of the circlet, a teardrop-shaped diamond flashed with light that came not from the sun but from within its own depths. At her waist hung a green-hilted sword in a green sheath, which he recognized as Támerlein, the same sword the elf lord Fiolr had offered him as a replacement for Zar'roc and that had once belonged to the Rider Arva. However, the hilt looked different than he remembered, lighter and more graceful, and the sheath appeared narrower.

It took Eragon a moment to realize what the diadem meant. He looked at Arya with astonishment. "You!"

"Me," she said, and inclined her head. "Atra esterní ono thelduin, Eragon."

"Atra du evarínya ono varda, Arya . . . Dröttning?" It did not escape him that she had chosen to greet him first.

"Dröttning," she confirmed. "My people chose to give me my mother's title, and I chose to accept."

Above them, Saphira and the green dragon brought their heads close together and sniffed one another. Saphira was taller; the green dragon had to stretch his neck to reach her.

As much as Eragon wanted to talk with Arya, he could not help staring at the green dragon. "And him?" he asked, motioning upward.

Arya smiled, and then she surprised him by taking his hand and leading him forward. The green dragon snorted and lowered his head until it hung just above them, smoke and steam rising from the depths of his crimson nostrils.

"Eragon," she said, and she placed his hand on the dragon's warm snout, "this is Fírnen. Fírnen, this is Eragon."

Eragon looked up into one of Fírnen's brilliant eyes; the bands of muscle within the dragon's iris were the pale green and yellow of new blades of grass.

I am glad to meet you, Eragon-friend-Shadeslayer, said Fírnen. His mental voice was deeper than Eragon expected, deeper even than that of Thorn or Glaedr or any of the Eldunarí from Vroengard. *My Rider has told me much about you.* And the dragon blinked once, with a small, sharp sound like a shell bouncing against a stone.

In Fírnen's wide, sunlit mind, planked as it was with transparent shadows, Eragon could feel the dragon's excitement.

Wonder swept through Eragon, wonder that such a thing had come to pass. "I am glad to meet you as well, Fírnen-finiarel. I never thought that I would live to see you hatched and free of Galbatorix's spells."

The emerald dragon snorted softly. He looked proud and full of energy, like a stag in fall. Then he returned his gaze to Saphira. Between the two of them, much passed; through Saphira, Eragon could feel the flow of thoughts, emotions, and sensations, slow at first, but then swelling into a torrent.

Arya smiled slightly. "They seem to have taken to each other."

"That they have."

A mutual understanding guiding them, he and Arya walked out from under Saphira and Fírnen, leaving the dragons to themselves. Saphira did not sit as she normally did, but remained crouched, as if she were about to spring onto a deer. Fírnen did the same. The tips of their tails twitched.

Arya looked well: better, Eragon thought, than she had since their time together in Ellesméra. For lack of a more suitable word, he would have said she looked happy.

Neither of them spoke for a while as they watched the dragons. Then Arya turned toward him and said, "I apologize for not contacting you sooner. You must think badly of me for ignoring you and Saphira for so long and for keeping such a secret as Fírnen."

"Did you receive my letter?"

"I did." To his surprise, she reached inside the front of her tunic and removed a square of battered parchment that, after a few seconds, he recognized. "I would have answered, but Fírnen had already hatched and I did not want to lie to you, even by omission."

"Why keep him hidden?"

"With so many of Galbatorix's servants still on the loose, and so few dragons remaining, I did not want to risk anyone finding out about Fírnen until he was large enough to defend himself."

"Did you really think a human could have snuck into Du Weldenvarden and killed him?"

"Stranger things have happened. With the dragons yet on the brink of extinction, it was not a risk worth taking. If I could, I would keep Fírnen in Du Weldenvarden for the next ten years, until he is so large that none would dare attack him. But he wished to leave, and I could not deny him. Besides, the time has come for me to meet with Nasuada and Orik in my new role."

Eragon could feel Fírnen showing and telling Saphira about the first time he caught a deer in the elves' forest. He knew that Arya was aware of the exchange as well, for he saw her lip twitch in response to an image of Fírnen hopping in pursuit of a startled doe after he tripped over a branch.

"And how long have you been queen?"

"Since a month after my return. Vanir doesn't know, however. I ordered the information kept from him and our ambassador to the dwarves so that I could concentrate on raising Fírnen without having to worry about the affairs of state that otherwise would have fallen to me. . . . You might like to know: I raised him on the Crags of Tel'naeír, where Oromis lived with Glaedr. It seemed only right."

Silence fell between them. Then Eragon gestured at Arya's diadem and at Fírnen and said, "How did all of this happen?"

She smiled. "On our return to Ellesméra, I noticed that Fírnen was beginning to stir within his shell, but I thought nothing of it, as Saphira had often done the same. However, once we reached Du Weldenvarden and passed through its wards, he hatched. It was nearly evening, and I was carrying his egg in my lap, as I used to carry Saphira's, and I was speaking to him, telling him of the world and reassuring him that he was safe, and then I felt the egg shake and . . ." She shivered and tossed her hair, a bright film of tears in her eyes. "The bond is everything I imagined it to be. When we touched . . . I always wanted to be a Dragon Rider, Eragon, so that I could protect my people and avenge my father's death at the hands of Galbatorix and the Forsworn, but until I saw the first crack appear in Fírnen's egg, I never allowed myself to believe that it might actually come to pass."

"When you touched, did—"

"Yes." She lifted her left hand and showed him the silvery mark on the palm, the same as his own gedwëy ignasia. "It felt like . . ." She paused, searching for the words.

"Like ice-cold water that tingled and snapped," he suggested.

"Exactly like that." Without seeming to notice, she crossed her arms, as if chilled.

"So you returned to Ellesméra," said Eragon. Now Saphira was telling Fírnen about when she and Eragon swam in Leona Lake while traveling to Dras-Leona with Brom.

"So we returned to Ellesméra."

"And you went to live on the Crags of Tel'naeír. But why become queen when you were already a Rider?"

"It was not my idea. Däthedr and the other elders of our race came to the house on the crags, and they asked me to take up my mother's mantle. I refused, but they returned the next day, and the day after that, and every day for a week, and each time with new arguments for why I should accept the crown. In the end, they convinced me that it would be best for our people."

"Why you, though? Was it because you are Islanzadí's daughter, or was it because you had become a Rider?"

"It was not just because Islanzadí was my mother, although that was part of it. Nor was it just because I was a Rider. Our politics are far more complicated than those of the humans or the dwarves, and choosing a new monarch is never easy. It involves obtaining consent from dozens of houses and families, as well as several of the older members of our race, and every choice they make is part of a subtle game that we have been playing amongst ourselves for thousands of years. . . . There were many reasons why they wanted me to become queen, not all of them obvious."

Eragon shifted, glancing between Saphira and Arya, unable to reconcile himself to Arya's decision. "How can you be a Rider as well as a queen?" he asked. "The Riders aren't supposed to support any one race above the others. It would be impossible for the other peoples of Alagaësia to trust us if we did. And how can you help rebuild our order and raise the next generation of dragons if you're busy with your responsibilities in Ellesméra?"

"The world is not as it used to be," she said. "Nor can the Riders remain apart as they once did. There are too few of us to stand alone, and it will be a long while before there are again enough of us to resume our former place. In any event, you have already sworn yourself to Nasuada and to Orik and Dûrgrimst Ingeitum, but not to us, not to the älfakyn. It is only right that we should have a Rider and dragon as well."

"You know that Saphira and I would fight for the elves as much as for the dwarves or the humans," he protested.

"I know, but others do not. Appearances matter, Eragon. You cannot change the fact that you have given your word to Nasuada and that you owe your loyalty to Orik's clan. . . . My people have suffered greatly over the past hundred years, and though it may not be apparent to you, we are not what we once were. As the fortunes of the dragons have declined, so too have our own. Fewer children have been born to us, and our strength has waned. Also, some have said that our minds are no longer as sharp as they used to be, although it is difficult to prove one way or another."

"The same is true of humans, or so Glaedr told us," said Eragon.

She nodded. "He is right. Both of our races will take time to recover, and much will depend upon the return of the dragons. Moreover, even as Nasuada is needed to help guide the recovery of your race, so too do my own people need a leader. With Islanzadí dead, I felt obliged to take the task upon myself." She touched her left shoulder, where her tattoo of the yawë glyph lay hidden. "I pledged myself to the service of my people when I was not much older than you. I cannot abandon them now, when their need is so great."

"They will always have need of you."

"And I will always answer their call," she replied. "Do not worry; Fírnen and I shall not ignore our duties as a dragon and Rider. We will help you to patrol the land and settle what disputes we can, and wherever it seems best to raise the dragons, we shall visit and lend our assistance as often as we can, even if it be at the far southern end of the Spine."

Her words troubled Eragon, but he did his best to hide it. What she promised would not be possible if he and Saphira did as they had decided during the flight there. Although everything Arya had said helped confirm that the path they had chosen was the right one, he worried that it was a path that Arya and Fírnen would be unable to follow.

He bowed his head then, accepting Arya's decision to become queen and her right to make it. "I know you won't neglect your responsibilities," he said. "You never do." He did not mean the statement unkindly; it was merely a statement of fact, and one for which he respected her. "And I understand why you did not contact us for so long. I probably would have done the same in your place."

She smiled again. "Thank you."

He motioned toward her sword. "I take it Rhunön reworked Támerlein to better fit you?"

"She did, and she grumbled about it the whole while. She said the blade was perfect the way it was, but I am well pleased with the changes she made; the sword balances as it should in my hand now, and it feels no heavier than a switch."

As they stood watching the dragons, Eragon tried to think of a way to tell Arya of their plans. Before he could, she said, "You and Saphira have been well?"

"We have."

"What else of interest has occurred since you wrote?"

Eragon thought for a minute, then told her in brief about the attempts on Nasuada's life, the uprisings in the north and the south, the birth of Roran and Katrina's daughter, Roran's ennoblement, and the list of treasures they had recovered from within the citadel. Lastly, he told of their return to Carvahall and their visit to Brom's final resting place.

While he spoke, Saphira and Fírnen began to circle each other, the tips of their tails whipping back and forth faster than ever. They both had their jaws slightly open, baring their long white teeth, and they were breathing thickly through their mouths and uttering low, whining grunts, the likes of which Eragon had never heard before. It looked almost as if they were going to attack each other, which worried him, but the feeling from Saphira was not one of anger or fear. It was—

I want to test him, said Saphira. She slapped her tail against the ground, causing Fírnen to pause.

Test him? How? For what?

To find out if he has the iron in his bones and the fire in his belly to match me.

Are you sure? he asked, understanding her intent.

She again slapped her tail against the ground, and he felt her certainty and the strength of her desire. *I know everything about him— everything but this. Besides*—she displayed a flash of amusement—*it's not as if dragons mate for life.*

Very well. . . . But be careful.

He had barely finished speaking when Saphira lunged forward and bit Fírnen on his left flank, drawing blood and causing Fírnen to snarl and spring backward. The green dragon growled, appearing uncertain of himself, and retreated before Saphira as she prowled toward him.

Saphira! Chagrined, Eragon turned to Arya, intending to apologize.

Arya did not seem upset. To Fírnen, and to Eragon as well, she said, *If you want her to respect you, then you have to bite her in return.*

She raised an eyebrow at Eragon, and he responded with a wry smile, understanding.

Fírnen glanced at Arya and hesitated. He jumped back as Saphira snapped at him again. Then he roared and lifted his wings, as if to make himself appear larger, and he charged Saphira—and nipped her on a hind leg, sinking his teeth into her hide.

The pain Saphira felt was not pain.

Saphira and Fírnen resumed circling, growling and yowling with increasing volume. Then Fírnen jumped at her again. He landed on Saphira's neck and bore her head to the ground, where he held her pinned and gave her a pair of playful bites at the base of her skull.

Saphira did not struggle as fiercely as Eragon would have expected, and he guessed that she had allowed Fírnen to catch her, as it was not something even Thorn had managed to do.

"The courting of dragons is no gentle affair," he said to Arya.

"Did you expect soft words and tender caresses?"

"I suppose not."

With a heave of her neck, Saphira threw Fírnen off and scrambled backward. She roared and clawed at the ground with her forefeet, and then Fírnen lifted his head toward the sky and loosed a rippling pennant of green fire twice the length of his own body.

"Oh!" exclaimed Arya, sounding delighted.

"What?"

"That's the first time he has breathed fire!"

Saphira released a blast of fire herself—Eragon could feel the heat from over fifty feet away—and then she crouched and jumped into the sky, climbing straight upward. Fírnen followed an instant later.

Eragon stood with Arya as they watched the glittering dragons ascend into the heavens, spiraling around each other with flames streaming from their mouths. It was an awe-inspiring sight: savage and beautiful, and frightening. Eragon realized he was watching an ancient and elemental ritual, one that was part of the very fabric of nature itself and without which the land would wither and die.

His connection with Saphira grew tenuous as the distance

between them increased, but he could still sense the heat of her passion, which darkened the edges of her vision and blotted out all thoughts save those driven by the instinctual need that all creatures, even the elves, are subject to.

The dragons shrank until at last they were no more than a pair of sparkling stars orbiting each other in the immensity of the sky. As far away as they were, Eragon still received a few flashes of thoughts and feelings from Saphira, and though he had experienced many such moments with the Eldunarí when they had shared their memories with him, his cheeks grew hot, as did the tips of his ears, and he found himself unable to look directly at Arya.

She too seemed affected by the dragons' emotions, although differently than he; she stared after Saphira and Fírnen with a faint smile, and her eyes shone brighter than usual, as if the sight of the two dragons filled her with pride and happiness.

Eragon let out a sigh, and then squatted and began to draw in the dirt with a stalk of grass.

"Well, that didn't take long," he said.

"No," said Arya.

They remained that way for a number of minutes: she standing, he squatting, and all silence around them, save for the sound of the lonely wind.

At last Eragon dared look up at Arya. She looked more beautiful than ever. But more than that, he saw his friend and ally; he saw the woman who had helped save him from Durza, who had fought alongside him against countless enemies, who had been imprisoned with him under Dras-Leona, and who, in the end, had killed Shruikan with the Dauthdaert. He remembered what she had told him about her life in Ellesméra when she was growing up, her difficult relationship with her mother, and the many reasons that had driven her to leave Du Weldenvarden and serve as an ambassador to the elves. He thought too of the hurts she had suffered: some from her mother, others from the isolation she had experienced among the humans and the dwarves, and still more when she had lost Faolin and then endured Durza's tortures in Gil'ead.

All those things he thought of, and he felt a deep sense of connection with her, and a sadness too, and a sudden desire came upon him to capture what he saw.

While Arya meditated upon the sky, Eragon looked about until he found a piece of the slatelike rock projecting from the earth. Making as little noise as possible, he dug out a slab with his fingers and brushed off the dirt until the stone was clean.

It took him a moment to remember the spells he had once used, and then to modify them so as to extract the colors needed from the earth around him. Speaking the words silently, he incanted the spell.

A stir of motion, like a swirl of muddy water, disturbed the surface of the tablet. Then colors—red, blue, green, yellow—bloomed on the slate and began to form lines and shapes even as they intermingled to form other, subtler shades. After a few seconds, an image of Arya appeared.

797

Once it was complete, he released the spell and studied the fairth. He was pleased with what he saw. The image seemed to be a true and honest representation of Arya, unlike the fairth he had made of her in Ellesméra. The one he held now had a depth that the other one had lacked. It was not a perfect image with regard to its composition, but he was proud that he had been able to capture so much of her character. In that one image, he had managed to sum up everything he knew about her, both the dark and the light.

He allowed himself to enjoy his sense of accomplishment for a moment more, then he threw the tablet off to the side, to break it against the ground.

"Kausta," said Arya, and the tablet curved through the air and landed in her hand.

Eragon opened his mouth, intending to explain or to apologize, but then he thought better of it and said nothing.

Holding up the fairth, Arya stared at it with an intent gaze. Eragon watched her closely, wondering how she would react.

A long, tense minute passed.

Then Arya lowered the fairth.

Eragon stood and held out his hand for the tablet, but she made no move to return it. She appeared troubled, and his heart sank; the fairth had upset her.

Looking him straight in the eye, she said in the ancient language, "Eragon, if you are willing, I would like to tell you my true name."

Her offer left him dumbstruck. He nodded, overwhelmed, and, with great difficulty, managed to say, "I would be honored to hear it."

Arya stepped forward and placed her lips close to his ear, and in a barely audible whisper she told him her name. As she spoke, the name rang within his mind, and with it came a rush of understanding. Some of the name he knew already, but there were many parts that surprised him, parts that he realized must have been difficult for Arya to share.

Then Arya stepped back and waited for his response, her expression studiously blank.

Her name raised numerous questions for Eragon, but he knew that it was not the time to ask them. Rather, he needed to reassure Arya that he did not think any less highly of her because of what he had learned. Nor did he. If anything, her name had increased his regard, for it had shown him the true extent of her selflessness and her devotion to duty. He knew that if he reacted badly to her name—or even said the wrong thing without intending to—he could destroy their friendship.

He met Arya's gaze full-on and said, also in the ancient language, "Your name . . . your name is a good name. You should be proud of who you are. Thank you for sharing it with me. I am glad to call you my friend, and I promise that I will always keep your name safe. . . . Will you, now, hear mine?"

She nodded. "I will. And I promise to remember and protect it for so long as it remains yours."

A sense of import came over Eragon. He knew there was no going back from what he was about to do, which he found both frightening and exhilarating. He moved forward and did as Arya had done, placing his lips by her ear and whispering his name as softly as he could. His whole being vibrated in recognition of the words.

He backed away, suddenly apprehensive. How would she judge him? Fair or foul? For judge him she would; she could not help it.

Arya released a long breath and looked at the sky for a while. When she turned to him again, her expression was softer than before. "You have a good name as well, Eragon," she said in a low voice. "However, I do not think it is the name you had when you left Palancar Valley."

"No."

"Nor do I think it is the name you bore during your time in Ellesméra. You've grown much since we first met."

"I've had to."

She nodded. "You are still young, but you are no longer a child."

"No. That I am not."

More than ever, Eragon felt drawn to her. The exchange of names had formed a bond between them, but of what sort he was unsure, and his uncertainty left him with a sense of vulnerability. She had seen him with all his flaws and she had not recoiled, but had accepted him as he was, even as he accepted her. Moreover, she had seen in his name the depth of his feelings for her, and that too had not driven her away.

He debated whether to say anything on the subject, but he could not let it go. After gathering up his courage, he said, "Arya, what is to become of us?"

She hesitated, but he could see that his meaning was clear to her. Choosing her words with care, she said, "I don't know. . . . Once, as you know, I would have said, 'nothing,' but . . . Again, you are still young, and humans often change their minds. In ten years, or even five, you may no longer feel as you now do."

"My feelings won't change," he said with utter certainty.

She searched his face for a long, tense while. Then he saw a change in her eyes, and she said, "If they don't, then . . . perhaps in time . . ." She put a hand on the side of his jaw. "You cannot ask more of me now. I do not want to make a mistake with you, Eragon. You are too important for that, both to me and to the whole of Alagaësia."

He tried to smile, but it came out more as a grimace. "But . . . we don't have time," he said, his voice choked. He felt sick to his stomach.

Arya's brow furrowed, and she lowered her hand. "What do you mean?"

He stared at the ground, trying to think how to tell her. In the end, he just said it as simply as he could. He explained the difficulty he and Saphira had had in finding a safe place for the eggs and the Eldunarí, and then he explained Nasuada's plan to form a group of magicians to keep watch over every human spellcaster.

He spent several minutes talking, and concluded by saying, "So Saphira and I have decided that the only thing we can do is leave Alagaësia and raise the dragons elsewhere, far away from other people. It's what's best for us, for the dragons, for the Riders, and all the other races of Alagaësia."

"But the Eldunarí—" said Arya, appearing shocked.

"The Eldunarí can't stay either. They would never be safe, not even in Ellesméra. As long as they remain in this land, there will be those who will try to steal them or use them to further their own designs. No, we need a place like Vroengard, a place where no one can find the dragons to hurt them and where the younglings and the wild dragons cannot hurt anyone themselves." Eragon tried to smile again, but gave it up as hopeless. "That is why I said we have no time. Saphira and I intend to leave as soon as we can, and if you stay . . . I do not know if we will ever see each other again."

Arya glanced down at the fairth she still held, troubled.

"Would you give up your crown to come with us?" he asked, already knowing the answer.

She lifted her gaze. "Would you give up charge of the eggs?"

He shook his head. "No."

For a time, they were silent, listening to the wind.

"How would you find candidates for the Riders?" she asked.

"We'll leave a few eggs behind—with you, I suppose—and once they hatch, they and their Riders will come join us, and we'll send you more eggs."

"There must be another solution besides you and Saphira and every Eldunarí abandoning Alagaësia!"

"If there were, we would take it, but there isn't."

"What of the Eldunarí? What of Glaedr and Umaroth? Have you spoken to them of this? Do they agree?"

"We haven't spoken to them, but they will agree. That I know."

"Are you sure about this, Eragon? Is it really the only way—to leave behind everything and everyone you have ever known?"

"It's necessary, and our departure was always meant to be. Angela foretold it when she cast my fortune in Teirm, and I've had time to accustom myself to the idea." He reached out and touched Arya on the cheek. "So, I ask again: will you come with us?"

A film of tears appeared on her eyes, and she hugged the fairth against her chest. "I cannot."

He nodded and took his hand away. "Then . . . we will part ways." Tears welled in his own eyes, and he struggled to retain his composure.

"But not yet," she whispered. "We still have some time together. You will not leave immediately."

"No, not immediately."

And they stood next to each other, gazing into the sky and waiting for Saphira and Fírnen to return. After a while, her hand touched his, and he grasped it, and though it was a small comfort, it helped dull the ache in his heart.

A MAN OF CONSCIENCE

W arm light streamed through the windows along the right of the hallway, illuminating patches of the far wall where banners, paintings, shields, swords, and the heads of various stags hung between the dark, carved doors that dotted the wall at regular intervals.

As Eragon strode toward Nasuada's study, he gazed out the windows at the city. From the courtyard, he could still hear the bards and musicians performing by the banquet tables laid out in Arya's honor. The celebrations had been ongoing since she and Fírnen had returned to Ilirea with him and Saphira the previous day. But now they were beginning to wind down and, as a result, he had finally been able to arrange a meeting with Nasuada.

He nodded to the guards outside the study, then let himself into the room.

Inside, he saw Nasuada reclined on a padded seat, listening to a musician strumming on a lute and singing a beautiful, if mournful, love song. On the end of the seat sat the witch-child, Elva, engrossed with a piece of embroidery, and in a nearby chair, Nasuada's handmaid, Farica. And curled up on Farica's lap lay the werecat Yelloweyes in his animal form. He looked sound asleep, but Eragon knew from experience that he was probably awake.

Eragon waited by the door until the musician finished.

"Thank you. You may go," said Nasuada to the player. "Ah, Eragon. Welcome."

He bowed slightly to her. Then, to the girl, he said, "Elva."

She eyed him from under her brow. "Eragon." The werecat's tail twitched.

"What is it you wish to discuss?" asked Nasuada. She took a sip from a chalice resting on a side table.

"Perhaps we could speak in private," said Eragon, and motioned with his head toward the glass-paneled doors behind her, which opened onto a balcony overlooking a quadrangle with a garden and fountain.

Nasuada considered for a moment, then rose from her seat and swept toward the balcony, the train of her purple dress trailing behind her.

Eragon followed, and they stood side by side, gazing at the spouting water of the fountain, cool and gray within the shadow cast by the side of the building.

"What a beautiful afternoon," said Nasuada as she took a deep breath. She looked more at peace than when he had last seen her, only a few hours before.

"The music seems to have put you in a good mood," he observed.

"No, not the music: Elva."

He cocked his head. "How so?"

A strange half smile graced Nasuada's face. "After my imprisonment in Urû'baen—after what I endured . . . and lost—and after the attempts on my life, the world seemed to lose all color for me. I did not feel myself, and nothing I did could stir me from my sadness."

"I thought as much," he said, "but I did not know what to do or say that might help."

"Nothing. Nothing you could have said or done would have helped. I might have gone on like that for years, if not for Elva. She told me . . . she told me what I needed to hear, I suppose. It was the fulfillment of a promise she made me, long ago, in the castle at Aberon." Eragon frowned and glanced back into the room, where Elva sat poking at her embroidery. For all they had gone through together, he still did not feel as if he could trust the girl, and he feared that she was manipulating Nasuada for her own selfish ends.

Nasuada's hand touched his arm. "You don't need to worry about me, Eragon. I know myself too well for her to unbalance me even if she tried. Galbatorix couldn't break me; do you think she could?"

He looked back at her, his expression grim. "Yes."

She smiled again. "I appreciate your concern, but in this, it's unfounded. Let me enjoy my good mood; you can put your suspicions to me at a later time."

"All right." Then he relented a bit and said, "I'm glad you're feeling better."

"Thank you. As am I. . . . Are Saphira and Fírnen still cavorting about as they were earlier? I don't hear them anymore."

"They are, but they're above the overhang now." His cheeks warmed somewhat as he touched Saphira's mind.

"Ah." Nasuada placed her hands—one atop the other—upon the stone balustrade, the uprights of which were carved into the shape of flowering irises. "Now, why did you wish to meet? Have you arrived at a decision with regard to my offer?"

"I have."

"Excellent. Then we may proceed apace with our plans. I have already—"

"I've decided not to accept."

"What?" Nasuada looked at him with incredulity. "Why? To whom else would you entrust the position?"

"I don't know," he said gently. "That's something you and Orrin will have to figure out on your own."

Her eyebrows rose. "You won't even help us choose the right person? And you expect me to believe that you would follow orders from anyone but me?"

"You misunderstand," he said. "I don't want to lead the magicians, and I won't be joining them either."

Nasuada stared at him for a moment; then she walked over and closed the glass-paneled doors to the balcony so that Elva, Farica, and the werecat could not overhear their conversation. Turning back to him, she said, "Eragon! What are you thinking! You know you have to join. All of the magicians who serve me have to. There can't be any exceptions. Not one! I can't have people think that I'm playing favorites. It would sow dissent among the ranks of the magicians, and that is exactly what I *don't* want. As long as you are a subject of my realm, you have to abide by its laws, or my authority means *nothing*. I shouldn't have to tell you that, Eragon."

"You don't. I'm well aware of it, which is why Saphira and I have decided to leave Alagaësia."

Nasuada put a hand on the railing, as if to steady herself. For a time, the splashing of the water below was the only sound.

"I don't understand."

So, once more, as he had with Arya, he set forth the reasons why the dragons, and therefore he and Saphira, could not stay in Alagaësia. And when he finished, he said, "It never would have worked for me to take charge of the magicians. Saphira and I have to raise the dragons and train the Riders, and that must take precedence before all else. Even if I had the time, I couldn't lead the Riders and still answer to you—the other races would never stand for it. Despite Arya's choice to become queen, the Riders have to remain as impartial as possible. If *we* start to play favorites, it will destroy Alagaësia. The only way I would consider accepting the position would be if the magicians were to include those of every race—even the Urgals—but that's not likely to happen. Besides, it would still leave the question of what to do about the eggs and the Eldunarí."

Nasuada scowled. "You can't expect me to believe that, with all your power, you can't protect the dragons here in Alagaësia."

"Maybe I could, but we cannot depend on magic alone to safe-guard the dragons. We need physical barriers; we need walls and moats and cliffs too high for man, elf, dwarf, or Urgal to scale. More important, we need the safety that only distance can provide. We have to make it so difficult to reach us that the challenges of the journey will discourage even our most determined enemies from attempting it. But ignore that. Assuming that I could protect the dragons, the problem would still remain of how to keep them from hunting livestock—ours as well as the dwarves' and Urgals'. Do you want to have to explain to Orik why his flocks of Feldûnost keep disappearing, or do you want to have to keep appeasing angry farmers who have lost their animals? . . . No, leaving is the only solution."

Eragon looked down at the fountain. "Even if there were a place for the eggs and the Eldunarí in Alagaësia, it wouldn't be right for me to stay."

"Why is that?"

He shook his head. "You know the answer as well as I. I've become *too* powerful. As long as I'm here, your authority—and that of Arya, Orik, and Orrin—will always be in doubt. If I asked them to, most everyone in Surda, Teirm, and your own kingdom would follow me. And with the Eldunarí to help me, there is no one who can stand against me, not even Murtagh or Arya."

"You would never turn against us. That's not who you are."

"No? In all the years I shall live—and I might live a very long time—do you honestly believe that I will never choose to interfere with the workings of the land?"

"If you do, I'm sure it will be for a good reason, and I'm sure we will be grateful for your help."

"Would you? No doubt I would believe my reasons were just, but that's the trap, isn't it? The belief that I know better and that because I have this power at my disposal, I have a responsibility to act." Remembering her words from before, he echoed them back to her: "For the good of the many. If I was wrong, though, who could stop me? I could end up becoming Galbatorix, despite my best intentions. As it is, my power makes people tend to agree with me. I've seen it in my dealings throughout the Empire. . . . If you were in my position, would you be able to resist the temptation to meddle, just a little, in order to make things better? My presence here unbalances things, Nasuada. If I am to avoid becoming what I hate, then I have to leave."

Nasuada lifted her chin. "I could order you to stay."

"I hope you don't. I would prefer to leave in friendship, not anger."

"So you will answer to no one but yourself?"

"I will answer to Saphira and to my conscience, as I always have."

The edge of Nasuada's lip curled. "A man of conscience—the most dangerous kind in the world."

Once more, the sounds of the fountain filled the gap in their conversation.

Then Nasuada said, "Do you believe in the gods, Eragon?"

"Which gods? There are many."

"Any of them. All of them. Do you believe in a power higher than yourself?"

"Other than Saphira?" He smiled in apology as Nasuada frowned. "Sorry." He thought seriously for a minute, then said, "Perhaps they exist; I don't know. I saw . . . I'm not sure what I saw, but I may have seen the dwarf god Gûntera in Tronjheim when Orik was crowned. But if there are gods, I don't think very highly of them for leaving Galbatorix on the throne for so long."

"Perhaps you were the gods' instrument for removing him. Did you ever consider that?"

"Me?" He laughed. "I suppose it could be, but either way, they certainly don't care very much whether we live or die."

"Of course not. Why should they? They are gods. . . . Do you worship any of them, though?" The question seemed of particular importance to Nasuada.

Again Eragon thought for a while. Then he shrugged. "There are so many, how could I know which ones to choose?"

"Why not the creator of them all, Unulukuna, who offers life everlasting?"

Eragon could not help but chuckle. "As long as I don't fall sick and no one kills me, I may live for a thousand years or more, and if I live that long, I can't imagine I would want to continue on after death. What else can a god offer me? With the Eldunarí, I have the strength to do most anything."

"The gods also provide the chance to see those we love again. Don't you want that?"

He hesitated. "I do, but I don't want to *endure* for an eternity. That seems even more frightening than someday passing into the void, as the elves believe."

Nasuada appeared troubled. "So you do not hold yourself accountable to anyone other than Saphira and yourself."

"Nasuada, am I a bad person?"

She shook her head.

"Then trust me to do what I believe is right. I hold myself accountable to Saphira and the Eldunarí and all of the Riders who are yet to be, and also to you and Arya and Orik and everyone else in Alagaësia. I need no master to punish me in order to behave as I ought. If I did, I would be no more than a child who obeys his father's rules only because he fears the whip, and not because he actually means good."

She gazed at him for several seconds. "Very well, then, I will trust you."

The splashing of the fountain once more achieved prominence. Overhead, the light from the sinking sun picked out cracks and flaws in the underside of the stone shelf.

"What if we need your help?" she asked.

"Then I'll help. I won't abandon you, Nasuada. I'll bind one of the mirrors in your study with a mirror of my own, so that you will always be able to reach me, and I'll do the same for Roran and Katrina. If trouble arises, I'll find a way to send assistance. I may not be able to come myself, but I *will* help."

She nodded. "I know you will." Then she sighed, unhappiness plain on her face.

"What?" he asked.

"It was all going so well. Galbatorix is dead. The last of the fighting has settled down. We were going to finally solve the problem of the magicians. You and Saphira were going to lead them and the Riders. And now . . . I don't know what we'll do."

"It'll sort out; I'm sure. You'll find a way."

"It would be easier with you here. . . . Will you at least agree to teach the name of the ancient language to whomever we choose to lead the magicians?"

Eragon did not have to think about it, since he had already considered the possibility, but he paused while he tried to find the right words. "I could, but in time, I think we would come to regret it."

"So you won't."

He shook his head.

Frustration crossed her face. "And why not? What are your reasons now?"

"The name is too dangerous to bandy about lightly, Nasuada. If a magician full of ambition but lacking scruples got hold of it, he or she could wreak an incredible amount of havoc. With it, they could destroy the ancient language. Not even Galbatorix was mad enough to do that, but an untrained, power-hungry magician? Who knows what might happen? Right now, Arya, Murtagh, and the dragons are the only ones besides me who know the name. Better to leave it at that."

"And when you go, we will be dependent upon Arya, should we have need of it."

"You know she will always help. If anything, I would worry about Murtagh."

Nasuada seemed to turn inward. "You needn't. He's no threat to us. Not now."

"As you say. If your goal is to keep the spellcasters in check, then the name of the ancient language is one piece of information that is better to withhold."

"If that is truly the case, then . . . I understand."

"Thank you. There's something else you should know as well."

Nasuada's expression grew wary. "Oh?"

He told her, then, about the idea that had recently occurred to him concerning the Urgals. When he finished, Nasuada was quiet for a while. Then she said, "You take much upon yourself."

"I have to. No one else can. . . . Do you approve? It seems the only way to ensure peace in the long run."

"Are you sure it's wise?"

"Not entirely, but I think we have to try."

"The dwarves as well? Is that really necessary?"

"Yes. It's only right. It's only fair. And it will help maintain the balance among the races."

"What if they don't agree?"

"I'm sure they will."

"Then do as you see fit. You don't need my approval—you've made that clear enough—but I agree that it seems necessary. Otherwise, twenty, thirty years from now, we may be facing many of the problems our ancestors faced when they first arrived in Alagaësia."

He bowed his head slightly. "I'll make the arrangements."

"When do you plan on leaving?"

"When Arya does."

"So soon?"

"There's no reason to wait longer."

Nasuada leaned against the railing, her eyes fixed on the fountain below. "Will you return to visit?"

"I'll try, but . . . I don't think so. When Angela cast my fortune, she said I would never return."

"Ah." Nasuada's voice sounded thick, as if she were hoarse. She turned and faced him directly. "I'm going to miss you."

"I'll miss you too."

She pressed her lips together, as if struggling not to cry. Then she stepped forward and embraced him. He hugged her back, and they stood like that for several seconds.

They parted then, and he said, "Nasuada, if you ever tire of being queen, or you want a place to live in peace, come join us. You'll always be welcome in our hall. I cannot make you immortal, but I could prolong your years far beyond what most humans enjoy, and they would be spent in good health."

"Thank you. I appreciate the offer, and I won't forget it." However, he had a feeling that she would never be able to bring herself to leave Alagaësia, no matter how old she was. Her sense of duty was too strong.

Then he asked, "Will you give us your blessing?"

"Of course." She took his head between her hands, kissed him upon his brow, and said, "My blessings upon you and Saphira. May peace and good fortune be with you wherever you go."

"And with you," he said.

She kept her hands upon him for another moment; then she released him, and he opened the glass door and exited through her study, leaving her standing alone upon the balcony.

BLOOD PRICE

s Eragon made his way down a flight of steps on his way
toward the main entrance of the building, he happened upon
the herbalist, Angela, sitting cross-legged in the dark alcove
of a door. She was knitting what appeared to be a blue and white hat
with strange runes along its lower part, the meaning of which was
lost on him. Next to her lay Solembum, his head propped up in her
lap and one of his heavy paws resting atop her right knee.

Eragon stopped, surprised. He had not seen either of them since—
it took him a moment to remember—since shortly after the battle
in Urû'baen. Thereafter, they had seemed to disappear.

"Greetings," said Angela without looking up.

"Greetings," replied Eragon. "What are you doing here?"

"Knitting a hat."

"That I can see, but why here?"

"Because I wanted to see you." Her needles clacked with swift
regularity, their motion as entrancing as the flames of a fire. "I
heard tell that you, Saphira, the eggs, and the Eldunarí are leaving
Alagaësia."

"As you predicted," he retorted, frustrated that she had been able
to discover what ought to have been the deepest secret. She could
not have eavesdropped upon him and Nasuada—his wards would
have prevented it—and so far as he knew, no one had told her or
Solembum about the existence of the eggs or the Eldunarí.

"Well, yes, but I didn't think to see you off."

"How did you find out? From Arya?"

"Her? Ha! Hardly. No, I have my own ways of gathering information." She paused in her knitting and looked up at him, her eyes

twinkling. "Not that I'll share them with you. I have to keep *some* secrets, after all."

"Humph."

"Humph yourself. If you're going to be that way, I'm not sure why I bothered coming."

"I'm sorry. I'm just feeling a bit . . . uneasy." After a moment, Eragon said, "Why did you want to see me?"

"I *wanted* to say farewell and to wish you luck on your journey."

"Thank you."

"Mmh. Try not to let yourself get too wrapped up in your head wherever you settle. Make sure you get out in the sun often enough."

"I will. What of you and Solembum? Will you stay here for a while and watch over Elva? You mentioned you would."

The herbalist snorted in a very unladylike fashion. "Stay? How can I stay when Nasuada seems intent on spying on every magician in the land?"

"You heard about that as well?"

She gave him a look. "I *disapprove*. I *disapprove* very much. I will not be treated like a child who has done something naughty. No, the time has come for Solembum and me to relocate to more friendly climes: the Beor Mountains, perhaps, or Du Weldenvarden."

Eragon hesitated for a moment and then said, "Would you like to come with Saphira and me?"

Solembum opened one eye and studied him for a second before closing it again.

"That's very kind of you," said Angela, "but I think we will decline. At least, for the time being. Sitting around guarding the Eldunarí and training new Riders seems boring . . . although, raising a clutch of dragons is sure to prove exciting. But no; for the time being, Solembum and I will stay in Alagaësia. Besides, I want to keep an eye on Elva for the next few years, even if I can't watch over her in person."

"Haven't you had your fill of interesting events?"

"Never. They're the spice of life." She held up her half-finished hat. "How do you like it?"

"It's nice. The blue is pretty. But what do the runes say?"

"Raxacori— Oh, never mind. It wouldn't mean anything to you anyway. Safe travels to you and Saphira, Eragon. And remember to watch out for earwigs and wild hamsters. Ferocious things, wild hamsters."

He smiled despite himself. "Safe travels to you as well, and to you, Solembum."

The werecat's eye opened again. *Safe travels, Kingkiller.*

Eragon left the building and picked his way through the city until he arrived at the house where Jeod and his wife, Helen, now lived. It was a stately hall, with high walls, a large garden, and bowing servants stationed within the entryway. Helen had done exceedingly well. By provisioning the Varden—and now Nasuada's kingdom—with much-needed supplies, she had quickly built up a trading company larger than the one Jeod had once owned in Teirm.

Eragon found Jeod washing up in preparation for their evening meal. After refusing an offer to dine with them, Eragon spent a few minutes explaining to Jeod the same things he had explained to Nasuada. At first Jeod was surprised and somewhat upset, but in the end, he agreed that it was necessary for Eragon and Saphira to leave with the other dragons. As with Nasuada and the herbalist, Eragon also invited Jeod to accompany them.

"You tempt me sorely," said Jeod. "But my place is here. I have my work, and for the first time in a long while, Helen is happy. Ilirea has become our home, and neither of us wants to pick up and move elsewhere."

Eragon nodded, understanding.

"But you . . . you're going to travel where few but the dragons or Riders have ever gone. Tell me, do you know what lies to the east? Is there another sea?"

"If you travel far enough."

"And before that?"

Eragon shrugged. "Empty land for the most part, or so the Eldunarí say, and I have no reason to think that's changed in the past century."

Then Jeod moved closer to him and lowered his voice. "Since you are leaving . . . I will tell you this. Do you remember when I told you about the Arcaena, the order devoted to preserving knowledge throughout Alagaësia?"

Eragon nodded. "You said that Heslant the Monk belonged to them."

"As do I." At Eragon's look of surprise, Jeod made a sheepish gesture and ran his hand through his hair. "I joined them long ago, when I was young and looking for a cause to serve. I've provided them with information and manuscripts throughout the years, and they've helped me in return. Anyway, I thought you should know. Brom was the only other person I've told."

"Not even Helen?"

"Not even her. . . . Anyway, when I finish writing my account of you and Saphira and the rise of the Varden, I'll send it to our monastery in the Spine, and it will be included as a number of new chapters in *Domia abr Wyrda*. Your story will not be forgotten, Eragon; that much, at least, I can promise you."

Eragon found the knowledge strangely affecting. "Thank you," he said, and grasped Jeod by the forearm.

"And you, Eragon Shadeslayer."

Afterward, Eragon made his way back to the hall, where he and Saphira had been living along with Roran and Katrina, who were waiting to eat with him.

All through supper, the talk was of Arya and Fírnen. Eragon held his tongue about his plans for departure until after the food was gone and the three of them—and the baby—had retired to a room overlooking the courtyard, where Saphira lay napping with Fírnen. There they sat drinking wine and tea and watching as the sun descended toward the distant horizon.

When an appropriate amount of time had passed, Eragon broached the subject. As he expected, Katrina and Roran reacted with dismay and tried to convince him to change his mind. It took Eragon nearly an hour to lay out his reasons to them, for they argued every point and refused to concede until he answered their objections in exacting detail.

Finally, Roran said, "Blast it, you're family! You can't leave!"

"I have to. You know it as well as I do; you just don't want to admit it."

Roran struck his fist against the table between them and then strode over to the open window, the muscles in his jaw clenching.

The baby squalled, and Katrina said, "Shh, now," and patted her on the back.

Eragon joined Roran. "I know it isn't what you want. I don't want it either, but I have no choice."

"Of course you have a choice. You of all people have a choice."

"Aye, and this is the right thing to do."

Roran grunted and crossed his arms.

Behind them, Katrina said, "If you leave, you won't be able to be an uncle to Ismira. Is she supposed to grow up without ever knowing you?"

"No," said Eragon, going back to her. "I'll still be able to talk with her, and I'll see to it that she's well protected; I may even be able to send her presents from time to time." He knelt and held out a finger, and the girl wrapped a hand around it and tugged with precocious strength.

"But you won't be here."

"No . . . I won't be here." Eragon gently extricated his finger from Ismira's grip and returned to stand by Roran. "As I said, you could join me."

The muscles in Roran's jaw shifted. "And give up Palancar

Valley?" He shook his head. "Horst and the others are already preparing to return. We'll rebuild Carvahall as the finest town in the whole Spine. You could help; it would be like before."

"I wish I could."

Below, Saphira uttered a throaty gurgle and nuzzled the side of Fírnen's neck. The green dragon snuggled closer to her.

In a low voice, Roran said, "Is there no other way, Eragon?"

"Not that Saphira or I can think of."

"Blast it—it's not right. You shouldn't have to go live by yourself in the wilderness."

"I won't be entirely alone. Blödhgarm and a few other elves will be going with us."

Roran made an impatient gesture. "You know what I mean." He gnawed on the corner of his mustache and leaned on his hands against the stone lip underneath the window. Eragon could see the sinews in his thick forearms knotting and flexing. Then Roran looked at him and said, "What will you do once you get to wherever you're going?"

"Find a hill or a cliff and build a hall atop it: a hall large enough to house all the dragons and keep them safe. And you? Once you rebuild the village, what then?"

A faint smile appeared on Roran's face. "Something similar. With the tribute from the valley, I plan to build a castle atop that hill we always talked about. Not a big castle, mind you; just a bit of stonework with a wall, enough to hold off any Urgals who might decide to attack. It'll probably take a few years, but then we'll have a proper way to defend ourselves, unlike when the Ra'zac came with the soldiers." He cast a sideways glance at Eragon. "We'd have room for a dragon as well."

"Would you have room for *two* dragons?" Eragon gestured toward Saphira and Fírnen.

"Maybe not. . . . How does Saphira feel about having to leave him?"

"She doesn't like it, but she knows it's necessary."

"Mmh."

The amber light from the dying sun accentuated the planes of Roran's face; somewhat to Eragon's surprise, he saw the beginnings of lines and wrinkles on his cousin's brow and around his eyes. He found the signs of encroaching age sobering. *How quickly life passes.*

Katrina laid Ismira in a cradle. Then she joined them at the window and placed a hand on Eragon's shoulder. "We'll miss you, Eragon."

"And I you," he said, and touched her hand. "We don't have to say goodbye quite yet, though. I'd like the three of you to come with us to Ellesméra. You would enjoy seeing it, I think, and that way we could spend another few days together."

Roran swiveled his head toward Eragon. "We can't travel all the way to Du Weldenvarden with Ismira. She's too young. Returning to Palancar Valley is going to be difficult enough; a side trip to Ellesméra is out of the question."

818

"Not even if it was on dragonback?" Eragon laughed at their surprised expressions. "Arya and Fírnen have agreed to carry you to Ellesméra while Saphira and I fetch the dragon eggs from where they're hidden."

"How long would the flight to Ellesméra take?" asked Roran, frowning.

"A week or so. Arya intends to visit King Orik in Tronjheim on the way. You would be warm and safe the whole while. Ismira wouldn't be in any danger."

Katrina looked at Roran, and he at her, and she said, "It would be nice to see Eragon off, and I've always heard tell of how beautiful the elves' cities are. . . ."

"Are you sure you would be up to it?" asked Roran.

She nodded. "As long as you're there with us."

Roran was silent for a moment; then he said, "Well, I suppose Horst and the others can go on ahead without us." A smile appeared under his beard, and he chuckled. "I never thought to see the Beor

Mountains or to stand in one of the elves' cities, but why not, eh? We might as well while we have the chance."

"Good, that's settled, then," said Katrina, beaming. "We're going to Du Weldenvarden."

"How will we get back?" asked Roran.

"On Fírnen," said Eragon. "Or I'm sure Arya would give you guards to escort you to Palancar Valley, if you would prefer to travel by horse."

Roran grimaced. "No, not by horse. If I never have to ride another horse in my life, it would be too soon by half."

"Oh? Then I take it you don't want Snowfire anymore?" said Eragon, raising an eyebrow as he named the stallion he had given Roran.

"You know what I mean. I'm glad to have Snowfire, even if I haven't had need of him for a while."

"Mm-hmm."

They stood by the window for another hour or so—as the sun set and the sky turned purple and then black and the stars came out—planning their upcoming trip and discussing the things Eragon and Saphira would need to take with them when they left Du Weldenvarden for the lands beyond. Behind them, Ismira slept peacefully in her cradle, her hands balled up in tiny fists beneath her chin.

Early the next morning, Eragon used the polished silver mirror in his room to contact Orik in Tronjheim. He had to wait for a few minutes, but eventually Orik's face appeared before him, the dwarf running an ivory comb through his unbraided beard.

"Eragon!" Orik exclaimed with obvious delight. "How are you? It's been too long since last we spoke."

Feeling a bit guilty, Eragon agreed. Then he told Orik of his decision to leave and the reasons why. Orik stopped combing and listened without interrupting, his expression serious throughout.

When Eragon finished, Orik said, "I will be sad to see you go, but I agree, this is what you must do. I have thought about this myself—worried about where the dragons might live—but I kept my concerns to myself, for the dragons have as much right to share the land as we do, even if we do not like it when they eat our Feldûnost and burn our villages. However, raising them elsewhere will be for the best."

"I am glad you approve," said Eragon. He talked to Orik about his idea for the Urgals, then, which involved the dwarves as well. This time Orik asked many questions, and Eragon could see that he was doubtful about the proposal.

After a long silence wherein Orik stared down into his beard, the dwarf said, "If you had asked this of any of the grimstnzborithn before me, they would have said no. Had you asked me at any time before we invaded the Empire, I would also have said no. But now, after having fought alongside the Urgals, and after having seen in person how helpless we were before Murtagh and Thorn and Galbatorix and that monster Shruikan . . . now I no longer feel the same." He gazed up through his bushy eyebrows at Eragon. "It may cost me mine crown, but on behalf of knurlan everywhere I will accept—for their own good, whether or not they realize it."

Again Eragon felt proud to have Orik as his foster brother. "Thank you," he said.

Orik grunted. "My people never desired this, but I am grateful for it. When will we know?"

"Within a few days. A week at most."

"Will we feel anything?"

"Maybe. I'll ask Arya. Either way, I'll contact you again once it's done."

"Good. Then we will speak later. Safe travels and sound stone, Eragon."

"May Helzvog watch over you."

* * *

The following day, they departed Ilirea.

It was a private event, devoid of fanfare, for which Eragon was grateful. Nasuada, Jörmundur, Jeod, and Elva met them outside the city's southern gate, where Saphira and Fírnen sat side by side, pushing their heads against one another while Eragon and Arya inspected their saddles. Roran and Katrina arrived a few minutes later: Katrina carrying Ismira swaddled in a blanket, and Roran carrying two packs full of blankets, food, and other supplies, one slung over each shoulder.

Roran gave his packs to Arya, and she tied them atop Fírnen's saddlebags.

Then Eragon and Saphira said their last farewells, which was harder for Eragon than for Saphira. His were not the only eyes with tears, however; both Nasuada and Jeod wept as they embraced him and offered him and Saphira their good wishes. Nasuada also said farewell to Roran, and she again thanked him for his help against the Empire.

At last, as Eragon, Arya, Roran, and Katrina were about to climb onto the dragons, a woman called out, "Hold there!"

Eragon paused with his foot atop Saphira's right foreleg and looked to see Birgit striding toward them from the city gates, gray skirts billowing, and her young son, Nolfavrell, trailing after her with a helpless expression on his face. In one hand, Birgit carried a drawn sword. In the other, a round wooden shield.

Eragon's stomach sank.

Nasuada's guards moved to intercept the two of them, but Roran shouted, "Let them pass!"

Nasuada signaled to the guards and they stepped aside.

Without slowing, Birgit walked over to Roran.

"Birgit, please don't," said Katrina in a low voice, but the other woman ignored her. Arya watched them unblinkingly, her hand on her sword.

"Stronghammer. I always said that I would have my compensation from you for my husband's death, and now I have come to claim it, as is my right. Will you fight me, or will you pay the debt that is yours?"

Eragon went to stand by Roran. "Birgit, why are you doing this? Why now? Can't you forgive him and let old sorrows rest?"

Do you want me to eat her? asked Saphira.

Not yet.

Birgit ignored him and kept her gaze fixed on Roran.

"Mother," said Nolfavrell, tugging on her skirts, but she showed no reaction to his plea.

Nasuada joined them. "I know you," she said to Birgit. "You fought with the men during the war."

"Yes, Your Majesty."

"What quarrel have you with Roran? He has proved himself a fine and valuable warrior on more than one occasion, and I would be most displeased to lose him."

"He and his family were responsible for the soldiers killing my husband." She looked at Nasuada for a moment. "The Ra'zac *ate* him, Your Majesty. They ate him and they sucked the marrow from his bones. I cannot forgive that, and I *will* have my compensation for it."

"It was not Roran's fault," said Nasuada. "This is unreasonable, and I forbid it."

"No, it's not," said Eragon, though he hated to. "By our custom, she has the right to demand a blood price from everyone who was responsible for Quimby's death."

"But it wasn't Roran's fault!" exclaimed Katrina.

"But it was," said Roran in a low voice. "I could have turned myself over to the soldiers. I could have led them away. Or I could have attacked. But I didn't. I chose to hide, and Quimby died as a result." He glanced at Nasuada. "This is a matter we must settle among ourselves, Your Majesty. It is a matter of honor, even as the Trial of the Long Knives was for you."

Nasuada frowned and looked to Eragon. He nodded, so with reluctance, she stepped back.

"What will it be, Stronghammer?" asked Birgit.

"Eragon and I killed the Ra'zac in Helgrind," said Roran. "Is that not enough?"

Birgit shook her head, her determination never wavering. "No."

Roran paused then, the muscles in his neck rigid. "Is this what you really want, Birgit?"

"It is."

"Then I will pay my debt."

As Roran spoke, Katrina uttered a wail and thrust herself between him and Birgit, still holding their daughter in her arms. "I won't let you! You can't have him! Not now! Not after everything we've gone through!"

Birgit's face remained as stone, and she made no move to retreat. Likewise, Roran showed no emotion as he grasped Katrina by the waist and, without apparent effort, lifted her off to the side. "Hold her, would you?" he said to Eragon in a cold voice.

"Roran . . ."

His cousin gave him a flat stare, then turned back to Birgit.

Eragon grabbed hold of Katrina's shoulders to keep her from flinging herself after Roran, and he exchanged a helpless look with Arya. She glanced toward her sword, and he shook his head.

"Let go of me! Let go!" shouted Katrina. In her arms, the baby began to scream.

Never taking his eyes off the woman before him, Roran undid his belt and dropped it to the ground, along with his dagger and his hammer, which one of the Varden had found in the streets of Ilirea soon after Galbatorix's death. Then Roran pulled open the front of his tunic and bared his hair-covered chest.

"Eragon, remove my wards," he said.

"I—"

"Remove them!"

"Roran, no!" shouted Katrina. "Defend yourself."

He's mad, thought Eragon, but he dared not interfere. If he stopped Birgit, he would shame Roran, and the people of Palancar Valley would lose all respect for his cousin. And Roran, Eragon knew, would rather die than allow that to happen.

Nevertheless, Eragon had no intention of letting Birgit kill Roran. He would let her have her price, but no more. Speaking softly in the ancient language—so that none might hear the words he used—he did as Roran had asked, but he also placed three new wards upon his cousin: one to protect the spine within his neck from being severed; one to keep his skull from being broken; and one to safeguard his organs. All else Eragon felt confident he could heal if necessary, as long as Birgit did not start cutting off limbs.

"It is done," he said.

Roran nodded and to Birgit said, "Take your price of me, then, and let this be an end to the quarrel between us."

"You will not fight me?"

"No."

Birgit eyed him for a moment; then she threw her shield onto the ground, crossed the few remaining feet that separated her from Roran, and placed the edge of her sword against Roran's breast. In a voice loud enough for only Roran to hear—though Eragon and Arya did as well with their catlike acuity—she said, "I loved Quimby. He was my life, and he died because of you."

"I'm sorry," Roran whispered.

"Birgit," pleaded Katrina. "Please . . ."

No one moved, not even the dragons. Eragon found himself holding his breath. The hiccupping crying of the baby was the loudest sound.

Then Birgit lifted the sword from Roran's breast. She reached down to take his right hand and drew the edge of the sword across his palm. Roran winced as the blade cut into his hand, but he did not pull away.

A crimson line appeared upon his skin. Blood filled his palm and spilled dripping to the ground, where it soaked into the trampled earth, leaving a dark blotch upon the dirt.

Birgit ceased pulling on the sword and held it motionless against Roran's palm for a moment more. Then she stepped back and lowered the scarlet-edged sword to her side. Roran closed his fingers around his palm, blood flowing between them, and pressed his hand against his hip.

"I have had my price," said Birgit. "Our quarrel is at an end."

Then she turned, picked up her shield, and strode back to the city, with Nolfavrell dogging her heels.

Eragon released Katrina, and she rushed to Roran's side. "You fool," she said, a bitter note in her voice. "You stubborn, pigheaded fool. Here, let me see."

"It was the only way," said Roran, as if from far away.

Katrina frowned, her face hard and strained as she examined the cut on his hand. "Eragon, you should heal this."

"No," said Roran with sudden sharpness. He closed his hand again. "No, this is one scar I'll keep." He looked around. "Is there a strip of fabric I can use as a bandage?"

After a moment of confusion, Nasuada pointed to one of her guards and said, "Cut off the bottom part of your tunic and give it to him."

"Wait," said Eragon as Roran started to wrap the strip around his hand. "I won't heal it, but at least let me cast a spell to keep the cut from getting infected, all right?"

Roran hesitated. Then he nodded and held out his hand toward Eragon.

It took Eragon only a few seconds to mouth the spell. "There," he said. "Now it won't turn green and purple and swell up as large as a pig's bladder."

Roran grunted, and Katrina said, "Thank you, Eragon."

"Now, shall we leave?" asked Arya.

The five of them climbed onto the dragons, Arya helping Roran and Katrina safely into the saddle on Fírnen's back, which had been modified with loops and straps to hold additional passengers. Once they were properly seated atop the green dragon, Arya raised a hand. "Farewell, Nasuada! Farewell, Eragon and Saphira! We will expect you in Ellesméra!"

Farewell! said Fírnen in his deep voice. He spread his wings and jumped skyward, flapping quickly to lift the weight of the four people on his back, helped by the strength of the two Eldunarí Arya was taking with her.

Saphira roared after him, and Fírnen replied with a trumpeted bugle before arrowing his way toward the southeast and the distant Beor Mountains.

Eragon twisted around in his saddle and waved to Nasuada, Elva, Jörmundur, and Jeod. They waved in return, and Jörmundur shouted, "Best of luck to the both of you!"

"Goodbye," cried Elva.

"Goodbye!" shouted Nasuada. "Be safe!"

Eragon replied in kind, and then he turned his back to them, unable to bear the sight any longer. Saphira crouched underneath him and sprang into the air as they began the first leg of their long, long journey.

Saphira circled as she gained altitude. Below, Eragon saw Nasuada and the others standing in a clump by the city walls, Elva holding up a small white kerchief, which fluttered in the gusts of wind from Saphira's passage.

PROMISES, NEW AND OLD

From Ilirea, Saphira flew to the nearby estate where Blödhgarm and the elves under his command were packing the Eldunarí for transport. The elves would ride north with the Eldunarí to Du Weldenvarden, and thence through the vast forest to the elven city of Sílthrim, which sat upon the shore of Ardwen Lake. There the elves and the Eldunarí would wait for Eragon and Saphira to return from Vroengard. Then together they would begin their journey out of Alagaësia, following the Gaena River as it flowed eastward through the forest and onto the plains beyond. All of them, that was, save Laufin and Uthinarë, who had elected to stay behind in Du Weldenvarden.

The elves' decision to accompany them had surprised Eragon, but he was grateful for it nevertheless. As Blödhgarm had said, "We cannot abandon the Eldunarí. They need our help, as will the younglings once they hatch."

Eragon and Saphira spent a half hour discussing the safe transport of the eggs with Blödhgarm, and then Eragon gathered up the Eldunarí of Glaedr, Umaroth, and several of the older dragons; he and Saphira would need their strength on Vroengard.

Upon taking their leave of the elves, Saphira and Eragon set off to the northwest, Saphira flapping at a steady, unhurried pace compared with that of their first trip to Vroengard.

As she flew, a sadness fell upon Eragon, and for a time he felt despondent and self-pitying. Saphira too was sad—she because of having parted from Fírnen—but the day was bright and the winds were calm, and their spirits soon lifted. Still, a faint sense of loss colored everything Eragon beheld, and he gazed at the land with renewed appreciation, knowing that he would likely never see it again.

Many leagues across the verdant grasslands Saphira flew, her shadow frightening the birds and the beasts below. When night came, they did not continue onward, but stopped and made camp by a rivulet that lay at the bottom of a shallow gully and sat watching the stars turning above them and talking of all that had been and all that might be.

Late the next day, they arrived at the Urgal village that had sprung up near the lake Fläm, where Eragon knew they would find Nar Garzhvog and the Herndall, the council of dams who ruled their people.

Despite Eragon's protests, the Urgals insisted upon throwing an enormous feast for him and Saphira, so he spent the evening drinking with Garzhvog and his rams. The Urgals made a wine out of berries and tree bark that Eragon thought was even stronger than the strongest of the dwarves' mead. Saphira enjoyed it more than he—to him, it tasted like cherries gone bad—but he drank it anyway to please their hosts.

Many of the female Urgals came up to him and Saphira, curious to meet them, as few of the Urgal women had joined in the fight against the Empire. They were somewhat slimmer than their men but just as tall, and their horns tended to be shorter and more delicate, although still massive. With them were Urgal children: the younger ones lacking horns, the older ones with scaly nubs upon their foreheads that protruded between one and five inches. Without their horns, they looked surprisingly like humans, despite the different color of their skin and their eyes. It was obvious that some of the children were Kull, for even the younger ones towered over their compatriots and, sometimes, their parents. So far as Eragon could tell, there was no pattern that determined which parents bore Kull and which did not. The parents who were Kull themselves, it seemed, bore Urgals of ordinary stature just as often as giants like themselves.

All that evening, Eragon and Saphira caroused with Garzhvog, and Eragon fell into his waking dreams while listening to an Urgal chanter recite the tale of Nar Tulkhqa's victory at Stavarosk—or so Garzhvog told him, for Eragon could understand nothing of the Urgals' tongue, other than that it made the dwarves' sound as sweet as honeyed wine.

In the morning, Eragon found himself blotched with a dozen or more bruises, the result of the friendly knocks and cuffs he had received from the Kull during their feasting.

His head throbbing, and his body as well, he and Saphira went with Garzhvog to speak with the Herndall. The twelve dams held court in a low, circular hut filled with the smoke of burning juniper and cedar. The wicker doorway was barely large enough for Saphira's head, and her scales cast chips of blue light across the dark interior.

The dams were exceedingly old, and several were blind and toothless. They wore robes patterned with knots similar to the woven straps that hung outside each building, and which bore the crest of the inhabitants' clan. Each of the Herndall carried a stick carved with patterns that held no meaning for Eragon but which he knew were not meaningless.

With Garzhvog translating, Eragon told them the first part of his plan to forestall future conflict between the Urgals and the other races, which was for the Urgals to hold games every few years, games of strength, speed, and agility. In them, the young Urgals would be able to win the glory they needed in order to mate and earn a place for themselves within their society. The games, Eragon proposed, would be open to every race, which would also provide the Urgals a means to test themselves against those who had long been their foes.

"King Orik and Queen Nasuada have already agreed to this," said Eragon, "and Arya, who is now queen of the elves, is also considering it. I believe that she too will grant the games her blessing."

The Herndall consulted among themselves for several minutes; then the oldest, a white-haired dam whose horns had worn away to almost nothing, spoke. Garzhvog again translated: "Yours is a good idea, Firesword. We must speak with our clans to decide upon the best time for these contests, but this we will do."

Pleased, Eragon bowed and thanked them.

Another of the dams spoke then. "We like this, Firesword, but we do not think this will stop the wars between our peoples. Our blood runs too hot for games alone to cool."

And that of dragons does not? asked Saphira.

One of the dams touched her horns. "We do not question the fierceness of your kind, Flametongue."

"I know that your blood runs hot—hotter than most," said Eragon. "That is why I have another idea."

The Herndall listened in silence as he explained, though Garzhvog stirred, as if uneasy, and uttered a low grunt. When Eragon finished, the Herndall did not speak or move for several minutes, and Eragon began to feel uncomfortable under the unblinking stare of those who could still see.

Then the rightmost Urgal shook her stick, and a pair of stone rings attached to it rattled loudly in the smoke-filled hut. She spoke slowly, the words thick and muddied, as if her tongue was swollen. "You would do this for us, Firesword?"

"I would," said Eragon, and bowed again.

"If you do, Firesword and Flametongue, then you will be the greatest friend the Urgralgra have ever had, and we will remember your names for the rest of time. We will weave them into every one of our thulqna, and we will carve them onto our pillars, and we will teach them to our younglings when their horns bud."

"Then your answer is yes?" asked Eragon.

"It is."

Garzhvog paused and—speaking for himself, Eragon thought—he said, "Firesword, you do not know how much this means to my people. We will always be in your debt."

"You owe me nothing," said Eragon. "I only wish to keep us from having to go to war."

He talked with the Herndall for a while longer, discussing the particulars of the arrangement. Then he and Saphira made their farewells and resumed their journey to Vroengard.

As the rough-hewn huts of the village shrank behind them, Saphira said, *They will make good Riders.*

I hope you are right.

The rest of their flight to Vroengard Island was uneventful. They encountered no storms over the sea; the only clouds that barred their way were thin and wispy and posed no danger to them or the gulls with whom they shared the sky.

Saphira landed on Vroengard before the same half-ruined nesting house where they had stayed during their previous visit. There she waited while Eragon walked into the forest and wandered among the dark, lichen-encrusted trees until he found several of the shadow birds he had encountered before and, after them, a patch of moss infested with the hopping maggots Nasuada had told him Galbatorix called burrow grubs. Using the name of names, Eragon gave both of the animals a proper title in the ancient language. The shadow birds he called *sundavrblaka* and the burrow grubs *illgrathr*. The second of the two names amused him in a grim sort of way, as it meant "bad hunger."

Satisfied, Eragon returned to Saphira, and they spent the night resting and talking with Glaedr and the other Eldunarí.

At dawn, they went to the Rock of Kuthian. They spoke their true names, and the graved doors within the mossy spire opened, and Eragon, Saphira, and the Eldunarí descended to the vault below. In that deep-set cavern, lit by the lake of molten stone that lay beneath the roots of Mount Erolas, the guardian of the eggs, Cuaroc, helped them place each egg into a separate casket. Then they piled the caskets near the center of the chamber, along with the five Eldunarí who had stayed within the cavern to help protect the eggs.

With Umaroth's help, Eragon cast the same spell he had once

before and placed the eggs and hearts into a pocket of space that hung behind Saphira, where neither she nor he could touch it.

Cuaroc accompanied them out of the vault. The metal feet of the dragon-headed man clanged loudly against the tunnel floor as he climbed to the surface alongside them.

Once they were outside, Saphira grasped Cuaroc between her talons—for he was too large and heavy to sit comfortably upon her back—and she took flight, rising above the circular valley that lay in the heart of Vroengard.

Across the sea, dark and shining, flew Saphira. Then over the Spine, the peaks like blades of ice and snow, and the rifts between them like rivers of shadow. She diverted north and crossed over Palancar Valley—so that she and Eragon might have one last look at their childhood home, if only from high above—and then over the Bay of Fundor, which was scalloped with lines of foam-crested waves, like so many rolling mountains. Ceunon, with its steep, many-layered roofs and sculptures of dragon heads, was their next landmark of note, and soon afterward, the leading edge of Du Weldenvarden appeared, the pines tall and strong.

Nights they spent camped by streams and ponds, the light of their fires reflecting off Cuaroc's polished metal body, while frogs and insects chorused about them. In the distance, they ofttimes heard the howls of hunting wolves.

Once at Du Weldenvarden, Saphira flew for an hour toward the center of the great forest, whereupon the elves' wards stopped her from proceeding any farther. Then she landed and walked through the invisible barrier of magic, Cuaroc striding alongside her, and again took flight.

League after league of trees sailed by underneath them, with little variation save for clusters of deciduous trees—oaks and elms and birch and aspen and languorous willows—which often lined the waterways below. Past a mountain, the name of which Eragon had forgotten, and the elven city of Osilon, and then trackless acres of pines, each unique and yet nearly identical to its countless brethren.

At last, in late evening, when both the moon and the sun hung low upon opposing horizons, Saphira arrived at Ellesméra and glided down to land amid the living buildings of the elves' largest, and proudest, of cities.

Arya and Fírnen were waiting for them, along with Roran and Katrina. As Saphira drew near, Fírnen reared and spread his wings, uttering a joyful roar that frightened birds into the air for a league around. Saphira answered in kind as she settled onto her hind legs and gently placed Cuaroc on the ground.

Eragon unbuckled his legs and slid down off Saphira's back.

Roran ran up, grasped him by the forearm, and clapped him on the shoulder while Katrina hugged him on the other side. Laughing, Eragon said, "Ah! Stop, let me breathe! So, how do you like Ellesméra?"

"It's beautiful!" said Katrina, smiling.

"I thought you were exaggerating," said Roran, "but it's every bit as impressive as you said. The hall we've been staying in—"

"Tialdarí Hall," said Katrina.

Roran nodded. "That. It's given me some ideas as to how we should rebuild Carvahall. And then there's Tronjheim and Farthen Dûr . . ." He shook his head and uttered a low whistle.

Eragon laughed again and started walking along the forest path toward the western edge of Ellesméra, they leading him. Arya joined them, looking every bit as much a queen as her mother once had. "Well met by moonlight, Eragon. Welcome back."

He looked at her. "Well met indeed, Shadeslayer."

She smiled at his use of the title, and the dusk beneath the swaying trees seemed to grow brighter.

Once Eragon had removed Saphira's saddle, she and Fírnen took flight—although Eragon knew Saphira was exhausted from their journey—and together they disappeared in the direction of the Crags of Tel'naeír. As they departed, Eragon heard Fírnen say, *I caught three deer for you this morning. They are waiting for you on the grass by Oromis's hut.*

Cuaroc set off in pursuit of Saphira, for the eggs were still with her, and it was his duty to protect them.

Through the great boles of the city, Roran and Katrina led Eragon until they arrived at a clearing edged with dogwood and hollyhocks, where tables sat laden with a vast assortment of food. Many elves, garbed in their finest tunics, greeted Eragon with soft cries, mellifluous laughter, and snatches of song and music.

Arya took her place at the head of the banquet, and the white raven, Blagden, rested upon a carved perch nearby, croaking and spouting occasional scraps of verse. Eragon sat by Arya's side, and they ate and drank and made merry until late in the night.

When the feast began to draw to a close, Eragon snuck away for a few minutes and ran through the darkened forest to the Menoa tree, guided more by his senses of smell and hearing than by sight.

The stars appeared overhead as he emerged from beneath the angled boughs of the great pine trees. He paused, then, to slow his breathing and collect himself before picking his way across the bed of roots that surrounded the Menoa tree.

He stopped at the base of the immense trunk and placed his hand against the creviced bark. Reaching out with his mind toward the slow consciousness of the tree that had once been an elf woman, he said:

Linnëa . . . Linnëa . . . Awake! I must needs speak with you! He waited but detected no response from the tree; it was as if he were attempting to communicate with the sea or the air or the earth itself. *Linnëa, I must speak to you!*

A sigh of wind seemed to pass through his mind, and he felt a thought, faint and distant, a thought that said, *What, O Rider . . . ?*

Linnëa, when last I was here, I said that I would give you whatever you wanted in exchange for the brightsteel under your roots. I am about to leave Alagaësia, so I have come to fulfill my obligation ere I go. What would you have of me, Linnëa?

The Menoa tree did not answer, but its branches stirred slightly, needles fell pattering onto the roots about the clearing, and a sense of amusement emanated from its consciousness.

Go . . . , whispered the voice, and then the tree withdrew from Eragon's mind.

He stood where he was for another few minutes, calling her name, but the tree refused to respond. In the end, Eragon left, feeling as if the matter was still unsettled, although the Menoa tree obviously thought otherwise.

The next three days, Eragon spent reading books and scrolls—many of which had come from Galbatorix's library and which Vanir had sent onward to Ellesméra at Eragon's request. In the evenings, he dined with Roran, Katrina, and Arya, but otherwise he kept to himself and did not see even Saphira, for she remained with Fírnen on the Crags of Tel'naeír and showed little interest in anything else. At night, the roars and bellows of the dragons often echoed across the forest, distracting him from his studies and making him smile when he touched Saphira's thoughts. He missed Saphira's companionship, but he knew that she had only a short time to spend with Fírnen, and he begrudged her not her happiness.

On the fourth day, when he had learned all he could from his reading, he went to Arya and presented his plan to her and her advisers. It took him the better part of the day to convince them that what he had in mind was necessary and, moreover, that it would work.

Once he had, they broke to eat. As dusk began to creep across the land, they assembled in the clearing around the Menoa tree: he, Saphira and Fírnen, Arya, thirty of the elves' oldest and most accomplished spellcasters, Glaedr and the other Eldunarí that Eragon and Saphira had brought with them, and the two Caretakers: the elf women Iduna and Nëya, who were the living embodiment of the pact between the dragons and the Riders.

The Caretakers disrobed, and—in accordance with the ancient

rituals—Eragon and the others began to sing, and as they sang, Iduna and Nëya danced, moving together so that the dragon tattooed across them seemed to become a single, unified creature.

At the height of the song, the dragon shimmered, and then it opened its jaws and stretched its wings and leaped forward, pulling itself off the elves' skin and rising above the clearing until only its tail remained touching the intertwined Caretakers.

Eragon called to the glowing creature, and when he had its attention, he explained to it what he wanted and asked if the dragons would agree.

Do as you will, Kingkiller, said the spectral creature. *If it will help ensure peace throughout Alagaësia, we do not object.*

Then Eragon read from one of the books of the Riders, and he spoke the name of the ancient language in his mind. The elves and the dragons who were present lent him the strength of their bodies, and the energy from them coursed through him like a great whirling tempest. With it, Eragon cast the spell he had spent days perfecting, a spell such as had not been cast for hundreds of years: an enchantment like unto the great old magics that ran deep within the veins of the earth and the bones of the mountains. With it, he dared to do what had been done only once before.

With it, he forged a new compact between the dragons and the Riders.

He bound not just the elves and the humans to the dragons, but also the dwarves and the Urgals, making it so that any one of them could become a Rider.

As he spoke the final words of the mighty enchantment, and thus sealed it into place, a tremor seemed to run through the air and the earth. He felt as if everything around them—and everything in the world perhaps—had shifted ever so slightly. The spell exhausted him, Saphira, and the other dragons, but upon its conclusion, a sense of elation filled him, and he knew that he had accomplished a great good, the greatest, perhaps, of his entire life.

Arya insisted on throwing another feast to mark the occasion.

Tired though he was, Eragon participated with good cheer, happy to enjoy her company and that of Roran, Katrina, and Ismira.

In the midst of the feast, however, the food and music suddenly became too much for him, and he excused himself from the table where he sat with Arya.

Are you all right? asked Saphira, looking over from her place by Fírnen.

He smiled at her from across the clearing. *I just need some quiet. I'll be back soon.* He slipped away and walked slowly among the pines, breathing deeply of the cool night air.

A hundred feet from where the tables lay, Eragon saw a thin, high-shouldered elf man sitting against a massive root, his back to the nearby celebration. Eragon altered his path to avoid disturbing him, but as he did so, he caught a glimpse of the elf's face.

It was no elf at all, but the butcher Sloan.

Eragon stopped, caught by surprise. In all that had gone on, he had forgotten that Sloan—Katrina's father—was in Ellesméra. He hesitated for a moment, debating, and then with quiet steps walked over to him.

As he had the last time Eragon had seen him, Sloan wore a thin black strip of cloth tied around his head, covering the empty sockets where his eyes had once been. Tears seeped out from under the cloth, and his brow was furrowed and his lean hands clenched.

The butcher heard Eragon approach, for he turned his head in Eragon's direction and said, "Who goes there? Is that you, Adarë? I told you, I need no help!" His words were bitter and angry, but there was also grief in them such as Eragon had not heard from him before.

"It's me, Eragon," he said.

Sloan stiffened, as if touched with a red-hot brand. "You! Have you come to gloat at my misery, then?"

"No, of course not," said Eragon, appalled by the thought. He dropped into a crouch several feet away.

"Forgive me if I don't believe you. It's often hard to tell if you're trying to help or hurt a person."

"That depends on your point of view."

Sloan's upper lip curled. "Now there's a weaselly elf-answer, if ever I heard one."

Behind him, the elves struck up a new song on lute and pipe, and a burst of laughter floated toward Eragon and Sloan from the party.

The butcher motioned over his shoulder with his chin. "I can hear her." Fresh tears rolled out from under the strip of cloth. "I can hear her, but I can't see her. And your blasted spell won't let me talk to her."

Eragon remained silent, unsure what to say.

Sloan leaned his head against the root, and the knob in his throat bobbed. "The elves tell me that the child, Ismira, is strong and healthy."

"She is. She's the strongest, loudest baby I know. She'll make a fine woman."

"That's good."

"How have you spent your days? Have you kept up with your carving?"

"The elves keep you informed of my activities, do they?" As Eragon tried to decide how to answer—he did not want Sloan to know he had visited him once before—the butcher said, "I guessed as much. How do you think I spend my days? I spend them in darkness, as I have ever since Helgrind, with nothing to do but twiddle my thumbs while the elves pester me about this and that and never give me a moment's peace!"

Again laughter sounded behind them. Within it, Eragon could make out the sound of Katrina's voice.

A fierce scowl contorted Sloan's face. "And then you had to go and bring *her* to Ellesméra. It wasn't enough just to exile me, was it? No, you had to torture me with the knowledge that my only child and grandchild are here, and that I'll never be able to see them, much less meet them." Sloan bared his teeth, and he looked as if he might spring forward at Eragon. "You're a right heartless bastard, you are."

"I have too many hearts," said Eragon, though he knew the butcher would not understand.

"Bah!"

Eragon hesitated. It seemed kinder to let Sloan believe that Eragon had meant to hurt him rather than to tell him that his pain was merely the result of Eragon's forgetfulness.

The butcher turned his head away, and more tears rolled down his cheeks. "Go," he said. "Leave me. And never trouble me again, Eragon, or I swear one of us will die."

Eragon poked at the needles on the ground, then he stood and stared down at Sloan. He did not want to leave. What he had done to Sloan by bringing Katrina to Ellesméra felt wrong and cruel. Guilt gnawed at Eragon, growing stronger second by second, until at last he reached a decision, whereupon calm settled over him again.

Speaking no louder than a whisper, he used the name of the ancient language to alter the spells he had placed on Sloan. It took him over a minute, and as he neared the end of his incantations, Sloan growled between clenched teeth, "Stop your accursed muttering, Eragon, and begone. Leave me, blast you! Leave me!"

Eragon did not leave, however, but began a new spell. He drew upon the knowledge of the Eldunarí and of the Riders whom many of the older dragons had been paired with, and he sang a spell that nurtured and fostered and restored what had once been. It was a difficult task, but Eragon's skill was greater than it had once been, and he was able to accomplish what he wished.

As Eragon sang, Sloan twitched, and then he began to curse and scratch with both hands at his cheek and brow, as if an itch had seized him.

"Blast you! What are you doing to me!"

Ending his incantation, Eragon squatted back down and gently removed the strip of cloth around Sloan's head. Sloan hissed as he felt the strip being pulled away, and he reached up to stop Eragon, but was too slow and his hands closed on empty air.

"You would take my dignity as well?" said Sloan, hate in his voice.

"No," said Eragon. "I would give it back. Open your eyes."

The butcher hesitated. "No. I can't. You're trying to trick me."

"When have I ever done that? Open your eyes, Sloan, and look upon your daughter and granddaughter."

Sloan trembled, and then, slowly, ever so slowly, his eyelids crept upward and revealed, instead of empty sockets, a pair of gleaming eyes. Unlike those he had been born with, Sloan's new eyes were blue as the noonday sky and of startling brilliance.

Sloan blinked, his pupils shrinking as they adjusted to the meager light within the forest. Then he jolted upright and twisted to peer over the top of the root at the festivities taking place between the trees beyond. The glow from the elves' flameless lanterns lit his face with a warm light, and by it, he seemed suffused with life and joy. The transformation in his expression was amazing to behold; Eragon felt tears in his own eyes as he watched the older man.

Sloan continued to stare over the root, like a parched traveler seeing a great river before him. In a hoarse voice, he said, "She's beautiful. They're both so beautiful." Another burst of laughter rang forth. "Ah . . . she looks happy. And Roran too."

"From now on, you can look at them if you want," said Eragon. "But the spells upon you still won't let you talk with them or show yourself to them or contact them in any way. And if you try, I'll know."

"I understand," murmured Sloan. He turned, and his eyes focused on Eragon with unsettling force. His jaw worked up and down for a few seconds, as if he were chewing on something, and then he said, "Thank you."

Eragon nodded and stood. "Goodbye, Sloan. You'll not see me again, I promise."

"Goodbye, Eragon." And the butcher twisted round to gaze once more into the light of the elven feast.

LEAVE-TAKING

A week passed: a week of laughter and music and long walks amid the wonders of Ellesméra. Eragon took Roran, Katrina, and Ismira to visit Oromis's hut on the Crags of Tel'naeír, and Saphira showed them the sculpture of licked stone she had made for the Blood-oath Celebration. As for Arya, she spent a day guiding them about the many gardens in the city, so they might see some of the more spectacular plants the elves had collected and created throughout the ages.

Eragon and Saphira would have been happy to stay in Ellesméra for another few weeks, but Blödhgarm contacted them and informed them that he and the Eldunarí under his charge had arrived at Ardwen Lake. And though neither Eragon nor Saphira wished to admit it, they knew it was time to leave.

It cheered them, however, when Arya and Fírnen announced that they would fly with them, at least until the edge of Du Weldenvarden and maybe a bit farther.

Katrina decided to stay behind with Ismira, but Roran asked to accompany them on the first part of their journey, for as he said, "I'd like to see what the far side of Alagaësia looks like, and traveling with you is faster than having to ride all the way out there on a horse."

At dawn the next day, Eragon said his farewells to Katrina, who cried the whole while, and to Ismira, who nursed on her thumb and stared at him without comprehension.

Then they set out, Saphira and Fírnen flying side by side as they headed eastward over the forest. Roran sat behind Eragon, holding him by the waist, while Cuaroc dangled from Saphira's talons, his body reflecting the sunlight as brightly as any mirror.

After two and a half days, they sighted Ardwen Lake: a pale sheet of water larger than the whole of Palancar Valley. On its western bank stood the city of Sílthrim, which neither Eragon nor Saphira had visited before. And bobbing in the water by the city's wharves was a long white ship with a single mast.

The vessel looked as Eragon knew it would, for he recognized it from his dreams, and a sense of inexorable fate settled upon him as he gazed at it.

This was always meant to be, he thought.

They spent the night in Sílthrim, which was much like Ellesméra, although smaller and more densely built. While they rested, the elves loaded the Eldunarí onto the ship, along with food, tools, cloth, and other useful supplies. The ship's crew was composed of twenty elves who wished to help with the raising of the dragons and the training of future Riders, as well as Blödhgarm and all of his remaining spellcasters, save Laufin and Uthinarë, who at that point took their leave.

In the morning, Eragon modified the spell that kept the eggs hidden above Saphira and removed two, which he gave to the elves Arya had chosen to safeguard them. One of the eggs would go to the dwarves, the other to the Urgals, and hopefully the dragons within would see fit to choose Riders from their designated race. If not, then they would swap places, and if they *still* did not find Riders for themselves . . . well, Eragon was not quite sure what to do then, but he was confident Arya would figure something out. Once the eggs hatched, they and their Riders would answer to Arya and Fírnen until they were old enough to join Eragon, Saphira, and the rest of their kin in the east.

Then Eragon, Arya, Roran, Cuaroc, Blödhgarm, and the other elves traveling with them boarded the ship, and they set sail across the lake, while Saphira and Fírnen circled high overhead.

The ship was named the *Talíta*, after a reddish star in the eastern sky. Light and narrow, the vessel needed only a few inches of water to float. It moved without sound and hardly needed steering, as it seemed to know exactly where its helmsman wished to go.

For days, they floated through the forest, first across Ardwen Lake and then, later, down the Gaena River, which was swollen with the spring snowmelt. As they passed through the green tunnel of branches, birds of many kinds sang and flew about them, and squirrels—both red and black—would scold them from the tops of the trees or would sit watching on branches that hung just out of reach.

Eragon spent most of his time with either Arya or Roran and only flew with Saphira on rare occasions. For her part, Saphira kept with Fírnen, and he often saw them sitting on the bank, their paws overlapping and their heads resting side by side on the ground.

During the days, the light in the forest was gold and hazy; during the nights, the stars twinkled brightly and the waxing moon provided enough illumination to sail by. The warmth and the haze and the constant rocking of the *Talíta* made Eragon feel as if he were half-asleep, lost in the remembrance of a pleasant dream.

Eventually, as of course it had to, the forest ended, and they sailed out onto the fields beyond. The Gaena River turned south then and carried them alongside the forest to Eldor Lake, the waters of which were even larger than those of Ardwen Lake.

There the weather turned, and a storm sprang up. Tall waves pummeled the ship, and for a day, they were all miserable as a cold rain and a fierce wind battered them. The wind was at their back, however, and it sped their progress considerably.

From Eldor Lake, they entered onto the Edda River and sailed southward past the elven outpost of Ceris. After that, they left the forest behind entirely, and the *Talíta* glided on the river, across the plains, seemingly of its own volition.

From the moment they had emerged from within the trees,

Eragon had expected Arya and Fírnen to leave. But neither said anything about departing, and Eragon was content not to ask them their plans.

Farther south they went, across more and more empty land. Looking about them, Roran said, "It's rather desolate, isn't it?" and Eragon had to agree.

At last they arrived at the easternmost settlement in Alagaësia: a small, lonely collection of wooden buildings by the name of Hedarth. The dwarves had built the place for the sole purpose of trading with the elves, for there was nothing of value in the area save the herds of deer and wild oxen visible in the distance. The buildings stood at the juncture where the Âz Ragni poured into the Edda, more than doubling its size.

Eragon, Arya, and Saphira had passed through Hedarth once before, in the opposite direction, when they had traveled from Farthen Dûr to Ellesméra after the battle with the Urgals. Thus Eragon knew what to expect when the village came into sight.

However, he was puzzled to see hundreds of dwarves waiting for them at the head of a makeshift pier that extended into the Edda. His confusion turned to delight when the group parted and Orik strode forth.

Raising his hammer, Volund, over his head, Orik shouted, "You didn't think I would let mine own foster brother leave without saying a proper goodbye, now did you?!"

Grinning, Eragon cupped his hands around his mouth and shouted back, "Never!"

The elves docked the *Talíta* long enough for everyone to disembark, save Cuaroc, Blödhgarm, and two other elves who stayed to guard the Eldunarí. The water where the rivers met was too rough for the ship to hold its position without scraping against the pier, so the elves then cast off and sailed farther down the Edda, in search of a calmer place to lay anchor.

The dwarves, Eragon was astounded to see, had brought to

Hedarth four of the giant boars from the Beor Mountains. The Nagran were spitted on trees as thick as Eragon's leg and were roasting over pits of glowing coals.

"I killed that one myself," Orik said proudly, pointing to the largest of the boars.

Along with the rest of the feast, Orik had brought three wagons of the dwarves' finest mead specifically for Saphira. Saphira hummed with pleasure when she saw the barrels. *You will have to try it as well*, she told Fírnen, who snorted and extended his neck, sniffing curiously at the barrels.

When evening came and the food was cooked, they sat at the rough-hewn tables the dwarves had built just that day. Orik banged his hammer against his shield, silencing the crowd. Then he picked up a piece of meat, put it in his mouth, chewed, and swallowed.

"Ilf gauhnith!" he proclaimed. The dwarves shouted with approval, and the feast began in earnest.

At the end of the evening, when everyone had eaten their fill— even the dragons—Orik clapped his hands and called for a servant who brought out a casket filled with gold and gems. "A small token of our friendship," Orik said as he gave it to Eragon.

Eragon bowed and thanked him.

Then Orik went to Saphira and, with a twinkle in his eye, he presented her with a gold and silver ring that she might wear on any of the claws of her forefeet. "It is a special ring, for it will not scratch, nor will it stain, and as long as you wear it, your prey will not hear you approaching."

The gift pleased Saphira immensely. She had Orik place the ring on the middle talon of her right paw, and throughout the evening, Eragon caught her admiring the band of gleaming metal.

At Orik's insistence, they stayed the night in Hedarth. Eragon hoped to leave early the following morning, but as the sky began to brighten, Orik invited him, Arya, and Roran to breakfast. After breakfast, they fell to talking, and then they went to see the rafts the dwarves had used to float the Nagran from the Beor Mountains to Hedarth, and before long it was nearly dinnertime again, and Orik succeeded in convincing them to stay for one last meal.

With the dinner, as with the feast the previous day, the dwarves provided song and music, and listening to the performance of a particularly skilled dwarf bard delayed the departure of their party even further.

"Stay another night," Orik urged. "It's dark and no time for traveling."

Eragon glanced up at the full moon and smiled. "You forget, it's not so dark for me as it is for you. No, we must go. If we wait any longer, I fear we will never leave."

"Then go with mine blessings, brother of mine heart."

They embraced, and then Orik had horses brought for them— horses the dwarves kept stabled in Hedarth for the elves who came to trade.

Eragon raised his arm in farewell to Orik. Then he spurred his steed forward and galloped with Roran and Arya and the rest of the elves away from Hedarth and down the game trail that ran along the southern bank of the Edda, where the air was sweet with the aroma of willows and cottonwoods. Above, the dragons followed, twining around each other in a playful, spiraling dance.

Outside Hedarth, Eragon reined in his mount, as did the others, and they rode on at a slower, more comfortable pace, talking softly amongst themselves. Eragon discussed nothing of importance with Arya or Roran, nor they with him, for it was not the words that mattered but rather the sense of closeness they shared in the confines of the night. The mood between them felt precious and fragile, and when they spoke, it was with greater kindness than usual, for they knew their time together was drawing to an end, and none wished to mar it with a thoughtless phrase.

They soon arrived at the top of a small hill and gazed down from it upon the *Talíta*, which sat waiting for them on the far side.

846

The ship appeared as Eragon knew it would. As it must.

By the light of the pale moon, the vessel looked like a swan ready to take flight from the wide, slow-moving river and carry him into the vast unknown. The elves had lowered its sails, and the sheets of fabric gleamed with a faint sheen. A single figure stood at the tiller, but otherwise the deck was empty.

Past the *Talíta*, the flat, dark plain extended all the way to the distant horizon: a daunting expanse broken only by the river itself, which lay upon the land like a strip of hammered metal.

A tightness formed in Eragon's throat, and he pulled the hood of his cloak over his head, as if to hide himself from the sight.

They slowly rode down the hill and through the whispering grass to the pebble beach by the ship. The hooves of the horses sounded sharp and loud against the stones.

There Eragon dismounted, as did the others. Unbidden, the elves formed two lines leading to the ship, one facing the other, and they planted the ends of their spears in the ground by their feet and stood thus, statue-like.

Eragon looked them over, and the tightness in his throat increased, making it difficult to breathe properly.

Now is the moment, said Saphira, and he knew she was right.

Eragon untied the casket of gold and gems from the back of his horse's saddle and carried it to Roran.

"This is where we part, then?" Roran asked.

Eragon nodded. "Here," he said, giving the casket to Roran. "You should have this. You can make better use of it than I. . . . Use it to build your castle."

"I'll do that," said Roran, his voice thick. He placed the casket under his left arm, and then he embraced Eragon with his right, and they held each other for a long moment. Afterward, Roran said, "Be safe, Brother."

"You too, Brother. . . . Take care of Katrina and Ismira."

"I will."

Unable to think of anything else to say, Eragon touched Roran once more on the shoulder, then turned away and went to join Arya where she stood waiting for him by the two rows of elves.

They stared at each other for a handful of heartbeats, and then Arya said, "Eragon." She had drawn her cowl as well, and in the moonlight, he could see little of her face.

"Arya." He looked down the silvery river and then back at Arya, and he gripped the hilt of Brisingr. He was so full of emotion, he trembled. He did not want to leave, but he knew he must. "Stay with me—"

Her gaze darted up. "I cannot."

". . . stay with me until the first curve in the river."

She hesitated, then nodded. He held out his arm, and she looped hers through his, and together they walked onto the ship and went to stand by the prow.

The elves behind them followed, and once they were all on board, they pulled up the gangplank. Without wind or oars, the ship moved away from the stony shore and began to drift down the long, flat river.

On the beach, Roran stood alone, watching them go. Then he threw back his head and uttered a long, aching cry, and the night echoed with the sound of his loss.

For several minutes, Eragon stood next to Arya, and neither spoke as they watched the first curve in the river approach. At last, Eragon turned to her, and he pushed the cowl away from her face, so that he could see her eyes.

"Arya," he said. And he whispered her true name. A tremor of recognition ran through her.

She whispered his true name in response, and he too shivered at hearing the fullness of his being.

He opened his mouth to speak again, but Arya forestalled him by placing three of her fingers upon his lips. She stepped back from him then and raised one arm over her head.

"Farewell, Eragon Shadeslayer," she said.

And then Fírnen swept down from above and snatched her off the deck of the ship, buffeting Eragon with the gusts of air from his wings.

"Farewell," Eragon whispered as he watched her and Fírnen fly back toward where Roran still stood upon the distant shore.

Then Eragon finally allowed the tears to spill from his eyes, and he clutched the railing of the ship and wept as he left behind all that he had ever known. Above, Saphira keened, and her grief mingled with his as they mourned what could never be.

In time, however, Eragon's heart slowed, and his tears dried, and a measure of peace stole over him as he gazed out at the empty plain. He wondered what strange things they might encounter within its wild reaches, and he pondered the life he and Saphira were to have—a life with the dragons and Riders.

We are not alone, little one, said Saphira.

A smile crept across his face.

And the ship sailed onward, gliding serenely down the moonlit river toward the dark lands beyond.

THE END

On the Origin of Names:

To the casual observer, the various names an intrepid traveler will encounter throughout Alagaësia might seem but a random collection of labels with no inherent integrity, culture, or history. However, as with any land that different cultures—and in this case, different species—have repeatedly colonized, Alagaësia acquired names from a wide array of unique sources, among them the languages of the dwarves, elves, humans, and even Urgals. Thus we can have Palancar Valley (a human name), the Anora River and Ristvak'baen (elven names), and Utgard Mountain (a dwarf name) all within a few square miles of each other.

While this is of great historical interest, practically it often leads to confusion as to the correct pronunciation. Unfortunately, there are no set rules for the neophyte. You must learn each name upon its own terms, unless you can immediately place its language of origin. The matter grows even more confusing when you realize that in many places the resident population altered the spelling and pronunciation of foreign words to conform to their own language. The Anora River is a prime example. Originally *anora* was spelled *äenora*, which means *broad* in the ancient language. In their writings, the humans simplified the word to *anora*, and this, combined with a vowel shift wherein *äe* (ay-eh) was said as the easier *a* (uh), created the name as it appears in Eragon's time.

To spare readers as much difficulty as possible, I have compiled the following list, with the understanding that these are only rough guidelines to the actual pronunciation. The enthusiast is encouraged to study the source languages in order to master their true intricacies.

Pronunciation:

Aiedail—AY-uh-dale
Ajihad—AH-zhi-hod
Alagaësia—al-uh-GAY-zee-uh
Albitr—ALL-bite-ur
Arya—AR-ee-uh
Blödhgarm—BLAWD-garm
Brisingr—BRISS-ing-gur
Carvahall—CAR-vuh-hall
Cuaroc—coo-AR-ock
Dras-Leona—DRAHS-lee-OH-nuh
Du Weldenvarden—doo WELL-den-VAR-den
Ellesméra—el-uhs-MEER-uh
Eragon—EHR-uh-gahn
Farthen Dûr—FAR-then DURE (*dure* rhymes with *lure*)
Fírnen—FEER-nin
Galbatorix—gal-buh-TOR-icks
Gil'ead—GILL-ee-id
Glaedr—GLAY-dur
Hrothgar—HROTH-gar
Islanzadí—iss-lan-ZAH-dee
Jeod—JODE (rhymes with *load*)
Murtagh—MUR-tag (*mur* rhymes with *purr*)
Nasuada—nah-soo-AH-dah
Niernen—nee-AIR-nin
Nolfavrell—NOLL-fah-vrel (*noll* rhymes with *toll*)
Oromis—OR-uh-miss
Ra'zac—RAA-zack

852

Saphira—suh-FEAR-uh
Shruikan—SHREW-kin
Sílthrim—SEAL-thrim (*síl* is a hard sound to transcribe; it's made
by flicking the tip of the tongue off the roof of the mouth)
Teirm—TEERM
Thardsvergûndnzmal—thard-svair-GOON-dinz-mahl
Trianna—TREE-ah-nuh
Tronjheim—TRONJ-heem
Umaroth—oo-MAR-oth
Urû'baen—OO-roo-bane
Vrael—VRAIL
Yazuac—YAA-zoo-ack
Zar'roc—ZAR-rock

THE ANCIENT LANGUAGE:

Agaetí Blödhren—Blood-oath Celebration (held once a century to
honor the original pact between elves and dragons)
älfa—elf (plural is *älfya*)
älfakyn—the race of elves
Atra du evarínya ono varda.—May the stars watch over you.
Atra esterní ono thelduin, Eragon.—May good fortune rule over
you, Eragon.
audr—up
böllr—a round object; an orb
brisingr—fire (*see also* istalrí)
Dauthdaert—Death Spear: name given to the lances the elves
made for killing dragons
Deloi sharjalví!—Earth, move!
Domia abr Wyrda—*Dominance of Fate* (book)
draumr kópa—dream stare
dröttning—queen
dröttningu—princess (roughly; it's not an exact translation)

du—the
Du Fells Nángoröth—The Blasted Mountains
Du Vrangr Gata—The Wandering Path
Du Weldenvarden—The Guarding Forest
ebrithil(ar)—master(s)
Eka aí fricai un Shur'tugal.—I am a Rider and a friend.
Eka elrun ono, älfya, wiol förn thornessa.—I thank you, elves, for
  this gift.
elda—a gender-neutral honorific suffix of great praise, attached
  with a hyphen
Elrun ono.—Thank you.
Erisdar—the flameless lanterns both the elves and the dwarves
  use (named after the elf who invented them)
fairth—a picture taken by magical means on a shingle of slate
fell—mountain
finiarel—an honorific suffix for a young man of great promise,
  attached with a hyphen.

flauga—fly (v.)
frethya—hide (v.)
gánga—go
gánga aptr—go backward
gánga fram—go forward
gánga raehta—go right
gedwëy ignasia—shining palm
Guliä waíse medh ono, Argetlam.—Luck be with you, Silverhand.
Helgrind—The Gates of Death
hvitr—white
íllgrathr—bad hunger
islingr—light-bringer/illuminator
istalrí—fire (see also brisingr)
jierda—break; hit
kausta—come
kverst—cut
Kverst malmr du huildrs edtha, mar fréma né thön eka

threyja!—Cut the metal holding me, but no more than
    I desire!

ládrin—open

letta—stop

Liduen Kvaedhí—Poetic Script

mäe—a fragment of a word that Eragon never finished saying

naina—make bright

Naina hvitr un böllr.—Make round white light.

Nam iet er Eragon Sundavar-Vergandí, sönr abr Brom.—My name
    is Eragon Shadeslayer, son of Brom.

Nïdhwal—dragon-like creatures that live in the sea, related to
    the Fanghur

niernen—orchid

Ono ach *néiat* threyja eom verrunsmal edtha, O snalglí.—You do
    not want to fight me, O snalglí.

Sé ono waíse ilia.—May you be happy.

Sé onr sverdar sitja hvass.—May your swords stay sharp.

Shur'tugal—Dragon Rider

slytha—sleep

snalglí—a race of giant snails

Stenr rïsa.—Stone, rise.

Stenr slauta!—Stone reverberate (sound)! (*slauta* is difficult to
    translate; it is a sharp, cleaving sound, like that of
    cracking stone, but it can also mean to make such a sound)

Stydja unin mor'ranr.—Rest in peace.

sundavrblaka—shadow-flapper

svit-kona—a formal honorific for a woman of great wisdom

thelduin—rule over

theyna—be silent

thrautha—throw

Thrysta vindr.—Compress the air.

thurra—dry (v.)

un—and

Vae weohnata ono vergarí, eka thäet otherúm.—We will kill you,

I swear it.

Vaer Ethilnadras—a brown, free-floating seaweed with gas-filled
    bladders along the joints of its branching stem

vaetna—scatter/dispel

valdr—ruler

vëoht—slow

verma—heat (v.)

vrangr—awry; wandering

Waíse néiat!—Be not!

yawë—a bond of trust

The Dwarf Language:

Az Ragni—The River

Az Sweldn rak Anhûin—The Tears of Anhûin

barzûl—curse someone with ill fate

Beor—cave bear (elf word)

derûndânn—greetings

dûr—our

dûrgrimst—clan (literally, "our hall," or "our home")

Erôthknurl—a stone of earth (literally, "earthstone"; plural is
    Erôthknurln)

Fanghur—dragon-like creatures that are smaller and less
    intelligent than their cousins, the dragons; related to the
    Nïdhwal (native to the Beor Mountains)

Farthen Dûr—Our Father

Feldûnost—Frostbeard (a species of goat native to the Beor
    Mountains)

grimstborith—clan chief (literally, "hall chief"; plural is *grimstborithn*)

grimstcarvlorss—arranger of the house

grimstnzborith—ruler of the dwarves, whether king or queen
    (literally, "halls' chief")

Ilf gauhnith!—a peculiar dwarf expression that means "It is safe and good!" Commonly uttered by the host of a meal, it is a holdover from days when poisoning of guests was prevalent among the clans.

Ingeitum—fire workers; smiths

knurla—dwarf (literally, "one of stone"; plural is *knurlan*)

Nagra—giant boar; native to the Beor Mountains (plural is *Nagran*)

thardsvergûndnzmal—something that appears other than it actually is; a fake or counterfeit; a sham

Tronjheim—Helm of Giants

Vor Orikz korda!—By Orik's hammer!

THE NOMAD LANGUAGE:

no—an honorific suffix attached with a hyphen to the main name of someone you respect

THE URGAL LANGUAGE:

drajl—spawn of maggots

nar—a title of great respect

thulqna—woven straps the Urgals use to display the crests of their clans

Uluthrek—Mooneater

Urgralgra—Urgals' name for themselves (literally, "those with horns")

ACKNOWLEDGMENTS

Kvetha Fricaya. Greetings, Friends.

What a long road this has been. It's difficult to believe that the end has finally arrived. Many times, I doubted whether I would ever finish this series. That I did is due in no small part to the help and support of a great many people.

I do not exaggerate when I say that writing *Inheritance* has been the hardest thing I have ever done in my life. For a variety of reasons—personal, professional, and creative—this book presented more of a challenge than any of the previous ones. I'm proud to have completed it, and I'm prouder still of the book itself.

Looking back on the series as a whole, I find it impossible to sum up my feelings. The Inheritance cycle has consumed twelve years of my life—nearly half of it, to date. The series has changed me and my family, and the experiences I have had as a result would take another four books to recount. And now to let it go, to say goodbye to Eragon, Saphira, Arya, Nasuada, and Roran and to move on to new characters and new stories . . . It's a daunting prospect.

I don't intend to abandon Alagaësia, however. I've put too much time and effort into building this world, and at some point in the future, I will return to it. That may not occur for another few years, or it might happen next month. At the moment, I can't say. When I do return to it, I hope to address a few of the mysteries that I left unresolved in this series.

Speaking of which, I'm sorry to have disappointed those of you who were hoping to learn more about Angela the herbalist, but she wouldn't be half so interesting if we knew everything about her. However, if you ever meet my sister, Angela, you can always try asking her about her character. If she's in a good mood, she might tell you something interesting. If not . . . well, you'll probably get a funny quip nevertheless.

Right, then. Onward to the thanks:

At home: both my mom and my dad for their constant support, for their advice, and for taking a chance on *Eragon* in the first place. My sister, Angela, for being a wonderful sounding board for ideas, helping with editing, once again allowing me to write her as a character, and providing invaluable support during the last quarter of the manuscript. I'm in your debt, Sis, but then you knew that. Also, Immanuela Meijer for keeping me company when I was dealing with a particularly difficult section.

At Writers House: Simon Lipskar, my agent, for his friendship and all he's done for the series over the years (I promise to start writing books a bit faster now!); and his assistant, Katie Zanecchia.

At Knopf: my editor, Michelle Frey, for her continued trust and for making all of this possible. Seriously, without her, you wouldn't be holding this book. Her assistant, Kelly Delaney, for making Michelle's life easier and also for helping to pull together a synopsis of the first three books. Editor Michele Burke for her keen eye on the story and, again, helping to get this book published. Head of communications and marketing Judith Haut, without whom few people would have heard of this series. Also in publicity, Dominique Cimina and Noreen Herits, both of whom have been of great help before, during, and after my various tours. Art director Isabel Warren-Lynch and her team for their beautiful design on the cover and interior (and also their work on the paperbacks). Artist John Jude Palencar for providing such a wonderful series of covers; this last one is a great image to end on. Executive copy editor Artie Bennett for his expertise in punctuation and words small, hippopotomonstrosesquipedalian, abstruse, and coined. Chip Gibson, head of the children's division at Random House. Knopf publishing director Nancy Hinkel for her immense patience. Joan DeMayo, director of sales, and her team (huzzah and many thanks!). Head of marketing John Adamo, whose team has continually amazed me with their creativity. Linda Leonard and her team in new media; Linda Palladino and Tim Terhune, production; Shasta Jean-Mary, managing editorial; Pam White, Jocelyn Lange, and the rest of the subsidiary rights team, who helped the Inheritance cycle become a worldwide publishing phenomenon; Janet Frick, Janet Renard, and Jennifer Healey, copyediting; and everyone else at Knopf who has supported me.

At Listening Library: Gerard Doyle, who does such a great job of giving voice to my story (I'm afraid I gave him a bit of a challenge with Fírnen); Taro Meyer for her subtle and moving direction of his performance; Orli Moscowitz for pulling all the threads together; and Amanda D'Acierno, publisher of Listening Library.

Also, thanks to fellow author Tad Williams (if you haven't, go read the trilogy Memory, Sorrow, and Thorn; you won't regret it) for giving me the inspiration to use a slate mine in the chapters on Aroughs. And to author Terry Brooks, who has been both a friend and a mentor to me. (I highly recommend his Magic Kingdom of Landover series.)

And thanks to Mike Macauley, who has set up and run one of the best fan sites out there (shurtugal.com) and who, with Mark Cotta Vaz, wrote The Inheritance Almanac. Without Mike's efforts, the community of readers would be much smaller and poorer than it is now. Thanks, Mike!

A special mention goes to Reina Sato, a fan whose reaction upon encountering escargot for the first time led me to create the snalglí on Vroengard. Reina, the snalglí are for you.

As always, my final thanks go to you, the reader. Thank you for staying with me through this story; I hope the stars shine brightly over you through the rest of your life.

And . . . that's it. I have no more words to add to this series. I have said what needed to be said. The rest is silence.

Sé onr sverdar sitja hvass.

Christopher Paolini
November 8, 2011